Bernice Rubens won the Booker Prize for Fiction for her fourth novel, *The Elected Member*, in 1970. She was also short-listed for the same prize for her ninth book, *A Five Year Sentence*, in 1978.

I Sent a Letter to my Love has been filmed with Simone Signoret and also made into a stage play in America.

In addition to numerous novels, Bernice Rubens has written for the stage, television and films. She lives in North London.

Bernice Rubens

BROTHERS

First published in Great Britain by
Hamish Hamilton Ltd 1983
Published in Abacus by
Sphere Books Ltd 1984
30–32 Gray's Inn Road, London WC1X 8JL
Copyright © 1983 by Bernice Rubens

Publisher's Note

This novel is a work of fiction, in which no reference is intended to any person living or dead, except that many historical characters are mentioned, and some occasionally appear on the scene.

Reproduced, printed and bound in Great Britain by
Hazell Watson & Viney Limited, Aylesbury, Bucks

CONTENTS

To
Joshua and Dashiel Lilley,
Brothers.

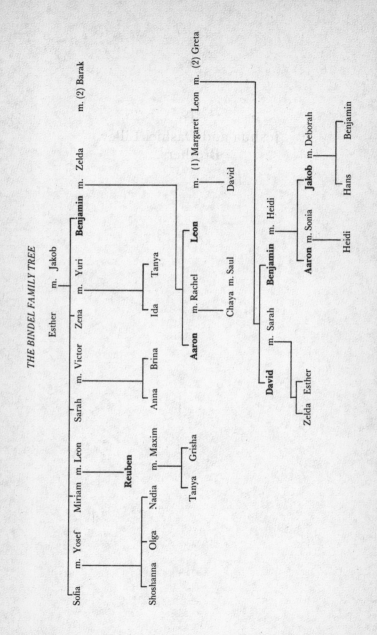

THE BINDEL FAMILY TREE

PROLOGUE

Come, stranger. Welcome to our Passover table. In the spring of each year we celebrate our flight from the bondage of Pharaoh. But this Passover festival of ours is much more than a homage to our history. Indeed it seems not history at all, for there is something disturbingly modern about its story, something offensively topical, a story that has a sour currency, as if no lesson had been learned from history at all. In the *Hagadah*, which is the service for the Passover eve, there is written a phrase which is the very core of the thanksgiving. 'In every generation each man must regard himself as if he himself had gone forth from Egypt.' Alas, we need no such reminder. Pharaoh has sundry names, and Egypt dwells in many lands.

Come, stranger, and hear the story of our constant flights from bondage and of that minstrel who sings the song that orchestrates our survival. A song that was heard almost a century and a half ago in a small tavern in the ghetto of Odessa.

Come, stranger, and warm yourself by our fire, for outside it is snowing.

PART ONE

The Book of Benjamin and Reuben

CHAPTER ONE

It must have been snowing.

Whatever else we know about Czarist Russia, whatever events punctuated its history, we can be pretty sure that it was snowing at the time. Snow fell on almost every Tolstoy page. Gorki's childhood was grievously gloved. Alexander Nevsky subdued the Teutonic knights in a celluloid battle on ice. The sun shone on the Odessa steps only because snow could not provide those stricken shadows. So we can safely assume that, on the day that the milk-brothers were born, it must have been snowing.

In fact, we know with absolute certainty that the temperature was well below freezing. We know it because it was historically recorded. Not that the birth of the milk-brothers merited a chronicle of any kind, but they chose to make their debut on that very day in the winter of 1825 when Czar Nicholas the First succeeded to the throne of Russia. On his inaugural way to the Palace of St Petersburg, it is recorded that one of the many horses drawing the royal carriage stumbled and fell on a mound of snow that had been carelessly left on an otherwise cleared highway. As a consequence, the royal carriage was delayed, a delay that did not improve the new Czar's habitually sullen temper. The negligent shoveller, leaning on his spade, was stationed by the wayside along with crowds of other pageant-fanciers, excited at the prospect of pomp and ceremony. When he saw the carriage falter, and realised its cause, he slunk away, with a haste and a tool that marked him as undeniably guilty. Poor Ivan Vassilevitch was the first casualty of the many thousands that littered Nicholas's reign and, before the royal carriage had reached the Palace, his powder-peppered body had been shovelled away to the side of the road together with the mound of snow that he had so dearly neglected. By evening, a vulture – at that time there were many such birds in the Russian skies – would gnaw poor Ivan out of recognition.

No Czar had ever been good news for Jews, and Nicholas the First upheld that tradition. He was a military man, with an unsurprisingly narrow vision and, in the course of his inaugural speech that day, he made reference to that time-honoured irritant to the Russian soul. 'The Yids run everything here,' he said. 'They are merchants, contractors, publicans, mill-owners. They are regular leeches, and suck our unfortunate provinces to the point of exhaustion.' So it would have seemed audacity, to say the least, that on that very day, and in the very echo of his words, yet two more affronts surfaced on the Russian soil to vex the Czar's mighty person.

The milk-brothers were born in snow-bound Odessa with ten minutes and one rickety storey between them. The first appearance was that of the only male offspring of Jakob and Esther Bindel, that partnership having already produced four daughters. Esther was forty when the boy was born. Her husband, two years her senior, knew that the child would be the last of his issue. Jakob Bindel, who all his married life had prayed for a son, cursing God behind his hand every time a girl dropped from Esther's fertile womb, now felt himself entitled to the status of Patriarch and, in keeping with his forefather, whose name he bore, he ordered the boy, this last child of his, to be called Benjamin, 'the son of my right hand'. He kissed his wife and left her bedside, making his way to the front part of the house, to that section which served as his tavern. It was five o'clock in the morning. Only one customer sat there – Faivel, the insomniac, Jakob's closest friend.

'*Nu?*' Faivel said as Jakob entered. There was little hope in his voice. A woman like Esther Bindel did not have the sinew for a man-child.

'Benjamin,' Jakob said softly, and he poured two glasses of kvass.

A tear fell from Faivel's eye. It might have flowed from sheer fatigue or from the two glasses of wine he had already consumed. But whatever its source, he meant it for joy. '*Mazeltov,*' he said. '*Le'chaim.*'

Jakob raised his glass. 'To Benjamin,' he said.

Esther Bindel put little Benjamin to her breast, and listened to her daughter Miriam's labouring cries from above. Sofia was with her, her oldest, still unmarried child. Esther began to sing softly, a song of joy and celebration, as much to welcome her own son, as to herald the arrival of her first grandchild. Then she heard a piercing cry, and she knew that the Bindel line had nudged itself a little further into continuity.

At the moment of her grandchild's birth, the child's father, Leon Wolf, was in the shed behind the tavern milking Devorah, the family cow. When Miriam had gone into labour, her sister Sarah had volunteered to replace him at milking-time. But the cow had kicked and whined at the touch of an unfamiliar hand. Leon was happy enough to be called away from the thrashing bedside. He could not bear his wife's pain, or his own embarrassment. Leon

Wolf was a shy man, and he was happier alone, his head resting on Devorah's warm flank as he pumped her teats to relieve her. When he heard his wife's piercing scream and, shortly afterwards, the undeniable cry of a new-born child, he quickly finished the milking, nuzzled Devorah's nose, and returned to his wife's bedside. Miriam had borne him a son and, as his father-in-law had called the last of his line by the traditional Benjamin, in that same manner Leon's first-born was to be named Reuben, which translated means, 'Behold a son'. So, whether it is the first or last born, it is the maleness of the child that is proclaimed and celebrated. Leon kissed his wife and went to join Jakob in the tavern. Man's work it was to toast one's sons.

Sofia ran to tell her mother of her new grandson, and returned to Miriam with the news of her baby brother. Both children, oblivious of their strange and almost synchronised kinship, sucked happily at their mothers' breasts.

Or at least did Reuben. Downstairs little Benjamin was having a tougher time. He sucked a little and then he stopped. He sucked again, and again he paused. Young as he was, he had an instinct for the notion of supply and demand, and there was no doubt in his mind as to a certain imbalance in that assumption. His mother was aware of it too, and without surprise. With her last child, Zena, she had heard the hollow echoes of a dried-up well. She clasped her new-born tightly to her breast, kissing him on his puckered bewildered brow, then she wrapped him in a blanket. 'Your sister will suckle you,' she whispered. She handed the bundle to Sarah who took it to the room above.

Miriam put her brother to her breast where he suckled till his brow was smooth. His nephew fed on the other side. Both children's eyes were closed. They neither saw each other, nor did they touch. Between them there was no sibling blood, but the bond of milk that coupled them was secured by an enduring and compelling love, a bond that was to remain unbroken throughout their lives.

*

On the eighth day the children were to be circumcised, and Jakob, who had never before been granted the privilege of such a ceremony, was determined to make of it some celebration. He was, too, and for the first time, a grandfather, a cause which on its own account called for commemmoration. So he sprinkled sawdust on his tavern floor, set up sundry wines and schnapps on his counter, and fussed about the stove as his daughters baked cinnamon cakes, honeyed rolls, and pots of peach and raspberry jam.

'Can we dance, Papa?' little Zena asked. 'Is it allowed?'

5

'We shall dance,' Jakob said. 'The Bindels shall dance and the Wolfs shall dance. Whether it is allowed or not,' he whispered to himself. There were enough restrictions on their daily lives, enough 'Thou shalts and shalt nots', whether they came from the Czar or from the rigid tenets of their own faith. More and more Jakob Bindel resented the restrictions that the elders of the community forced upon the ghetto congregation. Their taboo on the learning of anything but the scriptures, their insistence on speaking Yiddish, their sheer contempt for the Russian tongue. But he must refrain from argument. Esther got very nervous if he aired his views. They would be coming to the ceremony, some of those black-robed men of God. Jakob Bindel would hold his tongue. But, nevertheless, he would dance. And so would the women.

'Will you dance with me, Sofia?' he said. Sofia was his favourite. Of all the daughters, she, being the first, was the only one whose gender was forgiven. He wished he could see her married. But there were impediments to that, terrible obstacles that he dared not think about. She was different from the others, headstrong, like himself. She would be no man's lackey. Besides, she was cleverer than any young man he knew. She spoke and read Russian. She dreamed of getting out of the Pale. She even dreamed about Palestine. 'Russia isn't home,' she told her father once. 'It's exile.'

'Will you dance with me?' he said again.

'Dance with an old grandfather?' she teased him and, although she hugged him, pulling playfully at his beard, he felt her separateness for the first time.

Although it was not the Sabbath, the guests had put on their Sabbath clothes. The custom of circumcision, of cutting a covenant with the Lord, was a deeply religious act which called for appropriate attire. The men wore long black caftans with their brushed sable hats, and the women wore silk shawls under their woollen wraps. Reb Schlomovitch was the first to arrive, his wife three respectful paces in the rear. Crooked in her elbow, she carried his bag with the tools of his trade, his prayer-book and shawl, his knife and his roll of lint. Reb Schlomovitch was also the cantor in the synagogue, with a voice of operatic splendour, whose dulcet sonorous tones were occasionally at odds with the duties that were part of his calling.

Reb Schlomovitch sat down heavily on a corner bench and eyed the kvass on the counter. But Jakob made no offer. Reb Schlomovitch was getting old. His hands were already shaky.

'Afterwards, Reb Schlomovitch,' Jakob said. 'We'll drink like Czars.'

Then he went to the door to welcome Faivel. His friend's eyes were red-rimmed, athirst for the sleep that forever eluded him. His wife walked in his stooping shadow. One earful of Raisl explained Faivel's insomnia. It wasn't that she was an incessant chatterer. In fact she spoke little. But it was the tone of her voice. Its sound was of measured, monotonous, soporific tedium. It was like a continual drip which, given time, would wear away rock. Poor Faivel, Jakob thought, and he dragged him behind the counter and slipped him a measure of kvass.

From his stand, he caught sight of Mendel Meisels as he negotiated his large ungainly body through the tavern door. As always, when seeing Meisels, Jakob's spirits were clouded with foreboding. He did not like the man, and for good reason. Jakob owed Mendel a favour. And not just any favour. The nature of Mendel's pay-off was quite specific, though Mendel himself had never detailed it. But he would drop hints at every meeting and usually with a lecherous grin, so that it was clear to Jakob that there was only one means of squaring the debt. And that means was very costly. Sofia. Jakob owed Mendel Sofia, and nothing less than Sofia would satisfy him.

Mendel Meisels was the head of the Jewish Community Organisation, the *Kahal*. This body acted as liaison between the government and the ghetto and was responsible for collecting the crippling taxes and executing the sundry restrictions that the government thought might help efface that ubiquitous eyesore on their landscape. Some years before, Alexander the First, the then Czar, had ordered that Jews could no longer be licensed as tavernkeepers. Many lost their homes and livelihood. But Mendel Meisels had turned a blind eye on the Bindel holding. Government officials were always bribable. Part of the *Kahal*'s funds were earmarked precisely for that purpose. On his occasional visits to the Bindel tavern, Mendel Meisels had caught sight of Sofia. And for many years, since the death of his wife, and even before, if he were honest with himself, he had coveted her. But he had to admit to himself that he had little to commend him in Sofia's eye. He was older than her father. His body was ungainly. He had nothing but money and position and she would be attracted by neither. He needed Bindel in his debt. He needed Bindel beholden. Sooner or later he would have to pay his due. Neither man ever referred to the nature of the pay-off. Jakob was totally silent on the subject, but Mendel skirted around it from time to time, voicing his paternal concern with Jakob's daughters and inquiring as to their marriage prospects. 'Now that eldest one of yours,' he would occasionally say, with positive non-reference to her name, 'she's not getting any younger, you know.' And Jakob would cover with a smile, as his heart soured with the thought of what Meisels had in mind.

So when he saw him standing at the tavern door, he looked

7

quickly around the room for Sofia, as if with his glance he could protect her. And she, ignorant of the sacrifice that was expected of her, was approaching the door to welcome him, as she would any guest, with her smiles and greetings. Mendel eyed Jakob behind the counter. Sofia took his hand. She led him to her father. Jakob stared at Sofia's fingers, willing them to be disjoined from his guest's. The look was not lost on Mendel.

'How's business, Bindel?' he said, which, sub-titled, was a reminder that he was beholden to him to be in business at all, whether his profits were large or small.

'Business is good,' Jakob said, 'and today even better. For I have two heirs who will make it prosper.' He thought it as well to remind Meisels of the purpose of the gathering.

'As long as the tavern remains in Bindel's name,' Meisels said with a smile. He tightened his grip on Sofia's hand, and Jakob saw how she pulled it away, giggling a little to hide her embarrassment.

'Are we all ready?' Reb Schlomovitch sang from his corner. His eye had fallen on a dish of cinnamon rolls that Zena had carried to the counter. He was anxious to get on with the job and let the festivities begin.

'We're waiting for the Pinskis,' Jakob said.

'Then we'll wait for ever,' Reb Schlomovitch groaned.

The Pinskis were notorious for their lack of punctuality. But for the most part they were forgiven because, as Jakob pointed out, they were artists, and were therefore licensed to find the notion of time irrelevant except in so far as it referred to immortality. The Pinskis were music teachers, Dov of the violin, and Rosa of the piano. Almost every child in the ghetto had, at one time or another, passed through their kitchen/studio, and most of them without payment. Many of them were talented, but there was little in those days that a Jewish performer could achieve outside the teaching profession, and often the Pinskis regretted that they had unstopped a talent that had been better left dormant and at peace. The Pinskis were much loved in the ghetto, and pitied too, because they were childless, which was why many mothers were happy to share their children with them.

Little Zena ran to the door and looked down the street.

'They're coming,' she shouted, excited. 'And somebody else is with them.'

'It must be that nephew of theirs,' Raisl's tubular voice tunnelled through the tavern, turning the room into a vast echo chamber. 'He was driven out of his village.'

It took a little while for Raisl's reverberations to subside, by which time the Pinskis and their companion had reached the tavern

8

door. Jakob caught sight of Sofia's face, as she herself caught sight of the stranger's in the doorway. It was as if two stars had glided into her eyes and, in an instant, had burned out her childhood. He knew then that he would lose her, but he felt no sorrow. At least, not until he caught Mendel's eye and then his knees trembled. He looked to the tavern door.

Yosif Pinski was probably Sofia's age with a beauty that matched her own. In the restless line of his eyes and mouth there dwelt an equally unquiet spirit. The magnet that coursed between their two glances was almost tangible. Sofia did not move from the counter, nor Yosif from the door, even when the Pinskis moved into the tavern apologising for their tardy arrival.

'Dov was giving a lesson,' Rosa explained. 'The Bok's little girl. So talented. We didn't notice the time. This is Yosif,' she said, almost in the same breath, and looked around for him. 'Yosif,' she called, 'why don't you come in?'

And so Yosif was obliged to move and he lowered his eyes as if their mutual and compelling gaze could not contend with his mobility.

'This is Dov's brother's boy,' Rosa said.

'God rest his soul,' Reb Schlomovitch put in his kopek's worth. The boy's father was a no-good, a drunk and an idler, who'd been stupidly killed in a tavern brawl. But villain as he was, Reb Schlomovitch thought that he was still entitled to some blessing, perhaps even more so than those who had led a virtuous life, insuring their souls along the way. 'How's your poor mother?' he asked.

'She's not well,' Yosif said. 'The journey was hard for her.'

When Sofia heard his voice, she lowered her eyes for the first time. Its gentleness was almost unbearable.

'On Shabbos they did it. Of all days.' Raisl's pneumatic drill was at it again, and its whine shattered the caress of his voice that still echoed across the tavern.

'In the middle of the Shabbos service,' Dov Pinski said, 'they stormed into the *shul* and told everybody to leave the village. Just like that. No warning. Nothing. They walked out of the *shul* and took to the road.'

'It's getting worse and worse,' Faivel said. 'Where do they expect them to go? The ghettoes are overcrowded already.'

'What do you do for a living, young man?' Jakob said, and Sofia blushed for it was the time-honoured question of a father to a possible son-in-law. But Jakob had only meant it for conversation and he realised too late how others might interpret it.

'You lose no time,' Reb Schlomovitch laughed.

'I'm a farrier by trade,' Yosif said.

'In Odessa we have more farriers than horses,' Jakob said smiling. 'You'll have to look for something else.'

'I know Russian,' Yosif said. 'I could teach it.'

'Russian?' Mendel Meisels sneered. 'Yiddish isn't good enough for you? To learn Russian is the first step to baptism.'

'I don't agree,' Yosif started, but Jakob quickly interrupted him. You didn't argue with Mendel Meisels.

'Go and get the children, Sofia,' Jakob said loudly. And, for the first time since Yosif had arrived at the tavern, Sofia moved from the counter. Her step was unsteady. Her knees were trembling, and she stiffened them, walking slowly, her head bowed, anxious to hide the rapturous confusion in her heart. But once out of the tavern, she held her head high. 'He is for me,' she almost sang. 'Yosif is the man I shall marry.' She repeated it over and over again, until she reached the back room, then paused at the door to whisper it to herself yet again.

She opened the door. Her mother was holding both children who were sleeping, blissfully unaware of the price they were about to pay to be one of the chosen. 'You look so beautiful, Sofia,' her mother said, catching the glow on her face. 'I've never seen you more beautiful,' she whispered. Then Leon came and gathered the children in his arms, and still they were not disturbed. Sofia opened the door for him, and stayed behind with the women, while the men got on with man's work of going about God's business. Suddenly Miriam began to cry and rushed to her mother's side for comfort, but Esther, with all her mothering years behind her, was new herself to this man's game, and was holding back her own tears. It was Sofia who embraced them both with the strength and the love with which Yosif had wordlessly and remotely flooded her.

Leon carried the babies into the tavern. Benjamin who was the elder of the two, was the first to be initiated. Leon was to hold him as Reb Schlomovitch performed the rite. It was considered an honour to present a child in such an offering, but Leon could have done without it. It seemed to him to be a fruitless act of mutilation. He was a God-fearing Jew but he couldn't understand that his God could seriously demand such dire payment for His friendship. But he had never voiced any opposition. He cradled Benjamin in his arms, and he shut his eyes. He felt that if he was not a witness to such a procedure, he could not be held responsible. 'God forgive me,' he whispered to himself, though it sounded ridiculous to ask forgiveness for obeying a commandment. So he amended his prayer. 'I forgive You, God,' he said, and he held the child in his outstretched arms.

Reb Schlomovitch smeared the baby's lips with a little kvass, his small concession to anaesthesia. Then, holding his knife in a surprisingly steady hand, he sang a prayer and did what had to be done. Benjamin woke with a scream of affront, and as they linted his wound, he squirmed with reproach. He had been initiated, not so much into Judaism, as into the concept of pain, which, as he was to learn during the course of his life, added up to much the same thing. Leon gathered him into his arms and moved away, not wishing to see his own son submit to the ordeal.

Reuben had already awoken, warned no doubt by Benjamin's cries. He struggled a little in Jakob's arms, sniffing Benjamin's blood, and knowing the pain that was now his due. Jakob took a gulp of kvass, and kissed his grandson on the lips. Then, with joy, he held him out for the sacrifice. Reb Schlomovitch wielded his knife once more, accompanied by the same prayer. Reuben was silent. Not a whimper escaped him. Benjamin had wept for both of them, as Reuben would have done had he been first on the knife.

And so it was done. The knife was put away and the children removed to their mothers. It was in order for the festivities to begin. Leon returned from the back room behind the tavern with his accordion. Sofia and Jakob poured the wine, and Zena and Sarah handed around the cakes. Jakob held his glass high. '*Le'chaim*,' he shouted, and he looked around for his friend Faivel with whom he shared everything. But Faivel, who had with half an eye witnessed the first cutting, had closed it with disgust and desolation. He would die rather than witness another. And at that moment God gave him sleep.

Jakob leaned over the tavern counter. Faivel was sprawled on the sawdust floor, his arm crossed over his chest, and blowing through his parted lips a gentle childlike snore.

'A miracle,' Jakob whispered. 'Faivel is sleeping.'

'It's a good omen,' Raisl rasped, staring at her man with abject astonishment.

'Sh,' Jakob said. The last thing Faivel would want to hear, and possibly the only thing that would wake him up, was his wife's voice. 'We'll have some music,' he said. 'A lullaby.'

And as Leon stretched his concertina into a gently spread chord, Yankel, the *schnorrer*, as if on his music cue, appeared at the tavern door. His arrival was greeted with warmth and a certain relief, for no Jewish ceremony was complete without its attendant *schnorrer*.

There were four professional beggars in the Odessa ghetto, and Yankel was the doyen of them all. He was well over sixty, and his years, if not his calling, provoked a certain respect. The other operators were relatively newcomers to the district, and to the trade as well. Over the past years, they had been expelled from their villages and from their livelihoods and, out of necessity, and with a certain initial shame, they had taken to begging. Until their arrival,

Yankel had had a clear field, and their poaching posed a positive threat. Moreover they tarnished his profession. He had been a regular and highly trained *schnorrer* all his life. So had his father and his father before him. It was a calling that demanded qualifications, skill and apprenticeship. But Yankel was a generous man and he could not deny others a living. But it had to be orderly and non-competitive. So Yankel called them all to a meeting and together they formed what might loosely be called a *schnorrer's* union. They debated whose beat belonged to whom, and the rules pertaining to trespass. But most important of all was the principle that, whatever charity was offered, no services must be rendered in return. That code was unbreakable. A good *schnorrer* was one to whom it was a privilege to give, and that privilege, and that alone, was the only permitted feed-back. In view of Yankel's age and experience, he was accorded the larger slice of the charity cake. He was allowed to take his choice of weddings, barmitzvahs, circumcisions and funerals. The others could pick up on those that Yankel did not think worth his while. It was a good arrangement, for he very rarely went to funerals, and there were good pickings to be had at the graveside. And in those days in Odessa, there were more burials than nuptials. Besides, as a long-time professional *schnorrer*, Yankel had made his pile. In his line of work, there was always demand. Whatever the political or economic climate, wherever a Jew celebrated or mourned, wherever joy dwelt or sorrow, guilt was its eternal bedfellow. The most convenient and handy outlet for guilt is charity, and Yankel was always on the spot for the purposes of mitigation. A Jew in joy will always question what he had done to deserve such happiness, and that same Jew, in sorrow, will often blame himself. Guilt in the ghetto was a ubiquitous shadow. Even without the excuses of joy or sorrow, in the simple day-by-day grind of ghetto life, there lurked the self-reproach of survival itself.

'Welcome, Yankel,' Jakob shouted from the counter. 'Take a glass of wine with us and drink to our sons.'

Yankel kept his stand at the door. A glass of wine would be brought to him. He knew his place, and it was part of his professional skill to keep it at all times. Socialising was no part of a *schnorrer's* pursuit. And the guests knew their place too. Apart from the initial welcome, there would be no further conversational exchange. A *schnorrer* after all, was almost a divine messenger, a broker from God as it were, sent for the relief of them all, and his calling would brook no familiarity. Yankel would stand sentry at the door till the festivities were at an end.

Leon struck up an old Chassidic folksong, and Jakob rose to his feet. He was a tall man, of rock-like stature, and as he spread his arms to invite his guests to dance, it was as if he would embrace

12

them all. He clasped Reb Schlomovitch's shoulder and danced him to the centre of the floor. Dov Pinski joined them, and Yosif, unaware of Mendels's hostility, took his rival's ungainly arm, and linked the circle. Then each man took out a white handkerchief and waved it to the rhythm of the song. The women sat around the circle and clapped their hands. That, according to ritual, was the limit of their participation. Sarah, Zena and Sofia stood at the counter, their feet itching for the sawdust. If they'd been alone, with just their parents and the Pinskis, they could have danced too. But the presence of Reb Schlomovitch and, even more forbidding, of Mendel Meisels, chained their feet to the floor. Leon was playing his heart out and the singing grew louder as the dancers were transported in the love-words of the song, and, at its dizzy circling height, Dov Pinski waved his arm in Sofia's direction. 'Come,' he said. 'Join the dancing.'

Suddenly the circle lost its momentum. It was Mendel Meisel who skidded it to a halt. He stood stock still, horrified at Dov Pinski's suggestion, and he made to withdraw, not only from the dancing, but from the tavern itself.

'But it's not every day we have two sons,' Dov protested, looking to Jakob for some support.

Had it been anyone else but Meisels who had taken offence, Jakob would have stood by his friend. But to Meisels he was beholden, and today the presence of Yosif Pinski was a sad reminder of that debt.

'It's not done, Dov,' he said quietly, begging his friend to understand.

But Dov did not know of Jakob's obligation and he was more bewildered than hurt. He shrugged his shoulders and made to get on with the dancing. But now the music had stopped too, and Jakob had rushed to the counter to refill glasses. He sent the girls around with the trays of cakes, anxious to rekindle the light of good cheer that till that moment had filled the tavern.

'Play,' he shouted to Leon, but Leon was already drinking. It took very little wine to render Leon incapable. Jakob looked at his concertina shrivelling on the floor, and he knew that Leon would not play again that day. He looked over the counter and saw that Faivel was still sleeping. He wished he would wake up. Suddenly Jakob Bindel felt very alone.

At the tavern door Yankel had missed nothing of the preceedings, and had overheard Dov Pinski's outrageous suggestion, and in view of that he counted on a little extra from Pinski's pocket.

'Where are the mothers?' Rosa suddenly asked. Jakob went out. He was sad at the turn that the festivities had taken. He hated Meisels. The thought of him brewed an implacable rage in his heart. He wished him dead, and quickly, and he did not even ask God for forgiveness. Meisels's demise would be just and honourable. There were others in the ghetto who were bound to him in misery. The thought even passed through Jakob's mind that he might kill him himself. He shuddered. He went into the back room and gently embraced his wife. Hers was a cleansing love and it soothed his troubled spirit.

'Is Meisels still there?' she whispered.

He nodded.

'Has he said anything?' she asked.

'No.'

'What should he say?' Miriam said.

'Nothing,' Jakob said quickly. No one except himself and Esther knew of Meisels's blackmail. And Faivel. Jakob kept no secrets from his friend. 'Come,' he said. 'The guests are waiting.' He led them back to the tavern.

All the women had gathered together and Jakob led the mothers to their table. Their arrival was an excuse to propose another toast, and Jakob welcomed it, for it might well sweeten the scowl on Mendel's face and soften the bewilderment in Dov Pinski's eye.

'To Esther and Miriam.' Jakob raised his glass.

Reb Schlomovitch's mouth was full of cinnamon cake and he could only raise his glass to his lips. He swallowed quickly, coughing and choking on his mouthful of food. His wife slapped him on the back until he recovered, and when his mouth was empty he gave another toast to cover his embarrassment. He caught sight of little Zena with her tray of cakes. Her name would do as well as another. 'To little Zena,' he shouted, wanting to be part of the festivities once more. Then Dov raised his glass and gave a toast to Reuben and Benjamin, who at that moment were nursing at Miriam's breast. Then there was a pause, while the guests scratched in their minds for someone else yet to be toasted.

Then Mendel Meisels coughed and raised his glass. Jakob trembled.

'To Sofia,' Mendel said.

There was silence. No one echoed his words, for they were all mystified by his choice. Only Jakob understood, and Esther too, and she lowered her head into her lap. For in that toast both of them heard his undisguised proposal of marriage.

Sofia laughed. She thought it ridiculous that such an old and ugly man should toast her, but she thanked him out of kindness and pity.

Mendel took her thanks as a sign that she was not entirely indifferent to his person, and he translated her laughter as an embarrassed girlish giggle. He sat down and took another glass of wine. Let that Yosif feast his eyes on her, and she on him. Sofia was his, or she, with all the Bindel tribe, would be out on the streets, the tavern-door closed firmly behind them. No, he would not be moved by pity. Solomon Zemach, another inn-keeper on the edge of the ghetto, was also beholden. It is true that he already handed over to Meisels a large proportion of his monthly profits, but Zemach also had a daughter. Not as young as Sofia, and certainly not as pretty, but a woman for having children. But as he looked at Sofia, he knew that no one could ever match her, and that he could settle for nothing less. He would even offer to take her without dowry. He raised his glass once again. 'A toast to our future,' he said, addressing the company in general, then slowly edging his glass in Sofia's direction.

At the tavern door, Yankel made a note of the movement. He did not like Mendel Meisels and his hypocritical piety. He was a foreigner to the Meisels type of orthodoxy and, like a foreigner, he read the sub-titles of Meisels's ambivalent toasts. They spelt out nothing but his lechery. If men like Meisels heeded their conscience, men like Yankel would be millionaires. He hoped that the festivities, such as they were, would soon end. He had a wedding that afternoon, a rich wedding, a timber-merchant's daughter, and it was a long and tiring walk across the ghetto to the house of the bride.

'To our future,' the guests were responding to Meisels's toast, and Dov picked up Leon's accordion, and once again music filled the tavern. But there was no longer any dancing.

'Sofia, sing a little,' Dov shouted. He knew she had a good voice. When she had come to Rosa for piano lessons they had discovered it and now he played what he knew was her favourite folk-song. Sofia blushed and lowered her head. Normally she would have sung without any shyness. She was always singing. An audience made little difference to her. But Yosif's presence unnerved her. Yet she couldn't refuse for fear of betraying the secret in her heart. So she went over to Dov's side, turning her back on Yosif, singing to Dov's melody as if she were singing for Dov and Dov alone. When they reached the chorus of the song, Dov urged the rest of the company to join in. But only one voice obliged, a voice as beautiful as Sofia's. Dov caught Rosa's eye and they smiled at each other. At the tavern door, Yankel translated the smile. 'They are made for each other,' it said. Dov and Rosa Pinski, the match-makers.

When the song was finished the company cheered, and Sofia felt obliged to turn to her singing partner and acknowledge him. But her cheeks were on fire, and she dared not reveal to him such ardour. It was he who came to her. 'Thank you,' he said to her back.

Then she had to turn or else appear rude, and make a public issue of that very thing she wished to hide. But now everyone in the tavern knew how Sofia's heart was beating, and Sarah and little Zena didn't even bother to stifle their giggling. And all were happy for them both, except for Jakob and Esther, who knew the perils of such an encounter, and Mendel Meisels, who knew them too.

'We must be on our way,' Reb Schlomovitch suddenly stood up, shamelessly stuffing what was left of the cakes into his large cape pocket.

'For the children,' Mrs Schlomovitch explained, as she did at the end of every function. She had been saying it for so many years that she had overlooked the fact that her children had long since left home and had children of their own. She waited as Reb Schlomovitch extracted a few kopeks from another pocket to pay his exit money to Yankel. Farewells were given all round, and Yankel straightened his back for his first customer of the day.

'I must wake Faivel,' Raisl rasped, and made for the counter. But Jakob barred her way. He had an omen of an impending Meisels confrontation, and he needed his friend about him, even if his presence was a sleeping one. It would be a comfort to him, a silent support.

'Let him sleep,' Jakob said. 'He gets little enough. I'll send him home when he wakes. I'll bring him myself,' he re-assured her.

Nevertheless, Raisl insisted on at least looking at her man. Faivel in a state of sleep was such a rarity that it gave cause for anxiety: that perhaps it was something more than sleep, that Faivel had decided that there was nothing left in his life to keep him awake at all. Raisl knelt down beside him and stroked his forehead. Then she bent over and kissed him on the lips. Faivel did not stir. Jakob thought he saw a faint smile on his lips and he was convinced that behind those still-closed eyes his friend was as wide awake and as tired as ever.

As Raisl left the tavern, Yankel bowed to her, letting her pass without payment. It was a principle of his never to take alms from a woman. Women had other ways of squaring their guilts. Harder ways. Money, as long as you had it, was the easiest thing in the world to give. Women tended to acknowledge their guilt and attempt to do something about it. It took longer, sometimes a lifetime, and its cost was often blood, and always it was tears. Yankel looked to his next customer.

Mendel Meisels was putting on his coat. 'Have another glass,' Jakob said, anxious to delay his departure and the whispered demand that might well accompany it.

'No,' he said. 'I have business, and a little with you too, Bindel,' he said, 'if we could have a private word.' He motioned him to a quiet corner of the tavern.

16

Esther trembled. She watched Jakob as he followed Meisels to the darkened corner. Meisels's back was turned to the room and Esther could only see her husband's face. It was clear that Meisels was doing the talking. At first there was a great deal of it, for Jakob said not a word. As he listened, his face was grave, and his lips parted, wider and wider, as Meisels had his say. Then he spoke a few words and it looked to Esther like a timid and futile protest. She hoped she would never see begging in his eyes. Then he was shaking his head, not with adamant refusal, but as a signal of total disbelief. Suddenly Meisels turned and made for the door. He nodded a polite farewell to Esther, but the smile on his face she knew was not for her, but for himself and his envisaged future.

As Meisels approached the door, his face beaming with confidence, Yankel had the distinct impression that he had it in mind to walk straight past him, so gently he shoved his foot forward and barred the way. Then he put out his gnarled hand. To his surprise, Mendel had his money ready, and big money it was too, as a first downpayment to insure his future. He put a rouble into Yankel's hand, neatly stepped over his foot, and went out into the falling snow.

Esther looked at her husband. His face was grey. At his feet lay Leon, stirring slowly out of his drunken sleep. Jakob squatted and lifted him gently to his feet, leaned him over the counter and pushed a beaker of water into his hand. Then he pulled back Leon's head, and his face wore the beginnings of a smile. But the smile was not for Leon. It was for himself, that he had overcome a desperate desire on seeing Leon prone on the floor to kick him violently into some kind of sensibility, to vent his terrible spleen on anyone near to hand. Yet he had refrained. He looked at Esther and shook his head with despair. Sofia was collecting the glasses and the empty cake-dishes. He dared not catch her eye. He would never tell her. If she were to know the debt he owed, the debt for which he had never volunteered, she would settle it for him. She would not see him lose his livelihood. She was that kind of girl, his Sofia. So she must never know. He smiled at her as she looked across at him. He saw the glow on her face, and her happiness broke his heart.

Dov Pinski took his arm. It was a gesture of good will to show that he held no grudge against his host for his lack of support against Meisels.

'I can explain,' Jakob said, scratching in his mind for some excuse.

'It's not necessary,' Dov said, 'though I'd like to ask a favour of you.'

'Anything,' Jakob smiled, grateful for his friend's trust.

'It's about Yosif,' Dov said. 'You were right. There are more farriers than horses in the ghetto. D'you need help in the tavern? He's a good hard-working boy If only for his meals. That would help. Times are hard.'

Jakob shook his head. It hurt him deeply to refuse his friend, espcially as he had, only that morning, considered taking on another hand. What with his growing family, he could do with another cow, and some chickens perhaps, and even a vegetable plot, all too much for Leon to handle. But Yosif was out of the question. He must not see Sofia again. Perhaps if she married no one else, he might keep Meisels at bay. God forgive me, he whispered as he realised what pain such a suggestion would cause her. He knew that he could not do it. Again, and without any plea for forgiveness, he wished Meisels dead, and quickly, unmourned, unpardoned and a relief to them all.

'I have nothing,' he said to Dov Pinski and his voice was gruff and hostile, and once again Dov was bewildered, not so much at his friend's refusal, but as to its manner.

Jakob put his hand on Dov's shoulder. 'One day I'll explain everything,' he said.

'Is there anything I can do?' Dov said.

'Keep Yosif away from the tavern.'

The two friends stared at each other. 'I can't tell you why,' Jakob said after a while.

'I think he loves her,' Dov whispered.

'And she him,' Jakob said.

Dov moved away. 'Neither of us can do anything to change it,' he said.

Jakob watched and saw the Pinskis take their leave. He stood by and saw Yosif take Sofia's hand in farewell. He spoke words to her and she smiled at him. He was possibly requesting to see her again. Jakob looked on, helpless. He knew that if he had to choose between his livelihood and Sofia's happiness, he would not hesitate. But he had to consider the rest of his family who would be homeless and without means of support. He watched the Pinskis leave the tavern paying their exit dues into Yankel's outstretched hand. Then he himself went to the tavern door.

'You had a good day, I hope?' he asked, pressing money into the beggar's hand.

'Good enough to insure a long life for your children,' Yankel said. Then, like a courtier, he bowed, and stepped backwards to take his leave.

Jakob returned to the counter. The tavern was empty now. The women had gone to their quarters and only Faivel remained, sleeping peacefully on the sawdust floor. Jakob watched him. He remembered the stories they would tell each other as children, impossible stories which stretched one's belief. The story that was even now unfolding itself in his life would not have reached the heights of their boyhood fantasies. For it was as banal and as predictable as any hackneyed fairy-tale. But it was actually happening under Jakob's roof, and its happy ending was in no way guaranteed.

CHAPTER TWO

Jakob Bindel didn't know what to do. Despite the joy that the milk-brothers had brought to the family, a general gloom had settled over the inn-keeper's house, a gloom that was generated by Sofia's despondency. Sofia had always been the mood barometer of the family and her radiance was as infectious as her despair. No word was spoken about its cause, but conjecture centred it around the name of Yosif who had not been seen in the tavern since the celebrations over a month ago. The Pinskis has come of an evening, as was their custom, but always they were alone, and Sofia could have sworn they were avoiding her eye. When Yosif had left her, he had asked permission to visit her again. She gave it him with leaping heart. He would come the next day, he had said. She had dreamt of him that night, and all day she had waited and trembled. And every day since. Now she cried at night. Sarah and Zena could hear her sobs as she clung to the edge of the bed beyond their comfort. She feared he might be ill, but she dared not enquire. For if he were well, then there were others reasons for his absence, and those she dared not think about.

But Jakob thought about them. He thought of little else. Meisels had given him a week to apprise Sofia of his intentions. He proposed marriage within the month. Jakob had managed to get a stay of execution. He had explained to Meisels that it would take time to persuade a woman willingly to take a decision that would have to hold for a lifetime. He pleaded that it would be grossly insensitive to drive her to a marriage-bed so ill-prepared. He hinted that a move made with such unreadiness might well lead to disaster for them all. Mendel had relented. He had given Jakob another month.

There was barely a week to go, and Jakob's mind was in turmoil.

Esther's too. They discussed it endlessly. At night when everyone was in bed, they shut the tavern-door and talked in the darkness. The idea of marriage was unthinkable, but the alternative was even more sinister. It was an unsolvable dilemma that no amount of discussion could resolve. Yet they talked together well into the night, comforting each other with the belief, entirely groundless, that something would happen, some miracle, that would erase the villainy leaving no trace behind. And God is occasionally good.

The following day was a Thursday, market-day, and Jakob settled in his wagon and made for the centre of the town. For the first time in many weeks, no snow fell, and Jakob took it as an omen, a good omen of change. The roads were still icy, and he urged his horse gently on its way. He heard himself singing, a cheerful song of harvesting, and he wondered why such a song had seeped from his troubled heart. Yet he took pleasure from it and the clean biting air that sliced through his beard and whipped his cheeks into a rosy glow. He felt the slippery surface under the wagon wheels and he slowed the horse down, mindful of its fears, and from time to time he interrupted his song to comfort and encourage his horse on its perilous way. As he proceeded thus at a snail's pace, with an unbidden song on his lips, he heard someone call him by name. He looked around. There were many wagons on the road, both to and from the market-place, and it was difficult to decipher whence the sound had come. He heard it again, louder this time, and he stopped his cart. Then he saw Faivel. Faivel running. Running and calling his name. Although Jakob recognised him immediately, he could not equate his old friend with such an athletic pursuit. Faivel was always so tired he could barely amble, which was why he had chosen tailoring for a living, because it was sedentary, and his customers, such as they were, were obliged to come to him.

'Jakob, Jakob,' Faivel kept shouting, though Jakob was waving to him, and he was barely twenty yards from the wagon. Still he called, shouting and laughing at the same time, as if he had pressing news to impart, and tidings of great cheer.

Jakob watched him, and his heart warmed to the recollection of their long and affectionate friendship. For they had grown up together in the ghetto, and each had taken over their fathers' trades. Old Max Bindel had founded the tavern while, a few steps down the road which in those days was no more than a beaten path, old Meir Poliakov, Faivel's father, plied his needle to the already threadbare suits of the poor. Jakob and Faivel had grown up together, and the small terrain between the two family holdings was their childhood playground. They were both born in the same year, 1783, a year that still rumbled with the echoes of American

Independence, and the stirrings of the French Revolution that was soon to come. In their growing years they sniffed at freedom, which in those days, even in Russia, needed no longer to be a dream. The era of Czar Alexander the First started with a small measure of liberation for its Jews. They were allowed into high schools and universities. They could learn Russian, and both Jakob and Faivel had taken advantage of such liberalism. But such freedom was not to last. Their own children knew no alternative to the restricted life of the ghetto, and their fathers would reminisce about their Russianised youth in whispers, with nostalgia, and a certain shame.

At last Faivel reached the wagon, and Jakob helped bundle him inside. And even before he settled himself on the bench, Faivel panted, 'I heard a great story, Jakob, a story that will warm your heart. Let's go to Zemach's tavern.'

'Why Zemach?' Jakob asked.

'Because Zemach,' Faivel teased.

All that Jakob knew of Zemach was that his tavern too remained open despite the law of closure, and that most certainly Zemach must be in thrall to Meisels like himself. This tenuous connection excited him and he was more and more impatient for an explanation from his friend. He stopped the wagon.

'Come on, my friend. What's it all about?' Jakob spoke to him in Russian as a reminder of the bond between them, a bond in which Zemach played no part. 'Zemach can wait,' he said.

'It's a very sad story,' Faivel said, also in Russian in acknowledgement of the bond. 'D'you still want to hear it?'

'You said it was good news,' Jakob said.

'It's an ill wind,' Faivel answered.

'Then I'll listen and affect a sympathetic ear.'

Faivel smiled. 'Yesterday in Toloczka Street,' he said, 'you know, opposite the Pinskis' house. Well, one of the horses in the timber-yard cut loose and careered right down the street. There was no stopping it. It was quite wild, neighing, braying and rearing on its hind legs as if it were going off to war. Then a man stepped out of Mintoff's bank. He was the only one in the street at the time, because everyone else had fled for cover. Well, this horse just made for him, poor devil, crashed him down and stepped on him.' Faivel paused, then lapsed into Yiddish. 'Then the horse lowered its head, and nuzzled the old man's beard. Then it sang out a muted bray, like a mourner's *Kadish*, and turned and went back to the timber-yard at an orderly trot, as if its day's work were done.'

'Who told you all this?'

'Yankel the *schnorrer*. He was on his way to the bank and he was hiding in a doorway.'

'Was the man dead?' Jakob asked. His heart was singing, fluttering with a joy and excitement.

'As good as,' Faivel said. 'One of his legs was crushed. They took him off to hospital.'

'Poor devil,' Jakob said, and slowly he nudged his horse on his way.

There was a silence then between them, broken only by the clip-clopping of the horse's hooves and their distant echo through the cobbled streets.

'Someone we know?' Jakob dared to ask at last.

Then Faivel burst out laughing and took Jakob in his arms and hugged him. 'God is good sometimes,' he said. This last in Russian, for Yiddish was not the tongue of profanity. Russian could deal with all that. Let the language of their oppressors translate their curses, Faivel thought, and above all their illegal joy. 'Mendel Meisels,' he whispered in Jakob's ear.

Jakob stopped the cart. A great weight dropped from his heart. 'Will he die?' he asked softly. 'Will he most definitely die?' This last in impeccable Russian.

'Yankel's already preparing for the funeral,' Faivel said. 'He told me that's one burial he couldn't afford to miss. The crowd and the pickings would be legion. Come, let's get on to Zemach's and bring him the good news. We'll all celebrate together.'

But as they entered the tavern-yard they already heard noises of celebration. When Zemach saw Jakob and Faivel at his door, he was surprised, for they rarely came to drink at his tavern, nor he himself at Bindel's. Then he understood and afforded them both a great welcome, pouring them wine. Then he raised his glass to a nameless toast, and so did the others. Not once during their carousels was Meisels's name mentioned, but the object of their toasts was clear to them all.

It was well after mid-day when Jakob and Faivel left the tavern. By the time they returned to the market-place, everything was sold; then, out of his wine-haze, Jakob saw old Max Blomski crossing the square towards him. Blomski was another member of the *Kahal* and would no doubt have news of his colleague.

'You heard about Meisels, Bindel?' he said, when he reached the cart.

Faivel and Jakob nodded their heads with as much solemnity as they could muster.

'How is he?' Faivel said with manufactured concern.

Blomski shook his head. 'They saved the leg,' he said, 'but he's bleeding inside. He's not expected to last very long. So I'm told. Ach,' he said, moving away, 'we live in terrible times.'

Jakob smiled to himself. Runaway horses didn't make the times

22

terrible. It was riots, expulsions, restrictive laws and taxes which made ghetto life unbearable. Most Jews died from one or other of these causes. That way they died with some measure of distinction. It was just like old Meisels to succumb to such a non-Jewish way of departure. A horse, for God's sake! Unimaginative, Jakob thought, perverse, and an almost illegal way for a good Jew to die. But for Meisels it fitted superbly.

He dropped Faivel off at the square, and made straight for the Pinskis' tenement. Once there, he summoned them to his tavern, that very afternoon, and ordered that they should be sure to bring Yosif with them. Again Dov was bewildered but, by the look on his friend's face, he knew that the invitation was connected with celebration, and all no doubt would be explained.

Esther was waiting for Jakob in the courtyard, anxious because he was so late. But when she saw the empty wagon and smelt the liquor on his breath her anxiety gave way to anger.

'No, I didn't go to market,' he teased her. 'And yes, I have been drinking. Me and Faivel. We've been celebrating.'

'With all our troubles you found something to celebrate?' Esther said.

'All our troubles are over, Esther.' He put his arm round her and walked her into a quiet corner of the tavern. Then he sat her down, and quietly and soberly he told her the news. 'Poor Mendel,' Esther said, and clearly she was sorry for him. She was aware of the great fortune occasioned by Meisels's mischance but she regretted that it was at such cost. 'Well, poor man, he had no family at least.' For her, the lack of mourning kin was a distinct advantage. It took the edge off public sorrow.

'I've told the Pinskis to come,' Jakob said. 'They're bringing Yosif with them. I shall explain everything.'

'Are you sure?' Esther asked. 'Are you sure he will . . .?' She couldn't speak the word. It made her feel like Meisels's murderer.

'Blomski said he can't last much longer.'

'Perhaps we should wait,' Esther said.

'What difference?' Jakob said. 'Today, tomorrow or the next day. We are delivered, and so is Sofia. Where is she?' Jakob asked.

'In the kitchen.'

He got up, acknowledged his few customers, and followed Esther to the back of the house. Sofia was bent over the stove, and even though he couldn't see her face he knew its desolate look. It was not even perplexed. After the first few days of Yosif's absence, she had accepted it as one of rejection, and the bewilderment that had flickered in her face and had given it some semblance of life had vanished, and in its place was a numbed and frozen despair.

He put his arm around her shoulder. 'Sofia,' he said softly. 'Go and put on your best dress. This afternoon, the Pinskis are coming.'

She did not move. 'Why should I change for the Pinskis?' she said to the stove.

'They're bringing Yosif.'

Then she turned, her cheeks aglow, and the tears flowing freely. Jakob embraced her. 'Everything will be all right now,' he said. She rushed from him and out of the room.

Miriam was sitting by the stove, the milk-brothers at her breasts. He went over to them and took them in his arms. 'My little tavern-keepers,' he said.

Before the Pinskis arrived, Jakob took Leon aside and told him the whole story. Leon was to look after the tavern while the Pinskis and the rest of the family were being enlightened in the back room. Jakob was very fond of Leon, most fond perhaps of his timidity and shyness.

When Leon heard the story, he kissed his father-in-law on both cheeks. Although in his ignorance of the blackmail he had not been able to share in Jakob's distress, he was deeply aware of his relief. 'At Sofia's wedding,' he said softly, 'there will be no one to stop us dancing.' He took up his stand behind the counter, proud to be privy to such glad tidings. At the same time he was regretful. He comforted himself with the belief that it was God's will. Although he kept aloof from the social rumour of the ghetto, Leon knew that Mendel's adversity would bring joy to many a heart and that, though everybody would go to his funeral, nobody would mourn him. Perhaps that was God's will too. It was all very confusing.

When the Pinskis arrived, Leon called to Jakob who came out to the tavern to greet them. Yosif still wore his best and only suit. It had been multi-patched since Leon had last seen it, and it seemed to hang very loosely about its model. Yosif looked thin and pale, yet his eyes were feverish bright. They darted around the tavern, and closed for a second when it was clear that Sofia was not there.

'We're all in the kitchen,' Jakob said. 'Come,' and he led them through the tavern to the back of the house. He allowed Yosif to enter the kitchen first, and from the door he viewed the wordless exchange that passed between them. Then he ushered the Pinskis inside and they all sat around the table while Esther drew the samovar.

'I want to tell you a story,' Jakob began. Jakob was by nature and long practice a superb story-teller. He told a tale as if he himself were hearing it for the first time. He would tell it slowly, embroidering each event, sowing seeds of suspense and excitement in every turn of the tale. But he knew that the story which he was about to tell lent itself to no elaboration, to no adventurous detail and, above all, to no moral. He would tell it simply as it was, without judgement, without alibi, and in the simple language of truth. It was quickly over, and its brevity, and the bare bones of its telling, seemed to sharpen its cruel dilemma. His listeners stared at each other, but no one said a word. The silence was finally broken by Sofia.

'Poor Mendel,' she said, which remark called for a silence even longer than the first.

'And poor Sofia, if he would live,' Dov Pinski said at last.

'And poor Yosif,' Yosif muttered. He took Sofia's hand. It was a public gesture for them all to see. The private proposal of marriage had been wordlessly made at their first meeting. Now Yosif was asking her family for Sofia's hand.

'God bless you both,' Esther said. 'We shall all dance at your wedding.'

'We'll drink a toast,' Jakob said, and he went into the tavern to fetch some kvass.

Leon was doing a brisk trade. News of Mendel Meisels's accident had by now spread right across the ghetto, and men had need of a meeting-place to pick over his bones, even though they were as yet unburied. One brought a rumour that Mendel was already dead, but another had later news that spoke of his prolonged and painful dying. None was openly gleeful, but they seemed to be drinking more than was usual in the middle of the day, and a working day at that. They greeted Jakob with the news. He could not pretend he hadn't heard it, but he feigned indifference. He would not go as far as to assume regret. He whispered to Leon that he keep a sharp ear for the lastest bulletin on Meisels's condition. Then, with his bottles, he returned to the kitchen.

'And how will you provide for this beautiful daughter of mine?' Jakob teased Yosif, filling his glass.

'I teach a little. I already have some pupils. I'll get more.'

'One day, this tavern will be partly yours,' Jakob said. 'You should learn its trade. I give you Leon's job, and nobody will be happier than Leon. We'll buy another cow and some chickens. You can start tomorrow.'

And so toasts were given in quiet celebration.

In the circumstances, everyone consciously avoided discussion of practicalities, foremost of which was the date of the wedding. So they whiled the time away with endless toasts to people and things that they invented on the spot: toasts to a good wine harvest and to little Zena's plaits. They drank toasts to the health of everybody, all but that of Mendel Meisels, whose recovery would have nullified them all.

At milking-time, the Pinskis left the tavern, and Jakob took over

25

at the counter. Towards evening Max Blomski arrived, and when Jakob saw him he prayed to God for forgiveness for the joy in his heart, for Blomski was by no means a regular customer, and his arrival could only mean that he had brought news of Meisels's passing. For he looked doleful enough and in need of some sustenance to raise his spirits. He made straight for the counter. Jakob stiffened his knees and steeled his face to sorrow.

'Welcome, Mr Blomski,' he said. 'And how's Mr Meisels?' he said straight away, as anyone would have asked, whether he wished Meisels to live or to die.

'It's bad,' Blomski said. 'He's fighting, the doctors say, fighting like a lion. But there's little hope. We must all pray for him.'

When he's dead I'll pray for him, Jakob thought, I'll pray for his rotten soul, and he wondered why Max Blomski was in such despair. He had never been Meisels's friend. Mendel Meisels had no friends.

Blomski's distress was nothing to do with a possible loss of friendship. But Meisels's death would mean his inevitable promotion on the *Kahal*, and to be chairman of that association was a dubious honour that he could do without. To be a liaison between a vicious government and the people it oppressed was in itself a position of treachery. And even if one started in office with the most honourable intentions, it was very easy to backslide into the bribery, blackmail and corruption that attended the job on all sides. Over the years he had seen it happen to Meisels, though Meisels, aware of all the possible bonuses, had hankered after the job in the first place. Even at that very moment, lying so close to his death, he was availing himself of one of the perks of his position. For he was lying in a private ward in a State hospital, well beyond Odessa's Pale. Blomski could do without such favours. He would sooner take his health-chances in one of the alms-houses of the ghetto. 'We must pray for him,' he said again, and he downed an unaccustomed glass of kvass.

'Are you going to visit him?' Jakob asked. Blomski, as a member of the *Kahal*, would be entitled to a visitor's permit. Jakob needed someone for first-hand information. He could not rely on rumour and hearsay in the tavern. When Meisels died, please God, they would send his body back to the ghetto for burial, and that sight would be the final confirmation of his tavern-holding.

'He's not allowed visitors,' Blomski said. 'Not anybody. One day soon, the black wagon will cross over the bridge, and it will all be over.'

*

The days passed, and no word and certainly no wagon left the big house on the hill. In the tavern, Meisels was still the main topic of conversation, and Jakob was glad of it, for as long as that name was bruited about, his imminent death was possible, and Jakob himself would often promote it when that subject of conversation threatened to flag. But after a month had passed, it became harder to resurrect his name. Old Meisels was taking an unconscionable time to die, and speculation as to the exact timing was too boring a subject for conversation. At about that time, Zemach came to Jakob's tavern, a rare occurrence, and Jakob knew well the purpose of his visit. But between the two of them the name of Meisels was unmentionable. Blackmail, especially on the receiving end, was a private matter, and no matter how innocent the parties, there was always a public aura of attached shame.

'How is business?' Zemach asked, a question that he hoped was tangential to the matter that was pressing on both their hearts.

'It's good,' Jakob said, 'but who knows how long it will go on.' Jakob had expressed the fears of both of them and for the same reasons.

'Who knows, indeed,' Zemach said. He leaned over the counter. 'Come again to my tavern,' he said. 'We should keep in touch.'

'I will,' Jakob said, and intended to do so, for though he and Zemach had little in common the bond between them at that time was stronger than any family link. Meisels's name was now unmentionable. Perhaps in Zemach's tavern its terrible sound could still be aired, screamed aloud perhaps, tossed in the air, or shuffled. They could throw it around the tavern like a dice, taking their chances, raffling the name for death's first prize. It was the silence that Jakob could not bear. For as long as Meisels's was unspoken, there was life in it, and more life to come. To proclaim it aloud was to pass sentence, and Jakob longed for that relief.

'You've taken on a new counter-hand,' Zemach said, nodding in Yosif's direction. Sub-titled, his statement was an expression of admiration for Jakob's optimism. 'I was thinking of expanding myself,' he said. 'But I'll wait. I'll wait and see.'

'This is Yosif,' Jakob said, putting his arm round Yosif's shoulder. 'Zemach keeps the tavern at the edge of town,' he explained.

It crossed his mind to detail the introduction, to confirm Yosif as his prospective son-in-law. He knew that that suspicion was passing through Zemach's mind. Instead he said, 'We must all of us have hope, Zemach. We must go on living as if we shall live forever.'

'Not all of us,' Zemach said. It was the closest either of them had come to the mention of Meisels's name.

27

The rumourless days passed. Yosif had settled happily into his work, and the tavern clientèle increased under his caring service. Sofia kept her domestic place in the back rooms, and they would meet at the mid-day meal and look across the table at one another, and day after day the words multiplied between them. In the evening, Yosif would take supper before going home, and Sofia would be left alone to serve him. The other women were tending the children, and Leon would be in the yard. Jakob took over the tavern at this hour, a slow time for business, a change-over time between work and hard-won leisure. It was during one of these intervals that Jakob was in the tavern playing a game of chess with Faivel. There were no customers and the game was slow. It was Faivel's move. His chin rested on a clenched fist, and his eyes, never wide-awake, were almost closed. He was debating his next more, or so Jakob thought. Until he spoke.

'Any news?' he said.

Jakob shook his head. 'They say he's fighting like a lion.'

'To retain his power,' Faivel said. 'That's the only reason people linger against all laws of nature. People don't fight for love, not when they're dying, for they know that loving and dying is often the same, and they yield gladly to Death's embrace. Those who are monsters in life are monsters in Death too. A curse on him,' he shouted. 'I'll drink to his death,' he said, raising his glass, 'and to hell with the consequences.'

It was at this moment that a stranger appeared at the tavern door. He was dressed in soldier's uniform, of low rank. Even so, his so-Russian presence in the tavern inspired fear, and he leaned his young shoulder against the door with the arrogance of one who owned the place.

'Jakob Bindel?' he shouted with disdain.

Jakob trembled.

'Which one of you is Bindel?'

Jakob stood up and, for his support, so did Faivel, but his caring gesture only led to confusion.

'You can't both be Jakob Bindel.' The soldier did not conceal his temper, whereupon Faivel sat down, inadvertently knocking over the chess-board.

'You were in check,' he mumbled to Jakob, though lesser check, he thought, than his friend might be in now.

'I have a summons for you,' the soldier said. 'From the hospital. Meisels. Mendel Meisels. A Jew. He orders you to come. Here is your pass.'

He handed over a yellow star, the obligatory badge for those few Jews who were permitted to travel outside the ghetto. 'It is valid only for today,' the soldier went on. 'You should go at once.'

He pinned the badge on Jakob's blouse. 'I'll have a kvass before I go,' he said.

When he had gone, Faivel said, 'I'll come as far as the river with you.'

Jakob took off his badge and went into the back room to ask Yosif to take over the counter. He said he had urgent business in the town. His hospital visit would remain a secret and, if necessary, though Jakob trembled at the thought, its outcome as well. He returned to the tavern, replaced the badge and covered it with his coat, then he and Faivel climbed onto the wagon.

The journey was silent.

'D'you want me to wait for you?' Faivel asked, after a while.

'I may be some time,' Jakob said, though he knew that to offer his forgiveness to Meisels, or to accept his warning, would take roughly about the same time, and brief it would be at that. 'Come to the tavern later,' he said. 'Who knows, we may have cause for celebration.'

He said it with little conviction.

At the bridge, Faivel stepped down from the wagon, and stood waiting as Jakob crossed over. At the end of the bridge he saw the sentry coming out of his box, and he watched Jakob get down from his cart, open his coat, and reveal his passport to beyond the Pale. Then he mounted again and drove into the distance. Faivel waited until the wagon was out of sight. Then he made his way home.

It was many years since Jakob had visited this now-forbidden quarter of Odessa. When he was a child, there was no statutory law regarding the limits of the Pale, and the whole city was open to Jews and non-Jews alike. He had always lived where the ghetto was now confined, but often as boys he and Faivel would wander up the hill to view the harbour from the highest point in the city. Then they would run to the dock-side, and watch the timber-laden boats put out to sea, and wish themselves aboard. As he drove his wagon up the hill Jakob thought of those days, and how much less restriction had nudged at their lives. There was freedom too, in youth itself, whatever its location, or whenever its timing. Then he thought of his Sofia and her Yosif whose youth and happiness were immune to all restraint.

He remembered that the hospital was in a field at the top of the rise, but as the horse trudged up-hill he could see no greenery, and as he came closer to the top he realised that the field was no more. The building that in his youth had been the hospital had swollen over the grass. There was not even a tree on its perimeter to mark the spot of Jakob's boyhood. The sight depressed him profoundly. He hitched his wagon where a turnstile used to stand and recalled how he and Faivel would race towards it in an effort to vault it first.

He walked along, looking for an entrance, but he noticed that there were many doors, and none of them were marked in any way. He was wary of asking directions. His Russian was heavy with Yiddish accent, and he would have to display his star to prove his legality. Many people passed him by without a glance. He listened to their Russian talk and, though he loved the language and understood each word, though he trod the cobbles of his boyhood, he felt a stranger there, and fearful, as if surrounded by enemies. He wanted very much to be back in his tavern, finishing his game of chess. Esther would wonder what urgent business had taken him away and, though she would never ask, she would guess that it was on Meisels's behalf, for she knew that as the only urgency in his life. He prayed that he'd have good news for her on his return.

He opened one of the doors and found himself in a large public room, where many bare-footed men shuffled about aimlessly. They were dressed in grey hospital gowns, and were clearly patients; Jakob wondered why they were not in bed. They looked fit enough, he thought. Many of them were of good colour, but a pall of hopelessness hung about the room, as if it were more a prison than a hospital ward. But for some reason, he felt suddenly more free in this place than he had since leaving the ghetto. He felt he could talk to these men without shame for his broken Russian, without fear of his yellow star.

'Take your coat off, brother,' one of them called over to him. 'Make yourself at home.'

Jakob opened his coat and the bright sun of his faith was plain for all to see. They stared at him. Then one of them spoke.

'Welcome,' he said, 'and doubly welcome. You are our first Yid.'

Jakob was encouraged by his smile. 'Who are you?' he dared to ask. 'What is this place?'

'We are madmen,' a voice said from the corner of the room, 'This is a madhouse, and we are detained at the Czar's pleasure.'

Jakob was puzzled. He had seen mad people. There were plenty in the ghetto shuffling wild in the streets or lurching along the cobble-stones, mumbling their magic words, cleansing the polluted air with their beautiful dreams. They were incoherent, untouchable, almost holy. Not like these men at all.

'What's mad about you?' he asked.

'We have spoken against the Czar,' one of them said.

'But people go to prison for that,' Jakob said. 'They're called criminals, not madmen.'

'But our Czar is generous,' another man said. 'He thinks that anyone who is opposed to his office must, by nature, be a lunatic and should be treated as such. He sincerely believes that. They give us medicines to love the Czar with all our hearts and to have no other god.'

Jakob permitted himself a small smile. 'Are you getting better?' he asked.

'We shall die of our disease,' one of them said, 'and in this very place, till the end of our days.'

'But the door's open. You could walk away,' Jakob said.

'There's ice on the ground, and they have taken away our shoes. And there are dogs outside who are practised in our smell. But worst of all,' he added, 'we're used to it here.'

Jakob was overcome with depression. He wanted very much to be out of the room, but he felt that leaving them would seem like betrayal. In many ways he was one of them himself. He hated the Czar with all his heart, and so did all those who lived in the ghetto. But it was a private unpublished hate. It had to be. The Jews were the official victims. They were the legal scapegoat. They kept their mouths shut, as was befitting to their status. They survived only because they knew their place.

'What are you doing beyond the Pale?' the man asked.

'I was summoned by a patient to make a visit,' Jakob said. 'I thought this was the hospital.'

'It is,' the man said. 'But this is the asylum. All the low buildings are part of the asylum. In Russia, there are many lunatics,' he said, 'who, elsewhere in the world, would be treating the insane.' He returned to his seat in the corner of the room.

Jakob followed him. He wanted to be part of that circle of men. He felt them as brothers. Yet as he stood there among them, he felt himself a stranger. He was ashamed of his own rude health amidst their frailty, ashamed of his sheer height towering over their shrunken despair. He saw the grey stubble of their shaven heads and he was offended by his own protection of thick black hair. But above all else it was his boots that shamed him, that passport to the small freedom that he still owned, despite the confines of the Pale and the prison of his yellow star. He spread out his arms to embrace them.

'What can I do for you?' he pleaded.

Then they shrunk away from him. There was nothing he could do for them, and his concern disturbed them. His loving and his caring reminded them of those loves and cares they had left behind, and stirred those longings that over the years had been numbed in their hearts. Such feelings could find no accommodation in this place.

'The hospital is the old high building, the brown brick one, at the end of the road,' one of the men said. 'Someone there will tell you where to go.'

They were giving him permission to leave, yet Jakob was loathe to go. Despite the fearful visit he must make to Meisels, once he left this room he was going into freedom, at least a freedom of a kind. Eventually he would join his family, eat at his own table, quarrel and love with his kin. He wanted to know if these men had any visitors, if indeed their familes knew where they were. He wanted to offer them favours, some means of communication with the outside world, but he knew that he would be putting himself in jeopardy; for despite his yellow star he was still beyond the Pale, a Jew who, with a little patient investigation would be found in illegal livelihood. Then he remembered Meisels and the unknown purpose of his visit. He had troubles enough of his own. Yet he didn't know how to leave these men. 'Goodbye,' was too final. It was a confirmation of their life-sentence. 'I'll come again,' was impossible, because a visit to these renegades would be no ground for a yellow-star permit. Perhaps he should, after all, offer to do something for them on the outside, no matter what risk there might be to himself. He opened his mouth to speak.

'You can do nothing for us,' one of the men said, as if reading his thoughts and his hesitation. 'You and I are the same, brother,' he said. 'We receive the same kind of treatment, but on different sides of the Pale.'

Jakob went towards him and embraced him. There were tears in his eyes. His fears of the Meisels' visit ebbed quickly away; his own troubles were paltry and insignificant, compared with the life-long deprivation of these men. He turned away, sadly, buttoning his coat as he went, and he left the room without looking behind him.

He went into the street again, and passed the row of single-storeyed huts. He shivered. The thought crossed his mind not to visit Meisels at all. Meisels was as much the enemy to those men as the Czar himself. Let him rot in his dying, he thought, or, at worst, stew in his wretched recovery. But he needed Meisels to stamp his pass, as proof that the purpose of his permit had been fulfilled, else he would have trouble with the sentry on the bridge. He trudged along unable to wipe from his eye the misted vision of that loose circle of men. He felt still on his shoulder the print of their touch. Brothers, he thought, as brother to me as I am to Faivel, as Benjamin is to Reuben, as all men are to each other in the terrain of love. Meisels was a stranger to that land. He would grant him nothing, Jakob decided, not even a dying wish, and he hastened his step, anxious to get the visit over and done with it. Alive or dead, Meisels could not trouble him any more.

At the desk, he was directed to the third floor, where he was to ask directions once again. By the time he reached Meisels's ward, he was feverish with hate and indignation. He strode through the door. There were many beds in the ward, but he trusted his nose to sniff out the plague he was seeking. He stopped short, however, as he saw Meisels coming towards him, limping a little, but otherwise with the air of one in perfectly good health. Jakob made no attempt to hide his disappointment.

'You're better, I see,' he said coldly. 'You sent for me.'

'My recovery does not please you, I see. Come, sit down. This won't take long.'

Jakob followed him to a table at the end of the ward. They sat opposite each other, and Meisels got down to business straight away.

'I shall be leaving hospital in two weeks,' he announced, as if it were an order to lay the red carpet in the ghetto. 'You will make arrangments for the wedding. I have settled money on your daughter and she will want for nothing. On Sunday, in two weeks, I shall celebrate with my bride at your tavern. You will invite all the members of the *Kahal*, and we shall dance through the night. The men, that is.'

Jakob stared at him vacantly.

'D'you hear me?' Meisels whispered.

'Yes, of course,' Jakob said. He did indeed hear him, his voice, that is, and the sounds of his words, but he had long ceased listening. He got up to leave. 'I shall put everything in order,' he said. 'The wedding will take place on Sunday in two weeks.' And he meant it, with all his heart. On Sunday, in two weeks, Sofia would marry Yosif. They shook hands on what Meisels believed was their trading.

'I'm glad you're better,' Jakob said. He no longer minded if Meisels lived for ever, for never again would he figure in his life or livelihood.

He hurried out of the ward and down the steps and out of the hospital. His wagon was at the far end of the complex and he almost ran towards it, slowing down when he reached the low-slung huts. 'Brothers,' he whispered, and the word halted his step. He stood there for a while, and muttered a short, and, he knew, futile prayer for their well-being. Then he mounted his wagon and drove towards the bridge. He handed over his badge and his pass to the sentry. He felt it as an act of cleansing. Now he could go home, to his own kind. The whole of his life lay on the far side of the bridge. All but that small loose circle of men.

Half way across the bridge, he caught sight of a lone figure on the other side; on approaching, he deciphered Faivel, leaning his back on the iron rail. Jakob's heart was joyful. He would tell Faivel everything. And only Faivel. To Esther and the rest of the family, he would say nothing. They did not know that he had been summoned to the hospital. And Faivel would tell no one. They could all go on assuming that Meisels was nearing the end of his rotten days.

Faivel climbed onto the cart. 'I'm glad to see you,' Jakob said, and they drove for a while in silence. 'He lives still?' Faivel asked after a while.

But Jakob had forgotten all about Meisels. He wanted to tell Faivel about his brothers in the circle.

'I saw some men,' Jakob said. "D'you remember that field we used to play in. That turnstile? It's all gone now. All gone. The hospital has spread over the whole field. It's an asylum. I went into it by mistake.'

'Where we used to make up stories?' Faivel asked. 'All those blood-curdling tales? *That* field?'

Jakob nodded. 'They built a mad-house on our dreams,' he said, 'and inside I heard the most terrible story of all.'

Faivel recalled the field and the game they always used to play. He was usually the winner. He would fly into fantasies of horror, leaving Jakob incredulous at his side. 'I'm listening,' he said. He pulled the blanket more firmly across his knees. It was beginning to snow again.

'There are men who are called lunatics,' Jakob said. 'They don't have abnormal illusions; they don't think they're God or Jesus. They're not deeply depressed or jumping-crazy, and they don't scream or mumble.' Jakob tabled the categories of lunatic varieties he had encountered in his life. 'None of those,' he said.

'What makes them mad, then?'

'They're against the Czar,' Jakob said simply.

'That makes them mad?' Faivel laughed aloud.

'They actually get medicine for it,' Jakob said.

'God in heaven,' Faivel said after a while. 'Who in the world is sane?'

It was getting dark and there were few people on the streets.

'It's your turn for a story,' Jakob said.

Faivel was silent. Even he had no tale to match Jakob's vision of horror. He kept thinking of that distant, cowslip-carpeted field on which their boyhood dreams had spawned the most fearful nightmare of them all. He pulled the blanket over his shoulders. Although it had stopped snowing, he was feeling bitterly cold. He shivered as if his nerve-ends had been buried in snow. He shut his eyes, though not for sleep, but to raze that charnel-house to the ground, and sniff once again those innocent childhood lawns.

They were within a few yards of Faivel's dwelling, and then he spoke again. 'And the villain lives still?' he shouted. He, like his friend, now understood that one villain was very like another, and that between the Czar and Meisels, in their respective areas of power, there was very little to choose. Jakob stopped the cart.

'Not only does he live,' he said, 'he is better. He is walking about. In two weeks, he will be back amongst us.'

'What did he want from you?'

'He ordered me to arrange his wedding with my Sofia. On Sunday, in two weeks.'

'What will you do?' Faivel asked.

'I shall do as he asks,' Jakob said. 'I shall arrange a wedding on that exact day. And in my tavern. But Yosif will be the groom.'

Faivel clutched at his friend's arm. 'And after the wedding?' he said.

'We'll find something. We can all work. Each one of us.'

'But where will you live?'

Jakob shrugged.

'It will be hard on all of you,' Faivel said.

'D'you think I don't know?' Jakob shouted at him. 'D'you think I haven't thought of all that? But I think of Sofia's life too, and of those men I just saw on our field. We have to live with some kind of truth, Faivel,' he pleaded.

'I'll help you all I can,' Faivel said.

Jakob urged the horse forward once more, and stopped the wagon at Faivel's home. 'Not a word to anyone, Faivel,' he said. 'Not a word about the hospital visit. We don't know how Meisels is. We assume he is still in the business of dying.'

Faivel nodded and folded the blanket away. 'I'll come later and finish that game,' he said.

Jakob watched him into his house. 'Thank you for waiting,' he shouted after him.

*

It was the Thursday before the wedding was due to take place. And, as was his custom, Jakob was driving the wagon towards the market-place. The horse moved slowly, unurged by his master, who was in deep contemplation. By now, it was possible that Meisels had had rumour of the coming event that would secure his displacement. Jakob had heard from an excited Blomski that his chairman was due to return that very day. He dreaded the evening and a possible confrontation. But he had no doubt in his heart that he would brazen it out and take the consequences. Then he fell to thinking about what those may be, and as he tried to put such thoughts from his mind he heard someone call his name. He remembered how Faivel had called to him one market-day not so long ago and had brought him those glad tidings that had turned out to be not so glad after all. He looked round expectantly, and there, to his joy, was Faivel yet again, in the middle of a work-day week, bursting at his already risky seams with news of great import. And by the beaming joy on his face, news that would cheer them all.

'Jakob, Jakob,' he shouted, when still some distance from the cart. 'Have you heard the news? We must go at once to Zemach's tavern.'

Meisels is dead, once and for all, Jakob sang to himself. He hoped that Faivel in his excitement would not forget himself and scream the good news abroad, and thus publicise their joy.

'Get in first, Faivel,' he shouted. As he waited for his friend, the thought crossed his mind that Meisels's funeral would coincide with the wedding. There was a certain poetic justice in that, he thought, though it would pose a dilemma for poor old Yankel who, skilled in his profession as he was, could not hope to stretch his hand between graveyard and tavern.

He helped Faivel up onto the cart and, when he'd settled down, Jakob took up the reins once more.

'No. Don't let's move,' Faivel said. 'This is important. I want you to listen to every word.' And Faivel came straight to the point. 'The ukase regarding Jews and inn-keepers has been rescinded. As of today. Our Czar, God rot and bless him, is full of whims.' He grasped Jakob's shoulder. 'You're free, my friend,' he said.

'Where did you hear it?' Jakob asked, unbelieving. 'Who told you?'

'Blomski. It's written in their bulletin. He showed me. Signed by Nicholas himself. To Zemach's,' he shouted.

And so once again they made for the short cut through the woods singing their shameless joy to the trees.

'Old Meisels should live forever,' Jakob sang.

'For ever and ever,' Faivel chorused. 'And he should lose all his teeth, except one, so that occasionally he can still have toothache.'

'What a wedding we shall have,' Jakob said.

And so once again Jakob missed the market, and once more without fear of Esther's rebuke, for this time the news was good and would always be good and its value was irrevocable.

In the few days that remained before the wedding, Jakob kept himself indoors. He did not wish to risk an encounter with Meisels. In many ways he pitied him, and it was more for Meisels's sake than his own that he avoided a chance meeting. None of the customers in the tavern made mention of his return, or reported sight of him in the streets, so Meisels too was probably keeping himself indoors, stewing in a fury that Jakob dared not imagine.

*

The wedding took place in the ghetto's oldest and smallest synagogue. The Bindels did not want to advertise their triumph, and they did their best to call but small attention to their celebrations. But once the ceremony was over, and the tavern-doors closed on the wedding-guests, the festivities were loud, long and without scruple.

The long table in the tavern was laid out with meats and savouries. Faivel's Raisl, who was something of an expert in flower-arrangement, had gathered a wide variety of grasses that grew in the fields behind the tavern and had arranged them as harvest offerings. The guests crowded inside. Apart from Jakob's close friends, there were officials of the community, entitled by their standing to be invited to all joyful occasions and, though Jakob knew some of them only slightly, he accorded them an equal welcome. By this token, most of the members of the *Kahal* were present but for their Chairman, whose absence was discreetly unobserved. The thought of Meisels soured Jakob's joy. He thought of him, crouched over his stove, brooding and seething in his misfortune. He hoped some time would pass before he would see him again. In the corner he noticed Zemach, his wife and daughter at his side. He had been happy to invite Zemach to his celebrations. Between them, over the last few weeks, there had grown a firm bond based on their common hopes and curses. He went over to them and urged them into his circle of friends. Some of these had brought their hobby-instruments, and the balalaikas outnumbered the accordions. Leon gave them all his cue and random and partnerless dancing started on the floor. Even Miriam rose from her accustomed nursing position, and waltzed the milk-brothers around the floor while they slept, the two of them, their faces turned into the darkness of her flesh. And then Yankel arrived, sealing with his presence at the tavern-door, the legitimacy of the occasion. When Jakob saw him he felt relieved. He called for little Zena, and sent her with a plate of food and a beaker of wine to the tavern-door. Yankel acknowledged it, and raised his beaker to his host. The host/beggar exchange was now complete, and Yankel would keep his place at the door.

For many hours they feasted and wined and danced, and all at an unhurried pace. The Bindels were celebrating more than a mere wedding, and though none of the other guests, apart from Faivel and Zemach, suspected that there might be other cause for celebration, the Bindels' exaggerated joy was infectious, and Sofia and Yosif's wedding-feast would be recalled in the ghetto for many years to come. And not simply for its sheer enjoyment. For one other event was to make it memorable.

Dusk was falling. The music was soft and soothing, and the

guests spoke almost in whispers. They had returned to their seats to drink the various toasts of the day. The honour of the first toast had been given to Faivel, who was to propose the health of the bride and groom. He stood up and raised his glass. As he opened his mouth to speak, Jakob noticed that his friend turned suddenly pale. His wide astonished eyes were on the tavern-door, and Jakob, together with the rest of the party, followed his gaze.

And there, in the true tradition of any common-or-garden fairy-tale, the villain of the piece stood blazing on the threshold, screaming his revenge. Mendel Meisels's large ungainly frame filled the tavern-door, and poor and patient Yankel was forced inside the tavern, his right and proper place usurped. It was this displacement that disturbed Jakob even more than Meisels's sudden appearance, for it was as if, in Yankel's eviction, the whole natural order had been destroyed. Faivel put down his glass and stared at the late arrival, and so did all the others, and all were afraid, for his sudden raging presence was clearly uninvited, and it seemed from the fire in his eyes that he had come to curse them all.

'You will pay, Jakob Bindel,' he shouted. 'Mendel Meisels will bide his time, but the day will come when he will surely destroy you.' Then he turned, and was quickly gone.

And in the ensuing silence, the milk-brothers stirred and woke together, and together they started screaming.

CHAPTER THREE

Mendel Meisels waited. As he had promised them, he bided his time. He was a patient man, which was just as well, for he had to wait for ten long years before an opportunity presented itself for his revenge.

Much had happened in that time. Sarah and little Zena had married, and both had brought their husbands to the tavern. Behind the back of the inn, as well as the back of the official authority, Victor and Yuri had planted a vegetable garden whose produce fed the increased family and reaped a modest profit in the Thursday market. Between them they had five daughters. Sofia and Yosif had contributed two children to the Bindel table, daughters too. It was as if the birth of the milk-brothers had sapped all trace of male inheritance. The tavern was still the central meeting place of the ghetto and rang with the laughter of a new generation, despite the fact that in those days there was little enough to laugh about. The Czar's attitude had hardened towards the Jews. The Pale of Settlement was narrowed down, and expulsions from towns and villages continued at a greater pace. The Czar's intention was to make the holy earth of Russia Jew-free. He was still of the opinion that wholesale baptism could purify the Russian soil. To 'russianise' the Jew, to wean him from his Talmud and his Jewish gaberdine, were steps in that direction. But above all, to make a man of him. And to do that there was only one course of action. To conscript him into the Russian army.

Until 1827, the Russian Jew had been exempt from military service and was obliged to pay heavy taxes in lieu. The 1827 ukase annulled these taxes, and in their stead gave Jews the dubious honour of serving under their tormentor's flag. Jewish conscription was thorough and brutal. Unlike Russian soldiers, Jews were required to serve for twenty-five years, and again, unlike their Russian counterparts, they were recruited at the age of twelve. This last clause in the law was a veiled permit for child-murder.

It was the duty of the *Kahal* to provide the conscripts, or 'kantonisty', as they were called, on the basis of ten for every thousand of the Jewish population. In the Odessa ghetto, grossly overcrowded as a result of village expulsions, and overburdened with the very young and the very old, the toll was especially punitive. And it put a burden on the *Kahal* too, for if it did not fulfil its quota, its members were liable to fines or conscription. On the other hand, it was a devil-given opportunity for the extortion of bribes, and few members of the *Kahal* would forgo such gifts. So, unsurprisingly, it was the poor who had to pay the terrible price. They would often run away in fear and hide in the forests and the *Kahals* would employ 'khapers', or huntsmen, Jews themselves, to track them down. Thus a man like Mendel Meisels was kept very busy, filling his quotas and lining his pockets at the same time. Over the years, since the passing of the conscription law, Meisels had made his pile. But his appetite for revenge on Jakob Bindel did not cool, and he willed himself to live until such revenge were possible. The conscription law might well provide him with the key. Every week in the synagogue at the Sabbath services, he had seen the Bindel tribe, and noted how the milk-brothers were loved and cosseted on all sides. They were now ten years old, and Mendel had sworn, in the middle of the Sabbath prayer, and on that consecrated ground, that they would not live to see their barmitzvah.

*

It was the week before Passover, and Meisels's quota was almost due. He was sitting in the *Kahal* office, drawing up his conscript list, when a woman, black-shawled and weeping, stumbled into his room. Mendel was irritated. He was too busy for visitors, especially the poor, which this one surely was, with their endless complaints and pleadings. He had work to do. He had to copy out in a fair hand the full quota of conscripts which, after much manoeuvring, he had managed to assemble. But the woman had already sat down on the chair in front of him, and deposited a large bag on his desk.

'It's about my sons,' she blurted out. 'They're all I have. You're sending them to the army. I've come to beg you, honoured Mr Meisels. There,' she pointed to the bag. 'Look inside. It's all I have.'

Meisels looked at the leather hold-all with disdain. It was shabby enough, and possibly matched the paucity of its contents. He wondered whether it was worth his while even to bother opening it and looking inside. The woman must have read his thoughts, for she leaned over and opened the clasp herself, spilling the contents of the bag onto his desk. Four small bundles of rouble notes.

Meisels looked at them with contempt. 'You value your sons lightly,' he said.

'It's my life's savings,' the woman answered. Then she began to cry. She could not have known Meisels or have heard of his soul of steel. For tears could not move him. Indeed he found them a gross irritation. Yet the idea of holding someone in his power, especially a defenceless woman, was irresistible.

'What is your husband's living?' he said.

'He was a tailor. He's dead these ten years.'

'And what do you do for a livelihood?'

'I sew, I bake, I do people's washing. Anything in the house,' she pleaded.

Now it seemed to Meisels that she had something more interesting to offer than her miserable savings. A bribe paid in terms of service was always more exciting than one paid in simple coinage. It was more oppressive, more confining. 'Stand up,' he said to her. 'Let me look at you.'

The woman rose from her chair, trembling. She stood in front of him, straightening her body, holding her head high, even offering him a timid smile, for instinctively she knew that, whatever test she had to pass, it had to do with man's expectation.

Meisels looked her over. 'Take off your cape,' he said, enjoying his command and her obedience, the nature of which exchange was entirely new to him.

The woman dropped her cape from her shoulders, letting it slide to the floor. It was an instinctive and totally unconscious gesture of

40

seduction. But she wanted to please him, for his pleasure might benefit her sons.

'Turn round,' Meisels said. 'Turn slowly.' And when she obeyed, Meisels trembled with a specific sense of authority that he had never experienced before. He eyed her carefully. The woman was clearly beyond child-bearing, but she still had a good thigh on her.

'You will come to me every day,' he said, 'and serve me as housekeeper.'

'And my sons?'

'I shall cross them off my list,' he said.

The woman got down on her knees and crawled towards him. 'You have my life-long gratitude, Sir,' she said.

He trembled at the 'Sir'. Life had great joy in store for him. 'What's your name, woman?' he said, pocketing her life's savings.

'Lascevitch,' she said. 'Rachel Lascevitch.' She was still kneeling at his feet. She would stay there until his questions were over.

'And your sons?'

'Judah and Lev Lascevitch,' she said to his boots.

Meisels scanned his list until he found their names. 'Look,' he said.

She peered over the top of his desk, and saw how his finger-nail circled her sons' names. Then he took a pen and deleted them.

'Go home,' he said, 'and sleep in peace. Your sons are safe. As long as you serve me,' he added. 'You will start early tomorrow, and make my house fit for the Passover.'

The woman rose and pulled her cape around her. He handed her the empty leather bag.

'I shall never forget you,' she said, making her way towards the door. 'I shall speak your name in my prayers every night.'

Rachel Lascevitch would thus join a thousand other voices in the Odessa ghetto, but not to beg for God's blessings on Mendel Meisels, but His curses, loud and long, for having robbed them of their sons and their livelihoods.

When the woman had gone, Meisels laid his list out before him, and counted the names. Now with the loss of the Lascevitch boys he needed two more to complete his quota. Once again he went through his second list of eligible recruits, but he had already exhausted them either by blackmail or bribery. He was in something of a quandary. He had heard that in some cities of the Pale, the *Kahals* were kidnapping eight and nine-year-olds in a desperate bid to fill their quotas. Or sometimes, he had heard, they didn't even bother to kidnap them. They would forge a new date of birth on their papers, and recruit them legally. They were doing it in Vilna, Vitebsk and Poldava. He had heard it on the

Kahal grapevine. What was so special about the Odessa *Kahal* that it could not avail itself of the same manoeuvre?

Mendel Meisels had no problem with the selection of the two quota-fillers. Their names had been on his unforgiving lips for ten whole years. Their destruction had been in his nightly prayers. God had lent him His ear, and was now granting him a means for their annihilation. It paid to be a religious man, Mendel thought. He took out a clean sheet of official paper and dipped a new nib in the inkwell. And in his neatest and most official hand, he wrote, 'For the attention of the Recruiting Officer.' He could as well have donned a black cap and pronounced the death-sentence on them all. Dipping his pen once more, and licking his lips, he headed his list with the milk-brothers' names. Then he put down his pen. He would complete the list in the morning. That day, he considered, he had done more than a day's work. He had brought to fruition the result of ten years' travail, of carefully keeping his wound green. A decade of unrelenting rancour had at last come to an end. He opened the desk-drawer and took out a silver phial of kvass. He put it to his lips and downed it in one gulp. In the after-haze of the liquor, he pictured Jakob Bindel's face as the recruiting-officer presented the summons at the tavern-door. And that rewarding vision he kept in his eye for the rest of the day, and throughout his dreamful night, until it was erased by the sight of Rachel Lascevitch, eager and submissive, as she placed his waking glass of lemon-tea on his bedside table. He sat up in bed and considered himself a man truly blessed.

*

It was the Eve of Passover. The ghetto streets were deserted, and candle-light flickered from every window. The *Seder* service was about to begin, that feast that heralds the eight days of the Passover. Every household in the ghetto was celebrating, as they did every year, remembering with prayers and symbols the expulsion of the Jews from Egypt and their forty years' wanderings in the wilderness.

The Bindels were holding their *Seder* in the tavern, a room large enough to accommodate their family and friends. Miriam and Leon sat at the end of the table. The milk-brothers were seated in pride of place at the head of the table, Jakob and Esther beside them, together with the Pinskis and Faivel and Raisl, whose children had long left home. Esther lit the candles and said the blessings, and it was in order for the ceremony to begin. The tavern door was firmly closed. After the meal it would be opened, as would all the doors of the ghetto in order to allow the entrance of Elijah, that prophet of redemption, whose full cup of wine shivered on the table. Jakob rose to sing the first blessing of sanctification, and all those around the table drank the first of the four glasses of wine. It was time for the four questions, traditionally asked by the youngest member at the table. This year, the duty fell to Shoshannah, Sofia's youngest, who, though she could not read, had learned them by rote. Sofia proudly lifted her onto her chair. Shoshannah needed little prompting. For many days before, she had wandered about the house reciting the questions aloud. She had learned them in Hebrew, without understanding a single word. Her cheeks were flushed with excitement. She took a deep breath as she had been taught to do, and the first question was posed loud and clear.

'Why is this night different from all other nights?' she said.

And as soon as the question was out, there was a loud banging on the tavern door, as if the caller, whoever it was, had brought the answer.

And answer it was of a kind, of an updated history, from a minion of another Pharaoh, of an Egypt which was now called Czarist Russia.

Jakob paled. He knew that whatever was behind that door on such a holy night could only augur ill. Faivel too feared the worst, and so did Dov Pinski and Leon, and all three rose to support Jakob in his fear. Shoshannah burst into tears, her long-rehearsed recital so rudely interrupted. The milk-brothers stretched out their hands to each other, and clasped them. And they too rose, so that only the women were left seated.

'We must be calm,' Jakob whispered.

There was more banging at the door. 'Open up,' a voice cried. Jakob waited for some identification, though he knew from the authoritative and self-assured tone that it belonged to an official, and a hostile one at that. He turned and opened the tavern-door.

He opened it wide, as if he had nothing to hide, displaying the *Seder* table in all its quiet solemnity, hoping to indicate to the caller the peace he had shattered. But beneath his apparent calm Jakob was trembling, for he recognised on the intruder that hated uniform of the recruiting officer. And in the same moment he confirmed to himself that he and Leon were beyond recruiting age. Victor and Yuri carried forged papers, and were still officially registered in the village from which they had fled. That left only the milk-brothers, who, even according to that terrible law, were still minors. Over the years since the enforcement of the law, he had not unduly worried about the milk-brothers. He was rich enough to buy their exemption. But he had not reckoned with Meisels. Even Meisels, he considered, could not be that cruel. But Meisels must have lied about their age. For what other reason

43

could this officer be standing at his door? He pictured the two children swamped in army greatcoats. 'No, no,' he pleaded.

The officer handed him a document with the Czar's red seal emblazoned across the vellum. The summons was penned in Russian, and sub-titled in Yiddish in Meisels's gleeful hand. It ordered the appearance of Reuben Wolf and Benjamin Bindel at the conscription centre at eight o'clock the following morning.

'But it's a Holy Day,' Jakob mumbled, knowing how irrelevant was such a plea.

'A *Jewish* Holy Day,' the officer almost spat. 'Here we abide by Christian law.'

Jakob re-read the summons, and the false date of birth. 'But they're only ten,' he pleaded.

The officer looked at the document. 'Not according to the *Kahal*.' he said. '*Your* people. Your honest leaders.' Then he bent his mouth to Jakob's ear. 'Are they really only ten?' he whispered. His voice was gentle, as if he too were a father, and from it Jakob gleaned a measure of hope.

'I swear by all that's holy that they are ten.'

'The *Kahal*'s word is law,' the man said sadly. 'There's nothing I can do. In Vitebsk, they're taking them at eight. Hold their look, father,' he said, 'for it is a gaze that must last you for some twenty-five years. I hope you will live to see them again.'

Now Jakob broke down completely. 'And even if I live,' he said, 'with all my years, who knows that they will live to gaze on me?'

When the recruiting officer had gone, Esther came quickly to Jakob's side, and took his arm. She shut the door and led him back to the table.

'We will continue with the *Seder*,' Jakob said.

They returned to the table. Shoshannah was persuaded once more to be the *Seder* questioner. She stood high on her chair, but the old self-confidence would not return. She had to start once more at the beginning, since, having learnt all four questions by rote, she could not pick them up at random. 'Why is this night different from all other nights?' she asked again. But now everybody around the *Seder* table knew the answer, even little Shoshannah.

Jakob answered the four questions in turn, outlining the story of the Egyptian bondage, and the ten plagues that God visited upon the oppressors. And as they spilt one drop of red wine for each plague, Jakob prayed that each one be visited upon Meisels. 'Blood,' he mouthed, 'and frogs. Vermin and murrain; noxious beasts and boils; hail and locusts. And darkness. Let it shroud him for the rest of his days.'

A drop of wine trickled on his finger to pronounce the last and most terrible plague of all. The slaying of the male first-born. That curse he could not put upon Meisels, for Meisels had squarely laid it at his own tavern-door. He stood up, his *Hagadah* in his hand, and pointed with his blooded finger to the phrase that was the heart of the *Seder*. 'In every generation,' he sobbed, 'let each man regard himself as if he personally had gone forth from Egypt.' Then he sat down. He could pray no further.

Esther announced that they would eat, but they would forgo the eating of the bitter herbs, for they needed no reminder of the bitterness of bondage. It dwelt with them now and at that very table. The meal, which had been prepared with such care and such joy and was to be eaten with such celebration, was consumed in numb silence. After the meal, Jakob was to say grace. He rose from his seat and left the table. He was in no mood to thank God for the blessings on his house. He strode to the tavern door, and suddenly a flicker of life sparked within him. He opened the door wide, as all the ghetto celebrants were doing at the time, and he shouted the verse of the *Hagadah* into the silent cobbled streets.

'Pour out thy wrath upon the heathen who will not acknowledge Thee and upon the kingdoms that invoke not Thy Name, for they have devoured Jakob, and laid waste his dwelling.'

Then he closed the door softly, and leaned his head on the lintel, sobbing as if his heart would break.

The guests dispersed in silence, and all the children were sent to bed. Then the men of the house sat around the *Seder*-table, and made plans for the milk-brothers' flight from bondage.

Sofia had withdrawn to the kitchen with the other women. She knew, as all of them knew, that Meisels had manoeuvred the recruitment, and she knew too for what age-long reason he now sought his terrible revenge. She could not help feeling that she and she alone, was responsible for the milk-brothers' sacrifice. 'I need air,' she said to Zena who was sorting the dishes at the stove, and she threw on her cloak and left the tavern. The ghetto streets were deserted. Candles still flickered through some of the windows and from time to time she heard the closing songs of the *Seder* service. She made her way to Meisels's house. She had no idea of what she would say to him, or whether indeed he would receive her. But she knew that she had to go to him, to show herself to him in the hope that her beauty could still move him.

She waited for a while before his door, shivering as she recalled his ugliness and cruelty. Then she knocked with a strength and anger that astonished her. She heard his slippered tread behind the door, and she prayed that he was not already in his night-attire; and at that image of him, she trembled at the thought of what he might demand of her. She heard the bolt slipping inside and she caught sight of his white night-gown in the crack of the door. She was terrified and wanted to run quickly away, but her fear rooted her there. She felt faint and raised her arm to support herself on the door-frame.

Meisels gasped when he saw her and he stared at her for a long while. Her fear and trembling served to enhance her frail beauty, and his heart, withered as it was, opened to her, and in that moment, he would have granted her anything. But only for a moment. For then he realised the magnitude of his loss. Her beauty spelt that out to him too.

'What do you want, my child?' he asked, though he knew well enough why she had come. He took her arm and guided her into the house. He tried not to notice how she shivered at his touch. She would not move beyond the hall. She did not seek a greater intimacy. She was neither a guest nor a casual visitor. She was a supplicant, and the door-step would have done for her well enough.

'You can't take the milk-brothers,' she shouted at him. She regretted the hate that rang so clearly in her voice. It was not politic so soon to upbraid him. She needed a favour from him, and favours were pleaded for in gentle tones.

He took offence immediately. 'And why not?' he said. 'It's the law.'

'That's not your reason,' she shouted at him again. 'It's your revenge. You know it is.'

She was crying now and Meisels clenched his hands behind his back for the urge to take her into his arms was overwhelming.

'What can I do, my little Sofia?' he said.

How dare he address me in such a manner, she thought, but she held her tongue.

'What can I do?' he said again. 'I need to fill my quota.'

'There are others,' she said, and hated herself for saying so, but she could not bear her father's pain.

'Oh yes, there are others,' he said. 'I can think of one at least.'

'Then you . . .?' She looked him in the face for the first time, her tearful eyes full of hope.

'I'll make a bargain with you,' he said. 'I'll strike the milk-brothers off the list and replace them with the one I know. My quota will be short, but for your sake I'll take that risk.'

She fell on her knees then, and whispered her gratitude to the hem of his night-shirt.

'How can I thank you?' she said.

He raised her from the ground. Then he put his arm around her waist, and in that moment she knew that the price of his bargain was more than she would bear.

'I'll give you the milk-brothers for Yosif,' he said.

She stared at him unbelieving. He was bargaining for a

46

twenty-five-year tenure on her body. No more. No less. Her mouth oozed a well of saliva of contempt and outrage, and this she gave to him, spitting it squarely into his terrible face. Then she hurried to the door and let herself out into the street. She ran through the ghetto trying to muffle her footsteps on the cobbles, and she did not stop until she reached the back-door of the tavern. Then, before entering, she paused to catch her breath, knowing that the burden on her heart was now even heavier than it was before.

*

The following morning the Bindel household rose very early. Esther had packed a portmanteau of warm clothing and a store of food that would last for several days. Apart from the horror of the summons itself, its arrival was grossly ill-timed. The following day was a Holy Day in the ghetto. There would be no wagons on the road, which limited the possibilities of flight. The only avenue of escape open to the brothers were the forests behind the tavern, the very spot where the 'khapers' would go a-hunting. But on the first day of Passover, there was no alternative. On the second day, a few people would appear on the streets. Faivel had volunteered to cross the ghetto in his wagon and hide the brothers under bales of cloth. He would take them to the forests behind Zemach's tavern, where their whereabouts would not be suspect. Eventually, if, with God's help, they remained undetected, they could be smuggled in a timber-wagon to Vilna where Faivel had a brother. All night long Leon and Jakob prayed together, and so, in their separate dwellings, did Faivel and Dov Pinski.

At milking-time, Leon went to the yard, as was his custom, and the milk-brothers followed him. There was now three cows in the Bindel holding, and one was assigned to each of them. Both Benjamin and Reuben had Leon's gentle touch and it was the happiest time of their day when the three went together to the sheds. The brothers were especially quiet that morning. They had been told of their recruitment and the plans for their escape. They could not help but feel excited at the prospect of such an adventure, but they were also afraid. And sad, too, that they must leave the tavern and the laughter it contained. But what saddened them most of all was the desolate look in their parents' eyes, betraying a pain that in no way matched their own.

'We'll be all right,' the milk-brothers kept telling them, with such confidence and faith in their survival that it pointed to a total ignorance of how deeply that survival was threatened.

Leon finished his milking and lingered. He watched the milk-brothers at work, and prayed for their deliverance. In his own

47

heart he held out little hope for their escape, and he turned his face away from them and fought to hold back his tears.

'I've finished,' the milk-brothers said after a while, and both together for their rhythms were equal.

'I'll miss you,' Benjamin said, nuzzling the cow's cheek, while Reuben stroked his own farewell caress. Leon took their hands, and led them back into the tavern.

At the counter, Miriam and Esther were wrapping the parcel of food. Jakob sat at a table, his head in his hands. When he felt the children at his side, he lowered his hands from his face, and his eyes lingered on their faces. He drank in the image of them, etching their gentle beauty on his mind's eye, for he did not think that he would ever look upon them again. After a while he beckoned them to come to him, and to the others he said, 'Leave us a while.'

Leon and the women went to the back rooms, and the milk-brothers kept their eyes on the floor, because they could not bear Jakob's almost palpable pain.

Jakob gathered the boys into his arms. 'Look at me, children,' he said.

The boys shifted themselves and raised their eyes and stared at him, with a gaze of such intensity that they saw only around and beyond him, and thus avoided the film of tears that dimmed his eye.

'I want you to live,' he said. He gripped their arms. 'I want you to survive.' Then he paused, loosening his grip. 'You may be caught in the forest, and then you will have to be soldiers. You will be taken a long way from home, and sometimes you will be very sad. But every day you must think of us in the tavern, and think of our love for you, and that will give you strength. Life will be hard for you,' he said. 'They will give you strange food to eat, the food of the Christian. They will offer you pig, and you will eat it. Do you hear me? You will eat it because without food you will die.' Then he sank his head into his hands and wept uncontrollably.

'We'll be all right,' the milk-brothers whispered, and they kissed the top of Jakob's head and stroked his hair. He clasped their hands. 'They will force you into baptism,' he said, 'and you must not resist them. Let them sprinkle their holy water on your brows, let them flood your bodies with their purging priesthood. They cannot lay hands on your Jewish soul. You must survive, my children,' he said again. 'Listen to me.' He took them both in his arms. 'Beware of principles. Abandon them. You must if you are to survive.' Jakob knew that they could have no idea of what he was talking about, but he had to speak out if only for his own sake. Perhaps in the coming years, if they lived, they would recall his words, and know in retrospect how much he had loved them.

'There is no cause on earth worth dying for,' he said, 'no God worth one's dying breath, no country worth one's martyrdom, no principle worth one's sacrifice. Only in the name of love is Death worthy. And friendship. Therefore make no friends. Friendship seduces sacrifice. Avoid it.'

The milk-brothers looked at each other, and Jakob thought for one moment that they might have understood him. Then he gathered them in his large embrace.

'You must survive, my children,' he said again. 'Listen to me. Love each other as you have always done, and give each other your protection. Never go to bed in a state of quarrel. Settle your differences before sleep. Remember us all and all the love that binds us together. That will give you strength.'

Leon tip-toed into the cabin. 'We must go,' he said. 'It's getting light.'

Miriam and Esther stood behind him and the children rushed into their mothers' arms. No word was said. They held each other silently for a long time. Then Esther tucked the parcels under their elbows. They took Leon's hands and left the weeping tavern that echoed with the last moments of their childhood.

And so they went into the forest, fleeing their own Pharaoh, and to no promised land, their unleavened bread in their baggage, and terror in their heels.

Later that morning, Jakob and the women went to the synagogue. Their absence would have been conspicuous. Meisels, especially, would have noticed it, and suspected its cause. He would note, too, the absence of the milk-brothers and he would surmise that his vengeance was complete. In the women's gallery, Miriam and Esther stared vacantly into space, their limbs rigid with sobbing-control. The service of the first day of the Passover was no occasion for mourning, and their tears, if they had flowed, could not be attributed to the solemnity of the prayer. Below, Jakob sat next to Faivel. Meisels sat in a front seat, and a mere turn of his head would have forced some exchange. Jakob, for his part, had no intention of avoiding Meisels's eye. He would face him with pride and dignity, despite the torment in his heart. But Meisels kept his gaze ahead. He had no wish to look Bindel in the face, and he certainly did not wish to catch Sofia's proud eye. He recalled the visit of the previous evening, and he was enraged at the thought of how grossly she had humiliated him. Although he had no regrets for his actions, he knew that what he had done was terrible, that he had wrought a revenge of such magnitude that it was grossly out of proportion to the insult he himself had suffered. So he sat motionless, his eyes in the prayer-book, but with no prayer on his lips. In his heart, he relished the thought of Rachel Lascevitch, and the festive meal she would have prepared for his lunchtime diversion, and her constant servility and gratitude. He started to mouth the prayers, thinking all the time of Rachel Lascevitch's thighs, and a small spittle dribbled down his chin. He had it in mind to leave the synagogue immediately after the end of the service, to forgo the usual parleying in the courtyard, and to give Bindel a wide berth.

Jakob's eyes were also in the prayer-book, but the prayer in his heart was not written on the page. In his mind he was following the children through the forest, timing their progress, pacing their flight. At his side, Faivel was doing the same. He cursed the Holy Days. Escape on an ordinary working day, when the ghetto thronged with crowd and activity, would have been so much easier than the lonely obvious route of exposed forest. He feared the worst, and he clutched Jakob's arm in a gesture of support.

When the service was over, Jakob watched Meisels making his quick getaway. 'Come back to the tavern,' Jakob said to his friend.

As the two men crossed the synagogue courtyard and met up with their women, they noticed that many of the congregation turned away their faces, and shifted their positions to avoid them. News spreads quickly in the ghetto, and there was no doubt that Bindel's tragedy was known. Known too, or at least surmised, was the attempt to escape, and it was the need to keep that a secret that prompted Jakob's friends to avoid discussion. When the children were known to be safe, they would go to the tavern and share his joy, and if, God forbid, the children were caught, they would make the same journey to share in his mourning.

They walked slowly through the ghetto streets. Almost seven hours had passed since the children had left the tavern. The longer they stayed in hiding the better their chances of complete escape. If only they could remain undetected until the following day, they could be smuggled out of the ghetto and onto a wagon. And once the shouting had died down, Jakob would apply for a travel permit to Vilna and hold the children in his arms once more. A smile crept over his face at such a thought, but quickly froze as he heard and saw the marching feet along the cobbles. He rushed to his women and hid their faces in his cape, to shield them from the sight of what he was convinced was a nightmare in broad daylight. He tried to concentrate on the two uniformed figures walking on each side of the street, the guns slung on their shoulders. He stared at their faces, trying not to wonder why they marched so far apart, blinding himself to the pitiful struggle that squirmed and writhed between them. He kept his eyes on their faces, and a lump rose in his throat as he recognised the scum features of the 'khapers', and he wondered with disgust how they could go about their rotten work on such a Holy Day, a day when the first-born of their faith at least

50

was passed over. Then he forced himself to look at his children, and he uttered a loud wail of pain. The milk-brothers looked up and saw him and saw, too, his protection of Esther and Miriam. And at once they ceased their struggles and managed between them a wan smile. Jakob had ordered them to survive. They straightened their bodies, and they held their heads high, a pair of unhumbled 'kantonistys', and they fell into the 'khapers'' marching rhythm.

Jakob watched them out of sight, and when they'd turned the corner of the street he unwrapped his cape and held his women close. 'They have died, our children,' he wept. 'We must go home and say *Kadish*. We must mourn for them.'

The tavern door was open, and through it Jakob could see the hunched figure of Leon, leaning over the counter, his body shaken with sobs. On the walls of the tavern, the mirrors and pictures were already draped with white sheets. Leon had prepared for the mourning. When he heard them come into the tavern, he turned and went towards them. He linked his arms in their mourning circle. 'We didn't get very far,' he sobbed. Then they lowered themselves to the floor, as mourners do, humbling themselves to God's solace.

'Magnified and sanctified be Thy great name in the world, which He has created according to His will,' Jakob sang, his voice broken with anger and desolation. And Faivel joined in, and gradually a whole chorus of men from the synagogue, to whom the rumour and the wailing had spread, and who now gathered in Jakob's tavern to share in his sorrow.

'Oh Lord, what is man?' they wailed. 'His days are of grass; as a flower in the field, so he flourisheth. For the wind passeth over it, and it is gone.'

Suddenly Jakob rose, and made his stumbling way through the back of the tavern. Once in the yard he lifted his arms to heaven, and he let forth a sobbing scream of such grief and affliction that the fearful ghetto echoed with its sound, and was giddied by its heart's turning.

*

After the synagogue service, Mendel Meisels went straight home, hot with expectation. Mrs Lascevitch was waiting for him. As he opened his front door she hurried towards him to help him off with his cape. He tugged a little at the top button, thwarting her efforts. He wanted her to work at his service, and also to tease her a little. From the hall he could smell the aroma of her cooking and his nostrils flared with appetite. He went straight into his dining-room and sat himself at the head of the large mahogany table, where Mrs Lascevitch had set his place. He noted the shining display of his late wife's silver that his new treasure had rummaged from the cupboards and returned, as new, to its proper place. He noted, too, the bunch of fresh-cut flowers on the sideboard, the cut-glass vase reflected in its high polish. He sighed with satisfaction. It was like being married again. At least in the area of domesticity. The rest could be taken care of with a little manoeuvring.

He unfolded his napkin, fingering its white starched linen with relish. Then he spread it over his ample chest, and waited to be served. After a while, Mrs Lascevitch came in with a tureen of soup. She set it beside him and served him herself. He noticed her white apron-smock that covered her black dress to its floor-length. The thought crossed his mind to order her to wear thick black stockings, the uniform of the common servant of the time; as she ladled out the thick cabbage-borscht onto his plate, he wished profoundly to debase her. He watched her go back to the kitchen, her quarters, as he considered them, and imagined her preparing the next course of meat, garnishing it as a dish fit for her master. He slurped his soup noisily. Her borscht tasted even better than his late wife's. He gave a passing thought to Jakob Bindel and the blow that he had caused him to suffer that day. He did not let it trouble him. He had no doubt that the milk-brothers, poor devils, were safely in custody, and probably by now kitted out for army life. He had known that they would make an attempt to escape, and he had known, too, that on this Holy Day there was no way of getting through the ghetto unnoticed. Which was why he had ordered the summons for that very day. So that their futile attempt at flight was bound to be through the woods behind Bindel's tavern. Meisels had anticipated that escape-route, and had sent the 'khapers' there at cock-crow. Tonight the 'khapers' would come to him with their report, and he would relish every detail of their capture. He smiled into his now empty soup-plate, and raised his head, carrying the smile to Mrs Lascevitch, who was bearing a dish of meats. Quickly he wiped the smile from his face. Servants were not thus to be favoured.

She served him deftly, taking care with the lay-out on his plate, apportioning each item separately and heeding their symmetry. Not once did she look at him or speak one word, and when she was done she turned her back on him and walked away, on her face a look of contemptuous disgust. But Meisels only saw the stooped servile back of her, and he marvelled at the sudden surge of youth in his loins, and considered that never in his life had he struck a better bargain. Then, to his dismay, the thought of Sofia crossed his mind. No one could ever match her. Over the last years he had watched her grow in beauty. Motherhood became her, and each time he caught sight of her he was once again aware of his loss. So he had no scruple about the grief he had laid at Bindel's door. Not a single pang of conscience, he told himself, and he cut into his meat with fury.

In the kitchen, Mrs Lascevitch consoled herself with the thought of her sons' freedom. That morning, on her way to Meisels's house, she had heard from the butcher of the milk-brothers' summons. The news depressed her profoundly. She knew that, to take them at such a young age, they must have been desperate quota-fillers. Her sons' exemption had forced those children's recruitment. She tried not to feel guilty. Straight after work she would go to the Bindel tavern with her shame, and, on a low stool, she would mourn with them. For it could have been her own *Kadish*, for her own two sons. Meisels was an evil man, she thought, and she emptied the compote of fruit into a dish, and hoped it would choke him.

She took it into the dining-room. Meisels had cleared his plate, as well as the extra portion she had laid before him. He had a pig's appetite, she thought. She ladled the fruit onto his plate and left the bowl, so that he could not call her back for re-service.

'The fire is low,' he said. 'It needs another log.'

Mrs Lascevitch thought of her late husband, who had seen to their fire himself. It was not women's work to carry coals. But she did not complain. Instead, she concentrated on her plan to get herself and her children out of the ghetto, to flee to Kiev where she had a sister, and where her sons could hide unregistered. But for that she needed money. Both her sons worked as waggoners and it would take time to accumulate the wherewithal for travel and bribed papers. She herself worked well into the night on her dressmaking. It was a hard life, but Rachel Lascevitch was a woman who could count her blessings without any sense of abdication. She stole a glance at Meisels's wretched countenance. With all his wealth, she was better off than he. She had children and a host of good memories.

'Would you put on a log?' he said, 'before the fire goes out altogether.'

She skirted the dining-table and crossed over to the fire-place. That morning she had carried a pile of logs from the yard outside the house and stacked them on the side of the hearth. She bent down to lift a log and Meisels watched her, and with joy he noted that she was wearing black woollen stockings after all. He knew and did not care that he could no longer contain his excitement. He lowered the spoon from his mouth, removed the napkin from his chest, fiddled with his buttons, and made to rise. He waited until she had placed the log on the fire and was poking it into position, and then, unable to restrain himself any longer, he leapt on her, grabbing her from behind. The astonished woman did not move.

Her hand stiffened over the poker, and she stared into the fire in total disbelief. And in the flames she saw the flickering image of the milk-brothers in great army coats, overwhelmed by oppression, their linked hands hidden. Then she knew what she had to do. She turned quickly and stared at him. She was not in the least surprised to find him unbuttoned. Then she struck him on the chest with the hot poker that quivered in her hand.

Mendel Meisels fell backwards, catching the cup of his neck on the brass fire-fender. She watched him fall, and she listened to his howl of pain. 'I am sent from the milk-brothers,' she screamed at him. She waited immobile, until his eyes rolled to the ceiling and his writhing head lay still. Then she put the poker back in its place, took her coat and bag from the hall, and left the house.

That evening the 'khapers' came to Mendel's house to make their report. They banged on the heavy oak door, and were surprised when there was no response. They thought Meisels might be sleeping and they banged again. He had requested their report most earnestly, so it was unlikely that he was away from home. They knocked again, and their noise brought neighbours out of their houses. But when they saw the 'khapers' they quickly went indoors, for the sight of such officials brought fear and contempt into their hearts. One of the men then opened a side-window, and through it he could see the dining-table, and underneath a pair of boots, that were, without doubt, attached to a lying figure. He called to his companion. Between them they decided that this was a matter that called for a witness of a higher authority than their own, and they agreed to call on Blomski, who, as Meisels's deputy, was the natural recipient of news of his possible promotion. So one of the men stayed to keep watch, while the other went to Blomski's house. The street was silent. The neighbours still kept themselves indoors, but they peeped through their windows for any sign of change. For it was clear from the expression on the 'khapers'' faces, as they looked through Meisels's window, that something was radically amiss in the house, a house on which they had often prayed calamity to fall. They were excited. There was an indisputable air of foul and beautiful play abroad. They lay in wait for its final proof.

After a while, the 'khaper' returned with a worried Blomski hurrying at his heels. Blomski was invited to the window, and the neighbours caught his look of fearful concern. Then he was seen to nod, and one of the 'khapers' opened the window wide, and climbed inside. After a while, the front door opened and Blomski and the second 'khaper' went inside. The front door closed on the window-witnesses, and they waited hopefully for the blessed clap of thunder.

54

Once inside the house, the intruders hesitated in the hall. They smelt death there and each was loathe to seek out its source.

'We mustn't touch anything,' Blomski said, assuming the ridiculously inept role of detective. But he instinctively felt that murder was afoot. A man like Meisels, with so many enemies, stood little chance of dying of natural causes. 'Let's go inside,' he said, and he took each man's arm, and walked between them.

The sight of Meisels's corpse came as little surprise. It was the fact that it was unbuttoned that astonished them. The 'khapers' began to giggle. The sight of Meisels's pathetic purple member, drooping between his legs, was ludicrously incompatible with the power and the authority he had wielded during his lifetime. Blomski was silent and depressed. He already felt the burdensome mantle of chairmanship. He knelt down at Meisels's side, and buttoned him.

'He was on his way to relieve himself,' he said. 'And he fell. He knocked his head on the fender. It was a fatal blow.'

Blomski was taking upon himself the role of coroner. He had to. He suspected murder. And possibly he knew the murderer as well. He was privy to the deal Meisels had made with Mrs Lascevitch, and his unbuttoned state had clearly given her a motive. But such possibilities should not be rumoured abroad. There was no point in making a case of it. The man was dead and should be allowed to lie in peace. He looked up at the 'khapers', challenging their possible denial. 'It was an accident,' he said. 'There's no doubt about it. Go to Strachinsky's,' he said to one of the 'khapers'. Yossel Strachinsky was the ghetto undertaker. 'Tell him what's happened. He should come with the doctor. You will stay here,' he said to the other, 'and let no one inside. I myself shall go to make arrangements for the funeral.'

He looked at the corpse for a moment. It was not a pretty sight. 'Let us take off the table-cloth,' he said, 'and cover him.'

The 'khapers' removed the remains of Meisels's lunch from the table, and one of them could not resist a spoonful of Mrs Lascevitch's fruit compote. Then the other 'khaper' followed suit, and, though Blomski's mouth watered, he refrained, for it seemed irreverent to consume a dead man's meal.

'That's enough,' he said, and he took the cloth and spread it over the corpse. 'Let us go,' he said.

The neighbours saw the front door open, but no news could be read on the men's faces. They watched them down the street, then turned away. But some of them lingered and, shortly afterwards, were rewarded with the carnival sight of Strachinsky's wagon, covered with a black cloth outlining the coffin-shape beneath, and there was quiet joy in their hearts. In the wake of the wagon came

55

the doctor, and four men, recognisable as the ghetto washers, those who cleansed and shrouded the dead before burial. They watched Strachinsky as he off-loaded the coffin and took it into the house. The doctor and the washers followed him, and once more the heavy oak door was closed.

Then the neighbours left their houses and gathered in small groups on the street, whispering the good news abroad, scuttling it across the ghetto. It skirted Jakob's tavern, for that was already a house of mourning, but in its time it reached Faivel's dwelling. And Faivel wept. Not for the monster's death, but for its brutal ill-timing. Later when he went to the tavern, he said nothing to his friend, but Jakob's heart-ache was edged that evening with new bitterness, and Faivel surmised that he had heard the news. But neither man made mention of Meisels's name. It would have sullied the milk-brothers' memory.

Later that same week, Faivel broke the ghetto curfew, and went out in the dead of night, and made his way to the cemetery. And there, on his friend's behalf, he danced on Mendel Meisels's belated grave.

CHAPTER FOUR

Although Benjamin Bindel was older than his milk-brother by a mere five minutes, Reuben Wolf, the younger, regarded him as his protector. Even though Benjamin was the shorter of the two, Reuben, from his three-inch clearance, looked up to his twin with adoration and respect. Benjamin was his leader, and he, his willing apostle. Reuben had a striking beauty, and his large almost black eyes reflected that distant look of spiritual engagement that he took from Leon, his father. Benjamin, on the other hand, was like Jakob, of solid and stocky build. His mien and his gait spoke of utter reliability. When the boys were captured, it was Benjamin who stretched out his arms to shield his milk-brother, as if to offer himself to the 'khapers' for both of them. On the way out of the forest, Benjamin had whispered to Reuben to take his chances and run. He trusted that the guns their captors carried would not be fired on a Holy Day, and certainly not on one of their own kind. But Reuben did not want to leave his milk-brother. He knew that fear would lame his attempted flight. But it was more than that. Love and loyalty tied him to his brother's side. Even now, as their captors led them into the synagogue-yard, Benjamin urged him to run, but Reuben whimpered his refusal. Whatever hell lay in store, they would share it.

The 'khapers' shoved the boys towards the synagogue door. The Rabbi was just leaving, but when he saw the 'khapers' he knew why they had come, and at what gruesome ritual he was expected to officiate. He took the boys' hands and led them into the synagogue. He sat them down in front of the Holy Ark.

'I won't be long,' he said gently. 'Everything will be all right.' Then he disappeared through a side-door.

The milk-brothers were not unduly afraid, despite the sullen presence of the 'khapers' behind them. Nothing untoward could happen to them in a holy place and they smiled feebly at each other, hanging on to the thin remaining thread of adventure-promise that had quickened their forest-flight in the early hours, in that dawn which now seemed to them so many years ago. For, since leaving the tavern, they had become old men, and now the Rabbi re-appeared with old men's clothes to confirm it: clothes to which their young years were not entitled, long shroud-like robes, prayer-shawls and phylacteries.

'You must put them on,' the Rabbi whispered. 'It's the law. It's a bit like dressing up,' he added with a smile, trying to blunt the awful implications of the ceremony he was bound to perform. The boys donned the robes and shawls, and wound the phylacteries around their arms as they had seen their fathers do at their morning prayers. 'Let me try them, Father,' they had often pleaded. 'Time enough,' Jakob would say. 'After your barmitzvah.'

Now to wind them about their ten-year-old arms was premature, and there was some mischief in it and an element of adventure. They giggled and the Rabbi was glad of it. There would be time enough in their young life, if they lived long enough, to forget the sounds and tastes of laughter. He led them to stand by the Holy Ark. The 'khapers' approached and stood one each side of them.

'We are ready,' one of them said.

Then the Rabbi walked slowly and humbly to the Ark and drew the curtains. He was reluctant to let the holy Torah bear witness to the violence perpetrated against its children.

'Now repeat after me,' one of the 'khapers' said. 'One at a time. I, Benjamin Bindel.'

Benjamin echoed his words, and parrot-wise, with little under-standing, he repeated each phrase of the endless recital. 'I promise, in the name of God, our Father, and of His son, Jesus Christ . . .' Benjamin hesitated and looked at the Rabbi as if to ask his permission. Imperceptibly the Rabbi nodded, and raised his hand to shield the sacred Torah. Benjamin spluttered over the life-long forbidden words, while the Rabbi sadly nodded his encouragement.

'I hereby do swear,' the 'khaper' went on, 'an oath of allegiance to my Lord and Czar, Nicholas the First, to serve him in his mighty army, with loyalty and with courage, and with total obedience to his law.'

It took some time for the 'khapers' to elucidate what those laws were, including the sacrifice of young Benjamin's life in his Czar's service, and Benjamin echoed each word, without hearing or listening to his sounds, so choked was he still on the blasphemy he had uttered, and his bewilderment that the holy Rabbi had sanctioned it. He was drained now of all hope of adventure. For the first time he sensed the reality of their heathen and godforsaken future.

When Benjamin was done with, in thrall for life and death in His Imperial Majesty's service, the other 'khaper' started on Reuben. Reuben was prepared, and under his shroud his fingers were crossed against the blasphemy he knew he would be called upon to utter. And when it came, so oily-smooth out of the 'khapers'' mouth, that guilt-laden crucified name, he thought of his grandfather Jakob, and how he had abjured them, at whatever cost, to make it their supreme business to survive. Perhaps the utterance of that name was part of the price of survival; so when it came, Reuben pronounced it loud and clear, grasping it with his near-proselyte lips as if it were a life-line. Then he too promised to give his life for his Czar, though he was confident that, in that sacrifice too, there would be a loop-hole for survival. He knew well who the Czar was, the one they called Nicholas the First, for his rotten name was tossed daily about the tavern with loud curses and with words that children were not supposed to hear. And he, like Benjamin, knew now that their adventure was over.

The Rabbi patted the boys' shrouded shoulders, as if they had done their lessons well. Then he took up the ram's horn and put it to his lips.

Across the ghetto wailed the howl of lamentation, a mourning out of season, a requiem for orphaned sons, an elegy for fathers and mothers bereft, an offended sigh for an entire tribe, bewildered by the injustice of it all. And as its echo died away, the people left their homes and made their way to Jakob Bindel's tavern.

But Benjamin and Reuben saw nothing of their own obsequies. They were quietly disrobed and hurried into a covered wagon at the back of the synagogue. They huddled together, smelling each other's fear for the first time. They rode in silence for a long while. Even the 'khapers', who were wont to chatter endlessly between themselves, now fell silent, their faces drawn with such desolation that the milk-brothers almost felt sorry for them. 'This is the last time I'll do it,' one of them said, and they were the only words spoken throughout the whole journey.

At last the wagon halted, and the 'khapers' took the boys' hands. One of them actually said he was sorry, and Benjamin saw a tear start in his eye. 'Don't worry,' Benjamin said with little sympathy. 'Your Jesus will look after you,' he said with all his young disdain. He was astonished at how easily his lips could shape the word, and he was glad of it, for it meant a numbing of the senses, a steeling of the heart, an inert armour that would enable him to endure all the deprivations his father had woefully prophesied. He hoped that Reuben's heart would harden too, all of it, but for a small throbbing nest within, that would guard and shelter the love between them, and he prayed for that same sanctuary in himself.

In front of them was the low-slung building of an army barracks. The 'khapers', anxious now to take their leave, directed them towards the entrance and hurriedly returned to the wagon without any word of farewell. The milk-brothers watched them as the cart turned on its own axis and trundled out of sight. Reuben took Benjamin's hand, but Benjamin gently withdrew his support, smiling in an attempt to cover his cruel gesture. Reuben had to harden himself as he had done, for a hardened heart seeks no protection.

A drill-sergeant met them at the gate and shouted a command in Russian. The milk-brothers were fairly schooled in the non-ghetto language. Jakob had taught them, and occasionally Faivel with his stories. They obeyed the sergeant's command and rushed to his side as he marched them into the barracks and to a counter, where a line of young and new recruits were already waiting. They turned when they saw the newcomers, eager for conversation. Where did they come from? How were they taken? Did they too, have to utter that terrible word while the holy Torah stared down at them from the Ark? The friendly Yiddish tumbled from their frightened lips, and Benjamin and Reuben were stabbed with such a pang of home-sickness that both reached for the other's hand. Only a few of the recruits were from Odessa. Most of them came from the outlying villages and had been taken in much the same way as the milk-brothers. But they told their stories with no sense of adventure. From the very beginning, amid the wailing and the lamentation, they had seen their own deaths as inevitable. And as their parents in the villages were at that moment lamenting their loss, they were mourning for themselves, tugging at their ringlet side-locks for some measure of support. For all the village boys were orthodox *Chasidic* Jews, and the ringlet was a mark of their sect.

Though they were wont to worship with joy in their hearts, their prayers a splendid glorification of God, there was little joy on their faces now and less expectation. Benjamin was wary of them. They were losers, the lot of them, and he feared their contagion. He drew Reuben to his side.

'Why are we waiting?' Benjamin asked.

'They'll give us our uniform,' one of them said. 'What's your name?'

'Benjamin.'

'And I'm Reuben, his . . .'

He was about to say 'nephew', but he was too tired to accommodate the conversation that would ensue from the statement of such a paradox. 'His brother,' he said, and left it at that.

'I'm Yossel,' the ringlet replied. 'My brother's with me too,' he said. 'His name's Lev. He's got his uniform. They took him in that room over there.' He shook his ringlets in the direction of the door at the far end of the barracks and, as they looked, they saw the door open, and a herd of young children, swamped in noisy greatcoats, shuffled through the door. Their feet were invisible, but from the sound of them, they were clearly burdened with great boots, many sizes too large. All that was visibly human was a mass of tiny heads, each one seemingly like the other. It was a grotesque spectacle, as if a child, given a lump of clay, had made sundry blocks and stuck on each of them a round grey ball as a small concession to animation.

Yossel gave a little cry. He knew that his brother was amongst that herd yet there was no way of knowing him. For all were head-shaven, frameless-featured and identical. Any one of them could have been Lev. He looked searchingly at the sea of unsmiling faces, while one of the crowd shuffled towards him and feebly shrugged his shoulders under the weight of his greatcoat. Then he put his hand on Yossel's shoulder.

Yossel stared at him. 'Lev?' he said.

Lev's features formed a smile and a glimmer of recognition passed over Yossel's face. And his little heart heaved. He cringed, drawing himself away from this gentile creature, this hair-less head and ringlet-less face. He clasped his own curls with each hand, pressing them into his cheeks as if to groove them into his flesh, to root them there, entrenched for all time. For his ringlets were his very being, his inviolable entity, as much a part of his nature as colour is of negritude. He looked at his brother in horror. The hair-less Lev had already begun his dying. A tear fell from the corner of Lev's eye, as if in his own mourning.

Reuben and Benjamin had watched the painful encounter between brothers. Reuben put a sympathetic arm on Yossel's shoulder, but Benjamin made for Lev, grasping him by the thick wad of his shoulder-pad and shaking him. 'You can live without hair,' he shouted at him.

But Lev shook his head in abdication and Benjamin moved away, dragging Reuben behind him. Instinctively he knew that despair was contagious.

Though the barracks was now full of children there was scarcely any human sound. Weeping was silent, confined to the heart where the sin of hairlessness quietly hid its shame. Only the mourning murmur of greatcoats was heard, and the occasional shuffle of a large boot.

The door at the end of the barracks opened again and two sergeants entered carrying boots and uniforms. These they piled onto the counter and doled them out to the waiting recruits. There was no consideration of sizes, and the piles of clothes were given out at random. The recruitment of children had been a sudden and spiteful official decision, and there was no equipment. The uniforms had once clothed grown men, whose looted corpses lay snow-buried on sundry battlefields. The children's feet would be lost and blistered in dead men's shoes.

When the whole line had been catered for, the sergeants led the boys through the barracks door and across a tree-lined court, large and wooded enough to stifle whatever cries might plead from the bath-house to which the boys were now being led. In the centre of the vast hall was a large sunken tub of grey scum-topped water. The boys were told to undress, in gestures rather than words, for the sergeant had long since caught on to the village boys' Russian illiteracy. But they were friendly and laughed as they mimed their orders, trying to make an adventure of it all. Occasionally they helped a small frightened boy to unbutton his blouse, and gently, and with great respect, tidily fold the prayer-fringes that circled his waist. Most of the boys had never had a bath and were frightened at the sight of so much water. They saw no fun in it, only danger, and they had to be coaxed to put even a foot in it. But Reuben and Benjamin, re-capturing once more the smell of adventure, were the first to immerse themselves, jumping bodily into the bath, splashing each other and laughing all the while. They gave the village boys courage, who, one by one, risked the two foot depths. Once the boys were in the tub, the sergeant tossed them soap-slabs and mimed ablutions. They also mimed instruction that they need not bother about washing their hair. A slow silence gathered across the tub as the children realised the implications of that order. And, as whimpering gave way to wailing, the sergeants were seen to lose their playfulness, and they unhooked two hoses from off the wall, and ordered the boys out of the bath while they hosed them down. Then they were directed to a pile of dirty towels and, without miming, told to dry. Then naked, and shivering, they were lined up before their uniforms, and told to become soldiers.

The boys fumbled with their dressing, anxious to delay the unthinkable sacrilege that awaited them. Yossel kept one hand straddled across his face, pinning down his ringlets, while with the other hand he struggled with his blouse. But at times he was bound to use both hands in his dressing, and at those moments he crouched in a corner and shut his eyes, and prayed that he was invisible. And then, from habit, he reached out for his prayer-fringes, and so did the other village-boys, who wore them night and day like a second skin. The sergeant who, from experience, now knew the nature of their search, picked up a pile of prayer-fringes and shook his head. Then he threw them unceremoniously onto the fire that burned at the end of the bath-house. The boys turned away in horror. It was like setting fire to God.

Yossel drew on his trousers with his one hand. Now more than ever was it necessary to cling to that self in him. Though he felt naked and unclean without his prayer-fringe, it was less a part of him than his ringlets, those fingers of God that had, by sheer nature, caressed his cheek. Thus, one-handed, he managed to become a soldier, in a tunic that reached his knees, and breeches that hung over his huge boots. With one hand, he reached down to the floor for his cap. And many of the village-boys were doing likewise, anxious to provide some protection for their locks. But the sergeant roared out an order, and mimed it too, so that it would be clear that, at this stage, caps were premature. And at once he lined up the ringletted ones, knowing that they would give the greatest trouble, and herded them through the bath-house door that led to the clipping-room. Reuben and Benjamin were the last to enter, and they leaned against the wall, viewing the hair-strewn floor, and the ringlets that quivered on the quarried tiles like newly-diced worms.

'It's only hair,' Reuben said, picking up Benjamin's priorities. 'Such a fuss about hair.'

For those under the clippers were already screaming as the blades severed their God-lines. The ringlets were left till last, as if the barbers knew well the cream of the crop, and, when the heads were fully shaven, the ringlets were clipped and dropped like large black tears onto the stone floor. Then the wailing grew to such a volume of lamentation that the sergeant was obliged to strike out at the snifflers and to remind them of the honourable, if oversized, uniform they were privileged to wear. Reuben and Benjamin were clipped together, and managed to take some pleasure in each other's visual change. Their tearless faces did not go unnoticed by the two drill-sergeants who automatically singled them out as favourites.

For the next five years, the sergeants would be in charge of this motley crew. In the whole troop there were about two hundred children. Only a quarter of them were expected to survive their first year. When the winter snows came, they would drop like summer flies, those who had not already died of spring starvation and autumn fatigue. But those two smilers looked like survivors, the sergeant thought, especially the smaller one, whose large black eyes melted his knees with longing.

'What's your name?'

'Reuben,' he answered, 'Reuben Wolf.'

'And yours?' the sergeant turned to Benjamin.

'Benjamin,' he said, 'Benjamin Bindel.'

'I thought you were brothers,' the sergeant said.

'Well we . . .' Reuben stopped. Again he felt the explanation too complicated to offer. In any case, what would these blunt peasant soldiers understand of milk-brotherhood? Yet Benjamin saw in their possible friendship a positive aid to survival. He gave what his father had called his winning smile. The sergeant responded. In school, Benjamin recalled, the teacher's pet had been a friendless hated creature, but he was willing to play that role, and so, it seemed, was Reuben. 'We live together,' Reuben said. 'We're sort of related.' He had managed the whole conversation in his simple basic Russian.

The sergeants were impressed. The boys could be used as a liaison to bridge the language-barrier between them and their infant-troops.

The shaven children, threatened with beatings, were now quiet and subdued, and the sergeants led them back into the barracks. Yossel and Lev found each other once again, and like the others sought comfort in their common deprivation. Fatigue dulled the full realisation of their plight. When the sergeant tossed straw palisses into their midst, they were happy to lie down where they stood, brother seeking brother, and friend, friend, and, if without either, then a Jew like any other, hairless, fringeless, beyond the Pale of both Settlement and Torah, creatures of sin. 'God help us,' they dared to utter, fearing how unworthy they had become. But the milk-brothers fell asleep without scruple. Reuben did not even stir as the drill-sergeant folded the blanket around his shaven head. Throughout the night, the sergeants dozed on a wooden bench, occasionally waking at the cry of 'Mama' or 'Papa', a cry for home discernible in any language, and both of them stirred in their sleep, grateful that they had no children of their own.

In the morning, the children were woken by a crash of bells. They rubbed their sleep-filled eyes, looked at their surroundings and slowly realised the calamity that had befallen them. In the cold light of morning, it was proved to be no dream, a thought that had comforted them during their sleep. Some of them began to whimper for home, but most cried for hunger, for none of them had eaten since their breakfast the day before. And then they smelt what was in store for them. To most of them the smell was unknown, for, sheltered in the ghetto all of their young lives, they knew only the strictly kosher odours of their own meat, fish and fowl. This was an alien smell, and, as such, forbidden.

'You'll all feel better after breakfast,' the sergeant said, and motioned to Benjamin to translate.

Benjamin was surprised at the order, and glad of it, for it already gave him a status that for a time would be unassailable. He faltered with the translation but it was clear enough to the boys that their hunger would soon be assuaged.

'A nice piece of roast pork,' the sergeant went on.

Benjamin hesitated. It was all as his father had promised him. He looked at Reuben.

'You have to tell them,' Reuben whispered.

'You do it,' Benjamin said, more as a move to include Reuben in his new appointment than to shift responsibility of bearing such a monstrous piece of information. Reuben was hesitant. He himself was sickened by the thought of it, and he was frightened of speaking the terrible word aloud. So he whispered it in a small offended croak that was all that he could muster.

'You must fill your stomachs,' the sergeant went on. 'We have a long march ahead of us.'

Reuben translated and, before his words were out, the source of the blasphemous smell was evident in the barracks itself. Soldiers bearing trays of food and huge samovars placed the breakfast on the long counter, and ordered the boys to get into line. The sergeant put Benjamin and Reuben at the head of the line. He expected his recruits' pig-refusal, and hoped that his two favourites would set an example. Benjamin was first. With little hesitation, he took a slice of bread and placed the pork on top of it, then he lifted it high and showed it to the others. 'We must survive,' he said in Yiddish. 'God will forgive us.'

But the orthodox young recruits were not impressed. Many of them dropped out of the line altogether, and those who were left took only bread and a tin mug of sweet tea, and when breakfast was over the table still groaned with the scorned meat.

'Put some in your packs,' the sergeants said to Benjamin and Benjamin did what he was told, and urged Reuben to do the same, though both were retching on the devil's taste. They had forced themselves to swallow it and, after each mouthful, had asked God's forgiveness. For they knew that it was a terrible thing that they had done. Without doubt it was a step into baptism and thus into eternal limbo. After each forced swallow, they prayed feverishly, while the other recruits prayed too, but more for the involuntary loss of their ringlets than for any gratuitous sin.

The drill-sergeants did what they could to marshal the boys into some kind of formation. There were too many of them to handle, but that fact did not disturb them. They knew that, within a few days, with the slogging march ahead, their numbers would most certainly be halved and the troop become manageable. They herded them out of the barracks, putting Benjamin and Reuben in the lead, and marched them through the clearing onto the open road. They had gone only a little way when Reuben faltered and doubled up in pain. Then he rushed to the side of the road, where he freed himself of the devil that he had harboured. Benjamin followed him and did likewise, while the others stood and watched with little surprise, and were strengthened in their faith. But when the brothers re-joined the line, Benjamin took a hunk of meat from his bag, broke it in two, and gave half to Reuben. And with a preliminary prayer, both for forgiveness and for the strength to keep it down, they chewed on it numbly to the rhythm of the march. Not that there was too much rhythm. Most of the boys were stragglers, already weak from hunger. The sheltered ghetto lives they had led in no way equipped them for this unexpected and strenuous calling. They were mostly poor, and already ill-fed, and prone to infection. Their build was frail and their resistance low. Whatever energy they had, they used in prayer. The drill-sergeant looked back at the trudging line of great-coats, shunting their giant boots in sluggish tread, and he wondered how many of them would survive the day.

At noon, they were allowed to rest for a while. Most of them fell asleep on the road-side, and cared not if they never woke again. Lev and Yossel clung together in their misery, Yossel still clutching at his non-existent locks, ashamed of his bald heathen cheeks. When, an hour later, the drill-sergeant called them to order, there were some who could not rise, their frail bodies shivering, their brows feverish in cold sweat. Reuben and Benjamin trudged down the line and forced them to stand on their feet, with promises of hot cabbage borscht at their next holding-station. For that was what the drill-sergeant had told them. And so they struggled on, the sorry line of them, some near death, and mumbling that time-honoured Hebrew prayer that was a visa to Abraham's bosom. 'Shema Yisroel, Adonai Elohanu, Adonai Echod'. At night-fall, they reached the wagon trail, where soup and bread was brought to revive them. Then they were prodded into the wagons like cattle.

'Where are we going?' Reuben dared to ask.

'To the Eastern Provinces,' the drill-sergeant said.

The place name meant nothing, but it sounded like the other end of the world.

They travelled for days, on a diet of borscht, black bread and tea. Some of the village boys had compromised on the borscht, though they knew that what it contained was highly questionable. But most of the children took only bread and sweet tea, and there was much fever amongst them. And something more than fever, and much less. A fever that at last had cooled, a pain that had found peace, and a longing for home that was mercifully stilled. In all, twenty-three children died in the course of one night. Nobody knew their names, and in their huge boots and great-coats and shaven heads, even in Death they were identical. The survivors turned their faces away with not one mourning tear, their features hardened with the effrontery of their abduction and their hearts enraged with a bewildering adult fury. They did not look at the sergeants as they wrapped the bodies in blankets and ordered the wagon-train to halt. They waited while the soldiers off-loaded their burden and were silent as they heard the click of shovels outside. Then after a while, when all was still, they began the chant of *Kadish*. It was Benjamin and Reuben who led them in the mourning prayer, and when the drill-sergeants returned with blankets now empty they waited silently at the wagon-doors until the ritual was over.

The terrible journey continued but the deaths had wrought a great change. Now, one after the other, during the course of the next few days, children went to sleep and never woke again. It was as if, with the first deaths, permission had been granted to turn away from sacrilege, to subject the spirit to no further assault, and, in all simplicity to die, without offence, and without malice. So it was, that some weeks later, at the end of their wretched journey, one hundred and three of the young recruits had succumbed, and the wagon-trail was punctuated by their unnamed shallow graves. In the course of time, official time, that would amble at its own uncaring bureaucratic pace, word of their deaths would reach the villages. One hundred and three whispers would give shape to their holy names and wail them aloud. And God was cursed in one breath, and begged for forgiveness in another, and grief would wind its sheet round the ghettoes like a shroud.

Amongst those young recruits who survived, there dwelt a small sense of victory, as if in their first great battle they had acquitted themselves with honour. There was hope now that they might endure their twenty-five-year sentence. They had paid their price. They had eaten of forbidden flesh, they had suffered themselves to be shaven, from time to time they had spoken words in Russian, that language of baptism. Some of them had even been too ashamed to pray. They had offended God in all but their souls. They were convinced that the worst was over. But they had no notion of the horrors that were to come.

*

It was snowing. Every year on the milk-brothers' birthday it was snowing. But this snow was different, and so was the birthday on which it fell. For on that day, the milk-brothers were thirteen years old, barmitzvah-boys, without synagogue, without covenant, prayer-shawl or phylacteries, and all such improvidence in a wilderness of alien snow. For the Siberian snows were nothing like those of Odessa. Or rather like that of Odessa. For the snow of their childhood was singular, a one-time fall that softly served its snowballing purpose, that melted away before a second single coming. But the Siberian snows were plural in the extreme, with no pause for thaw or gentle snowmanship. There, in that distant howling desolation, the winter terrain was mean, its covering rock-hard, violent and menacing.

Benjamin and Reuben lay entwined on their narrow cot, and woke together as they did each morning. And as was their custom they whispered a morning prayer, which, over the years of their recruitment, had never varied. 'Thank God,' they said, their eyes still closed and bleary with sleep, 'God be thanked that we have survived another day.' Then slowly they opened their eyes and knew what that day was. They smiled at each other with remembered joy of Odessa birthdays, and knew that on this day they must do something very special to celebrate their entry into manhood.

'Where's our knife?' Benjamin said.

Reuben reached into the deep pocket of his great-coat, took out the knife and extracted one blade. He knew what Benjamin had in mind. He made a small incision in his left thumb and handed the knife to his milk-brother. Benjamin cut his thumb likewise, then they clasped each other's hand.

'Now we are blood-brothers,' Benjamin said. 'Happy birthday.'

From the room beyond came breakfast smells of roasting pig, an odd aroma for a barmitzvah feast. The boys sniffed, as they sniffed at it every morning on waking. For so long now they had eaten of it, and always with the same disgust, but always with Jákob Bindel's injunction on their larded lips that they were to survive. In the beginning, after their first taste of it, they had asked God's forgiveness after each retching mouthful. But they had never acquired a taste for it, and concluded that that must be God's doing. 'Eat,' it seemed He was saying to them. 'Eat, but by no means enjoy.' So they no longer asked for forgiveness. Their survival, at whatever cost, was an unspoken contract between them and the Lord.

67

They got out of bed and pulled on their boots, rejoicing in their snug fit. They tried not to think of how they had acquired them. It was on one of their long marches, a regular part of their training, and a dreaded routine, especially in the winter. The dead men's shoes, that shuffled around the tiny feet of the marchers, were more an impediment than an aid, and often the child-soldiers, who perhaps were beginning to think that survival was hardly worth the price, would throw them away and walk barefoot on the ice, sooner than drag the weight of them. Many of them faltered and lay on the roadways, starving and full of tears, and died where they lay. Once on these marches, in the last hard winter, the milk-brothers, in outsize shoes like the others, skirted the corpses and quickly learned the lesson of being snugly shod. They learned another lesson too, as part of their survival kit. Looting. They scanned the dead children's feet for smaller sizes, but they took care to replace the shoes they had taken with their own and, without looking back, they continued on their god-forsaken way.

Like most of the recruits in their platoon, the milk-brothers were billeted in a farm house, one of many dotted over the snow-covered wastes. They had three billet-companions. Lev and Yossel Abromovitch, despite the thousand assaults on their bodies and spirits, had yet managed to survive. And pray too, with daily fervour, while little Yossel still clutched at the non-existent ringlets on his sunken cheeks. Each of them had celebrated his thirteenth birthday as a time of prayer and mourning, and they had both fasted throughout the day. Yet, in their rest periods, after a long day's training, their shrunken stomachs sated and their weary feet at rest, they would sit around the farm-house fire with still enough spirit to sing songs of home, to tell their village stories and, above all, to laugh at the ridiculousness of their present situation. Over the years, they and the milk-brothers drew close to each other and a frightening bond of friendship grew between them. Each time brothers hugged brothers with the relief of being alive and together, Benjamin and Reuben would recall Jakob Bindel's admonition: Make no friends, for friendship and love are the only causes worth dying for.

The fifth lodger in their billet was one Sergei Ash. He was fifteen years old and something of an outsider. He didn't sleep with the others. Farmer Pankov had allotted him a small space above the hayloft, so that his presence, even if it were a sleeping one, would deter thieves in the night. Unlike the others, Sergei had not been forcibly kidnapped. His recruitment had been legitimate. But, despite the poverty of his childhood and his illiteracy to boot, Sergei Ash was tough. Never in his three years of army life had he touched meat of any kind. He lived on bread, tea, any vegetables that he could find, and eggs. He was the most deft egg-thief in the platoon. But most of all, he lived on prayer. He adjusted his orisons to the rhythm of his marching steps, to every manoeuvre of his drill. His lips were constantly on the move, and if you caught their motion in a side-long glance, he would smile at you. Sergei Ash dreamed a lot, and always of victuals. And he talked a lot too, and his subject was always the same. Food. Food was an obsession with him, that came a close second to his compulsion for prayer. When he talked about his parents or the people in his village, it was not about what they did or how they lived. It was simply about what they ate. Night after night, he would lead his fellow-lodgers on a gastronomic tour of his village, an excursion into 'haute cuisine' that was wholly of his own invention. Caviare was the staple diet, heightened with 'blintzes', sour cream and smoked sturgeon. When pressed to offer what exactly it was that he, Sergei, used to eat around his own family table, he would confess to salt herring, and blackcurrant tea. And at that moment his lips would salivate and tremble with longing.

One night, during one of Sergei's culinary recitals, the drill-sergeant, Likov, called in at the billet, ostensibly to give an order for the following day but, in truth, to feast his eyes yet again on Reuben's face, a vision that nightly haunted his restless dreams. He arrived in time to hear Sergei's dissertation on the inestimable value of the simple, common-or-garden salt herring, and it sowed the seeds of a monstrous plan in his already sickened mind.

Orders had come from the highest quarters, in fact from the mighty Czar himself, and pressure had been brought to bear on all platoon commanders to confront and to conquer the Jewish menace once and for all. And with the final weapon. That of baptism. The directions as to how this was to be done were clear. In the beginning, baptism was to be propagated by persuasion, gentle but firm, and failing that by sheer blackmail. And that failing too, force was to be administered. The mighty Czar would brook no Christ-refusal.

The matter was urgent and put the platoon commanders in a dilemma. It was all very well for the Czar to dictate orders from his royal palace in St Petersburg, a million miles from the smell of any Jew and his intransigence. Could he conceive of the flesh and blood of Benjamin Bindel, Reuben Wolf, Abromovitch, Lev and Yossel, and Sergei Ash? Could he hear their monotonous prayers, their whispered Christ-cursing, and sniff their stubborn resistance to Him they had crucified and who had died for them on the Cross? But orders were orders. At first they tried the gentle persuasion suggested. 'If you become Christians like the rest of us, life would be much easier for you. For one thing, you wouldn't have such trouble with the food,' they tried.

The boys laughed in their faces. A drop of holy water on their shaven heads would in no way numb their taste-buds, and when that night a priest came to the Pankov billet, ostensibly to pay a social call, the boys claimed a sudden ignorance of Russian, and tried to school him in the Yiddish tongue. The priest left in a rage of defeat and confusion. Every week came another directive from the highest quarters, stressing the imperative nature of baptism, that it was the bounded duty of every God-fearing Christian soldier to show the 'Yids' once and for all that there was only one true way to Heaven, and it was not via Abraham's bosom. As it became clear that apostasy was not to be achieved through persuasion, gentle or otherwise, stronger measures were ordered and, moreover, prizes were to be awarded for every conversion. A bonus of two roubles was promised for the saving of each Jewish soul. Fifty Jewish souls, retrieved from the wayward path, merited promotion in rank and extra privileges. It was the very spur that the men needed. Investment in the Christ-business had suddenly become profitable, and they went about their dealings with ruthless efficiency.

One night Sergeant Likov dropped into the boys' billet and listened once again to Sergei's salivating soused-herring stories. He put his arm around Reuben's shoulder, and, as casually as he was able, he said, 'Treats for you tomorrow, Ash. Herring for breakfast. Just like home.'

'For us too?' Yossel's eyes brightened and, for one moment, with this hopeful sniff of home, he dropped his hand from his ringlet-less cheek.

'For all of you,' Likov said. 'It'll be just like being back in the ghetto.'

That night, Sergei slept without dreaming, and when he awoke his mouth was already watering. His fantasy was about to be realised.

When the boys entered the kitchen they were astonished to find that Sergeant Likov's promise was indeed fulfilled. The table was loaded with black bread and salt herrings of all kinds, ruled by the steaming samovar in the centre. But most surprisingly of all was the presence of Sergeant Likov himself, already seated at the head of the table, with an air of jovial but veiled authority. Surprisingly too was the frightened face of Anna Pankov, the farmer's wife who usually attended breakfast with a bustling happy-go-lucky air. Benjamin looked around the room and smelt conspiracy. He knew that that mouth-watering herring was bait and he must by all means urge his companions to avoid it. Reuben needed no persuasion. Lev and Yossel protested in whispers for a while, but finally bowed to the milk-brothers' judgement.

But Sergei was immovable. He could barely wait to get to the table. His mouth was screaming for a taste of home. And so they sat

70

down and listened, as they did every morning to Anna Pankov's thanksgiving prayer. Normally she tossed it out of her mouth while doling out the hot oatmeal and hunks of bread. But this morning she sat upright in her chair and said it with her idle hands, thanking God for what they were about to receive in a tone of deep earnestness, as if she meant every word. For the last time Benjamin tried to dissuade Sergei by silently shaking his head in his direction. But Sergei did likewise. He would not be diverted. After the blessing, Anna Pankov dealt out the bread and forked a juicy herring onto each boy's plate. Sergeant Likov was awarded two herrings, but she took care not to look him in the eye. He lifted up his fork and it was permission for them all to begin. Yossel and Lev and the milk-brothers concentrated on their bread, turning their faces from the fatally seductive aroma on their plates. Their eyes watered with their loss.

'Don't you like herring?' Anna Pankov said, and there was an unmistakable measure of relief in her voice.

They shook their heads, begging her to understand.

'There's nothing else this morning,' she said gently.

'Bread is enough,' Benjamin said. 'Bread and blackcurrant tea.' He glanced across the table and winced as the sergeant re-loaded Sergei's plate. 'You're lucky,' he said. 'You can have their share,' and he shovelled fillet after fillet before him. Sergei did not take his eyes off his plate. The look on his face had little to do with relish. It was as if he had undertaken the most important mission of his young life. After a while of feeding, he reached out his tin mug for tea. And then the whole point of the exercise became crystal clear. The sergeant shook his head vigorously, and so did Anna Pankov, as she had been strictly instructed. She opened the samovar tap and filled the tin mugs of all at the table. All except Sergei, who looked at her at first with profound disbelief, and then, very slowly, with the realisation of what torture he had brought upon himself. Sergeant Likov drank his tea noisily, leaning over and slurping it next to poor Sergei's parched ear. Then he shovelled more herring onto his victim's plate. Sergei feebly shook his head, defeated.

'You'll eat it,' Likov shouted. 'Every last bit of it.' And he picked up Sergei's fork and shoved it into his hand. 'Eat,' he said, forcing his shaven head down onto his plate.

The others watched in silence, and Anna Pankov hid her face fearing the treacherous pity in her eyes. The terrified Sergei chewed and chewed, his soul crying out with hatred for the food he had once loved so well. Each time he paused, the sergeant stuffed another fork-full into his mouth and continued to do so, until only the perfidious smell of the herring remained.

'You want some tea?' Likov asked.

Sergei nodded eagerly but with little confidence.

'If you go to the priest he will give you tea. Lots of it. And lots of cold water to quench your thirst,' he slurped. 'And holy water too,' he added, 'to cleanse your herring-infested soul.'

This last, Benjamin was forced to translate, though it was obvious from Sergei's crest-fallen look that the gist of the message was clear. He had just enough energy left to shake his head. And shake it again and again till the tears rolled down his cheeks.

'It's herring for lunch then,' the sergeant said, 'and for supper, and for tomorrow and for every day after that. There will be no drink of any kind. Except at the house of the priest.' He looked around the table menacingly. 'If any of you give Ash water,' he threatened, 'you will be shot.' He looked at all of them in turn, including Anna Pankov, but when his eyes rested on Reuben, he gave an almost imperceptible shake of his head.

They left the table and were marched to the drilling-yard for their daily routine. For lunch and supper that day, Sergei was made to eat his herrings alone under the watchful eye of Sergeant Likov.

At the end of the third herring day, Likov wondered how the boy managed to survive at all. So did the Pankovs and their other lodgers. But none of them knew that Sergei had found a watering-hole. If one could call it that. It was, at its best, a mere source of liquid. Outside the barn-door which led to the hay-loft in which he slept, there was a permanent puddle. Its least ingredient was rain-water. For the most part it consisted of liquified mud and horse urine. After each stealthy mouthful, Sergei suspected that it was more than likely that he would die from the cure than from the disease. Yet it was a juice of sorts, and temporarily assuaged the raging thirst inside him, though its after-effects were as nauseating as the thirst itself.

Each day Likov kept his startled eye on him, and he wondered how long the stubborn boy would hold out, and how soon he could collect his ransom. But Sergei plodded through his herring filled days. Six of them in all. And on the seventh day, like any good Jew, he rested. And yielded too. His body was athirst, raging, dry as a desert. For a gulp of cold clean water, he would have given, for what it was worth, his entire herring-soaked kingdom. In a faint dry whisper, he asked to see Likov, who took him gently by the hand and led him to the priest's quarters. Sergei tried not to think that the day was a Sabbath, *his* Sabbath, and in view of his impending baptism, his last. Thereafter he would rest on *their* Lord's day and desecrate the Sabbath of his fellow-lodgers. He tried not to think of the consequences of it all.

Reuben, Benjamin, Lev and Yossel gathered in their sleeping-hut and silently prayed for Sergei's soul. He was still a Jew to them, and always would be, whatever kind of water was poured upon his head. And in God's eyes he would remain one of His chosen, because the water could not rinse his soul. They waited for his return, untroubled by the length of his absence, for they knew that neither a minute nor a thousand years could rid Sergei's gentle spirit of the Torah.

When he returned, they were at supper. Anna Pankov was sitting silently, ashamed of her involuntary complicity, and when she saw the door open, and Sergei's sudden Christian presence in the kitchen, she turned her face to the wall. The boys stared at him, as if they expected a change in his appearance, a halo perhaps about his head. Sergei looked at them warily, gauging their response. With one hand he was clutching at something around his neck, and his white little fist was tight and angry and ashamed.

'Hullo, Sergei,' Reuben said. 'Come and sit down.'

He stared at them without moving. 'I don't want to talk about it,' he said. It seemed that their silence was a condition of his joining them at the table.

'Neither do we,' Benjamin said, and went towards him and took his arm.

Still Sergei clutched at the curse around his neck, and without removing his greatcoat he sat down. Anna Pankov served him a bowl of soup and at the same time drew him a large mug of tea from the samovar. Sergei gave her a feeble smile. 'It wasn't your fault,' he said, and Anna Pankov was so overcome that she knelt by his side and took him in her arms. 'My little Jew-boy,' she said. 'Always will be. Now get some food inside you,' she said gruffly, fighting back her tears.

Sergei picked up the soup-spoon with one hand, and was obliged to put it down every time he reached for his bread. His was clearly going to be a one-handed supper.

'It doesn't matter,' Benjamin said after a while. 'Let it go. It doesn't mean anything. Just a string around your neck.'

'A mill-stone,' Sergei whispered.

Benjamin leaned over the table and held Sergei's clenched fist. 'It's only what it is,' he said, and gently he opened Sergei's hand. Sergei turned away as the metal crucifix fell from his throat and draped itself across his presumedly repentant Jewish breast.

'Benjamin's right,' Reuben said. 'It's only what it is.'

But Sergei would not be comforted. He could not erase from his mind's eye the smile on the face of the priest as he draped the cross over his wet forehead. 'Now you will walk in the ways of Jesus Christ, our Lord,' the priest had said, 'and that way, and only that way,' he said, prodding Sergei's lately Jewish ribs with the crucifix, 'only that way will lead to Paradise.' It was a vision that Sergei would carry behind his eyes for the rest of his life. Even the long glass of water that the priest had thereafter placed in his hand as a pay-off for his newly-cleansed soul gave him little pleasure. He drank it swiftly and asked for more and more, but less to assuage his gigantic thirst than for his own desperate need for purification. He went to bed early. There was now no point in sitting around the fire and listening to Lev's and Yossel's village stories. They would only gnaw at the raging hole in his heart. Neither did he want to listen to their Yiddish songs. He no longer felt himself worthy of the tongue or of its melody. He lay down on his cot, clutching the Christ in his hand as if to hide it from his God's all-seeing eye.

The other boys retired early as well, with little appetite for their nightly nostalgia. They slept fitfully without understanding the Sergei-dreams that troubled their rest.

In the morning Sergei did not appear at breakfast and Reuben was sent to the hayloft to wake him. At the top of the ladder, he hesitated. A sudden fear had gripped him and he wished that Benjamin was with him. He peered over the edge of the loft and saw the silent hump of Sergei lying in the hay. He listened. He prayed for a small sound of breathing, a whispered sigh, an imperceptible butterfly-stir, but the loft was silent and as still as a tomb. He wondered whether he should run and fetch Anna Pankov, but he knew that what had happened in that loft was no outsider's business, that it was strictly a 'family' affair, of which unit Sergei was an undeniable part. He crept warily towards the still great-coated hump.

Sergei was lying on his back, his eyes staring wide at the overhead beams. His hands lay open on his coat, and in one of them the Christ lay, his chain broken and dangling in the straw. A manger death, Reuben thought, and he took up the cross and for no reason that he could understand he carefully mended the broken chain and laid it tidily on the straw. Then he closed Sergei's eyes with the palm of his hand, and rested his head on Sergei's chest and wept long and silently. He wept for Sergei, for Lev and Yossel, for Benjamin and himself, and for all those children of his tribe so rudely weaned from warmth and comfort. He cradled Sergei's shaven head in his arms, and in his ear he sang the prayer for the dead. Then he covered his friend's young face, and returned to the kitchen and told them what he had found. They did not ask or wonder why young Sergei had died. They knew. The priest had injected Jesus into Sergei's stubborn little Jewish heart. He had simply rejected it. It was the least and the most that he could do. The cause of death was wholly natural; a fitting way for a Jew to die. And as a Jew, they mourned him. They insisted on their own burial rights, and they insisted too on their own mourning rituals. And Likov, who had already collected his bond, saw no reason to deny them, especially since it was Reuben they had sent as their spokesman. So they washed and prayed over their friend, and on the very next day they buried him in Farmer Pankov's fallow field. And for seven days, between their regular routines, they sat on the floor and mourned him.

Sergei was not replaced in the billet, and the young recruits drew even closer together, bound now by their common bereavement.

Sergeant Likov did not look upon Sergei Ash as one of his failures. He ascribed his death to his overlong thirst but at least, in his eyes, and in his pocket, Sergei Ash had died a Christian, despite all that mumbo-jumbo they sang over his grave. Besides, he'd had greater success, and certainly a better survival rate in other billets, and the pieces of silver itched his greedy palm. He'd heard of a travelling fair that was due to arrive in a near-by village, and with a certain amount of manoeuvring he managed to give his troops a week's rest, confined of course to their billets, and to take himself off for a well-earned spree. On hearing the news, a delighted Farmer Pankov put the boys to work. Benjamin and Reuben begged for and were given charge of the cows, while Lev and Yossel were delegated to the kitchen to help Anna Pankov bottle her fruits and vegetables for the winter. It turned out to be the boys' happiest time since they had left home, so much snow, so many foot-slogs, so many *Kadishes* ago.

When, years before, the farm had been commandeered by the army as a billeting-post for child soldiers, Anna Pankov had been apprehensive. Her husband had petitioned the army commander to be relieved of the duty. Like any good Russian peasant, he hated the sight of Jews who were the cause of all the troubles in Holy Russia and he did not want them contaminating his land. Neither Farmer Pankov nor his wife had ever seen a Jew in their lives so when the farmer, his petition denied, had been forced to reduce part of his holding to an army billet, he and his wife had waited hand in hand in their yard in fear and trembling for their first lodgers. When the bedraggled pathetic group had arrived at their gate, they had watched as the sergeant syphoned off five of their number and pushed them up the path.

'They're not too bad,' Sergeant Likov had shouted to the farmer, 'and they speak a bit of Russian. We'll make Cossacks of them yet,' he had laughed, and he had led the rest of the herd away.

The Pankovs stared at their uninvited guests, looking for some mark that by all accounts and hearsay distinguished them from the rest of the young humanity they had known. But they could find nothing.

'Are you Yids?' Farmer Pankov asked after a while.

Benjamin nodded on everyone's behalf.

'Lift up your coats from the ground.' Farmer Pankov was sceptical. He no doubt expected cloven hooves. The boys did as they were told, revealing only boots many sizes too large for them.

'Come in,' Anna Pankov said timidly, and she led the boys into the kitchen.

Farmer Pankov followed them, sizing them up from behind and no doubt looking for tails. Then he sat down on a kitchen chair and ordered them to take off their coats. In their blouses and breeches they looked the same as any school-child of the region, but for their shaven heads, the mark of their conscription. Still he was not satisfied, and resolved to have them strip entirely to discover the exact spot on their bodies where the devil had left his print. So he ordered them to gather around the fire – he did not want to appear punitive – and to take off all their clothes in order to wash themselves down. He bade his wife prepare hot water and he himself unhooked a large tin-bath that hung on the brick side-wall of the hearth. The boys undid their buttons nervously, fearing the tell-tale mark that they knew he was seeking. They left their breeches till last, then, naked to the waist and bare-foot, they had no choice but to drop their final defence. Farmer Pankov looked hard at their bodies, staring from one to the other. Then he took Benjamin's genitals gently in his hand and examined them closely. He did likewise with the others. Then he wiped his own hand down the side of his breeches, threw back his head, and roared aloud.

'Anna,' he shouted, 'come quick,' he said, as if the vanished foreskin would suddenly re-appear. 'Come and look, Anna,' he shouted.

Anna Pankov bustled back to the kitchen laden with steaming kettles. She put the pans down and stood by her husband's side.

'Look,' he roared, pointing to Benjamin's parts, and then to the others', 'here and here, and here. That's why they're different. That's what all the fuss is about.'

Anna Pankov blushed scarlet, as much for the boys' embarrassment as her own, and she busied herself filling the bath and reaching for the slabs of soap. The spectacle had put Farmer Pankov in good humour and he urged the boys to stand in the bath and to wash that part on behalf of which millions of Jews in his Holy Russia had been, and were at this very moment, uprooted, maligned, tortured and slain. He splashed them gently as his heart filled with pity for their whole tribe. 'We'll make Cossacks of you yet,' he echoed the sergeant's words, but he meant them kindly. He was a simple man and he devoutly believed that to arrive at Cossackdom was the height of any good Russian's achievement. He meant well for his lodgers. He knew it would not be hard to love them.

Anna Pankov rubbed down their backs and gave them her husband's white linen night-shirts to sleep in. As the boys settled in their cots that night, they thought that in some strange way, and in some alien land, they had come home. And so for the last two years or more, despite the terrors of their army routines, their billeting had been happy enough, and the prospect of a week's freedom with the Pankovs was like a longed-for holiday. And that's how it turned out to be. Soldiers turned farmers' boys, and closer to their own childhood then they had been in many years.

*

After a week, Sergeant Likov roared back into barracks, drunk and penniless. It was high noon when he rolled into Farmer Pankov's billet and ordered food and vodka. During their happy freedom the boys had forgotten all about him, and all that he stood for, and his sudden re-appearance cast a gloom over the farm and all its inhabitants. He drank himself into a vodka-stupor and dropped his head onto the table, snoring himself into oblivion. The boys withdrew to the kitchen and the cow-shed and dreaded his wrath on the following day. And, as it turned out, they had plenty of cause for terror, though it was kept secret from them. For during the sergeant's absence, word had come from on high that His Imperial Majesty was by no means impressed by the conversion figures. Besides, the rewards he had promised for saving Jewish souls had been a drain on his Exchequer, and the troublesome administration of single conversions in no way merited the small returns. The Czar expressed a wish for quicker results and on a larger scale. So the order went out for wholesale baptism. An enforced measure without preliminary persuasion. A rider was added to the effect that His Majesty would be visiting that region for an inspection of his young recruits, and would expect on that day, in a month hence, to witness a wide-spread baptism in the River Ural which bordered the area.

The barracks were thrown into confusion. A visit from the Czar was a menacing prospect. They were not too worried about the baptism for that presented few problems of organisation. The River Ural was waiting and willing, and so were the priests. So were the children, though innocent of the conspiracy. It was the inspection that was worrying. The children's drilling and soldiership were hardly up to the expected standard of His Imperial Majesty. So the drill-sergeants went to work with a vengeance and the poor children couldn't understand the sudden brutalising panic. The long foot-slogging marches were now unending, the dress parades, the marathon runs. Every night Anna Pankov would rub her boys' feet with spirit of alcohol to soothe their blisters and sores. Rumour of the Czar's visit had spread around the camp, and this increased the boys' terror. They had the impression that a raging battle was at hand and that the Czar was coming to lead his infant troops into the bloody fray as one sure and certain way of getting rid of the lot of them. In the last week of their brutal training, their rations were increased to feed the energy expended in such exercise, but at the end of the day their fatigue and apprehension had blunted all appetite and the morning prayer of thanksgiving for their survival was as fervent and as zealous as if it might be their last.

On the appointed day, the Pankovs gave their boys a special breakfast, and embraced them as if they were seeing them for the last time. Sergeant Likov was meticulous in his troop inspection, and clearly very nervous of his performance. When he was satisfied with the appearance of his troop-section, he marched them onto the barracks square. There the few hundred of them were assembled and stood to attention until the entourage of His Imperial Majesty appeared on the brow of the overhanging hill, and led their sovereign to the platform that had been erected on the square. The children stared at him with a raging hate, seeing in his terrible person the cause of all their sufferings, and their trigger-fingers itched on their unloaded rifles. And their hatred acted as a spur to their parade, each marching tramping foot a revengeful treading on the tyrant's grave. The drill-sergeant did not know what had so suddenly inspired them, and he could only imagine that it was the awe of Majesty. When the long parade was over, they were allowed to stand easy for a while in preparation for the marathon formation-run to the river bank some nine versts distant. But the Czar was impatient for the river spectacle, so the rest period was curtailed and the children ordered into formation.

The marathon run began. Sergeants and officers rode along the way, their eyes on the troops, while the Czar and his entourage were carriage-driven towards the river bank. Benjamin and Reuben, Lev and Yossel ran abreast, encouraging each other in low whispers, and it seemed to each of them that their drumming hearts would burst. Yet there was no let-up. The officers urged them on from the side-lines, whipping the odd straggler into line. Occasionally a sergeant would number off their striding steps from one to four to keep them in running rhythm. After a while the little legs moved of their own accord, and left the heart to deal with its own agony. At last the river bank came into view, and the horse-soldiers whipped again in case there was any let-up in the running rhythm. In the last spurt towards the river, some forward officers galloped to the bank and arranged themselves in a row to mark the finishing line, while the sergeants conducted and graded a tidy slow-down. At last the whole troop came to a halt, and in their ranks there were now noticeable gaps, once filled by children whose hearts could not bear the strain. Their whipped bodies lay somewhere on the roadside, trampled on, dying, or mercifully dead. The roll call at the river bank registered twenty-five child-soldiers missing. The news was transferred to the Czar's aide, who shrugged his shoulders with disdain.

After the roll call, the commanding officer stood the boys at ease and told them that they had done well. And as a reward for their labours they were going to be given a treat. A sigh of young and monumental disbelief rose from the platoon, and the officer took it as one of relief.

'You can throw off all your clothes, and cool off in the river,' he said. 'Enjoy yourselves,' he commanded, and gave them the order to strip.

For the young 'kantonisti', that order, under whatever circumstances, spelt danger. To undress was to reveal their difference. They hesitated, suspicious.

'You can't go in with your clothes on,' Sergeant Likov laughed. 'I'm going for a swim. Follow me.' And he began to unbutton. Thus encouraged, many of the children followed suit. But Reuben and Benjamin hung back. They knew that for a poor 'kantonisti' in the Russian Imperial Army, nothing was for nothing. Treats were always costly and they wondered now what price they would have to pay for this one. Around them, naked children, holding their mark of difference, were running towards the water. But Lev and Yossel held back too, sniffing conspiracy.

'What shall we do?' Lev whispered.

'Just not go,' Benjamin said. 'It's a trap.'

And his fears were confirmed at the sight of a troop of Orthodox priests who loomed out of nowhere, earnest in their sacerdotal robes and wading into the shallows, their holy books held high above their heads. And what was His Imperial Majesty himself doing there on his horse on the river bank awaiting spectacle?

'It's baptism,' Benjamin whispered, and the four of them turned and walked away.

'Come on, boys.' It was the commanding-officer's voice and its tone was order. 'Get undressed.'

They turned and he himself walked towards them. 'Just get into that water,' he said.

There was no way out. Benjamin grasped at his time-honoured release, means which, even in this extreme and terrible circumstance, might justify the ends. 'It's in the name of survival,' he whispered, then a little louder in Lev and Yossel's ear, 'We have to survive. It's God's will.'

Lev shrugged his shoulders as he unbuttoned his blouse. Not *his* God's will, he thought, nor Yossel's. He did not know what he was going to do. Neither did Yossel. But both of them knew that Benjamin's price for survival was beyond their spiritual means. Yossel put his little hand to his cheeks, and once again clung to his non-existent ringlets, a habit he had slowly grown out of in the last few months; while Benjamin, already stripped himself, undid the button of Yossel's blouse. Then the four of them walked slowly towards the river.

Sergeant Likov, paddling in the shallows, encouraged them into the water, and the sight of so many children laughing and splashing was so innocent and so devoid of malicious intent, despite the sombre priest-presence, that Reuben was heartened and he started to run, clutching Benjamin's hand. 'It's all right,' he shouted back to Lev and Yossel. 'It's only water.'

But Lev and Yossel were not pacified. In their eyes, Christians could pollute anything, and most of all water. Especially water, by pretending it was holy. For them the river was no playground.

The commanding officer yelled at them again, and they slunk, terrified, into the shallows.

The water was undeniably refreshing after their long run. They dog-paddled a little, encouraged by the joy of the other recruits around them. And so they besported themselves for a while, until the commanding officer ordered them to the bank. They looked and saw a troop of soldiers line up behind an equal line of priests, their naked bayonets in their hands. And they knew, each child amongst them, that God's back was turned. They looked round. Behind them there was a far distant bank, and, far beyond that, the sea. In front of them, the gate to Hell.

The priests took them in turn. The priest bade each child immerse himself and, on coming up for air, a prayer was recited over his head, and the sign of the cross was the final seal of conversion. After a while, Reuben and Benjamin, hand in hand, reached the priestly line, and both were baptised simultaneously. They held hands all the while and, when it was over, they walked silently out of the water and sat alone on the bank. 'Shema Yisroel,' they both began together. 'Hear, O Israel.' Just in case God had been looking, they wanted to reassure Him.

There was a small commotion on the river bank. And much shouting. Two single shaven heads were seen across the river, and two pairs of hands were clutching the cheeks. 'Come back,' Sergeant Likov shouted, fearful of yet another failure. Yet he made no attempt to save them. The other recruits looked on, helpless. Then the heads were seen to move close to each other as if the bodies below were clasped together. There was a terrible silence across the water, as they all watched the Abromovitch brothers from the bank, the children not knowing whether to pray for their deliverance or their peace. And uncertain too of to whom now, in their recent baptism, to address such a prayer. Then across the water like a ghostly spondee supplication, came the cry of the 'Shema', as Lev and Yossel Abromovitch made their final covenant with their God, and its unconquerable faith echoed across the river and onto the heathen bank, in a fragile peal of glory. The young recruits shivered with shame. They watched as the twin heads submerged, rose once, then again, and finally were seen no more.

'That's two Yids off our hands,' Reuben heard one of the officers say, and the other by his side laughed.

'I wish their whole tribe would be so obliging,' he said.

Benjamin and Reuben stared at the now peaceful patch of water that sheltered their friends, and from their throats yet again came the opening chorus of 'Kadish', that mourning prayer which, over their bereaved years, had found a permanent lodging on their lips, and the other recruits, baptised as they were, took up the song, and pealed it across the water. Then His Imperial Majesty was seen to turn away in anger. 'Horse-whip them,' he shouted, then he rode off to his carriage.

The commanding officer ordered silence, and the command that the naked boys were not to move from their places. Then the drill-sergeants took their whips and wrought havoc with their naked flesh. The Czar watched from the door of his carriage then, satisfied, he ordered the coachmen to drive away. The whipping ceased, and the boys, wincing with pain, yet sustained by their small triumph, crawled along the ground for their clothes.

That night, Farmer Pankov and Anna wailed the loss of their children and clung to the milk-brothers in their common sorrow.

'We'll miss them,' Anna Pankov cried.

'I hate them,' Reuben suddenly said, his grief heaving with anger. 'Both of them. My grandfather said there was no God worth one's martyrdom. They were not *supposed* to die.'

'Everybody has to do what they have to do,' Farmer Pankov said. 'It doesn't make them heroes, and it doesn't make you cowards.' He took them both in his arms. 'Tomorrow is Sunday,' he said. 'We'll go together and look after the cows.'

He knew that to be a possible source of solace for the milk-brothers. But they trembled. If tomorrow was Sunday, they suddenly realised that this day was the Sabbath. They had submitted themselves to baptism on their Holy Day, and on that same day Lev and Yossel had committed the most cardinal sin of all. All the brothers in their own way had desecrated their Sabbath, and in some strange way it made them all equal.

CHAPTER FIVE

It was snowing. Odessa snow. Manageable. And once again it was the milk-brothers' birthday. Jakob Bindel woke early, knowing the day from the tail-end of his dream. He smiled on waking, as one would on a birthday, although there was no one on whom to shower his greetings, but he smiled nonetheless, because he knew with absolute certainty that, somewhere in the vast Eastern territory of this hated land, two people whom he loved more than his own life had survived yet another year. He knew it because there was no reason to know otherwise.

Every night since the children's recruitment, he made his fearful way to the offices of the *Kahal*. Over a year ago, the *Kahal*s had been abolished, but their offices remained, staffed now by police and local officials, as corrupt and as bribable as were their predecessors. Yet even now, after so many years, Jakob's heart soured with Meisel memory as he approached the bulletin board and scanned the register of missing child-soldiers. All were very young. Few were over the age of thirteen and, though they were presented as having sacrificed their lives for His Imperial Majesty, the bereaved would find no honour in such citation. As the years had passed, Jakob had read the list with less fear, for his children were children no longer, and had learned to eat with tongue in cheek, and to accept Christ likewise, for today, undeniably so, they had reached their twenty-first year. Jakob Bindel had not missed one moment of their growth. In their absence he had lived with them daily. He had stood by their side in front of the Holy Covenant, and had coaxed that survival word out of their throats. He had attended their weaning from their home, their ghetto, their warmth and comfort and with them had suffered all the terrible pains of withdrawal. On the day of their barmitzvah he had gone to the synagogue, and on their behalf had initiated them into manhood. He had feared their eventual baptism, and daily he had reasoned and argued and finally defied God in the name of survival. He felt the growth of their limbs, the stirring in their loins, and he prayed that their gross deprivation would not forever freeze love in their hearts. And each day he thanked God, even though he had quarrelled with Him; nevertheless, he thanked God for their survival.

And of this he had had proof. It had happened at the end of the milk-brothers' barmitzvah year. It was late evening in the tavern and he was playing chess with Faivel. A uniformed soldier had appeared at the door. Jakob's heart had faltered as it always did at the sight of a uniform, recalling the dreaded call of the recruiting officer and that fatal visit that had changed all their lives. Now he reminded himself that he had no more seed for the Czar's sowing and blessed himself for his unassailable granddaughters. Besides, this soldier did not look to be the bearer of ill tidings.

'Jakob Bindel?' he enquired from the tavern-door.

Jakob stood. The soldier came towards him, and put his hand into the inside of his greatcoat.

'I have a letter for you,' he said. 'From Benjamin and Reuben.'

Jakob was forced to seat himself again. The mention of his children's names always overwhelmed him. Now they came from a stranger's mouth, and in such loving tones that Jakob was shaken with emotion.

'Sit down,' he said to the stranger, 'and welcome to my tavern. Will you take a kvass with us? This is my friend Faivel,' he said, almost in the same breath. 'He knows the children well.' He was thinking of the letter that the soldier had promised and the words that tumbled out of his mouth were for the purpose of postponing that unspeakable pleasure that lay in store.

But Sergeant Likov was not disposed to stay, or to make any kind of production of a mission that simply required letter-delivery. He had almost not bothered to come at all. But the letter had itched in his pocket ever since he had come home on leave almost a month ago. Yet he couldn't bring himself to throw it away. He was anxious to catch a glimpse of the family which had sired that body which, with such sulking resistance, had given him so much pleasure. For nothing was for nothing. For when, before his leave, he'd promised the boy anything he could name in return for lying by his side, Reuben's simple request had been for him to deliver a letter to his family. Then Reuben had paid the postage price. Likov's loins still burnt with the lingering memory of that love, unrequited as it was, and it was to rekindle that joy that he had turned his steps towards the ghetto. But he did not want to stay. Despite the years he had spent in Jews' company, he still felt ill-at-ease in their presence. Besides, he was beginning to find them human and that was not good for a Russian soldier who aspired to Cossackdom. So he declined Jakob's invitation.

'I must be leaving,' he said. 'I just came to bring the letter.' Then he turned to go.

'Tell me about them,' Jakob pleaded. 'When did you see them? Are they well? Are they happy?' he dared to ask.

'Who is happy in the army, Mr Bindel?' Likov laughed. 'But your boys are well. I saw them only a month ago. They are a credit to you, your children,' he said. 'They know how to survive.' He clicked his heels, nodded to both men, and left the tavern.

The echo of his last words throbbed in Jakob's ear, and he prayed to the God he wasn't speaking to, to give him life long enough to see his children once more.

'They will survive,' he said to Faivel, as his finger trembled on the envelope in his hand. 'I will open the letter with all my children,' he said. 'You come too, Faivel. I shall need a man's support,' he laughed, and he led him into the back room of the tavern. The women were all assembled around the huge stove, Miriam, Sofia, Sarah and Zena and all their little daughters, and Esther, who clung to Jakob's sleeve. Then he showed them the envelope.

'I have a letter from Benjamin and Reuben,' he said simply.

'They are alive?' they whispered.

'They are well,' he said. 'A credit to us. They know how to survive.'

'Open the letter, Father,' Sofia said softly.

They waited in silence as Jakob prised the envelope with his trembling thumb, and when it was open two sheets of paper were visible. Jakob rested as if after a long labour. The pleasure that lay in store was to be savoured and prolonged. It was almost four years since word had come from the milk-brothers, and the breaking of such a silence was to be relished slowly, stage by stage. After a while, he took out one of the sheets, and laid it squarely in the centre of the table. At that angle it was not readable for all members of the family circle, but it was an opportunity to view the script, and the paper that had been touched by their children's hands. Then Jakob picked up the sheet, and read aloud.

'*Our dearest grandparents, parents, sisters, uncles, aunts, cousins, Faivel and Raisl, Dov and Rosa.*' Jakob paused again, and watched each face around the table as it beamed at its calling. '*And the cows too,*' Jakob read on, and paused yet again, and smiled. '*We love you all very much,*' he went on, '*and we think of you every day. Life here is not so miserable. We live for the time being on a farm with Farmer Pankov and his wife, who are very kind to us.*' At this point in the reading, Jakob had to pause to accommodate the lump that was rising in his throat. And for the sudden surge of love he felt for those unknown, unseen peasants. '*Sergeant Likov,*' he read on, '*who is our drill-master, has promised to deliver this letter when he goes on leave. Do not worry about us. We have come to terms with many grievances. We have whispered the Kadish many times for friends we have lost, but we know we shall live to see you all again. We kiss you all. Love from Benjamin and Reuben.*'

'Again, again.' Esther said quietly for she feared a flood of tears round the table. And Jakob obliged quickly, and for the same reason, and so they read the letter over and over again, each one in her turn until they all knew it and chorused it by heart. And as if for a second course in their delights, Jakob withdrew the other sheet of paper. He looked at it quizzically, trying to connect the unknown signature with the handwriting he knew so well.

'It's from Farmer Pankov,' he told the gathering, 'and look, Faivel,' he said, showing him the paper. 'It's written in Russian, but it's in Benjamin's hand.'

'Translate, Father, please, quickly,' Miriam said.

Jakob held the letter at a respectable Russian distance and adjusted his voice to a formal tone that had no part in his prior reading of the milk-brothers' Yiddish. The sound was almost declamatory. *'My respected Mr and Mrs Bindel,'* he recited, *'and honoured Mr and Mrs Wolf. I cannot read or write, but I want to talk to you in some way, and Benjamin will write down for me what I have in my heart. I love your two children as if they were my own. My wife Anna says the same. They have suffered much, but they are strong and enduring. They meet every obstacle with courage. Today was their bravest day of all. They submitted themselves to baptism.'*

Esther gave a small scream, and the other women wailed in sympathy. Then suddenly Jakob raised his voice, and shouted, 'Be quiet, all of you,' with such anger and with such trembling of his lip that they were cowed by his fury. 'Listen,' he said. 'Listen to the rest of it. *"They submitted themselves to baptism,"'* he repeated, *' "but"'*, he shouted the word, and paused, so that its significance should be lost on none of them, *' "but,"'* he repeated, *' "they are still your loving sons."'* He looked around the table, and touched the women's hands. 'They're alive,' he whispered. 'Isn't that all that matters?'

'They did it to survive,' Faivel said. 'We should all be proud of them.'

Jakob picked up the letter again. *'My wife and I send our respects to you and all your family, all of whom, from the children's stories, we now know so well, and we hope that the times will soon be better for all of us.'*

Benjamin had then signed Farmer Pankov's name, and under-lined it as if to give it the importance and the dignity he felt it deserved.

Jakob laid the two sheets of paper on the table and then touched them in silence for a while. Then he called for a second sitting for the men of the house. Faivel offered to take Yosif's place at the tavern counter, and Leon was called in from the sheds. Victor and Yuri left the wagon they were loading for the next day's market and gathered around the kitchen table. Once more Jakob performed his recital, and once more the men learned it by heart, and in the safe absence of the women they embraced each other with their mutual embittered joy. Then Jakob wrapped the letters in a silk handkerchief and put them in a leather bag which he kept under his bed. And every morning since, he had taken them out of their silk wrappings, as he was doing now, on this, their twentieth birthday. He needed to look at them as he said his morning prayers. Years ago, before the children had been recruited, his morning-prayer ritual had been irregular due to the gradual waning of his faith. When the milk-brothers had left the tavern, he had put away his phylacteries as his first gesture to God that he was not at all pleased with Him. And until the day of Sergeant Likov's visit, they had lain untouched in the drawer. But with the news of the children's baptism, he took them out again and wound them lovingly about his arms, but he made it clear to God that it was solely on his children's behalf that he worshipped, and that he himself was still displeased with His Almighty's bewildering business methods. With his eyes on the letters in front of him, he went earnestly about his devotions, and when he had finished he folded the letters once more into their silk wrapping.

*

During the pre-Passover days, the women were busy preparing for the feast, and Jakob spent much of his time with Leon, and always in Leon's place of work, in the cow-sheds, where Leon was most at his ease. Over the years Jakob had come to value his silences, and the worth of his unspoken words. He spoke of the milk-brothers rarely, but when he did it was as if he had seen two sudden pillars of fire and there was glory in their sound. He loved to go about his work while Jakob hovered about him and spoke of their children, recalling memories of their childhood. From time to time he would nod, smile and even laugh aloud, and in the extremes of his emotion he would caress his animals with an itching rage. Then Jakob would leave him, and it was in those moments, when Leon was alone, and Jakob, frayed with memories, returned to the tavern, that the two men came closest to loving and to touching each other.

There were rumours that Passover in the ghetto. Rumours of unrest. The ghetto-dwellers heard tell of even more restrictions on their lives, higher taxes and the closure of Jewish schools. But they were used to the pre-Holy Days ferment. The Jew-hate that seethed in the Russian soul throughout the year was wont to boil over on Jewish feast days when the difference between the true-blooded Russian and this alien irritant became more apparent. Especially was this so at Passover when the old belief, that Jews used Christian blood in the preparation of their unleavened bread, once more found its seasonal credence. And at the same time it presented a God-given solution to the problem of one Victor Pandowska.

Pandowska was a serf on a large holding of an Odessa landlord.

86

His daily life was miserable enough, and now made even more wretched by the misfortune that had befallen his daughter Tanya, fifteen years old, who at that very moment was giving birth to a poor bastard a passing soldier had planted inside her. He'd hidden her lying-in in the tool-shed, keeping watch from the outside and listening to her labouring cries. And when they ceased, he cocked his ear for a baby's cry. But none came. He waited, and still there was silence from behind the door. He peered inside. Tanya lay there on a bed of straw, her legs spread-eagled and a lifeless shape between them. He could not hide his relief that the child was dead. But where, in God's name, could he hide the body? The sight of his daughter's weeping despairing countenance filled him with pity and rage against all the injustices of his life, against all his deprivation, his poverty, enslavement and his abject misery. His only avenue of relief was to find someone to blame, someone on whom to pin the causes of his wretchedness. And that scapegoat name that lodged on every Christian lip now found utterance. Let those rotten Jews pay for his daughter's shame, and the misery of his own life. He looked at the child and was pleased that it was a boy. He turned his back on his daughter and quickly he incised the child's member with his knife. It was a crude cutting. A little blood flowed and soon congealed, then he wrapped the baby in a tool-bag that lay on the floor and he left the shed.

It was almost dusk in the ghetto, a good light for subterfuge. Not that Pandowska felt that he needed any camouflage. In all his poverty and his deprivation, he was still rich in comparison with these ghetto-dwellers, for he at least was of the Christian faith, and in these pagan surroundings he felt almost legally entitled to any misdemeanour of his choice. He lorded his feet over the cobbles, strutting like a master, the parcel of dead child under his arm. He had made no plan as to where to deposit it. One Jew as a victim was as good as any other. At that moment he was passing a tavern, and saw beyond it and behind it a field, and in that field was a cow-shed. He made his mean way over the grass.

The door of the shed was open, and the cows were lowing in their stalls. He sought out a mound of hay and threw the parcel in that direction. Its dead weight landed on the mound and was clearly visible from the door, so he stepped inside and buried it lightly in the hay. The action of interment stirred a prayer in his heart and he committed the child's body to the earth and returned its soul to God in the way of any priest. Then he left the shed and sauntered down the street.

He had it in mind to go to the police, but he had to make his way there at a leisured pace, so that he could rehearse to himself some believable story. It took him a little while to sort out the sequence of events, and when he reached the station he stood outside and whispered it to himself. 'My master wanted some cord for his bales and the ghetto shops are open late, especially before their Passover. As I walked past the tavern, I saw a man hurrying towards a field with a parcel under his arm. He looked suspicious so I followed him, and I watched him as he tossed the parcel into the cow-shed. Then he went inside. Of course, it may mean nothing at all, but you know officer, with those Jews and their Passover . . .' He opened the station-door.

*

Leon was making his way to the sheds. He was humming one of those songs they would sing at the *Seder* table. 'Only one kid, only one kid, which my father got for two farthings,' and as he sang it he saw the milk-brothers' ten-year-old faces, and he tried to imagine how they would look now in their twenty-first year. But he postponed it until he should reach his cows, when, sitting on a stool at their flanks, he would while away the milking-time with story-telling. Leon's tales for Reuben and Benjamin grew more and more adult as the years passed by. It was in their thirteenth year that Leon had put away their childish things, and his tales became those of manhood, and they varied with the season and the Holy Days in the Jewish calendar. It was his way of being with them, of holding them close to his silent breast. He hurried to the sheds in anticipation of his nightly encounter with his children. But that night, when he entered, he shivered and he did not know why. He sat on his stool and set to milking, but the cow was restive, and he heard the others lowing uncomfortably in their stalls. He continued at his work, but he could not begin his nightly tale. Or rather, he would not. He didn't want his children in the shed at this time. There was malevolence in the air and he feared it, and his fear would give the children little welcome. So he spoke softly to the cows to calm them, though he himself was shivering with apprehension. As a result, his milking was clumsy, and the cows moaned with his uncertainty. He tried to re-assure them with his caressing hand, but he noted how it trembled on their flanks. For the first time in his life, Leon Wolf did not want to be alone. He would go quickly to the tavern, he decided, and fetch Jakob, on the pretext of needing some milking help. Perhaps Jakob too would feel the evil eye about him, and find some explanation for its intrusion. He patted the cows once more as his signal that he would soon return. Then, sweating, he turned and made for the door. But when he saw the posse of police sergeants standing there and watching him, looking as if they had been there for some time, the sweat poured from his forehead. Two of them pounced on him, and held his arms rigid behind his back, while the others began a search of the shed.

Pandowska stood at the door, avoiding Leon's gaze, and watching the men as they scrambled the hay, resisting his great temptation to guide them to their quarry. They were far off it, rummaging in the stalls as the cows lowed in terror of their violent presence. Pandowska shifted from one foot to another, impatient to have done with it, and to go back to his miserable hut and tend his daughter. He dared to steal a glance at Leon, who was ashen-faced and looked as if he was about to vomit. The police were impatient too, and wantonly damaged the stalls in their fury, kicking down the wood partitions, as if some treasure were to be found in the grain. Silent and enraged, they destroyed all in foot's range, until one of Leon's keepers left his post and joined in the search. To Pandowska's relief, he went straight to that part of the shed that the others had ignored and, rummaging in the hay, he came across the quarry.

'I've got it,' he shouted.

The others left their havoc and gathered around him, while the cows bellowed, full of fear and pain, their udders bursting.

'Let me milk them,' Leon managed to whisper to his guard. Whatever terrible charge they held against him, whatever appalling evidence their booty revealed, he was concerned with the well-being of his animals.

'He wants to milk his cows,' the guard laughed across the shed.

'He won't be milking cows for a long time to come,' one of the policeman said.

'On the milky way perhaps,' another laughed.

Then they stood aside and revealed the parcel's contents on the straw.

Leon stared at it, and the full implication of the accusation was crystallised in three earthquake words. *Passover. Ritual murder.* A wave of nausea overwhelmed him. Then a scream escaped his throat. 'Reuben, Benjamin,' he shouted, and he broke into terrible sobs, knowing now that never in his life would he see them again.

'Is this what you saw?' one of the policeman asked their informant. Pandowska dared to enter the shed, keeping his eyes firmly on the ground. Then he looked at his parcelled grandchild.

'That looks like the packet I saw,' he said.

'You can go now,' the officer said. 'You have done a good service today.'

'A true Christian,' another said, and Pandowska touched his forelock and retreated, his back to the door. Then once outside the shed, he turned and made his hurried way back to his hovel.

The policemen rewrapped the parcel. 'Murderers,' he muttered.

'The whole tribe of them,' and he motioned Leon's guard to take him away.

Outside, the guard kicked Leon into the wagon, and the posse and their parcel piled inside. Then they clattered off over the cobblestones. Above the din of the wagon-wheels, Leon could hear the cows bellowing. He knew Jakob would hear them.

*

Jakob went every day to the police-station, and after a week, and the end of the Passover, there was still no claim to the baby's body.

'How long will you wait?' Jakob asked.

'Until someone claims him.'

'But the child must have been missed by now,' Jakob said.

They were not interested in his opinion. One day some distraught woman would arrive, screaming for revenge on the murderer of her child. She had to, else their case was threadbare.

But, not surprisingly, no such claimant appeared and, after a month's incarceration, Leon was brought to trial. It didn't matter, they said, that no one had claimed the body. It was enough that the child was dead, mutilated, and found in Leon Wolf's cow-shed.

The prosecution's case rested heavily on Pandowska's evidence, and he lied his rehearsed tale. He had acutely elaborated his initial story. He had had time and the help of the prosecutor himself who fed his mind with sundry tit-bits of narration that spot-lit the honesty of its teller. Pandowska gave the impression of being an upright Russian peasant, who didn't want to get anybody into trouble, but at the same time felt that he was bound to do his Christian duty.

The stuffy room was crowded, and most of the spectators were shrieking for blood. Jews were wary of attending such proceedings. All Jews in Russian eyes were guilty, so they kept to their homes, and kept their ears alert for the latest bulletin. But Jakob was in court, and so was Miriam. She had been adamant even though Jakob had tried to dissuade her. She sat next to him, under his protective arm, while on her other side sat Faivel, and their three faces were masks of despondency. Miriam kept her eyes on Leon. Occasionally he looked in her direction, but neither of them could manage a smile. He was barely recognisable. His face was gaunt, and his shoulders stooped with the burden of another's guilt. His clothes hung about his wasted frame, no longer familiar with the contours that once gave them a shape and a form.

The defence, such as it was, offered no witnesses. Any testimony as to the whereabouts and the doings of the accused at the time of the crime could only be confirmed by the prejudiced party of his family. He was in the tavern, they would claim, and they were all preparing for Passover. But it was the mention of those monstrous preparations that Leon's supporters wished to avoid for they only confirmed suspicion that no Passover could be prepared without Christian blood. So it was only Leon who was called in his own defence. He was frightened, and his voice was barely audible. He had been in the tavern all day, he whispered. He was helping to bottle the wine from the barrels, he said.

'Red wine?' the prosecutor asked with a sneer, and someone tittered.

He was asked to give the timings of his movements, of when he woke, ate and milked the cows. But Leon's life was not guided by a time-piece. He woke when he was no longer tired, he ate when he was hungry and he milked his cows when, by some telepathic magic, he knew they needed him. The only time that he kept was the length of the milk-brothers' absence, and he could have told them that to the day. He looked helplessly round the court. His shoulders were seen to shrug under the loose blouse.

'I don't know about the times,' he said, and he meant it in the general as well as in the particular. 'The only thing I know is that I am innocent.' He shuddered, and slowly he straightened his shoulders and held his head high. Miriam gripped her father's arm. A reddish glow suffused Leon's face as he opened his mouth to speak.

'I have two beautiful children,' he said, 'who at this moment are serving in the Russian army. They were taken away from me when they were ten years old. I do not know whether they are alive or dead. It is your Czar who is in the business of killing children,' he said. 'My hands are clean.'

The room was hushed. Then the spectators began to hiss their horror; and Jakob, Miriam and Faivel knew that Leon had now condemned himself out of his own mouth, that gentle mouth of so few words and of so many long silences.

The judge called for order, and it was in anticipation of the death-sentence that the crowd obliged. Then a lawyer was called to pick up the pieces and make what he could of Leon's blasphemy. But the man did not refer to it. He thought it better to let it lie. Instead he concentrated on the threadbare case for the prosecution, and particularly on the lack of a claimant to the body. He suggested that this pointed to a conspiracy. The child was unwanted, he said, and some villain, riddled with medieval prejudice, had seen it as an opportunity for persecution, and had planted the corpse on the Jew's property. His words were addressed to Pandowska who kept his eyes on the floor.

'Thank you,' the judge said, and the lawyer sat down, and it was clear to the crowd that the judge fully agreed with what had been suggested. Jakob, Miriam and Faivel clasped their hopeful hands.

'But what about the Czar?' one of the spectators shouted, and his indignant cry was taken up by the others, whose peasant lives had been oppressed by that Majesty, in whose name they were now so outraged. The judge called for silence again, and set about to sum up the case. He prefaced his remarks by congratulating the prosecution in bringing the case to the attention of the courts. One could not be too careful, he said, especially in the period of the Jewish Holy Days. But in this case, he went on, there was little evidence of guilt, and he was bound to agree with the points made by the lawyer who had put the Jew's case. He therefore concluded that, on the charge of ritual murder, Leon Wolf was not guilty.

Jakob held Miriam close as she broke into sobs of relief, but Faivel, smelling the judge's rider, laid a restraining hand on Jakob's arm. The Czar's name once more hissed across the room, and this time the judge did not ignore it.

'However,' he said, 'I cannot overlook the supreme insult against His Imperial Majesty, and for that breach of the law I sentence him to ten years' hard labour.'

On the whole, the crowd were appeased, and some of them even cheered. Miriam, her eyes wild with disbelief, rushed over the benches in an attempt to reach her husband, to touch his hand with a ten-year hold, to print his face on hers in a decade's etching, but they were already taking him away.

Leon turned and saw her and he smiled.

'I shall live,' he shouted, 'and so shall the milk-brothers.' This last to Jakob.

Jakob watched as Leon's back shrivelled down the stairway. 'We'll wait for you all,' Jakob whispered. Then he turned and led the way through the court.

Pandowska was the first to make his getaway. But for the defending lawyer's speech, and its implied accusation, he might have hung around to reap the fruits of his Christian act. But the crowd's admiration had been shaken, and he shrunk from the court and made his way back to his hovel. In a way he was relieved that Leon Wolf's life had been spared, but he was bewildered by the crime for which he had been so heavily sentenced. For how often had he himself cursed the Czar and the yoke of serfdom that he had burdened him with. He was very sorry for Leon Wolf, but he was confused too, because he didn't want to share his bed of oppression with a Jew. It was all his daughter's fault for getting into trouble in the first place. He would give her a beating, he decided. That way, his anger and his confusion might be stilled.

By evening when news of the trial had spread around the ghetto, Leon Wolf had become its hero. He had spoken for them all. Together with the Bindels they would await his return, as many of them already waited for their lost sons. The years would pass, the birthdays, the Holy Days and all the landmarks of the year, and each new day would swell the sound of their distant voices, and the passage of time would shorten the shadows of their long march home.

But for Leon Wolf they would wait in vain. For nine solid years he broke stones on the Siberian wastes. He worked alone, talking to himself all the time, telling stories to the milk-brothers on each back-breaking shift. Perhaps he thought that, in their thirtieth year, they were now too old for his tales. For one day he sat down on the rubble and laid down his pick, as a minstrel would put aside his harp. He died because he had run out of stories, and his own was too monstrous to tell.

CHAPTER SIX

It was snowing. Siberian snow, as mean and as unyielding as it had always been. But now it didn't matter any more. On their wagon-trail across the Siberian wastes, the milk-brothers were seeing it for the last time. For they were going home.

They still could hardly believe it. A few months before, there had been rumours in the camp. Nothing specific, just hear-say of an event of great import. It was said to have happened in St Petersburg, and its very location gave it a certain urgency. It was hard to tell whether the news was good or bad, such was the ambivalence of its rumour-tone. It appeared that what had happened was cause for rejoicing, but that the cheers must be behind the hand, and the laughter stifled in the throat. And as it turned out the news required just such a reaction, and when the milk-brothers heard it they feigned sorrow, but their hearts were bursting with joy. For the tyrant was dead. His Imperial Majesty had proved his final fallibility, and like any one of his forty million serfs had qualified for mortality.

Alexander the Second, who succeeded him, was a lesser tyrant of spasmodic liberalism. In one of his generous episodes, sundry restrictions on Jews and Jewish life were lifted. Child-recruitment would soon be abolished, and, in random pockets of the Czar's army, those who had soldiered twenty years were released from service. The milk-brothers had been given an hour's notice to pack their kit. They were stunned. Unlike their family, who took account of their years of absence rather than the soldiering years to come, the milk-brothers had concentrated on the latter, and when suddenly, from one moment to the next, five whole years were knocked off their reckoning, in a strange way they felt cheated. The phrase, 'We have survived', had waited for twenty years in the wings of their tongues, awkward, unripe, unrehearsed. Now it was called upon for utterance and it dried in shyness and total disbelief. Others would have to say it for them, all those waiting for them at the tavern, and as they imagined the welcome they would receive, it did not occur to them that each and every member of their family would not have survived as well.

During the course of their homeward journey they rehearsed their return to the tavern. The days were spent in arguments for and against surprise. There were ways of letting the family know that they were on their way home. A few days' notice would give them the joy of anticipation and lessen the shock of their sudden arrival. But it would detract from the milk-brothers' pleasure, which depended largely on its shock value. They analysed each choice like two philosophers, stretching out the argument beyond its merits. For in truth, they were both apprehensive of their return. They had changed, and with far more than the natural changes of growth. They did not know how they could tailor themselves to a life which, in their adult memories, had become so alien. They had travelled in lands never inhabited by any Jew. Over the past ten years even their fellow-recruits, those who had survived, had been dispersed. It had been twenty years since they had celebrated a single Jewish Holy Day. But most worrying of all was the fact that they were floating in a language limbo. They had left Odessa with a ten-year-old's Yiddish, a language in which they wrote, spoke and, most important of all, dreamed. They were returning with an adult's Russian, which alphabet they could not decipher, which imagery was not of their blood. For many years now neither of them had dreamed, for want of a language for their adult fantasies. The occasional nightmare had startled their sleep, but it was wordless, full of images of despair and sounds and smells of fear. Even now, as with each day they neared their home, they spoke together in their flat Russian, as if this banal exchange would exorcise the Odessa ghosts whom they no longer had a language to confront.

'It seems so long since I milked a cow,' Reuben whispered one night, but even this childhood memory could not prompt his childhood tongue.

'How many cows now in that cow-shed?' Benjamin said.

'I'll lay you a rouble on ten.'

'Done,' Benjamin said, stretching out his hand.

They looked at each other for a long while. Then Benjamin clasped Reuben's shoulder. 'We have survived,' he whispered.

They were woken by a sudden change in the wagon-wheel music. Instead of cobble-stones, the wheels were passing over wood, and Benjamin and Reuben peered into the dim light and saw the wagon's reflection in a dawn river.

'It's the Dnieper,' a soldier behind them said. 'By dusk we'll see the ships in Odessa harbour. How long are you from home?' the soldier asked.

'Twenty years,' Benjamin said.

'A lifetime,' the soldier muttered.

'And you?' Reuben asked.

'Four years,' he said. 'I've got a girl in Odessa. Said she'd wait for me.' There was little confidence in his voice. 'But by now she probably thinks I'm dead. Maybe she's married somebody else.' He paused and peered into the half-light. 'I'm a bit afraid of going home,' he said.

They turned into their blankets while the wheels took up the cobble-tune again and wound their relentless way to the site of all their fears.

'Will you marry, Benjamin?' Reuben whispered after a while. They had rarely spoken about such things. In all the years of their recruitment, neither of them had known a woman, and Reuben's enforced connection with Sergeant Likov was a secret that he had kept from Benjamin.

'I'd like children,' Benjamin said. 'Two boys like us.'

'Then you'll continue the Bindel line,' Reuben said and there was an unmistakable relief in his voice.

'What about you?'

'I'll never marry,' Reuben said. He had never admitted it even to himself, but now that it was out, and moreover shared, he felt suddenly unburdened. He knew his decision never to marry was unnatural, and he knew its cause.

'Why not?' he heard Benjamin say.

'I want to spend my life learning,' he said. 'I want to study the Talmud.' His future ambition, now so freely stated, did not surprise him. He had lost twenty years of his inheritance and, with each day of his recruitment, that loss had been confirmed. Now he would go home and spend the rest of his life redressing the balance of language and heritage.

Benjamin put his arms around Reuben's shoulder. He would accept it if his milk-brother wished to make a hermit-like withdrawal. 'Then I shall have sons for both of us,' he said, 'and between us we shall guide their growth.'

Then they slept the whole day through, and were woken by the hooters of the Odessa ships. This time, on waking, they felt less fearful. The certainty of their investment in the future, both in the body and the spirit of the Bindel family, had given them peace. The wagon-convoy slowed down as it reached the harbour, and the screeching of the gulls almost drowned the groaning of the wheels. Then they creaked to a halt, and the men inside stared at each other, rooted to the rough floor of the cart, unable to deal with that moment of freedom they had dreamed about over so many years.

'What's the matter with you all?' the coachman shouted. 'D'you want to go back to Siberia?'

They laughed feebly, astounded that that word, that for so long had crystallised all their sufferings, could so soon be the subject of a joke. They trundled out of the wagons and assembled loosely at the port-side. Some of them said their farewells, others were shipbound for the Bessarabian port of Ismail. So each embraced their comrades-in-arms, those men with whom they had for so long shared such hardships, those men who, in the course of time, they would forget, because they could not afford to remember them.

Benjamin and Reuben lifted their kit from the quay-side and walked along the waterfront. They were a good six versts from the tavern. If they hurried they would reach it by evening. After some time they reached the limits of the ghetto and, there, their feet faltered. From open windows the suddenly familiar cooking smells teased them. They sniffed, breathing deeply, unclogging their throat of all the years' foreign nourishment. But the more familiar the smell, the more alien they felt. They trod the cobble-stones warily like intruders on a foreign soil. They matched nothing in their surroundings. Everything was out of joint and the only fitting thing about them were their great-coats, into which they had finally grown. Those same great-coats that had swaddled their young limbs so many *Kadishes* ago.

'It must be near to supper-time,' Benjamin said, and he spoke in Yiddish, as if the ghetto cobbles had dictated that language. And Reuben responded likewise, plucking the syllables of their mother-tongue into a distant familiar melody. And through those magic words they were gently shipped back into the past of their childhood, and its comforting sound eased their passage home.

*

It was Thursday, market-day in the ghetto. That morning Jakob Bindel had woken with a strong sense of elation for which he could find no cause. As was his habit, he took the milk-brothers' letter out of its silk wrapping, and as he unfolded it he was startled to find that the folds of the letter had split in two, and he had to piece

96

together its four parts to make it whole. The breakage did not dismay him, for in some way he felt it connected to his feeling of elation. He wound his phylacteries about his arms and made his peace with God. He saw the broken letter as a sign that he need not pray on the milk-brothers' behalf any more, but that he must pray for himself, and give thanks for his renewed faith. And this he did, as his spirits rose, and by the time he reached the kitchen and sat down for the family breakfast he was in a state of euphoria.

'We must cease suffering this day,' he announced to the table. 'The year of mourning for Leon is over. We have all wept enough. We need to tutor our talent for joy in order to welcome our children home.'

'You still hope for them,' Esther said sadly. 'There's been no word of them for seven years.'

'I don't ever want to hear talk like that,' Jakob said. His anger reddened his face, and his clenched fists were white under the knuckle. 'We must restore order in our lives.'

Then he left and hitched his wagon and made his way to market.

On his way, he made a detour to Faivel's. His friend was stitching away on the pavement outside his shop. Though he would not admit to it, Faivel's sight was failing, and whenever the weather permitted he would take his work outside and profit by the light.

'Come, Faivel,' Jakob said. 'Come with me to market. We'll spend the day together.'

Faivel caught his friend's happy mood. He wrapped up his sewing and wheeled his machine indoors. Jakob waited while he made his excuses to Raisl and he heard the echo of Raisl's rasp as it dogged Faivel's fluttering steps from the house. He shrugged his shoulders in mock despair and hauled himself onto the wagon.

'To Zemach's?' he said, his eyes twinkling.

'Of course to Zemach's,' Jakob said. 'But first we must go to market.'

Jakob found himself buying food far in excess of his weekly needs, but he did not wonder at it for it seemed naturally dictated by his continuing high spirits.

'Are you expecting an army?' Faivel asked, helping to pile the provisions into the wagon.

Jakob looked at his friend. That word was no accident, he thought. 'To Zemach's, Faivel, and we shall tell stories to while away the time.'

'I dreamed of the milk-brothers last night,' Faivel said suddenly.

Jakob stopped the wagon and clutched Faivel's sleeve. 'Is that the truth, my friend?' he said.

'Have I ever told you a lie?'

97

They journeyed in silence and soon they saw the tavern through a clearing in the woods. Outside the entrance Zemach was sitting, a white table-cloth tucked into his collar. He was having a hair-cut, and Zelda, his granddaughter, was barber. When he saw Jakob's wagon, he jumped up to give them welcome, and Zelda scolded him for the disturbance.

'It will wait, my little cabbage,' he said. 'Friends are first,' and he strode towards the wagon. Over the years, his family and the Bindels had grown close. His wife had died shortly after the milk-brothers' recruitment, and the Bindels had made his daughter's wedding in their tavern. Esther Bindel had acted as grandmother to Zelda as she was growing up and Jakob had told her the stories he would have told the milk-brothers. To Jakob, she had been yet another granddaughter, but now as he looked at her he saw her for the first time as a woman, and this realisation was somehow connected with his present happy mood.

'What news?' Zemach asked. 'Is it a holiday that Faivel doesn't work and that you don't return home from market?'

'It's not good to work all the time,' Jakob said.

They went into the tavern. 'We'll open one of my best,' Zemach said, and he went behind the counter and drew out a bottle of red wine which he held up to the light. 'It's from Georgia,' he said. 'It's rare in these parts. It's fit for a celebration.' He paused and looked at his friends, and taking the glasses down he asked, 'What are we celebrating.'

'To life? To the future?' Jakob said. 'Isn't that enough?'

'There's life and future in every day,' Zemach said.

'But in some days,' Jakob countered, 'they seem more possible.'

Zemach poured the wine. 'To life,' he said, and so the three friends sat and soberly celebrated Jakob's unspoken hopes and Faivel's wish-fulfilment dream.

That night the family supper in the kitchen was light-hearted and carefree. They had all been infected by Jakob's mood. Esther had cooked his favourite dessert, and he noted that she had made more than could possibly be eaten by the family. 'You cook for an army, Mama,' Sofia laughed, and as she said it, there was a muffled knock on the tavern door.

In that moment, Jakob understood each presaging moment of his day. His knees trembled. They looked at each other around the table. No one of them moved into the tavern. Not that they were afraid. There was nothing authoritative about the knocking. There was no summons in its tone, no punishment. It was gentle, pleading almost, like a child begging shelter. Once more they heard the knocks and then Jakob rose on his trembling legs and left the table. He shuffled through the tavern, the tears already starting in his eyes. When he reached the door, he would not ask who it was. One did not question the identity of one's own children. He leaned against the door before opening it, gathering his own strength and wishing with all his heart that the gentle Leon was still alive. Then he braced himself and lifted the latch and opened the door wide.

The door-frame was filled with great-coat and he looked from the hem to the collar of them and then at their faces before he could allow himself to accept that his daily prayers over the past twenty years had been answered. They looked exactly as he had imagined them, as he had seen them growing day by day. Reuben was the taller of the two, as he himself had prompted in their imagined growth. He looked very much like Leon, and Jakob was glad of it for it would help mitigate Miriam's loss. When he looked at his own, Benjamin, it was as if in a mirror. He stared and marvelled, afraid to touch them.

They, for their part, saw an old man, and in his worn wrinkled features all the years of his parental loss. Then Benjamin spoke.

'We survived, Father,' he said.

Jakob grasped them both in his arms. He could not speak and he would not sob, but he thought his joy would break him in two. They led him gently into the tavern, noting on the way how small it had grown, or how greatly their nostalgia had enlarged it. They hesitated at the kitchen door, and then stood still. They were too frightened and too excited to take a step further. Jakob gently pushed them aside, and he himself opened the door and shut it behind him, while the milk-brothers stood outside and listened to his voice which had the holy resonance of a prophet.

'What did I tell you?' He thundered to the astonished table. And again. 'What have I always told you? What? What?' The tears were streaming down his face. 'Did I not have faith in it every day?' he whispered.

They stared at him.

'God is good sometimes,' he said. Then he stood away from the door and opened it wide.

The milk-brothers stood on the threshold, their eyes slowly circling the table, identifying brother, sister, niece, parent. And once again they surveyed the faces, their lips muttering each name they knew. Throughout this silent scrutiny, that painful patent gap at the table, that seat unoccupied, that space unstaked, seemed to stretch out its ghost-like arms for remembrance.

'Where's Father?' Reuben said.

Jakob wished that all that could have been saved till the last. That they could have rejoiced in the homecoming, that they could have celebrated with untrammelled joy, and then, after that, and only after that, Reuben would have asked for his father; and Jakob was suddenly seized with a rage against Leon because he had not chosen to survive.

'He's dead,' Miriam said. 'He died a year ago.' She did not cry. She did not wish to give her son a cue for weeping. Leon had been gone from her life these ten years and she was used to his absence. He had gone from his son's life for much longer. She did not want Reuben's tears. 'Leon died a hero,' she said and she stretched out her arms for her son's embrace.

He moved towards her, as Benjamin did to Esther. Gradually, around the table hands, small, large, and all trembling, touched the milk-brothers' faces, as the blind would seek out and welcome their kin. For the rest of that evening, they sat together, silent for the most part, not knowing what questions to ask of each other, undecided as to whether the relevance of the answers was lost in history. Questions about army life would be too large and too general, and their replies could give no adequate picture of their twenty-year sentence. That would have to be drawn slowly, and all that would take time, time for rage, disbelief and wonder, and finally time to prepare its proper place in their heritage. Mostly that evening, they looked at each other while Esther plied them with food.

'You always cooked for an army, Mama,' Benjamin said.

*

The news of the miraculous return of the milk-brothers spread quickly around the ghetto, and the following night, after the beginning of the Sabbath, there were celebrations in the tavern. Like most close-knit families in close-knit communities, the Bindels kept their friends for life, and the guest-list for the welcome home party, with a few additions, was exactly the same as for the parties that had marked the milk-brothers' circumcision and Sofia's wedding. Death had carried off a few of their number. Reb Schlomovitch had gone to his grave and his wife had followed shortly after. There were no officials of the community present for, with the abandonment of the *Kahals*, there was no longer need to curry favour. The absence of Meisels was especially toasted since, for all his malevolence, the milk-brothers had finally outwitted him. Over the years, the true nature of his death had been discovered. Mrs Lascevitch, his reluctant housekeeper, had courageously let it be known, and now Faivel told it as he had told it a hundred times before with much relish and ornament. As he came to the end of his tale Yankel appeared at the tavern-door. He was incredibly old now, and long since retired, but in the Bindel household he had graduated to the status of guest and it was in this capacity that he was now welcomed to the tavern and given a much-needed chair and glass of kvass. No '*schnorrer*' would attend a celebration where Yankel was a guest. Despite his changed status, they would still have regarded it as poaching. For, notwithstanding his retirement from the begging profession, he was still considered by most of his fellow-guests to be God's insurance broker, and they had to restrain their hands from their pockets as they passed him by and took their leave.

The last to arrive, because they had the furthest to travel, were Zemach and his family, his daughter, her husband, and his grandchild, Zelda. Zelda went straight to Esther and kissed her, and then went to help with the dishes on the counter. Benjamin stared at her and wondered who she was, and by what right she was so readily accepted into the Bindel family. He resented her a little. She struck him as flighty and presumptuous. Jakob looked at Benjamin looking at Zelda, and so did Faivel and so did Zemach, and so, out of his long professional training, did Yankel, and all of them chose to misinterpret the look as one of profound curiosity that might well grow into love. They waited for Zelda to catch sight of him, and when she did, turning with a dish of honey-cakes, her eyes were drawn by his staring, and for one second were caught, and then lost in her blushes. The witnesses were satisfied. The mere exchange of glances between Benjamin and Zelda was enough in their eyes to set in motion a marriage contract. It was only a question of time and, if they had learned nothing else in their lives, they had learned, all of them, patience, in whose name this present party was being celebrated.

In his corner, Reuben had witnessed it too, but he knew his milk-brother's heart, and he understood that, like his own, it was closed to loving. To open one's heart was to allow a breach in one's defences. Their bulwarking talent, gleaned and honed by so many years of exile, was not so easily discarded. It saddened him profoundly and more for Benjamin than himself. For his resolve never to marry had been strengthened by the news of his father's death. That morning, his mother had quietly told him the story of Leon's death trial and heroism, and he had decided to devote the rest of his life to study of the Talmud and the Torah, for he knew that in their pages he would find some meaning in his father's silences and in the passion to which he had finally given tongue.

CHAPTER SEVEN

In the months following their return, the milk-brothers withdrew more and more from the family circle. Adjustment was not easy. Over the twenty years of their absence, in their day-dreams the tavern-door had swollen into the vast wrought-iron gates of heaven, and in its portals the whole Bindel tribe had lined up with its welcome. But on their return all images had shrunk. The tavern-door was narrower than their combined greatcoats, and scarcely higher than the top of their shaven heads, and, behind it, the impudent truth of an old shrivelled man, the wrinkles on his face notching each year of their absence, and in that focus, so suddenly and so professionally sharp, they were rudely shunted into the truth of the twenty years that had passed. But the most damning proof of that loss lay behind the tavern-door, through the dark hostelry, shrunk now to their boyhood, and into the back rooms beyond, where lay all the pent-up love that over the years had fed upon its fragile hopes and expectations, a love that, given the smallest avenue of release, would flood the earth. It was that love that the milk-brothers had not reckoned on. In their dreams the tavern of their return was a palace, and such love does not dwell in palatial dimension. It belongs to confinement, to the anchorage and root of family life. It knows no breathing-space, no formality. Any time, any place will do for its artless release, undressed for all occasion. Confronted by this sudden surge of loving, the milk-brothers, for so long untouched, uncaressed, unheeded, longed to withdraw, and to share in the only safe loving that they knew, that of the one for the other. They were like two conspirators who shared the filthy secret of survival, a secret they could share with no other.

In the months after their return, they withdrew in such fashion, taking endless and silent walks through the ghetto, each familiarising himself once again with his past. But one day, during a forest walk, as they strolled through a clearing, Benjamin put a hand on Reuben's shoulder.

'We've lost the talent of loving,' he said.

Reuben paused and stared at his brother. He nodded. Benjamin had fully spelt out the final cost of their survival, and he could not gainsay it. The love that they had for each other was real enough, but its routine skills were not transferable. It was their inalienable property. It was based on a sharing of a past, a past that was sharable with no other. For, despite the endless tales with which they had regaled the tavern-table, they remained only stories, that in no way conveyed the cost of their telling. Sergei Ashe had chosen to die, and so had the Abromovitch brothers, as had those hundreds of ringlet-less boys who had dropped into Abraham's bosom by the wayside. But Benjamin Bindel and Reuben Wolf had *not* died, because that was not what they had chosen, and there was no story that could convey the shame and the guilt of their survival. And so they had to tell it to each other, over and over again, in quiet and private places, sharing the images of their guilt like dirty pictures.

'You should marry Zelda,' Reuben said after a while.

'I do not love her,' Benjamin said. 'Zelda nor any other woman.'

'I have watched her,' Reuben said. 'I have seen her love for you. Such love can open your own heart. Such love will give you children, and your children will justify your survival.'

'And you?' Benjamin asked. 'How will you learn to live with yours?'

Reuben did not answer. He took his brother's arm and walked him across the clearing into the safety of the forest where the trees were a natural orchestration to silence. But after a while Benjamin stopped and held his brother close.

'How will you come to terms with it all?' he asked again. 'You have more to assuage than I.'

Reuben stared at him. 'What do you mean?' he said softly. Benjamin guided him once more into their walking, then he stopped under a tree. 'I know about Likov,' he said. 'Anna Pankov told me. She saw you.'

Reuben trembled. Benjamin's reminder had, with rude speed, shipped him back into that hay-loft, that tabernacle where Sergei Ashe had died. Likov had deliberately chosen that spot, and had led him there to desecrate Sergei's tomb. He recalled hearing some rustling in the hay. At the time he had thought it was a rat.

'She went up there to get some preserving bottles,' Benjamin was saying. 'That night she told me.'

'What stopped you from killing him?' Reuben asked.

'Survival,' Benjamin said. He spat out the word with bitterness. 'Was it worth it?'

'It has to be, brother,' Benjamin said. 'For both of us.'

Reuben smiled. A surge of relief overwhelmed him. Part of the pain of the Likov encounter had been its terrible enforced secrecy. All their lives he and Benjamin had shared everything. Likov had erected the first stake in a barrier between them, and it was this slow and threatening isolation that had pained him most of all. Now that that stake had collapsed, now that his shame was known and understood, his body seemed to cleanse itself a little, to lose its odour of contagion.

'I'm glad that you know,' he said, but, though he was indeed greatly relieved, he knew, as well as Benjamin knew, that this shared secret only served further to reinforce their conspiracy of isolation.

*

Over the next few months, Benjamin grew restless. He longed for anchorage. The need to settle down and raise another Bindel generation became in him a survivor's obsession, and he sought out Zelda as he would any woman who would offer him that haven. On their occasional meetings in the Bindel or Zemach taverns, he had found her fickle and flighty, but it was that very quality that attracted him against all his nurtured principles. For Zelda, as yet, knew nothing about pain or loneliness. She couldn't understand Benjamin's preoccupation with guilt, so she scoffed at it. 'It's all over now,' she said to him. 'It's all in the past, and you must think of your future,' and she turned away to hide her blushing.

'Would you share that future with me?' he asked. He hadn't meant to propose to her. He was simply obeying the logic of her argument. But he made no attempt to withdraw, nor even to dilute his proposal with a suggestion of a long engagement.

'We'll marry in the summer,' he said, and, as he took her trembling hand, he prayed with all his heart that he would learn to love her.

So Zelda and Benjamin were married and, contrary to custom, they made their home not in the bride's house, but in the Bindel tavern. Benjamin was loathe to live apart from Reuben. Besides, Zemach had no land, and Benjamin and Reuben had already enlarged the cow-herd and had started a small trading in dairy produce. Their way of life and way of work had become a repetition of the life-style of their past, always together, ever-dependent on each other, and almost always alone, but now it was a life without fear, and over the years they talked less and less about those evil days in the slow process of self-forgiveness.

*

It was not until Benjamin's first son was born that he was able to open his heart to Zelda. She had promised him a future, and here was the fruit of that promise. He called the boy Aaron after him who saw that promise fulfilled. A year later, a second child was born, another son. It was as if the milk-brothers' return, after such a lengthy female holding, had licensed the renewal of male dynasty. Reuben was still unmarried, and, though he was no longer averse to husband-status, he made little effort to achieve it. The possibility of a family of his own grew more and more remote. So Benjamin named his second son for his milk-brother, calling him Leon, as Reuben would have named a son of his own in his father's memory. Reuben would be a second father to the child, as Benjamin's own sister had been his mother.

The two boys grew up in the tavern with all the privilege, patronage and entitlement of a new generation. Every woman in the household was their mother, and each man their father, but it was to the milk-brothers that Aaron and Leon instinctively turned for parenthood as if for the reliability of a mirror-image. All their free time was spent in the cow-sheds, and as Benjamin and Reuben watched them at the milking, it recalled for them their own pasts that were as yet untainted by survival.

When Aaron reached his barmitzvah year, the Bindel family rightly considered that it was cause for great celebration. Not since Jakob Bindel's own initiation over seventy years ago, had the tavern celebrated that admittance to manhood. Except silently and vicariously, when, on the milk-brothers' thirteenth Siberian snow-bound birthday, Jakob Bindel had gone to the synagogue in proxy celebration.

It was snowing. Aaron's birthday fell a few weeks before Christmas, a safe enough time, for no Jewish festival, either of mourning or rejoicing, fell within its shadows. That barmitzvah morning would mean a slow and precarious walk to the synagogue, but despite the cold the congregation, mindful of the very special Bindel celebration, filled the hall to overflowing. Aaron was nervous, and so was Leon on his brother's behalf. But most nervous of all were the milk-brothers. Not that they doubted Aaron's skilful acquittal of his role, but they were wary of their own. This specific ceremony was unknown to them. On the day of their own barmitzvah they had breakfasted on Farmer Pankov's pork, their tongues already well-tuned to its tasting. Baptism was not far behind, and as they watched Aaron ascend the platform to read his Portion of the Law, they felt like gate-crashers at a stranger's feast, and for a moment they were assailed yet again with that hungry need for withdrawal, to go together to a dark and secret hide-out, and share their shame. But Aaron's song soared in their ears, claiming his entry into that realm of manhood to which he was now, by his years, entitled, and his voice was strong and entreating enough to gain a tardy admission for the milk-brothers as well.

After the ceremony they returned to the tavern where the women busied themselves with preparations for the evening's festivities. The men were ordered out of the tavern. Benjamin took his sons into the forest, and Reuben went with them. The forest was a favourite withdrawing ground for the milk-brothers. Aaron and Leon had their own use for it too, as a playground, but this was the first time that the milk-brothers had shared the forest with the children. It was not a deliberate choice. Their steps had turned quite naturally in that direction. Aaron and Leon took the lead, making for that part of the forest that was their habitual rendez-vous. Benjamin and Reuben followed, and as they covered the route their legs tingled with a strange recall, and they broke instinctively into a running pace, as if that was the tempo that the path dictated. And when they saw the huge oak-tree where Aaron and Leon were resting, they remembered that it was that very tree that had marked the end of their escape-route and their final capture. Aaron and Leon had never been told that story. Neither had the milk-brothers taken that particular forest route since their return. Both had quite consciously avoided it, fearing the rage of its recall. But now it seemed as if the children were licensing that memory, for their own sharing, as if, on this day above all others, Benjamin's eldest son was claiming his part of the Bindel heritage.

'Now is the time to tell them,' Reuben said as they approached the tree. 'Till now it would have been a fairy-tale.'

They reached the oak and leaned against its vast trunk, their backs tingling with recalled youthful fear.

'Is this where you always come?' Reuben asked.

'Yes,' Aaron said. 'Don't we, Leon? We always end up here.'

'Why *this* tree?' Reuben said.

'It's big. You can always find it.'

'There's a story attached to this tree,' Benjamin said after a while.

'A true story?' Aaron asked doubtfully, as if he was prepared on this day to listen to no other.

'It's true all right,' Reuben said. 'Every word of it. It happened to me and your father.'

'Tell us, Papa,' Aaron said eagerly, settling himself down on a fallen pine-log nearby. He moved along for the milk-brothers to sit beside him. Which they did, Reuben taking Leon on his knee.

'We were younger than you both at the time,' Benjamin began. 'We were ten years old. I have to tell you a little of the history of that time.'

Thus Benjamin Bindel let his children into his truncated child-hood, leading them through the dark and perilous journey that, together with Reuben, had robbed them of their youth and natural growth. As Benjamin set the stage for the forest-capture, Reuben saw the lean and gentle back of his father, hunched with anxiety, tip-toeing through the trees, turning occasionally to urge the children's speed and silence. When they'd reached the tree, he'd motioned them to sit and rest. 'You must go to the river,' he had said. 'It's about three versts from here. I shall come with you. But if we get separated, you must make for the willow-tree. It's the largest tree on the bank, and its branches spread half way across the water. Make for its trunk. At that point, the water is shallow, and you can cross the river direct. There's a hut on the other side. Stay there. Eat some food and wait till one of us comes for you.' Then suddenly, as he was speaking, they heard the distinct crunch of foot-steps through the leaves. Reuben recalled the sickly pallor on his father's face. 'Go at once,' he had said, and he'd lifted them both from the ground, kissing the tops of their heads and holding them still for a moment to say goodbye. Then he'd pushed them away, turning his back on them, holding his ground with courage enough in his heart to stem an army. Reuben had taken Benjamin's hand, and heedless of the noise they had scrambled through the trees, their spirit of adventure soured by fear. After a few moments running, Reuben had turned and looked upon his father for the last time. Leon was standing where they had left him, his legs apart, his arms spread-eagled, his fists clenched, an immovable bulwark against any attack. So it was with horror that Reuben watched his father crumble to the ground, like a poorly-packed snowman, as with one disdainful flick of the wrist the huntsman cast him aside.

'You are named after that man,' Benjamin was saying, taking young Leon's hand, and the boy turned on Reuben's knee and clung to his neck. Benjamin smiled at his milk-brother. It was a proper sharing of fatherhood.

Benjamin continued his story. The light in the forest was failing as he reached the last chapter, the knocking on the tavern-door, and their grandfather's unstartled joyful face in its frame. And when the story was fully told, Aaron took his father's hand.

'How did you both survive?' he said, using for the first time that word that day by day had coloured the calendar of the brothers' long absence from home.

And then Benjamin realised that, although he had told the story of their survival in its entirety, he had not told them how that word was first spoken, how it had reverberated in their childish ears, and out of whose angry and loving mouth it had first thundered. It was because of Jakob Bindel and his farewell oratory that the milk-brothers had survived at all, and he had told his children the story without mention of its central theme. He wondered now whether he could give it to Aaron in answer to his question, to give him in answer Jakob Bindel's farewell, which he and Reuben knew word for word. But the present times were calm. No racial threat lurked in their childish corners. Jakob's words would be less pertinent now.

'We were lucky,' he told Aaron. That was all at this time that his son needed to know. 'Come,' he said. 'It's time to go back to the tavern.'

As they turned their steps towards home, they heard the sound of men's voices, and the crunch of fir-cones on the ground. In the clearing they came face to face with a group of woodmen, state foresters with the Czar's insignia on their green caps. Benjamin and Reuben looked at their faces, and in the echoes of their recent story they saw the features of the old 'khapers' who had hunted them down. Even Aaron and Leon trembled at the connection. The men stared at them sullenly, then turned back to their work, that of singling out the trees that would be felled for the Christmas celebrations. But the milk-brothers and the children did not move. They could not. Some unnameable fear had frozen their steps. They watched as the men tapped at the tree-trunks, and from time to time marked one of them with a chalked cross, marking the wherewithal to rejoice in His birth with the mark of His crucifixion.

'What are you staring at?' One of the men turned suddenly from his chosen tree, the chalk dust dripping like blood from his hand. He turned on them angrily as if they had caught him in a depraved act. Benjamin and Reuben were silent and afraid. The woodman turned to his companions.

'The Yids don't like what we're doing,' he shouted.

'Christ-murderers,' another yelled back. 'What d'you expect from them? Look,' he shouted. He strode across to Benjamin and grabbed him by the sleeve. 'Watch me,' he ordered. 'I'll do you a favour.' He took his chalk out of his pocket and went to the nearest fir, and on its trunk he chalked the six-pronged Star of David. 'Is that better?' he laughed. 'Does that suit you?' he sneered, and he took his axe and notched each arm of the Star in turn, destroying, storey by storey, the mansions of their Father's house. Then he raised his axe as if to blind a seventh star, and strode towards the children.

Aaron and Leon took to their heels, and Benjamin and Reuben, in their already practised flight, ran after them, hearing the men's laughter die away in the echoing branches of the trees. No, Benjamin thought. The present times were not as calm as he supposed. Jakob Bindel's valedictory counsel was as pertinent now as it had been over thirty years ago.

They had reached the path that led to the back of the tavern. Benjamin called to his children, and, together with Reuben, the four of them sat on an old wooden bench not far from the cow-sheds.

'I have to tell you something,' Benjamin said. 'You asked us how we survived those terrible army years. I told you we were lucky.

108

But that was only a small part of it. We survived because your grandfather Jakob had shown us the way.'

'How?' Leon asked, 'and why didn't you tell us before?'

'Was it because of those men in the forest?' Aaron said.

Benjamin smiled. 'There are always such men,' he said. 'And always will be. Wherever you are. As long as you are a Jew. Such men will attack you in many disguises. They will do it in the name of the Czar, or they will assault you in the name of freedom. They will try to destroy you on the principle of purification. They will use all kinds of ideologies, but whatever they are called, and with whatever sweetness, they are made, each one of them, of Jew-hate and oppression. Listen to me,' he said. 'When we went into the Czar's army, your grandfather gave us the wherewithal to survive. And I want now to give it to you, as you must give it to your children and they to theirs. Look at me, my sons,' he said, as his own father had addressed them so many years ago. The children stared at him, wondering at the urgency in his voice.

'I want you to live,' he said. 'I want you to survive.'

Reuben chorused him, as if in a litany, recalling all those terrible moments of death-temptation, when anything, on or in the earth, seemed preferable to the life they were forced to live at that time.

'Listen to me,' Benjamin whispered. 'In times to come, the enemy will force you into baptism, as they did to me and your uncle Reuben. Do not resist them. Let them sprinkle their holy water on your brows, let them flood your bodies with their purging priesthood. They cannot lay hands on your Jewish soul. You must survive, my children,' he said again.

Then he and Reuben recited together. 'Beware of principles. Abandon them if you are to survive. There is no cause on earth worth dying for,' they said, 'no God worth one's dying breath, no country worth one's martyrdom, no principle worth one's sacrifice. Only in the name of Love is Death worthy. And friendship.'

When it was over, Benjamin, like his father before him, wondered whether his children had any idea of what he was talking about. But he had to speak out, for his own sake, as his father had for his. From generation to generation there would be a minstrel to sing that stubborn song of survival, in ghetto streets, at wailing walls, in synagogue choirs, and even, and still with throbbing hope, in the changing-rooms of gas-chambers. Everywhere and at all times, there would be a minstrel, and somewhere, someone would hear his song. It was the least and the most that the milk-brothers could bequeath their children. That song was their sure and sublime inheritance.

CHAPTER EIGHT

The next years in the Bindel household were happy ones and the twenty-year interval of mourning and pain was soon numbed and muted in history. The tavern was crowded and over the years the men had built make-shift extensions to house themselves. The Bindel holding was by no means prosperous, but between the tavern, the cows and the vegetables, they managed to eke out a living for them all. Jakob still controlled each area of their livelihood, but his work was confined to the care of the cows. It was that work that he loved the most. Besides, it was the least demanding, for since the return of the milk-brothers Jakob had aged considerably. It was as if their miraculous home-coming had at last given him licence to submit to the natural process of ageing. Until that time he had punished his body in his struggle to survive, to live until they came back to the tavern. Now he was more gentle with himself. He allowed himself shrinkage, as nature dictated. There was little left now of his thick wad of black hair. It was sparse and grey, as was his beard, which he tugged at from time to time, because he knew that that was a mannerism of old men. He still walked with the old pride and stubbornness, though his gait was slower. But he was not submitting to his years. He was simply acknowledging them, bowing to those ways of nature that for so many years he had defied.

There was a certain relaxation of laws pertaining to Jews, a greater freedom of movement beyond the Pale, and entry into certain professions. But these concessions only applied to what was known as 'useful' Jews, those who were wealthy and educated, and Jewish society in general remained unaffected. Indeed a certain schism arose in the community amongst those who propagated assimilation and those who stubbornly adhered to their faith, and it was the latter who remained the constant target of Czarist oppression. Jewish schools were closed, and those who taught in them lost their licence. The wearing of ritual clothing was forbidden as was the wearing of ringlets on the cheek. All were signs of Jewish particularism, their unassimilitability. The Bindel family were not particularly orthodox Jews, so many of the restrictions did not basically affect them. But nonetheless, they remained part and parcel of the butt of Russian anti-semitism. They remained Jews, not for orthodoxy's sake, neither for ritual's, but because the notion of apostasy was treacherous. Besides, they knew that being Jewish is as much in the eye of the beholder as in the Jewish eye itself, and that when the chips were down, no raging, looting, raping Cossack, rampaging through the ghetto, would pause to peruse a certificate of baptism. Nevertheless the Czar's policy was one of 'fusion', and it was plainly unworkable. The more he screamed 'assimilate', the more the Jews cultivated and found shelter in the Mosaic Law, and awaited the coming of the Messiah, and fed the Czar's fury with their stubborn intransigence. It now seemed to them that he was as great a tyrant as his hated predecessor. But for forty million Christian serfs under his rule, Alexander the Second *was* the Messiah, for in 1864 he freed them, allowing them to rent or even own their land. For many Jews this emancipation had drastic repercussions. In their livelihood as middlemen in agricultural goods, they were now redundant. Some of the more prosperous ones invested in the growing railway boom, but for the most, the prospects were pitiable. The Bindel household managed to maintain a steady livelihood, but Jew-baiting was a daily irritant in their lives, and no authority interfered to hinder it. There was no law that sanctioned anti-semitic riot, yet equally there was no law that forbade it. Until that time, throughout the Czarist regime, attacks against the Jews were unorganised, unprepared and erratic. But in 1871, a new word surfaced in the Russian lexicon and sullied it for all time. In the years to come, its utterance would shock the ghettoes of all the major cities of Russia, where the blood would run cold in its echo. It would reverberate in the synagogues of Elizavetgrad, Kiev, Brody and Balta. Finally it thundered in Kishinev and shook the world. The word was 'pogrom', and it was born in Odessa.

*

In 1871, the festivals of Easter and Passover did not coincide, a happy lack of synchronisity, since it diluted the myth of blood libel. The celebration of Christ's death and resurrection would be over and done with before the Jews would celebrate their ironic freedom. And that year, for the first time, the Bindels were to feast at Zemach's tavern, for the *Seder* fell on Zemach's eighty-fifth birthday. Benjamin took Zelda and their sons across the ghetto. She was going to help her mother during the preparations. Benjamin and the rest of the Bindel family were to join them for the *Seder*.

Benjamin drove back alone. It was the Sabbath eve, and late. The streets were quiet, with an ominous silence, Benjamin thought,

111

broken only by an occasional grunt which Benjamin at first could not identify. It sounded as if it came from a stray pig, but Benjamin dismissed that possibility, because the presence of a pig in the ghetto was so unlikely that it could not be considered. Yet he was uneasy. He went inside the tavern and said nothing, but he was very restless that night and he regretted his separation from his wife and children. He heard Jakob's tottering tread on the floor above him and, next door, in a cubicle, the continuous creaking of Reuben's unquiet bed. He was glad when morning came.

It was Sabbath and it was their custom to go to the synagogue. The men of the family left early, Benjamin heard once again an isolated grunt. He looked at Reuben who showed no reaction. Neither had deaf old Jakob. But each of them had heard it and smelt the warning in the sound, and each kept their fears to themselves. At the corner of the synagogue, there was another omen, this one visible, in a group of furtive-looking men in the uniform of the Members of the Sacred League, whose presence, wherever it might be, boded ill, and on such a holy corner could only spell calamity.

'Don't hurry,' Jakob said, as the younger men quickened their pace. 'We must show no fear,' and they walked past the group and each heard the other's heart beating.

Inside the synagogue there was loud murmur among the congregation, and its tone was not that of prayer. Jakob and his family took their seats as the Rabbi stepped into the pulpit and called for order. He looked up to the women's gallery and seemed relieved to find that it was empty.

'Please listen, all of you,' he said. 'This is very urgent. They are preparing an onslaught on our people. The Greeks have spread the story that we have stolen the cross that decorates their church.'

A sigh of fearful disbelief rose from the congregation, and they surged forward towards the Holy Ark as if for protection.

'They are screaming that the Jews have penned up cattle in the Russian cemetery. But there is worse, my friends,' the Rabbi went on. 'A rumour is abroad that a Law has been proclaimed from St Petersburg that allows these hordes to attack our people in every way, and that the Easter festival should be observed with this in mind. I fear the worst,' the Rabbi said in a whisper. 'Go home, all of you, and keep to your homes. Protect your women and children,' he said. And he started to sing the hymn that normally concluded the Sabbath service, *Lord of the World*. The congregation joined in, and their fears quickened its tempo. Even during the singing, they were folding their prayer-shawls in preparation for leaving. The Rabbi nodded, signalling their departure, and they sang their way out of the synagogue while he watched them from the pulpit.

'God be with us all,' he said.

There was no dawdling in the courtyard that Sabbath. Everyone was anxious to get home. As the Bindels neared the tavern, Benjamin heard the grunting once more, and at last the source of it was visible. A large pig was snorting his way over the cobbles towards them. It moved its huge head from left to right as if looking the form over, an alien invader of the Sabbath, an advance guard of an approaching horde. Jakob was hurried by his family into the tavern, and there they remained all day in a state of siege and terror, fearful of the silence in the streets outside, and more fearful still that that silence might be broken. Benjamin prayed for his family on the other side of the ghetto, with the sickening terror that he would never see them again.

They were all afraid to go to their beds that night, and they sat in the tavern watching the gathering dark, and listening to the thunderous silence of the night. As dawn broke, they heard the grunts again, and they peered out of the windows and saw a flock of swine making their way past the tavern, unherded, and with no command, yet in their growing numbers was a vast authority. And then the church bells tolled their Palm Sunday chimes and, as if their peals were signal to attack, the Odessa pogrom began. It lasted for one whole day and night, punctuated with false lulls, feigned retreats, and bogus truces.

During the morning of that day, the Bindels kept themselves indoors and watched the straggling hordes of peasants, labourers and professional agitators march past the locked tavern doors. For the most part they were armed with crude weapons, sticks and truncheons and iron bars. They were singing national songs of Holy Russia, with the kind of patriotic fervour that has to have an enemy in mind. Jakob held his breath while they were passing the tavern, praying that they would ignore his family and his holding and asking at the same time for forgiveness. For he knew that all their swagger, all their patriotism, must find a target somewhere, their weapons some quarry, their anger some goal. Some family or many would have to pay the price for the Bindel by-pass, but not Faivel's he prayed, not the Pinskis, and above all, not Zemach's. And on exactly that account, Benjamin was fraught with anxiety. He had to find some way of being with his children. He knew it would be madness to risk driving through the ghetto and its invading army, yet he could not stay where he was, while his family probably at this moment shuddered at the sound of the rabble's approach.

'I've got to go,' he said suddenly.

'It's madness,' Jakob said. 'But you must,' he added quietly. 'Your place is with Zelda and the children.'

113

Benjamin looked at Reuben. His place, he owned, was equally by Reuben's side, and Reuben's by his.

'I'm coming with you,' Reuben said.

Esther tried to restrain them, but they went quickly and, deliberately, without farewell.

Around the tavern the lanes and by-ways were empty. The horse was restive in the eerie stillness of the streets. They drove off in silence, but not for long, for shortly they could hear the singing again, and the cheering cries of the mob. They saw smoke too in the distance, lying in the very path they had to take to Zemach's tavern. Yet they pressed on. Soon they saw the site of the fire, a group of small tailoring stalls which heralded the beginning of the main shopping street. The wagon was already in the shadow of the mob, when suddenly the horse, sniffing danger, pulled up sharply, and neighed with fear and apprehension. Its bellowing alerted the rabble, a handful of whom turned swiftly and made for the wagon. Benjamin tugged on the reins in an effort to turn the horse, but it was obstinate in its fear. The wagon-wheels creaked helplessly on the cobbles while Benjamin and Reuben could do nothing but await the attack. There was no time to get down from the wagon. The first of the mob were already clambering on the wheels, while others set about restraining the horse.

'You won't need this wagon any more,' one of them shouted, while another beat Benjamin about the head with his stick.

Reuben, raging in fury, kicked the attacker in the groin, and he fell back onto the cobbles groaning with pain. The others looked on, dumb-founded that a rotten Jew should dare to put up resistance of any kind. Reuben stood on the wagon, his legs apart, as if daring another challenge to his authority. He had, after all, served twenty years in their rotten army and, if it had given him nothing else, it had bred in him a consummate skill in survival, together with the brute strength to ensure it. He helped Benjamin to his feet. He seemed a little dazed by the blows he had received, but he took his place by Reuben's side, and shared the same aggressive stance.

'We don't want the wagon,' one of the men shouted. 'We'll just take the horse.'

Reuben made a movement to grab the reins but Benjamin restrained him. 'You don't die for horses,' he whispered.

So they had to stand there and look on helplessly, while the beast was roughly unharnessed. There was no point in trying to get down from the wagon. Their elevated position offered some defence advantage, and they would risk a mob assault were they to descend. So they held the challenging look in their eye, even though their attackers had transferred their interest to the horse. At last the animal was loose, and there was some squabbling amongst the men as to whom had the right to possession. Finally one of them settled it by mounting. As he clambered up the horse's flank, he was reaching for the heights of Cossackdom. Never again in life would he have such a moment of glory. But it was short-lived, for the horse, sensing a hostile hand, reared and threw him to the ground. His companions laughed and led the horse away, pleased enough with their trophy, with not even a backward glance at the stranded waggoners.

Benjamin and Reuben waited till they were out of sight, then slowly they descended and made their way back to the tavern. Benjamin was distraught. Now, even if it were possible to get through the ghetto, they had no means of transport.

'If we can get to Faivel's,' he said, 'we can borrow his wagon.'

But Faivel, God help him, lived in the heart of the ghetto, that area where fires were burning, and God knows what else.

'Let's wait till night-fall,' Reuben said. 'It may be quiet by then.'

Esther bathed Benjamin's head, and vainly urged him to sleep. Jakob had ordered his household to sundry tasks, so that they should be continually occupied. The women were in the kitchen. Food was a sustainer, Jakob had said, and they might well be in for a long siege. The men were in the outhouses and market-garden, armed with crowbars, and keeping watch for intruders. The cows were milked and the sheds locked and barred. All the while, Jakob and the milk-brothers kept watch at the tavern windows, and the silence and the emptiness outside unnerved them; they half hoped for some sign that would break the endless waiting. Then suddenly there was the sound of hurried footsteps which stopped for a while, and they heard a desperate panting and reaching for breath. The sound seemed to come from a fugitive seeking shelter. The watchers waited and they heard the footsteps again, hurried, painful, breathless and full of years. Then they saw a ghost-like figure approaching the tavern. At first, the lone runner was unrecognisable, yet there was something familiar in its silhouette, a familiarity that was friendly and eased the watchers' hearts. They saw him approach the tavern door, and watched him as he knocked with a timid despair, his old body bent with the exertion of his flight. Jakob rushed to the door and unbarred it.

Faivel stood, or rather bent, there, moaning with an anguish more related to sorrow than pain. Jakob clasped him in his arms and helped him into the tavern. Reuben reached under the counter for some kvass, and together they settled Faivel on a bench and tried to calm him. His breathing was easier now, but he kept mumbling in a demented fashion as if it were his mind that was out of breath. Jakob put his ear to Faivel's mouth.

'What is it, my friend?' he asked.

'I must bury her,' Faivel said. 'I have to bury her. Do you hear me, Jakob?' He looked up at him. 'I must bury her.'

'Who must you bury?' Benjamin said.

There was a silence, and then Faivel said, 'She's lying in the street. But the Rabbi's dead, and who will bury her?'

They did not press him further. They sat by his wild side and held his hands. It was clearly a ghastly tale that Faivel had to tell, and he would tell it in his own time. They sat in silence for a long while until Esther came to the back door of the tavern, bringing food for the sentries. She saw Faivel sitting there, his old head in his hands. She put down the food and went over to where he sat.

'What is it, Faivel?' she said softly.

He looked up at her. The tears were streaming down his face. 'Raisl,' he managed to splutter. 'They killed her. She's lying on the street. Next to the Pinskis.'

Esther said nothing. She looked at the men, and they clearly shared her disbelief. Faivel was hysterical, they thought. He was frightened and hallucinating in his fear. Yet the specific nature of Faivel's tale lent it credulity; but the thought of Raisl being dead, and perhaps Dov and Rosa Pinski, their life-long friends, and the Rabbi too, that abiding pillar of the faith, seemed to spell out the end of all their days.

'I must bury her,' Faivel said again.

They tried once more with him.

'Tell us slowly, Faivel,' Esther said. 'Tell us everything that happened.'

His hands were trembling and they filled his glass once more, and as he put it to his lips he shook his head in disbelief. 'The shop is gone,' he said slowly. 'They burnt it down and we ran into the street for safety. Safety,' he laughed. 'One of them picked up Raisl and threw her onto the fire. I ran and dragged her away, but it was too late. She's lying in the street, and all her hair's gone,' he wailed, 'and I have to bury her.' His voice was calm now, detached, as if he were recalling a story that someone else had told. 'I ran away then because there was nothing more I could do. I saw the Pinskis further down the street. At least they looked like the Pinskis. They were burnt too. I passed the synagogue. It's on fire,' he said simply. 'The Rabbi was lying on the steps outside. He must have gone inside to save the Scrolls, because he was lying on the steps still holding them in his arms.' He looked up at Jakob. 'I think it's the end for all of us, my friend,' he said. Then he began to weep again, hearing the echo of his own words and knowing their undeniable truth.

Benjamin turned away and grieved too for, if the fires had

116

reached the synagogue, there was no reason why the maurauders should not be making their way through the ghetto to Zemach's tavern. At first he could not understand why the Bindel tavern was spared. Now he realised that the mob were saving the taverns till the last when they would loot and pillage at will, and drink themselves into a free stupor to celebrate their victory.

Reuben read his thoughts. 'Is this why we survived?' he said.

'We should leave,' Esther said. 'All of us. We should go into the forest. I shall get the food,' she said, 'and gather the children.' As she spoke, the church bells pealed the close of the Palm Sunday evening service.

'Perhaps it will be over,' Jakob said. 'They started with the bells, and the bells are tolling the end of the pogrom. They will go home now,' he said.

'But on their *way* home,' Reuben said, 'past the tavern.'

'I think in any case we should go,' Esther said again, and as she spoke they heard the singing and the shouting in the distance, and they knew that it was now too late for flight.

'Bring the family into the tavern,' Jakob said. 'we must all stay together. To keep watch,' he added, for he had to give a reason for the assembly, feeble as it was. For there was no point in keeping watch since against a mob they were defenceless, but Jakob feared their end, and he wished his family together. Poor Benjamin, he thought.

The women set the table in the tavern, and the family assembled. The men had come in from their posts in the gardens and the children had been brought from their beds. They sat bleary-eyed and bewildered at the table and, when Jakob saw them, he regretted that he had taken them from sleep. He had opened their eyes only to witness their own deaths. 'Let them go back to sleep,' he said quickly, and he picked up two of them in his frail old arms and took them to their beds. The other children followed, and Jakob watched them as they closed their eyes and he prayed that they would sleep right through the pain of Death's calling. He went back into the tavern, and sat by Faivel's side at the table.

'I must bury her,' Faivel kept saying, over and over again, and nobody stopped him, because the words bandaged his wounds and kept the life-blood within him.

Despite all the food that had been prepared, nobody ate very much, but the ritual of the blessings over the bread and the wine, of serving, created a core of order in the chaos that surrounded them. It was to be their last supper, though neither traitor nor Lord was at their table. Both were outside on the cobbled streets, in the rioting mob and in the pealing of the holy bells that orchestrated their destruction. They could hear the shouting and the singing, though still at a distance, and occasionally the sound of shattering glass. And they waited, restive and fidgety, almost willing a swift and painless end. All except Faivel who sat motionless, his face rinsed of any expression, with the infinite calm and patience of one who had lost everything, and now had nothing more to lose.

The hours passed, punctuated by the shouts and the screaming, until the shadows of first light limped across the tavern walls. And then, as if fuelled by the cold morning sun, the singing grew louder and the marching feet nearer, and the screaming was drowned by the crackling fires. And then, suddenly, the tavern was surrounded.

Jakob went to the window and crouched beneath the sill. Men were sitting on the grass verge in front of the tavern, at least a hundred of them, and others were joining them, shouting and singing, and rolling about as if drunk.

'They're on this side too,' Benjamin whispered from his stand at the back-window.

'And around the sheds,' Reuben said. 'They've got torches.'

It seemed that the whole invading army had gathered at the Bindel tavern as their last port of call. Yet they seemed to have no purpose in mind but to loll on the grass, sing, shout and wave their torches and it was their insulting inactivity that was the most frightening of all.

'They will go away,' Jakob said, trying to instil some confidence into his voice. 'In time they will all go away. And then we shall go out into the streets and bury the dead.' He went over to Faivel and sat by his side.

It was then that they heard the lowing of the cows. Yosif automatically rose, but Jakob shook his head. 'No one must leave this room,' he said. He knew that the appearance of any one of them would be provocation. Then suddenly the singing stopped and all in the tavern held their breath.

'Go and see to the cows,' one of the rabble shouted.

Yosif rose again, and again Jakob shook his head.

'Don't you rotten Yids care?' another voice bellowed through the tavern. Then there was laughter and the singing started again and muted the cows' lowing. But Benjamin and Reuben heard it, even through the raucous voices, and the thought crossed Benjamin's mind that if he went out and relieved the cows, God would save his children. He knew it to be a ridiculous thought but he was obsessed by it. Reuben stared at him. Whatever Benjamin chose to do, he would follow him.

The time passed and the singing outside could no longer mute the cows' call for attention. They were bellowing now, with moans of such anguish that the women stopped up their ears, and covered their faces as if the terrible moaning was visible. And in that moment, the three men rose from their seats, Jakob, Benjamin and Reuben. And had Leon been alive, Jakob thought, he would have joined them. All their lives they had chosen how to live and how to survive. How to die lay within their choice as well. The three men left the tavern.

Outside, in the half-light, they discerned a body of men leaning against the shed-doors. As they approached, the men dispersed and bowed mockingly, ushering the milkers into the barn. The noise inside was deafening. The men hurried to the stalls and set to work, resting their heads on the throbbing flanks, while out of the confusion of their minds burst a lightening bolt of clarity which lit the by-ways and the high-ways of their separate journeys into the past.

Of them all, Jakob had the furthest to travel. Eighty-eight years of survival. There was no chronology in his recall, but each event had a clarity and a containment of a separate drama. He remembered the baby carriage of his infancy, and under his fingers he could feel the smooth cane of its weaving. He played with Faivel in the nursery lands between their houses and then made snowmen on that lullaby field that now rocked men into sanity. Then Esther flashed across his eye in her white wedding-dress that slowly clothed Miriam and then Sofia. But blotting the vision was Meisels, and Jakob clutched at the cow's teats in a spasm of bitterness and rage. He looked across at the milk-brothers and he had to calculate their age. As long as they had been in the army, he had known their calendar as intimately as his own, crossing off the years they had served from childhood through adolescence to manhood. Once released from that detested army life, he considered them immortal in view of the miracle of their survival, so he had not bothered to count any more. He had to drum his fingers on the cow's flanks to tally their earthly years. Forty-six, he concluded. His own father had died at almost twice that age, and, like himself he supposed, he had died a-milking. He recalled now how they had missed him at breakfast, and how all around the stove had stared at him, Jakob, as if confirming his succession. He had gone to the cow-shed. There had just been one cow in those days, Devorah, he remembered, the milk-brothers' favourite. He had taken his time getting there, fearing what he would find, and in no rush for orphanhood. His old father lay slumped on Devorah's half-milked flank, his lips grazing the limp teat. Jakob paused in his milking for a while as he held the image of his dead father in his eye. He thought of Esther again and of all those around the fearful tavern-table, and how, after a while, they would know he would never return, and no heir could be sent to look for him. As no heir had gone to the shed to look for Leon. As no heir would seek out Benjamin or Reuben. This day would mark

119

the end of the rugged Bindel line and he prayed for the lives of those in Zemach's tavern.

As Benjamin was doing by his side. His journey through his past was a backward one, and started with his last memory of Zelda and his children as he left them waving at Zemach's tavern. But the image quickly faded, and when he tried to recapture it it was blurred by the memory of his escape into the forest when he was a child. He recalled his capture, but he would not allow himself to think of his army life. With Death so patently by his side, he would not give those years of his life the dignity of recall. 'Aaron, Leon,' he whispered, for they were the names he must etch into the future, to whom in his memories and his blessings he must give the gift of survival. His own father had given him that gift and he had done his best to honour it, which thought rekindled the memory of his army days which he tried to put aside. He tried to imagine himself at his children's present ages and again it was in the Czar's service on the mean Siberian snows. He recalled it with a cold shudder. If he were to die this day, he thought, he would have given almost half his life in the service of that power that was about to destroy him. He could not help smiling at the ridiculousness of it all.

After a while, the three men moved to the other stalls and soon the cows stopped lowing and there was silence in the sheds. Reuben's face was calm, glowing with a peace that he soon expected to be his. Now he and his milk-brother were about to die together, and in the closest intimacy. Soon he knew, it would all be over. He looked at Benjamin by his side, and Jakob too, and he knew that whatever journey awaited them, he could find no better companions. Death would stand before them, face to face, because they were grown men, but with Aaron and Leon, because they were children, he would stand behind their backs, and in one embrace he would consume four Bindel generations. God is almighty thorough in His work, Reuben thought, as diligent and as prompt as those who executed His will, and he cast a sidelong glance at the barn-door, and saw them all assembled there, waiting. Soon the Bindels would finish their milking, and there would be no more to do but to abandon once and for all their life-long clutch at survival, and walk with calm and with grace to their lynching.

But the mob had something else in mind. They waited for the milking to be done. They watched as the men put the buckets aside. Then three of them rushed into the barn and pinned the men's arms behind their backs. None offered any resistance. Three others, armed with knives, poured the buckets of milk on each man's head, as if to anoint them, then they passed their blades across each throat and the blood mingled with the milk, their life-blood incarnate. Then the cows were led from the barn and no one bothered to close the doors.

The murder of the head of the Bindel household was the signal to destroy it whole, root and branch. The mob burst into the tavern and there, in one contained holding, lay the three targets for their violence – pillage, rape and murder. But their priority was the tavern stock, and to this they helped themselves liberally, so that the fumes of the wines would perfume the knife on the throat and translate their lechery into the name of love. Although there was no one outside the tavern to witness the slaughter within, one of the rabble closed the door behind him. Perhaps for him it was a God-bothering moment, or perhaps it was a gesture of politeness. Then he grabbed Sofia by the waist, threw her on the floor and tore her legs apart. Soon all the women in the tavern were spread-eagled on the sawdust. Esther's heart had mercifully stopped before her violation so she did not know of the succession of men who took their pleasure upon her lifeless body.

Yosif, Victor and Yuri and even Faivel, had grabbed bottles from the counter, and had managed to lay low a half-a-dozen men before they themselves were slaughtered for their impudent challenge. And then, when all the Bindels were disposed of, or so the rioters thought, the children, those who threatened yet another generation of irritants to the Russian soul, gathered in the back doorway, woken by the noises and screams and shattering glass.

'Go back to bed,' one of the men shouted, and the children, terrified by what they had already seen, fled to what they thought was the safety of sleep, and they comforted each other with the theory of nightmare, because the murdered bodies of one's parents had to be the stuff of dreams. So they huddled together on Jakob's and Esther's large and gentle bed, amongst those feather pillows on which all of them had been born. They too, like Jakob and the milk-brothers, but with their young geometry, were completing their own circle.

Downstairs the mob was withdrawing, taking what was left of the Bindel cellars. And they closed the door firmly behind them. Then they gathered paper and oil-soaked rags, lighting them one by one, and they placed them with a drunk's care at intervals around the tavern. They stood back and watched as the flames quickly fed on the tavern-wood, and sprouted and spread until a vast carnival conflagration consumed it whole. If the children screamed, their cries went unheard, drowned by the chanting and the cheering of the mob, who saw in the Bindel furnace the climax of their long day's toil. The pogrom was over, at least for the time being, and slowly they made their drunken ways home, rehearsing the tales they would tell their children. Defenders of the Czar they were, heroes, each and every one of them. Thus they muttered to themselves on their way back to their hovels and some of them wondered whether all the filth, congestion and poverty therein spelt out a home fit for good Christians to live in.

*

When the bright morning light fully asserted itself, the police, who had stood by and seen order destroyed, now set about to restore it. Those still alive in the ghetto stirred themselves, thanked God for their survival, and dared the streets. Amongst them, one Simon Paritsky, ripe in his ninety years and shamefully unscathed. Paritsky was the beadle of the synagogue, everybody's willing lackey, who, in his menial role had never sought preferment or promotion. It was God's will that he should spend his life in humble service. God's will too, he supposed, that He had spared him in that terrible day and night, so that he could be His chosen witness to the hell that remained of the ghetto. He wandered through it like a ghost close to the peace that he knew would soon be his, once he had recorded with his mind's eye all the havoc and the devastation. He turned his unsteady steps in the direction of the synagogue. On his way he noted that many of the small shops had been raised to the ground. A tailor's dummy stood idly against a broken wall, its canvas chest pierced with a farrier's tool. He shrunk at the occasional body on the cobbles, and looked around for something to cover the dead astonished faces. He heard a wagon approach, and as it neared he discerned old Zemach the innkeeper at the reins, with Zelda and her two sons behind him. He supposed they were making for Bindel's tavern. He turned the corner of the synagogue street and he wondered whether he had lost his bearings. For that same temple where he had become a man, where he had married, rejoiced, mourned, and all his life given service, was now a shell, blackened by smoke, doorless, windowless, deserted. On the steps a handful of pigs were lolling, taking the cold morning sun, and in their midst lay a body. Paritsky approached and saw the Scroll of the Torah which had rolled open down the steps. The pigs were feeding on its parchment and velvet trimmings. He looked at the body and, with a cry, he recognised the Rabbi. He took what was left of the velvet covering and laid it over the old man's face, then he turned away. At the bottom of the steps he turned round and saw a pig gnawing at the Rabbi's right arm. Then, for all his ninety years, he fell onto his knees and prostrated himself on the ground. And with Elijah's heart-rending cry, 'It is enough, O Lord,' he whispered. 'Now take away my life.'

Some time later, a large hearse-wagon drew up by the synagogue steps and collected two bodies. In its wake came Zemach's wagon, moving at a hearse's pace with two new coachmen at the reins: Aaron and Leon Bindel. Behind them, on the wooden bench, Zelda, shaken with sobs and disbelief, lay on Zemach's shoulder. Her grandfather's great years had dried up his well of tears. He sat erect, dry-eyed, with no release for his profound grief. All he felt was a shudder of shame that he had survived. In the driving seat, Aaron clutched tightly at the reins, his fists clenched, as were his eyes to stop the tears, as if they were no part of the new status that his father's death had so brutally bequeathed him. But Leon, at his side, could still afford to be a child, and he sobbed for himself and for his brother too, silently, with the occasional whine of despair.

'What are we going to do?' he asked.

Aaron recalled his father's words in the forest. Everywhere, and at all times, he had said, there would be a minstrel, and somewhere, someone would hear his song. Aaron heard it now, loud and clear across the cobbles of the broken ghetto. He put his arm round Leon's shoulder.

'We must survive,' he said.

PART TWO

The Book of Aaron and Leon

CHAPTER NINE

There were only three of them now at Zemach's tavern. Zemach had died shortly after the pogrom. On his return from the Bindel ruins he had taken to his bed and willed himself to die. It had taken him less than a week and with his dying breath, he had thanked God for his passing. Zelda's mother survived a little longer, refusing all the time to believe that anything had changed in the ghetto. Even after her father's funeral, she had returned to her kitchen and continued to prepare for his 85th birthday. Occasionally she grumbled that the Bindel family were late in arriving and she fretted for her honey-cakes that grew stale and mildewed with the waiting. She was irritated by her daughter's tears and laughed at her plaintive claims on widowhood. The Bindel family had not arrived because they were lazy and insensitive and she would prepare for them no more. Nevertheless, she remained stubbornly in her kitchen all the day long and later on throughout the night, cooking and baking with a demented vengeance. Zemach's funeral sweetmeats slightly depleted her vast store, but she quickly replaced it with her next night's baking. Shortly after her father's death, she began to sing at her work in a tone of careless joy that would suddenly dissolve into one of mourning. And all the time she baked, stacking the shelves with a disordered array of cakes and tarts and cursing the Bindels for their tardiness. Zelda did nothing to hinder her. Her mother was crying in her own way, each tray of unbaked tarts, a thrust into the raging heat of her grief. After a while her mother acknowledged that the Bindels would never come, that they had forgotten in their careless fashion, and that they were celebrating selfishly in their own tavern. Then one day she suddenly closed the kitchen door behind her, and went, barefoot, into the woods behind the tavern. She wasn't missed until Zelda smelt burning from the kitchen. On the stove, a tray of honey-cakes had charred to a cinder. Their ashes were her mother's final signature. Aaron and Leon found her in a clearing in the forest. She was asleep. Or so they had to think. And as they carried her back to the tavern, they tried not to notice that she had stopped breathing. Together with their mother they laid her on the bed, and

Zelda closed her mother's eyes. The three watchers looked from one to the other.

'No more of us must die,' Zelda said quietly.

So they linked their survivors' arms and once more went wearily to the burial-ground. After the funeral they ate no sweetmeats, but they took the hordes of honey-cakes and buried them at the back of the tavern. For the customary seven days they sat on low stools and they mourned, and when it was over, Zelda and her sons threw themselves into work and the bustling trade of the tavern. Now that the Bindel holding was no more, much of the drinking-trade of the ghetto was diverted to Zemach's tavern. They worked hard, dividing the counter and the cellar between them. It was a bereaved life, with little laughter and many silences. But they were not disturbed when others broke that silence. Indeed it was a relief of sorts when the tavern filled up in the early evening and the sound of men's singing and laughter astonished the prim walls.

One such evening a stranger came to the inn, a man in his middle years, unknown to any of the customers and clearly a new-comer to the ghetto. He stepped warily to the counter and ordered a kvass. Zelda served him.

'You're a stranger here,' she said, 'but you are welcome.'

'I thank you,' the man said. His voice, his manner, unlike his clothes, were elegant and well-turned. He had clearly known better times.

'My name is Khasina,' he said. 'Pavel Khasina. I am come from Kherson.'

'I am Zelda Bindel,' she said. 'Bindel,' she said again, caressing that much-buried name. 'My husband and his family died in the pogrom. But these are my sons,' she offered, calling Aaron and Leon to her side.

'They are fine boys,' he said. 'Too fine for the Czar's cannon-fodder. What will they do when their time comes?' The man had voiced that burning question that the three Bindels had strangled with their frequent silences. It was a relief to them all to hear it spoken aloud.

'We shall survive,' Aaron said repeating his father's catechism, though he knew that such a phrase would find short shrift with the recruiting officer.

'They should leave,' the man said to Zelda. 'You too,' he added. He looked round furtively. 'As I am doing,' he whispered.

'Where are you going?' Leon said, whispering too, understanding that it was not politic in front of patriots to advertise desertion from the land of their Holy Mother Russia.

'To Wales,' Khasina said. 'I have a sister there. She was wise. They left some years ago.'

'But you have somebody to go to,' Zelda said.

'There are many of our people over there,' Khasina answered. 'They will welcome you.' He paused and drank from his glass. 'You must leave,' he said, and there was no mistaking the urgency in his voice. He spoke like a prophet-messenger. 'You have learned a hard lesson in Odessa,' he said. 'There are harder lessons to come.' He reached into his pocket for a pencil and note-book and, tearing out a sheet, he wrote down an address. He took his time with it, concerned with its neatness and legibility, familiarising himself, for his own sake, with the strange letters and shapes, so alien to his Russian hand. He handed the paper to Zelda. 'Look after it,' he said. 'You will find me there and I shall help you.' He downed his glass. 'I take the train at midnight.' He took each of their hands in farewell, then he turned quickly and left with no formal leave-taking, and the three Bindels stared at the space he had so recently occupied and all of them wondered whether he had been a fleeting vision in their fearful eyes. Yet they heard the echo of his warning words and saw on the counter the undeniable proof of his recent presence. They read the address without understanding it. Wales, he had said. A place in England, they surmised, which was where his train and his boat were taking him. Wales, they said to each other, laughing at its strange sound, realising that that laughter was the very first they had given voice to since the epidemic of death in their families. And in that laughter there was hope, as if the visitor had, with his calling-card, sanctioned them to have faith once more. That it was not enough to chant 'We must survive', without finding the wherewithal to do so. That it was permissible to leave the graves of husband, parents, grandparents, that their memory lay not in tomb-stones, memorial candles or flowers, but in the consummate impertinent act of their own survival. Zelda folded the piece of paper and put it in her blouse.

'He's right,' she said softly. 'Aaron has two years before he is called. In that time we must try and sell the tavern.' She looked at her sons with little confidence. 'Well, we must try,' she said.

'But who will buy it, Mama?' Aaron asked.

'We must try,' she insisted, though she knew that the possibility of a sale was very remote. Tavern-keeping was a Jewish trade, and no Jew in Odessa would stake a future in that town of his mourning. But she must try.

'We shall make our future in England,' she said.

'In Wales,' Leon laughed.

She hugged them both. Their long mourning was over.

Although they knew it would be some time before they would be able to leave the country, they started their departure preparations the very next day. Aaron and Leon started to clear the loft and the cellar of all the jumble that had accumulated over the years of Zemach's holding. Every market day, Aaron would load the wagon with dispensable pieces of furniture and household goods, and he would sell them in the market-place and marvel at his wealth on his return home. Within a month, the tavern was stripped to its bare essentials. There was now nothing more to do but to wait for a buyer. Zelda did not want to publicise the sale. With two sons nearing conscription age, there would be too many questions, and besides, it would be bad for her business and good-will if her clients suspected a change of management. But she would speak to the casual customer, the traveller, the irregular passing trade, and hope thereby that word would spread beyond Odessa. But for a whole year there was not a single enquiry. Every night before sleeping Zelda would unfold the piece of paper that Pavel Khasina had left behind, reading the address aloud, assuring herself that a safe and hopeful future was real and possible. But as the weeks went by, she began to wonder whether she would languish for ever in this hated land, grieving for her soldier sons. Many of her friends in the ghetto had already left. Occasionally when she went to the synagogue she noticed their vacant places. But they had not been encumbered with property. They were tailors, bakers and craftsmen and they travelled abroad with their trade. That was their wealth, their future, a portable skill that would ensure them a living anywhere in the world. But she and her sons had no trade but that of tavern-keeping, and such a skill did not travel well. It required a new language, a knowledge of strange money, and in England, she had been told, it was not a trade for Jews. She knew she had to sell the tavern. Money was the only wealth she could acquire.

One day in early winter, a few weeks before Aaron's nineteenth birthday, the vintner's wagon drew up in the courtyard of the tavern. It was the first of the month, delivery date for the tavern stock. Usually there were two porters on the wagon who would carry the goods to the cellar. But this time, Zelda noted a third man who, by his elegant dress, was clearly no porter, but possibly the vintner himself. Zelda stood at the door of the tavern and watched as he alighted from the wagon, firmly setting down his silver-knobbed cane in the crevice of the cobbles. He smiled as he saw her standing there and came straight towards her.

'Mrs Bindel?' he said.

She was nervous as she always was with strangers. Especially with men, and those who were so Russian and so un-Jewish as this one.

'May I speak with you?' he said.

She was frightened, frightened for her children, her livelihood. 'What's the matter?' she said. 'What's happened?'

130

'Nothing's happened, Madam. I just wished a word with you. Your respected grandfather, Zemach, was a friend. It's many years now since I have visited this tavern.'

'Mr Fedorov?' she asked recalling the name from her childhood.

He nodded. 'I remember you as a little girl.'

She led him into her sitting-room and offered him refreshment. But he declined.

'I am here on business,' he said.

She wished her sons were with her, but Leon was serving in the tavern and Aaron was helping the porters. She presumed Mr Fedorov wished to change his selling terms for supplying her with liquor, and she was not confident that she could bargain with him.

'Shall I call my sons?' she asked.

'Let me state my business first,' he said, 'and then if you are interested, you can talk to your sons.'

She folded her hands in her lap, her knuckles clenched. 'I'm listening,' she said.

'While I was arranging your order this month,' Mr Fedorov went on, 'it occurred to me that you might be relieved to find a buyer for your tavern.'

Zelda tried to hide her excitement. She knew she must not appear too eager.

'It's a very hard trade for a woman, Mrs Bindel,' he said. 'Your sons will soon be in the army, and then it will be impossible for you.' He paused, staring at her. 'I thought perhaps you might be grateful for a buyer.' He wanted to make his position quite clear. He was doing her a favour. It was his mission in life to concern himself with widows and orphans. He would offer her a helping hand.

'Did you hear that I wanted to sell it?' she asked, keeping her voice steady, trying not to think of the three of them on board ship, spitting on the hated land that they would leave behind.

'No. I heard nothing,' he said. 'Why? Were you thinking of selling?'

'Sometimes I think I would like to be rid of it,' she parried. 'But only on some days. I've talked to people about it sometimes. Why do you want it?' she said. She was suspicious. Tavern-keeping was a Jewish trade. A Russian, and a rich one at that, would consider it unseemly.

'I'm concerned with your welfare,' he said with a smile, and the smile told her he was lying. 'Your family have been my good customers for many years. Besides, it's a good little business. I would expand it. Build a good restaurant as an extension. I would give you a fair price,' he said.

'I must talk to my sons.' Zelda half-rose from her seat.

'Of course,' he said. 'There's time. But not too long.'

'Would you like to see my accounts?' She went over to her cupboard.

'Of course,' he said quickly, 'but only when you have decided to sell.' He had no interest in her accounts. He didn't care whether she made a vast profit or an equally vast loss. He didn't care about her stocks or her good will. He was totally indifferent to the tavern and its trade. It was the land he wanted, that ground on which the tavern stood which, according to his inside information could well prove to be a gold-mine. For among other voluntary activities, natural in a man of his standing, Mr Fedorov was a member of the Odessa Railways commission, and was thus privy to the decision that the Zemach tavern holding was to be the site of the new railroad station, linking the line from Kishinev to Odessa. Whoever owned that land owned a fortune.

'I'll come again next week,' the vintner said.

Zelda was confused by his haste. He had told her there was time, but a week was hardly time enough to make a decision that would affect their whole lives. Yet in truth she had already made up her mind and, but for a certain business acumen, would have sold the tavern there and then.

'A week is not long,' she said, knowing that delay would be a bargaining factor.

The vintner kept the smile on his face, but in his heart he was grossly irritated by this Jew-woman who wouldn't let him have his way. 'I'm leaving for Leningrad next week,' he lied. 'I have to have your decision before I leave.'

He rose and held out his hand. But Zelda did not take it. She was beginning to tire of the smile on his face, and to spite him a little, she said, 'I don't think my sons will want to sell.'

'They will be making a mistake,' he said, the smile at last fading, 'but in any case, I shall call on you in a week.'

In four days, the vintner returned, excusing his haste on account of pressure of other work. He'd brought his smile with him, and wore it fixed over his cheeks, masking his fury at the woman's delay. This time she had her sons by her side, and both showed a marked lack of enthusiasm for the sale. Zelda had rehearsed them in their attitudes and both crossed their fingers as they expressed their indifference to his offer. But the vintner, crossing his fingers too, decided to call their bluff. He knew those two Jew-boys were perilously near conscription age. He knew that they would shirk their patriotic duty and, like the rest of their rotten tribe, would run like rats to save themselves. But to run, they needed money. 'I'm sorry,' he said, his smile fixed. 'I'd hoped we could do business together.' He turned to go, and with unhurried pace, waiting for their recall. It came as he reached the door.

'We might be interested if you made a larger offer,' Aaron said as Zelda trembled in her chair.

Fedorov turned. Now he had them, he knew, and he could play with them as long as he wished. 'I think my price is fair,' he said, not moving from the door. He was beginning to resent the offer he had already made. Why should he, a good Russian patriot, finance these Yids' desertion? He watched them look at each other and he smelt the hesitation between them. It was that hesitation that proved their bluff. And with total confidence he said, 'My offer is more than fair. Yes or no.' He spread the smile on his face a little to off-set the finality of his terms. He put his hand on the handle of the door.

'All right,' Aaron said after a while. 'We agree, as long as you can complete arrangements within the month.'

'My lawyers will draw up the contract immediately,' the vintner said and he returned from the door and took Aaron's hand.

'We shall drink a kvass on it,' Leon said, uncrossing all his fingers behind his back.

And so the deal was done, to everyone's huge satisfaction, while each of the celebrants assumed on their faces a look of sublime indifference to an event that would radically change each and every one of their lives.

'Where will you live?' the vintner dared to ask.

'We will go to Kiev,' Zelda said quickly. 'I have a brother there.' Now it was she who handed him a fixed smile and it was clear to all parties that such a smile, no matter on whose face, was a natural accompaniment to any falsehood that dropped from the lips, and that only when that smile was removed, could the truth be told.

Fedorov, in his own exploitative interest kept his word. Within the month the tavern deal was completed.

Zelda went to the railway office. A woman travelling abroad with two friends, and even on a single ticket, would be less suspicious than young men whose body and spirit was mortgaged to the Czar.

'Where to, Madam?' the ticket-seller asked.

'To Wales,' she said.

'Where is that? I've never heard of such a place.'

'Near England, I think,' Zelda said, wondering whether Mr Khasina had lied to them.

'I can only give you tickets to Hamburg,' he said. 'From there you can buy tickets to anywhere you like. England, America, even Wales,' he laughed. 'Will you be coming back?' he said.

'Oh yes,' Zelda answered over-hastily. 'I have two sons here.'

'When do you want to go?' he asked.

'Tomorrow.' She wanted her sons away, and quickly, for she trusted nobody.

The official gave her three rail tickets. 'I hope you have a nice holiday,' he said. 'I hope you find Wales too.'

She left the office quickly. That night she closed the tavern early, and the three of them sat down to a celebration.

'To Wales,' Leon kept raising his glass, and laughing too, for there was something faintly unreliable about a country that even the ticket official had never heard of. That night they went to bed early, and it was early morning when they took their leave. The cocks were crowing as they left the tavern-courtyard, and they looked back at their home and their livelihood with no regret. Zelda spat on the ground.

'Come for them now, you recruiting swine,' she hissed. 'Go, find my children over the high seas.' Her laughter was almost hysterical. Indeed, it soon dissolved into tears. For there was much to weep for. Not for the tavern, nor for the livelihood, nor for the hated country that they would never see again, but for those whom that same cruel land had consumed, whose great love that cruel land had buried. They left the tavern courtyard and at no one's suggestion, made instinctively for the burial grounds to visit the Bindel and the Zemach families for the last time.

They walked in silence to the cemetery, and there they picked their way over the stones to where Zemach held domain with all his kin. Zelda held her children's hands, but she did not weep. All her life she had been so thoroughly schooled in grief that she was expert at its timing. She had already given her family its due season of mourning. Together with her sons she built a pyramid of pebbles on the Zemach graves. Then when it was done, they turned their steps to where the Bindels lay. Or rather, their ashes, pogrom-leavings, heaped together under a stone which listed the four generations consumed by the fire. Aaron and Leon stood by the side of the tomb, holding their mother's arm, and read the names aloud. Hardest of all was to say goodbye to one's dead. They stayed by the tomb for a long while, loathe to leave, reluctant to yield that certain proof of their history. Now all they would have would be memories and a list of alabaster names to tell their children. Now they themselves would be pioneers, would start a history in a new country, would create their own dead for their children's memories, new monuments for their myths, new legends for their inheritance. But one legend they would bring from Odessa — that of Jakob Bindel and his catechism of survival. They crouched by the tomb and made a castle of pebblestones at its base, each stone for a future visit they would never make, a pyramid of advance payments of their respect.

'We shall not be buried here,' Aaron said. 'Our bones shall break new ground elsewhere.'

They linked arms and together they left the cemetery.

It was still early morning as they made their way to the wagon-station. They were burdened with luggage and their travel was slow. Food for the long journey formed the bulk of their luggage. Zelda had diligently concerned herself with that provision. It was something she could deal with. And her sons lent their willing hands, each of them busying themselves with matters of little problem in order to avoid confrontation with the real obstacle that lay ahead. They had money, they had provisions, but only Zelda had a passport. She had received one straightway on application. But it would have been dangerous for the brothers even to apply. Their age would betray their intended desertion. So they busied themselves with journey preparations, with food and drink, and blankets for the crossing. But none of them spoke about passports. It would be a problem that they would deal with at the frontier post.

The wagon-trail left for Kishinev at midnight. There they were to take the train across Galicia and into Prussian territory. It would be early morning on the following day when the passport problem could no longer be ignored. It was when they changed from the wagons to the train that Zelda realised the enormity of the move they were making. It was the train that first set off the fear in her, that machine that moved along so swiftly and seemingly without anyone's participation. As they gathered speed, the nature of the landscape changed, and its strangeness confirmed the farewell they had made to a land that, for all its cruelty, was at least known and familiar. The houses they passed were strange too, and the people who went about their business in the streets. All about the terrain was alien and threatened the proximity of a frontier town. The Bindels avoided conversation with their neighbours. None were Jews and they feared awkward questions. They feigned fatigue during the whole journey though none was able to sleep. In the early hours of the morning, the train came to a halt, and its sheer unexpectedness provoked a swift and shrieking silence. After a while an official entered the compartment and told the passengers to alight. They were within walking distance of the frontier post. There they would be able to buy refreshment and wait for the passport official. In two hours another train would take them across the border and on to Hamburg. The Bindels rose with the other passengers but, unlike the others who renewed their interrupted conversations, they kept their silence. Words between them would have forced them to face the hurdle that confronted them. They followed the other passengers off the train, and gathered in a waiting-room that adjoined a tavern. Aaron took a seaman's cap out of his luggage, and placed it firmly on his head. Zelda had never seen it before, and when she saw how it transformed his look, 'russianising' his features, she understood that, despite his silence, he had, on his own account formulated a plan to confront the passport hurdle. She dared not ask what it was, and when Aaron told Leon to wait in the waiting-room with their mother, while he went about his business, she was happy to remain ignorant of what he was about.

Aaron left the room and dawdled for a while outside the tavern, watching the comings and the goings of the passengers and railroad officials. From the occasional furtive enquiries he had made among the taverns in Odessa, he had learnt, and not to his surprise, that all officials were bribable. Sometimes sailors came to those taverns, and he would encourage them to tell stories of smuggling and stowaways. Apart from the details of their stories, their underlying message was always the same. Every official, however petty, however powerful, was corruptible. But in no way could Aaron elicit details of the measure of the bribe. It was of vital importance that he find out, for to offer less than the expected sum might expose him to greater peril than illegal voyage. His near-conscript age would spell out the reason for his departure and he would spend the rest of his life hard-labouring for premature desertion. He had, somehow or other to find out the present bribery rate. He straightened his cap and, with a rolling gait, he entered the tavern.

His Russian, though fluent, was laced with Yiddish accent, and he had decided to pass himself off as a seaman who had spent most of his youth on the high sea, where his Russian sounds had been scored to the accents of each port. He was on his way to Hamburg, he would tell them, to pick up a ship. He ordered himself a kvass, and the same for a lone neighbour who stood beside him at the counter. Thus he was able to enter conversation with the stranger and he was delighted to discover that he was a railroad official whose job was to check passengers' numbers against collected tickets. He was no doubt the stowaway's friend, and his knowledge of bribery rates in all departments of corruption would be absolutely reliable. Aaron slipped easily into conversation, remarking on the numbers of passengers who seemed to be taking holidays abroad. It was a fruitful opening, for his companion was a bitter man, who all his life had served and with little reward, who was full of envy and malice, and needed little encouragement to vent his spleen on those who were better off than he.

'Plenty of rich people in this country,' he said with disdain. 'Landowners, bankers and the rest.'

Aaron trembled, waiting for the Yids to join the contemptible company. But the official was satisfied with the exploiters he had already mentioned.

'Living off my sweat,' he said, 'and thousands like us. When did you ever see the likes of me going on holiday?' he asked. 'Or you, my friend?'

Aaron ordered another round of kvass. He warmed to the man's company, not only for the information he could yield, but because he had extended a hand of friendship in his ready willingness to accept him as one of his kind. Aaron's life had been isolated and sheltered. Sometimes in their tavern he had conversed with such a man, and always he wanted to know more of his life, to enquire further into his angry discontent, his sudden rages, and equally sudden spasms of raucous laughing joy.

His companion put an arm around his shoulder. 'Come, my friend,' he said. 'This is a time for drinking. Let's get drunk together, you and I, and dream of the holidays we shall never take. Let's get drunk, my friend, and curse those who oppress us, the landlords, the bankers –' Aaron waited, his knees trembling ' – and the Czar.' This last in a whisper, followed by such seditious laughter, that Aaron put his mouth to the man's ear, and, sealing their friendship, he echoed, 'And the Czar.'

If they had nothing else in common, no language, no tradition, no sustaining myth, they did at least have a common enemy, and his destruction was worthy of a toast. His companion drew a wad of grubby rouble notes from his pocket, licked his forefinger, and drew one note from the pile. 'Enough of these pretty little glasses,' he said, and he shouted to the bar-tender to bring a bottle. Then grabbing it, he took Aaron's arm and guided him to a table at the far end of the tavern in the midst of a crowd of revellers concerned with their own toasts and curses, all of which, in their raucous echo, were exactly the same. The exploited were cheered, those who exploited them were cursed. They seemed to be in general agreement that the arch-exploiter was the Czar, but that agreement was whispered and cheered behind the hand. It took little time for Aaron to be accepted as one of their number. He hoped they wouldn't ask him too many questions. So, to pre-empt their curiosity, he himself was the questioner. He asked about their work, and once again brought the subject around to the other passengers.

'How do they all get passports? Do they have to buy them?' he asked innocently.

His companion laughed. 'Anyone can get one,' he said. 'It's the ticket you have to buy.'

'Except conscripts,' another man joined in.

Aaron was delighted. The man had turned the conversation very neatly.

137

'But on some of the ships I've served on,' he said, 'I've seen young men travelling. How do they manage without a passport?'

'Everyone's palm itches,' his companion said. 'The passport official's itches to the tune of fifty roubles.' He laughed and put the bottle to his lips.

Aaron smiled. He now had the information he had sought. One hundred roubles would see himself and Leon into freedom. 'They must make a good living,' he said.

'Money buys everything.' A drunken reveller raised his glass in their direction. 'Passports, exemptions from the army.' he shouted. He was becoming aggressive and Aaron badly wanted to get out of the tavern. 'Landlords' sons, the rich scum of the earth,' the man threw out the words with contempt. Then he crowned his shabby catalogue. 'And Yids,' he spat. 'Always the Yids.' He lurched over to Aaron's side, and grabbed his arm. 'What d'you expect from them, my friend?' he asked.

'What indeed?' Aaron said. His father had told him to survive, and he had just made his first down payment on that order.

'I've got to go,' he shouted, trying to keep his voice steady. He no longer trusted himself with these men, and he resented the warmth he had first felt towards them. They had nothing in common. Not even an enemy. For when the Czar was on a Jew-baiting binge, they would be firmly behind him. Not so long ago, his own father had been killed by such a mob.

'I'm going back to the waiting-room. I left my girl there,' he added, feeling the need to give some excuse for his sudden departure. For he was afraid of them.

'You can be with your girlfriend any time,' one of the men said, and there was trouble-making in his eye.

'She doesn't feel well,' Aaron improvised. Perhaps they would make allowances for sickness. And they did, grudgingly, urging him to return with the latest bulletin on her health. He promised he would, and, smiling all the while, he made for the tavern door, disguising his haste, and when he was outside in the open air, he breathed freely, as if he had escaped with his life. He made his way back to the waiting-room, and there he appraised his mother and Leon of his findings.

Zelda turned her back on the waiting passengers, and extracted the bribe from her portmanteau She handed fifty roubles apiece to her sons. Then suddenly, as if from a signal, the passengers rose and made for the door. The train had shunted into the station. Aaron and Leon sent their mother ahead of them, while they themselves hung back, waiting for the crowd to thin. Already many passengers stood in line outside the passport shed, fearless in their legality, their passports ready in their hands. Zelda stood amongst them, with the occasional backward trembling glance at her sons. Aaron and Leon waited until almost all the passengers had crossed the barrier and then they joined the line. Leon was insistent on going in front of Aaron, as a protective measure, with instructions to his older brother that, if the bribe did not work and if the official called the police, he, Aaron should disappear to escape arrest. Leon would take whatever punishment they would mete out to him. At least he was well under conscription age.

Aaron's heart was thumping as Leon moved into his turn. The official looked at his ticket and then at Leon.

'Passport?' he asked.

The notes shivered in Leon's trembling hand. He offered them to the official. The man made no attempt to hide the bribe. Indeed he flourished the packet, counting the notes openly and aloud. When he had finished he folded them and stuffed them into the back of his boot, and Aaron noted that the space between the man's sock and the boot lining, was already packed with bribery. Then it was Aaron's turn. The official looked at him, then back at Leon. 'Brothers?' he asked.

Aaron nodded.

'Passport?' The man's voice was far from friendly.

Aaron handed him his fifty roubles, and again he counted them out loud. Then he smiled and put his hand on Aaron's shoulder. 'What's your name, son?' he said gently.

Aaron smiled at him, melting with this gesture of friendship. 'Aaron,' he said. 'Aaron Bindel.'

The smile lingered on the man's face, but he tightened his grip on Aaron's shoulder. 'Yids,' he spat. 'It's a pleasure to be rid of scum like you.' Then he stuffed the money in his bribe-lined shoe, and booted Aaron through the barrier.

Leon took his brother's arm, anxious to put some distance between themselves and the official. 'We're through,' he whispered. 'We're safe. Now no one can insult us like that any more.'

'D'you remember what Papa said in the forest?' Aaron reminded him. 'There will always be men like that, he said, as long as there are Jews.'

Zelda was leaning out of the train window, scanning the platform, and when she saw them, she called their names aloud, shrill and clear. 'Aaron, Leon,' she shouted, and for good measure, 'Aaron, Leon Bindel.' And the undeniable Jewishness of those names echoed shrill on the alien platform, and for the first time since she had left the tavern, she felt the rising fever of freedom.

They rushed onto the train and settled together in a crowded compartment. The character of the train seemed suddenly to have changed. The faces were different, the talk was loud, laughing, and

139

above all, unguarded. And it was Yiddish, all of it, unashamed, raucous and free. Each passenger had a tale to tell, and was intent on telling it, even if nobody listened. It was enough for them to hear it themselves in affirmation of their new-found freedom. Amongst them, sitting alone in the corner, was a middle-aged man, holding himself rather aloof from the others. Zelda stared at him, and so did Aaron and Leon, and all for the same reason. He bore an uncommon resemblance to Benjamin Bindel. A little younger perhaps, but with the wisdom of Grandpa Jakob about the eyes, and he had Benjamin's squareness of build and the same laughing mouth and stern chin.

'He looks like Papa,' Aaron said, for it was a fact easier to be declared between them than privately considered and contained. Zelda smiled and Aaron saw a look of joy on her face that he had not seen since the Bindel tavern fire. She leaned across the space between them, drawn by that uncanny resemblance to a sorrow now blunted by the passing of time. 'Where are you from?' she asked.

'Kiev,' he said. 'But that's of the past.' There was a finality in his voice as if he was unwilling to dwell on what was gone for ever.

'We're from Odessa,' Leon cried, anxious to keep the conversation alive.

'You must forget it,' the man said, almost angrily. 'Odessa, Kiev, Balta, Kishinev. Every rotten syllable of them. For us Jews, they were regions of hell.'

The man spoke in learned Yiddish which pointed to a fluency in Russian as well. He had the self-assurance of an educated man, and the smouldering fire of an orator. 'In the whole infested country,' he declaimed, 'in all that rotten blood-soaked soil, there is but one holy spot.'

The man's eyes began to water. Aaron and Leon watched as the tears stood on the rim, immobile, becalmed, aloofly declaring themselves before going back where they came from, milked back into the eye of the storm. Aaron and Leon stared at him. Grandpa Jakob had sometimes cried like that, with the same stubborn stagnant tears, when nudged by the bruised memory of a sorrow. Then Grandpa Jakob would speak of it slowly and with well-armed detachment, as if it was a story that belonged to somebody else. And in such manner did their fellow-traveller tell his tale. 'So many years ago, it was,' he said. 'My son Uri. They took him for a soldier. He was twelve. Can you imagine? Twelve little years of life, and they took him for a soldier.' He paused, wiping the sleeve of his coat across his dry eyes. 'Somewhere between Kiev and the Eastern Provinces, there's a small piece of holy ground. His mother died of mourning,' he said. He folded his hands across his lap. 'It's over,' he said. Then he turned his body into his small corner and stared out at the passing landscape.

In the course of his story, the rest of the passengers had fallen silent and it was a silence that they now maintained. It was as if he had spoken for them all. And above all, for Zelda who heard in his words the final validation of their flight into freedom.

The night passed. Most of the passengers slept and many of them dreamed, and some cried out in their dreaming and shivered at the thought of their unpardonable desertion of their dead. It was late morning when the train drew into Hamburg station and disgorged its weary passengers onto the wagons that would take them to the harbour.

CHAPTER TEN

The dock-side was like a market-place, but more in sound than in sight. For there were very few stalls, but innumerable traders stood about and proclaimed their invisible wares. Those of the passengers who had Yiddish as their mother-tongue heard faint rings of familiarity in the German sales-talk of the traders. For they were languages from the same gnarled root. Certain words were picked up and understood: soup, blankets, beds, hostelry, and above all, tickets. Almost every trader it seemed, was selling tickets for the boats and they shouted out a choice of destination too, '*America, England,*' they sang, wandering through the market-place, touting for trade. Zelda, who never trusted a bargain especially when it came from an unofficial source, made straight for the licensed ticket-booth, dragging her sons after her. There she purchased three single tickets to England. She was given no choice of class. The boat carried only steerage but the agent assured her in his broken Russian that the accommodation was adequate. The boat would not leave until late afternoon, he told her, but they were permitted to embark at their leisure. There was little else for them to do. They had no need to buy provisions. They had a full portmanteau of food. They had a blanket a-piece, and, thus equipped, they made their way to the dock-side. The sight of the ship was not a heartening one. It was little more than a cattle-boat and, despite the fact that it was not due to sail for some hours, it already appeared pretty crowded. They made their way up the gangway. A seaman directed them to the steerage-cabins, shrugging his shoulders as he watched them go, no doubt wondering where on earth they would find to seat themselves, and for how long they could bear the stench of those nightmare quarters.

It hit the Bindels as soon as they entered the cabins, like a wall of foul-smelling heat from the bodies of the emigrants as they lay haphazardly on the wooden benches, their clothes torn, their faces haggard and yellow with dirt. There were many children amongst them, but all of them looked like old men. Zelda shrunk back at the entrance.

'We'll get used to it,' Aaron said, and he urged them forward and sought out a bench for them to sit on. He found space enough at the very end of one of the platforms, where the boat narrowed, and on it he deposited their luggage on which they sat. Except for the money valise which Zelda held forever at her side. Over the platform an oil-lamp was slung, and in the semi-darkness, it illumined the terrible shadows of the figures sprawled around them. It was like an entrance into hell. But for many of those who lay there, the present circumstances were as paradise to what they had endured over the last few months. For, unable to pay for trains, they had walked their way to freedom, picking up a generous wagon here and there, some from the far Ukraine, others from Poland, robbed on their journey of their money and possessions. For the roads were full of pitfalls. Frontier towns were the worst, for the peasants had learnt to exploit those illegal migrants without papers. Having come so far, the travellers could hardly return, so they were easy prey for the swarms of parasites on the borders. When they had run out of money, they had offered their luggage and possessions, and perhaps after that, one dared not speculate, except perhaps that they sold that, which after selling, they would still have, to sell it again and yet again, until its sale had become obligatory to survival itself, and thus carried with it no shame. At Aaron's feet a woman lay sleeping, her body draped in faded and torn finery. She had clearly sold everything, yet her pale face glowed with a serene innocence.

Crowded as it already was, the newly-embarked passengers squeezed into the cabin area. On their faces was a look of dismay and horror at the sight which confronted them. Some made to turn back, but the sailors forced them through, for the open decks were only available to passengers during the daylight hours. And so the cabins burst with the stream of passengers, all fighting for what little space was still available. Among them, Zelda caught sight of their fellow-traveller on the train, that Benjamin-image that had so drawn her. Despite the horror of his surroundings, he still maintained his air of self-assurance. Indeed it seemed to be heightened for there was actually a smile on his face, a smile of achievement, filtered with rays of hope. He looked around for somewhere to place himself. Then his eye caught Zelda's and she waved to him, signalling him to come over to their small territory, and he picked his way over the bodies to where they sat. Somehow they found room for him, and he settled himself with great dignity, then turned to thank them.

'The past is over,' he said. 'There is now only the future.' He dug into his pocket and brought out a small bottle of grappa. He unscrewed the top which acted as a cup and poured a measure. 'We will drink to freedom,' he said. 'Madam,' he handed the cup to Zelda, and as she raised it to her lips, he said, 'To America. Our new world.'

Zelda looked at her children. 'To America?' she said.

'We're going to England,' Aaron said.

'But this boat goes to America,' their companion insisted, while the cup of cheer idled in Zelda's hand unsure of the destination of its toast. Then Zelda opened her portmanteau and gave a ticket each to her sons.

'What does it say there?' she said, nervous now that the ticket-official had cheated her, which explained why there were so few clients at the licensed booth. Aaron read the legend on the ticket. It was simply a permit to embark at Hamburg, but it gave no port of call. Their companion's ticket was the same.

'It goes to America,' he said. 'The ticket-man told me in the market-place. This boat goes to America. No doubt about it. Lots of people were buying tickets from him and they all came on this boat. I've got a brother in America. It's the only place I can go.'

The Bindels were wary of the man's confidence. They did not wish to go to America. That was a land that, over the past years, had been granted no mention in Zemach's tavern. It was the sound of England, chorused by Wales, that echoed daily in the inn, and Pavel Khasina was their anchor there. There was, in Wales, a small street, they imagined, no bigger than Tolocksa Street in Odessa where the Bindels had tavern-traded. It was there, under Khasina's patronage, that they would settle, it was in that small street that they would marry and raise their children, and there, in their due season, their bones would be laid, a new foundation of burial, an offering of myths and legends for their grandchildren. All that was arranged. America had no part in it.

'It can't be true,' Aaron whispered. He rose and made his way to the end of the cabin where a group of seamen were gathered, admitting the passengers who were still embarking. He managed to get their attention.

'Where does this boat go?' he asked.

'To Tilbury,' one of them said, then seeing the look of noncomprehension on Aaron's face, he clarified, 'To London. England.'

Aaron returned to his family with the news. Zelda, far from being relieved, was now deeply concerned for her companion. 'How much did you pay for your ticket?' she asked.

'It was a bargain,' he said. 'The trader said it was half the official price.'

'How much?' she insisted.

'Fifty roubles,' he said.

It was more than she had paid for the three of them. She was enraged. 'Come,' she said. 'We shall find him on the market-place. We shall demand our money back.' She now felt herself part and parcel of her friend's campaign. 'What's your name?' she asked, feeling that it was time that she knew the identity of her companion-at-arms. She hugged her money-portmanteau to her breast and took his arm. She was incensed by the injustice of it all.

The man took time to raise his hat. 'Rubinov,' he said. 'Barak Rubinov.'

'Leon, you come with me,' Zelda said. 'Aaron, you will stay and keep our seats.'

Aaron rose. 'Goodbye, Mr Rubinov,' he said. 'I wish you well,' and to his mother, 'Come back soon. We sail in an hour.'

'Don't worry,' she said. 'You just hold our seats.' She was anxious to be away, to right the terrible wrong that had been done to her friend. For now he was more than that. He was a cause, and she was going to fight for it come what may. Leon looked at Aaron and shrugged his shoulders, then he followed his mother and Mr Rubinov into battle. As Aaron looked after them he prayed that they would not miss the boat, and he was already restless for their return.

They fought their way down the gangway off the boat. The fresh air was an astonishing relief.

'You are very kind, Madam,' Mr Rubinov kept saying, trying to keep up with his crusader, for Zelda was tearing along the dock-side on fire with vengeance. Leon paced her at her side, looking back from time to time to ascertain that the gangway was still attached to the boat. When they reached the market-place it was, unsurprisingly, deserted. No unscrupulous trader would hang around to take the consequences of his cupidity. All those invisible wares had now been sold by their now invisible vendors. Zelda stood in the empty market-place and seethed with fury.

'There's nothing we can do,' Mr Rubinov said. 'I shall stay in Hamburg and tomorrow I shall find him. You must get back to the boat.' He took Zelda's arm. 'You are a good woman,' he said. 'What a pity that we go our separate ways.'

Leon instinctively stood to one side as if not wishing to eavesdrop on what threatened to be a proposal.

'Perhaps one day you will decide to come to England,' his mother said.

'D'you know what's so terrible?' Mr Rubinov said after a while. 'The man who sold me the ticket. He spoke a good Yiddish. He was a Jew. He told me so. He called me brother.' It was clearly that aspect of the deception that pained Mr Rubinov most of all, and far more than the extortion of his money. 'Come,' he said. 'I'll take you back to the boat.' He took Zelda's arm with the ease of a long-standing escort. 'What a pity,' he said again, 'that we are to part. And I don't even know your name.'

'Zelda. Zelda Bindel,' she said. 'I am a widow. My husband was killed in the Odessa pogrom.' She was surprised at how calmly she had related an event that had shattered her whole life, and for the first time since her widowhood she knew that perhaps now her life was not beyond repair. 'My husband was a "kantonisti",' she said. 'Like your little boy.'

'And in the end they conquered him,' Mr Rubinov said. 'I'm very sorry.'

They walked the rest of the way in silence and when they came to the gangway they found that an official had taken a stand at the dockside and was examining the credentials of the late, straggling passengers. Zelda and Leon had their tickets at the ready. Zelda gave Mr Rubinov her hand. 'I'm glad we met,' she said, then she handed her ticket to the official. He clipped it and let her pass. It was Leon's turn. His ticket presented no problem but, for some unknown reason, it entered the official's mind to ask for Leon's passport. Leon called to his mother. 'He wants my passport,' he said.

Zelda paled. She opened the bribe-bag and handed the official a few rouble notes. The man ignored them. 'Passport,' he insisted.

'I haven't got one,' Leon said simply.

Zelda took a few more notes out of her bag and pushed them under the man's nose. He flicked away her hand with disgust. 'We Germans cannot be bribed,' he said.

Zelda wanted to scream at him about what his compatriots were doing on the market-place and what pageant of sin was being enacted there. But she didn't have the language to make herself understood, and in any case she realised how futile would be her protest or her insults.

'What shall I do?' Leon said.

The official shrugged. 'Go back where you came from,' he said, 'and get yourself legal papers.'

Leon froze. The official smiled at him. He shouldn't have smiled,

Leon was to recall later. If he hadn't smiled, Leon would never have raised his gentle hand. But it was the official's smile that armed him, armed him for every single rage of his burning Bindel inheritance. It armed him to avenge Grandpa Jakob's death, to avenge the monstrous service that his own father and uncle had given to the Czar. It fired a vengeance for that gentle Leon after whom he himself was named. It armed him to settle the account of the Bindel fire and the four generations that had been consumed in the flames. It fed a sweet revenge even on that swindler in the market-place, and on all the oppression and anger that drove one Jew to persecute another of his tribe. In sum, that smile armed him for the final retribution for all the pain that had knifed the thousands of ghetto hearts in Odessa, Kiev, Kishinev and in every single town and village within the Pale. It was a titanic vengeance that he sought and it fused him with a mighty strength. He felt a tingling pain in his hand and his shoulder and at his feet he saw its cause. The official lay on the dock-side, his nose bloodied, his eyes closed. Then out of nowhere, a posse of officials appeared, and rushed to his side. Mr Rubinov, who had stood by and witnessed the whole swift encounter, took Leon's astonished arm. Zelda rushed down the gangway to her son's side, and within seconds they were all overwhelmed by the uniformed indignation. A wagon drew up alongside, and the three of them were herded into the cart, while a stretcher bore away the injured body of the official who should have known better than to smile.

*

On the boat Aaron paced the spread of his small territory. He was now restless indeed. The sailors had withdrawn from the cabins and he feared that the ship was about to sail. He feared too that, if he left his spot, he would lose his holding, to say nothing of their provisions and luggage. He turned to a man who sat alongside. 'I must go away for a minute.' he said, 'and look for my family. Will you look after my things?'

The man stared at him. He looked at the space and its furnishings as if trying to assess their value. 'It will cost,' he said coldly. 'Fifty kopeks.'

Aaron would gladly have struck him. But he had no choice but to accept the deal. He nodded. 'I'll pay when I come back,' he said.

'Now,' the man said, holding out his hand.

'We're Jews,' Aaron said. 'Both of us. You can take my word. My mother has the money.'

'When you come back,' the man agreed. 'And then, no money, no space.'

At least he didn't smile. It's possible that he hadn't smiled in

146

many months, Aaron thought, as he picked his way across the cabin trying to forgive the man his meanness of spirit. He fought his way onto the deck and was surprised at how dark it was. He went to the ship's rail and to his horror he saw the gangway being shunted along the dock-side. He heard the ship's hooter and his heart froze. Apart from a few officials and sailors the quay was deserted. One of them raised his hand as if in farewell, and even as Aaron stood there he felt the boat move on its creaking way. He panicked, not knowing what to do, not knowing who or where to ask for advice, and already with an aching longing for his family. Then he realised suddenly that, although he had the food and all their clothing, it was Zelda who held all the money.

A sailor came towards him and ordered him off the deck. He went down the wooden stairway to steerage, and as he entered the cabin he caught sight of his creditor, and he of him, and the man stretched out his hand, awaiting his due.

'I've lost my mother,' Aaron said. 'I don't know what's happened to her.'

In answer the man stretched his whole body over Aaron's holding as if he would commandeer his luggage as well as his site. Aaron contemplated the two days' and nights' journey that confronted him and he wondered how he could survive. Then he remembered. 'I have some food,' he offered.

The man raised his body and shifted back to his own small site. Aaron re-took his place and opened the food portmanteau. In his anxiety he himself had lost all appetite. He handed his companion a hunk of bread, a cucumber, some cheese and an apple. The man was more than pleased with his payment. 'Thank you, brother,' he said. 'I've not eaten for some days.' And Aaron immediately forgave him, for hunger, he knew from his father's tales, could drive the gentlest of men into malice.

'Won't you break bread with me?' the man said.

'I'm not hungry.' Aaron would not allow himself to believe that his mother and brother were still in Hamburg. He talked himself into believing that they were somewhere on the boat, that they had found a more comfortable cabin. But he feared that that was not possible, that if they had re-embarked, somehow or other they would have found each other. He kept his eye on the steerage door, but with little hope of their arrival. He couldn't understand what had happened to them, and therefore he found himself imagining the worst. They were ill or they were dead. He sighed aloud.

'Don't worry, my friend,' his companion said. 'You will find them again. Have you schapps in your bag?' he asked.

Aaron nodded. 'Then drink some,' the man said. 'Drink of it

147

well. Drink yourself into a sleep. Our people deserve forgetfulness for a while.'

Aaron was glad to take the man's advice for he could not bear his terrible imaginings. He poured a measure for his neighbour and he himself drank from the bottle. They finished it off between them, and both fell into a drunken and merciful sleep. But for most of the passengers, unnumbed by alcohol, fraught with fears of the future and terrors of the past, the night passed with appalling slowness. Although the seas were calm and the weather fair, the boat heaved and rolled with the misery of its cargo, and in the morning the stench of sickness, sweat and sheer human despair was intolerable. Aaron woke to it and wished to sleep again, but the thought of his missing family, which had never entirely left his mind even during his drunken sleep, now drove him on deck in the vain hope of finding them. His bed-fellow was still half-asleep, and Aaron whispered into his ear. 'Keep our places,' he told him. 'Stretch out. I'll be back soon, and we'll take something to eat.'

The man grunted, gratefully stretching his body over Aaron's vacant seating, and with the holding secure in his whole body's possession, he fell back into sleep. Aaron picked his way through the groups of crouching passengers, those without the strength to reach for the open air. His own body was stiff and painful, his bones were frozen and his nerve-ends itched. His brow was fevered and he was afraid. Above all he needed his health at this time, and like a small boy, he longed for his mother. He reached the deck and leaned on the rail, gulping the fresh air. His eyes watered with the wind and alibied his tears with the thought of his total aloneness and the bleakness of his future. Then suddenly his mind monitored Khasina's address and the vision of the small card he had left on the tavern counter. Pavel Khasina, 24 Bute Street, Cardiff, Wales, England. He repeated it in the phonetic version they had taught themselves in the tavern, over and over again, then screamed it aloud across the sea, as if appraising his sponsor of his arrival. The recollection of the name much heartened him, and he turned from the rail and walked briskly about the deck. He had little hope of finding his mother and brother, but he scanned the deck for them all the same. He fretted less now about their absence. He had no doubt that somewhere soon, they would find each other. He felt a little hungry, so he returned to the cabin and his breakfast companion, who was still stretched out over their holding, undisturbed by the moans and sighs of sickness, of crying children and the stifled sobs of old men. Aaron shook his shoulder.

'Aren't you hungry, friend?' he asked.

The man stirred at the suggestion of food, roused himself, looked around and once again closed his eyes.

'Well I'm hungry,' Aaron said, 'and you're lying on the food.'

He sat him up gently, picked up the food hamper and sat himself down. As he opened it, he was conscious of a sudden silence around him, and he knew its cause. He regretted now that he had so brazenly displayed the layers of rolls and cheese and honey-cakes that Zelda had packed with such loving and such care. He looked up and saw the eyes staring, or rather the mouths, salivating with astonished and rude appetite. He gauged the amount of food in the case, and the number of miserable travelling hours ahead. They would reach England in two days, so a sailor on deck had informed him. There was certainly not enough food for everybody. There was no question in his mind that he must share it. His problem was to ration it out most fairly. While he was debating his allotting method, a man crawled to his side. He looked up at Aaron, his eyes begging.

'I have something to exchange,' he said. 'It cost me my last rouble, but I'll give it you in exchange for food for my children.'

'The food is for the children in any case,' Aaron said. 'We have to share it as fairly as we can.'

'You are a good man,' the traveller said, and he drew a small knife from his pocket and handed it to Aaron. Then he helped him divide the food. Aaron cut small portions, on the premise that a little food was better than none at all, and as he did so, the children, urged by their mothers, crawled towards him, their little hands outstretched for their portion. When they were all provided for, Aaron was glad that there was still food left over, but he did not touch it himself and he quickly closed the lid of the hamper so that he would not be tempted. There was still one more bottle of schnapps. He would keep it till nightfall, he decided, then share it with others desperate for sleep and oblivion. He returned the knife. The man still crouched at his side.

'I'm Aaron Bindel,' Aaron said, holding out his hand. 'What's your name?'

'Abraham,' the man said. 'Abraham Bok. From Vilna,' he smiled. 'What a life this is,' he said.

'What was it you paid a rouble for?' Aaron asked.

'Letters on a piece of paper,' Bok said. 'Here,' he dug his hand into his blouse pocket. 'I will give it to you.'

'I cannot pay,' Aaron said.

'I give it to you in any case. Because I want you to live. A good man must survive.' He handed the paper to Aaron. It looked like an address.

'What is it?' Aaron said.

'You must copy it out and keep it until we arrive. Then you must show it to an Englishman.'

'Yes, but what is it?' Aaron insisted.

'It's the address of the Jew's Temporary Shelter in London. They keep it a secret and you have to pay to get it. Because it will save our lives. It will give us money, somewhere to live, work with which to earn a living, and a synagogue where we can pray.'

'You *paid* for that?' Aaron asked. 'Who sold it to you?'

'A Jew,' Bok said. 'A brother-Jew. He probably paid 50 kopeks for it himself. My friend,' Bok said, laying his hand on Aaron's arm. 'Nothing surprises me any more. Did I not try and sell it to you? You, a brother-Jew? And, if you were hungry and your children, you would sell it too, and for the highest price. We are all in the survival business, my friend,' he said, 'and it is the most cut-throat business of all.' He handed him a pencil. 'Have you paper?' he asked.

Aaron searched his pockets. His ticket was the only paper. On the back of it he copied the letters of Bok's one-rouble life-line.

'I know how to say it,' Bok said. 'A sailor taught me,' and he ran his finger along Aaron's lettering. Then like a child reading his first lesson, he pronounced slowly, 'The Jewish Temporary Shelter, Leman Street, Whitechapel, London, England.'

Aaron smiled. The sounds were similar to his sponsor's dwelling-place and gave him reason to hope that Whitechapel was close to Wales.

Bok rose. 'I must go to my wife. Perhaps we shall meet again,' he said.

Aaron looked at his site-holder. He was sitting upright but still fast asleep, as he had slept during the whole food-distribution and threatened to sleep the day through. At his feet the young girl stirred herself, she whom Aaron had noted the night before, dressed in torn silks, faded clues to a better time than now. She sat up and shivered. Aaron took a blanket and put it round her shoulders. 'Are you hungry?' he said.

She nodded with an attempt at a smile.

He delved into the case for a roll of bread and gave it to her. She did not snatch it, but took it daintily, and ate it with an exaggerated leisure and grace to hide her hunger.

'What's your name?' Aaron asked when she had finished eating.

'Ida,' she said.

'I'm Aaron.' He stretched out his hand.

She took it in hers, and he noted how each finger of her hand was ringed, some twice over. He stared at the dazzling stones.

'It's everything I have,' she explained as if in apology.

'Are you alone?' he asked.

'Yes,' she said. 'We came from Kiev, my brother and I, but we were caught at the frontier. He's twenty. So they took him back.

But they let me go. I had rings on the other hand then,' she said. 'I was lucky. They only took the rings. Honestly,' she said. 'D'you believe me?' She was eager for his approval.

'Of course I believe you,' he said. 'But if they would have taken more it wouldn't have been your fault.'

She gripped his arm. 'They did,' she said. 'On the train to Hamburg. They offered me a ticket. I thought they were being kind, but I had to pay and they didn't want rings. I don't mind,' she said shrilly. 'It's not so terrible.'

Aaron put his arm about her. 'Of course it isn't,' he said feebly. She turned to face him, her eyes blazing. 'What do you men know about it?' she screamed at him, and she took his hand and bit it with all her rage. He forced her head away and laid her down once more. He thought he understood her but he didn't know what more he could do, so he moved away and went once more on deck and longed for his mother and Leon, and felt more and more alone, and totally ill-equipped to deal with all the injustice that he met at every turn. Once again he repeated to himself Mr Khasina's address. He took his ticket out of his pocket and tried to spell out the location of the Shelter. He could make nothing of the strange lettering. But it was enough to look at it, and see in its strange hieroglyphics, some kind of haven, a place for food, sleep, work and living, but above all a place where his mother and his brother could eventually find him.

He turned back to his cabin, and when he reached his site, the space on the floor was empty. He scanned the benches all around him but could see no sign of her. All that day she didn't return, although Aaron stayed there trying to convince himself that he was not waiting for her. At evening, the children drew around him, knowing his corner as a source for food, and he rationed out what was left in the portmanteau. He himself took a drink of schnapps from the bottle and shared it with his site-holder, who all day had sat at his post, sleeping, waking, and preferring to sleep once more. Between them they finished the bottle and Aaron was weary with hunger and numbed with drink. Most of the passengers were sleeping. More calmly this night, more resigned perhaps to the hunger and the thirst they could not assuage, and soothed perhaps with the hope that the morrow would bring a new land and hope for the future. When Aaron finally closed his eyes, she still had not returned. During the night he thought he saw her, or the faded silk of her dress. He heard it rustling at the cabin door. And he thought he saw a sailor's blouse in its folds. Or perhaps he was only dreaming.

When morning came, the passengers woke from their fitful sleep, and noticed that the boat was not moving. The sickness of the night and days before had suddenly left them, and they felt a sense of well-being which might well have been the euphoria of hunger. The sailors were moving along the compartments of the cabin, urging the passengers to leave the ship. They needed little encouragement but many were weak with hunger and the despair that comes with waking. They shuffled to their feet, collecting their children and their scant luggage, and allowed themselves to be pushed and shoved to the cabin-door. Once there, some of them tasted their first fresh air in two terrible nights and days and they reeled with the blow of it, hanging onto the rails for support. Somehow or other they stumbled to the gangway and the surge of the mob carried them to the quay-side.

Aaron stayed for a while on the boat, leaning over the rail. He still hoped for a miraculous appearance of his family amongst those who disembarked, and from his vantage-point he had a precise view of every passenger and as they touched English soil he wondered how many of them, hoodwinked on the Hamburg market-place, thought they had arrived in America.

The dock-side was bustling with activity. He saw many small stalls, but from where he stood, he could not decipher their wares. But he heard a lot of shouting from the traders, and most of it was in Yiddish. And then he caught sight of Ida. She was standing alone on the quay-side. A man approached her, raised his hat, and bowed politely. A few words passed between them, then he took her arm and guided her through the crowds. For a moment Aaron lost sight of her, but he was glad that there had been someone to meet her, someone concerned, who would look after her and heal the terrible wounds of her journey. Then he glimpsed her again. Her escort was helping her into a carriage where there were four or five young girls already seated and Aaron knew instinctively that that carriage was not good for Ida, and he was no longer glad that she had been so graciously met and accommodated. The boat was quiet now and it seemed that most of the passengers had disembarked. Aaron turned from the rail and made his way to the gangway.

He must have been the last off the boat, for the crew were coming off at the same time. Now Aaron knew for certain that his mother and brother were still in Hamburg. He wondered whether he would ever see them again. As he reached the end of the gangway, a man approached him and asked in Yiddish if he wanted some hot soup. The question reminded him of his raging hunger. He nodded his head weakly and the man took his arm and led him to one of the stalls.

'I have no money,' Aaron thought fit to tell him before he was served.

'It's free from the Jewish Board of Guardians,' the man said, and he pointed to a banner with that legend above the stand.

Aaron accepted a bowl of soup and a large hunk of bread. He took it slowly and relished the taste, and especially the gift of it. He didn't know what or who the Jewish Board of Guardians were but he knew that he would be indebted to them all his life. There were other emigrants enjoying the Board's hospitality, and all were too engrossed in their food for conversation. Aaron stood alone and thought of Ida, then quickly put the thought of her from his mind. And as he did so, a woman approached him and asked him in Yiddish if he was enjoying his soup. He nodded, smiling and glad of company. She was a middle-aged woman with a gentle voice. Her hair was grey and wound in thick plaits about her ears. 'Have you lodgings?' she asked. 'Work? Relatives?' She was offering him all that a man could need.

He shook his head, hope singing in his heart.

'If you come with me, I can give you shelter,' she said. 'Come unto me,' she dared to add, 'and I will give you rest.'

But Aaron, whose schooling had not included the New Testament, was ignorant of her illusions. He put his empty soup-plate on the counter. 'Thank you,' he said with overwhelming gratitude. He bent down to pick up his portmanteau.

'I will help you,' the woman said. She stooped to pick up his valise, and as she did so, a pendant slipped from inside her blouse and dangled in Aaron's line of vision. He gasped when he saw it and deciphered the figure at the end of the chain. The Christ swung between his eyes like a pendulum of doom. He raised himself and so did the woman at the same time, his valise in her hand. Then she noticed the mark of her calling that had so rudely and so untimely revealed its double-cross. She blushed with shame. Aaron took the valise from her hand, and without a word he turned his back on her and moved away, trembling with the joy of one who had been saved. He smiled at the woman's sheer audacity, that, under the very banner of the Jewish Board of Guardians, and in its mother-tongue, she was plying her Christian trade. He looked about him, not knowing now where to turn. But he was no longer depressed. His body's needs were sated for the time. Then he heard someone call his name. He knew it could not be Leon because it was 'Bindel' that the voice called and he turned around and saw his one-rouble Jewish Shelter friend Bok running towards him.

'They are here,' he cried ecstatically. 'The Shelter have come to meet us. I came to find you. That was a waste of a rouble,' he laughed. He put his arm round Aaron's shoulder. 'Come,' he said, 'they are waiting.'

They began to walk towards the dock gates. Aaron looked

around and saw the Christ lady accost an immigrant as he relished his Board of Guardians' soup.

'Wait a minute,' he said to Bok. He put down his cases, and rushed to the immigrant's side. 'Come,' he said. 'The Jewish Shelter is waiting. Finish your soup and come.'

Aaron and the rescued immigrant went back to where Bok was waiting.

'It's a new life,' Bok said taking their arms. 'We should all have joy of it,' and he helped them into the horse-drawn bus that would take them to the Shelter. I'm in England, Aaron thought as they drove through the strange streets and by-ways of east London. Occasionally he saw something that reminded him of home, a sewing-machine on the pavement, an old man's foot on the treadle. Shops had Yiddish signs painted on their windows and groups of Chasidic boys, their ringlets trembling on their young cheeks, carried large loaves from the bread-stall. He could have been back in Odessa. He thought perhaps that in whatever country, in whatever tongue, Jews were much the same all the world over, and that thought comforted him a little and blunted the edge of his loneliness.

CHAPTER ELEVEN

The massive exodus from Eastern Europe began in earnest in the late seventies, and continued until the passing of the Aliens Bill in 1894. During the first wave of trickling immigration, of which Aaron Bindel was a part, the Jewish Temporary Shelter was able to cater for all the needs of the improvident immigrant. There were beds, food, clothing, holy books for prayer and help in finding employment. For many of the immigrants the Shelter was used as a stop-over haven until relatives could be traced. Aaron fell marginally into this catalogue for, though Mr Khasina was no relative, he was a known 'landsleit', or fellow-countryman. So, after a day's rest and feeding, Aaron was given enough money for his travel to Cardiff and the address of the Jewish Board of Guardians in that city. He had told the officials at the Shelter about his mother and brother. They assured him that contact would eventually be made. The Shelter was inevitably the centre and postal address for all new immigrants. They copied the address of his Cardiff sponsor and they wished him well. A Shelter official took him to the station, and instructed one of the train guards to put his passenger off at Cardiff. Aaron felt like a child and was close enough to childish tears.

The journey took many hours. The other passengers in the compartment were very talkative and they tried to include him in their conversation. He shook his head and told them in Yiddish that he didn't understand. Whereupon one of them set about giving him his first English lesson, the names of colours, features of the face and body, and all manner of emotions which they affected with charade, and in this fashion the journey passed with much enjoyment and lightened Aaron's spirits. By the time he reached Cardiff he was equipped with a minimal English vocabulary, enough to savour the sounds of the language and to accept that it would be that music that would orchestrate his future. One of the passengers offered to take him to Mr Khasina's address. He himself, he mimed, lived in the neighbourhood. It was dark when they arrived in Cardiff and Aaron feared that it might be too late to make such an unexpected call. But his companion indicated that he need not worry and he urged him along the narrow streets checking the numbers on the doors against the piece of paper in Aaron's hand. At last they reached Khasina's dwelling. Aaron bade farewell to his companion, thanking him. Then he pulled the bell at the side of the door. He listened as the echo died away but he heard no footsteps towards the door. He wouldn't ring again, he decided. He would wait a while, then go away with a certain relief. He would somehow find his way to the Board of Guardians. He was about to turn from the door when it opened. A man stood there, slippered, Aaron noted, which accounted for the silence of his approach. His father would have been the man's age, Aaron thought, and for that reason, immediately resented him, so he gave his name coldly and asked for Pavel Khasina. The man smiled and turned his head indoors.

'Pavel,' he shouted. 'A "landsleit".'

Shortly afterwards Pavel himself appeared at the door and scrutinised the caller. After a while he cried out, 'Odessa. The tavern. The widow. Two sons. Come in, my friend. You took my advice.'

The welcome was lavish. They led him through the front room which Aaron could discern as a shop of sorts, but it was dark and it was difficult to decipher what was sold. At the back of the shop were the living-quarters, not unlike the lay-out, Aaron thought, of Grandpa Jakob's tavern. And the kitchen was similar too, where all the living took place, the cooking and the eating, and there was even a small truckle-bed in the corner.

155

'For you,' Pavel Khasina said, and he took Aaron's bags and put them on the bed. Then he introduced his sister, Hinda, his brother-in-law, Max, the slippered one who had opened the door, and two or three friends, 'Landsleit' too, Khasina explained. And just like the tavern, the samovar stood in the centre of the table.

All were eager of news of home. They knew no one in common, no friends, no relatives, but that was not where their interest lay. Their nostalgia was for the land, the language, even the cruelty; they needed to hear about it, to reminisce each chapter of their own survival and to celebrate the fact that they were now beyond its reach. But they kept silent. They wanted him fed and fortified. Then, when he was sated, they could sniff out the land on him, that land which had borne and bred them, hated and abused them, and in which they had left their dead. Aaron ate in a watchful silence and when he had done, Pavel poured wine for them all, and they drank a toast to his welcome.

Then 'What news of home?' one of them asked, giving Aaron an opening and making it as general as possible. But Aaron had only his own personal story to tell, but that was general enough, for it could have happened to any of them. He told it from the beginning, back-tracking occasionally when questions were asked which called for clarification from the past. So that when the long recital was over, he had told them not only his own tale but that of his father's and Grandpa Jakob's as well. During the telling, they nodded with signs of recognition because many of the events had coloured their own lives too. They drank another glass of wine together, and then they spent much time speculating on what could have happened to Zelda and Leon. Their prognoses varied, but fundamentally they were all the same. 'Soon you will all be together again,' they said.

The phrase had a familiar ring. From the stories Grandpa Jakob had told him, it was with exactly those words that he had bade farewell to the milk-brothers. Had not the gentle Leon used that phrase too, he after whom his brother was named? It was that hope and conviction of family reunion that Leon had shouted from the dock before his one-way Siberian journey. And finally his own father had said it, as he kissed them and sent them off to Zemach's tavern to prepare for his eighty-fifth birthday. 'Soon we shall all be together again,' he had said. Aaron did not like that phrase, and he wished that those around the table had not voiced it. 'Please God,' he whispered. Perhaps if he appended a prayer, it might come true.

The following morning, Aaron was awoken by the bustle in the kitchen. Hinda was making breakfast for the family. Two little girls materialised; they had obviously been in bed when Aaron had arrived. They stared at the new-comer on the cot, then turned away, giggling. Aaron rose and dressed quickly. Soon Max came to the table and Pavel. Aaron was invited to sit between the children who were chattering freely in English. Pavel explained that in front of the children only English was spoken. The children were their teachers and would be Aaron's teachers too. So for Aaron it was a silent meal until the children left for school. Then it was Yiddish again around the table with plans for Aaron's future. His first move, they suggested, and on that very day, was to go to the Jewish Board of Guardians and register his immigrant status. They would help him with money until he could find work. His lodgings on the kitchen bed would be free, they assured him, until he found his feet. The Board held classes for English too. It would be somewhere for him to go during the day. As to the prospect of work, Pavel offered to train him in the job that he did himself. Pavel was a credit draper. This was a trade most favoured by those immigrants who did not have a particular skill. Its great advantage was that it required little initial capital and even that could be credited. The trade itself was concerned with the sale of clothing to lower income groups at the minimum payment of a shilling a week, and the main hunting-ground for such clientèle was the Welsh mining valleys. The tally man would buy his goods on credit from the wholesale merchants, then make the rounds of his customers. The profit margin was narrow, the work-hours long and arduous, but it already provided Pavel with a living, as it did many of his 'landsleit'. Some of them, after a year or two, had bought their own houses, and some, like Max, had used the profits to set up a shop of their own.

Max's shop was sited on the long busy thoroughfare that led to the docks. The docks at Cardiff were a harbour for cargo from all over the world and the wagons of imported grain would pass the out-going coal-wagons as they trundled to and from the dock-side. The area was rich in passing trade. Many of the early immigrants set up small businesses there, catering for the needs of sailors and ship personnel. Max's shop sold men's clothing and luggage, and wooden chests and tin trunks stood on the forefront. Tailoring establishments were sandwiched between ale-houses and brothels. At first sight the area could have been any port in the world. Only the line of coal-wagons shuttling down Bute Street gave a clue to its Welsh location.

It was into this confusing and alien thoroughfare that Aaron was launched, on his first morning, a carefully drawn map in his hand, to make his way to the Jewish Board of Guardians. As he walked he worried about Zelda and Leon and wondered what had become of them. Such thoughts always led to the image of some calamity that had befallen. Perhaps he should go back to Hamburg. But, even if he had the money to get there, where and how would he start

157

looking? Perhaps the Jewish Board had a representative there. He quickened his pace, and from time to time, he checked on the map in his hand. He was so concerned about his family's welfare, that he had little curiosity about his strange surroundings. He would have felt guilty to find a possible pleasure in their novelty. He considered that all his energies must be channelled into the search for his mother and brother.

In time he reached the offices of the Board where a member, noting his immigrant garb and confusion, spoke to him in Yiddish and welcomed him. Aaron sat down on the chair that was offered him but he declined a glass of lemon tea. He was anxious to appraise the official of the loss of his family, to seek help in finding them. The official was baffled by the story. But he would make enquiries, he promised, taking their names and particulars. He then concerned himself with Aaron's personal financial needs and gave him the address of a school where every evening he could attend classes in the English language. Aaron left the offices of the Board, his spirits lightened. Now someone else, someone in authority, would share with him the responsibility, if not the concern, for finding his family.

That evening he attended his first English lesson. There were a dozen or so pupils and most of them were older than Aaron. A new-comer was assured of welcome because the smell of home still lingered on his gaberdine, and although most of them, as it turned out, hailed from Poland, their mother-tongue was common, and all had fled from like oppression. One of the group, the youngest, was a girl who introduced herself as Rachel and who had recently arrived from Lodz. She offered Aaron a seat on the bench beside her. It was a rule in the class that once a lesson had begun no Yiddish was to be spoken, so for Aaron it was a silent hour. But he was able to learn a little and to begin to draw the letters of a strange alphabet. When the lesson was finished, he found himself walking into the street with Rachel at his side. Out of politeness he offered to see her to her home, an offer which she accepted on condition that they spoke no Yiddish on their way. So once again Aaron was driven to silence. And so it was, night after night, after the English lesson, until in time, as the weeks passed, he was able to talk to her, and to share with her his cares and occasional hopes. And with words now between them, he began to grow fond of her.

A few weeks after his arrival in England, he accompanied Pavel on his valley rounds. The job required little skill except that of book-keeping. Its major demand was on physical strength and endurance. Pavel set out on his journey encumbered with large parcels. He would travel by train to the central town of the valley, and from there would walk or wagon along the roads to the outlying villages and hamlets. It was back-breaking work, and especially hard in the winters. But there was always a welcome in the valley and the great bonus of the trade was the friendship and warmth of the mining communities. As Pavel's companion and apprentice, Aaron was slowly accepted into their circle. In time he would have his own round. Meanwhile his English found a surer footing, as did his friendship with Rachel.

*

It was about three months after his arrival that he returned home from his English lesson to find a letter from Hamburg. It shocked him profoundly. Its surprise was disturbing for, over the past few weeks, his family had ceased to be his waking thought. That place had been taken by Rachel, and he hadn't realised until that moment that any displacement had occurred. He stared at the letter chiding himself for his negligence. He was wary of opening it, and he sat for a while staring at its much-marked and re-directed envelope, while Pavel and Max stood behind him eager for its news. Then after a while they realised that Aaron wished to be alone and they withdrew. The writing on the envelope was in his mother's careful hand. The address was clear but the town of Cardiff was omitted, which explained the delay in its delivery. He slid his thumb slowly under the envelope flap. There were two closely-written pages inside, and both in his mother's hand. He looked in vain for his brother's scrawl, then fearful, he spread the pages on the table and began to read.

His mother prefaced the letter with her deep love for him, her concern with his penniless condition, and a plea for a swift reply to an address that was written with great clarity at the top of the page. Then after such preliminaries, she gave him the explanation for their absence, and each stage of it was spelt out factually and unadorned. She wrote of the unfortunate incident at the dock-side, stressing their good luck that the official had only been slightly injured. However, Leon had been taken to court and charged with assault, together with illegal entry. This latter charge the Court was willing to overlook, and his mother thanked God for that because Leon could well have been returned to the border. But on the charge of assault, their judgement was severe. Leon had been sentenced to one year in prison.

Aaron put down the sheet of paper. His mother's method of narration had cushioned the final shock. She was at pains to stress that matters could have been much worse, so that the year's sentence when it came seemed less devastating. But when Aaron began to think about it, he could not help but reduce it to months, and then to weeks and days, and after that to calculate how much

159

of his sentence his brother had already served. It was three whole months, and, like his Grandfather Jakob before him when he estimated the milk-brothers' absence, Aaron concentrated on those months, ticking them off in his mind, rather than admit to the many months to come. He pictured his brother in his cell, and his heart heaved for his solitude and his despair. He hoped that he was sleeping. How could his mother be faring on her own in a strange land? He turned again to the letter. And again it was full of hope and even a measure of excitement. She wrote much about Mr Rubinov. They had returned to the market-place, she wrote, to retrieve the money he had spent on his ticket, but everyone had disappeared. He had been most helpful in dealing with the police on Leon's behalf, and had decided to stay in Germany, at least until Leon was released. He had found a small house near the prison so that they could visit Leon regularly. They found Leon well, she wrote, and in good spirits. Meanwhile Mr Rubinov had found work in his old trade, that of a furrier. She wrote that she found him a wonderful companion and that they spent much time together. There were many beautiful things to see in the city, she wrote, and their pleasure was only marred by Leon's incarceration. 'The language is not difficult,' she added. 'It is so much like our own.' There followed another passage about Mr Rubinov's helpfulness and solicitude and the letter ended with practical matters. She was anxious to send him money but wanted first to make sure where he was living. She wanted too to know *how* he was living, and whether he would consider Germany as a future home. She wanted to know everything about him, and quickly. She loved him with all her heart.

Aaron put the letter down. *All* her heart? he wondered, when patently much of it was on its way to Mr Rubinov. He was glad for her. His mother was still a young woman with much love to give and much grief to overcome. He recalled her now as he had seen her with his child's eye, and all the fun-loving gaiety with which she seasoned the tavern. Those high spirits had been dampened by the fire, and he was happy that they might now be rekindled. He was glad too for himself, for it helped excuse the displacement of his waking thought. But around the thought of Leon, there was nothing but sadness; Leon's isolation from any possibility of happiness, such as he and his mother had found, gnawed at Aaron's heart. He took pen and paper and set immediately to writing. He described to her his journey to England, his night at the Shelter, and his eventual meeting with Pavel Khasina. He told her about his life and his work and his English lessons. But he made no mention of Rachel. Neither did he comment on her suggestion that he should live in Germany. Most of his letter related to his concern

160

for Leon, urging her to write to him after each prison visit and tell of his brother's condition. He wanted no money, he wrote. Soon he would be earning his own living. He sent his regards to Mr Rubinov and his thanks for taking care of his family. He did not re-read the letter, needing to post it immediately. He was anxious that his mother know about him. Anxious too that she should write again, and quickly, for in his next reply he would tell her about Rachel. He went out immediately and posted the letter and when he returned he told Pavel and Max and Hinda, who were hovering in the kitchen, the news that he felt they were entitled to. He did not mention Mr Rubinov and afterwards, when he was in bed, he wondered why he had omitted his name.

One evening, shortly after the receipt of the first letter, Pavel and Max suggested that it was time that Aaron started his own drapery round. They showed him a map and circled an area that was as yet untouched by tally-men of their kind. Aaron read out the village names with difficulty. They were the mining villages of Caerphilly and Senghenydd. The following morning, he took the train with Pavel who was travelling in the same direction. He carried no parcels. His mission was to find his first orders. He was nervous as he walked up the strange valley road. On his way he rehearsed the speech he would make at his first door. When he reached the summit, he saw the now familiar sight of the pit-head and heard the grinding toll of its wheel. In his apprenticeship days with Pavel, he had met some of the men who worked below the ground, deaf to the wheels turning, their ears cocked for other noises, hearing hopefully only those they made themselves. Alert too, for the canary's song in its cage and in its melody the assurance that they were safe. He'd warmed to those men he had met, for he had smelt courage on them, laced with a terrible acceptance of their own wretched lot. Their poverty was extreme yet he did not pity them. Their pride forbade pity. They held the rich and their masters in splendid contempt, but those who struggled like themselves would find friendship amongst them. They accepted Pavel because he too, struggled for a living, and they trusted him because of the poverty they had in common. Aaron hoped that they would extend the same trust to himself.

Aaron knocked on his first door and, when it was opened, all the words of his rehearsed speech deserted him. The woman called him in after he had managed to mumble the purpose of his visit. She sensed his shyness and his need. He was handsome too, she thought, with a face unlike any other in these parts. She was Mrs Williams, she said, one of ten Mrs Williams in the village and none of them related. 'You'd better call me Myfanwy,' she said, and a cup of tea was made ready to ease the frightened words from his throat. There'd never been a tally-man in the village before, she told him. There were insurance men and never-never men for food and furniture, but none like him for clothes. But they'd heard about clothes-men from the other valleys. Yes, they needed clothes. All of them. Four children she had, and all dressed in charity hand-me-downs, with nothing for a Sunday, and a wedding coming in the village and a family christening too. But how could she pay for all these things? She was asking his advice, some magic manoeuvring of her stubborn budget. She took herself a cup of tea and sat at the table opposite him. And with no hesitation she told him her husband's earnings. Aaron took a pencil and paper and wrote a column of her weekly expenses. She was poor indeed, Aaron thought. She could hardly afford to invest in a pair of shoes. He worked out a small savings budget for her, and offered to let her have the clothes on a higher credit than was normal. She was his first customer and she might bring him luck. He knew that that was no way to make a living; he had chosen a business in which he would never make his fortune and the realisation did not in any way trouble him. Mrs Williams gave him a list of the village women who would be interested in his call. She herself accompanied him to the first house. Aaron fared better with his second customer, also a Mrs Williams, who had savings put by for such a purpose. By the end of the day, Aaron had a full order book and he returned home light-hearted and in time to attend his evening lesson. When afterwards, he took Rachel home, she asked him, for the first time, to come inside and meet her parents.

Rachel's father was a tailor, a trade he had brought with him from Lodz. Mr Ruboff had a brother in America, who had emigrated from Lodz some years before, and it was to America that the family had intended to travel. Like most immigrants from the east, they had set sail from Hamburg and it was possible that Mr Ruboff was served by the same trader on the Hamburg market-place who had, to his gross profit, mis-routed Mr Rubinov. Mr Ruboff had not uncovered the swindle at the time. Indeed he had walked the streets of Whitechapel for almost a week, under the impression that he was taking the air in New York. When appraised of his misconception, he had taken it in his stride, and had made for Cardiff where he had 'landsleit' . He and his wife spoke very little English, but they were proud of Rachel's achievement. She was their only child and they looked to her for interpretation of the strange ways and mannerisms that they daily encountered. They invited Aaron for a glass of lemon tea. The talk was Yiddish, the language of home. Aaron told them of his life in Odessa and of their flight from the city. He told them of the events in Hamburg, and his present situation. In return Mr Ruboff gave

162

his own story, much of which Aaron had already heard from Rachel. But Mr Ruboff's account was of a different style mainly because he shared the narration with his wife who filled in those details that she felt would highlight the drama. It was a poet and peasant recital, that betrayed a marriage of initial inequality but one which, over the years, had, through tolerance and affection, found a level of harmony. The evening passed with ease and pleasure and, as Aaron was leaving, they asked him to come again. He returned to his little truckle-bed, elated.

It was a few days after this visit that a second letter arrived from Zelda. Aaron was loathe to open it, for any reminder of his brother's deprivation could only cloud his own happiness. He put the letter in his pocket and walked to the harbour where he could find some privacy. Once there he found an empty bench, and though the docks were noisy, raucous with sailors and gulls, for Aaron it was private enough, for those around him had no curiosity or concern for his state. He looked at the date on the envelope. It had been on its way only ten days. Whatever news his mother would reveal would be new indeed. He slid his thumb under the envelope flap and spread the two pages on his knees, holding them down against the wind. The opening phrase of the letter heartened him. *Good news, my dearest*, his mother wrote. As a result of Leon's appeal, his sentence had been reduced by half. He would be free in two months' time. His mother spent almost the whole of the first page rejoicing in this piece of news and sharing it with her eldest son. The second page began with words of sudden urgency and importance. *There is something which my heart bids me to do, and for which I very much want your permission.*

Aaron looked out on the sea, and let the wind fan his face. He needed time to absorb the good news about Leon but, even more important to prepare himself for the matter of the permit that she asked. What impressed him was that she asked for permission at all, and he was reminded again of his exact status in the family and the duties which attended it. He thought of the death of his father and of the confusion as well as the grief that it had wrought, how it had upset the natural order, turned mothers into children and given sons the power of permit. He turned back to the letter.

The mention of Mr Rubinov did not surprise him, nor did the fact that, during the course of the letter, he became Barak. He was kind, gentle, solicitous and lonely, and he had asked her to marry him. For her part she owned a true affection for him, and gratitude, too, that he had sustained her during Leon's troubles. He had enough money, she added, for their comfort, and his business prospered. They had it in mind to make their home in Germany. She had made no mention of his proposal to Leon, for she felt that

163

Aaron as the eldest son should be the first to be told, and it was his permission that she sought and by whose decision she would abide. She eagerly awaited his reply. Whatever his decision, she declared, they could look forward with joy to a family reunion in the near future. She sent her best wishes and her thanks to Pavel Khasina and his family, and her longing love for him. *My son*, she wrote, *I am happy for the first time in many years.*

Aaron folded the letter and quickly put it in his pocket. He was anxious to get home, to write to her quickly, to give her the permission she so ridiculously sought, to wish her joy of her future. But most of all it was the news of Leon that so heartened him. He would write her of that too. And when all that was written, he would tell her about Rachel. He ran all the way down the dock road, and when he reached home, Pavel, Max and Hinda, as he expected, were hovering at the door for the news. But first he explained, he had to write a letter, and only when it was done and posted, did he tell them. He told them in the order of his mother's priorities, of Leon's reduced sentence and of his mother's intended re-marriage. But he kept silent about Rachel, and would remain so, until his mother was privy to his news.

He waited daily for her reply, for, in telling her about Rachel he was, in his turn, seeking her permission for his eventual marriage. It was three weeks before the letter arrived. He was too impatient even to seek privacy, and then and there, on his truckle-bed, while the family were preparing supper, he read of his mother's joy in the prospect of his engagement. *We shall be together soon,* she wrote, *to celebrate your marriage and Leon's freedom.* She added that she and Barak would marry quietly in Hamburg. She hoped then that they could arrange to come to England, at least for a little while. Aaron pocketed the letter and smiled at the hovering faces around him. 'All is good,' he said, then he put on his best suit, pomaded his hair, and took himself to Rachel's house to talk with her father.

On his way down Bute Street he rehearsed his address of proposal. He knew he had little to offer Rachel in terms of material goods. He had entered a trade in which he could see little financial reward. He had no home of his own and little prospect of one in the near future. He loved her, and his love was all that he had to offer. He wondered whether in her father's eye that would be enough.

Rachel was not at home when he arrived, a fact for which her father apologised when he welcomed Aaron inside.

'But I can offer you my company,' he said. 'Come into the workshop. I'm pressing a suit.'

'It's you I've come to see, Mr Ruboff,' Aaron said to his back as he followed him upstairs.

'Then take a seat,' Mr Ruboff said without surprise, 'and talk to me while I work.'

The steam rose from the heavy iron, and from time to time it cast a mist over his face and it was not easy for Aaron to put forward a serious proposition to a face that swam in and out of clouds of vapour. It was like talking to a ghost. He fidgeted in his chair.

'I remember when I was a boy in Lodz,' Mr Ruboff said. 'I used to sit in my father's workshop and watch him at his sewing-machine. Sometimes he let me turn the wheel or he would give me a box of buttons, and I'd sort out the sizes. That's how I learned how to count.' Then, without a pause, and with the heavy steam masking his features, he said, 'You've come to talk to me about Rachel.' Then he put the iron aside, the smile in his face now slowly coming into focus. 'Come, my friend,' he said. 'Say your piece.'

'I want to marry her,' Aaron said, heedless of his rehearsal, without overture or elaboration.

Mr Ruboff moved away from the pressing-table and clasped Aaron by the shoulders. 'My blessings on you both,' he said softly. Aaron opened his mouth to list his inadequacies, his lack of livelihood or position, and to state his willingness to wait for their betrothal. But Mr Ruboff did not let him speak.

'I know,' he said. 'You have no living and you have no house. But all these you shall have in time. I would like to teach you my trade. There's good business in tailoring,' he said. 'Think about it. There's time. Come, we'll make ourselves tea. Rachel will soon be home.'

They went downstairs to the kitchen where Mr Ruboff busied himself at the stove. 'You know,' he said, 'when I wanted to marry my wife, I was afraid to ask her father. He was a great Rabbi, full of learning, and I felt I was not good enough for his daughter. For a whole year I tried to give myself courage. Then one day the old man came to me himself. "In the Hagadah that we read at Passover," he said, "there is the story of the four sons, the wise one, the wicked one, the simple one and the one who does not know what or how to ask. You are like that fourth son," he said, "and I shall answer you as the Hagadah instructs. To the son who does not know what to ask, the Hagadah says, 'thou shalt open the subject to him." Then he put his old hand on my shoulder and he said, "You want to ask for my daughter's hand. You have asked and it is given."'

Mr Ruboff took the pot from the stove and topped up the samovar on the table. They heard the front-door open and footsteps in the hall.

'David?' Rachel's mother called.

'We're in the kitchen,' Mr Ruboff shouted.

Rachel followed her mother and, when she saw Aaron sitting

there, and her father's face wreathed in smiles, she sensed a contract between them to which she was central. She blushed and turned her face away, hiding it in the large shopping-bag that she was carrying. Mrs Ruboff too sensed a gentle conspiracy between the men, and she too knew its matter.

'Only tea?' she said, 'for such an occasion?' and she went to the cupboard and brought out a bottle of shnapps. 'Rachel,' she said, 'get the glasses.'

Thus Rachel was forced to turn, and Aaron dared to go to her and take her hand. As he did so he realised that, of all the words that they had shared over the past months, marriage had not been spoken, yet he knew that its notion was as much her waking thought as it was his own.

'Your father has given his blessing on our marriage,' he said. He spoke in Yiddish for her parents' understanding. She smiled at him, then kissed her father and mother in turn. Then without a word, she took the glasses and held them for her mother's pouring.

'To our children,' Mr Ruboff said, raising his glass, taking his wife's arm, and they drank together.

'To you both,' Aaron said, raising his glass in his turn. He could not call them his parents. His mother was still alive and his father was irreplaceable. It is possible that Mr Ruboff read his thoughts, for he raised his glass once more. 'To the memory of your father,' he said, and with that toast he endowed their joy with the solemnity that was proper to the occasion for, at a celebration of continuity, at each avowal of the future, there must be in attendance an acknowledgement of the past, a homage to those who had made the present possible. For the rest of the evening, they sat in quiet reminiscence of that past, of both Aaron's and Rachel's, and despite the grief and the rage that had attended almost every event in their history, it was remembered now with quiet acceptance, and for the first time since he had left Odessa, Aaron felt himself free to let his father lie quietly in his grave.

That night, when he reached home, Aaron wrote immediately to his mother, telling her of his evening's visit. It was a short letter, but he enclosed a longer one to Leon asking that it should be delivered to him in the prison. To his brother he wrote little of Rachel. He still felt unentitled to his own happiness. His letter was a confirmation of the fraternal love he bore him, of all his hopes of the future that they would share. He reminded him of stories of their childhood; he talked of their father, and every syllable of his recollection was a song of joy. He tried to infuse his brother with that peace and serenity that he himself had suddenly found in his father's memory.

*

166

For the next few weeks, Aaron met with Rachel every day, and every day too he went on his round to Senghenydd. He had not yet decided on Mr Ruboff's offer of tailoring apprenticeship. His little credit drapery was prospering in a small way, and he wished to consolidate it. When he thought about it he knew that he was doing it for his brother's sake, that he was establishing a foothold for Leon who would eventually make his home in Wales. Once Leon was settled, Aaron could begin his tailoring apprenticeship. He longed to see his brother again. He tried not to think of him in his prison-cell. His mother wrote of her re-marriage and, in reply to that letter, Aaron had a certain difficulty with the mode of address. It was natural for him to write 'Mrs Bindel', and only when he had completed the address did he realise that in truth, he had not given her permission to re-marry at all. He thought he might cross out 'Bindel' and replace it with an acknowledgement of her new status, but that seemed to him like a re-burial of his father. So he took a new envelope, and with a careful hand, he wrote, 'Mrs Zelda Rubinov' and it was as if he were writing to a total stranger. He began to be apprehensive of their reunion. Leon was due to be released in two weeks. In less than a month they would all be together again and, though he longed for it, Aaron was nervous for its success. In the last months the Bindel family had lost much of its cohesion. The absence of two of its members, and the foreign grafting of another threatened the possibility of a return to that love and mutual support that the Bindel family had always known. The fact of living together under the same roof, as the Bindel family had always done in each generation in Odessa, such a fact was crucial to family cohesion. For a moment Aaron dreamed of a huge house in Bute Street where the Bindels would regroup once more, and live out their lives in shared joy and sorrow. But when he envisaged them in such a setting, with the stranger Rubinov at the head of the table, and his now stranger of a brother with whom he had not shared those first steps into exile, and his own Rachel whose childhood was known to none of them, it seemed to Aaron that there was little left that could hold them together. The songs of the Bindel tavern in Odessa did not travel well. They belonged to the discords and harmonies of an era that had passed. Aaron had accepted that passing. His love for Rachel had enabled him to put it aside. Perhaps his mother, for like reasons, had done the same. But there remained in Aaron's mind the figure of Leon in his cell. He hoped, as always, that Leon was sleeping, but not, Aaron prayed, to dream of the Bindel tavern, to hear its songs in the hope of ever hearing them again. He must help Leon to limp out of the trap of his history, to tune his ears to other songs and voices, but above all, to lead him away from his dead and leave them to lie in peace. Aaron was overcome by a sudden longing to take his brother in his arms, and it was this thought that helped him allay his fears of the impending family reunion.

CHAPTER TWELVE

Aaron had decided against going to Tilbury to meet the boat from Hamburg. What little money he had managed to save, he put by for his marriage. Pavel was insistent on making a reception to welcome them and Max and Hinda were more than happy to open their home to new 'landsleit'. The Ruboffs had readily offered sleeping accommodation. Aaron was dispatched in good time to the station to meet the train and he had to idle nervously on the platform for a good hour before the train would arrive. So he took himself to the nearest hostelry and ordered himself a beer which he had been told was the national beverage. It was the first time since his arrival in England that he had been into a tavern. Often on a Friday night, the mining men of Senghenydd had urged him into the corner public-house, but he had always pleaded his haste to be home. He liked the miners' company but he had no taste for their beer, and now he wondered at himself that he had ordered the glass of ale that was by his hand. He remembered the last time he'd been in a tavern, one like this, adjacent to a railway station, on the Prussian border. He recalled his encounter with the angry reveller, and his first strategy in the battle for survival. All that now seemed so many years ago, a continent ago, and since that time there had been much confusion. His mother was no longer a Bindel, and both he and his brother had passed through adventures unshared. He felt profoundly alone. He lifted his glass in unspoken toast to the stranger beside him. It was a contact without touch, but it was enough for the moment to blunt the edge of his isolation. He downed his glass and left the tavern.

The platform was now peopled with those waiting to meet the London train, and Aaron was glad of the company. Their presence might help dilute the panic of the Bindel meeting, open it to the public view, enforce formality and thus reduce its agitation. In the distance he caught sight of the signal-pointer, its arm extended, immobile. Then suddenly it dropped and there was now no reason why a train should not approach the platform and launch that drama that Aaron both longed for and dreaded. He heard the train's hooter and saw the high column of smoke as it belched skyward. He planted his feet firmly together and stiffened his limbs to still the tremblings in his body. When the train creaked to a standstill, he stood rooted to the spot, unable to move. In the distance he saw them distinctly. Mr Rubinov first, as he held out his hand to help his mother from the train. And some moments after her, his brother Leon, lagging behind as if he were a lone traveller. The crowd on the platform surged forward to greet those who had arrived, and it was only their movement that propelled Aaron into stirring, and he allowed himself to be swept along the platform with the human tide until he found himself face to face with his kin. Mr Rubinov stepped aside as if knowing his place, allowing a mother-and-son embrace. His presence affected the proceedings with some formality. When the embrace was done, timed as it were by Mr Rubinov's stage prompting, they separated and Zelda stepped aside for Leon's entry. One look at Leon's face told Aaron that in his brother's eyes he was already a total stranger. His look was cold, angry and bitter, and when Aaron put his arms around him, in that embrace that had so often scored his day-dreams, he was aware of a deadness in his arms. Leon's hands hung loosely by his side with no attempt to seal their brotherhood. Aaron shivered at the rude lack of response. Then he held him at arms' length and stared at him. On the whole of Leon's face, in no crevice, in no contour was there a hint of a smile.

'Hullo, Aaron,' Leon said, and his voice too, as well as his mien, was that of a stranger.

Aaron didn't answer. He just took his brother's hand and held it in both of his own. I understand, his caress was meant to say. I understand it all. But though Aaron knew that Leon's body and spirit cried out for understanding, he had no notion at all of the meaning of his pain.

Aaron helped Mr Rubinov with the luggage. He noticed that they had brought little with them, as an indication that they did not have it in mind to stay very long. Aaron was ashamed of his relief. But not Leon, he thought. Leon must stay, and he would help ease the pain that troubled him. He was frightened that his brother might be ill. He wanted desperately to talk to him, but he feared that Leon would give no clue. In any case his instinct prompted him that Leon's recovery would take time and many silences. He reached out to his brother's arm and held on to his sleeve, and the cold rub of serge had caught the torpor of the limb it clothed.

As soon as they were settled on the tram, Zelda took Aaron's arm. 'Now tell me,' she said. 'I want to know everything.' She gave

169

no pause for his reply, but preceded to regale him with an account of their journey from Hamburg, detailing every small trivia of their passage. She seemed to be talking for the simple sake of filling the space between them and in utter dread of the silence that was the alternative. Because she feared that Aaron might whisper a question concerning Leon, and whatever question he had in mind, she knew she could not answer. Whatever the reason for Leon's indisposition, she herself felt the cause, and her heart was a trough of guilt fermenting in bubbles of inconsequential chatter. She told Aaron about her marriage and described in great detail the small synagogue where it had taken place, and the Rabbi who had performed the ceremony. She described the house Mr Rubinov had bought, itemising every single room and piece of furniture. It was a large house and in her manner took some time to survey, and by the time they alighted from the tram in Bute Street, she was almost hysterical with her catalogue. It would be a relief to pass on to others the butt of her incessant tongue, and when on arrival at Max's house, Aaron made introductions all round, he withdrew quickly into the darkness of the shop. He needed to be alone, to rinse out of his ears his mother's hysteria. After a while he returned to the living-quarters and was not surprised to find his mother holding court with an agitated recital of her life and times in Hamburg. Perhaps, Aaron thought, there was nothing wrong with Leon at all. It was Zelda who was out of countenance. For his own protection from her garrulousness, his brother had assumed a feigned deafness that was in danger of becoming a reality. Mr Rubinov took his mother's arm and Aaron noted his look of concern. As he touched her, his mother drawled her tale to a halt as if her spouse had gently unwound her mechanism. Max took advantage of the interval to pour wine into the glasses already set on the table and Hinda passed around the cakes.

'The Ruboffs are late,' Max said.

In his anxiety, Aaron had forgotten that his future family were to be present at the welcoming reception and now he heartily wished that they would not come. Much as he wanted to see Rachel, he did not look forward to presenting her to his family. And moreover they were to stay in the Ruboffs' house. He heard the bell-push in the hall. It was altogether too much for him. He felt like a child in need of protection but those to whom he would have naturally turned, were themselves afflicted.

He felt a sudden cold presence by his side, and he looked up and he saw Leon.

'Let me stay here with you,' his brother said. They were the first real words that Aaron had heard from his brother's mouth, and he wanted to embrace him, just for the sound of them and for their great gift of contact. Then he wondered what they meant. By staying, did Leon mean for ever, and in Wales, or just that night in Pavel's dwelling-place? He put his hand on his brother's shoulder. 'Of course,' he said. 'You must. There's no question of it.' Then he followed Pavel into the hall to greet Rachel.

The Ruboffs entered the room shyly, unused to strangers' company. But they were all 'landsleit' of a sort, and some of them would soon by marriage, be related. It was Mr Rubinov, in many ways more of a stranger than the others, who eased the company into conversation. He was anxious to give no pause for his wife's renewed recital, and he was eager to ask Mr Ruboff of his background and his immigrant experience. Mrs Ruboff slipped easily into the conversation, and stretched out a hand for Zelda to join them. Aaron urged his way into the circle putting Rachel by his side. He wanted at that moment to avoid a face-to-face meeting between his mother and his intended bride and he hovered in the women's circle for the protection of both of them. Pavel had approached Leon, and Aaron strained one ear to listen to whatever conversation would ensue, while with the other, he monitored the tenor of the women's exchange. Between the two he kept his perilous balance, fearfully anticipating a breakdown on either side. But for a while both parties seemed at ease and Aaron felt that it would be safe to move to Pavel's side and perhaps through him to engage in conversation with his brother. But what conversation there was, was mostly one-sided with a hard-pressed Pavel reminding Leon of their last meeting in the Odessa tavern with very little response or encouragement from Leon's side. For Pavel's relief, Aaron contributed his own elaboration of the scene. When it was done, Pavel scratched in his mind for a new topic of conversation. Suddenly Leon said, 'I'm so very tired.'

Both Pavel and Aaron knew that Leon's weariness had nothing to do with fatigue.

'When they are gone,' Pavel said, 'you can be alone here.'

For the first time since their reunion, Aaron saw the smallest hint of a smile on his brother's face. He clutched Pavel's arm in gratitude for his understanding. Then Pavel turned to the company. 'I think our guests must be very tired. I shall prepare the wagon to take the Ruboffs home.' He left the room but there was no let-up in the conversation.

'Have you spoken to Rachel?' Aaron asked his brother.

Leon shook his head. 'Tomorrow,' he said.

Aaron nodded and made to move away, when Leon touched his sleeve. 'She's beautiful,' he said.

'It's important to me that you should like her,' Aaron said. 'It's the most important thing of all.' He smiled at his brother with the

171

relief of the conviction that nothing was wrong with him. A man couldn't spend six months in prison and expect to emerge laughing. Gradually around his person there would be a gentle thaw. He looked at the group of women.

His mother was silent and had been so since Mr Rubinov had wound her down, and, though her eyes darted from one face to the other, it was clear that she was not listening. He went over and took her arm, linking the other with Rachel's, while Hinda and Mrs Ruboff compared their housekeeping problems and marvelled at the strange English ways. After a while Pavel announced that the wagon was ready. He would first load the luggage. Capes and cloaks were donned, thanks and farewells were given, and it only remained for Pavel to return. In that waiting time was silence, with eyes on the door and feet shifting.

'He won't be long,' Max said after a while, and there was silence yet again. Aaron wished that Pavel would return quickly. The silence was uneasy. Then suddenly, to break it, a small voice pleaded, 'He doesn't talk to me any more.'

It was the voice of a ghost and Aaron wondered whether only he had heard it. But Rubinov put his hand on his wife's arm.

Max looked questioningly at Hinda and Rachel looked at the floor. And Leon turned his back and walked from the room.

Then Mr Ruboff spoke. 'You're very tired, Mrs Rubinov,' he said. 'Tomorrow all will seem different.'

Then mercifully Pavel re-appeared. Aaron kissed his mother good-night. 'We shall talk tomorrow,' he whispered. 'When you are rested.'

'I have no sleep in me,' she said.

'Come, my dear,' Mr Rubinov held her hand and she squeezed it like a child. Aaron saw them all to the door and helped them into the wagon and watched it out of sight. On his return through the shop in the darkness, he called Leon's name.

'I'm here,' Leon said and his voice came from the corner where the window was and the stacks of tin-trunks of the window's display. Aaron groped his way to Leon's side and sat beside him, silent for a while, accustoming himself to the half-light in the shop, lit by the gas-light outside the window. He did not particularly want to talk or ask questions. It was enough for him to have his brother at his side. The silence between them was no embarrassment. It seemed to be Leon's wish as well. Then after a while Aaron spoke.

'D'you like Barak?' he asked. He suspected that Barak, kind and concerned though he was, was the core of both his mother's and his brother's discontent.

'Barak is fine,' Leon almost shouted, and his extreme protest could not mask his jealousy.

172

'He makes her happy,' Aaron said, and as he heard his own words, he heard the lie of them too.

'You call that happy?' Leon mocked.

There was a silence then between them, and after a while Aaron asked,

'Then what do you think's the matter with her?'

'She's murdered her past,' Leon said, 'and she doesn't know what to do with the body.'

Aaron was astonished at his brother's turn of phrase. His solitary confinement had nurtured in him a philosophical frame of mind. Aaron had difficulty in accepting that Leon was his younger brother.

'It was all right before she was married,' Leon was saying. 'She was a widow, and honourably widowed by our history, and the past had its proper untainted place in her heart. Grief had made her strong and independent. She had no need to marry again.'

'Is that why you're angry with her?' Aaron asked as gently as he could.

Leon turned away. 'I cannot go back to Hamburg,' he said. 'I must stay here.' There was no pleading in his voice. Not even anger, and though Aaron could not see his brother's face, he knew that there would be no betrayal on his features of whatever confusion reigned in his heart.

'Of course you will stay. You will make your home here. With me and Rachel. And there is work too. There's a good life here, Leon. We are safe here. We can all die in our beds.'

'I would like to talk to Rachel tomorrow,' Leon said tonelessly.

Aaron held him in his arms. He no longer minded the limp hands at Leon's side or the almost imperceptible stiffening of his brother's shoulders in his embrace. In his long and alien isolation, his brother had become untouchable. But he would learn to love again, not least for his own sake, but for his mother's pure and simple survival. 'We shall sleep now,' Aaron said, 'and tomorrow we shall all begin again.'

When they returned to the kitchen, the tables had been cleared and a second cot was set up in the corner. The oil-lamp still burned on the table, and they left it burning for Pavel's return, but neither of them woke with his coming or were disturbed by the dimming of the lamp, and when Pavel looked at them, he was surprised at the peace on their faces, as if nothing on earth could trouble them. He wished well for both of them, but especially for their mother, whose troubled spirit, despite its long journeyings, had never left Odessa.

Pavel had offered to make Aaron's round collection during the visit of his family, and the following morning he offered to take Leon with him and show him a little of life in the valley. He sensed

173

that Aaron was establishing the Senghenydd round for Leon's sake. But more than that. He sensed too that Leon would be more at ease in strangers' company than in that of his family, and this belief was confirmed by Leon's gratitude at his suggestion. So the two of them left for the valley by the early train, sharing the parcels between them.

Aaron made his way to the Ruboffs. He was surprised to find his mother still a-bed. Mrs Ruboff had decided not to disturb her. Sleep was remedial and, though she did not know the nature of Zelda's condition, she was certain it needed cure. But Mr Rubinov had breakfasted and seemed bright enough and eager to walk and talk with Aaron. Which Aaron welcomed. As non-kin, his step-father could admit him to his mother's heart without any sense of betrayal. Mr Rubinov expressed a wish to visit the synagogue which was a happy choice, for it was a long enough walk to encourage the growth of intimacy, and promised a destination of quietude and contemplation, which Aaron had no doubt would be called for after their discourse. Aaron spent a few moments with Rachel before leaving, and as he turned to the door she said, 'Don't worry about your mother.'

'But I do,' he said. 'I can't help it. With what miracle can she be cured?'

'Forgiveness,' Rachel said.

'But she has done no wrong.'

Rachel put her hand on his arm. 'She thinks otherwise,' she said.

'Then who can forgive her?'

'Only herself, but with our help.'

Aaron kissed her on her forehead. 'You are a woman of worth,' he said.

Mr Ruboff's house was situated on the riverside, and they walked in silence along its embankment to the steps that led to the bridge. From there they crossed over the fields and had a clear half-mile in front of them before they reached the main thoroughfare.

'The Ruboffs are fine people.' Barak broke the silence between them. 'When will you marry their daughter?'

'I have to save first,' Aaron said. 'We need somewhere to live.'

'Your mother has money for you,' Barak said. 'And you must take it. It would be your grandfather Zemach's wish. Your father's too.'

'But my mother has need of it,' Aaron said.

'We have enough,' Barak answered him. 'My business prospers. It's not money that your mother needs.' Barak dug his stick into a small clump of grass at their feet. For a moment he kept it there, screwing it deep into the soil. Then he sighed and retrieved it and walked on in silence.

'What does she need then?' Aaron asked, though he knew the question was unanswerable.

Barak shook his head and continued walking. Aaron grabbed his shoulder. 'Tell me,' he said. His voice was almost weeping. 'What's the matter with her?'

'Survival,' Barak said. He stood still and turned to face Aaron. 'For some people,' he said, 'like you, like your father, and his father before him, survival is a state of health, and in its confines they bloom and they prosper. For others, like your mother, it is a disease. They are maimed by its symptoms and sometimes the malady is mortal. My own wife died from survival,' he whispered.

'I don't understand,' Aaron shouted.

Barak took Aaron's arm and guided their steps over the fields. 'Let me explain it to you,' he said. 'Your mother is consumed with guilt, and it gives her no peace. She blames herself for everything. She insists that Leon's imprisonment was her fault. She should never have left that boat in Hamburg, she says. If she had sailed to England with you, with no care of my dilemma, all would have been well.'

'But she did care,' Aaron said.

'Yes, I know. Your dear mother acted in accordance with her nature, but the consequences of her act were unfortunate, at least as far as Leon was concerned.'

'And you?' Aaron dared to ask.

'I love her,' Barak said simply, 'but I am another symptom of her survival. I have replaced a man whom she refuses to accept as dead. She cannot confront that overwhelming sorrow. So in our marriage, she sees herself as an adulteress, and she must punish herself because she survived. That's how my first wife died,' Barak said. 'She too was convinced that she was responsible for our son's death, simply because she had survived him. Do you understand now?' Barak said quietly. 'It is guilt your mother is suffering from. The guilt of survival.'

'But how can she learn to forgive herself?' Aaron said, echoing Rachel's words.

'I talk to her a lot,' Barak said. 'I try to explain things to her. She knows the root of her despair. But there are two ways of knowing. Knowing with your head where the knowledge will lie with no call for disturbance. But hardest of all is to know with the heart, for that knowledge behoves us to react, to behave in different ways, to make decisions to live and love once more. We can do nothing for Zelda,' Barak said, 'except to love her and it is our love that will plunge her into the perilous depths of self-esteem.'

They had reached the edge of the fields that led to the road, one of the main thoroughfares of Cardiff. It was called Cathedral Road, so named for the temple of worship to which it led. But the road was paradoxically named, for half way along it the synagogue was sited, as if some mason, on his way to the Cathedral, paused for a while, and built a tabernacle in homage to the Founder of that faith whose own particular God held sway at the end of the road. The two men crossed over the main street and once again there was silence between them. When they reached the gates of the synagogue, Aaron stopped and turned to face Barak.

'My father would have called you friend,' he said. Then he opened the gates and let his step-father into the courtyard.

Morning prayers were over and the synagogue was closed. Unlike an ever-open church, one could not just drop in on the Jewish God. Appointments had to be made. Appointments for morning and evening prayers, *Kadish* for the dead, and festival celebrations. 'Let us sit a while,' Barak said, and they found a bench in the courtyard where they rested themselves.

'Leon told me he would like to stay in Wales,' Aaron said after a while.

'I hoped he would want that,' Barak said. 'He needs to be with you.'

'Will Mama be angry?' Aaron asked.

'I think she might be relieved,' Barak said. 'When we go back to Germany, we shall move. The fur-trade is well-established in Leipzig. It is the centre for world trade. With the money I have I could open a business there. The change would be good for Zelda too. Hamburg has hard memories for her. And Leipzig, they tell me, is a beautiful city. You and Leon will come to visit us there when we are settled.'

Then he rose, and both men left the courtyard and crossed the fields once more. When they came to the bridge they paused and leaned over the rail, following the shallow waters of the river Taff as they lurched over the pebbles and grooved the slime between the stones. 'If you think about it,' Barak said suddenly, 'we are born with a status of survival. Out of the millions and billions of spermatazoa that flood the womb, only one can fertilise the egg. Can you imagine the struggle to achieve that victory? Yet each and every one of us on earth are conquerors. We have, all of us, survived the others. And that victory, in the moment of fruition, pricks our consciousness with culpability. Man is *born* guilty, my friend.' He turned from the rail. 'Let us go to your mother,' he said.

*

176

When Aaron returned that evening to Pavel's dwelling, they were all at supper. As he threaded his dark way through the shop, he heard laughing chatter from the kitchen. And the voice that dominated it all was that of his brother. He paused for a moment to check on his hearing. His brother was actually laughing. He waited for the laughter to subside before entering the kitchen, and when he did so, he saw his brother's smiling countenance and he was amazed at the day's transformation. Even when Leon saw Aaron, that link with his family his smile did not fade, but when Aaron went to the table and embraced him, he tried not to notice the shrivelling of Leon's shoulders, or feel his clenching fists, for he knew without looking that his brother's smile was fading. I must not touch him any more, Aaron thought, not until he himself is ready to move towards me. Thereafter the conversation was subdued. Aaron's arrival had clearly dampened Leon's spirit, and the others had taken their cue from him who hitherto had been their star.

That night when the brothers settled in their beds, Aaron made an attempt at conversation. But Leon pretended he was sleeping. Aaron tossed on his bed, sad and restless. And as was his custom at such moments, he thought of his father, then of Reuben and of the glorious milk-brotherhood between them. He and Leon were linked by blood, yet between them now was no fraction of the love that sustained the milk-brothers throughout their lives. Yet only milk had bound them. Between himself and Leon, bound by blood, there was a Siberian distance. Perhaps, Aaron thought, it was the blood that was the curdling factor. More even than Rachel's love, he needed Leon's, and he feared that it was that love that would forever elude him.

The following day Leon joined the family and in their presence he became again withdrawn. Once again Zelda had set off on an unstoppable recital of their Hamburg life-style. Sometimes during her narration, she dared to look at Leon, but each time he turned his face away and, at each rejection, the pitch of her voice was raised, and all one could do was to stand aside until she had had her hysterical say. 'You like Hamburg, don't you, Leon?' Zelda dared to ask.

Leon made no answer. He did not even shrug his shoulders. Aaron caught the pained look on his mother's face, and for the first time in his life he tasted the sour bile of hatred and to his horror it was directed at his blood-brother. That night when they were alone, he again tried to talk to him, and again Leon feigned sleep. But Aaron ignored that ploy. He had to speak out, even if only to hear the words himself.

'Why don't you talk to her?' he hissed. 'It's all that she wants.

You can't hate her just because she married again. You can't never ever speak to her again just because of that.'

Leon made no answer, but, as Aaron heard his own words, he realised how threadbare a reason he had given for Leon's silences. That the re-marriage was but a trigger to the pent-up anger that must have resided in Leon's spirit long before the Hamburg adventure, and that his poor mother was but a convenient target for his spleen. And so Aaron set about to wonder at the source of his brother's rage. When he recapped their life since their childhood in Odessa, it could have been one of so many griefs that could have scarred his spirit, griefs that he himself had endured without the consequent fury. The incident of his imprisonment was the only event of their lives that they had not shared.

He got out of bed and went over to his brother's cot. 'Leon,' he whispered. Then, when there was no response, he shouted his name in his ear.

Leon turned on his pillow. 'What d'you want?' he said sourly.

'What happened to you in that prison?' Aaron asked.

Leon sat bolt upright in his bed. 'Nothing happened,' he said. 'I was in prison. That's all. Now let me get some sleep.' He laid his head on his pillow and closed his eyes.

'Something happened,' Aaron insisted. 'Why don't you tell me?'

Leon turned over on his cot and put his hands over his face. Aaron was weeping with anger, and despite his former decision not to touch his brother, he gripped one of his shoulders and shook him violently. 'Why don't you talk to our mother,' he shouted at him. Then he heard Leon's muffled sobbing. He knelt down by the bed.

'What's the matter, brother?' he said softly.

Aaron waited, for he knew by the sound of the sighs, that put a brake on the sobbing, that an answer would come. And when it did, he reeled at its blasphemy.

'Why do we have to be Jews?' Leon said.

Aaron remained kneeling for a long while. He did not trust his legs to take him back to his bed. He crawled to his cot and sat on the edge and tried not to think of what Leon had said. But it was impossible to rinse that profanity from his ear. So he crawled into bed and covered his head with the sheets, so that the thought of Leon's sacrilege should lie in the darkness to which it belonged. Aaron did not believe that ever, in the whole line of Bindel heritage, had one single member of the kinship uttered such an oath. Though their family history had been strewn with corpses and griefs of many a kind, they still considered it a privilege to be born one of the chosen. Indeed, not to be so born was to be deprived in all manner of ways, but above all in the realm of the spirit, that which sustained their faith through all adversity. Aaron wondered where such a thought could lead, but he feared its conclusions, and tried once again to put them from his mind. But it insisted there, every syllable of its heresy, so that he had to face the question that would naturally follow. If one wished one wasn't a Jew, as Leon had so patently implied, then it would follow that to be Jewish was not a state to which one aspired. And following that would be a conviction of Jew-hatred. Each stage followed upon another with a terrible logic. What, with or without the help of God, was to become of his brother? These thoughts were not such on which one could sleep easily, and he tossed and turned on his bed till the morning light filtered through the kitchen window. Then, as if that light had smoked out the unhallowed company of his bed, he fell asleep, and did not wake again, despite the kitchen preparations, until late morning, and for the first time in many months, his waking thought was light-years away from Rachel and their love, but surfaced bumpily on Leon's loss of faith.

In the next few days, they completed the arrangements for the engagement party. Zelda and Barak would return to Hamburg shortly afterwards, and Leon would remain in Wales. His intentions were forwarded to his mother via Aaron. She seemed in no way upset that Leon was remaining, and Aaron noticed that she was at pains to hide her relief. Occasionally during her bouts of hysteria, she would turn to Aaron and whisper, 'Why does he not talk to me?' But with such repetition the phrase had lost its meaning, doubtful that it had ever had one. For Zelda knew that Leon's communication would not give her peace, any more than her continued widowhood would have eased Leon's distress. Both of them were escape-routes that dictated the detours of their spirit, the ring-road round the cities of their pain, circuiting that core of madness and confusion that neither of them could face. For in Aaron's eyes it *was* madness, certainly Leon's, who was on the brink of apostasy.

*

Most days Leon accompanied Pavel on his rounds and twice a week they went to Senghenydd. Each time Leon returned with light and laughter in his eye which dimmed at the sight of his brother, or any mention of his family. Since that night when Leon had declared his lack of faith, the brothers had spoken little to each other. It seemed that Leon's statement had frozen conversation for ever. Aaron was relieved when his engagement day arrived, for it hastened his mother's departure. He loved her now no less than he had ever done, but he could not bear her desolation, each sign of which nurtured in his heart an irrational hatred of his brother. Leon for his part, would gladly have spent the day in Senghenydd

179

where he warmed to the unencumbered welcome that the families offered him, especially the women. But one above all would welcome him, and he her, though he did not know her name, yet in her eyes was a knowledge of his longing, and in her fiery looks an anger that matched his own. Pavel had to persuade Leon to forgo the valley on the day of the party. Leon gave in reluctantly and his face and mien were even more sullen than ever.

The synagogue hall was crowded with 'landsleit'. An engagement, espcially between immigrants, was a cause for everyone's celebration. It spelt settlement, stability, and above all, continuity. It took them back to synagogue halls all over the Pale. So they dwelt for a while in the land of their fathers, in Odessa, Kiev, in Balta and Vilna, and they loved once again and were loved in turn, and even if that love was now lost, or had, over the years, turned sour, it was still good to remember that there had been a time when it was alive and true. Mrs Ruboff and Zelda between them, had prepared the food and in Mrs Ruboff's kitchen each woman had dwelt in Odessa and Lodz. But though each cuisine was different, marginally influenced by the different nationalities of the ghettoes, they were basically the same: survival food, which was the essence of Jewish cooking. So, even when the pressures were lifted, when there was no longer any need to run for one's life, no fear of the fugitive's short notice, the prerequisites of the food remained the same. Durance and portability. Apart from the wines, the menu for Rachel and Aaron's engagment differed little from the fare that Esther and Miriam Bindel had packed for the milk-brothers for their vain flight from the services of the Czar.

The conversation was nostalgic and reminiscent. The guests came from all the cities of the Pale, with common stories, griefs and joys. Amongst them was a family from Kishinev, who would live to thank God that they had left in time. Mr and Mrs Nekrasov, with their daughter Galina. A celebration such as this one, which concerned itself with continuity, was a ready-made mis-en-scène for match-making. In those days there was little opportunity for social intercourse and, at an engagement party, it was almost incumbent on the hosts to ensure that the seeds of another such celebration would be sown. Mr Ruboff, who knew the Nekrasov family through business, for Mr Nekrasov was also a tailor, took upon himself the duty of affecting an introduction between Galina and Leon. He himself had little hope of a match between them. That Leon was an unknown factor. He was withdrawn, given to melancholy and seemed to find little pleasure in the company of others. He was young, too, barely eighteen, but though that was old enough for marriage and responsibility, it seemed that Leon was a lot older. That he had achieved the lack-lustre of an old man. That he was too old for marriage, children and loving, and perhaps even for life itself. Yet he would try to put the two young people together, and Mr Ruboff made his way to the corner where Leon stood alone. 'Come,' he said. 'Meet my friends from Kishinev.' He took Leon's arm and guided him across the hall, steering his way through the dancers who had already taken to the floor. The Nekrasovs stood in a group with others of their countrymen, recalling weddings in the old country, and when Leon was brought into their circle, each one of them knew the purpose of the introduction. Galina blushed and looked away, even when Leon, out of politeness, took her hand to make her acquaintance. All were at pains not to let the conversation flag and they continued with the discussion that Leon's introduction had interrupted. Then, when a new subject was called for, they turned to him and asked him about himself, his background and his prospects. There was nothing amiss about their questionings, neither was their timing too hasty. It was clear to all concerned what business was afoot, and the questions were light-hearted and in public, and to the background of music and song, all of which took the edge off their formality.

Leon wanted very much to get away. All those people were reminders of home, and such memories sickened him. The facts of the death of his father, of his loving Uncle Reuben, and his cherished Grandpa Jakob, had only recently overwhelmed him. Until his lone sojourn in the Hamburg gaol, he had considered himself merely as an orphan, with an elder brother to look after him. It was in the nature of things that fathers, uncles and grandfathers died, and he did not allow himself to think, in their case, how unnatural that nature was. He had cried for their loss, but had found some excitement too in being a survivor. It was only when he was stranded, alone in his cell, far from his protectors, that he realised for the first time, the earthquake proportions of his loss. Not only had most of his family died, but they had died burning, and every night before what little sleep they allowed him, the flames insisted before his eyes, stinging the tears on his face. And sometimes he could even smell their burning flesh. The privations he suffered as part of his imprisonment, did in no way touch him, for his nights and his dreams were agony enough. After a few weeks of his incarceration, the pain eased and gave way to an anger of titanic proportions. And at the height of that anger, he asked himself the question, or rather his wrath asked it of him, What was it all for? Why did they have to insist on being the Chosen, and therefore so much better than everybody else? Why couldn't they mix with proper Russians, live and marry amongst them, and learn their ways? Why, in whatever God's name, did they persist in being Jews? His whole family had died in that name. He himself languished in his cell on account of that name, too. When was it all going to stop? Some weeks later, to ease his pain, he began to hate them, all those ghetto martyrs, their trappings and trimmings, their distinctiveness, their beards, their ringlets and their suffering gaberdine. Over the remaining weeks of his sentence, he nurtured in his heart such a hatred of all those who had sired and loved him, so that by the time he was released, he had achieved a rehearsed indifference to the whole of his tribe, both dead and alive, and that indifference had served to ease his pain. All that had stood him in good, if unpleasant, stead until his arrival in England and his meeting with Aaron. When his brother had embraced him at the railway station, his touch had acted as an inconvenient, importunate trigger for the old love, and he'd had to resist it, for he knew that if he should yield, his surrender would force him back into his family and all the desperate cult of suffering of their tribe. And now, as he looked at the Nekrasovs, he sensed again that old pull of home and again he wished himself away. But out of politeness he gave answers to their questions, though there was little enough of himself that he was willing to give, and they ascribed his reticence to shyness and modesty.

'Have you started English lessons?' they asked.

Leon shook his head.

'Galina has a very good teacher,' Mrs Nekrasov said. 'She is looking for new pupils.'

Leon turned to looked at her daughter. She had that very special beauty that belonged to the Pale, that pallor of inherited suffering and resignation, that very beauty that symbolised all that he needed to discard. Her long black hair framed a face that was vowed to submission, a head bowed to God, man, and oppressor. There was a frightening promise of pogrom in her eye. She was nothing like that fiery one in Senghenydd, a rebel in every bone of her, who knew of suffering too, but who did not intend to make it her life's mission.

'I would like to meet your teacher,' he said out of politeness, and Galina whispered that she would talk to her.

Leon was grateful when Aaron and Rachel joined their circle and in time allowed him to withdraw. And as he turned to leave, he came face to face with his mother.

'Leon,' she said, without looking at him. 'Are you enjoying yourself?'

He nodded, staring at her averted face. He felt deeply sorry for her. He understood why she had married Barak, and on that account he had forgiven her. But he had used her re-marriage as an excuse to cover his withdrawal from family. Both he and his mother faced the same dilemma, the problem of acknowledging the past.

With a gesture that he felt he could afford, he touched her arm. 'Are you enjoying it?' he said.

Zelda turned to look at him and she felt her arm shiver under his touch. For her part she did not hear the words he had said to her. She heard only the sound of his voice so patently aimed at her ear. She was overwhelmed by it and did not know how to deal with the relief of it. She scarcely believed the sound she had heard, and wished she had a witness at her side. She nodded in her turn. 'I grieve that your father isn't alive to see it,' she said and dared to touch him, then wished she hadn't, for his revulsion was unmistakable.

It surprised even Leon himself, but her reminder of his father symbolised all that gloom that would darken her future. He didn't want that darkness. He wanted the light to see where he was going, even if that light should lead him into hell. Such light would find no admission in his mother's as yet untrodden ways. He was glad she was soon going back to Germany.

'Papa is dead,' he said. 'We have mourned him. We have left his bones behind. The past is over.' Then he touched her again, hearing the cruelty of his words. 'You must begin to live again,' he said.

'And you, my son?'

He shuffled off the chains of her appelation. 'I shall find a way,' he said. He was glad when Barak approached them and, once again, escape was possible.

Barak had watched their encounter from the side of the hall, and had deliberately given it a little time before offering his services if they were required. For he knew that eventually Zelda would need his support.

'Are you all right, my dear?' he said, taking her arm.

She smiled at him, and as she turned her face to look at him, Leon slipped away. She watched him go. 'He spoke to me,' she said, as if in a dream.

'It's a beginning,' he said. He did not ask the matter of Leon's words. Like Zelda, he valued the simple fact that sounds had been exchanged.

Zelda and Barak were leaving on the following day, and the newly-engaged couple would follow them as far as Tilbury to see them safely onto the boat. Leon was persuaded to accompany them all to the Cardiff station. Farewells were difficult. In Leon's mind his farewell to his mother was a leavetaking of all that history to which he was bound, that link with the past that he wanted so much to break. They leaned out of the window as the train drew out of the station, and the steam from the engine slowly misted their features and made them indistinguishable from all the other faces that peered through the mist at those they had left behind. Leon raised his hand and waved to them, smiling, in the safe knowledge that he could have been waving and smiling at strangers. As the train moved out of sight, those on the platform turned and went away, leaving Leon alone, watching the trail of smoke in the distance. The smile, that he had offered to departing strangers, still lingered on his face, but now it was on account of his sudden feeling of freedom. He was, for a short time at least, completely without family, and he straightened his shoulders and breathed deep, as if a great burden had been lifted from his heart.

Chapter thirteen

It was in the spring of 1887 that Aaron finally took Rachel for his bride, roughly at the same age as his father had taken his mother. The long years of their patient courtship had in no way dimmed their love for each other. Barak was not well enough to travel to the wedding, so the honeymoon was spent in Leipzig. Barak's fur business prospered with many employees, though Barak himself, in his failing health, took little part in it. Zelda cared for him with a loving tenderness. When she asked after Leon, hungry for his news, her question was private, for Aaron's ear alone, for she feared the tears that would greet his answers. Aaron was filled with a deep hatred for his brother for the hurt he caused with his neglect, and he resolved to confront him on his return. But Leon grew more and more distant. When Aaron moved into the Ruboff house after the honeymoon, he invited Leon to lodge with them, and Rachel too did her best to persuade him. But Leon declined their offer and kept to his own strange quarters, and the 'landsleit' community looked with some bewilderment on this arrangement and wondered yet again, what would become of that younger Bindel who shunned their society and was not like a 'landsleit' at all. Their doubts were confirmed when Leon finally moved his person into the valley. With his savings, and his share of the tavern inheritance, he bought a small miner's cottage in Senghenydd, far from Jew or synagogue, with only Pavel to keep a weekly eye on him and hold his tongue when Aaron asked for news of his brother's welfare. For such news was untellable.

Leon had fallen in love with one Margaret Davies, not the red-headed one of Leon's first exile dreams, but one very much of her kind. A coal-miner's daughter, a million miles from Odessa, close to Eisteddfod and chapel, and to whom the word pogrom was meaningless and would remain so all her life. Leon kept Margaret a closely guarded secret, except from Pavel in whom he confided. But though Pavel was sympathetic he was deeply appalled by Leon's treachery. Leon too was aware of the monumental sin he was committing but he rationalised it as part of his personal method of survival. Even so, he feared Aaron's reaction, and at Pavel's suggestion he resolved to see more of his brother and repair those bonds of fraternity that were so frayed. So thenceforth, every Tuesday when he travelled to Cardiff to collect his goods for sale, he called at his brother's house. On one such visit, he was given news of Rachel's pregnancy. He rejoiced with them both, but he was fighting envy in his heart. After each visit to his brother's house, he was gnawed by feelings of jealousy. For he too wanted a home and a family, and he wanted to make that home with Margaret. Now that his brother would become a father, the need to make a decision regarding his own future was paramount, and he resolved that whatever consequences might ensue, and he knew that they would be catastrophic, he would propose to Margaret at their very next meeting, and hope that she would accept him. He knew it as his only way to happiness. Suddenly he thought of his mother, and with that thought, he understood for the first time, the magnitude of his transgression. Such an act that he had in mind would be for ever beyond her forgiveness, and perhaps would finally sever the bond between them, that bond that he had for so long teased and imperilled. He would keep his marriage a secret from her, for if the truth were told, she would mourn him as though dead, and she herself would possibly die of imagined sorrow. He loved her enough to keep that secret, and Aaron, out of the same love and within that same mourning, would do the same.

It was not long before news travelled to Cardiff, along the credit-drapery grapevine, of Leon's impending engagement, and everyone was at pains to keep the report from the ears of Aaron Bindel. But Pavel was uneasy with his secret. He sincerely thought that if Aaron were told, he might be able to change his brother's mind. Moreover he had a right to know, a right to intervene, a right to try, and a right, too, to fail. One evening, his heart trembling, he made his way to Aaron's house.

They were at supper, Mr Ruboff, Rachel and Aaron. Rachel was already big with child, though her movements were graceful and her face radiant with happiness, a joy that spread across the table. Pavel sat with them wondering how on earth he could begin. He decided to wait until the meal was over, and then, in privacy with Aaron, he would gently shatter his joy.

'Shall we take a walk?' he suggested to Aaron when the meal was finished.

Aaron was glad of it. At this time of the year, the river was at full tide and it was pleasant to walk along the embankment in the direction of its flow, to contemplate its journey towards the sea, and to tune one's spirit to its tempo. They set off briskly along the bank. It was Aaron who dictated the pace, and Pavel was at pains to slow him down, for the news that he had to tell was not appropriate to speed. It fitted, if it fitted at all, with an ambler's pace, that could suddenly in total shock, root itself to the ground.

'Slow down, friend,' Pavel said. 'We have time.' Yet Pavel was aware of what little time there was. Only that morning he had heard that Margaret Davies was preparing for a spring wedding. They reached the bridge and crossed over to the fields that skirted Cathedral Road. It was a favourite evening walk for many 'landsleit' strollers, who would cross the fields, circle the synagogue yard and return home. But that evening there were few people about and Pavel was glad of it. Near the road's verge there was a wooden bench and Pavel reached it and sat down. He motioned Aaron to sit by his side.

'I have something to tell you,' he said.

Aaron noted the seriousness of his friend's face. 'Not bad news, I hope?' he said, fearing first for the welfare of his mother though there was no reason why Pavel should be privy to such news. So it must be about Leon who saw more of Pavel than he himself.

'Is something the matter with Leon?' Aaron asked fearfully. 'Is he ill?'

Pavel decided to tell Aaron without preamble for he knew of no overture that could make such news more palatable. 'He intends to marry,' Pavel said, then before Aaron could question it, Pavel gave him the object of his brother's intent. 'Her name is Margaret Davies,' he said, as steadily as he could. 'A coal-miner's daughter.' He watched the colour drain from Aaron's face, and he gripped his arm fearing that he might faint away. After a while Aaron managed to speak.

'Our mother must never never know,' he said. Then he rose, leaning on Pavel's arm. 'I'm grateful that you told me,' he said. 'Tomorrow I shall go to the valley.'

That night Aaron feigned a restlessness and a wish to sleep alone. But he did not sleep. All night he prayed for his brother's soul, and in the morning, telling Rachel that he was visiting a client, he went to the station and took a train to the valley. He had never been to Leon's house, but from his brother's description of it,

186

he knew its location. He trudged up the hill concentrating on the impending birth of his first child to offset the heavy sorrow in his heart. A woman was coming towards him stumbling under a large basket of washing. He offered to help her, but she declined with a look of both amazement and gratitude. He asked her directions to his brother's house.

'Over by there,' she said, pointing behind her with her head. 'That one with the pink door. It's open.'

He thanked her and went on his way. When he reached his brother's door, he knocked, but there was no reply from within. He went inside, calling Leon's name, then sat on a chair in the sitting-room and waited. He was not interested in looking at his brother's house, or indeed at the furniture or objects in the room in which he sat. He was in a foreign land, alien, isolated, a land in which no Jew had ever lived, had ever prayed, had ever chosen to lay his bones. Yet this was Leon's land, and he prayed to God to give him the strength not to hate him. After a while he heard footsteps on the cobbles outside. He had left the door open as it was found and from where he sat he could see his brother's shadow as it fell across the threshold. He opened his mouth to signal his attendance at his brother's house, but no words came, and shortly Leon appeared in the doorway of the sitting-room and paled at his brother's presence.

'Aaron,' he said, and he did not move from the doorway.

Aaron stood. 'I wanted to see you,' he said, and he was relieved at the steadiness of his voice.

'Would you like some tea?' Leon said.

Aaron shook his head, then regretted that he had declined the offer. A cup of tea between them might have softened the anger and hatred in his heart.

And Leon too, who had guessed at the purpose of Aaron's visit, wished for a similar diversion to ease their encounter. He moved into the room and took a chair opposite his brother. 'How is Rachel?' he said.

'You can't do it, Leon,' Aaron whispered. 'You just cannot do it.' His voice was no longer steady.

There was silence between them until Leon said, 'I love her, Aaron.'

'You delude yourself, brother,' Aaron said. 'How can you love someone who is none of our kind? Come away from this temptation, I beg you. You can live with us,' his voice was raised now, and it gathered speed. 'We have room. I have enough money. I can teach you the tailoring trade.' He stopped. He knew that what he was saying was futile, for his brother was looking at him with pity. 'You're a murderer,' Aaron screamed at him.

'Whom have I killed?' Leon said softly.

'You break all our hearts,' Aaron said.

'Won't you at least meet her?' Leon pleaded.

'Never. She is not of our kind. Never,' he shouted. 'Is this how you revere the memory of our father, our grandfather, and of all of those who died for being Jews?'

'It is time that all that had a stop,' Leon said as gently as he could. 'I am marrying out in order to survive. Our own father baptised himself for survival.'

'But this isn't Russia,' Aaron sobbed. 'Do you read what's happening in our country? The hundreds who are murdered day after day? Is this how you pay them for their faith?'

Leon put his hands on Aaron's shoulders feeling for the first time like an elder brother. 'It's a payment that over the years will ensure that such madness will never happen again. My children will not be the Chosen, either by God or the Czar.'

Aaron shrugged his shoulders away. 'Don't touch me,' he said. Then he looked him squarely in the eyes. 'You are dead for me, brother,' he said, and he turned and walked from the room. Then he left the house through the still open door.

On his mourning way down the cobbled street, he met the washerwoman. She smiled at him. 'Did you find him all right, your brother?' she asked. He had no smile for her, nor words, and she knew that he had quarrelled with that foreigner, Mr Bindel, and she also had a shrewd idea of what that quarrel was about. Leon came to the door of his cottage and watched his brother as he walked slowly down the valley. His back was hunched and he looked like a very old man. Leon turned and went inside, and though there was no one about to watch him, he shut the door and buried his face in his hands.

All the way down the valley, to the station, on his train, and along the embankment, Aaron muttered the *Kadish* prayers, and when he reached home, he said them aloud, over and over again, as he took sheets from the linen cupboards and covered the pictures and the mirrors on the wall.

Rachel watched his wild grief. 'Who has died?' she said.

'He that was my brother.'

'Leon?' she screamed.

He turned towards her, then took her in his arms. 'Never mention his name again in this house.' He told her all that he knew, then he sat slippered on the floor, and his father-in-law sat with him and shared his shame and his sorrow. And thus Aaron sat for seven days as was the custom amongst mourning Jews. And on the eighth day he went back to his workship and his machines and he knew that his pain would never cease. Time would not heal such a wound, for though for a whole week of days he had mourned his

188

brother's death, he had, every one of those days, prayed for his life too.

Leon, who had known what his brother would do, waited for the period of mourning to be over. Then he took Margaret to the small registry office in Caerphilly and there he married her, and for the first time in many hundreds of years of their wanderings, from the Ukraine to Bessarabia, a Bindel married out of his kind. That same day, Rachel gave birth to a daughter. They called her Chaya which, translated, means life. Her second name was Esther, in memory of Rachel's mother, which also served to revere the memory of Aaron's paternal grandmother, Esther Bindel. As Aaron and Rachel rejoiced in their parenthood, Aaron mourned the loss of that sole person with whom he wished to share his joy. And in the valley to which Pavel the messenger had brought the news, Leon asked for and was refused a sight of his brother's child.

*

Aaron wrote to Zelda about the birth of her first grandchild. She replied post-haste, urging them to bring the child. Barak was not well enough to travel, she wrote, and she was loathe to leave him. To which suggestion Rachel and Aaron would have happily responded, but Mr Ruboff was now too ill to be left. And they dreaded that Zelda should come, for once in the midst of family and community, the secret of Leon's sin would out, and Aaron dared not think of the consequences of that revelation. So he wrote to his mother of his father-in-law's indisposition, and urged her to wait until he had sufficiently recovered for them to leave him for a while. He sent his best wishes for Barak's health.

But Zelda was impatient to see her grandchild, and made arrangments for Barak's care in her absence. She wrote in haste that she was preparing a visit in two weeks' time. *Give Leon my love too*, she added. *I long to see him.*

On receipt of this letter, Aaron was greatly agitated, and he went straight to Pavel's little house. He thanked God for Pavel, who, without any encouragement from Aaron, had appointed himself as a liaison between the brothers. He knew of the love between them that a million words of *Kadish* could not destroy. Hinda and Max took a different view. They were sorry for Aaron, but Leon was dead for them. They had children of their own, and they did not want his contamination in their house. And, though Aaron understood them, he turned away from them in his heart.

Pavel was not one to give advice. He merely offered suggestions which he now proceeded to do. On his next journey to Senghenydd, which was to be on the following day, he would tell Leon and allow him to make the decision whether or not to greet his mother. If he should decide to come to Cardiff for that purpose, then Aaron would have to compose himself to treat him as if nothing untoward had happened. That would not be easy for him, Pavel warned, but on no account must his mother be privy to the catastrophe. During her visit they would make sure that she called on only himself, Max and Hinda who, even without his heeding, would hold their tongues. He promised that he would visit Aaron the following evening to inform him of Leon's decision. As Aaron was leaving, Pavel said, 'How is the child?'

'Beautiful,' Aaron said. 'She sleeps all night without a feed, and she smiles all day.' He was itemizing all the titbits of news that he knew Pavel would convey to his brother. He himself did not ask for news of Leon. Pavel understood the rules.

'He is very well,' he said. 'He seems to be happy.' Pavel had difficulty in pronouncing Leon's name.

Aaron returned home with a small relief that he had shared his problem with another.

The following evening, as he had promised, Pavel called at Aaron's house, and Aaron took him to the workshop at the top of the house where they would not be disturbed.

'He's not very helpful I'm afraid,' Pavel came to the point right away. 'He's quite prepared to meet your mother, he says. Indeed he would look forward to it, but he insists on bringing his wife with him. Any acceptance of him, he insists, must include his wife.' Pavel threw up his hands. 'It is impossible,' he said.

'What shall I do?' Aaron said helplessly.

'We must tell her he doesn't want to see her. It will hurt her terribly, but it will be less hurtful than the truth. D'you know,' Pavel said after a while, 'I'm beginning to feel very sorry for him. The other day in the clothing market, Goldstein turned him away from his store. So did Lepcovitch. No Jewish merchant will serve him. He is a pariah. He had to buy dear at the big emporium.'

Aaron was sorry for him too, but his compassion was blunted by his anger, for the hurt that he had caused them all. For a moment he prayed that his brother's wife would suddenly die, and it would be as if nothing had happened at all.

'His wife didn't agree with him,' Pavel said suddenly. 'She tried to persuade him to go. She said it was a son's duty to his mother. But he is stubborn, your brother.'

'Will you come with me to the station to meet her?' Aaron asked.

'Gladly,' Pavel said, and as he went, he deposited a small packet on the work-table. He did not refer to it, neither did Aaron for he knew it as one of Pavel's messages. When he had gone, Aaron opened the package. A tiny pair of baby's shoes wrapped in tissue-paper. Aaron examined the wrapping. Each fold was neatly turned

190

and symmetrical. He pictured Leon measuring each fold with his thumb, donating to the wrapping as much love and care as he had given to his choice of gift. It was a wrapping to be respected and Leon knew that his brother would acknowledge it and he would unfold it as slowly as he himself had assembled it. Aaron took the shoes and re-wrapped them. Then he hid them at the bottom of his button-drawer. Leon had spoke to him, but it was a voice from the dead.

*

A week later, he and Pavel went uneasily to the railway station. They dawdled on the way with little appetite for the encounter. As a result, when they reached the station, the train had already arrived, and Zelda was waiting bewildered on the platform. It was not a good beginning. Aaron ran towards her and he hugged her with genuine warmth. He was surprised at how happy he was to see her. She looked well, and younger than he had remembered her.

'No one would believe you were a grandmother,' he laughed.

Then Pavel came forward and shook her hand, but she did not look at him. She was staring at the empty space around him. 'Where's Leon?' she said, then looking at their faces, regretting that she had asked. 'He's all right, isn't he?' she panicked.

'Oh yes.' Aaron was quick to reassure her. The only good news about Leon was that he was alive, at least in his body's sense, and Aaron was at pains to stress his brother's well-being.

'Where is he?' She knew she shouldn't have asked. She knew that it didn't matter where he was. He simply wasn't at the station because he had no wish to see her.

'He's in the valley,' Pavel said.

'Will I see him?' she whispered. Again it was a question better left unasked. It seemed she wished to torture herself with his neglect.

'I thought you came to see your granddaughter,' Aaron laughed, and he picked up her portmanteau and took her arm. They hired a wagon to take them home, and during the journey Aaron and Pavel pumped her for news, their questions always at the ready. Barak was comfortable, Zelda said. He went to the store only once a week, but he had a good manager there. The doctor had told him that he must take life a little easier. Leipzig was a beautiful city, and she enjoyed the peace of it after the noise of Hamburg with its unhappy memories. 'That prison,' she said, suddenly dropping the statement into a description of the Leipzig Museum. 'It was all my fault.'

'Of course it wasn't your fault,' Aaron said, and ached to give her proof that on that score Leon had never blamed her. He suddenly thought of Margaret, thinking of her by name, by that same name

191

that his brother no doubt called her with his love. The thought disturbed him. He could not afford to identify her by name. She was that woman, that anonymous one, who had set a cross before his brother and taught him how to kneel. She was unmentionable, and always would be, for she never was, else Leon would be dead for ever.

Rachel was at the door to meet them, with Chaya in her arms. Mr Ruboff had risen from his bed for the occasion. He knew the problems that attended her visit, and he intended to offer his company for Zelda's diversion, and his talk to fill the gaps of questions that she dared not ask. Rachel had brightened the home for her visit and the table was set for the Sabbath that evening with the unlit candelabra in its centre. Zelda was delighted with the welcome and at once took Chaya in her arms. She stared at the child. 'She's a Bindel,' she announced. 'She looks like Sofia. D'you remember your aunt Sofia, Aaron? She was a rebel.' She smiled. 'She died in the fire,' she added, 'with the rest of them.'

Wherever his mother went, Aaron thought, she took that fire with her, charring her heart along the way, as Barak took that holy piece of Russian ground where his son lay buried, as he himself portered his father's loss. All of them cleaved to their holy luggage. All but one. And with the thought of Leon, he shuddered.

It was Chaya's feeding time, and Rachel took the baby upstairs.

'I'll come with you,' Zelda said, rising.

Rachel looked at Aaron helplessly, but there was nothing he could do. There was no reason on earth why his mother shouldn't spend time with her daughter-in-law and grandchild. The men watched her follow Rachel out of the door.

'Rachel won't say anything,' Aaron said when they were gone.

The three men sat there in silence, no doubt expecting at any moment the clap of thunder. But all they heard was laughter, Zelda's laughter as she played with Chaya, changed her, mocking herself with her clumsy handling.

'Aaron was such a good baby,' she recalled.

'Tell me about him,' Rachel said. 'About when he was a child.' She grasped at a topic of conversation, anxious to avoid a silence that shrieked for the mention of Leon's name.

But Zelda needed no interval of silence. 'Have you seen Leon?' she said. She was casual with the question, concentrating on the pinning of the baby's napkin as if the whereabouts and welfare of her younger son were of little matter to her.

'We see him sometimes,' Rachel said, rummaging in the drawers to hide the lie that might show on her face.

'Is he well?'

'Yes,' Rachel said weakly.

Zelda caught the hesitation in her voice. 'What's the matter with him?' Zelda whispered. 'You must tell me.'

'Nothing,' Rachel fairly shouted. 'Nothing at all.' And she was seized with a need to tell her mother-in-law everything. It was not fair that Aaron had to bear the brunt of the terrible secret. It needed to be shared. Besides it was Zelda's right to know. It was a grief to which she was as entitled as her widowhood. It was extra luggage, which accumulated load would finally kill her. But it had to be told for the relief of them all. But she dared not speak. There was only one who could rightfully tell her, and that was Leon himself.

With Rachel's insistent denial that there was anything amiss with her son, Zelda became more and more suspicious. She began to convince herself that he was ill. The true cause of his absence would never in a lifetime occur to her. Such thoughts were too monstrous even for nightmare. 'I wish I could see him,' she said. To which there was no reply that Rachel or anyone else could give.

'I'll take the baby downstairs,' Rachel said, anxious for company. She dreaded the week that Zelda would stay with them, and she feared that Aaron's anger was in danger of loosening his tongue.

Pavel left before supper. He was very troubled. Tomorrow was the Sabbath and there were no trains to the valley on a Sunday. It would be two days before he could reach Leon and beg him to come alone to his mother's side. He had little hope of his mission but he would try.

At supper that evening, when Rachel had lit the candles and Aaron had said the blessing, Zelda expressed her wish to go to the synagogue on the following morning. It was the anniversary of the fire, she said, and she wished to join in the prayers of remembrance. Mr Ruboff was quick to make an alternative suggestion. He knew that a visit to the synagogue was out of the question. There, without doubt, in the gossip of the women's gallery, far from the protection of the men below, the secret would be out, and her shame pitied. She would have more than the fire to mourn. Her heart was a wailing-wall, into the crevices of which the worshipper sent messages to God. In that crumbling structure, she would yet another cranny to accept her grief, a grief without anniversary, without calendar, a grief for all eternity.

'On Sabbath I take my one walk of the week,' Mr Ruboff said. 'Rachel usually comes with me and I am allowed to wheel the pram. I thought that this week you would accompany me. I've looked forward to it.'

It was an unrefusable invitation, and Zelda readily accepted it. She had suggested the visit to the synagogue precisely for the reason they had all feared. She wanted news of her son. She had even dared to hope that he would be there for prayer, and they could have a chance meeting. But that she feared, so she was grateful for Mr Ruboff's invitation.

'I would like that,' she said. 'We could go to Sofia Gardens. I remember them from my last visit. They are so pretty.' What she most remembered about the gardens was their proximity to the synagogue. Perhaps Leon would stroll there on his way to prayer. But Mr Ruboff had no fear of such an encounter. It was unlikely that Leon would enter a synagogue ever again. And if they should meet any congregants, he would know how to deal with their tongues.

They went to bed soon after supper, for Zelda was much fatigued after her journey. But Aaron lay awake all night and heard his mother moaning and tossing on her restless bed. Yet she looked bright on the following morning and was ready for Mr Ruboff's company.

Aaron left early for the synagogue. He was not a regular worshipper, but this Sabbath he knew was the anniversary of his father's death without any reminder from Zelda. When she heard that he had gone, and for that very purpose, she was glad of it for Aaron would pray for all of them. Without her knowledge Aaron would pray for his brother, not with the regular Sabbath prayers, but with the *Kadish* he would use for his father, words to which Leon, in his brother's heart, was now sadly entitled.

When Mr Ruboff was ready, Rachel prepared the pram, and she set them off on their way, glad not to be with them, but fearful of the waiting, and the perils of their journey. But as it turned out, their way had been smooth, as Mr Ruboff had reported at the lunch table. Chaya had slept all the way and they had been able to converse without interruption. Mr Ruboff declared that he now knew Leipzig as if he himself had lived there, Zelda's description of that city was so graphic. He had also learned much about the fur trade. For her part, Zelda had returned from their promenade with a tourist's acquaintance with the city of Lodz. Both had reminisced on the subject of their respective departed partners and had seemingly found pleasure in so doing. The sore matter of Leon's absence had not ruffled their companionship and Aaron had hopes that his mother had accepted Leon's neglect and that his name would not be mentioned again. That afternoon Pavel came to visit, accompanied by Max and Hinda who had been well primed to silence. The afternoon passed pleasantly in conversation. Aaron ticked off in his mind the one day out of seven that had passed without incident. But that day was not yet over.

When the visitors had gone, Zelda insisted on helping Rachel prepare the supper. The kitchen had never been the domain of Bindel men and Zelda would have been horrified to see her son reduced to domestic tasks. So once again Rachel found herself alone with her mother-in-law, and quickly she put her to preparing the soup in the hope that if she busied her hands her tongue would lie still.

'Now I feel really at home,' Zelda said as she pared the vegetables, and seemed happy enough without conversation. Rachel busied herself with the meats and slowly her anxiety ebbed. Until someone pulled the door-bell. Rachel froze and she didn't know why. People often came to their door, usually customers for fittings or collection. And especially once the Sabbath was over, there could be one or two business calls. But for some reason she feared that ring and she moved over to the kitchen-door and quietly closed it.

'Who could that be?' Zelda asked, and there was no mistaking the hope in her voice.

'Probably a customer,' Rachel said. She moved herself nearer the door, straining her ear for some clue. Then she heard Aaron's footsteps in the hall and the unlatching of the front door.

Aaron had gone to open it without any wonder as to who it might be. There were two suits ready in the workshop and he expected either customer to collect. He was glad of it and he went smiling to the door. But the smile faded as he recognised the caller. Leon stood there. On his face was a look of anger, of expected rebuff and one that was pre-empting it with aggression.

'I've come to see our mother,' Leon said. His voice matched his face with its gruffness, and Aaron thought his brother might be close to tears. Aaron had sworn that he would never see him again, yet in his heart he welcomed him. He was sorry that Chaya was sleeping. The thought crossed his mind that he should question Leon as to whether he was intent on telling their mother that which was untellable. But suddenly he didn't mind any more. The burden of that secret was heavy, and it was with some relief that he invited his brother into his house.

He ushered him into the dining-room, because Mr Ruboff was in the sitting-room and he felt that Leon would prefer privacy. The table was already set for supper, one setting on each side of the rectangle. Another place-setting would disturb the symmetry, but Aaron would welcome such a disturbance. Suddenly he saw it as Leon's permanent placing, for he allowed himself to imagine that his brother had left the unnameable one and had at last come home.

'Where is she?' Leon said without looking at him.

'In the kitchen with Rachel.'

'Would you tell her I'm here?' he said tonelessly. 'I'd like to talk to her alone.'

Then Aaron knew that his brother had not come home at all. He had come simply to confirm his leaving of it. He had come to appraise his mother of what he had left it for. Aaron looked at him in horror.

'Why are you waiting?' Leon said coldly. He had not forgotten the last words his brother had spoken to him in the valley. 'I am dead for you, don't you remember?'

Aaron left the room and closed the door behind him. Then in the hall he gripped the bannister to steady his tremblings. He knew that he no longer had any control over the situation. He opened the kitchen door. Rachel saw the pallor on his face and knew at once the caller's identity. She gripped his arm.

'Mama,' he said his voice breaking. 'Leon has come to see you. He's in the dining-room.' He could not bear the look of joy on her face as she rushed past him into the hall. He watched her open the dining-room door and his heart filled with pity. He took Rachel in his arms and wept like a child.

Zelda did not immediately embrace her son. She stood at the door and looked at him, savouring that face that haunted her dreams, that uneasy face, that disturbed spirit. As she looked she noticed the agitation about his mouth, his clenched fists and she wondered why he was not smiling. She went towards him, kissing him tenderly.

'I knew you would come today,' she said. 'You would not forget the anniversary of Papa's death.'

'It's almost twenty years since Papa died,' Leon said and there was no mistaking the anger in his voice.

'You went to the synagogue?' she asked, knowing even as she said it that the question would not be welcome.

'Mama,' he said. 'I have to tell you something.'

'What's the matter, my son? Are you not well?' Now she knew that something was very wrong. That his health was failing. That he had contracted some incurable disease. That her son's days were numbered. 'O God,' she prayed in her heart. 'Anything, anything but that. Anything on earth,' she prayed.

Then Leon gave her the alternative she seemingly sought. 'I am married, Mama,' he said.

Now she was in total confusion. Her son was not ill. He was not dying. She would not survive him. Had she not asked God for that? Then she must thank God for His deliverance. Yet what gift had He given her in its stead? Her son's health. Should she not thank God for that? And something else. Marriage. Was that not a gift too? Not this way, her heart faltered, married without ceremony, without warning, and now with apology. Did Aaron know? Did Rachel? Then when she had exhausted all irrelevant questioning, she could postpone her pain no longer. So she asked that final one, the answer to which she knew would tear her heart in two. She sat down, trembling. 'Who have you married?' she said.

'Her name is Margaret Davies. Her father is a coal-miner.' It was the clearest and the kindest way he could tell her that his wife was not one of their kind.

Rachel and Aaron heard the screaming. In Rachel's ear it was an echo of the cry she herself had made when Chaya was born. The birth pang. Yet to what had Zelda given birth but to the death of the Bindel tribe? But, unlike Rachel's cry, it did not cease for there was no end to her sort of pain. No cure, no compensation. Rachel rushed into the dining-room and held her. Aaron stood at the door, staring at his brother with a look of such wild hatred that Leon thought his mind unhinged. 'She had to know,' he said quietly. Then he made to leave. As he reached the door, Zelda found some semblance of a voice. In her heart she was screaming, though the sound was a whisper. But her words were swords. 'In time she will look at you and call you a bloody Jew,' she said.

Leon shrugged and left the room, while Aaron and Rachel helped Zelda to her feet and took her to her bed. Rachel sat with her for a while holding her hand. There was nothing she could say to her. But as she sat there listening to Zelda's grieving, she could not help questioning whether what Leon had done merited such sorrow. It was a blasphemous thought, she knew, and must never be spoken aloud. Aaron would disown her.

Zelda squeezed her hand. 'My son is dead for me,' she said. 'Tomorrow I shall begin to mourn him.'

But he is alive, Rachel thought, and his health is good. He is even happy. Was it possible that Zelda preferred God to her children? She sat with her until she slept, then she crept from the room jarred by thoughts that were out of her time, her gender, and most of all, her faith.

*

When Leon reached home, Margaret was anxiously awaiting him. When she saw his drawn face in the doorway, she knew that the meeting with his mother had failed. She was glad then that she had kept her news until that time, had not blurted it out that morning when she knew, had saved it for just this eventuality so that it would cheer him and take the edge off his disappointment.

'I am dead for her,' he said from the door.

She kissed him, took his coat and set him at the table where his supper was waiting. She took the pot from the stove and poured tea for them both and she waited for him to speak. But he said nothing about the meeting. He was staring at the tea-pot. Then after a while he said, 'When next I go to Cardiff, I shall buy a samovar.'

He had told her all she needed to know. She now feared for the baby inside her, but she held her tongue. The time that she had thought to be ripe, seemed now not so ripe after all. They finished the meal in silence. As she cleared the table, Leon buried his head in his hands. She sat beside him and held him close. Now was the time perhaps. The news would calm him, delight him even. It would give the lie to whatever his mother had prophecied, and she had a shrewd idea of her auguries. It would confirm their future together.

'Leon,' she said. 'We're going to have a child.'

He raised his head and looked at her, and though she searched the map of his face, she could find no contour of a smile.

'Are you sure?' he said.

'The doctor confirmed it yesterday.'

'If it's a boy, we'll call it Benjamin.'

'Benjamin?' she said. 'That's a . . .'

'That's a what?' he shouted.

'Well it's so . . .' She hovered. 'It's not Welsh,' and she prayed that he would settle for that.

Then at last he smiled. But it was not a smile of joy. It was a bitter recollection of his mother's parting words, and that smile told Margaret in fearful terms that she had begun to lose him.

*

The week of Zelda's visit passed very slowly. Most of the time she kept to her bed, reading the morning prayers. In the evening visitors came. It was a relief that the secret was out, so that friends could come and officially share her sorrow. Throughout this time Mr Ruboff was a source of great comfort. He refused to share Zelda's anger, and without words he did not condone her grief, and when Rachel looked at him, full of her own profane thoughts, she wondered whether they shared the same impious doubts, and she realised how little she knew of her own father. One night, shortly before Zelda's departure, when she and her father were alone, she dared to ask him.

'Is it so terrible, Papa, what Leon has done?'

'Yes,' he said. There was no hesitation in his voice. 'What is not terrible is that you have questioned it. For times will change and so will men's hearts, and then it will not be so terrible. But yes, yes,' he said. 'Now it is terrible.'

'As bad as dying?' Rachel insisted.

'It's a death of a kind,' Mr Ruboff said. 'It's the death of a life that we know and have suffered to preserve. When Zelda mourns Leon, it is her own small death that she mourns, for the death of one of the tribe infects them all with mortality.' He spoke to her in Yiddish as he always did and for a moment Rachel was glad that he had never wanted to learn the language of his exile, because the matter of his words belonged inalienably to his mother-tongue.

*

Aaron had counted the days to his mother's departure and when it arrived he didn't want her to go. More for her sake than his own, for she would be leaving for a land without family to comfort her. Barak would be sympathetic of course, but it was not his blood that had been so cruelly diluted. He could only hold her while she wept. It was out of this pity that Aaron offered to take her as far as Tilbury Docks, and it was clear that she was very grateful, for she felt more alone and burdened than ever. The night before she left, Rachel made a farewell supper, and invited Pavel, Max and Hinda. There was little to celebrate, but it was an occasion to confirm their friendship and their support.

During the course of the meal, Zelda turned to Pavel.

'I don't want any news of him,' she said. She knew that Pavel was the self-appointed messenger between her sons, and with her negative declaration, she hoped to include herself in his service.

He smiled at her. 'I understand,' he said.

That night before she went to bed, she took Aaron on one side. 'How did he come to Cardiff from the valley?' she asked. She had already buried Leon's name.

'He came by train,' Aaron said.

'He rides on the Sabbath?' she said. There was a hint of relief in her voice as if she had discovered for herself a small sin on her son's behalf, a sin that God in time would find forgivable, and for a while that sin seemed to erase the monstrous transgression that was beyond pardon.

In the morning, Aaron and his mother took the train to London. They took a tram-ride to Whitechapel and there Aaron found a restaurant that he had noticed when he had first arrived in London. The restaurant was in a busy thoroughfare, and the area of pavement outside served as a kind of unofficial employment agency. People scurried about. Tailors looking for pressers, boot-makers for seamers, bakers for kneaders, and the crowds of workless looking for anybody who could offer them a living. And girls too. Lining the thoroughfare in their faded finery. As Aaron guided his mother towards the restaurant, he was obliged to pass the line. He tried not to look at them, but one face caught his eye. He knew her. He had seen her before, and in similar attire. When she averted her gaze, reddening beneath her rouge, he remembered who she was. The last time he had seen her was well over ten years ago when she was boarding a carriage to join others of those who would be her kind. Ida. He wanted to smile at her, but he sensed that she would have preferred his lack of recognition. But he smiled nonetheless. She was, after all, a survivor, surviving in her own orphaned, untutored way. Was she not the same as his own brother who had chosen his way too? If he could look at Ida without censure, he could surely forgive his brother.

'Come,' his mother said. 'Why are you dawdling?'

'I thought I saw Leon,' he said, testing his name on her.

'Did you?' she asked anxiously. 'Where? Where?'

'It wasn't Leon,' Aaron said. 'It was just someone like him.'

He smiled for then he knew that her son was no more dead for her than his brother was for him. And once alive, he was available to pardon.

CHAPTER FOURTEEN

The years passed and quietly the century turned. It was Easter Sunday in the spring of 1903, and the bells tolled all over the world in cathedral, church and chapel. In the town of Kishinev in the province of Bessarabia, they were tolling too, and were a signal to the onset of the most bloody pogrom of all. In his cottage in Senghenydd on that day, Leon Bindel was as yet unaware of the events which decimated the tribe he had foresworn. Later he was to hear of them and their awesome facts would exacerbate the guilt that had soured his heart and had been so doing for many years. That day he was aware of another event, for it was the barmitzvah birthday of his son. They had called him David as something of a compromise. Margaret had drawn the line at Benjamin, insisting that it was no name for a son of Wales, so they had settled on David, which conveniently doubled for the country's patron saint and the King of Israel. They had had no more children, which Leon considered was a blessing, for the marriage had begun to sour shortly after David's birth. Leon's fractured English which had so attracted Margaret when they had first met now irritated her profoundly. Every aspect of his foreignness was a source of her displeasure. The sharp differences between them, the tribal and cultural barriers, seemed more and more insurmountable as the initial passion waned. Leon had never sought to tutor her in his history, and had not insisted on the boy's Jewish upbringing. But he had drawn the line at baptism. Margaret had grudgingly acquiesced. Leon, for his part, had done his best to become part of the life of the valley for he warmed to the mining community who, for the most part, accepted him. As his domestic strife became more and more acute, he often thought of leaving his marriage but it was the mining community that kept him there. That and David, from whom he would not be parted. Besides, his pride forbade a separation from his wife even though legally he would have had grounds. For Margaret was still a beautiful woman and was much sought after by bachelor miners. He could hardly blame her for her pursuit of pleasure since her life at home was miserable and silent. Leon's mood was unusually gloomy. She did her very best to enliven him, but she couldn't understand his guilts and his sorrows. He would laugh only with David, and in the Working Men's Club in the High Street, she was told. But at home he was disposed to melancholy. He went to Cardiff twice a week to collect his goods and always returned in sullen mood. He longed to see Aaron but he was too proud to call. Four years before, Mr Ruboff had died, and Pavel had brought message that Rachel would be especially pleased if he would attend the funeral. He had gone and stood by the graveside, trembling in the echoes of his childhood tongue. Nobody spoke to him. Aaron had shaken his hand. That was the last time he had seen his brother. His brother's daughter he had never seen. He longed for a meeting between Chaya and David, but he was too proud and too wary of refusal to drop hint of it in Pavel's ear. That same kind ear was privy to news from Leipzig too and Leon learned that his mother was well and sending him her thoughts. That Barak still lived and that his condition was stable. Leon knew that, at this stage, only he could make the move to return to his family, but that return had to be alone, and though he longed for it, his pride would allow no move in that direction.

With such thoughts he sat in his cottage that Sunday in the spring of 1903 and wondered where Margaret and David had gone. Sunday morning Margaret was usually at home cooking the traditional Sunday dinner, and David was playing with a school friend. That Sunday Leon had risen late and had found the house deserted. In the kitchen there were no signs of dinner preparations and the breakfast things still lay in the sink. He tried not to think of his wife as a slut, simply because that was the name by which his mother would have called her. And when he thought in such terms about his mother, he wished that Margaret were there on the spot,

201

so that he could touch her, caress her, and stir within her and himself those old longings that had, in such taboo, bound them together. And, as if in answer, he heard steps behind the door, and David's hob-nailed boots that she'd insisted he wear so that he wouldn't be different from miners' sons. They came into the kitchen and Leon noticed that she was dressed in her best attire, her Sunday best she called it, and David was wearing his proper suit. There was an unnerving aura of 'saved' about them.

'Where have you been?' Leon shouted.

Margaret opened her frightened mouth.

'Our Mam took me to Chapel,' David said. 'For my birthday.' He spoke in an accent a million miles away from Bessarabia and the content of his words rattled untold Bindel bones, and every nerve in Leon's body writhed with insult. He was white with rage.

'For his barmitzvah?' he shouted.

'Dad?' David said, thinking that his father's mind had turned and in a language which to his ear was gibberish. But Margaret understood, for once in their courting days Leon had told her of his own initiation in Odessa and the word now rang a distant bell, at that time tuned to their loving, but now as distant and as dreary as those that tolled from the chapel high up in the fold of the mountain.

'What difference?' Margaret dared to say. 'There's nothing Jewish about him. He's the grandson of a Christian coal-miner.'

And of a Jewish taverner, Leon thought to himself, though there would have been no acceptance from that quarter. 'Your father would understand my rage,' Leon said. 'Better than you will ever know.' And Leon was right. David Davies had always been on Leon's side regarding the boy. 'For God's sake, no religion,' he had sworn at his birth. Mr Davies was a socialist. Dai the Red they called him in the valley. His time was spent, in and out of the mine, in organising his work-mates into some form of union. He was a bit of a poet too, and those who did not like his politics but valued him as a friend, called him Dai the Bard. Between his poetry and his politics he had no time nor inclination for God and though he sang hymns in the colliery choir, he did it for the melodies.

'The way I bring up my son is none of my Dad's business,' Margaret said. She stood her ground, unafraid. Her man was not like those others from the pit, those others who beat their wives into submission. Leon had never raised his hand to her, and often she'd boasted about it in the wash-house, so that the women of the village thought Leon lily-livered, and the men of the village felt ashamed.

'It's my business though,' Leon said. 'I didn't give up one God to exchange it for another.'

'You never gave up anything,' Margaret said.

She was right, Leon thought. From the beginning he had

wronged her to invite her into his wilderness of faith. He had given up nothing. His body dwelt in a god-forsaken Jew-less village, and his heart still lingered in Odessa. Margaret was right. He regretted how he had used her. He took his coat and left the house, wandering down the hill to the village square. He had it in mind to walk to the head of the valley beneath the Sunday-still winding gear of the pit-head. There he would meet miners and their families, who, despite the six perilous days that they spent underground each week, would often view its stillness on a Sunday with an assurance of safety. Only two years before, eighty-one men on the night-shift had died in a mine explosion. Now those who survived and took their Sunday stroll in the shadow of the harmless wheel remembered the friends they had lost. Sometimes on a Sunday the Salvation Army Band would gather there with their choir, and sing hymns and songs of praise. Being Easter, they were there that Sunday, and Leon dawdled for a while listening to the haunting melodies, and turning away his ear from the name of the Son of God whom they praised. He recalled his father's stories of his recruitment, and how the utterance of that name had been his first bid for survival. That taboo was part of his inheritance, that legacy that he had chosen to forgo, yet he stood here on alien soil amongst men who were strugglers and survivors like himself, and still that name jarred his ear. He smiled to himself. Whatever past one had, one was saddled with it, one had to accommodate it as best one could. Once again he had longings to go home, to embrace his brother and his family, to sit in a synagogue amongst his own kind. But pride and love of his son forbade him. He made his way to his father-in-law's house opposite the colliery.

David Davies lived in a row of terrace houses known as the Huts. They were one-storey buildings with corrugated iron roofs and had been hurriedly constructed just over ten years ago when the sinking of the Senghenydd colliery had begun. Their purpose was to house the men who were shaft-sinkers and those who worked on the railway extension that took the coal to Cardiff. David Davies had been one of the shaft-sinkers and he and his family now lived permanently in the Huts. The terrace was located directly opposite the mine. It was a dangerous siting, and often David Davies had thought of moving. But over the years the terrace of Huts had become a community in itself and was the centre of dissent and protest against the working conditions in the mines. David Davies was their spokesman, and a change of address would have seemed like a small desertion.

When Leon arrived at the Huts, he was given, as always, a great welcome. Mrs Davies had always regarded him as a bit of a catch for a son-in-law. He had a clean, tidy and safe job. He'd had an education and he could speak a foreign language. The fact that he was a Jew did not disturb her. She regarded the Welsh as part of the lost tribes of Israel. He was a good father to her grandson. He'd actually bought a piano first thing after they were married and insisted that David have lessons. He wanted the best for the boy, but Mrs Davies had to acknowledge that in Senghenydd the pit was the best that could be had. David would be a miner like the rest of them, and no shame in that, she kept saying to a protesting Leon. The salt of the earth down the pits, she would say. Men didn't come any better. 'You wait,' she said. 'In two or three years conditions will improve. More money, more safety. You just leave it to my Dai. They don't call him Dai the Red for nothing,' she laughed.

'Go in the parlour,' she told him. 'They're meeting now. Starting the revolution.' She grinned and showed him into the front room and the men rose to greet him. It was a deference that made Leon feel slightly uneasy, for it confirmed the acknowledgement of the difference between them.

'Sit down, Leon boy,' Dai said. 'And listen. You'll learn something.' He drew a chair to his side and motioned Leon to sit by him. Before the meeting continued he leaned over and whispered in his ear. 'Morgan Jones here tells me his wife said our David was in Chapel today. I'll tan our Margaret's backside for her I will,' he said. 'I promise you. Chapel for God's sake. What next?' Then he returned to the business of the meeting.

Leon looked at the men's faces. Morgan Jones, he whose wife was chapel-inclined, was a fireman in the pits and lived in one of the first Huts in the terrace. He had five children, all of them girls, except the youngest, Gwilym, fourteen years old, and a colliery boy working his father's shifts at his side. Morgan was a tenor in the Male Voice Choir of the valley, and every Thursday night at the Workmen's Institute, Leon would enjoy their concerts. Richard Hunt sat on the other side of Dai. He was Dai's neighbour in the Huts and a collier too. He was the youngest of the men, as yet unmarried, but he was courting Morgan Jones' youngest daughter, Mary. He lived in the Huts with his father, once a miner in a nearby colliery, but now confined to his bed coughing away a silicosis retirement. The last man in the group was Gilbert Whitcombe who lived in the last Hut in the terrace. His father and two brothers had been killed in the pit explosion two years before and his concern in the protest group was as much for better safety measures as for improved wages. For every time a collier went below, he put himself at risk. Most of them accepted that risk as part and parcel of the job, and it was this very acceptance that blunted their protest. They lent more support to the wages claim. At the time, miners' wages were based on a sliding-scale that was regulated by the current selling-price of coal. It was a deeply unfair system, since coal prices were an economic factor over which the miners had no control. It was a scheme that ensured that the management would always be in profit. For Dai Davies, the abolition of this system had become something of a crusade. Wherever he was, and whatever subject was under discussion, underground or in the village square, in the Institute or public house, he would always make it relevant to the wages issue. Around that table they were discussing a method of campaign.

Leon listened and felt at ease in their company. In many ways he knew them intimately, as he did most of the colliers in the valley. For he had seen them naked. One of his collecting-days was a Friday and he tried to time his calls shortly after their return from the day-shift. On Friday they would bring home their pay-packets. Leon would knock on the open terrace door. 'Bindel,' he would shout. Then, without waiting for answer, for he knew he was welcome, he would make his way into the kitchen. The tin-bath, brought in from the back yard, was filled with hot water from the kettles, and placed in front of the roaring fire and in it the collier would make a vain attempt to scrub the years' accumulated coal dust from his body. Whoever was available, wife, daughter, son, would scrub his back and often he would ask especially for Leon, who instinctively knew the itching parts, and whose touch was gentle as a woman's. Once one had viewed a man's body, touched it, known its particular symmetry, one cannot help but care for that man, because, naked, he is as innocent as when sleeping. He looked at the men around the table. He had scrubbed each one of their backs in his time while waiting for their weekly shilling payments on trousers, coats, boots or shirts, that had probably long been worn out of service. Often, during a short wage period, Leon would forgo the payment, which was why after ten years of valley business he had managed to save so little. He didn't mind his poverty. He had enough to keep a decent home. But he minded for his son. He minded for his son's future and he knew that the only way to make that future brighter was to get him out of the valley. But the opposition to such a move would be insurmountable. Margaret's roots were in the Aber valley through countless generations. She could no more leave it than Jakob Bindel would have willingly left his tavern in Odessa. Leon did not relish such thoughts and he tried to concentrate on the discussion around the table.

Dai was in favour of sending a representative of the miners to see Edward Shaw the manager of the mine. There was no question of who that representative should be. Dai Davies was indisputably the miners' spokesman. But Gilbert wanted the matter of safety to be on the agenda of their discussions.

'My father and brothers needn't have died,' he said. 'Nor any of those they brought up from the bottom, or who are still there. It's a dry mine. That's why there was fire. It's *still* a dry mine. Shaw's done nothing about it.'

The Senghenydd colliery was a comfortable one to work in simply because it was dry. But being dry made it less safe, more vulnerable to fire and explosion. After the enquiry following the recent tragedy, the investigating committee had suggested that the mine-roofs be regularly watered, together with the rail-tracks that linked one district seam with another, and that the full coal-trucks plying from seam to seam should be covered to prevent the spread of dust. That was two years ago and still nothing had been done.

'Do we have to wait for another explosion,' Gilbert asked, 'before he gets off his fat back-side? What's the point in better wages if you can't live to enjoy them?'

As Leon left the Davies Hut, he felt the acute isolation of the outsider. These men in the valley struggled daily for their survival as his father and grandfather had done. But now he himself was safe. His life was not daily imperilled and he stood a good chance of a fairly non-Bindel death, that of dying in his bed of natural old age. He was not part of their struggle.

When he reached home they were already at their mid-day meal. Margaret was clearly in a sullen mood. When she saw him at the door, she rose from the table and went into the kitchen then returned with his hot dinner and put it at his place on the table. She had a stern look of duty on her face, a look not condusive to conversation. So the meal was eaten in silence.

'I'm going to work on my ship,' David said when the meal was done. David had a hobby common to the pitboys in the valley, that of making models out of matchsticks. Most of the boys were content with making copies of their own cottages or the pit-head wheel, sights with which they were safely familiar. But David had chosen to model something he had never seen, nor even the sea on which it sailed, and Leon thought that some insistent Bindel gene in him nudged him into preparation for flight. He made to go upstairs to his room.

'What about a walk in the woods afterwards?' Leon said. 'The bluebells are out. We could pick a bunch for our Mam and our Gran.' Leon had picked up scatterings of the Welsh vernacular and they always sat uneasily on his tongue. At least for his listeners who found their native idiom strange when laced with an accent so foreign.

'All right Dad,' David said. 'When I've finished with the sticking.'

When he'd left the room, Leon picked up his plate and made to take it into the kitchen. Margaret snatched the plate from him.

'I don't want any man of mine doing women's work,' she said.

'Well at least I got you to open your mouth,' Leon said.

She went into the kitchen and he followed her. 'Margaret,' he said. 'I want to talk to you.'

She turned her back on him at the sink. 'I'm listening,' she said.

'I want us to leave the valley,' he said, coming to the point straight away. 'I want us to live in Cardiff. There are better opportunities for our David there.' He said it almost in one breath, fearing her interruption.

She did not pause to consider what he'd said, and shouted, 'No,' even before he'd finished. 'You're not getting me to leave Senghenydd. David neither. He's staying with me and his Gran and his Gramp. He was born in the valley and in the valley he'll stay. If you want to go to Cardiff, then that's your doing. And I'm not going to stop you. But you'll go on your own.'

She was shouting at him, and in his ears it sounded like an order to leave. He had often thought of it. He would have forfeited his friends in the valley and his occasional sense of belonging to their community. He would have given it up even though there would be nothing in Cardiff to replace it. Indeed in that hostile city, he would suffer nothing but censure and exclusion. That he would endure. But he would not give up his son. 'Won't you think about it?' he said softly. 'It would be better for you too. There's more to do in a big city.'

'I've been there once,' she said, 'and I hated it. It's full of noise and traffic and nobody talks to you. Anyway, I want to be with my Mam and Dad.' She turned to face him. 'I'm not going,' she said. 'They might be your people but they're not mine.'

They weren't his either, he thought, or if they were, they would not receive him. But there were schools there, proper high schools for David.

'And don't you try and take him,' she shouted.

He smiled. He imagined an army of angry colliers' wives descending on Cardiff to reclaim one of their own. Abduction was out of the question. 'What will become of him when he leaves school?' he asked.

'He'll go down the pit like my father does, and like his father did in the other valley.'

'But I'm his father,' Leon shouted. 'And I'm not a miner.'

'More's the pity,' she said.

He stared at her, hearing the terrible reverberations of regret in her voice. 'Did you make a mistake then?' he dared to ask her after a while.

'No more of a mistake than you made,' she said. 'It couldn't work from the start. We're different, you and me, and it's not just

207

religion,' she hastened to add, 'whatever your narrow-minded mother and brother might have said.' It was the first time she had spoken ill of either of them and Leon had always given her credit for her silence on that score.

'They haven't helped,' she said bitterly. 'My Mam and Dad took you in like one of the family. But who have I met from yours? Our David's got a cousin in Cardiff he's never seen.'

She was angry now and Leon feared the terrible fulfillment of his mother's prophecy.

'Who do they think they are?' she screamed at him, the tears starting in her eyes. 'The chosen bloody people?'

He turned away. He could not deny what she had said. She was entitled to say much worse, yet he could not hate his brother for the neglect he had meted out to him.

'It doesn't work,' she said. 'We're both of us unhappy.'

He loved her then, for all the words that over the years she had left unsaid. 'If we lived in Cardiff,' he said, 'it would help us. They would come round eventually.' He knew there was little likelihood of it, and he was being less than honest in suggesting it. He had the impression that she was going to leave him, and it disturbed him that it did not hurt him. It was only David whom he wanted, his share of him that she would not deny.

'What shall we do?' he said.

'I'm going back to the Huts,' she said. 'With David. We'll live with our Mam and Dad. You can come whenever you want. I've thought about it for a long time. That's why I went to Chapel today, to ask God for forgiveness.'

Leon sighed. The bleakness of his future blinded him. He was now tied to Senghenydd for ever. 'D'you want a divorce?' he said. He had heard of such a measure on very rare occasions. He knew it was a shameful thing to do, but both of them had a chance of happiness.

She looked at him in horror. 'There's never been that sort of thing in my family,' she said with a certain pride. 'I made my bed and I'm going to lie on it, but I'll lie on it in my Mam's house.'

'But you're young,' he said. 'And still beautiful.'

She laughed with a certain bitterness. 'And soiled goods,' she said. 'That's what they call us women in the valleys. You're better off widowed. Not that I want to be,' she said quickly. 'I don't bear you any grudge. You always treated me well. But it's better for both of us if I go.'

He didn't know what more to say to her. He felt he could keep her with a little persuasion but his appetite for their marriage was as sickened as her own. He went to the foot of the stairs and called David. 'We'll pick some bluebells,' he said to Margaret. 'You can take them to your Mam.' He was sanctioning his wife's departure and it was like buying flowers for his own funeral.

'She'll like that,' was all Margaret said.

They walked towards the woods at the bottom of the valley. At home David was a silent boy, though his school reports declared that he was very talkative in class. Leon knew most of his son's friends and had noted how they chatted endlessly with their families. He wondered what hurdles stilled David's tongue between school and cottage. Dai Davies said that when he came to the Huts he couldn't stop talking. On and on he chatted, as if he was making up for many silences. Leon could only suppose that he himself was the cause. Even when they took walks together he said very little, and usually in answer to questions that Leon asked. But this time he was more forthcoming.

'We're going to live at Gran and Gramp's,' he said.

So she had already told him, and he resented that breach of his fatherhood. He tried to hide his anger.

'Will you like that?' Leon asked.

'Yes,' he said. 'But you'll come every day, won't you? Mam says you will.'

'D'you want me to come?'

David gripped Leon's sleeve. 'You've got to come, Dad.'

It was a rare show of emotion from his son. Leon could see he was on the verge of tears. He took his hand, but at the same time quickened his pace as if to alibi his gesture which a thirteen-year-old boy might find embarrassing.

'What's the matter, Dovidle?' Leon said. It was his Yiddish name for him, the name by which his own father and grandfather would have called him had they lived.

'I wish you were a miner, Dad,' David said after a while. 'So's I could go down the pit with you when I leave school.'

'D'you want to go down the pit?'

'Of course,' David said. 'All my friends are going to be colliery boys.' The thought of an alternative had clearly never occurred to him, and Leon was careful not to suggest one for he knew that Margaret's decision had annulled all choices. He was deeply depressed at the prospect of his son's bleak future. Perhaps he should have been more firm with Margaret, he thought. He had been weak in acquiescing to her decision. But during his long sojourn in the valley he had learned the strength of its women. 'I'll have to ask my Missus,' was a phrase he'd heard countless times in the Institute or on his rounds. Under the earth the men reigned supreme, but above ground was women's domain. 'You'll like it with Gran and Gramp,' Leon said.

'Will Mam let me go to Cardiff?' he said suddenly. 'Just for a visit.'

'Why d'you want to do that?' Leon asked.

'See my cousin. Mam's told me about her. Chaya or something. It's not a Welsh name, is it Dad?'

'It's Jewish,' Leon said.

'Like you?'

'That's right. You've got a Jewish name too. David was King of Israel.'

'It's Welsh too,' David said. 'Patron Saint.'

They reached the woods. Through a clearing they could see a haze of blue, and David darted to its centre and started picking. 'You pick for Mam,' David called, 'and I'll pick for Gran.'

Leon stood watching him and he trembled with sudden and total recall of the Odessa forest behind the tavern. The scene played before his eyes with such clarity he actually heard his father's voice, undeniable, insistent, as if it dictated Leon's turn to hand down his survival legacy to his son. But this is Senghenydd, Leon thought, a sleepy village in the Aber valley, far from Czar, ignorant of pogrom, a village in which he, Leon Bindel, was the only Jew. What relevance was his legacy to a child to whom his barmitzvah day was no different from any other birthday?

'We used to have a forest like this,' Leon began. 'Behind our tavern in Odessa.' Leon had told his son very little of his own childhood. Beyond its geography he knew practically nothing. Margaret had never encouraged Leon's childhood tales. They only served to accentuate the differences between them.

'Did it have bluebells?' David asked.

'No,' he said, rather sharply. He wanted to get on with the story. He could afford no diversion. 'We went there once on your Uncle Aaron's thirteenth birthday,' he said. 'Just like yours is today. We had quite an adventure there.' He paused. 'But first, I have to tell you a little of the history of that time.' He started to pick the bluebells which gave a rhythm to his story and he told his son of his grandfather's childhood. Half way through, David paused in his picking, so engrossed was he in the adventure his father had to tell. And when he came to the end of it with an account of the milk-brothers' return to the tavern, David asked a question that echoed those very words that he himself and his brother had posed in the Odessa forest all those years ago. 'How did they survive?' he said.

Leon thought of Grandpa Jakob, and that litany of survival that had been the milk-brothers' inheritance. That same litany that his own father in his time had bequeathed his two sons in the forest. And now the burden of that inheritance was his and his alone. For Aaron had no son and, in the Jewish ethic, survival lay in male domain. He looked at David and wondered what he would make of Grandpa Jakob's bequest. He knew every word of it by heart, as

Aaron knew it, and as Benjamin and Reuben had known it. It was a hymn that had to be heard from generation to generation, a hymn that would have no stop, that no one could stifle, and even a stray from the tribe could be its minstrel. He put his arm around his son, and in his mind he recited the litany. There was no point in declaring the threat of baptism. His son was already half way to the Cross. But there was point, ample point in abjuring his survival. And mindful of the seeming irrelevance of his homily, its anachronism in both place and time, he laid before his son, word by word, the Bindel inheritance. 'You must survive, Dovidle,' he said. 'But beware of principles. Abandon them if you are to survive. There is no cause on earth worth dying for, no God worth one's dying breath, no country worth one's martyrdom, no principle worth one's sacrifice. Only in the name of love is death worthy. And friendship.'

When he had done, Leon, like his father before him, and his grandfather too, wondered whether his son had any idea of what he was talking about. But he had to speak out for his own sake, as his father and grandfather had for theirs. But to whom would his son bequeath that minstrel's song of survival? Then for the first time he realised the monstrous penalty of his desertion from his tribe. Despite all his efforts he himself was still inextricably tied to the burdensome Bindel inheritance, but he had effectively cut off his son from all of his father's history. In his heart and in his soul, he held a gift of sublime splendour, that of the spirit of survival, but now it was a gift, unbestowable, untransmittable. With his own desertion he had disinherited his son, and such a mean act of dispossession appalled him.

David put his hand on his father's arm. 'You know Trevor, Dad? Trevor Evans, my friend?'

Leon nodded.

'Well, you know his Dad was killed in the pit explosion?'

Leon nodded again.

'Well, Trevor told me,' David went on, 'that his Dad was saved. Ready to go up in the cage he was. But he looked in the cage and he couldn't find his friend. John Llewellyn it was. Owen's Dad. So Trevor's Dad went back to look for him. Then there was a fall. Killed him it did. So Trevor said. Him and Mr Llewellyn.' He gathered his bunch of bluebells and stood upright. 'Let's go, Dad,' he said.

And, as his Grandpa Jakob before him and, as Benjamin his own father, Leon thought that his son had understood him after all.

When they returned to the cottage, the table was set with the Sunday high tea. The fact that that day she would be walking out on her marriage would in no way upset Margaret's routine. Her duties as a wife would continue as long as she and her husband shared the same roof. But it was their last meal together as a family, and mindful of that, Margaret had put herself out to make it memorable. She had baked Welsh scones and pikelets, that were both Leon's and David's favourites, and there were tinned salmon cutlets, which were the staple fare for every Welsh high-tea Sunday table. Margaret put Leon's offer of bluebells in a jar and placed them in the centre of the table. She would leave them there, Leon knew, not as a rejection of the gift but because she would wish some cheer to take the edge off his loneliness.

'Can I go to Cardiff with Dad one day?' David asked suddenly. 'Just for a visit,' he added seeing the look of dismay on his mother's face.

She relaxed a little. 'As long as your Dad brings you back,' she said with a laugh masking her fears of his abduction.

'You know I'll bring him back,' Leon said. 'This is his home.'

She was grateful for that acknowledgement. 'It could have been yours too,' she said. 'If you'd put your mind to it.'

'It is mine now,' he said. 'It has to be.'

She did not want to pity him, but she could not be indifferent to his isolation. 'You should patch it up with your brother,' she said.

She insisted on clearing the table and washing-up before she left. She made no production of leave-taking. As she pointed out, they were only going down the valley and no doubt they would be seeing him in the morning. Leon offered to escort her, to carry her case. But Margaret declined. She was leaving of her own free will. She was not entitled to a porter.

Leon waved them goodbye from the door-step, and when he returned to the empty cottage, he looked around and noticed the sudden absence of all her traces, her sewing-box on the side-board, her brown exercise-book of recipes, her white bible, things whose presence before had never impressed themselves on his eye, but whose removal shrieked her absence. He wandered from room to room, wooing his loneliness. In the kitchen he noticed that she had set out his breakfast tray. On it was a glass in a holder and inside the glass was a piece of lemon. It was the only concession she had ever made to his Bindelhood, one of the few Odessa legacies he himself had retained with ease. He filled the kettle and boiled it on the open fire. Then when it was ready, he made a very weak tea and poured it over the lemon. He opened the larder and found the final flavour that would transport him back to the Bindel tavern. Blackcurrant jam. Then he sat at the table and sipped it slowly. As he drank he made the decision that after so many years of fraternal silence, he would make a bid to see his brother again.

212

Pavel Khasina, the Bindel brothers' intermediary, had retired some years before, retired that is from his drapery round. He was no longer strong enough to carry parcels and to make the strenuous uphill climbs in the valleys. With his savings, he had set up his own small store a few doors away from Max's in Bute Street. There he sold haberdashery and notions, soaps and powders and registered aids to health. He had sold the good-will of his valley round to a 'landsleit' who had recently emigrated from Odessa. He had had sundry offers for his round, and that which determined the ultimate buyer was whether he could successfully execute the message-service for the Bindel brothers. So each applicant was assessed for his loyalty, his tact, and his aversion to gossip. The lot fell to one Victor Zubko, who carried out his tasks as go-between with diligence and skill. It was Victor who brought Aaron the news of Leon's estrangement from his wife, and some days later, of Leon's wish to see his brother once more.

The news of his brother's separation from his wife did not surprise Aaron. Indeed he wondered why it had taken so long. He did not consider it as a matter for his concern or his compassion. But he was delighted that Leon had expressed a wish to see him again. This delight he conveyed to Victor, who then divulged the second instalment of Leon's message. He wished to bring his son with him. Victor was quick to note the look of displeasure that clouded Aaron's face at the mention of this request, but that look would not be part of his return message. Over the years Victor had taken a liking to Leon and would not hurt him. In his heart he thought Aaron a stern ungiving man and he wished Leon well of the meeting. 'I have to consider it,' Aaron said. 'I will let you know tomorrow.' Neither would Victor convey to Leon his brother's hesitation.

Aaron consulted with Rachel.

'Of course,' she said, 'he must bring his son. Chaya has never met her cousin.'

'Cousin?' Aaron said. The notion of blood between his wholly Jewish daughter and a child who, by Jewish law, was Christian, he found faintly displeasing. But he did not want to argue with Rachel. He had noticed in the past that on the subject of Leon, her thoughts were sometimes dangerously close to approval.

213

It was Rachel who, on the following day, charged Victor with the message that Leon and his son would be very welcome, and Victor would take exactly that message back to the valley. Except that he would say that it was Aaron himself who had issued the invitation. Victor knew the cost of Leon's request, the cost to his pride, his dignity and self-respect.

'Aaron would be glad to see you. And David,' Victor said to Leon the following day. 'He will make you most welcome.' Then they sat together at the cottage table drinking blackcurrant tea and sharing stories of Odessa.

Later that week, on a Sunday, David put on his suit and tie and went with his father to Cardiff.

Leon was nervous and tried to hide his apprehension from his son. He had not seen his brother for almost five years. That meeting had been formal and fleeting. Its place the graveside, at Mr Ruboff's funeral. He had not been invited to return to the house of mourning, though he had the impression that Rachel would have wished it. He had slunk away like a pariah, while the men about him whispered and the women turned their faces away. On his way back to the valley he had tried not to think ill of his brother. He tried to understand him. Over the past years Aaron had become something of a leading figure in the growing Jewish community. He was an official of the synagogue and an organiser of charities. He had a position to maintain. The acceptance of a tainted brother into his life could only threaten that position.

David was agog with excitement. On their way from the station he had seen a trolley-tram for the first time, and he gripped his father's hand in fear and joy. Leon wondered whether Aaron had given Chaya instructions on how to behave, what names must not be mentioned, and what questions must not be asked. On his side, he had given no instructions to David. He hoped that he would be allowed to be himself, for they had to accept the truth of him with no apology. As they walked down the bridge steps to reach the embankment, Leon said, 'You can see your Uncle Aaron's house from here,' and he pointed it out from where they stood. He felt a sudden sweat on David's hand as he clutched his own. The boy stopped, suddenly nervous. 'Do I look all right, Dad?' he asked.

Leon looked at him and smiled. 'Fit to meet a king,' he said, responding to the nature of David's fears. But Leon knew that however David looked, Aaron would see him as that little half-Jew boy, in his posh chapel clothes on his way to a pit-future like all of his kind. He put his arm around his son as a pre-emptive move of protection. David, by the same instinct, did likewise with his father. 'We'll survive, Dad,' he said.

They stood for a while before Aaron's door. David nervously

patted his hair and pulled at his unaccustomed tie. 'Let me pull the bell, Dad,' David said. He came from a village of ever-open front doors, and he was in awe of this heavily barred and locked one, and he wondered why his uncle was so afraid. He pulled on the metal chain and listened to the hollow echo of the bell inside the door. It was sometime before it was opened. Leon hoped that Rachel would answer, or even Chaya whom he had never seen. But it was Aaron who opened the door and bade them welcome. Through the doorway Leon could see a little girl peeping around a door into the hall, and he sent David into the house so that he could be alone with his brother.

'I'm glad to see you, Leon,' Aaron said, with what sounded like a rehearsed formality.

Leon embraced him and, at his touch, Aaron melted a little, and arm in arm they entered the house. Rachel was introducing Chaya to her cousin. Her hand was on the boy's shoulder in total and immediate acceptance. Then she greeted Leon. 'Come and say hello to your niece. This is your Uncle Leon, Chaya,' she said.

'Uncle Leon,' the child repeated, two brand new words in her little world, unheard before in this house, unpractised, astonishing. 'Uncle Leon,' she repeated and went up to him and took his hand.

Leon hoped that the children would stay with them for the rest of the day. Their presence diluted the tension he felt between himself and his brother. Rachel led them into the dining-room where lunch was ready. David went to his father's side and stayed there, clinging. He was fiddling with his tie. 'You can take it off if you like,' Leon said. He realised that a tie would make little difference to their impression of his son. He noted that Aaron had not yet touched the boy or addressed one word to him. He felt David clinging to his sleeve as if to confirm their dual outsiderness, evidence of which was all around him. The white table-cloth on the table, and all that silver. Chaya's dress, clearly not her best, probably a school one, and him, strait-jacketted in his Sunday suit, yet it was she who was the posh one. Perhaps food would thaw them all, Leon hoped, and he guided David towards the table.

Rachel sat David by Chaya. She meant well, but David was loathe to leave his father's side. The abundance of cutlery on the table frightened him, and his total ignorance of all their uses seemed to put him firmly in his lowly place. He wished he were back in Senghenydd at his Gran's table, where one knife and one fork did for everything. He watched his father unfold the linen napkin and tuck it into his collar. He did likewise wondering how his Gramp would manage, whose neck was always scarved above an unbuttoned shirt. He dared to sneak a look at his Uncle Aaron who was carving a chicken at the end of the table. He reminded him of his headmaster. Leon too was looking at his brother. He noticed how fat he'd grown, with a fat that sat ill on his naturally lean structure. It was a fat of prosperity and safety, and had thus never framed a Bindel before.

'Did you have a good journey?' Aaron said, making conversation.

'Yes,' Leon said. 'David had never been on a train before.' He wanted to include his son in their exchange, making it clear that the one was not acceptable without the other.

'Did you like it?' Rachel said, addressing herself to David.

He swallowed. His face was on fire. He did not trust his voice so he nodded in her direction and hoped that she would be satisfied.

'No tongue in your head?' Aaron asked. They were the first words he had addressed to him, and they were by no means friendly.

'He's shy,' Leon whispered to his brother. 'Give him a little time.' He dared to look across at his son and saw the tears in his eyes and at that moment Leon too wanted to be back in the valley. He sought in his mind for some topic of conversation to divert their attention from a child whose lineage his brother clearly could not forgive. But before he could think of anything, Aaron was once again at his questioning.

'What school d'you go to?' he said, not looking at him.

His name's David, Leon thought. His brother should have no difficulty pronouncing it. It was Jewish enough to slip easily off his tongue.

Now David had to say something. A nod or a shake of the head would no longer do. He raised his head and decided to brazen it out. He looked Aaron straight in the eye and was glad that he wasn't his father. 'Senghenydd Boys' School,' he said, then he looked back at his plate and wondered how he could deal with the chicken leg, that had suddenly appeared on it, without using his fingers. He looked across the table at his father and Leon gave him a smile which told him he had acquitted himself well.

'And what will you be when you grow up?' Aaron was relentless.

'I'll be a collier,' David said proudly. 'Like my Gramp.'

Chaya giggled. She had not heard that word before.

'Like Zeder,' Rachel explained, using Chaya's word for Mr Ruboff. Then it was David's turn to laugh at a word as foreign to him as Gramp was to his cousin. Leon looked across at him tenderly. He's a true survivor, he thought. The score was now about equal around the table.

'There are better things to be than a miner,' Aaron ploughed on.

Perhaps he was trying to get near the boy in his own ham-fisted fashion, Leon thought. He wanted to make some contact. In Aaron's eyes, Aaron was doing the right thing.

'Like what?' David asked. He was now perfectly at ease. The smile his father had flashed him was ammunition enough to confront his uncle's hostility. Now he felt he and his father were hosts, and the others rank outsiders.

'Well,' Aaron pressed on, 'you could be a doctor or a solicitor or a dentist. You're young.' His voice was raised in an anger that seemed to reflect a resentment of his own loss of youth. 'You can do anything.'

David found his catalogue of possibilities quite fantastical. 'That's daft,' he said with no adornment. 'I'm going down the pit with my Gramp.'

'I want Chaya to be a teacher,' Aaron said proudly.

David was not impressed. From his small personal knowledge of the teaching profession, he considered them the enemy, and he couldn't understand why everybody didn't want to be everyone's friends. He wished his Uncle Aaron would stop examining him. He was hungry and he wanted to eat, and even he knew that you mustn't speak with your mouth full. He looked at his chicken, checked on the tool that his father was using, and did likewise.

'How's your business, Aaron?' Leon said, offering himself as a second front for Aaron's line of fire, so that David could get on with his dinner.

'I'm busy,' he said. 'Lots of new immigrants have settled in Cardiff. Everyone wants a new suit and they all seem to come to me. There just isn't enough time.'

'What a pity,' Leon laughed. 'I was thinking of placing an order.'

Aaron looked up at him. 'For you I'll find time,' he said. 'After lunch I'll show you some new materials.'

He was thawing gently. Perhaps soon he would be ready to talk about their childhood, that conversation for which Leon longed, and which dialogue he'd had with himself night after night in the cottage.

'We'll go up to the workshop,' Aaron was saying, and Leon wished the meal quickly over to begin his craven journey back to the Odessa tavern.

'D'you have any hobbies, David?' Rachel asked, carefully waiting until his mouth was empty.

'Matchstick models,' David said. 'I'm making a ship. My Dad's been on a ship,' he said proudly.

'So have I,' Aaron said. It was a journey he would have preferred to forget, but he wanted to make himself part of Leon's adventure.

David was not pleased with that news, though he tried to hide it. He wanted his father to be someone special. If he couldn't be a miner then he had to be able to offer something that his friends' fathers had never experienced. Besides, he'd hoped that his father would have something special that he didn't have to share with his brother. David had been in that house long enough to notice the

217

inequality in the brothers' ways of life. Uncle Aaron lived in a big house. He was rich and he had a happy family life. His father had none of those things. It was not too much to hope that, on that ship on the high seas, he was a lone traveller.

'But your father's done something none of us has done,' Aaron said. Leon trembled. He knew that Aaron meant well, but there was no way David would accommodate a gaol-bird as a father. 'He's been in prison,' Aaron went on.

David paled. 'Dad?' he said, and there were tears in his voice.

Now Aaron was confused and regretful. How was it possible that his brother had never mentioned that episode to his son? Then he realised that the cause of that imprisonment was part and parcel of all the heritage that Leon had foresworn. Aaron tried to make amends. 'It was for a good cause,' he said. 'Your father was very brave. Any brave man would have done what he did.'

'What did you do, Dad?'

'I hit a man,' Leon said. 'A ship's officer. Because he made insulting remarks about Jews.'

There was silence. It was clear that David did not think that was a good enough reason. Why should he, Aaron thought, since he had clearly been told nothing about the events that preceded the flight from Odessa? 'There's a long long story behind it, David,' he said.

It was the first time he had used the boy's name.

'Have you not told him our story, Leon?' his brother asked.

'No,' Leon said. 'Not all of it. But I have told him of Granpa Jakob's legacy. I have told him about survival. He has inherited.' Aaron touched his brother's arm and smiled.

'Tell him the whole story, Papa,' Chaya said. She turned to her cousin. 'It's full of blood and fighting and running away,' she said.

Aaron took a sheet of paper from his pocket-notebook and drew a little map. 'Come here,' he said. 'I'll show you where it all began.'

And so the tale of survival unfolded. The brothers shared it between them, laughing at times, reminding each other of omissions, encouraged by the excitement of the two children. Much of it Chaya had heard before, but for David most of it was new, and he kept asking if it was all true, and all the time he wanted repetitions. It was tea-time when the brothers came to the end of the story, to that event that provoked it in the first place, the striking of the ship's officer.

'You should have killed him, Dad,' David said with indignation.

Leon was glad that his son had so fully understood his father's history, and for the first time in many years he felt the relief of one who no longer lives a lie.

Rachel made two cups of lemon tea for the brothers and they took them upstairs to the workshop. They sat by the cutting bench and sipped their tea in silence. Then after a while Leon said,

'Thank you for helping me to tell him.' He spoke in Yiddish since that was their boyhood tongue, and it was the togetherness of their childhood that he wished to recapture.

'Come, let me measure you for a suit,' Aaron said, also in Yiddish. He wanted to talk to Leon but he needed to busy himself with work which always eased his conversation. He drew the measure round Leon's chest. 'What are you going to do?' he said. 'Are you staying in the valley?'

'I must,' Leon said. 'David is there. Margaret won't leave, and I won't leave David.'

'But you're young,' Aaron said. 'You should marry again. A proper marriage this time.'

'Margaret won't hear of a divorce,' Leon said. 'And it was a proper marriage. As long as it lasted. It wasn't a mistake at the time. I changed. That's what went wrong. It was not her fault.'

'But she must free you.' Aaron was insistent.

'A divorce would destroy her,' Leon said. 'There's nothing I can do about it. When David grows up, please God, and marries, then perhaps I'll come and live in Cardiff. But while he's growing I cannot be apart from him.'

'Is he really going to go down the mine?' Aaron asked.

'You must try and understand him, Aaron,' Leon said gently. 'David has a history almost as long and as oppressed as our own. His grandfather was a collier, so was his father before him. The pit is the whole fabric of the valley life. It's what he wants. It's his only honest way of growing into a man.'

'But aren't you ambitious for him?' Aaron asked. 'If I had a son, and, alas, I shall not have a son . . . Rachel cannot bear more children.'

'I'm sorry,' Leon said. Then with a shock he realised that his son, his David, would be the only Bindel of the new generation, and that it was he who, out of his renegade loins, had sired him.

'If I had a son,' Aaron went on, 'I'd want him to have all the opportunities that we never had. But Chaya will be a teacher. I have decided on that. It's a prestigious profession. Of course, it doesn't matter so much with a girl. She'll marry and have children. But they won't be Bindels. He mustn't be a miner,' Aaron said.

How different they both were, Leon thought. In many ways, he himself had stayed closer to the Bindel tradition than had his brother. Aaron had been infected by freedom and safety. It had bred in him ambition, a greed almost, for prestige and status, a greed he was foisting on his daughter. He had become a different kind of Jew, whose priorities were no longer those of survival. Parental expectation was the crippling disease of freedom. He thought of the Odessa days. When Grandpa Jakob had said

219

farewell to the milk-brothers, when his own father had spoken in the forest, neither had said, 'Go, my sons. Be doctors, be teachers, be lawyers.' All they had said, and with all their love, was, 'Go, my sons. Survive.' That was the limit of their parental hopes. Survival. To do that was to do more than enough. That was the blessing from children. It was that that he hoped for his own son. That and no more. Just the miracle of survival. Had Aaron learned nothing from their history, that history he knew by heart? Had it not taught him to be immune from the virus of freedom? They were two very different kinds of Jew, his brother and himself. Yet despite this ironic difference he had never felt so close to Aaron. He watched him circling his body, measuring and writing down the lengths. He was humming to himself as he worked, as their father Benjamin would do at his milking, as Grandpa Jakob sang softly to himself as he took the stock of his tavern cellars. 'It's good to be with you again,' Leon said.

Aaron squeezed that part of his arm that was under the measure. 'You must come every Sunday,' he said.

*

Over the next year, Leon and David came every week to Cardiff and, with each visit, David gleaned more and more of his inheritance. Like his father, he looked forward to Sundays. Margaret willingly gave in to these visits. She and Leon often met in the public-house where she would go with her father, and she would drink a stout with them, and the people of Senghenydd slowly got used to their strange relationship.

One evening, the messenger Zubko called in at Leon's cottage. He brought news. Aaron had received a letter from their mother in Leipzig in which she wrote that Barak had died. She had been expecting it for many months. He had been in no pain and his death was peaceful. He had left her very comfortable. During the last months of his illness he had been cared for by a young nurse called Greta whom she now kept on as a companion. She was anxious to see her sons once again, and announced that she and Greta would be coming to Cardiff within the next month, once she had cleared Barak's business affairs.

'Are you sure she said sons?' Leon asked. 'Not just Aaron?'

'Aaron had written to her of your separation,' Zubko said.

'What did she say?'

'She's never mentioned it in her letters. But she did write "sons". I saw the letter myself.'

'Then she will have to meet her grandson too,' Leon said. He did not give it as a message, but Zubko would know how to deal with it.

*

220

When Zubko arrived at the cottage with news of Zelda's arrival, Leon indicated that he would meet her alone on the following day. It was almost fifteen years since he had seen his mother and their last meeting had been bitter and painful. In his moves to re-unite with his family, he felt no disloyalty to Margaret. She had, after all, left him. It was her choice, and her leaving was almost an instruction to him to return to the fold. He wore the suit that Aaron had made for him so that she could take pride in her son's handiwork and in its symbol of fraternity.

When he arrived at his brother's house, it was Zelda herself who came to the door. She embraced him straightaway. 'Where's David?' she said.

'He's coming on Sunday,' Leon said, delighted with her ready acceptance.

'Let me look at you,' she said, holding him at a distance from her. As she appraised him, he did likewise with her. She had shrunk a little, but there was a brightness in her eye, and a general radiance about her features that was surprising in a face so recently bereaved. He knew that his mother had always had qualms about her re-marriage, although her years with Barak had been happy. But it was as if his death had wiped her slate clean once more. Now she was Zelda Bindel once more, and widowed in that name. He followed her into the dining-room where the family were assembled. Lunch was set, and Rachel urged them to table.

'This is Greta,' Zelda said, taking the hand of a girl who stood at the far end of the room.

Greta held out her hand, looking him squarely in the face. There was no shyness about her, and Leon had the impression that he was no stranger to her, that his mother had talked much about him, as compensation for the pain of him in her heart. She looked at Leon as if she knew his childhood, his growth, his rebellion, and although he found her attractive and friendly, he felt slightly at a disadvantage, and he resolved to get to know her as intimately as she seemingly knew him.

'Your mother has told me a lot about you,' she said. She smiled at him, and he at her, for the pleasure of the knowledge that his mother had never fully rejected him.

Aaron was in a jovial mood and so were Rachel and Chaya, each taking their cue from Zelda who took such pleasure in the long-delayed family reunion.

'What a pity my grandson isn't here,' she said as they all sat down.

'Sunday, Mama,' Leon said.

'Three Bindel generations around one table,' she said. 'It's just like the old days in Odessa.'

And that was the cue for nostalgia and a texture of conversation that Leon so delighted in. He felt strangely elated, a feeling not wholly due to their reminiscence. It was the presence of that girl who sat opposite him, and who, like a leader of a Greek chorus, prompted each of their memories, although she was an outsider to them all. Later when they withdrew to the sitting-room, Zelda told them about her life in Leipzig and she sang Greta's praises for the care she had given to the ailing Barak. 'I loved him,' Greta said. 'He was like a father. Mine died when I was little. Oh it's no cause for sorrow,' she said quickly. 'I have no recollection of him at all. Nor of my mother, who died when I was born. I'm an orphan,' she laughed. 'I've never had to love anybody because of blood.'

Perhaps that was the real meaning of freedom, Leon thought. He warmed to the girl and smiled at her, and Zelda noted the exchange and was glad of it. Ever since Greta had come to them in Leipzig, she had day-dreamed of a union between her and her son. The notion of Leon's divorce, or whatever problems it presented, in no way ruffled her. In Jewish terms the marriage had been illegal from the start. In Jewish law it would not be countenanced therefore its dissolution was irrelevant. She took no account of the Christian law of the land. All their Bindel lives they had broken that kind of law. Grandpa Jakob had run an illegal tavern. Benjamin and Reuben Bindel had attempted army desertion, although they had failed. Leon Bindel, blessed be his memory, had died in protest against the Czar's law. Her own sons had run away from legal recruitment, and their travelling-papers were by no means legitimate. Since the beginning of time, the Bindels had been chronic law-breakers, and she saw no reason why they should change. Her dream was that Leon should return to Leipzig with both of them, marry Greta and make his home there. 'I don't intend to sell Barak's shop,' she said suddenly, envisaging that one day Leon would take it over. 'There's a good manager there,' she said, 'and it brings in a useful income.' Her sons applauded her sense of management.

'You must visit one day,' she said, directing her remark at Leon. 'Leipzig is a beautiful city.'

'I'll show it to you,' Greta said.

In anyone else, her manner might have been construed as forward, but Leon and the others saw it as a refreshing openness from one who had never been trained in social cunning.

'I have a short end of a lovely suiting upstairs,' Aaron said suddenly. 'It will make a suit for David.' Now that his mother had not expressed her displeasure at meeting her grandson, he could afford to publicise his acceptance of the boy.

'Can you imagine,' Zelda laughed, 'a son of mine a tailor.' Which set her to remembering the insomniac Faivel and once again they boarded the Odessa carousel.

The following Sunday David met his paternal grandmother for the first time. The encounter was less uneasy than Leon had expected. The presence of the rest of the family, and especially Greta, eased the first moments between them. 'He looks like you, Leon,' Zelda said, though David clearly looked like his mother. Zelda put her hand on David's shoulder. 'You're a Bindel,' she said.

He felt an awe in her touch, as if she had loaded him with an enormous responsibility. 'Your children shall be Bindels,' she added.

Leon realised how little his mother knew of his son, how the boy, through his father's own straying, had left the tribe far far behind. How he had a tribe of his own, not unlike hers in some respects. The thought crossed his mind that he might take his mother on a visit to Senghenydd, but it would be the moon to her, Jewless, unearthly.

After lunch David and Chaya went walking in the park together. It had become a Sunday post-prandial habit with them. At first Aaron had had qualms about letting them go off on their own. David was a boy, but he was less worried about that than the fact that he was only half Jewish, and therefore in his mind, only half to be relied on. Yet he could not voice his fears for fear of hurting his brother. Often the children would wander as far as Llandaff fields, and then they would bring back flowers or leaves according to the season. Which left the adults alone in the house. Greta and Rachel cleared the kitchen, but Zelda hung behind, keeping her seat in the dining-room, a position which, out of politeness, kept her sons at table. Aaron pleaded a suit to finish, so his leaving was legitimate and Zelda gladly excused him because she wanted to talk alone to Leon. Leon was nervous of such an encounter, though he knew it was unavoidable. His mother would ask questions and would not be pleased with their answers. And no doubt she would make impossible demands. He waited for her preamble, for she was not one to come straight to the point, especially when that point was controversial. So she skirted it, as he expected.

'You have a lovely son there,' she said. 'A very attractive boy.'

He thanked her, and said that he was a good son and had always given him pleasure.

'What is his future?' she said. Again she was skirting, for it was his own future she wanted to talk about. He saw no point in lying to her. 'He'll follow in the tradition of all his family. He will be a collier.'

She gasped. 'A Bindel a collier?' She was unbelieving.

'He is only half a Bindel,' Leon said.

'And what about you, a whole Bindel. What's to become of you?' The gentleness had gone from her voice and Leon was glad of it for it now excused his cruel honesty. 'My future is bound up with my son's,' he said. 'I shall stay in the valley.'

'You will bury yourself there,' she shouted at him.

'What do you want me to do, Mama?' he said helplessly. He hadn't meant it as a question. It was a simple statement of his own lack of choice. But she took it as a request for her advice.

'I want you to come back to Leipzig with me. I want you to make your home there. Take over the fur business. It will be yours one day.' She paused. 'I want you to marry,' she said. It had all, till then, been a preamble, Leon realised. At last she had come to her point. But at least she had not mentioned Greta's name.

'But I'm already married, Mama,' Leon said as gently as he could.

'That's not a marriage,' she said with disdain.

He did not want to dislike her, and he prayed that she would not mention Margaret's name for it would be a curse from her lips.

'You can get a divorce,' she said.

'My wife won't give me a divorce,' he said, and he dreaded her response. But she was clever enough not to malign her. 'In Leipzig no one would know that you were ever married before.'

He let that pass and asked her the unanswerable question. 'What about my son?' he said.

She looked at him with infinite pity, and then to his great surprise, she put her arms around him. He had spoken words that had finally touched her heart. 'How old is he now?' she asked. 'Thirteen,' he said. Any other year would have been preferable for thirteen in the Bindel tradition was heavily loaded. 'I took him into the woods, Mama, like Papa took us into the forest. And I told him what Papa told me, and what Grandpa Jakob told him. I told it to David, Mama. He has inherited.'

'You know,' she said, still holding him, 'children grow up, they marry, they have children of their own. Will you stay with him then?'

He smiled at her. 'No,' he said. 'Then I shall come to Leipzig.'

'Greta is a young woman,' she said. Even if there had to be an unavoidable delay, she saw her plans for the future amply fulfilled.

That evening before he left, Leon asked Greta if he could show her a little of Cardiff during her visit. He would gladly come from the valley for that purpose. She was delighted to accept his offer having first asked Zelda's permission which was gladly given. So over the remaining weeks of Zelda's stay, Leon came often to

Cardiff for the sole purpose of seeing Greta. They walked a lot, and talked as much. Greta told him all that she knew about him from his mother, and how she had been right in every particular. She knew the Bindel history so intimately, she might have been born in the tavern. It was as if his mother had laid the foundations for his wooing. Greta knew about his marriage too, and she wanted to know about Margaret and his life in the valley. Leon was happy to talk about such things, for never before had he found a listener for that Senghenydd tale.

Slowly he grew more and more fond of Greta, and, at night, alone in his cottage, he dreaded the day of her return. He day-dreamed of taking David out of the valley, and to Leipzig to learn the fur-trade. But it would be too cruel even to suggest it to Margaret, much less to Gran and Gramp. David Bindel, however he was sired, was a son of the valley and like all its sons, in the valley he would live, marry, bear children and lay his bones. He thought of Greta and knew that he would miss her terribly.

They were due to leave the following week and Leon had decided to take them to Tilbury. Margaret gave her permission for David to take off from school and go as far as Cardiff to say goodbye to his grandmother. But she drew the line at London, fearing the docks and their wherewithal for flight. It was arranged with Aaron that David would spend two nights with them and wait for his father's return. Margaret bought him a new pair of pyjamas. It would be the first night he had spent away from home. 'Will you miss your old Mam, cariad?' she said to him.

He nodded for her sake. He was excited at the prospect of having a room of his own, of sleeping in his own bed like he used to do at the cottage. Now in the Huts he slept with Gramp, while his Gran and Mam slept on the couch in the parlour downstairs. He loved his Gramp, but sometimes when he was dozing off to sleep in Chaya-dreams and Chaya-imaginings, he wished he were alone.

His father called at the Huts early on Thursday morning and David was waiting for him at the door. He was wearing the suit that Aaron had made him and, when Leon looked at him, he noticed that he did indeed resemble a Bindel and, when he looked closer, he saw that Aaron had cut the suit in their childhood Odessa style. The thought crossed his mind that he might there and then spirit him away to Leipzig. 'Keep an eye on our boy, Leon bach,' Gramp said suddenly as he appeared at the door. 'I need another man in this house,' he laughed. That colliery chain was as sacred and as unbreakable as that of the tavern.

When they arrived at Aaron's house there was only time for lunch before leaving for the station. The whole family came to see them off. As the train drew out of the station Leon saw the lone figure of his son as he stood slightly apart from Aaron and his family. He was frantically waving one of Gramp's white Sunday handkerchiefs, and as Leon watched his small blurring figure, he knew that his Leipzig dream would remain a dream for ever.

They did not reach London till late in the evening and Leon booked into a hostelry that was well on the road to Tilbury Docks. That evening, before going to bed, Greta and Leon walked the silent cobbled streets in long and sad farewell. They exchanged promises to write to each other, to hold each other in their hearts. Such promises Leon made freely because they could be honoured. But neither mentioned his possible home-making in Leipzig. Greta too had seen David's lone figure on the Cardiff platform and knew how that figure, despite the years that would pass, would remain in Leon's eye forever that of a child.

At the docks the following morning, Greta held out her hand in more formal farewell. But Leon took her in his arms while Zelda stood to one side. Then he gathered his mother in his embrace, and kissed them both.

'It's been the happiest time I've spent in many years,' Zelda said. 'Soon we shall all be together again.'

And that phrase, that Bindel phrase though each generation, that overture to sadness, startled his ear, and confirmed that it was unlikely that he would see Greta again.

The journey back to Cardiff was endless and depressing. It was late when he arrived, but there was still time to collect David and take the last train back to the valley. He hurried to Aaron's house. As he pulled the bell, he had a premonition of something amiss and his fear was confirmed by the stern look on Aaron's face as he opened the door. 'What's the matter?' Leon said as he followed his brother into the kitchen.

David stood in the corner, white-faced, close to tears, his overcoat buttoned and his little cardboard case in his hand. He was clearly being sent away.

'What's happened?' Leon said.

'I don't want him in this house again,' Aaron said. 'You yourself are welcome, but not your son.'

'In that case,' Leon said, 'I am not welcome either.' He wanted to get that very clear before investigating the cause of David's exclusion. 'What has happened, Dovidle?' he said.

But Aaron gave him no space for reply, even if David could have made one. He came to the point straight away. 'He's been telling my Chaya stories,' Aaron said.

Leon noted the possessive. So was his Chaya, his possession, not to be touched with alien tales? 'What sort of stories?' Leon was impatient.

226

'He learns them in his scripture class, he says. You know, the usual stories. He told my Chaya that we Jews killed . . .' he hesitated then, and settled for the least incriminating name. He still had Bindel problems with that word that had stuck in his father's throat. 'He says that we Jews killed his saviour,' he said.

'Has she not heard that before?' Leon said softly.

But Aaron ignored him. 'She's in tears,' he said. 'Rachel is with her. I can't have her exposed to such damage. I was too free with my hospitality in the first place.'

Now it was all out, and Leon wondered whether he should stay to argue, whether he should plead David's youth and lack of understanding. But that would have been to apologise for his son.

'That's what our scripture teacher told us, Dad,' David whispered from his corner. 'I only said what she said.'

'Come,' Leon said. 'We have time to catch the train.' He took his son's hand. 'Goodbye, Aaron,' he said.

'You are always welcome in my house,' Aaron said.

Leon looked at him. 'I'm sorry for you, brother,' he said.

CHAPTER SIXTEEN

For many months after that unhappy meeting Zubko was extra-busy in his carrier-pigeon work. Both brothers feared that their break was final and both of them, especially Aaron, were frenzied in their messages. Thus Leon learned that his mother was well, that Chaya had passed a piano exam and, in Zubko's whispered parenthesis, that she missed David very much. He heard too that the tailoring business was profitable and that he, Leon, was always welcome in his brother's house. From the valley, information was scant. Leon said nothing about his constant correspondence with Greta, but he did convey the news that David had won a prize for his model ship and that soon he would leave school and start as a collier boy. In reply to each of Aaron's invitations, he sent his polite refusal. He missed his Sunday visits, and so, at first, did David, but Aaron's price for brotherhood was too costly.

It was a Tuesday in mid-October, Leon's day for his Cardiff buying and also David's first day in the mine. All week he'd been trying on his helmet and his overalls that Gramp had brought home from the pit-store. On that Tuesday he would relinquish his boyhood, and opt for manhood that thereafter would be imperilled with each shift and would never vary until his dying day. Leon left his cottage very early that morning because he wanted to see David before he went underground for the first time. When he reached the Huts, David was ready to go, nagging his Gramp to hurry.

'There's time, Davy bach,' Dai Davies said. 'You'll be down there soon enough. And every day of your life too, bar Sunday, and Saturday too if I get my way with the management.' Dai Davies was still optimistic about a miner's future, though in the past years he had made little headway on the wages issue, and none at all on the matter of underground safety. 'Just wait for me to fill up my jack,' he said.

The jack was the miners' metal tea-carrier. Dai's was scratched and mis-shapen from its long years' service, but David's was brand new and was stopped with a champagne cork that the man in the ironmongery shop had given him for good luck.

'Come on, Gramp,' David said again.

Leon wanted to kiss him, but what with his overalls and his jack and his helmet, he was too old for that sort of thing. So instead he grasped his shoulder. 'Good luck, son,' he said. He watched the pair of them cross the road and up to the pit-head, and he saw that Gramp took David's hand half way up the slope. It looked like a gesture of partnership, and Leon watched them out of sight then he made his way to the station.

He was early for his train so he sat on a bench and re-read the last letter he had received from Greta. She wrote of her daily life in Leipzig in the smallest detail. She had a gift for enjoyment and there was pleasure in every syllable. Everything she had done she wished to share with him. She asked him to write in similar detail of his own life in the valley and not to think that it was too ordinary or too mundane to record. Nothing's ordinary, she wrote, if it is you who experiences it. He resolved to write to her that evening after he had seen David, and tell her about his son's first day in the mine. He put the letter away and looked up at the station-clock. It read ten minutes past eight. He wondered why he did not hear the ticking as he did every time he waited for the Cardiff train. He had a strange and frightening notion that time had stopped. Then he heard the hooter and his heart froze.

He had heard it before, that sound, some years ago when the pit exploded, that premature funeral bell that tolled in rehearsal for the obsequies to come. His knees seemed to be melting. He looked back at the village and saw a column of dirt and smoke rising from the pit and in its occasional clearance in the wind he saw the pit-head winding-gear like a black cenotaph in the sky. Then he found

228

himself running with the speed of a stag fearfully seeking its imperilled young. On his way to the pit he prayed with fervour. Please God, not David. Not my David. Along the railroad tracks he was alone for a while, and then suddenly and silently, he found himself amongst a vast crowd stumbling up the slope to the pit-head with inward prayers and panting hope. Not my Dai, not my Owen, not my Evan, not my Trevor. Please God, not any of those. But could God, even that almighty Almighty, exclude them all? He was nearing the Huts now, and what he saw appalled him. They in no way resembled the buildings he had left only a short while ago. For what had been Dai Davies' dwelling was now a mass of rubble together with the Huts on each side, wrecked by the blast of the explosion. Thank God David was out of there, Leon heard himself say, but then he realised what other hell David had left them for. He realised that somewhere, underneath that heap of stones and steel armature, lay the woman for whom he had left his tribe. Her mother too, since both of them were still abed when he had called to say goodbye to his son. Not goodbye, he screamed to himself and he hurried up the slope to the pit-head.

The whole village was assembled there, mostly women and children. Those men who were there were old and coughing and had seen it all before. Other men, those who had shortly before come off the night-shift, had risen from their day-beds to go down once again in the hope of rescue. Three ambulances pulled up at the foot of the slope and waited. Back in the village Jones the undertaker went into his timber-yard behind his house, and silently took stock.

They whispered around the pit-head, as if the lives of their men depended on their silence. The black and red uniforms of the Salvation Army filtered amongst them, but for the most part they were given a wide berth. It was too soon for their kind of comfort. Much too soon. There was still everything to hope for.

The first cage of men went down. In it Leon recognised the pit-manager, Edward Shaw, whom he had once seen at a meeting. It can't be that bad, he hoped, if the boss is going down. He wouldn't put himself in any danger. The others took the same hope from the sight of him, and slowly they began to talk to neighbours and share with them all their sudden illogical and desperate reasons why all would be well. Leon looked down the slope at the Huts. A crowd of men were attempting to clear the wreckage. He felt he should go down and help them, but his heart was pinned to the pit-head, where at least there was still some hope of life. Down there amongst the Huts all hope had already been abandoned.

They waited.

When, some time later, Mr Shaw emerged from the cage and

made his way to his offices, nobody approached him. Nobody wanted to know the state of affairs underground or how the rescue work was progressing. They wanted to cling to their hopes. Nothing on earth could crush their hopes, no word of caution from any management, no premature comfort from the Salvation Army. They would hold these hopes in their hearts, if necessary day after day of their waiting and only the sight of the lifeless bodies of their men and sons would shatter them.

It was early in the afternoon when the first bodies were brought up from underground. The women waited, their feet itching to run to the stretchers, yet fixed by fear to the ground. Leon hovered. He did not have a woman's fortitude. He moved trembling and on tip-toe to the stretchers. The bodies were long, too long for children, and he uttered a shameful cry of relief.

'I'll go home and tell his wife,' he heard one of the rescuers say. Then the man saw her in the crowd, and hung back for the blame she would heap on him as news-bearer.

'I'll come with you,' another said.

Leon saw them walk like mourners through the crowd. Then they stopped before a young woman, a baby in her arms. They said nothing to her for she knew what they had to say. Then a Salvation Army woman took her hand, and offered her comfort, which she now accepted because it was in season. She took her down the slope and back to her man-less home.

They brought up forty more bodies that day, and with the appearance of each sorry batch, Leon tip-toed to the cage, his heart bursting. As night fell, rumour spread that there were fires below, unreachable, unquenchable. The west district of the mine was the worst. There all ventilation was blocked. There was little hope of any survivors from that quarter. The women didn't know where in the mine their men worked. Underground was underground and all of it was dangerous. Now they did not care to enquire of the management where their men were stationed. Death could not be muted by its location. Only a little bit dead your son, Mrs Evans. Not much suffocated your husband, Mrs Williams. Whether in the west quarter, east, north or south, death was a word that could not be gently spoken. When night fell, a woman's cry of 'Murder' rang through the crowd for word had spread that the explosion had been caused by gas from a naked light., That in itself could have been controlled, but the fires were fed by the coal-dust, that ominous word that had for years been on the tip of Gilbert Whitcombe's tongue, a tongue that probably now lay shrivelled and charred in the dust.

'Murder,' the woman screamed, but few took up her cry for they clung to hope still and her accusation was unseasonal. A Salvation

Army woman comforted her and gave her a cup of tea, as if that would solve everything.

The crowd thinned out as night fell. Women took their children home, numb with despair. Leon stayed and would stay there until David came to the surface. He had nothing to go home for, not yet. He prayed incessantly. He prayed first for God to forgive him, to forgive his desertion, and his neglect. He needed to be pardoned for that, before he could ask for His favours. With this thought, a bile of guilt rose in his throat, that if David died it was God's punishment for his own heresy. He waited and he prayed. His legs began to ache with fatigue and he realised he'd been standing all day. He made for a bench further up the slope, and as he sat down a cramp shot from his ankle to his calf. He stretched his leg, then relaxed, and almost immediately fell into a sleep. He was woken by a gentle tap on his shoulder.

'What's happened?' he cried, his waking thought on his son. Had they come to tell him that he need wait no longer? It was still dark. He had slept only a little while and he peered at the Salvation Army lady who stood by his side, a bowl of soup in her hand.

'Have some soup,' she said. 'It will warm you.'

He could have blessed her for having no news to give him. He took the soup and realised that he'd had nothing to eat all day.

'I'll bring you a ham sandwich,' the woman said.

'No,' Leon almost shouted. Not that. Never in his life had he touched the meat of the pig. His desertion had not included that. If Margaret had wanted to eat it, she would go to Gran and Gramp's, but she would never bring it into the cottage. Then he remembered Margaret, and chiding himself for his negligence, he hurriedly drank his soup and went down the slope to the Huts. The wreckage was almost clear. A few men, working by the light of miners' lamps, were boarding up windows and doors. When Leon approached the light, they recognised him, and he them, for they were customers. Jenkins, who was the village blacksmith, was the only one who could look him in the eye. 'She's gone, Mr Bindel,' he said gently. He didn't know how to call her. She hadn't been his proper wife for a long time. 'She's gone,' he said again. 'Her and her Mam. Six of them died in these Huts.'

'Where are they?' Leon said.

'In the funeral parlour on the hill. Nice and tidy. Couldn't have felt a thing. In bed they were. It was all sudden like.'

'Thank you,' Leon said and he moved away. He wondered whether he should make arrangements for their funeral. But quickly he dismissed the thought. It was a husband's job to bury his wife, a father's job to bury his daughter. When Dai Davies came up from the pit, he would break the news gently and he would hold

David in his arms and tell him about his mother. Though Leon had a deep affection for both women, his eyes remained dry and he was glad of it, because in this moment of his waiting agony, he did not trust his tears. He returned to his bench and accepted the cup of tea that was brought to him. Then he dozed fitfully until morning light.

Over the next hour, the women of the village came to the hill and so began the second day's vigil. It began with hope. Four survivors stumbled out of the cage. They were black with smoke and coal and fear, and their cold unbelieving eyes, strained by the sudden light, told of the hell they had seen below. Some women rushed to greet them, and some plied them with questions. But they were silent, all of them. What they had to say was untellable. Leon watched them as they emerged. They were all too large for children. Later that morning the reporters from the South Wales press converged on the pit-head. They were seen to go straight to the management. Then after a while they mingled with the waiting crowd, taking names which many were loathe to give, but finally offered them in return for information they had gleaned from the invisible and silent administration.

The fires were still raging. That fact was evidenced by the appearance of fire-engines and firemen who had come from all over the valley. Ventilation to the west district of the mine was still blocked. Much rubble had been cleared. There was still hope of survivors. And so the day passed. Many bodies were brought up that day, and in several shifts. No one of the crowd counted, for each of them was counting for her own, a husband, a father, a son, a brother, or sometimes all of them, for mining in the valley was a family pursuit. But rumour had it that over a hundred bodies came up that day, many of them charred beyond recognition. As the earth gave up its toll, Leon tip-toed towards the cages, and gauged the measure of each body for childhood. There were many boys amongst the dead that day, and some of them unrecognisable. He wondered whether he should go to the manager's office. But he was afraid. He would sooner wait and hope. During the day an official approached a board in front of the pit-head and pinned on it a large notice. Then he walked shamefully away. The crowd stared at it. They knew what it was, and they did not want to see it. At least not publicly, because their possible grief was private. But Leon was drawn towards the board with the same force that pinned his feet to the ground. He rubbed his hands over his face and felt the stubble around the chin. He remembered the Odessa ghetto then, and the sudden stubble on men's faces when they were in mourning and that thought prompted his first tears. Almost blindly he crept his way to the notice-board.

The names of the dead were in alphabetical order. So he did not have far to scan for Bindel. It was clearly not there, but he did not trust its absence. Perhaps Margaret had registered him as Davies. A little further down, the Davieses began. About twenty of them for it was a common name in the valley. There were two David Davieses and either of them could have applied to his son or Gramp, and Leon's heart froze. He looked quickly at the addresses in the opposite column, but both David Davieses lived in Stanley Street. Then he scanned the address column. Only one lived in the Huts. He looked at the name. Morgan Jones, the tenor in the Male Voice Choir. He turned away, the tears flowing freely now, and he did nothing to restrain them. He went back to his bench and he waited. More men were brought up that day, and a few of them were alive. Those who could walk were fortified by soup and tea, and besieged by reporters. But none of them wanted to speak. For their own reasons they had joined the conspiracy of silence that covered the subject of events underground. Their reasons were not those of the management, whose silence alibied the long history of their negligence. The rescued men held a survivor's reticence, that silence of embarrassment and shame. They took their women's proffered arms and made their ways home. But none of them, either of the dead or the living, were Dai Davies or David Bindel.

Leon waited. He would not leave the pit-head. The waiting women came and went, for they had children to see to, meals to serve, brass to polish, door-steps to scrub. Somehow or other, life had to continue. As they left, some burdened Leon with their waiting. 'Keep your eyes open for my Morgan, my Trevor, my Gwylim,' and he felt he was keeping vigil for them all. The Salvation Army lady kept a special eye on Leon. She plied him with soups and teas. Over the last few days she had learned his history, and once she had sat by him on the bench and offered up a special prayer for his son. The Almighty listens to all of us, she had said, and Leon had thanked her, hoping that his prayers and hers would not lead God into confusion.

On the third day, Mr Shaw finally made an appearance. He stood on crates of orange-boxes which the colliers had hurriedly erected in front of the notice-board, and as he mounted the wooden platform, the women surged towards him. He had news, and they could no longer postpone its hearing.

Leon moved with them, taking the arms of two women to help them up the slope. It was the third day and they were still dry-eyed, and no dire managerial predictions would release their tears. They looked angry, defiant and unafraid of the unease on Mr Shaw's face.

'I have to tell you,' he said, without any preamble, 'that the prospect of any more survivors is very dim. The fires are still smouldering underground, and those districts that are accessible have already been cleared. We are doing our very best to tunnel through to the west quarter, and to unblock the ventilation areas, but we cannot any longer hope that anyone trapped in that quarter is still alive. I'm very sorry.'

He stepped down quickly from the make-shift platform and made for his office as if he feared a lynching. Still they waited there, as if they had not heard one syllable of what he had said. After a while they heard the creaking of a cage, and they drew back, fearful of its cargo. They waited until the cage bar was lifted, and out of it two rescuers led a horse. It was unsteady on its legs and had to be urged along. It neighed a little, disgustingly alive.

'The horses live,' a woman shouted. 'Men come cheap.' She rushed to the poor animal and pounded it with her fists, until a Salvation Army woman restrained her, and led her to the eternal tea-urn. Later on that day, they brought up more bodies and at night-fall an extra list was pinned on the board. Leon made his weary trembling way towards it, peering in the light of the miners' lamps for the Bindel name. His finger trembled over the Davieses, but none of them lived in the Huts. There was still hope, he decided. He went back to his bench and he waited.

Night and day he stayed there, as the stubble on his chin grew bearded and the lists on the notice-board multiplied. On the seventh day, he looked down over the valley and it was black with funeral. The women had begun to bury their dead. That day, the bodies of another eighty men and boys were brought to the surface, but no Bindel appeared on the lists, and no Dai Davies either. They were sticking together, old Gramp and little Dovidle, Leon thought. They would look after each other and emerge alive. Then he began to wonder how he would break to them the news that Gran and Margaret were dead. He would take them home first, he decided, back to his cottage, and he would make them sleep the day away. He wondered whether there were clean sheets in the linen cupboard and what was in the larder for them to eat. He would go shopping while they were sleeping, he decided, he might even buy a bottle of wine to celebrate their return. Then when they had toasted their survival, he would gently break the news. He did not allow that they would ask for their kin before the celebrations. That would not be the time for questioning. Everything had its own order. Then he recalled his father's story of the milk-brothers' miraculous return from the dead. And how Reuben Bindel had not waited for the celebrations to be over, before he had asked for his father. Some people simply did not know the right order of things, Leon thought, and he wiped his forehead which was feverish with his fantasy. All day he sat there waiting, while his fever grew and his nerve-ends trembled, and anxiety and hopelessness gradually overwhelmed him.

When he woke up on his bench on the morning of the eighth day, it was already late, and he heard the noon chimes from the church bell in the valley. He had slept overlong and he chided himself. He had to go shopping. He had to put clean sheets on the bed. There was so much to do. The fever was still on him, and he shivered in its delirium. Another notice had been put up on the board while he was sleeping. He trembled at the silence about him. His eyes were still half-closed and he had the impression that he was alone, and when he opened them wide he saw that the pit-head was almost deserted. Even the Salvation Army had left with their tea-urn, and it was the final proof to Leon that all hope had been abandoned. He tip-toed across the slope to the notice-board, his trembling finger Bindel-seeking. Nothing. Nothing of Davies of the Huts either. A rider was appended to the latest bulletin. It announced a tally of four hundred and six bodies of men and boys recovered. Thirty-three bodies of men and boys were buried underground in the west wing and could not be retrieved. All rescue attempts had been abandoned. A list of their names was appended. But that list Leon refused to read.

He would not believe it. He returned to his bench and he waited. And there he sat, most of the day, looking at the motionless winding-gear of the pit, and the occasional collier who passed by in the gloom. Late in the afternoon, one of them approached him. 'Mr Bindel?' he said sadly.

Leon nodded.

'I'm sorry about your boy,' he said. 'I was down there. They were in the west quarter. Him and his Gramp. Other men from the Huts too. They didn't have a chance.' He put his hand in his pocket and thrust something into Leon's hand. 'We joked about it,' he said, 'when we were going down in the cage. I found it in the rubble on the west side.'

Leon opened his palm. On it lay the champagne-cork that had stopped up David's tea-jack. Then he knew the truth of it all.

'My David's dead,' he said to the man. 'And buried.'

He would wait no longer. He clutched the cork and made his way down the slope. He felt the fever leaving him, but his eyes were still dry. He knew he must busy himself and drive his raging body about the valley until it calmed itself. He went to the funeral parlour in the village, and made his dry-eyed arrangements for the funerals of Gran and Margaret. Then, still raging, he walked to the bluebell woods tramping his feet on the ground where they grew, ensuring that they would never never never grow there again. Slowly his rage was spent and he returned to his cottage on the hill. He denuded the parlour table of its cloth and its flowers and he placed the champagne-cork central on the wood like a naked shrine. Then he took sheets and cloths from the cupboard and covered the mirrors and the pictures on the walls. Then, because he had no low stool, he sat on the floor and offered himself to God's solace. Thus in the Jewish tradition, he began his seven days' mourning for his uncircumcised son. In the act of placing himself in God's hands, the tears flowed freely and his fever abated. All night he sat, dozing from time to time, and in his waking moments murmuring the *Kadish*, embracing all the lost of the valley in his prayer. When morning came, he looked up and saw the figure of his brother in the doorway. Aaron came towards him, and gave him the traditional Jewish greeting to one who is bereaved. 'I wish you long life,' he said. It was an order to survive at whatever painful cost. Then he crouched down by his brother's side, and took him in his arms. Then Aaron broke completely and he sat on the floor by his brother's side, and shared the days of his mourning.

During that week, Zubko came from time to time and even Pavel made the journey to the valley, and they recited the *Kadish* together. Women came too, many of them greenly windowed. They shared their own mourning with Leon. They thought his ways were strange, with the sheets on the walls and him, a grown man, suddenly bearded, sitting on the floor like a child. And his brother too, whom they had never seen before, doing likewise. They saw the champagne-cork on the table, and all of them knew its meaning, for the story had spread around the valley. But they were different from Leon Bindel. They had had the relief of burying their men and their sons. There were graves they could visit, and the good earth for flowers, stations of remembrance. But David Bindel was buried without ceremony, with no hymn, with no prayer. Leon Bindel had nothing that proved anything except a gnawing pain in his heart that would never cease.

For seven days Leon sat there, and on the eighth day he rose.

'We shall go home,' Aaron said, though he knew it was a meaningless term for his brother. For home is with one's kin, and a child is the closest kin of all. Leon picked up the champagne-cork, then went to his room and filled his suitcase with his few possessions. Then he and his brother left the cottage, closing the ever-open door behind them. He stood on the threshold and took one last and longing look at the valley, that site of his painful rebellion. His eyes wandered over the dips and the climbs of the dales, but he did not look towards the woods. Then he closed his eyes as if to gather all his visual strength to imprint for ever on his eye, his son's memorial. He turned towards the pit-head and opened his eyes. He stared at it for a long time, then he turned and let his brother take his arm and lead him to the station.

CHAPTER SEVENTEEN

Some years before, when he was alive, Barak had told Aaron that Leon would return to his mother when he had found his own happiness. Barak had been wrong. It was tragedy that drove Leon home. He had made his sad peace with his tribe. He went to Leipzig because it was a way of returning to his father's house, and to the mother who had never left it. He needed to see her. Unlike Aaron, she had accepted his son with understanding and without reservation and now only she could comfort him. He stayed only a few days with Aaron, then he left for Leipzig. His brother took him to the station. 'You're still young, brother,' he said to him. 'You will marry again and have children.'

Leon nodded without a word. He means well, he tried to think, though his brother's advice was untimely. But Aaron was not one who could deal with another's grief. His own pain he could endure, as Leon remembered when their father had died in the fire. It was his mother's and his brother's heartbreak that he could not bear. It irritated him because it threatened him with disintegration.

'Come and see us soon,' Aaron said, as the train was drawing out of the station. But not too soon, he hoped, not until Leon had recovered from a grief that his brother did not have the courage to face. For it was he who had turned David out of his home and, for that rejection, he felt painfully unentitled to the relief of mourning.

Some wounds do not heal, even given an eternity. The scars they leave are permanent and can only be accommodated into the sad fabric of one's future. Over the years that passed, Leon responded to such partial healing, and two years after his arrival in Leipzig, to his mother's boundless joy, and his own sense of sad inevitability, he married Greta. Their first child, a boy, was born a year later, and was called, from the moment of his known conception, by the name of David. Two years later, a second son was born and, by the same unspoken understanding, was named Benjamin. It was an affirmation of sorts, an act of atonement that would once and for all settle the differences between Leon and his compelling tribe.

The years passed. Once during that time, Zelda and Leon made a visit to Cardiff, leaving Greta behind with the children. There were many visitors to Aaron's house, amongst them Victor Zubko, the brothers' erstwhile go-between, to whom Leon had bequeathed what was left of his Senghenydd drapery round. He came with a mouthful of news from the valley, but Leon wanted none of it. There was no news Victor could bring of the valley's dead, and he had no interest in those who had survived. He declined Victor's well-meaning invitation to accompany him back to the valley. David's tomb was forever in his mind's eye, an image that needed no nurturing. Though Aaron's welcome was lavish and unstinting, Leon was not at ease with him. Despite their reconciliation, Leon was ever mindful of its terrible cost. But what depressed him most was Chaya, and the sight of Chaya growing. David would have been about her age now, almost twenty, and each time he looked at her, he had to invoke God's blessing on her life, for he feared the evil eye in his heart. He was glad when they returned to Leipzig. He decided that many years would have to pass before he could meet with his brother again.

Events enforced his decision. A year after that visit marked the beginning of the first Great War. Aaron, for the first time since Chaya's birth, considered himself blessed that he had no sons. And in enemy country Leon rejoiced in his son's young years and he thought of his first David who, had he lived, would at this time be again imperilled. But there was little comfort in that. But the thought that he and his brother had now by law been declared enemies, gave him a strange satisfaction, for it legitimised his frayed fraternal feelings.

Apart from the general restrictions that war imposes on its civilians, neither Leon nor Aaron were greatly inconvenienced by the hostilities. On the contrary. Both brothers prospered. Leon's fur business was turned over to the making of army coats for the winter campaigns. Aaron too had obtained a similar government concession in American officers' uniforms.

By that time, Chaya had qualified as a teacher. Her growing had not been easy. After David's death, she had slowly become estranged from her father. She became rebellious. She joined the Women's Suffrage movement. She actually took part in sabotage, being part of a group that was engaged in cutting telephone wires. For this offence she was sent to prison for two months, during which time Aaron kept himself indoors and resigned from all his community positions, so great was his shame. But he did not complain. He considered it as part of his atonement. After Chaya's release, the school re-instated her on condition that she played no more part in politics. This she agreed to do. She had made her point, and the beaten look in her father's eye confirmed it. Aaron heartily wished her married and off his hands. But Chaya was headstrong and independent, and few men could match her intelligence. When war had broken out, she was already at marriageable age, yet despite her beauty and her expected dowry, men were frightened of her. In their parochial orthodox eyes, her prison sentence had left a faintly whorish stain on her. Sometimes Aaron feared that she might marry out, and that thought drove him to distraction. Rachel understood her daughter better than her husband, and was secretly very proud of her rebellion. But such pleasure she had to conceal from Aaron, and Chaya found herself in a limbo between their conflicting loyalties. She was not a happy girl.

One day, she was coming back from school, dawdling as was her wont, for she was never eager to reach home. Her relationship with her father was strained and silent and she avoided him as much as possible. Meal-times were the worst, when confrontation was unavoidable. Her father's looks were a mixture of anger and despair, and her mother's verged on pity. Both feared for her future, but neither so much as she herself. Almost all her friends were already married and, though she had little time for their husbands, she envied them their married state. But not for the security that it offered, or the children that it allowed. She envied them because they had been able to leave home. That, for Chaya, was an over-riding ambition, and she knew that her only escape-route was through marriage. But where could she find a husband? She had long since given up her dreams of an ideal partner, considering him now the stuff of fantasy, and she was beginning to accept that, with certain reservations, almost any man would do. It would be the most supreme betrayal of all her principles. But what use principles, she thought, if they could find such little expression in the stifling confines of her home. Yes, anyone will do, she decided, and the decision cheered her a little, and she quickened her pace, humming softly to herself. She saw a young man approach. He was wearing an American Naval uniform and he was looking about him as if he were lost. He walked slowly, occasionally stopping to study a piece of paper in his hand. Chaya had time to appraise him. In the light of her recent decision, she imagined that he would be suitable enough. If he was nothing else, he was certainly very handsome. She thought she might smile at him but, despite her rebellious nature, Chaya was a shy girl, and deeply conventional. She lowered her eyes as he approached, and she was startled when he stopped to speak to her. She felt herself blushing at her previous thoughts, and she wished that he would go away.

'Excuse me,' he said, 'but I'm a stranger here. D'you know where I can find this address?' He handed her the piece of paper. She did not look at it straightaway. She was still too surprised by the encounter. She was sorry that he had stopped speaking, for his accent attracted her with its promise of a thousand miles from home. He smiled at her, embarrassed by her lack of response. Then

239

she was forced to look down at the paper, and what she saw there only served to make her blush again. She felt her heart racing.

'It's where I live,' she said to the paper.

'Is your father the tailor?' he asked.

She nodded.

'And are you going home?'

She nodded again, and started walking.

'May I come with you?' he asked, walking by her side.

'If you like,' she said. She hoped he did not notice the spring in her step or the infuriating blush that burned her cheeks.

'You're the first Welsh girl I've talked to,' he was saying. 'Are they all as shy as you?'

She did not answer.

'Not so fast,' he said. 'I can hardly keep up with you.'

She felt two of his fingers on her elbow, and her skin seared beneath his touch. She slowed her pace and he dropped his hand.

'What's your name?' he said.

'Chaya.'

'My name's Saul. Saul Weinberger.'

What a relief that name would be to her father, Chaya thought. Her house was now in view and she hurried once again. 'This is where I live,' she called back at him.

He ran, laughing, and joined her at the door. She pulled the door-bell and hoped that her mother would answer. And when Rachel did, she caught the radiance on her daughter's face and welcomed the stranger into her house. 'My husband's with a customer,' she said, assuming from his uniform that he had come as a client. And then for Chaya's sake, she added, 'Won't you have a cup of tea while you're waiting?'

'I'll make it,' Chaya said quickly. She wanted to leave her mother alone with him. She needed to know the answer to so many questions which, if she were to ask them herself, would seem brash and forward. Where did he come from? Was he on leave? Would he be going away soon? And would he ever come back? She could leave such queries to her mother. She took her time preparing the tea, then she carried the tray into the living-room. 'A lawyer?' her mother was saying. 'And will you follow in your father's footsteps?'

He rose, seeing Chaya enter the room, and helped her with the tray. 'Probably,' he said. 'I'm interested in law. But the war has to be over first.'

'Are you on leave?' Rachel asked.

'Just a few days,' Saul said, 'and then I go on manoeuvres for a month. Which is why I hope for a fitting before I go.'

'I'm sure my husband will find time for you,' Rachel said.

They had barely started their tea before Chaya heard the front-door close on her father's customer. She'd hoped he would have been delayed much longer. But he came into the sitting-room and joined them for tea. Saul told him how he had met his daughter in the street and the happy coincidence of her address. Aaron tried to hide his pleasure, so he appeared over-business-like and asked his prospective customer how he could help him.

'I need an extra uniform, just like this one,' he said. 'I leave at the end of the week. Then I shall be back in a month.'

'In a month a fitting will be ready,' Aaron said. 'Then it will be finished in a few days.'

'I'm much obliged,' Saul said. 'You have been highly recommended.'

Aaron actually blushed with pleasure. He was always delighted when his work was praised, and especially in front of his daughter, whose respect seemed so hard to win. He rose as a signal that he was ready to begin. 'Would you come upstairs?' he said.

Saul rose, then hesitated, then addressed himself to Rachel. 'There's a small gathering at the Jewish servicemen's club tomorrow night. It will be over quite early,' he assured them. 'May I take Chaya with me,' he asked, 'if she is willing?'

'Of course,' Rachel said, without needing to look at her daughter.

He turned to Chaya. 'Then I'll call for you at six o'clock,' he said.

And so the courtship of Chaya and Saul began. Chaya was at first diffident. She did not wholly trust her feelings. She felt very close to Saul and she questioned the ease with which she was beginning to love him. Before meeting him, she would have settled for much less. Much less than his tenderness, his humour, his intelligence. It seemed like a miracle that he should have happened to her at all. So at first she was wary. But Saul was patient. During his first month on manoeuvres, she missed him terribly, and when he returned, she accepted in her heart that she loved him. Thereafter, he was often away on duty, and his leaves were few. This heightened the tenor of their wooing. The eternal fear of his non-return and the relief of his re-appearance, gave an artificial colouring to their relationship. It was one of extremes and Saul often feared that it might collapse under the strain. He decided to put it on a surer footing. He asked her to marry him as soon as the war was over.

For Chaya, the proposal was an overwhelming relief, for sometimes she dreaded the end of hostilities.

'I shall talk to your parents,' Saul said.

'Where shall we live?'

'In America of course.'

'I'll miss them,' she said, and meant it. But it pleased her nonetheless, for she realised that through her own happiness she had learned to forgive her father.

*

The following year the armistice was signed, and shortly afterwards, the first letter for many years came from Zelda, crossing one that had been sent by Aaron. Zelda wrote that they had suffered little in the war years except for that lack of contact with those she loved. She expressed a wish to visit them very soon. Leon and Greta were well, she added and the two young boys flourished. *It is strange,* she wrote, *but it is young David who looks so like Benjamin Bindel.*

Aaron's letter told her of Chaya's impending marriage with an invitation to them all to share in the celebrations. Zelda was delighted. She was now in her seventy-fifth year, and though she was still sprightly, she knew that this would possibly be her last journey to England. Aaron might well go to America to be near his daughter, so her wedding was perhaps the last possibility of a family reunion. She began to pack on the receipt of Aaron's letter. She was anxious too for the reunion of her sons. She knew that between Aaron and Leon there existed an uneasy no-man's land, a land of cross-fire, unprotected by law or morality. Aaron, as the accused, was trapped in that land, and there he would remain until Leon, with his pardon, would give him free passage. She urged Leon to make arrangements for the journey while she busied herself with her own preparations. But as the days passed, she noticed that Leon made no move.

'I'll do it tomorrow,' he kept saying, when asked about train tickets and boat reservations, arrangements at the store, and permission for the children to take time from school.

'It's only a week to the wedding,' Zelda said one evening at supper. 'When *are* you going to get the tickets, Leon?'

'I'll do it tomorrow.'

'You've been saying that every day,' Zelda said.

Leon rose from the table. 'I'm not hungry,' he said, and he left the room.

'He doesn't really want to go,' Greta said after a while.

'I know,' Zelda said. 'But can't you persuade him?'

'I wouldn't try,' Greta said. 'It's his own decision.'

In his bedroom Leon looked at the empty suitcase that Greta had placed at the foot of the bed. It was her gesture of non-interference and he was grateful for it. For in truth he was reluctant to go to the wedding. It wasn't because of Aaron. He had forgiven him in so far as that was possible, but he did not feel close to him. He could not understand his bigotry or his intolerance. Now, after his 15-year rebellion, he felt himself to be far more Jewish than Aaron, but in the old tradition of his father and Grandpa Jakob. His reluctance for the journey was related to Chaya. Chaya's growth. Every time a letter came from Aaron, Zelda would read it aloud at the breakfast table, and at each Chaya item, Leon would stop up his ears. Her growth was a confirmation of each one of David's lost years and, against all his innate goodness, he could not help but resent her sheer existence. He was glad that she was soon to be married and go to America. It was unlikely that he would ever have to set eyes on her again. He hated himself for such a thought, for Chaya was innocent. He did not know what to do. He did not trust himself. He did not trust his anger or his tears, for, despite his happy marriage with Greta and the delight that he found in his sons, the memory of his first David, that child of his revolt, was at times as painful and as nagging as it had ever been. Perhaps if he had been able to bury his body, he could in time, have overcome his grief. But the lack of a body made the death a non-event, as immaterial as his own rebellion. He had to find some way of burying David in his own heart. Then he realised that his only chance lay in a return visit to his memorial. He began to pack. He would go back to Senghenydd, and on his way, he would attend Chaya's wedding.

And so they made that familiar journey from Hamburg to Tilbury once more. Familiar to them all, that is, except to David and Benjamin who had never been on the sea before. They were very excited and, once on board, Greta and Leon gave them free range to wander at will. Leon watched their wonder. Both of them looked like Bindels, and he was glad that his first David had resembled Margaret. For the first time in many years, he thought about her. He had no difficulty in recalling her features, and he was glad of that, because his long neglect of her memory troubled him. He had loved her in his way at that time. Now he knew in hindsight that his manner and his season was then out of joint. But Margaret was blameless of all that. He would go to her grave too, he decided, and was astonished at the sudden relief in his heart. He went and joined his sons and walked with them over the deck. Zelda watched them from the rail. Leon was talking to them, and she presumed that he was telling them the story of how he had missed the boat from Hamburg so many years ago. Now would have been its time and its place. But she was wrong. Most certainly it had crossed Leon's mind to tell them that story, but he had decided against it. For it was a story that could not be told in a vacuum. It had to be told in the context of the whole Bindel history, and that story he was reluctant to relate. Although it was his son's inheritance he was loathe to bequeath it. Once already in his life as a father, he had assigned the burden of the Bindel history. Already he had bequeathed the survival legacy, which sadly turned out to be so ironically futile. He was wary of repeating such a bequest. So instead he told them all that he could remember of their cousin Chaya whom his sons would be meeting for the first time, in much the same way as he had told his first David as they travelled together from the valley. He remembered how the boy had fiddled with his Sunday chapel suit, forever straightening his tie and smoothing his hair, and how Leon knew at the time, that, no matter how clean and proper his son appeared, he could never be clean and proper enough for Aaron. Now his sons, his rough-and-tumble David and Benjamin, with no care for their appearance and no fear of rejection would, in their pure Bindeldom, be wholly accepted in his brother's house. I must not feel bitter, Leon told himself. His brother had been punished enough. So he told his sons what he remembered about Chaya, and it all concerned her life as a child, for he could not countenance her adulthood.

Aaron was waiting for them at Cardiff station. It was a joyful reunion. He especially welcomed David and Benjamin, giving them his exclusive attention on the way home, and since they had no common language, their exchange involved much mime and gesture. Aaron did his inhibited best.

'It's good to see you,' Aaron said. 'You don't know how happy I am that you came.'

Leon nodded. 'You must be very busy,' he said.

'I have been,' Aaron laughed. 'Everyone wanted a new suit for my Chaya's wedding. But now all is ready.'

He still possesses her, Leon thought. Aaron had learned nothing.

*

Leon left on the first train early the following morning, and as the train drew into the valley, he sensed the excitement of one who, after a long absence, was going home. He had expected the sight of the valley to fill him with gloom, but his feelings were quite otherwise. As he got down from the train at the Senghenydd platform, he looked up at the station clock. It showed ten minutes past eight, a time deeply grooved in his memory. At first Leon thought that the clock had stopped, and out of respect had never ticked again since the pit explosion. Then Leon checked on his own watch and saw that the station clock was functioning. The hour it showed did not depress him. He considered that it timed the ripeness of his return.

He made his way to the pit-head. It had been fourteen years since he had last seen the valley, and he did not recognise the few faces that passed him in the street and no one seemed to recognise him. He was glad of that for he had not come on social business. He

244

had two calls to make, two accounts to settle in his heart. He made for the pit-head. From a distance he could see that the winding-gear was still, and he wondered whether the day was a holiday. As he approached the slope, he noticed that where the Huts had once stood was now a playing-field. The slope of the pit-head was covered with grass, and Leon's heart faltered as he caught sight of a clutch of bluebells. Grass grew even where once the manager's quarters had been sited, and it was clear to Leon that it was not a working-mine any more. The bench was still there, where, for over a week, he had trembled and waited. He went towards it and sat down in the silence and stared at the pit-head. He was glad that it was closed, that no man went down to tread on that burial ground. The silence around him, the grass, the occasional flowers, the head-stone of winding-gear, were all attendants at a graveyard. The pit was closed, as closed as a grave could ever be, and he was glad of it. He walked up to the pit-head and stood at the foot of the winding-gear. There he recited the *Kadish* and for the first time since David had died, he buried him, and was able to honour his grave. He stood there for a while, and looked towards the valley. He followed the paths he had trod years ago, burdened with parcels and fears for his living. His eyes wandered to the head of the valley, and he dared to look at the bluebell woods, that futile schoolroom, where his dead son had learned his lesson in survival. He walked down the pit-head slope, picking bluebells from the grass, and he made his way to the little cemetery on the hill, for he had to bury Margaret too. He wandered round the churchyard noting how many hundreds of head-stones bore the same death-date. *Died in the explosion*, was the epitaph of them all. It took him some time to find Margaret's grave. She was lying beside her mother, and both with the same epitaph. He crouched on the ground and laid the bluebells between them. The champagne-cork, which had stopped David's tea-jack, was always in Leon's pocket, wherever he went. Now he took it out and consigned it to where it belonged. With his fingers he dug a gentle hole in Margaret's grave, and put the cork inside. It was his final act of burial. Then he stood up, caressed the head-stone with his hand, and turned away.

As he walked along the adjacent path, his eyes caught a small black head-stone. It was graveless, and stood there as a memorial. Its legend astonished him, and he read it aloud. *'In memory of David Bindel, aged 14, son of Leon and Margaret Bindel. And of his Gramp, David Davies. Both killed in the explosion. 1913.'*

Leon stared at it for a long time, reading its epitaph over and over again. He wondered who could have put it there, and he could only conclude that it was Pavel or Victor Zubko, who had executed their messenger service to the last. He was overwhelmed with gratitude and now he was anxious to get back to Cardiff, to meet them and to thank them and to tell them of the peace that he had found.

When he reached Senghenydd station, he stood on the platform and turned to take a long last look at the valley, and he knew that he would never have to visit it again.

When he reached Aaron's house they were all busy with preparations for a pre-wedding supper. Rachel was in the kitchen and he offered to give her a hand. Quickly she found him something to busy himself with. They did not talk till suddenly Leon said, 'Are Pavel and Zubko coming this evening?'

'Of course,' she said. 'They both look forward to seeing you.'

'And I them,' Leon said. 'Very much.'

'Has Senghenydd changed?' She broached the subject gently.

'Not much,' he said. 'The pit is closed.'

'Did you go to the little cemetery on the hill?' she asked.

He looked at her, and she was smiling.

'Did you see it?' she asked.

Then he knew that it was neither Pavel nor Zubko who had placed that memorial. 'Aaron?' he said softly.

She nodded.

Once again in his mind he read the epitaph which he now knew by heart. In it, Aaron had at last acknowledged his brother's marriage, and, moreover, with '*Gramp*', David's lineage. He could have done no more. He left the kitchen and went to find his brother. Aaron was alone in the dining-room arranging chairs. He went to him and embraced him. 'Thank you, Aaron,' he said. 'You have helped me to bury him.'

That night, at the party, Leon was able to talk to Chaya for the first time.

In the Cardiff Jewish community, Chaya Bindel's nuptials were the event of the year, and when they were over, Chaya and Saul left for their new home in America. Leon stayed on with his family for a week and it was clear that, when they left, his brother would be very lonely. Zelda sensed it, too, and she declared that she would like to stay in Cardiff for a while. Perhaps Aaron would make her a new coat, and she and Rachel could spend some time together. Aaron was grateful for her offer, and they both enjoined her to stay as long as she wished.

At the end of that week, Aaron took Leon and the little boys to the station.

'Do you think of going to settle in America?' Leon asked.

'I don't know,' Aaron said. 'We shall miss her of course, but I think the Bindels have wandered enough. It's a pity that we are all so far apart.'

But that's the accident of Jewish history, Leon thought. Chaya was in America only because Saul Weinberg's father had found an honest ticket-merchant at the Hamburg docks. Aaron was in Wales, only because one night Pavel had dropped into Zemach's tavern in Odessa. He himself was in Germany simply because Barak had encountered a dishonest salesman. Their locations were all accidents of history.

'Will you stay in Germany?' Aaron asked.

'It's my home, my accidental home,' Leon said. 'Like Wales is yours.'

'And your children?'

Leon bundled the two boys onto the train. Then he embraced his brother.

'Don't worry, Aaron,' Leon said. 'We shall survive.'

That age-long chorus.

Then he, too, boarded the train. He held his children's hands. Thus David and Benjamin Bindel, of the fourth of the generations of Bindels from the Ukraine to Bessarabia, from Odessa to England, and from England to Germany, set forth on their journey, to a land where their time-honoured survival-minstrel would soon be screaming.

PART THREE

The Book of Benjamin and David

CHAPTER EIGHTEEN

Germany. The accidental home of the fourth generation of the brothers Bindel. Germany is not a good word for the Jews, and never will be. For what happened in that land in the time of the fourth traceable Bindel generation was a pageant of horror beyond any human imagination. Thus that performance does not fall within the realm of human forgiveness. And for that lack of pardon, until the end of time, there need be no apology. Never.

But that pageant was yet to come, and the post-war years in Germany were spent in its rehearsal. In the 1920s, the country was suffering from a post-war depression that adversely affected the whole of the defeated race. For Leon and Greta Bindel, who in their own and in their forefathers' time had lurched from one catastrophe to another, the deprivations were not unduly disturbing. Leon Bindel did not feel personally diminished by the defeat, as did most of his compatriots. For Leon had never been a patriotic German. If he felt patriotism at all, those feelings centred round the land of his childhood, cruel that it was, for in that land lay the bones of those he had loved. And sharing that Odessa patriotism, and for the same reason, was the little village of Senghenydd. Greta was of the same unpatriotic mind, and their life together was smooth, happy, and unfettered by the frustrations of the conquered spirit. The fur-business, even in the post-war years, still earned Leon a good living. David and Benjamin were well settled in their school, and within two years they could look forward to David's barmitzvah.

Only one event marred the even tenor of their lives. A short while after Chaya's wedding, a raging epidemic of Spanish influenza had spread throughout the English ports, and Zelda, in her rugged health and prime, had been one of its first victims. Leon had returned to Cardiff in response to Aaron's urgent telegram. On the train, on the boat, and on the train again, he had prayed that she would keep her dying until his arrival. He had been deprived of farewell to his father, and that deprivation had fed his disbelief and prolonged his grief. He prayed to see her alive once more, so that he could hold her hand into her dying. To see that hand loosen as her life ebbed away, to know, to see, to hear, to feel, beyond any shadow of future doubt, that his mother was dead. And then, in that painful knowledge, to give time, time to heal. He'd reached his brother's house, and the front door was open, so that no obstacle should delay his arrival. The house smelt of mortality, and he nosed it out, rushing upstairs to its source. She lay there, struggling and bursting with death, but keeping it in until he came. He took her hand and she gripped it, a small smile labouring on her lips. 'I love you, Leon,' she said, and he watched as the smile faded, and her hand grew limp, and her head turned and stared unseeing at the wall. His mother had given him much to wonder at in his life. Her strength, her fortitude, her quiet pain, and her talent for joy. But the manner of her dying was the greatest and most wondrous gift of all.

He looked up and saw Aaron and Rachel for the first time. They were standing at the foot of the bed. Rachel held Aaron's hand, and she stretched her arm towards Leon, and together they embraced their loss. The following day they buried her. Now Aaron no longer thought of joining Chaya in America. Once in his lifetime he had left his dead. He would not do it a second time.

When Leon returned to Leipzig, he found it hard to enter his mother's room. But every day Greta left the door open, and over the months she refurnished it, keeping those small intimate things that Zelda had loved. The children began to play in there, and slowly the room lived again and Zelda's memory was housed with ease and affection.

Leon missed Zelda terribly, together with his first David, whose death her own death recalled, and it was many years before he could think of either of them without a gnawing desolation. But he took great joy in his sons, and curiosity too, for both, though equally loveable, were very different from each other. David was open, responsive and affectionate, while Benjamin maintained a reserve that could sometimes be construed as coldness. He was studious too, far more diligent than David, who treated school as a continuing holiday and did little more work than was necessary to get him by. David had many friends, and whether or not his choice was deliberate, they were all of them Jewish. The school was a state establishment and though the numbers of Jewish pupils were small, they all seemed to congregate together, in isolation from the others, in some sort of united front. But Benjamin was a loner. He had one friend in the school, a non-Jew. Hans Dreiser. Hans was the son of a truck-driver, but it was not Hans' intention to follow in his father's footsteps, although Kurt Dreiser thought he could do no better. This intention little Hans shared with Benjamin who was equally determined not to enter the fur trade. He had set his sights on becoming a doctor and Hans had decided on a career in electronics. Each of them went their own lone ways, coming together from time to time in a state of firm and enduring friendship that Leon knew would last a lifetime. When David's friends came to the house, Benjamin would withdraw to Zelda's room and stay there until they had gone.

'They think they're so special,' Benjamin told his father. 'They stick together. They're asking for trouble. They've just got to be so different from everybody else.'

In his son's words, Leon heard the distant echoes of his own futile rebellion, and it did not please him.

'Who are *they*?' he asked.

'Jews,' Benjamin said, loud and clear and with no hesitation. He felt no sense of betrayal. 'Especially the religious ones. The "Ostjuden",' he added.

Leon shuddered. 'Those "Ostjuden",' he said, trying to control the anger in his voice, 'they're you yourself, me, your mother, your grandfather. We are all of us "Ostjuden", Jews from the East, and if you despise them, you despise yourself.' Yes, he thought, that, in sum and substance, was the lesson he had learned from his own tribe-desertion. The alarming lesson of one's own identity. He had learned it well, and his return to the fold had been as unequivocal and as assertive as his straying. Since the death of his pit-boy son, he had embraced Judaism with a passion, compensating for all those lost years of his neglect. He looked now at his younger son, his Benjamin, that son of his right hand, and he sniffed the Jew-fear in him and it saddened him profoundly. He wondered whether this was the time to tell him Grandpa Jakob's story, and the story of his own grandfather after whom he himself was named. But Leon held his tongue. He would not burden his children with Grandpa Jakob's song of survival. Not again. There was no Czar in Germany. Even in Russia, the Czardom and all its tyranny had been overthrown. His children would grow up freely and survive in the natural order of things, without the heavy onus of obedience to a legacy.

So instead, he held Benjamin by the shoulders and said, 'You are a Jew, Benjamin. Remember that. In our history, there have been enough people who have hated us and persecuted us. That is no reason for Jews to hate themselves.' He held him in his arms. He could not be angry with him, for those same feelings of self-hate and shame had assaulted him in a Hamburg cell all those years ago. He did not want his son to experiment as he himself had done. He could not tell him that story either. Nothing was more burdensome to a son than his father's grief.

Benjamin detached himself from his father's hold. 'I'm going over to Hans',' he said.

'Wear a scarf,' Leon said helplessly. 'It's cold outside.' At least he could deal with his son's bodily health. But he feared for his spirit.

*

His fears were given further confirmation, almost two years later, in 1922, when the family prepared for David's barmitzvah.

'It will be your turn next, Benjamin,' Greta said, as they all set out for the synagogue.

'I don't want a barmitzvah,' Benjamin said. And then, with some determination, 'I'm not going to have one.'

Greta looked at Leon and shook her head. There was no point in discussing it. 'Let's not spoil David's day, Benji,' she said.

Once again Leon thought of Grandpa Jakob. Throughout the Bindel generations, it had been the barmitzvah day of the eldest born that had timed the bequest of Grandpa Jakob's legacy. His own father had taken his sons to the forest on Aaron's day of initiation; he himself had taken his first David into the bluebell woods on his thirteenth birthday. Now was surely the time to tell his second David, and more for Benjamin's sake than for David's. But Leon was loathe to speak those words again, for the Welsh explosion had embittered each and every one of them.

After the ceremony, the party was held in the house. The guests were close friends, who happened too to be business associates, those in the fur trade. There were publishers too, a trade that flourished in Leipzig at that time and, like the fur trade, was mainly pursued by Jews. There was a small sprinkling of non-Jewish guests, David's form-master, who was invited at David's request, little Hans Dreiser and his parents, invited likewise by Benjamin. It was the first time that Leon had met Hans' father and he warmed to him immediately because of his resemblance to Dai Davies of Senghenydd. Like Dai, Kurt Dreiser was a fighter, a strong union man, and he lost no time in putting his case to the sundry furriers and publishers around the buffet-table. Any platform would do. He found a ready if hostile ear in Dr Georg Fuchs, the Bindel family doctor, not a Jew, who bristled at any premise that hinted of communism. But he loved a good argument, and the two of them spent some time together. David and his friends had retired to Zelda's room for their own private celebrations, but Benjamin and young Hans kept themselves to themselves in a corner of the dining-room. The other topic of conversation, confined to the Jewish guests, was Palestine and Zionism, a relatively new and exciting concept that fired the imagination and nurtured the seeds of whatever patriotism lay dormant in the heart of the exiled Jew. Five years before had seen the Balfour Declaration which had favoured the establishment in Palestine of a national home for the Jewish people. There were those among the guests who felt that the Jews had a duty first to the country of their birth. This notion was held by those Jews who had been born in Germany, and their fathers and grandfathers before them. But those of the Bindels' history were of the opposite opinion. They had had personal experience of futile patriotism in the land of one's birth. They knew all there was to know about scapegoating. It was at this point of the argument that Kurt Dreiser offered his opinion that anti-semitism had nothing to do with race or religion, but was simply due to economic causes. 'There's no anti-semitism under communism,' he said.

Leon knew that Kurt Dreiser was wrong, but he did not have the information to gainsay him. 'Even in a communist country,' he said, 'whenever anything goes wrong, they need to find someone to blame and hold responsible. It's usually the Jews,' Leon said.

Kurt Dreiser smiled. 'On that,' he said, 'we must agree to differ.'

*

When Benjamin's barmitzvah approached, he was adamant in his refusal. Leon knew better than to compel him. He could not learn to love his tribe by force. But he would need to learn to love them, or at least to belong to them. For in that same year of Benjamin's refusal, in that same month of May 1923, a young man sat in a cell in a Münich prison writing a book. And in that book, which he called, *Mein Kampf*, he was making it clear that Benjamin and his kind would have little option but to belong. That, for non-Aryans, there would be no choices.

This basic difference of opinion between the two brothers nagged at each of their schoolboy years, and was only relieved when Benjamin left home to study medicine at the University of Dresden. Young Hans went with him to study electronics, and in that same year, David entered his father's business.

During his lifetime, old Barak had built up a profitable fur-business. Under Leon's subsequent management, the business had prospered further. With Greta's help and encouragement, Leon had discovered in himself an untapped business talent that had for so long lain dormant in his Senghenydd days. By the time young David entered the business, it was thriving, and the Bindel household lived unsparingly on its profits.

*

The year was 1929, and Germany was in a state of economic crisis. There were over three million unemployed, and already one could hear the scapegoat rumblings. Moreover there was a man ready and willing to orchestrate that discontent, and a band of willing followers to interpret his score. The conductor was called Adolf Hitler, and his players, the brown-uniformed S.A. and black-coated S.S. But despite these forebodings the Bindel family that year found cause for celebration. For David Bindel married. Since his late teens, he had been a member of a group of young Zionists who met every week and debated different aspects of Zionist history and discussed the possibilities of settlement in the Promised Land. Already hundreds of pioneers from Eastern Europe had forsaken their urban pursuits to opt for a life on the soil, and there was much romanticism attached to that pioneering spirit. Already the young movement had gathered a repertoire of nationalist songs and it was the custom of David's group to meet on a Sabbath to sing, to dance, and to dream of settling in their ancient home. It was on one of these Sabbath gatherings that David had met Sarah, Sarah Bieder-mayer, daughter of a tailor, who lived in the poorer quarter of Leipzig, a district that approximated to a ghetto. Her father like David's, was from Russia, but from Kiev, and he, too, had ridden the train through Prussia to Hamburg. There, the family had run out of money, and had had no option but to stay, and for Mr Biedermayer to ply his portable trade. But there were hundreds of others doing likewise in Hamburg at the time, and many of them had arrived carrying a sewing-machine. Sarah's father had heard of the fur-business in Leipzig, and the shortage of fur-cutters in that city. With a little training, he could adapt his tailoring skills. So he had come with his family to Leipzig. But he discovered that fur-cutters in Leipzig were as plentiful as tailors in Hamburg, so Mr Biedermayer had settled for a poor living in his old and known trade. Sarah was his only child. She worked as a clerk in a printing firm. Both Sarah and David shared the dream of going to Palestine, and it was this fantasy that formed the basis of the loving between them.

The wedding was set for the summer, when Benjamin would return from Dresden. Leon dispatched invitations to Aaron and Rachel, urging them to share in his celebrations, as he had done with them at Chaya's wedding. Aaron replied that they would both be happy to make the journey.

It was a very hot day at the end of July. The synagogue was crowded with the Bindel and Biedermayer connections; though there was much disparity in their classes, their history and their tradition were common, and so strong was this binding factor, that there was no unease between them. When the marriage ceremony was complete, and David trod the glass under his foot, a great cry of '*Mazeltov*,' rang through the synagogue, and Leon was suddenly troubled by that old and nagging concern. My son is married, he thought, and he has not yet inherited. He will have children of his own, and he will have no story to tell them of his past. In his grandchildren's life, wherever they may be, a minstrel might well be singing that song of survival, and their ears will not be tuned to hear its stubborn melody. He was assailed by guilt.

They adjourned to the house after the ceremony. In Leon and Aaron's memories of the Odessa tavern, there had been many births to celebrate, but only one wedding. The fire had quenched all the loving that might have been. But as the brothers looked around the room, they thought that a tavern wedding would have been much like this one, with the same menu of portable and durable food, the same timid segregation of the women and the men and the daring fraternisations of the younger generations who, in their own time and ripe season, would assume the separateness of their present elders. Even a *schnorrer* was there, and though the Odessa Yankel had died long before Leon and Aaron's time, they had heard stories of him from Grandpa Jakob. It seemed to them that the status of *schnorrer* in Odessa was considerably higher than that which the present incumbent enjoyed. Yankel's standing was fed by poverty and insecurity, fed too by a sharper awareness of, and a familiarity with, God, Whose business was part of their own concern. But here, away from the ghetto, God was distant, and had no representative on earth. Here, away from Czar and threat, the *schnorrer* was reduced to the status of simple beggardom. With the rest of them, he had brought his portable trade from the Ukraine, but such a trade did not travel well into a land of comparative prosperity. Seligmann was the Leipzig *schnorrer's* name, and nobody knew how his mother had called him, nor sought to enquire, such was his anonymity. Seligmann kept himself to himself in the corner of the room, not like Yankel out of pride of his place, but out of shame of his poverty. And unlike Yankel who, at the end of the ceremony, would stand at the door like the Prince of guests, Seligmann would not care to wait until the proceedings were over. He would collect his dues, between mouthfuls of hors d'oeuvres, and he would actually count them publicly and voice aloud his approval or otherwise. Seligmann was a social embarrassment, but as necessary to any Jewish ceremony as Yankel had been, for whatever else the Jews had relinquished in their journey to prosperity, they had kept their guilt firmly by them, and Seligmann, in his gross and crude fashion, was at hand to unburden them.

The talk turned to politics and the inevitable discussion of the new Nazi party. Most of the guests preferred to dismiss it as an overnight phenomenon, but their dismissal was desperate and hid their fears of its possible success. For Hitler was a name no better for the Jews than the Czar. Those of the guests who were *Ostjuden* refrained from discussion, as experts might do in the company of laymen. For they had long been schooled in alarm and the recognition of omens and they did not want to disquiet their new compatriots who had lived on German soil for generations and who counted themselves as true Teutons. Benjamin who, until that time had stood on the sidelines of the argument, now voiced his opinion. 'We would have nothing to fear if only we would assimilate,' he said.

It was a courageous suggestion to make in such a gathering, and, though many of the guests agreed with him and were attempting that very assimilation in their own private lives, they did not think it was a timely argument for such an occasion. Leon was incensed at his son's suggestion, and again he thought of Grandpa Jakob's legacy and again he put it aside.

'It takes two to assimilate,' he said quietly. 'In Odessa, those Jews who baptised themselves, did not escape pogrom.'

'But this is not Odessa, Papa,' Benjamin insisted.

And then the glass shattered.

The guests did not move. But they turned their heads slowly and viewed the large bay windows, now open wide onto the streets, the huge brick that had landed on the buffet-table, and the group of young blackshirts framed in the shattered glass.

'Down with the Yids,' they crowed, over and over again, gloating over their handiwork, and celebrating it with their chanting.

Miraculously no one was hurt. Most of the glass had fallen back into the street. The silent shock of the guests shuddered across the room.

'Rich bloody swine,' one of the hooligans pierced the silence.

'Me?' Mr Biedermayer could not help but ask himself, and the same question hovered on Seligmann's lips. Then the *schnorrer* turned to the guests and smiled, a sudden sense of undeniable equality flooding his heart. The guests noted the smile and learned its silent lesson.

Greta had left the room meanwhile, and returned with two screens that Aaron helped her assemble to shut off the room from the street. Then, when that was done, she removed the bricks from the table and re-arranged the food that had not been touched.

Young Hans Dreiser had also left the room, and the guests could hear him outside on the street shouting at the ruffians and ordering them away. It took some heroism, Leon thought, to go out there alone, armed only with courage and indignation.

'*Jew-lover*,' they heard them baiting. 'You'll get it too when the time comes.'

Leon looked about the room. His guests shuffled there, all

supposedly close friends, yet none but Hans had moved to make a protest. He ascribed their inertia to cowardice, for there was nothing wrong with being afraid.

'He ought to come inside,' Dr Fuchs said. 'He'll get hurt.'

Greta urged the guests to take more food and to carry on as if there had been no disturbance, but it was difficult to pretend that nothing had happened. David put his arm around his bride in a gesture of protection. Benjamin was standing white-faced at his side. David turned to his brother, and in the silence of the room, he shouted, 'Go, Benjamin. Assimilate.'

'They're just a hooligan minority,' Benjamin said. 'It doesn't destroy my argument.'

Leon could contain himself no longer. The voice of Grandpa Jakob and his minstrel song of survival screamed in his ear. 'Come here, Benjamin,' he said. He was at pains to control his voice, which was trembling with his rage. 'Come here,' he almost shouted. 'You too, David.'

They went to his side, hearing the urgency in his voice and fearing his wrath.

'Excuse us a moment,' Leon said to the assembled company. His eye caught Aaron's across the room, and Aaron knew his brother's business, as in the old days, Reuben had known his milk-brother's, and he made his way through the guests and followed Leon out of the room. No Christmas tree forest for his sons, no bluebell wood, no tavern table. But location was irrelevant to Jakob Bindel's legacy. Zelda's room as a setting, would do as well as any other.

The young men followed Leon inside. Aaron shut the door after them, and with no preamble, Leon began to speak. 'I have to tell you a story,' he said. 'It has to be told,' he shouted, 'and you're going to listen. Both of you. Especially you, Benjamin, d'you hear me?'

'I'm not a child, Papa,' Benjamin said. 'Neither is David.'

'But you'll listen all the same,' Leon said. 'It's a story for grown men's ears as well as for children's. I should have told you years ago.'

So he began, sharing the story with Aaron, and they told of the milk-brother years, of Meisels and the *Kahals*, of the child-recruitment and the milk-brothers' miraculous return. Leon looked at his sons and saw them once again as children and as he related the story of the milk-brothers' return to the tavern, he recalled his first David in the bluebell wood and the great light of wonder in his eye. That same childish light now flickered in the eyes of his grown sons, and for some reason it angered him, for it was no adventure story he was telling them. He wanted to shatter that fairy-tale dream in their eye. So he told them about the fire. When it was all told, and only the Bindel ashes remained, he told them of Grandpa Jakob's song of survival. And they sat there, the Bindel brothers of the fourth traceable generation, and syllable by patient syllable, they inherited.

When it was over, they returned to their celebrations. The non-Jewish guests had left, leaving their hasty apologies with Greta. All except the Dreisers who would not be counted amongst the deserters. Leon was grateful that they had stayed and he was mindful of young Hans' support, yet he wished now that they would go away. He needed desperately to be exclusively with his own people, to be silent with them, in a language which they all understood, to share their fears and their desperate hopes that all would be well. For many of them, those who believed that it would never happen, were deeply shaken by the events of the afternoon. What had troubled them most was not the actual act of vandalism. That could be ascribed to the barbarism of a lunatic fringe. It was the sudden and silent withdrawal of those non-Jews that disturbed them, those whom they considered friends. They had sloped off in a pack as soon as the street was clear, fearing the stain of their acquaintance.

*

When the summer was over, Benjamin went back to Dresden with Hans. Leon took him to the station, and as they were waiting for Hans to arrive, Benjamin said, 'I've been thinking about what great-grandpa Jakob said, Papa, about friendship and love. Hans is my best friend, you know, and I firmly believe that he always will be. How would great-grandpa Jakob have viewed Hans?'

'He did not confine friendship to those of his own faith,' Leon said. 'He was not that kind of Jew. If the time should ever come, God forbid, that Hans is to be tested, he will not fail. He, like any other friend, would be a cause worth dying for. But let's not be morbid,' Leon laughed. Then, after a pause, 'Have you got a girlfriend, Benjamin?'

'I was going to tell you, Papa, but I was going to wait until after I am qualified. She's a nurse in the Dresden children's hospital.'

The question burned on Leon's lips, but he dared not ask it.

If, as he feared, she was not of their kind, he dared not decry it, for it would have been to deny his own Margaret and their son. Margaret had never been in season for a Bindel, except in futile rebellion, but now, in this place, and at this time, with the brown and black shirts loose on the streets, with 'Yid' salivating on their lips, now was no time for a Margaret, no time for such rebellion. Yet he held his tongue. He would not even ask her name.

'She's called Heidi,' Benjamin said.

Leon's heart sank. A name as alien to the tribal ear as Margaret.

'Heidi Chernick,' Benjamin went on for his father's relief, and smiled. So did Leon, and from that name he guessed her background. Born in Germany of the first generation, he supposed, out of parents from the Pale. Her forename was their bid for security. Much good might it do her, he prayed, when and if a fire should rage.

'Why don't you bring her home next time?' Leon said.

Then Hans came panting along the platform as the Dresden train puffed behind him.

'Good luck,' Leon said, shaking both their hands.

*

Benjamin qualified as a doctor in the following year, and in that same year he married Heidi. The wedding took place in Berlin, where Heidi's parents lived. Once again Aaron and Rachel came to join in the celebrations and to rejoice in Leon's first grandchild, Esther, born to David and Sarah a few months before Benjamin's wedding. Aaron was also a grandfather, and doubly so, for Chaya had borne two children by this time, a son and a daughter.

'D'you realise,' Aaron said to his brother, 'that we have both outlived our father in years?'

'Let us hope for a more peaceful death,' Leon said.

'Why don't you come back to England?' Aaron asked suddenly. 'It's not safe here. I have terrible feelings about this country. I haven't easily forgotten David's wedding.'

'There's been nothing as bad as that since,' Leon said. 'They'll never come to power. Besides, how could I leave here? My children are here, my grandchild, my living, though, like you,' Leon said, 'I shall shortly retire.'

'I don't mean just you,' Aaron said. 'I mean your whole family. You are all in danger here.'

'You worry yourself too much,' Leon said. 'We shall die in our beds. Both of us.'

Later, when Leon went back to Wales for Aaron's funeral, he wished he hadn't said that. Dying in one's bed was to die of ripe old age, and Aaron, at seventy-four, still strong and agile, despite his increasing weight, was still too young for that natural death. Shortly after Benjamin's wedding, only a week after their return home, Aaron, without warning, had suffered a sudden heart-attack, and had died before Leon could reach his side. They had buried him next to Zelda, a rich Bindel investment in Welsh soil.

'What will you do, Rachel?' Leon asked when the burial was over. 'You're welcome in our Leipzig home.'

She thanked him. 'There is nothing to keep me here now, except graves. And I want to spend the rest of my life with the living. I shall go to Chaya and be with my grandchildren.'

And so, with Rachel's departure, the Bindel connection with England was severed, as Leon's own flight from Odessa with Zelda and Aaron had cut its own cord. He prayed that once and for all he could live and die in Leipzig, and that his children and his grandchildren would never have to wander again. But as his train drew into Leipzig station, he heard singing on the platform, and looking out of the window, he saw a boys' choir waiting there, their black jack-boots gleaming in the sunlight, their swastika armbands raised in Nazi salute. They were clearly there to greet one of their leaders. Leon walked down the corridor to the back of the train, and when it stopped, he slunk off onto the siding and crept up the embankment to the road. What in God's name am I doing? he thought to himself. Aaron was right. We should all get out of here. Then he realised that England was now Bindel-empty, and that there was nowhere on earth that they could hide.

When he reached home, he was happy to see Benjamin there. He had been offered a job in a Leipzig hospital. This news greatly lifted Leon's spirits. He hoped that within the proximity of his family, Benjamin would come back into the fold. For his younger son still flirted with notions of assimilation. Heidi, too, whose feelings, at her parents' promptings, had always been much the same as Benjamin's. They never went to synagogue, had few, if any, Jewish friends, and moved almost exclusively in the rarer air of Christian Leipzig society to which, as a doctor, he had access at that time. He had ceased to argue with David, but he mocked his attempts at Zionist fund-raising, and he pitied his obsession with the Promised Land.

'It will lead you into trouble,' he told him once, 'if you're not careful. And the rest of us as well. We're Germans,' he kept saying, over and over again, and David thought his endless repetition of that phrase was by way of convincing himself.

*

The next few years in Germany were a period of severe economic crisis. Unemployment rose to over six million, and many businesses went to the wall. Though David maintained Leon's fur concern, they had greatly to reduce their standard of living. Despite the worsening conditions, and the time's ripeness for a new and ruthless political leader, they refused to believe that the Nationalist Socialist party would ever assume power. Only Kurt Dreiser feared it, and knew with certainty that it was possible. When Benjamin came to visit his family, he brought Hans with him, as if for his protection, David thought. Hans was now one of the few non-

Jewish guests who came to the Bindel house, and Leon no longer invited others. He did business with them still, or rather David did, for nowadays Leon rarely went to the store. He and Greta spent much of their time indoors, except when Greta was shopping for food. Then she would return with as much as the shops could offer, and she would start cooking as if preparing for a siege. One day David approached his father with the suggestion that they should all migrate to Palestine. In the shop that day, a rowdy gang of brownshirts had been his only customers. They had stormed in, unhooked a sable wrap from the window display and one of them had mincingly modelled it, to the great amusement of his colleagues. David had made a small effort to retrieve the cape, but he was too frightened to do battle with them.

'It's my mother's birthday tomorrow,' one of them said, and his friend tossed him the wrap and they left the shop swinging it between them.

David would not tell his father of the incident, but the threat of it hung over him all day. He no longer wanted to uproot himself and journey into a land itself troubled by domestic strife; he didn't want to change his language, and above all he could not see his family adapting themselves to the agricultural life which would be expected of them. For David, despite the pioneering passion of his youth, had come to look upon Zionism as an ideal, but one not to be realised, a cause that must remain a dream, a dream for which funds must be continually raised. Palestine was a place for others to settle. Yet, with all these drawbacks, he felt it imperative that the family should make their home there, for Leipzig threatened to turn into Odessa.

His father sympathised with his suggestion, but he sensed the lack of urgent commitment in his proposal. 'We're too old, Greta and I,' he said, 'to uproot ourselves again. And Benjamin would never leave. But for you and your children. That is something you should think about.'

'I would never leave you, Papa,' David said.

The matter of emigration was not discussed again for many months, although conditions in Germany worsened. At about this time, Hans Dreiser was preparing for his wedding. His bride, Inge, was a hospital almoner whom he had met through Benjamin in their Dresden University days. The whole Bindel family were invited to the wedding. Leon and Greta were wary of accepting the invitation. They did not want to offend Hans, but the presence of Jews in a strictly non-Jewish ceremony would be something of an embarrassment to them all.

But Benjamin insisted that they accept the invitation. 'His friends are not like yours, Papa,' he said. 'They have no prejudices.

263

They are communists, most of them, and anti-semitism is just not part of their thinking.' Leon was doubtful. That ideology had sprouted and flourished in the land of his birth, and he could not imagine that, out of that hated soil, anything beautiful or just could flower.

'He's my best friend,' Benjamin kept saying and, on that account, Leon could not deny him.

So the invitation was accepted. Benjamin was delighted and, as he left the house that evening to return to his own, he said, 'By the way, don't wear anything too showy.'

He was at the door when he said it, slinking out of its echo of which he was ashamed. Sadly Leon watched him go. Despite his inheritance, Benjamin was still uneasy with his tribe, and it was only the undeniable and compelling family tie that kept him from denying them altogether.

In their bedroom, they dressed for Hans' wedding. The bed was strewn with outfits that Greta had tried and discarded. Benjamin's word 'showy' rang in her ears. 'Wear what you like,' Leon suddenly shouted at her out of his own anger. 'We must not tailor ourselves to other people's expectations, especially when those expectations are false and unjust. Wear your mink,' he dared her. 'Let Benjamin eat his heart out.'

He took the coat from her wardrobe and laid it on the bed. 'What is Sarah wearing?' Greta asked nervously.

'She'll wear what she pleases,' Leon said.

When they assembled downstairs in the living-room, Sarah was also mink-attired. Neither women was fond of furs; they wore them only for business occasions. But, for this event, their fur-attire was an act of defiance, at least on their husbands' parts, if not on their own.

'You look beautiful, Sarah,' Leon said, and David complimented his mother likewise.

'Are we ready?' Leon said. They linked arms and each of them feared that they were going into battle.

They had by-passed the church ceremony. Never in his life, even during his marriage to Margaret, had Leon entered a church. David had inherited the same instinctive aversion, but Benjamin had no such scruples. Indeed he had consented to be the best man at Hans' wedding and Leon wondered whether he was kneeling with the rest of them, his eye on the Christ, unblinking. He shuddered.

They decided to walk to the reception hall, for they did not wish to arrive too early. None of them had any appetite for the festivities, aware as they were of their own fears and Benjamin's admonitions. When they entered the hall, the first person who greeted them was Benjamin. On his face was a look of pained disgust.

'There's a cloakroom downstairs,' he hissed. 'Take them off.'

Sarah and Greta were ready enough to oblige, but Leon held their arms. 'Is it warm enough in there?' he asked, as a last desperate stand for his family's identity.

'Everybody's left their coats,' Benjamin said.

Leon let the women go, and he watched them down the stairs, divesting themselves as they went.

Heidi was not at the ceremony. She was shortly to give birth and, in Benjamin's eyes, looked too ungainly to make a public appearance. Leon prayed nightly that Heidi would deliver a girl, and thus release Benjamin from a decision regarding circumcision. For Leon knew that Benjamin would ignore that rite out of pure bravado.

'Was it a nice ceremony?' David asked, feeling the need for conversation, however trivial, for the three of them stood together in public view and were clearly, even without mink, outsiders. For the other guests swept past them, having glanced sideways at their patently Jewish features. Leon very much wanted to go home. Greta and Sarah re-appeared and Benjamin led them into the reception hall. Hans and his bride were waiting to greet them. There were many other guests in front of the Bindels and Leon waited anxiously for their turn. He was wary of the welcome they would receive, and he watched Hans' enthusiastic greeting of his guests. When Leon's turn came, he let Benjamin go before him, as if Benjamin's introduction would act as a testimonial to their presence, and he resented his need for reference. Hans introduced his wife and welcomed them as effusively as his closest friends. He even left the greeting line and escorted them to a group of people in the hall with whom he felt they would feel at ease.

'This is Dr Luber,' he said. 'Benjamin's Professor of Medicine from Dresden. And Mrs Luber.' Then having introduced a topic of conversation, he left them and rejoined his bride. Benjamin had left them too, and out of the corner of his eye, Leon could see him, hanging on to the end of the greeting-line, affecting a great bonhomie with Hans' parents.

'So you taught my son,' Leon said to Dr Luber.

'Indeed. I hope I made a good doctor of him. He and Hans used to come often to our house in Dresden.'

Leon was surprised at Dr Luber's German. It was no purer than his own and sang distinctly of the Pale.

'Where are you from, Dr Luber?' he asked innocently, hoping for a more firm basis for conversation than his academic acquaintance with his son.

'I am from here, of course,' Dr Luber said with some indignation. 'I was born in Dresden. So were my parents. And their parents before them.'

'That's interesting,' Leon said. He decided to let it pass. He did not think there was a Jew in the world who could trace three generations of ancestry through a single vein of soil. He was sorry for the man who had to lie so poorly about his own provenance. His question and Dr Luber's hasty and indignant response had somewhat halted any further conversation.

'Are you living in Leipzig now?' David practically shouted, anxious to keep the Lubers at their side because the alternative was complete isolation. He too wished they had never come.

'No,' Dr Luber said. 'We are here only for the wedding. No, Dresden's my city. I wouldn't leave it. I was born there, and I expect that's where I shall die.'

He was really making quite a production of that false birth certificate of his, Leon thought, but he made no comment. 'I suppose you could say the same for us,' he said, 'though I myself wasn't born here. Nor my wife. But no doubt we shall stay here all our lives.'

'Well as long as the lunatics don't take over, this will be a fine country to live in, given time.'

'Is there any chance of that, d'you think?' Leon said.

'I sincerely hope not,' Dr Luber said quickly, 'and certainly for your sake, Mr Bindel. They are not so well disposed to your kind.'

Then David had the courage to call Luber's bluff. 'Are you not of our kind, Dr Luber?' he asked.

Dr Luber blanched. 'You are mistaken, Mr Bindel,' he said, and he took his wife's arm and guided her out of the ghetto.

'He was stupid to leave,' Greta said. 'It's only proof of what he's trying to hide. I'm sorry for Jews like that,' she said.

'D'you think Benjamin ever denies it?' Leon asked fearfully.

'He is too much of a coward even for that, I'm afraid,' David said, and Leon was saddened by the rift between his sons. He thought of Aaron then, whom he missed terribly, and of those painful Pavel go-between years. They had finally come together in some kind of loving, but the cost had been appalling. He prayed that David and Benjamin would not have to pay such a price.

Benjamin, from the edge of the room, caught sight of his family's isolation and after some hesitation, he joined them. 'What happened to the Lubers?' he said.

'They went to talk to some friends,' Leon said quickly. He was suddenly afraid of his son.

'Then come and have some food,' Benjamin said. Their isolation would be less conspicuous if they were eating. He led them through the hall and to the buffet at the far end. To their dismay, the Lubers were standing there, eating alone, and David quickly deflected their passage so that they could station themselves at the far end of the table. Benjamin did not notice the diversion or, if he did, he refrained from any comment. He stayed by their side, and ate a little himself, feeling their need for his protection.

'Have you thought of any names yet, Benjamin?' Greta asked.

'Gretchen, if it's a girl,' Benjamin said. 'And Hermann if it's a boy.'

Leon swallowed. What a long way they had come from Bessarabia. Gretchen, the Aryan ideal. And Hermann. Together they were German purity incarnate. He said nothing. He just hoped for a girl, however she was called.

The Bindels spent a good deal of time eating, though none of them were particularly hungry. There were many dishes on the table that were taboo in their cuisine, and Leon noticed how Dr Luber was making a feast of the suckling pig, but with little relish on his face. Luber's self-deception could not have given him much pleasure. They were relieved when the speeches started. That was an occasion in which they could be seen to be occupied, at least as listeners. Almost everybody who proposed a toast used the platform as a means for political statement. Reference was made to the black-shirt scum that threatened to take over the country. But there was no fear of that, the speakers said, for their party was strong and united and would not be overruled. No one of the speakers mentioned the party by name, but it was clear to the Bindels what faction they had in mind. And out of Leon's history, he wondered which was the worse of the two evils.

In time, the celebrations came to an end, and it was late enough to leave decently and without excuse. They left without Benjamin. He stayed behind, not wishing a post-mortem with his family. But Leon would not have wished that either. He hoped that Hans' wedding would never be a subject of conversation between them.

When they reached home, Greta fetched him his slippers.

'Oh Greta,' he said, 'it must have been so much easier in the ghetto to keep a family together. When there were no doubts, no temptations from outside.'

'But it was too costly,' Greta said. 'Besides, look at David. He has no doubts. They're not all like Benjamin.' She kissed his cheek. 'Anyway,' she said, 'you were a Benjamin once.'

'I hope Heidi has a girl,' Leon said.

'We already have one granddaughter,' Greta said. 'A grandson would be welcome. Besides, there must be Bindels of the next generation.'

But Leon had a terrible foreboding that the Bindel line would end in Germany. The encounter with the Lubers, at Hans' wedding, had deeply depressed him, far more than any outward display of anti-semitism. The assault at David's wedding had been less painful. 'If our own people are our enemies,' he said to Greta, 'what will become of us all?'

A few weeks later, Benjamin rang his father very late one night to announce the arrival of his first grandson. Leon tried to hide the disappointment in his response, and hoped that, if Benjamin heard it, he would ascribe it to the lateness of the hour.

'How is Heidi?' Leon asked. 'How much does the baby weigh?' All answerable questions. Playing for time. Then, 'What will you call him?'

'Hermann,' Benjamin said. 'And Aaron, after Uncle.'

It coated the pill a little. 'That pleases me,' Leon said. Then he dared to ask about circumcision for, with a name like Aaron, the rite could not be denied. He heard the hesitation on the other end of the line.

'I'll talk to you about it,' Benjamin said.

Leon was sickened. 'Talk to your mother,' he said, and he handed the phone to Greta.

They tried to get back to sleep, but Leon's mind was feverish. He realised for the first time how deeply hurt Aaron and Zelda must have been by his rebellion. He wondered whether Dr Luber was circumcised. The following day he visited the hospital with Greta. It was the hospital where Benjamin worked and he was with Heidi much of the time. He was beaming with pride when he saw them, and rushed them excitedly to the bedside to view his son. He bundled him from his crib and proudly placed him in his father's arms.

Leon looked at the screwed-up little face. 'Aaron,' he whispered.

'We're calling him Hermann,' Heidi made it clear from the bed. 'Aaron's only his second name.' She was confirming that 'Aaron' was an insertion only for form's sake. 'It's in memory of your brother,' she said. Heidi would always do the right thing.

'I'm very moved by that,' Leon said.

She stretched out her arms and took the child. 'Hermann, Hermann,' she whispered in his ear. She did not want her baby confused.

Leon looked at her. There was something different about her hair, he thought, and the change, for some reason, offended him. Normally her fair hair hung loosely about her shoulders. Now it was parted and severely plaited, as if in homage to the myth of Heidi, that eternal small heroine of German schoolgirls. She, too, he thought, had turned from her tribe with a vengeance equal to his own in his valley days. He took Greta's hand and they sat there for a while, both stifling the question of circumcision that hovered on their tongues.

'How long are you staying in hospital?' Greta asked. The length of stay might open a discussion of that vexed question. The eighth day of life was the usual timing for the ceremony.

'About a week,' Heidi said.

'Don't worry,' Benjamin said. 'The baby will be circumcised, but in hospital. And a doctor will do it. We don't want a religious ceremony. It will be done medically, and simply for the sake of the baby's health.'

It was a typical Benjamin compromise, in the same way as he had bracketted Aaron in the baby's name. Leon was not dissatisfied. It was the most he could hope for.

So a week later, without Rabbi and without ceremony, in the sterile confines of the hospital ward, with Hans Dreiser as godfather, little Hermann was cut for the sake of his health and cleanliness. And let no one think otherwise. But with all that camouflage, Leon thought, with all of Benjamin's apologies, he had done more for his son than he himself had done for his first David.

As the weeks passed, Leon grew to know his little grandson, and he nurtured a growing hope for the continuance of the Bindel line. The family drifted back once more into that state of complacency, based on the certainty that nothing would change. Even David had stopped mentioning Palestine, and Leon was confident that he would keep his family about him all his days.

And then on January the 30th, in the following year of 1933, everything changed. They were all in the family house that night as they listened to the news on the wireless. The announcement was cold, detached and unsurprised. Adolf Hitler had been appointed Chancellor of the Third Reich.

CHAPTER NINETEEN

Benjamin said that it wouldn't last. He insisted on it. Germany was his home and always would be, and when a year later, his second son was born, he named him Heinrich, as a testimony of faith in his German future. Hans was once again the godfather. Heinrich, like Hermann, was cut in hospital for the sake of his health and cleanliness, and like Hermann, was given a second name for family appeasement. This time it was Jakob after that grand Odessa dispenser of inheritance. David had increased his family too, and now had two daughters, Esther and Zelda who, because of their gender, did not qualify for Bindel inheritance. Women, it was considered, survived by osmosis. It was only man who needed to know the wherewithal.

In the first few months of the Hitler regime, there were rumours of many arrests and disappearances, especially amongst the intelligentsia. This category Hitler considered as enemy-potential. They were the thinkers and therefore the doubters, and finally those who would not be led.

One evening Benjamin came to the house with the news that Dr Luber had been arrested. 'They're rounding up the communists,' he said.

That same evening Hans came to the Bindel house. He was looking for Benjamin, and Heidi had sent him to Leon's.

'They've taken my father,' he said. He was trembling and they made him sit down and gave him a drink. Then they asked him what had happened. About twenty of them had come to the house, he said. They'd broken down the front door and stormed straight into the living-room.

'My father was reading the paper,' Hans said, 'and I was fiddling with the radio. They asked him if he was Kurt Dreiser. I saw my father tremble. Then they grabbed him and took him away. Just like that. Twenty hooligans to take one defenceless old man.'

'Where have they taken him?' Leon asked.

'I asked them, but they wouldn't tell me,' Hans said. 'They just laughed. "Keep out of trouble", they said, "or you'll go the same way".'

'Dr Luber was taken too,' Benjamin said. 'D'you think the arrests are connected?'

'They have to be,' Hans said. 'Could you come home with me?' Hans looked at Benjamin. 'Inge and my mother are terrified. We need company. I need some help too with the front door.'

Leon opened his mouth to urge Benjamin not to go. In these times, a house that was the scene of an arrest was a contaminated place, for any person seen entering could be involved in the same offence for which the arrest was made. Especially for a Jew was it dangerous, for he had already offended. But Hans' plea was one for friendship, and Leon would not forbid his son to offer that. But he feared for him.

'I'll come, of course,' Benjamin said. 'You have never hesitated to come to my house. We are both lepers in this society.'

It was the first time that Leon had heard his son admit to the offence of being a Jew.

'Inge and your mother can come here any time,' Greta said. 'We criminals must stick together,' she laughed.

270

As they left, David touched Benjamin's arm. 'Be careful,' he pleaded. 'Please be careful.'

Leon noted the rare sign of loving between his sons and, though it pleased him, he was sad that it was the stress of the times that had brought them close.

Benjamin responded gently. 'Don't worry, David,' he said. 'I will survive.'

'Please let us know if you have news,' Leon almost begged, for it was news of Benjamin he wanted as well for, with Benjamin's going, it seemed he was involving himself in the Dreiser catastrophe. But a few days later, Benjamin visited once again, with the news that Hans' father, together with Dr Luber and many others who belonged to the same communist cell, had been taken to a camp near Munich. It was called Dachau, and was the first concentration camp established by the new regime. Nothing more than that was known. The police at headquarters would give no information as to the charge, laughed in their faces at the mention of a trial and gave no hint of when they would be released, or indeed if they would be released at all. Hans had always been a communist sympathiser, but after his father's arrest he resisted showing the smallest outward sign of sympathy. Every day he went to his place of work at the Siebel Aircraft Corporation in Halle some twenty miles from Leipzig, where he was an electronics specialist. He went to his work and he came home and he saw nobody outside these two places except for Benjamin. He no longer knew whom to ask about his father, and if he had known, he would have been afraid to enquire.

Winter gave way to spring and early summer, and there was still no word of Kurt Dreiser. In May of that year there was a great fire in Leipzig, not one that was accidental, or one that destroyed life and property, but a fire which incinerated the spirit. The grand square of Leipzig was the scene of the burning of the books, books concerning Judaism, or those written by Jewish authors, and those which were opposed to Naziism. The auto-da-fé drew a great crowd, who watched for hours as the words burned away, and those Jews who happened to pass by, were stung away from the crowd as if their own flesh had been charred. David Bindel happened to find himself in the crowd that day, for his fur store was on the corner of the square. He rushed back to his shop, but he was afraid to stay there, so he bolted the doors and shuttered the windows and left for home. In the morning, he found the shop looted. The windows were daubed with the yellow star of David, and there was absolutely nothing that he could do about it. Once more he thought of going to Palestine, and once more he broached the subject with his father. But Leon would not leave Benjamin

271

behind, and David would not leave Leon. Thus in the name of their family bond, the Bindels colluded in their own destruction.

Over the next few months there was a lull in anti-semitic attack. Jews even dared to hope that Hitler would lose his power, and things would return to normal. It was the extreme hope of desperation. Slowly and without violence, the Jews found themselves forced into a state of isolation. For many German Jews, who had always considered themselves patriotic Germans with an incidental Jewish faith, it was a terrible blow to be so ostracised. Leon Bindel had never been such a German. He had learned from his own history the lesson of the outsider. But Benjamin Bindel knew no such lesson except from hear-say, and he was deeply hurt one morning when a letter arrived from Dr Fuchs, their family doctor, he who had brought him into the world, requesting the family to find a practitioner of their own kind. It had become inconvenient, he wrote, to include Jews amongst his patients. Benjamin was incensed but there was nothing that he could do. Leon received a similar letter; he read the news with less anger, for it did not surprise him. For a long time he and Greta had noticed how their few non-Jewish friends would cross the road or look the other way when a meeting seemed inevitable. He did not blame them. He was grateful at least for their embarrassment. Only Hans Dreiser and his wife continued to be regular visitors to the Bindel house, and, though Leon urged them not to come for their own safety, Hans would not listen. His father had been taken almost six months ago, and there was still no news of a possible release. Every fearful enquiry at Gestapo headquarters produced the blanket response. He is being dealt with. The words echoed with maltreatment and torture. Sometimes in the semi-dark hours of early morning, Kurt Dreiser's family wondered whether they would ever see him again.

Then on Christmas Eve of that year, without any notice, Kurt Dreiser came home. Almost at once, after their astonished reunion, Hans insisted on bringing him to the Bindel house. The Bindels had sustained the whole Dreiser family during the absence of its head, and Kurt was anxious to thank them. Besides, Kurt was so overcome with seeing his family again that he could barely accommodate the strain, and he needed neutral ground and the presence of a third party to dilute those emotions that threatened to become unmanageable. He wanted to tell his family what had happened to him during his imprisonment. But he had refrained, fearing to relive it in the telling. Neither had they asked. They looked at him and they knew it all. It wasn't just the gross loss of weight. That they could have expected. It was his sunken abdicated eyes that told the story of how they had tried to break his spirit. Indeed, probably succeeded, Hans had thought, but he didn't care, for his father was alive and home. There would be time to renew that spirit and to wreak revenge. Hans had to think in those terms, though he knew revenge was impossible. But only if he was armed with such thoughts could he bear to look at his father.

Benjamin and Heidi were sent for, but Benjamin came alone. Leon was not surprised. He knew from Greta's hints that Benjamin and Heidi's marriage was fraying. Heidi was an outgoing woman, highly dependent on social intercourse, and, with the wave of ostracism, she grew depressed and, for no logical reason, she blamed Benjamin for their isolation. They had few Jewish friends and, having neglected them for so long, she was too proud to seek them out now. Whereas Benjamin was changing. He no longer had the confidence that all would be well. He had been dismissed from his duties at the Leipzig general hospital and he was now working in the Jewish Infirmary. He had been lucky to obtain the post for, after the purification measures, the hospital was besieged with applicants from discharged Jewish doctors. He was grateful that they had taken him in, and, though he still winced at their separateness, both in their manner and their dress and in their survival ghetto vision, he no longer found them a threat to his own safety. Indeed they had saved his livelihood. But he had another problem. The house where he lived was tied to his old hospital post, and within a month he would have to find other accommodation. He did not have enough money to buy a house, and people were now wary of letting accommodation to Jews. It was logical that he should return to the Bindel family home where there was room in plenty. Benjamin would have welcomed that return, but he dared not suggest it to Heidi. Nowadays he spent more and more time at his father's house and it had become an unspoken agreement that Hans should meet him there. Now he was overjoyed to see him and to share his relief that his father had come home.

It was a champagne occasion and they toasted Kurt's return, and as they grew mellow in the wine, Kurt was eased into telling part of his story.

'They are not of the human species,' he began. 'I don't know who makes them or where they come from. They are primitive.' He paused. 'That really is the whole of the story,' he said. 'What more can I tell you? We got up at four in the morning, and there was a roll-call. Even when it was over, we had to stand there, barefoot and shivering. Sometimes they made us kneel with the palms of our feet upwards and the guards would run along the line behind us, beating our feet for their pleasure.'

Kurt's wife uttered a small scream. 'I don't want to hear any more,' she said.

Kurt put his arm around her. 'I'll tell you one more thing,' he said. 'D'you know where I was last night?' He was smiling and they couldn't understand what happy memory he could have of his incarceration.

'I was being wined and dined in Nuremburg,' he said.

'Wined and dined?' Hans asked. He was not curious about the location.

'Julius Streicher,' Kurt went on, 'that beast who publishes *Der Stürmer*, he's the provincial governor there. He entertained twelve of us to dinner, twelve of us who'd been released that day. There were SS officers at the table. We were a kind of Christmas gift for them. "Repentant racial comrades", Streicher called us. And they sang *Heilige Nacht* with tears in their eyes. It was nauseating. They are a strange mixture, our people, of cruelty and sentimentality.'

'Did they talk about Jews?' David was bold enough to ask.

'No,' Kurt said quickly.

Too quickly, Leon thought.

'Not a word,' Kurt said, and then the Bindels knew that the future of their kind had been discussed at that table and they were afraid.

'Is there any news of Dr Luber?' Leon asked. 'Were you together?'

'He's still there, I'm afraid,' Kurt said. 'He's Jewish. Did you know? The guards said they wanted to play with him a little longer. Those were their very words.' Kurt put his hand on Leon's arm. 'My friend,' he said. 'You must leave this country. All of you. There is no future for you here.'

When the Dreisers had gone, David decided to profit by Kurt's warning and Benjamin's presence by bringing up once again the subject of Palestine. He pleaded with them.

'Kurt is not necessarily right,' Benjamin said. 'It will never be so bad that we have to leave. In any case, people who work in commerce or the professions are essential to the German economy. They'll leave us alone.'

'What's essential about the fur-trade?' David asked.

'Exports,' Benjamin said, but with little conviction.

'We have never exported,' Leon said. 'There's nothing essential about us.'

'If you listen to Hitler's speeches,' David said, 'it's clear that Jews are dispensible whatever their profession. At least let our children go,' he pleaded.

'I won't be parted from my children,' Benjamin said.

Then David wondered for the first time whether he himself would send his children away, and the possibility appalled him.

'All my life I've been running,' Leon said. 'Running to survive.

I'm too old now to run any more. What do you say, Greta?' he asked.

'I think we must all stay together,' she said. 'Whatever we decide.'

'Mama's right,' Benjamin said.

'She said *whatever* we decide,' David reminded him.

'Heidi will never leave,' Benjamin said. 'I am tied to Germany.'

With a shock Leon recalled a similar bond that had rooted him in Senghenydd and he shivered at the recollection of the event that had finally loosened that tie. But Benjamin's bond fettered them all.

If the German Jews at that time were unsure of their status, oscillating between complacency and despair, the passing of the Nuremburg Laws in 1935 made their position legally clear. Those laws reduced them to second-class citizens. They were deemed persons of inferior status, non-Aryans, of impure blood. They were forbidden marriage or congress with an Aryan. It was only a matter of time before their property would be confiscated and their isolation would be complete. Once more David introduced the now weary subject of emigration, and once more it was Greta who ruled that they must all stick together, which, in view of Leon's ageing years and Benjamin's marital strife, decreed that they would stay in Germany. Over the months, at regular intervals, David would air the subject yet again, but now it had become a ritual that had lost all its meaning and purpose. But as long as they kept the possibility of flight in their minds, they would be saved. Not one of them, not even David, considered that, in time, it would be too late.

Benjamin's housing problem became acute. They had moved into an apartment building, but now that whole complex had been sold to a party official, and he wanted it '*Judenrein*'. The Jewish families who lived there were thus obliged to leave and, in many cases, it prompted their emigration. But in Benjamin's case there was the alternative of the Bindel family home. It was the only alternative, since Heidi's family lived n Berlin. So, with much reluctance on Heidi's part, and much welcome on Greta's, Benjamin and his family moved into the Bindel home. Now in Greta's sense they were all truly together. But in many ways, the togetherness, that they had enjoyed until that time, was splintered by Heidi's presence. She was in all ways unaccommodatable. Greta had always kept a Jewish house. Zelda had been responsible for that. After her death Greta had relaxed the Laws a little, but they still honoured all the festivals and the Sabbath. The Friday night ceremonial supper was the high point of the week, especially for David's children who were allowed to stay up late. But Heidi sat at the table like a stranger, her children safely tucked up in bed, away from their grandfather's constant 'Aaron' and 'Jakob' that he insisted upon when he played with them. Her little Hermann and Heinrich were fast asleep upstairs, undisturbed by the shennanigans of these outsiders who insisted on their differences, and thus made difficulties for them all. Greta tried to reason with her, but she sulked and was silent. Between Benjamin and herself there was little communication, and it seemed that the marriage was virtually at an end. But they would stay together as reliably as they would stay in Germany. Leon viewed it all with desolation, and in those times he often thought of Margaret.

Benjamin's children were in kindergarten, and David's in the primary department of the same state school. One day, Sarah went to collect the children, both her own and Benjamin's. Little Zelda appeared tearful at the gate, and seemed to Sarah to look somewhat lop-sided. She had left home that morning with two bright plaits over her shoulders, and one of them was missing. Sarah knew immediately what had happened, and she knew too that there was no one to whom she could complain. She took the children home and comforted Zelda as best she could. She cut her second plait and gave her hair an equal length all round. She took care not to ask how it had happened. There was no need for Zelda to re-live the experience. Zelda did not want to go back to school on the following day, but Sarah and David insisted, though they were not sure whether they advised wisely. That day it was Esther's turn. She came home with a torn smock and a bruise on her cheek. She wore her scar with some pride, for it equallised her with Zelda. Meanwhile little Hermann and Heinrich remained unscathed. Heidi was triumphantly convinced that their names protected them, until one day, letters came to both Sarah and Heidi from the headmistress of the school suggesting that they withdraw their children for their own safety. She could not be responsible for any injury they would suffer. She added that she was very sorry, but that her powers were restricted. The letter came as a tremendous shock to Heidi. For the first time she realised her lack of immunity. The children had to be schooled elsewhere, and the only alternative was the Jewish school in the Jewish quarter of the city. For Heidi it was a terrible humiliation, and she tried to persuade Benjamin that the children would be better off without schooling. But Benjamin was adamant. For the first time he berated Heidi in front of his whole family. Leon dared not look at his son, for he saw a terrible hatred in his eye.

The following morning it was Benjamin who took the children to their new school across the city and David went with him. They had to join a queue for registration. All over Leipzig Jewish children had been eased out of the state school system. The children were excited at the prospect of a change of scene. But on the whole, their parents, who waited with them, looked downcast and defeated. It was mid-morning before Benjamin and David were ushered into the headmaster's study. He apologised for the delay, and expressed his regret that their children's schooling had been so rudely interrupted. Zelda and Esther were registered first, and then it was Benjamin's turn to give the names of his sons. As he spoke them aloud, he felt deeply ashamed.

'Have they got other names?' the headmaster asked him.

'Aaron and Jakob,' Benjamin said, and in that instant he decided that henceforth that's how they would be called, at home as well as at school, whatsoever Heidi's objections. He wondered whether he ought to leave her.

The children could not start till the following week so they all returned to the Bindel house. David had hoped that he and Benjamin could talk on the way home, but the presence of the children in the car inhibited a private conversation. For he needed to talk to him, or rather, he wanted to give Benjamin an opportunity to talk, to open to him his confused heart. For confused he knew it to be. Assimilation, which Benjamin had once promoted, had now been proved to be of no avail, and he was faced with a total re-adjustment of his values. Heidi had been a good companion in those days of self-deception, but now he could find no place for her in his life, for she clung so stubbornly to her old ideas, despite all the proof as to their failure.

When they reached home, Benjamin's children proudly announced their new titles. Leon refrained from showing his delight, but Heidi was appalled by the name-changes that had, at one stroke, turned her children into strangers.

'No more Hermanns and Heinrichs,' Benjamin said.

Thereafter Heidi never called her children by name, and when she needed their attention, she would gently prod them.

Greta suggested that Benjamin and Heidi take a holiday, leaving the children in their keeping. But Heidi would not trust her children to the elder Bindels. They would convert them totally beyond her recognition. But she did suggest that she'd like to visit her parents in Berlin, and take her children with her. But Benjamin disallowed that, with the excuse that the children should not miss school, but in truth he was afraid that once out of the Bindel hold, with her children Hermann and Heinrich once more, she would not return. So they all stayed together in the Bindel family home, but because of Heidi's sulking presence there was little togetherness in the house.

Lately the men of the household, even Benjamin, had taken to going to the synagogue on the Sabbath. The need for community amongst the Jews became more acute in those years. The synagogue was the centre for news and rumour of their brethren throughout the country. And that news was always depressing. But most depressing of all, were the vacant seats in the synagogue. Week by week, they emptied, and the untenanted seats shrieked with warning. In that same year of 1938, a law was passed which enforced the registration of all Jewish property, and the Jews knew it was a preliminary to total confiscation. Emigration increased day by day, and each Sabbath as Leon left the synagogue with his sons, he wondered whether they were being foolhardy to stay, and whether if he, as the elder, were to insist on it, even Heidi could be persuaded to go. He broached the matter at the Sabbath lunch. Heidi gave a rare laugh. 'You go if you want to,' she said, 'but I'm staying here with the children.'

Leon looked at Benjamin hoping for some show of resolve. But Benjamin had little appetite for battle, especially in front of his family. Besides he was not yet too sure himself that emigration was necessary. He still clung to the hope that the real German people would see the folly of their acts and, in time, decease. But there were no signs that Germany was coming to its senses. In fact, it was preparing for war.

That year in the spring, Germany annexed Austria and anti-Jewish measures became more oppressive and widespread. Synagogues were destroyed in Münich and Nuremburg, and passports belonging to Jews were invalidated. There was no question that events were closing in on German Jewry and that in time they would be trapped beyond any possibility of escape. But the Bindels stayed. Nevertheless, David quietly made discreet enquiries.

Hans Dreiser was still a regular visitor to the Bindel home. He brought news that Dr Luber had finally been released. He had of course been deprived of his University post, and he was leaving Dresden because he couldn't bear to be ostracised by his erstwhile friends. He was coming to settle in Leipzig, where he knew nobody, and rejection would not offend him. Hans also brought news of his father whose health was failing. Ever since his release from Dachau he had had trouble with his lungs. He had caught a chest infection while at the camp and it had never cleared. Now there were days when he could barely leave his bed, so laboured was his breathing.

'Why haven't you told me all this before?' Benjamin said angrily.

'My father wouldn't allow it,' Hans said. 'He knew you would insist on coming regularly, and the house is under constant surveillance. It would endanger you.'

'I'll take you home,' Benjamin said.

Thereafter Benjamin visited Kurt Dreiser every evening after his hospital rounds. He reported back to the Bindels that his condition was worsening, and that he was not likely to recover. He told Greta that Mrs Dreiser would be very happy if she would visit and be with her for a while, and that very evening, after supper, Greta went to the Dreiser house.

It was the night of the ninth of November, 1938, that in historical hindsight would be known as the *Kristallnacht*, the night of glass. That was the night that Greta Bindel did not return home. At midnight, the family started to worry. Benjamin phoned Hans and learned that Greta had left an hour earlier. 'Perhaps she had to wait a long time for the bus.'

Benjamin heard anxiety in his friend's voice. 'I'll go out and look for her,' Benjamin said.

Benjamin took the car and David went with him. They lived in the residential area of the town and as they drove through the streets, the silence unnerved them.

'It's so quiet,' Benjamin said.

'It's midnight. Everyone's in bed.' That would explain the stillness, David thought, the natural silence of sleep. But he too was disturbed by it. It was oppressive, menacing, reflecting the brothers' fears for their mother's safety. They were nearing the town centre when the silence broke. It broke with the shattering of glass. In the main thoroughfare, the centre of the fur-trade, the pavements were littered with the shattered remains of shop windows. Venetian shutters stuttered along the kerb. What remained of the Bindel shop, and the one next to it, was the bare steel armature of its erstwhile design. Fires had been started further down the street, and a crowd of fur-lined looters helped themselves to the pickings under the very noses of the police, themselves, sable-capped, directing the one-sided battle like kindergarten generals. Benjamin drove through the crowd as quickly as he could. It was no place for a Jew to be abroad, and certainly no time to claim ownership of the damaged property. There would be no redress or reparation. To claim it would be to put their lives in jeopardy. Now their fears as to their mother's well-being multiplied. They suddenly didn't know where to look for her. Benjamin pulled up at a phone box in a deserted street to ring home to find out whether she had arrived. A distraught Leon answered. There was no sign of her, but a friend had phoned to say that the synagogue was on fire. 'What's happening?' Leon almost cried.

'I don't know,' Benjamin said, and he wiped the word 'pogrom' from his lips. For that perhaps was what was happening, evidenced now by the clanging of fire-engines and ambulances that seemed to be going in all directions. 'Don't worry, Papa,' he said. 'We'll find her.'

279

They drove towards the bus-station, having to make many detours on route, avoiding the mobs of storm-troopers who seemed to have taken over the streets. A group of them marched along the shop-fronts, pausing occasionally, and then daubing, in yellow paint on sundry windows, the Star of David. Then out of nowhere the gangs would come and with bricks and stones they wrecked according to the markings.

When the brothers reached the bus-station, it was deserted. 'Mama,' Benjamin called into the darkness, as if she might be hiding there in the shelters, fearful of the streets.

'Benjamin?' It was Hans' voice, and he came out of the darkness towards them. 'She's not here,' he said. 'She must have taken the bus.'

'What's going on, for heaven's sake?' David said.

'It's a pogrom,' Hans answered. He had no problem with the word, no historical hangover that would have curbed his tongue. 'It's on the radio. I heard it in the bus-station office.'

'Have people been killed?' Benjamin asked. He was not concerned with the burning of property or synagogues. All that was replaceable.

'Yes,' Hans said tonelessly. 'They didn't say how many.'

What did numbers matter, David thought. Only one mattered to them at this time.

'I don't know where to look for her,' Benjamin said.

'Let's follow the bus route,' Hans suggested.

They got into the car.

'We should ring home first,' Benjamin said, but he made no move towards the kiosk. He was loathe to hear his father's anxiety yet again. 'You phone, David,' he said.

Hans and Benjamin waited in the car.

'I'm frightened,' Benjamin said.

'You should leave. All of you. Go to America, England, even Palestine. You can still get passports.'

'You're right,' Benjamin said. 'But first we have to find her. Then we'll leave.'

Their emigration now depended on Greta's discovery, and Benjamin feared that it was yet another excuse to stay, and then he truly feared that she would not be found at all. From the look on David's face as he returned to the car, it was clear that there was no news from home. Heidi and Sarah were doing their best to restrain Leon from going out himself and looking for her. David got into the car and they drove off.

It was difficult to get through the town and dangerous, too, because of the flying glass and missiles. Besides, their journey suddenly seemed to them to be quite pointless, for Greta was unlikely to be walking the streets. The presence of so many ambulances was unnerving. They had to swerve to give one of them right of way. Hans told Benjamin to stop the car.

'This is useless,' he said, voicing the thoughts of them all. 'Was she carrying identity?'

'Of course,' Benjamin said. 'It's the law.'

'Then let's face it,' Hans said softly. 'Let's presume the worst. If she's hurt, they would have taken her to the Jewish hospital. That's where we must go.'

It was an obvious place to investigate, and the thought had crossed Benjamin's and David's minds as soon as they had started the search. But neither of them had wanted to suggest it, because it would have seemed such a negative view. Now it was the only avenue open to them. Benjamin turned down a side-street and made his way to the Jewish Hospital.

It lay on the edge of the Jewish quarter, and Benjamin was wary of driving through the area for fear of what he would find. But it was difficult to avoid the cobwebs of little streets and alleys that threaded the quarter. And what they saw and heard was appalling. As they approached the central street of the area, Benjamin was obliged to park the car, for the road was strewn with glass. The windows of almost every house were broken, and, lacking glass, the yellow star was daubed on each front door. There was wailing in the streets and, from the little synagogue on the corner, they could see the Rabbi carrying the sacred scrolls to the comparative safety of his own home.

'This is what Odessa must have looked like,' David said, 'after the fire.'

'This is not Odessa,' Benjamin practically screamed at him, not so much in defence of his German birthright, but in fear of the death that was the fire's aftermath.

The hospital courtyard seethed with ambulances, and the foyer with crowds of frightened relatives seeking news of their kin. Benjamin, in his authority as hospital doctor, was able to by-pass the reception desk and go straight into casualty. David and Hans followed him. On their way, Benjamin acknowledged a colleague who was hurrying past in the other direction. But the man did not acknowledge his greeting. Benjamin turned and rushed after him, sweating with fear, for he knew that his friend's avoidance had to do with his mother.

'Michael,' he shouted.

The man turned.

'Didn't you see me?'

Michael was flustered. 'Yes,' he said. 'I just . . . God, this place is a nightmare.' And he hurried on.

Benjamin was not convinced by his excuses. In his friend's hesitation, he suddenly knew that his mother was dead.

The reception desk in casualty was besieged by enquiries. He forced his way through. The girl looked up at him and paled.

'Dr Bindel,' she said. 'I was just going to phone your home.'

Then he knew for certain. 'My mother?' he whispered.

She nodded. Then there was a silence between them. The question hung in the air. Alive . . .? Injured . . .? Or . . . no, not that.

'Where is she?' he said.

'In the morgue.'

All hovering questions answered. He trembled.

She rose from her desk, took his arm, and led him into the registrar's office behind reception. David and Hans followed him. 'Dr Bindel,' she said, as she opened the door. Then she let them inside, and returned to her desk, relieved of the burden of bearing his sorrow.

'What happened?' David asked the registrar. There was panic in his voice, as if the knowledge of how she had come to die, once known, and acted upon, would resurrect her.

'The reports are very confused, Benjamin,' Dr Segal said. 'It seems that the buses couldn't get through and the passengers had to walk. The storm-troopers were taking identities of all pedestrians. They beat her up, it seems. I wouldn't look at her, if I were you.'

'Well, you're not me,' Benjamin shouted, and he put his head in his hands and cried aloud. 'I'm sorry,' he said after a while, then turning to Hans he said, 'You don't have to come if you don't want to.'

'I thought of her as my family,' Hans said, and the three of them left the room and made their way to the basement of the hospital.

Benjamin had never worked in pathology and he rarely went to the morgue. The basement was a tangled network of corridors and anti-rooms and there was no sign-posting. A few orderlies were about, wheeling empty trollies, but Benjamin was loathe to ask directions. He didn't want to enquire of strangers where his mother lay. As her son, he should know and he tried door after door with his search. Then they heard the rattle of a trolley as it trundled laden down the corridor. They followed the stretcher-orderly to the morgue.

Inside, the room looked like a vast sterile filing-cabinet with long drawers along each wall. 'Dr Bindel?' the morgue-attendant said as Benjamin came through the door. He led them to the far wall and placed his hand on one of the metal drawer-handles. He left it there for a while. 'Are you sure?' he said.

Benjamin nodded. Then the man pulled out the drawer and gently withdrew the sheet around the face. David took Benjamin's arm, and Hans stood aside, feeling an intruder. David did not look at Greta's face. He saw the mirror of it in his brother's horror. Benjamin put out his hand to draw the sheet down over the body.

'No,' David said. 'We have seen enough.'

'We must see it all,' Benjamin said, and his voice was strangely calm. 'We must know what they have done.'

He drew the sheet away. It seemed that almost every limb in Greta's body had been broken. The flesh was bruised and bloody. He touched her arms and legs gently, smoothing them in a caress, as if to re-set them. Both brothers knew that their mother's death had been terrible, slow and infinitely painful. Benjamin lifted her up by the shoulders and took her in his arms. He kissed her, then he passed her gently to David. But David held her tightly, as if willing her to live again, and there was a terrible creaking of bones as he pressed her spine against his large hands. They had broken her to pieces, and her sad and bruised skin was a fragile wrapping for the fragments of shard and bone within. He laid her down on the drawer and covered her.

'I'm sorry, Dr Bindel,' the morgue attendant said. 'We live in terrible times.' He shut the drawer and its echo clanged across the chamber.

'We must go home,' David said, though neither of them knew how they would tell their father. Hans did not offer to go with them. In the beginning their mourning would be private.

Benjamin parked the car a good way from the house so that Leon would not hear their approach. They walked slowly and silently along the street and almost tip-toed to the front door. As David reached for his key, the door opened. Leon stood there. He had sensed their coming. There was no need to say anything. He looked at them for a moment and smelt the mourning on them. David took him in his arms.

'We must leave this country,' he said. 'We must save ourselves, Papa.'

Heidi appeared in the hall.

'What's happened?' she asked.

'They killed her,' Benjamin said. 'The storm-troopers. It's a pogrom.'

'But those things only happen in Russia and Poland,' Heidi said, protecting her native land from such sullied words.

'They're happening here,' Benjamin said coldly. 'And it's only a beginning.'

But as it turned out, it was a beginning on quite a large scale. Many synagogues all over the country had been destroyed, 7,000

Jewish shops were looted and wrecked. 30,000 Jews were arrested and sent to concentration camps, and according to the official figures, 91 Jews were killed.

They buried Greta a few days later. Leon had asked for her to be laid next to Barak. She had always looked upon Barak as a father, and it seemed fitting that she should lie by his side. When they reached the cemetery, they were horrified by the devastation. The wreckage of the burial-ground had been part of the Kristallnacht celebrations. Barak's headstone lay in two pieces on top of his grave, and each piece was daubed with a swastika. At the graveside, the Rabbi intoned the customary burial prayers and, when it was over, he did not turn away, but stayed and stared at the ground for a long time. Then he lifted his head towards the mourners and almost in a whisper, 'You must leave this country. All of you who can,' he said. Then he turned and made his way out of the burial ground.

The Bindels returned home and mourned for the customary seven days, and when it was over David broached yet again the subject of emigration. 'We must go, Papa,' he said. 'All of us. There is nothing left for us in this country.'

'There are bones,' Leon practically shouted at him. Greta's death tore at his heart. 'There are bones,' he said again. 'Bones of one I loved. All my life I have run away from my dead. There must come a stop to such a running. This time, I shall not run. Not even in the name of survival. I am old enough. In God's eyes I have survived already. I shall not leave Greta,' he cried. 'I shall be buried at her side.'

A few days later, Leon went to the offices of the burial board of the synagogue, and reserved for himself the vacant plot alongside Greta. But Leon Bindel was never to lie there. His tomb would be a wide trench, dressed in quicklime, hundreds of miles away from this place, and he would lie there with countless others of his kind, related only by their common faith and their jagged creed of survival.

CHAPTER TWENTY

A few weeks after Christmas Kurt Dreiser died. Hans mourned him as naturally and as deeply as a son would mourn a father he loved, and that mourning bred his appetite for revenge. How, or when, he had no idea, but day after day, for many years, he nurtured that appetite until it became a means of survival. Mrs Dreiser insisted that the funeral be private. Kurt had had many friends, most of them politicals, and Mrs Dreiser did not want to put them at risk in a gathering, however solemn the occasion. The SS were everywhere, with their wary eyes and notebooks. It must be a family funeral, she insisted. But she made an exception with Benjamin. She loved Benjamin as she did her own son. He had attended her husband daily during his illness. She regarded him as part of the family.

Kurt Dreiser was to be cremated according to his wishes and the ceremony was to be performed in the afternoon. Benjamin took time off from the hospital. He said not a word to his family. He knew that Heidi and David would try to stop him. He knew, too, that his father would let him go his way, but with a great deal of anguish. It was better than he tell nobody. They gathered in the courtyard of the crematorium. Mr Dreiser, Hans and Inge. A stranger was there who was introduced to Benjamin as Kurt's younger brother. There were also two sisters of Mrs Dreiser together with their husbands. Benjamin, the only non-relative, completed the small party.

'Everything is ready,' Hans said. 'Shall we go inside?' He took his mother's arm and led her into the small chapel. Benjamin and the others followed. The mourners arranged themselves in the first row, a pew of concentrated grief. The coffin, wreathed in flowers, stood on its ball-bearings directly in front of them. The priest stood at the lectern, his head buzzing with hurriedly acquired data of the deceased's life, much of which was politically unspeakable. All men are human, and deserving of God's grace, he kept telling himself, and that could be the theme of his sermon. Meanwhile, echoing through the hollow chapel, came the sounds of a distant choir, and when the hymn was over, the priest asked the mourners to stand. While he was reciting the funeral prayers, there was a disturbance at the back of the chapel. The doors were flung open and were heard to close behind stamping feet. Booted feet, the mourners knew, and jack-booted too, and each of them was afraid to turn and look at the intruders' faces. But they saw the priest look towards the door. His voice faltered a little, then settled into the comfort of the prayer. When it was over, he asked the mourners to sit, and he cast a second nervous glance towards the door. Still the mourners dared not turn. The priest spoke about Kurt Dreiser in the terms of a brother. The presence of the SS guards in this holy place angered him, but he was not afraid. Indeed their belligerent presence moved his tongue to speak out on Kurt Dreiser's behalf, to celebrate and to applaud his life, his courage and his principles. And when he spoke in this manner, the mourners trembled. They were glad when his eulogy was over. 'Let us pray,' he said.

The Dreiser family knelt down in the pew. But Benjamin's knees stiffened with that time-honoured resistance that had dwelt in the Bindel soul for so many generations, and despite the jack-booted stares of those behind him, he sat on his wooden seat and crouched a little, hoping to make his lack of genuflection less conspicuous. The prayers continued silently until a long and solemn 'Amen' from the priest signalled their end. 'Let us say farewell,' he said, 'to our brother Kurt Dreiser, who leaves us with our grief and the memory of his courage and his glory.'

Slowly the coffin moved backwards on its bearings, and the slow movement of a Schubert quartet filtered through the chapel. But only for its first opening phrases, for suddenly it was rudely broken. From the back of the hall came the loud yet harmonious singing of the Horst Wessel song, its words and its music a monumental affront to the memory of a man who, all his life, had fought against the evil of which it sang. '*The flag is high, the ranks are closed, / The SS march with calm and steady stride.*'

Mrs Dreiser broke into sobs and Hans' face was purple with rage. Benjamin was glad that Hans had his mother by his side, to whom he must give comfort, else his hands might well have wandered and killed. But Benjamin's hands were free. He turned without fear and, with no hesitation, he walked to the back of the chapel. They waited for him, laughing. He went to where they stood.

'How dare you, you scum,' he hissed at them. 'Get out of here.'

'Identity,' one of them said, as if he hadn't heard, while the other two guards grabbed Benjamin by the shoulders and kicked him behind the knees. They buckled to the ground.

'So you *can* kneel,' one of them said.

Benjamin's ears were burning with pain and his hand trembled as he withdrew his card of identity from his pocket. The storm-trooper snatched it from him, then the other guards took his hands and forced them upwards behind his back. Hot tears of anger and pain rolled down his cheeks. He turned his head then and managed to see the tail-end of the coffin as it rolled towards the fire. 'Farewell, comrade,' he whimpered.

The guard struck him across the face. Then he held the card up to the light. 'A doctor,' he said. 'We need his kind. I know just the place for him. Take him away.'

The two guards relaxed their hold and gripped Benjamin's arms.

'Where are you taking him?' Hans was suddenly at Benjamin's side.

'You'll be told,' the leader of the gang said. 'But it would be better for you and the likes of you if you don't enquire.' He raised his hand in salute. '*Heil Hitler,*' he said, and he goose-stepped out of the chapel.

They bundled Benjamin to a darkened van and threw him onto the floor, while they sat one on each side of him, their boots resting on his neck. Benjamin felt his bowels empty, but he would not let it humiliate him. This place would do for a sewer, and the storm-troopers for sewer-attendants. He had to think that way, else he would have crumbled in his shame. He was relieved to be lying down, despite the yoke on his neck. He relaxed his muscles and tried to breathe deeply, and slowly his pain ebbed. He was sorry when the van came to a stop. He had begun to doze and he would have wanted to sleep for ever, for he dreaded what fate awaited him. They dragged him from the van, keeping their distance.

'God, he stinks,' one of them said.

'What d'you expect?' his companion said. 'He's a Yid. Smells like all of them.'

They threw him in a cell and they left him. Benjamin lay on the stone floor and did not move, while his eyes grew accustomed to the darkness around him. He could smell himself, and in a strange way it comforted him. For the smell spoke of his indignation, his weakness and his fear, and all that made him more human than his attackers. He would sleep in that smell and wake in it too, and it would not offend him. He looked at his watch and noticed that the glass was broken. He put it to his ear and heard its comforting tick. Four o'clock, it said, and he wondered whether it was morning or afternoon. Then he remembered the funeral, only a short time ago it seemed, so he knew that the darkness was only in his cell. He closed his eyes. When he awoke, or rather, was suddenly awakened, he felt he had slept for hours. But his watch showed ten minutes to five. He heard a voice telling him to get up and, when he tried, his knees buckled once again and a sharp pain shot through his arms. But he forced himself to stand and to look at his captors. There were two of them this time, but he couldn't tell whether or not they were the same as the others. He had noticed on the streets of Leipzig how all storm-troopers looked alike as if they had been cloned, but not from a human cell, but from the germ of an idea that was evil incarnate. He looked at his guards with contempt.

'We're going on a little trip,' one of them said. 'You'd like that, wouldn't you?' He kicked him on the shins.

Benjamin breathed deeply, fighting the pain, and allowed himself to be dragged from the cell and into the blinding light of the street. But not for long. For once again he was bundled into a van, a different one this time, one with windows, one, too, with company. For there were already many men standing inside, pressing against each other for lack of space. And still others came after Benjamin, forcing their reluctant way inside in order to escape the kicks of their guards. Then soon the van doors were locked and barred and the men stared at each other, but no one spoke, as they shifted this way and that to try and find a firm hold on the floor of the truck. Then suddenly the van took off, and they could not fall because there was no space for their collapse, so they rocked and lurched until, in that rhythm, they found from each other's bodies some means of support. After about an hour of travelling each of them had found a pocket of support in his neighbour's person. They had woven themselves, body by body, into a web of common fear and apprehension, and none of them spoke, each one of them concentrating on his own contribution to the warp and the woof. They could not bear to think of what would become of them. They travelled so for many hours. Benjamin, who was taller than most, could see out of the windows, and as it grew dark, he deciphered a signpost, lit by the headlight of a following car. It signalled that 20 kilometres hence lay the town of Weimar, of which kingdom, Benjamin recalled, Goethe had once been chief minister. He hoped that they would by-pass it, and go far, far away, miles from that place that had once spelt out his country's glory.

The van turned into a side-road, and after a few miles, the road was unmade, and the van heaved its way over the bumps and the dips while the web of men inside held to its perfect symmetry. It was very dark now, and it was impossible to see the terrain through which they passed. Benjamin caught sight of a lone star and, for the first time since the chapel, he thought of home, of his children, of his father, David and Heidi. And in that order. And for the first time too, he felt despair, not on his own account, but on theirs, for their anguish, and the pain of his absence. He looked at the men around him and he knew that all of them were thinking of home. The night had urged that recall, the gathering dark had prompted their weary thoughts towards their separate firesides. The gleam of imagined firelight was flickering in their eyes, and some of the men were crying. But still nobody spoke. Nobody wanted to know his neighbour's name, where he was going and why, for any speech would have given credence to their present situation. They preferred to consider it as a nightmare from which they would soon awaken.

The van pulled up sharply and they opened their eyes, but still the nightmare clung. The door was flung open and the human web disintegrated. They were herded into a group outside the truck. It was dark, and difficult to decipher their whereabouts. They could see the silhouette of barracks of a sort and the shadows of many trees.

'Get in line,' one of the guards barked at them.

They shuffled themselves into some kind of order, and then were led through a clearing to a line of buildings at the entrance of the camp. A few guards stood there and ordered the men to run. Mercifully the distance to the barracks was short and, when they reached there, they were directed to a shed and told they could sleep till morning. Work would begin at four a.m. For all the men, the offer of sleep was a gift indeed and, though they needed food and warmth, their need for oblivion was greater than either. There were serried rows of straw beds on the floor, but no blankets, and the men lay where they stood, and shut their eyes against the horror of it all. As the guards were leaving, one of the men dared to ask where they were.

'This place is called Buchenwald,' he said, 'and you're not likely to forget it.'

The Buchenwald concentration camp had been opened a year before and was, at the time of Benjamin's imprisonment, in the last stages of its construction. It was sited five miles from the city of Weimar in the wooded area of Ettersberg. Its siting was deliberate. Weimar was the cultural centre of Germany, the hub of its classical spirit. It seemed fitting to the rulers of the Third Reich that the new spirit of Germany should unfold in its environs. Thus Goethe's oak-tree, the Goethe-Eich, which inspired Germany's greatest minstrel, became the central feature of Buchenwald concentration camp, the only tree spared in that black wooded landscape. The job of the first prisoners had been to clear the jungle of bracken and roots that was to be the camp site. At the time of Benjamin's arrival, a road-building scheme was under way, and the construction of drainage. It was back-breaking work, with inadequate tools, and it was this work that the new prisoners would be forced to undertake during their camp stay. Nobody knew when that stay would end or whether it would end at all. Benjamin was excluded from this detail. He was designated as the Prison Doctor and in the morning he was called into the Commandant's office. SS Colonel Koch was in charge of the camp, assisted by one Major Rödl and Captain Weissenborn. Benjamin was greeted with unexpected respect.

'Your work is vital to our Organisation,' Colonel Koch told him.

Benjamin was horrified. He didn't want to be any part of their organisation and certainly not a vital one.

'A doctor's work is important wherever he practises,' he said indifferently. 'I would like to see the hospital,' he added.

The Colonel smiled. 'We are not yet so grand,' he said. 'We call it our medical room. But first go and collect your uniform. Then I myself will show you your work quarters. He raised his right arm. '*Heil Hitler*,' he said.

Benjamin stared at him. Did the man actually expect some response?

Colonel Koch smiled. 'It's very simple you know,' he said. 'You just lift your right arm to about 120 degrees from your body. It's really very easy. Try it.'

Benjamin didn't mind lifting his arm, but he was not inclined to the words that accompanied such a gesture. His hand lay limp at his side.

'Aren't you willing to try?' Colonel Koch said, and Benjamin noticed that the smile had gone from his face.

'My heart is not in it,' Benjamin said, finding courage.

'Then Major Rödl will help move your heart,' he said. He signalled to his assistant who grabbed Benjamin's right wrist and forced his arm upwards. 'Now keep it there,' he ordered, letting the wrist go.

Benjamin looked at his outstretched arm and imagined himself as a policeman on point duty, and this image held his arm where it had been ordered.

'Now say *Heil Hitler*,' Colonel Koch said.

But such a statement was no part of a traffic policeman's work. Benjamin's lips were firmly sealed.

The Colonel signalled to the Major once more, who pinched Benjamin's nose so that his mouth had to open.

'Now let the words out,' Koch said. '*Heil Hitler*.'

Still nothing came. Rödl twisted the nose so that the tears started in Benjamin's eyes. His ears rang with his father's words from the minstrel of Grandpa Jakob's legacy. Survive, There is no cause on earth worth dying for, no country worth one's martyrdom, no principle worth one's sacrifice. Survive.

'*Heil Hitler*,' Benjamin shouted with zeal.

Koch was impressed by his enthusiasm. 'That's a good beginning, Bindel,' he said. 'What a pity you're a Jew.'

A guard took him to the shower rooms. 'A shower is a privilege,' he told him. 'It's only because you're a doctor. Not that it will make much difference. You stink like a Jew.'

Benjamin had forgotten the incident of his capture. He had become used to his smell and no longer found it offensive. But the prospect of a warm shower was heartening and he stood under it and wiped the dried faeces from his flesh. The guard took away his clothes promising their return on his release. 'If that day should ever come,' he added. Then he took him to the store-room.

He was given a torn vest, a pair of socks, and boots, with no regards as to fit. Then he was led to a counter on which lay separate piles of jackets.

'Jew,' the guard said to the attendant.

The man pulled the top jacket from a pile, one marked with a yellow star. Benjamin looked along the line at the other piles. Jackets with purple stars, with red, with green.

'What do those colours stand for?' Benjamin asked.

'You'll learn,' the guard said. 'All you need to know is your own. Yellow's for Jew. He's a doctor,' he added to the attendant, who then went to a cupboard at the end of the store-room and returned with a none-too-white coat. He handed it to Benjamin. It was very much larger than the jacket, and Benjamin noted that if he buttoned it all the way up it would hide his yellow star. So he left it open. He had nothing to hide in this place. Indeed the yellow symbol had given him some pride. He wondered whether an equal pride could be felt in the other colours.

He was taken into the barracks-yard and told to wait for the Commandant. It was very cold. The torn vest next to his body did little to comfort him, and he longed for his funeral suit, stinking as it was, for its warmth and familiarity. It seemed to him that he had been years in this place and he had to remind himself that Kurt Dreiser had been buried only the day before, and he winced at the recall of his obscene obsequies. A line of men was waiting at the barracks. They were probably his companions in the van that had brought them to this place. He could not recall any of their faces. In any case, in their prison uniforms and now shaven heads, they looked very similar, and the only feature that distinguished them was the colour of their stars. Benjamin wandered over in their direction. He stood apart from them, at a distance, ashamed of his white coat and its mark of difference. He looked at them keenly, not at their faces, but at the jackets they wore. He was seeking out another yellow star for his comfort. He smiled. All his life, he and Heidi had run from that identity and here, in this bleak and desolate place, he was seeking it out for friendship. But he could not spot one yellow star among them. Most of them were red, with the occasional purple. He was afraid to approach them. There were guards all around. At night in their sleeping-quarters he would seek out their categories. He watched the guard as he moved them off. 'Left, right, left,' he barked at them, and they fell into some kind of marching rhythm, their stars flashing in the cold morning light. He watched them into the distance, and saw how some stumbled and fell, and how the guard whipped them upright, and how they fell yet again. He wondered whether any of them would become his patients. He went back to the spot where he had been told to wait. He scanned the perimeter of the camp, and he could see no building that could pass as medical quarters. He began to fear what his duties as a doctor might be. He saw Colonel Koch coming towards him, and as he drew near, he raised his right hand in salute. '*Heil Hitler,*' he said.

Benjamin was glad that the other prisoners had gone, and that there was none of his kind around who could witness his response.

'*Heil Hitler,*' he said, raising his arm, and he was surprised at the ease with which he could respond, because he knew that its only meaning was that it guaranteed his survival. At least for the time being. Then he would find other means, he decided, no matter how base, how demeaning. He owed it to his great-grandfather Jakob of Odessa.

'Come,' Colonel Koch said. 'I'll show you your working quarters. You will keep three paces behind me,' he said. He called two guards to his side, and instructed them to walk in front of his prisoner. With all his power, Benjamin thought, Koch was frightened, and the thought pleased him.

He was led to an out-house on the perimeter of the camp. From outside it looked like a vast white-washed shed but, once inside, Benjamin saw that it was sub-divided into many rooms. There was little to indicate that it was a hospital. In one room, where they now stood, there was a table on which were spread out the rudimentary medical instruments. A blood-pressure gauge, a stethoscope, an eye and ear torch, and a pile of swabs and spatulas. In one corner stood a weighing machine. On a wall in a small annexe to the chamber were written figures to measure the height of a man. It seemed to be a room for preliminary examination, a diagnostic room perhaps, before the serious business of treatment began.

'These are your quarters,' the Colonel said.

'Where are the wards?' Benjamin asked.

'There are no wards. All treatment is given in here.'

'But if people are ill and need beds?' Benjamin asked.

'Your patients will not need beds,' Koch said. 'In here they are given special treatment.'

Benjamin shivered.

'Don't worry,' Koch said. 'I will show you how it works.'

But he's no doctor, Benjamin thought. How can he tell me my job?

But this so-called medical room had nothing to do with medical treatment. Its purpose was murder, and Koch, by profession and long standing, was a murderer. This room was his job, a job of which Benjamin knew nothing.

'I'll show you what you have to do,' Koch said. 'Come with me.'

Once more Benjamin followed him while the two guards placed themselves between the parties for Koch's protection. He crossed the room. The far wall was open at one end, giving out to an ante-room, the floor of which was covered with sawdust. The room smelt of death, like a morgue. But the most terrifying feature was the drain that ran through the centre of the floor, probably the only efficient drainage system in the camp.

'What's the drain for?' Benjamin dared to ask.

'Blood,' Koch said. 'What else?'

'Whose blood?' Benjamin persisted.

'Criminals',' Koch said.

Benjamin knew that in Koch's opinion all men who were not Nazis fell into that category. This room could well be his own death-chamber.

'It's all very simple,' Koch was saying. 'This annexe is the killing-room,' he said. He was as phlegmatic as an estate-agent showing a property to a prospective client, 'and here, if you look closely at the wall, there is a hole large enough for the nozzle of a gun. Behind that hole is where the marksman takes his stand. You will place your patient alongside this embrasure, so that his temple is aligned with the hole. He will suspect nothing, for here, as you see,' he pointed to the wall, 'is a measuring scale for his height. Rather neat, don't you think?' Koch turned to Benjamin. He was not asking his opinion. He was simply stating his admiration of an ingenious device that he himself had probably invented.

'Of course,' he said, 'there will be certain formalities before the criminal is dispatched. Those formalities are your job. You will not bring your patient into this annexe until you have weighed him, taken his pulse, his heart-beat and blood-pressure. When that is done, and you have taken your notes, you will direct him to this annexe ostensibly to measure his height. When you have lined him up against the wall – there are three small steps here, you will notice – ' he said, pointing to the floor, 'you will have to adjust his height to the embrasure. And then you will say, "Stand there for a moment. I'll get my notebook." That will be the marksman's cue to fire. You yourself will have quickly withdrawn from the chamber.'

He turned and walked back to the medical room. 'Is that all clear?' he asked.

Benjamin stared at him, incredulous. 'Why do you need a doctor?' he whispered.

Koch smiled. 'Everything about our party, all our operations, are totally professional and authentic. Now I would like you to try out the scheme,' Koch said. 'The guard will stand in as your patient. You can regard it as a dress-rehearsal,'

'You,' he nodded to the second guard, 'you will be the marksman. Go to your stand.'

The guard withdrew to the shooting gallery, while the other waited for his examination.

'I omitted an important fact,' Koch said. 'It is imperative that you require all patients to strip naked before your examination. You will have a guard present at all times, and he will sort out the clothing and possessions after the patients' disposal. Now you may begin.'

293

'Benjamin did not trust the words that would come out of his throat, and when they came, they squeaked with fear and disbelief. 'Would you undress?' he said to the guard. 'Take everything off.'

The guard made no move. He just smiled and looked at the Commandant.

'A member of the Nazi party does not undress in front of a Jew,' Koch said. 'This is only a rehearsal, remember.'

Benjamin walked to the table, stiffening his legs to hide his trembling. He picked up the stethoscope and hung it round his neck. Then he went towards the guard and made to open the buttons of his tunic.

'You don't have to touch him,' Koch said gruffly. 'I appreciate your zeal, Bindel, but this is only a rehearsal.'

Benjamin put the stethoscope in his ears, and placed it over the guard's breast-button. He waited for a while, then he took it away and returned to the table for the blood-pressure gauge. 'Would you sit down?' he said to the guard.

'What about your notes on his heart?' Koch said.

'I'm sorry,' Benjamin said, and he picked up his note-book. It sounded so silly to apologise, especially since he didn't know what he was sorry for. He was angry with himself for failing to refuse this monstrous assignment. He kept thinking of his great-grandpa Jakob, and wondered whether he himself had any notion of the cost of survival. Then he recalled the story of the milk-brothers, and the price they had been forced to pay. But had either of them connived at murder, as he was doing? 'I'm sorry,' he said again, almost to himself, but even as a self-apology, it sounded so grossly inadequate for the enormity of the crime he was about to commit in the name of his own survival. For a moment he was tempted to down his sham tools and to refuse to participate. But then he realised that he was replaceable, a thousand times over, and that his refusal would not save a single life.

He wound the black bandage around the guard's arm and made as if to take his blood-pressure. Then, with his torch, he looked into his eyes and his ears, and with a spatula he examined his throat, taking notes after each stage of examination, as he was directed. He dallied with his note-taking, delaying the dénoument of his act, anxious to postpone his unpardonable collusion.

'Hurry up, Bindel,' Koch said. 'I appreciate your conscientiousness, but I have work to do.'

Was this not his work? Benjamin thought. The core of all their works? Was not murder their divine purpose?

'I'd like to take your height,' Benjamin whispered, and he directed the man to the annexe. Every limb in his body was trembling, as he gauged the guard's height in relation to the embrasure. He instructed him to stand on the second step, and noted that he had rightly chosen, for the guard's temple fitted neatly against the hole in the wall.'

'Well done, Bindel,' Koch laughed. 'Right first time. Beginners' luck, perhaps,' he said.

And then Benjamin realised he'd forgotten his line, that cue he was to give to the marksman. That line that would put his own person out of shooting-range. Perhaps he had never listened to it, finding the whole performance so grotesquely unbelievable. He turned to Koch. 'I've forgotten what I must say,' he said. There was no apology in his voice, nor helplessness.

'It's the most important part of the procedure,' Koch shouted. 'Write it down, man, and learn it by heart. "*Stand still for a moment. I'll get my note-book*".'

Benjamin turned back to the medical-room to fetch his pad.

'You can write it down later,' Koch thundered. 'Just say it.'

But it had gone again, so loathe was Benjamin to utter it. He hesitated.

'*Stand still for a moment*,' Koch tried to be patient.

Benjamin repeated the words in a whisper.

While I get my note-book,' Koch said, and Benjamin echoed the words.

'Now again. On your own,' Koch said.

This time Benjamin remembered them, for their terrible echo still hung on the air. He looked at the guard's face as he felt the cold nozzle nestle his temple. He looked decidedly uncomfortable. Benjamin was rooted to the spot.

'Get out of the way, man,' Koch yelled.

'Bang, bang,' the marksman bleated from behind his screen.

The guard fell to the floor, a huge grin on his face, and the rehearsal was over.

'How many a day?' Benjamin dared to ask.

'It varies,' Koch said. 'Depends on how the prisoners adapt. Some of course,' he said, 'are given a medical examination as soon as they arrive. We are not interested in their adaptability. But you will be here on duty, even when there are no patients. But I think we can keep you pretty busy. You start tomorrow,' he said, and made to leave the room.

There was one question that burned on Benjamin's tongue. What had happened to his predecessor? But he was too frightened to ask it. He knew that no man who had seen such things could be allowed to live. He thought of his children, but he could not recall their faces. Nor their heights, their weights, their heart-beats, their pulses. Nothing. To recall all those things in this place would have been to confirm their mortality. All he could remember was the fact that they had not inherited, and that omission, which meant their ignorance of the means of survival, grieved him far more than any thought of his own certain death. Suddenly he felt very hungry, and he realised that he hadn't eaten since before Kurt Dreiser's funeral which now seemed so many years ago. He was ashamed of his sudden appetite, that appetite that belonged to the vibrant and the living, when he himself was engaged in the business of murder.

'It's time for breakfast,' the guard said, as if reading his thoughts, and he grabbed his arm and led him out of his quarters.

In all other ways apart from that of his work, Benjamin was treated like the other prisoners. He slept in the same doss-down barracks, covered by one thin blanket; he ate at the same slop-table, and presented himself at roll-call four times each day. Breakfast was a hunk of bread and some thin soup. The bread ration for the whole day was distributed the night before, but prisoners were so hungry that they often consumed it during the night. The work they were obliged to do was back-breaking. At the time of Benjamin's imprisonment, they were constructing the sewerage system, and the men, most of whom had never in their lives bent their backs to hard labour, were now forced to break stones and hump them by hand from the quarry. It was an exceptionally cold winter that year and, for lack of food and warm clothing, it was unlikely that they would survive. If they must die, Benjamin prayed, let them die in the quarry. For no matter how painful or how unjust that death, it was cleaner and more natural than the fatal disease of unadaptability.

He sat at the table in as isolated a position as he could find. He wanted to be alone, yet at the same time he had a hungry need to tell others of the horrendous duties that he was obliged to fulfill. Yet he made no attempt to talk to them and he certainly would not look them in the eye. He did not ever want to see their faces, much less to know the nature of their pain. He did not want to learn of their work, or of their families that they had left behind. He wanted to know nothing about them. As they sat there, bent with their fatigue and their despair, each one of them showed the frightening symptoms of unadaptability. Any one of them, at any time, could be led into his medical room, with all the guard's solicitude, and offer himself for treatment. He dared not learn to know them, and through them the widows he would make, and the orphans. Yet he needed so desperately to reach out a hand for friendship. Perhaps if he could find a yellow star, that bearer of their common guilt, such a man would understand. But most of the stars in the barracks were red. He had to discover the colours' meanings. He would ask one of them, he decided. He would keep his eye on the man's star, but never once would he look into his eyes. A red one sat next to him, as intent, it seemed, on his separateness as Benjamin himself.

'What does the red star mean?' Benjamin asked, staring at the man's jacket.

'Political.' The man gave a sideways whisper.

'Green?' Benjamin asked.

'Criminal.'

'Purple?'

'Jehovah's Witness.'

The conversation was over, and neither men would ever connect the other's voice with a face.

Every day Benjamin went to the medical room and waited, trembling at every footfall outside the door. He began to believe that Colonel Koch's little pageant was a huge joke designed to frighten him, and that for the rest of his time in the camp he would live in daily fear of its truth. So that when on the fourth day, his first patient arrived, he thought that Koch had carried the joke too far. But one look at the guard's face told him that he was at last in business, the serious business of extermination.

He heard the prisoner enter the room, and as long as he could he avoided looking at the man's face. The voice was young and trusting. Twenty-eight years old, it said. Profession? Married? Children? Any previous illnesses? Questions to put the man at ease, to authenticate the purpose of his visit, to erase from his mind any doubts or suspicions.

'Let's have a look at you then,' Benjamin said, as he would have addressed any patient at the Jewish hospital in Leipzig. Though in the hospital he would have known the man's face and the nature of his complaint long before the undressing stage. 'Take your clothes off,' he said. He looked at the man's attire as it dropped to the floor. He had been brought straight from the transport, so he wore no prison-uniform, no star. Benjamin would never know for what so-called crime he was sending this man to his death. He weighed 155 pounds. A healthy weight, if his height was average, but Benjamin dared not think of that factor, for it was that measurement that would signal the cock of the trigger. He looked at the young man's body. Uncircumcised, he noticed, and he was ashamed at the sudden surge of relief in his heart that he was not sending to his death one of his own kind. He put a stethoscope to the man's chest and was hurt at the rude health of the young heart. His blood-pressure pulse was like a boy's, ripe for living, his eye bright with hungry vision, his young ears tuned to vibrant sound. No malady, no disorder, just too healthy, too young, too innocent to survive.

'Let's see how tall you are.'

'Five foot eleven,' the man said.

'I must check it,' Benjamin said helplessly. He took his patient's hand in a gesture of farewell. The hand was cool, fearless and trusting. Benjamin squeezed it as a token of his love. He instructed the prisoner to stand on the second step. Until that time he had not seen the man's face, but now he would have to look at it, to measure his gentle temple's adjustment to that hollow chamber of his death. He raised his eyes and looked at the man's face for the first time. His young trusting years stabbed at his heart.

'You'll see I'm right,' the man said. 'Five foot eleven.'

Benjamin eyed the hole and found its adjustment exact. He would not smile at the man. Instead, he took both his hands in his own.

'Wait here,' Benjamin said. 'I have to fetch my note-book.' He turned quickly away and shuffled back into the medical room. Then he heard the explosion and the thud of the falling body.

'Well done,' he heard the guard say.

Benjamin put his face in his hands and wept like a child.

'The first one is always the worst,' the guard said. 'You'll get used to it.'

But never, never would he get used to it, Benjamin knew, or rather hoped, for he feared that the guard may be right, and that the only way to survive the overwhelming shame and guilt of what he had done was habituation.

The whistle blew for roll-call, the second of the day. He staggered out of the medical room, but the fresh cold air of the morning brought no relief. He was a murderer and the label shrieked from every pore. And he would have to get used to it, or die. The second roll-call of the day was always the longest and the most punishing. The men, most of them unused to physical labour, had already broken stones since the cold dawn. They were hungry too, and shivering. Benjamin noticed that a feverish sweat poured from many a forehead, and he prayed that if they had to die, it would be from the natural cause of pneumonia. He waited while the names were called. In front of him a man fell forward onto his face. Benjamin knelt down by his side. 'You must try to stand,' he pleaded.

'Let me die,' the man said.

'No.' Benjamin was outraged. He who had just sent a man to his death, who had, in all deception, prepared his body for that final celebration, now concerned himself with survival. And for what? he thought: So that this same man should one day come to his quarters and submit himself to innocent measurement? He turned the man over and cradled his head in his hands. He noted the purple star on his jacket. A Jehovah's Witness. Where, in God's name, was his God witnessing now?

'Leave me,' the man said.

Benjamin stood and returned to his place, turning his face from the jack-booted guard, clenching his teeth against the kicking on the ground, but forcing himself to watch, for after all, what he had done that morning was far gentler than this. He had touched no man's body except with love. He had gathered human hands in his own and had felt in their trusting pulse the very last throb of their earthly lives. He had listened with love to the curtain-call of their heart-beat. His own face had been fanned by the patient's last breath. He had gone with him into death as far as he was able. And then he had turned away and tried not to hear, and to wipe from his eyes the vision of that face that he had had to confront. I did not put the gun into the guard's hand, he kept telling himself. Yet he had put his target squarely and neatly, and oh so skilfully, into the line of fire. What difference between him and the marksman?

The guard in front of him had at last exhausted his appetite. He dragged the prisoner to his feet and ordered him to stand. Benjamin knew that the man could not support himself, so he grabbed the back of the man's jacket with one hand, while with the other, he supported one shoulder, and held the man as upright as he could. Soon the roll-call would be over. But how could a man in such condition go back to work? 'He is beaten, hungry, feverish and, as Jehovah is his witness, probably dying. Let him die of pneumonia,' Benjamin prayed, for already he had the rash of unadaptability. 'Please, O God. Not my department.'

The roll-call was over, and the men were led off once again to their work. Benjamin had to release his hold on the man, and as he did so, he fell at his feet, shivering and crying and praying for death. As Benjamin made to kneel by his side, the guard laid a hand on his shoulder.

'Leave him,' he shouted.

'But he will die,' Benjamin said, and wondered again why he was so concerned with the continuation of life, since they were all going to die in this place anyway, and what point was there in prolonging a living death?

The guard led him back to his quarters. Once inside, he noticed how clean it all was, how warm, how innocent. The floor of the killing-room had been spread with sawdust, and fresh clean water trickled through the drain with the sounds of a mountain stream. He sat at his desk and he waited, shivering with every footfall outside, the volunteering hoodwinked footsteps of the condemned.

'There's a new transport tonight,' the guard promised him. 'Communists from Dresden. You'll be kept pretty busy.'

That night, after dark, the van drove through the camp gates. There were seven prisoners. Each man took his last breaths of fresh air in the short walk from the van to the medical room. The men were kept in the van until their turn came, so that they were out of ear-shot of the final examination. 'To spare their feelings,' the guard had told Benjamin, with sudden obscene compassion.

That night, Benjamin listened to seven hearts, seven pulses, and looked into seven innocent faces. Each one of them was unique, and none of them would he ever forget. He went to bed that night with eight murders on his gentle hands, and he prayed to God for his own death. The following night, the tally was twenty, and no face yet blurred into another. As he closed his eyes for the sleep that would not come, each portrait loomed, separate, gallows-framed in the gallery of his mind. And there were spaces that he knew would soon be filled, filled with new unblurred faces, and one of them, he prayed, would soon hang with his own.

For a whole week there were no new arrivals at the camp. Every day Benjamin was escorted to his medical quarters where he waited for patients and prayed that they would not come. There was nothing he could occupy himself with. He was allowed no reading matter or writing materials, and all he could do was to contemplate the instruments on the desk in front of him that had, each one of them, become tools of his fraud and deception. He doubted, even if he survived this place, whether he would ever practise medicine again. At the end of the week and a whole seven days of blessed unemployment, Benjamin began to have hopes that the slaughter was over. Until that time, all his victims had been civilian-clothed, star-less, journey-weary, so he began to convince himself that at least those men, whose restless faces he viewed each night, tossing on their filthy beds, would never be candidates for his fraudulent diagnosis. Perhaps now he could risk their friendship and dare to search for a confidante amongst them, one to whom he could confess his sins, one who would justify them in the name of survival. And as it turned out, he was freed into their daily company. For after a week of idleness he was sent to work on the sewerage, until new one-way transports would arrive.

He welcomed the work as one would a holiday. As he picked over the stones, his back aching with the unaccustomed work, he celebrated each moment of his absence from his usual quarters and he tried not to think that he was party to the construction of blood drainage. He kept telling himself that he was helping to build a system that would enhance the sanitary conditions of the camp. That the make-shift open-air latrines could be disposed of, and in their places men could find privacy, where no one could eavesdrop on their despair. No longer would the prisoners have to squat over the open latrine pits, fearing the prodding of the SS boot, that for its fun and diversion, would often hurl the squatting prisoner into the cess-pool below, in the very act of his elemental confirmation that he was alive and could of his own volition, dispose of his waste.

Benjamin worked with zeal and celebration. After the medical quarters, he found in the punishing labour, the searing cold, and the jeers and kicks of the guards, something of a paradise. He covered for the other prisoners, while they took a little rest from their labours. From time to time, and in whispers, he sang to them, his inherited song of survival, a true Bindel minstrel in that desolate waste. But still he did not look into their faces. He still feared that one day, he would have to measure the height of one with whom he had broken bread and stones.

He had been in Buchenwald for three whole weeks, and that night, after his day's back-breaking labour, was the first time that sleep came swiftly to comfort him. The following morning, he noticed that some of the beds were empty, and he learnt that some men had been released and sent back to their homes. Benjamin's heart surged with hope, and he dared once more to think of his children. For another week he worked in the sewers, and every morning, when he awoke, he noticed and blessed the absence of those faces he had not dared to view. Rumour spread that the camp would slowly be cleared to make room for a large contingent of prisoners that was expected after a nation-wide political purge. They would need a doctor, Benjamin could not help thinking. But a white coated guard would do. Each night he prayed for a day's work in the sewers. He would settle for that, even for a lifetime, rather than dispense one more diagnosis in his quarters. A week passed and the barracks slowly emptied. Roll-calls were reduced to two a day, but there were still casualties who fell in the line.

'Hang on,' Benjamin urged them in whispers. 'Our freedom cannot be far away,' and he began to wonder whether the empty morning mattresses signified death rather than freedom.

At the end of that week, marking almost two months of incarceration, he was told to wait in the barracks square at the end of the evening roll-call. He dreaded the order for his return to the medical room. He stood alone on the parade-ground, shivering with cold and fear. It was dark when the guard approached him, his own personal guard from the medical quarters. 'You will be released in the morning,' he said. 'You will go now to the store-room and collect your clothes.'

It was some time before Benjamin could move from the spot, so overjoyed was he. For a moment he forgot the nightmare that would travel home with him, and without separateness, because it had inhabited his body as irresistibly as any vital organ in his frame.

'Go on,' the guard shoved him with his stick.

Benjamin ran to the store-room. He waited at the counter while the attendant sifted through the piles of clothes. He withdrew a bundle wrapped with string, and checked on the label. 'Bindel?' he shouted. 'Doctor?' he sneered.

Benjamin would not acknowledge that profession. He had forfeited all his rights to practise it. 'Bindel,' he said, and that was all. The attendant put the bundle on the counter.

'Thank you,' Benjamin said.

'You're welcome to that stink,' the attendant said.

Then Benjamin recalled his arrest in the crematorium chapel, and he longed for that smell again, that smell that had belonged to his last moments of freedom. He held the parcel to his chest. Then, the attendant gave him an envelope with his wallet, his handkerchief and his keys. Benjamin took them without thanks, and left the room. Outside the guard was waiting, and he escorted him back to the barracks. 'I'll miss you, Bindel,' he said. 'You're different from the others. The last doctor we had was very unadaptable.'

Benjamin refrained from asking what had happened to him, for he knew that the disease of unadaptability was terminal. He had yet not succumbed to it, but he was ashamed of the price he had paid.

Before he went to bed, he put on his suit., He wanted no delay in his freedom. He would get up in the morning and straightway leave the camp. The suit was crumpled and caked with his own faeces, but it did not offend him. It was an honourable stench, and lingered still with the odour of survival. He did not bother to brush it down with his hands, and he lay down in it, sniffing the promise of freedom in its creases.

He did not sleep that night. Once again he stalked his mind's gallery like a ghost, viewing the faces that time had not blurred. And now there was another face, the most haunting of all, and one that he had never seen. He shivered at the wearer's white jacket, that mark of his own profession. He prayed fervently for forgiveness. He buried his face in the mattress, deafened by the silence around him.

Then suddenly the silence was shattered. The rumble of a lorry droned in his ear. He trembled and prayed that it would echo into the distance. He could hear his heart beating against the rough mattress-ticking, willing with its pulse that the lorry-rumbling never stop. Benjamin prayed feverishly, though he knew that the road to Buchenwald was a cul-de-sac, and that at the end of it, all transport must have a stop. Then he heard the screeching of brakes and the slamming of doors. No more doctoring, he prayed, and even as he whispered his prayer he felt a hand shaking his shoulder.

'Patients,' the guard's voice said. 'Get up.'

Benjamin could not move. He simply couldn't face that medical room again. The guard pulled the thin blanket off the bed, and poked the end of his gun between Benjamin's shoulder-blades. Benjamin crawled out of his straw, reached for the white coat, so-long unworn, and tried to believe that he was dreaming. But the cold night-air outside in the yard quickly shattered that illusion.

'Hurry,' the guard said. 'They're waiting.'

Death will not be offended by unpunctuality, Benjamin thought, and wearily he opened the medical room door and sat at his desk. Within seconds his first patient had arrived.

Benjamin fully expected that he would have forgotten the routine, and he was horrified by his total recall of every single manoeuvre. The comforting questionnaire, the heart-beat, pulse, blood-pressure, and the final alignment with the lattice where lurked the gun. He had lost none of his dexterity. His timings and his bearings were exact. His skill shamed him profoundly. Six more patients visited him that night. Six new bullets, six fresh sluices through the drains, six new layers of sawdust on the killing-room floor.

'One more,' the guard said, 'and that's the lot. Tomorrow you'll go home.'

One more, Benjamin thought and the nightmare would be over, that nightmare that, on waking, would never cease to be.

He heard the man enter the room, and he asked him to undress, keeping his eyes on the floor as was his custom.

'Benjamin,' the man said.

Benjamin trembled. It was a long long time since anyone had addressed him by that name. The voice was gentle, like his father's, and he thought he must be dreaming.

'Don't you know me?' the voice insisted.

Then Benjamin had to raise his eyes, and see in the face of his last patient an old and respected friend. His former mentor, Dr Luber. He could not stop the tears that burned in his eyes.

'You know this man?' the guard said.

'He is a friend,' Benjamin answered, taking Luber's hand.

'Then be quick,' the guard said.

His advice was gentle and exact, and Benjamin would have done well to heed it. But his shock was devastating, and it took some time to recall those manoeuvres that he had so lately carried out with such consummate skill. Why had he been arrested? Had he an appointment as Communist or Jew?

'I'm in reasonably good health,' Dr Luber was saying as he undressed. 'A little chest congestion perhaps, as you will hear. The tables have turned,' he laughed, 'that a pupil should examine his teacher.'

Benjamin could not understand his professor's composure. Was it possible that he had no notion of what was to become of him?

That the state of his chest, congested or otherwise, could grant him no reprieve? After all, the man had spent time in Dachau. He must be well versed in the lexicon of Nazi euphemism. Benjamin decided to say nothing, to recite the weary questionnaire, as if Dr Luber were a stranger. Now, on the brink of his grave, was no time to renew their familiarity. He took his heart-beat, pulse, blood-pressure and weight, but all the time he looked him in the eye. It was the least that he could do. To look one's dupe squarely in the face, was to lessen the lie a little, he hoped. He picked up his eye-torch from the desk and put it to Dr Luber's eye, caressing his cheek as he steadied his torch.

'You are very thorough,' Dr Luber said. 'A credit to my teaching, I like to think.'

How innocent he is, Benjamin thought. He has no notion of how I so appallingly abuse all that he ever taught me.

'Why do you examine my vision?' Dr Luber asked. 'Is it necessary to know the opthalmology of a Communist? And my blood-pressure? My pulse-rate? Are they indications of my political stand? If my heart-beat is irregular, am I therefore unreliable? Does my vision affect my faith? If my pulse is racing, am I diagnosed as a fanatic? And my weight. What secrets does my weight reveal? Unless of course,' he laughed, 'you are measuring me for the gallows.'

He knows, Benjamin thought, and he is trying to make it easy for me. He turned back to his desk. This man taught me all I know, he thought. I have supped with him, I know his wife, and I have played with his children. All the other patients were strangers. With them I obeyed orders. But this man is a friend. This is murder. Nothing extenuate. He thought of his inheritance. Only in the name of love is death worthy, great-grandpa Jakob had said. And friendship. But if he were to offer his own life now, it would be no replacement for Dr Luber. Dr Luber would die, whosoever would place him in the line of fire. I must not waste my death, Benjamin thought, for it will give life to no one.

'I must check your height, Dr Luber,' he said. He used his name. He wanted him to know that he was fully aware of sending a friend to his death. He was meticulous about the placing on the step. This alignment had to be exact, the death swift and painless. He looked him in the eye.

'I understand, Benjamin,' Dr Luber said. 'You are innocent. You are innocent, Benjamin,' he said again. 'You must never believe otherwise. Never.' He held out his hand in a gesture of farewell. Benjamin mounted the step and embraced him. Then he turned away. 'I must get my note-book,' he sobbed his cue, then he returned to the medical room and waited for the explosion. When it came, he rushed back to the slaughter-cell. Dr Luber lay on the floor, his brains blown. He forced himself to look at what was left of his mentor's face, and he heard the echo of his merciful farewell.

'That's the lot,' the guard said, and Benjamin was suddenly conscious of his presence. There was a rule that the doctor must not talk to his patients, apart from the utterance of the rehearsed lines. It was a rule that, hitherto, Benjamin had been eager to obey. But the guard had turned his ear from this last encounter, and Benjamin was grateful.

'Thank you,' he said. He made to leave.

'Wait until the marksman leaves,' the guard whispered, and Benjamin wondered why there was this sudden change of procedure, and he was frightened. The marksman strutted through the killing-room, pausing for a while to view his most recent handiwork.

'A very brainy one,' he said with disdain. As he passed Benjamin on his way to the door, he said, 'You won't be needing your coat any more, Doctor.' Then he laughed. 'Good luck, mate,' he said to the guard, and he sauntered out of the room.

Benjamin took off his coat, and the guard threw it into the killing-room. Benjamin shivered at the knowledge that shortly he would follow it. With little confidence and with melting knees, he made for the door, but the guard put a hand on his shoulder.

Benjamin trembled at the touch. He knew it as a gesture of authority, yet there was tenderness in it. He turned and saw how the guard drew his gun with his other hand. His first thought was one of gratitude that he would be killed with a semblance of affection and a hint of remorse. How stupid he had been ever to have believed in his freedom. They had to kill him, he knew, as they had no doubt disposed of his predecessor. After all he had learned in this place, how could they let his tongue loose? He thought of his children and the tears rolled down his cheeks. He was not ashamed of his weeping but he felt he owed the guard some explanation. The man had shown consideration for him while they had worked together. Perhaps he too had children. 'I have two sons,' he said. 'I was thinking of them.'

The guard raised his gun. 'This bullet is meant for you,' he said. Then he levelled it at Dr Luber's brain-spattered body and fired into its dead limbs.

'Go quickly,' he said. 'At the back of the hut there's a path that leads to a field. It runs parallel to the road. Creep along it and the sentry won't see you. I'll tell them I buried you with that one.'

Benjamin stared at him. 'Why have you done this for me?' he asked.

The guard shrugged. There were a thousand reasons and every one of them would have sent him to the firing-squad.

'I don't know,' he said.

Benjamin embraced him swiftly and tenderly and the tears that he had shed for his children now flowed freely for this man's great and troubled heart. The guard had roughly to distance him and urge him to be on his fugitive way. He himself then went to the door to ascertain that there was no one about, then he motioned Benjamin to leave. Once again Benjamin took his hand, then he stole through the darkness into the field.

When he reached the road, he stood upright. He was not afraid. He considered himself a dead man, and therefore he must be invisible. He remembered that, on that road, the van had swerved to the right for the camp. He turned left, and after a few miles he saw a sign-post to Weimar. He walked in that direction. He was hungry, cold, tired and, despite the official entry in the camp files, shamefully alive. He kept repeating to himself Dr Luber's farewell. 'You are innocent, Benjamin. You must never believe otherwise. Never.' But no matter how often he repeated them they gave him no consolation.

It was late in the afternoon when he reached the railway station, some miles from Weimar. He had just enough money to buy his ticket to Leipzig. He no longer worried about his hunger. It was now so acute that food would have sickened him. When the train pulled into the station, he found an empty carriage and slumped into a corner-seat, and sniffed at his mortality. 'You are innocent, Benjamin,' he said to himself, over and over again, until its repetition sent him into a merciful and dreamless sleep. He was woken by the guard who demanded his ticket.

'I am innocent,' he said, as a hangover from his sleep, and the guard looked at him and sniffed him too, and thought it better to move quickly away.

Out of the window, Benjamin could see the factory buildings that fringed his home town. He felt no excitement or longing. In many ways he never wanted to go home again. He didn't want to see his father, children, brother, wife, all of whom, in their own gentle ways, would smell the murder on him. You are innocent, he said to himself yet again, and he thought that in time he would become mad with his not guilty plea. It was that madness, he now realised, that would be his future weapon of survival.

CHAPTER TWENTY-ONE

Leon's father, Benjamin, had told his sons the story of the milk-brothers' return from Siberia. He had told them of great-grandpa's premonition on that day, and his conviction that the brothers were alive and would soon come home. On the day of his son's return from Buchenwald, Leon Bindel had a like premonition. So when, late at night, he heard the key in the lock, he got up from his bed, and shuffled with an old man's steps to the door.

'Benjamin,' he called. It was no question, for he knew it was he.
'Papa?'

He heard his son's voice and he winced at its pain. Carefully he made his slow way down the stairs and, once in the hall, he stared at his son, confirmed that he was alive and, only later, as he took him in his arms, did he know of his hunger, his fear and his shame.

'I love you, Papa,' Benjamin said.

Leon started. It was not a phrase that came easily to his younger son. Indeed he had never heard it from his lips before and certainly not in his own ear. He had never doubted his filial love, but Benjamin had never been free enough to express it, and the fact that he did so now, pointed to more than a declaration of affection. It was an expression of manic reparation. He knew that his son's declaration was a plea for forgiveness and, out of some divine paternal instinct, he held his arm and said, 'You are innocent, my son.'

Benjamin embraced him, his tears flowing. His father, with his forgiveness, had given him a licence to loosen his tongue. He could, unashamedly, tell those he loved of all that he had done. It was the second liberation of his day, and it was the greatest freedom of all.

Soon the hall was filled with family. Benjamin ran to his children and passed by the astonished Heidi as she stood at the top of the stairs. She had clearly never expected his return, and he tried to greet her without bitterness. David, Sarah and their children leapt down the stairs to welcome him.

'You're hungry,' Sarah said, appalled by his painful loss of weight.
'I need to bathe myself,' he said.
'Then we will prepare a feast,' Leon said. 'And champagne too.' He was giggling like a child, unable to contain his joy.
'Not a feast, Papa,' Benjamin said gently. 'Just a little to eat, and a little more tomorrow, perhaps.'
'Shall I come with you?' Heidi asked as he walked up the stairs.

'Bring the children,' he said without turning. He was disturbed at the coldness in his heart for Heidi. Never once during his stay in Buchenwald had he thought about her. She belonged to that part of his life that had been a living lie, a lie that Buchenwald had more than confirmed. He wondered whether his absence had shaken her, touched that stubbornness of hers in any way.

'How skinny you are,' she said as he undressed.

'We have to leave this country,' he said.

She laughed. 'You haven't changed at all,' she said. 'They won't take you again. No one gets taken twice.'

He wanted to tell her about Dr Luber, but he did not love her enough to share that story with her.

'Everyone says there's going to be a war,' she went on. 'Hitler won't have time to harass Jews. He'll be too busy fighting.' He did not have the strength or the inclination to argue with her. 'Nevertheless, we're going,' he said. He turned to go to the bathroom, where the children were waiting, fluffing the foam in the water.

'You can go if you like,' they heard their mother shouting, 'but I'm staying here with the children.'

Benjamin shut the bathroom door behind him.

'Where are you going, Daddy?' Jakob asked.

'Nowhere,' Benjamin said. He was distressed that the children had heard their argument. He began to feel that it was indeed nowhere that he would go. He would gladly leave Heidi behind, but never his children. But it was the children above all who must be saved, and he wondered whether he would have the strength to let them go without him.

Downstairs Sarah had set the table with an assortment of light foods for Benjamin's choice. They opened champagne to celebrate his return. Like the return of the milk-brothers, Benjamin's homecoming was silent, a drinking-in of faces and gestures that had belonged to another life, with a piercing awareness that nothing had changed in that past, nothing except oneself, and that the problem of adjustment would probably be insurmountable.

Later Heidi asked him if he wanted to sleep alone. He was grateful for her understanding. But he did not sleep at all. He tossed on his single study-divan as Dr Luber's farewell sang in his ear. Towards morning, he fell asleep, and when he awoke, he looked around for his camp-companions and, when he realised where he was, he missed them with an aching longing.

He got up and dressed. The children had already gone to school and David had left for the store.

'Hans is here,' Heidi said as she saw him coming downstairs. Benjamin rushed into the living-room, and welcomed his friend.

They embraced, and Hans tried to joke about Benjamin's spare frame.

'You always wanted to lose weight, my friend,' he said. Then he looked at him and saw in his face the hell he had known. 'You needn't talk about it,' he said. 'Only if you want to. My father didn't want to talk about Dachau.' He paused, then after a while he said, 'I came to thank you for what you did at his funeral.'

'Dr Luber was in Buchenwald,' Benjamin said suddenly. He hadn't meant to speak about it. But Dr Luber was a friend whom he had shared with Hans, and Hans had a right to know his story.

'Is he still there?' Hans said.

'He died yesterday.' Was it only yesterday Benjamin wondered, that he had measured his mentor for the scaffold?

'Did they kill him?' he heard Hans say.

Benjamin looked Hans in the eye. 'I killed him,' he said.

All this while Leon had sat silent in his armchair by the fire. Now he suddenly shouted, 'No, you didn't kill him.' He knew nothing of the Luber story until now. 'If you killed him it was because they forced you.'

'What happened?' Hans said.

'He was my last patient,' Benjamin began, and slowly he unfolded the nature of his medical practice. He told the tale without adornment. The simple facts of it were horrifying enough. When he'd finished he said, 'Today I must go and tell Mrs Luber.'

'No,' Hans said, and his voice was a command. 'She'll be told soon enough and she need never know the details. His death had nothing to do with you. He told you so himself. You must begin to believe him. Today you go back to the hospital and arrange to start work as soon as you feel well enough.'

'Hans is right,' Leon said.

'We must leave this place, Papa,' Benjamin said suddenly.

'You must leave perhaps. You and Heidi and the children,' Leon said. 'And David too. But I am too old now to sow the seeds of a new past. I am tired of running. I have done my surviving.' Benjamin knew that he would never leave his father. Perhaps his father was right. He had done his surviving and, perhaps, he himself, his younger son, had done his surviving too. Both had paid their dues to their common inheritance.

'What about some breakfast?' Leon said. 'I've been waiting for you. And Hans too. He took the day off when he heard you were home.'

Benjamin put his arm round his friend's shoulder, and he took his father's arm and they went into the dining-room.

After breakfast, Hans walked with his friend to the Jewish hospital. Benjamin was glad that he did not have to walk alone into his hospital medical room, and view all those instruments that he had so lately abused. He picked them up one by one, handling them with excessive care, concentrating on their orthodox use, trying to wipe from his mind the fraud and the swindle that they had so recently embodied. But one instrument he removed from his room, for never again could he use it without memories of its final deception. He took the measuring rod from the wall, with its irrelevant markings of inches and feet and he put it outside his room for disposal. Then he went to see the hospital director, while Hans waited for him in reception.

The Director urged him to start work as soon as possible. Part-time to begin with, he suggested, until his health was completely restored. Benjamin thanked him and arranged to start work on the following day. Then he and Hans took the tram to the fur-store to see David.

From the outside the shop looked closed. The windows were boarded up as was the front door. A hand-written sign, declaring that it was open, was the only indication that Bindel Furs was still in business. The shop was empty. David sat behind the counter checking a ledger-book. He greeted them warmly, locked the door after them, and led them into his office at the back of the shop.

'As you see,' he laughed, 'I'm not very busy. I don't know that we can stay in business much longer. There are rumours in any case that they are confiscating all Jewish property. I'm not buying any more stock. Don't tell Papa, but it's all very depressing.'

'I think your father knows,' Hans said. 'He hears from other traders. But he says nothing.'

'The fight has gone out of him,' David said. 'He is content to stay here until he dies.'

'And you?' Benjamin broached the subject straightaway.

'How can I leave him?' David said. 'But you could go. You could go with Heidi and the children.'

'I wouldn't leave Papa,' Benjamin said. 'And Heidi won't go. We are all digging our graves in this place.'

'Not all,' David said. 'I'm making arrangements to send Sarah and the children to Palestine. Her parents will go with them. But not a word to Papa. If only you could persuade Heidi, Benjamin,' he said.

'I've tried,' Benjamin said. 'Besides, she won't leave her parents, and they are as stubborn as she is. They think that rich Jews will be exempt from persecution. Can you imagine such crazy logic?'

'How will they get there?' Hans said. 'Entry to Palestine is illegal.'

'There are ways,' David said. 'Illegal ways. By the end of next week I shall have made all the arrangements. They shall leave within the month.'

'So soon?' Benjamin said, visualising the emptiness of the house without Sarah and her children.

'There's not much time,' David said. 'By the end of the year, this country will be at war. They're hungry for it. And once that happens, we'll all be trapped.'

'Shall I try talking to Heidi?' Hans volunteered. 'I'm not Jewish,' he laughed. 'She might listen to me.'

'I'd be grateful,' Benjamin said. 'But I doubt if you could move her.'

'But the children, for God's sake.' Hans was bewildered. He himself was childless. Inge had had a series of miscarriages and finally they had reconciled themselves to a life without family. Hans' marriage was a happy one, but both partners were sadly aware of their lack. All attempts at adoption had failed. Hans' political heritage was considered unworthy of parenthood.

*

In March 1939 German armies occupied Czechoslovakia. And still Sarah and the children lingered in Leipzig. There were hold-ups in the arrangements for departure. There was the problem of co-ordination. In the organisation of *Aliyah Beth*, as illegal immigration into Palestine was called, there were a limited number of ships. Many of them were far from sea-worthy, and all of them, when they sailed, were overcrowded. In last-minute panic, thousands of refugees were leaving Europe. Most countries had imposed refugee quotas, and the doors of many countries remained firmly closed. Only the gates of Palestine were open, or rather, illegally ajar, for British policy towards refugees was punitive. But despite these restrictions, boats sailed stubbornly into Haifa harbour, or along the dark beaches, and with luck, were sometimes able to empty their weary cargoes onto the forbidden shores.

One day, after weeks of waiting, news reached David that a boat would be leaving Venice in the first week of July. He had a month in which to make his final arrangements. With Hans' persuasion, he had decided to tell his father, and to tell him straightway, so that he would have time to anticipate the children's absence. Leon welcomed the news, and urged David to go too. But David preferred to stay with his father, and in that preference he had no sense of sacrifice. He loved his father as well as he loved his wife and his children. And as long as they were safe he would have the peace of mind to remain with the man he loved most.

'What about Aaron and Jakob?' Leon asked. 'They must go too.'

'Heidi refuses to leave,' David said.

'Tell Benjamin to come to me,' he ordered.

It was a Sunday, a day which Benjamin liked to spend in the

garden. It was planting and pruning time, a season which envisaged fruit and future. Since his return from Buchenwald, Benjamin spent many hours in the garden, hoeing a feverish stake in a future in which he would probably play no part. Nor even his children. Yet he planted, and nurtured, weeded and hoed as if his life depended on it, and he was loathe to leave his work when he heard David's call.

'Papa wants you,' David shouted. He went out into the garden and they both returned to the living-room. David had already told Benjamin of the impending departure, and now Benjamin had an inkling of why his father wished to talk to him.

'You want me, Papa?' he said.

'Heidi must go with the children. The Biedermayers will take care of them all. You cannot miss this opportunity. It won't come again.' His voice was raised in anger, as if he anticipated Benjamin's objections.

'Heidi refuses to go,' Benjamin said. He noticed the vein of anger that projected on his father's brow.

'So she stays,' Leon shouted. And then, in a whisper, 'But not Aaron and Jakob. David will take them to Venice with the others. When they have gone, you will tell her. The Bindels must survive.'

Leon at that moment was back in Senghennydd standing at the pit-head of his first-born's memorial. He knew that there was no profit in regretting one's past, but he knew too that one must learn from it, else all of one's history was folly. He knew now, in his present time, and in the autumn colours of his maturity, that he should have taken his first David and rescued him from the dangers of the valley. That he should have cared less for Margaret's feelings, that he should have insisted on the boy's future. Now in his own drawing-room, hundreds of miles from that memorial, so many griefs ago, was an exact re-enactment of that drama. It had to have a different ending.

'They must leave the valley,' he said, suddenly confused.

'The valley?' Benjamin asked.

'I was thinking of a long time ago. They must leave. They must go with the others.'

'Do I have your blessing to such a deception, Papa?' Benjamin asked.

'My blessings on you and your children,' Leon said.

It took a little planning. Passports had to be applied for, and to that end they needed photographs. Benjamin could not take Aaron and Jakob to a studio, for they would have told their mother and it would have been unjust to enjoin them to secrecy and thus conspire against one whom they loved and would forswear to leave. So that afternoon, while the children were playing in the garden, Benjamin

312

took his camera and amongst many family portraits, he took singles of each of the four children. The following day, he and David went to the passport office. There were many people waiting there and had been so doing for some hours.

'My God,' Benjamin said. 'I had no idea so many were leaving.'

'We should bring Heidi here,' David said.

'She would scoff,' Benjamin answered. 'Possibly she would call them cowards.'

'You must try not to think ill of her,' David said. 'She loves her children.'

'I know,' Benjamin said. 'I know too that I'm doing a terrible thing. She will never, never forgive me.'

They waited and it was late afternoon before their turn came. The official was gruff. He talked to his desk without once looking at their faces. But Benjamin would not blame him for that. He himself had used that kind of evasion. It had been out of his own sense of shame. Was it possible that this official, in some part of his uniform, harboured that same guilt that had strait-jacketed Benjamin's whole being from response?

'How many passports?' the bureaucrat asked his desk.

'Five,' David said. Sarah's parents were arranging their own.

The official took some forms from his tray. 'Jews?' he asked his desk.

'Yes.'

He took a large and clearly well-worn stamp and rolled it on a pad of ink. With it he stamped each form with the initial 'J'. 'Names?' he said.

David gave his list first. Names, addresses, ages, together with photographs. The official was slow. His writing was meticulous and he curved his tongue around each pot-hook and hanger. Then when the particulars were noted, he stapled a photograph to each corresponding form and once again stamped the face underfoot with his 'J'.

'You must sign here,' he pointed out the dotted line, 'and your wife on the line below.' Then he turned to Benjamin and repeated the same routine. He handed him the papers for his signature. 'Your wife must sign too,' he reminded him. 'Or whoever is the children's mother,' he sneered.

'I'll bring it back tomorrow,' Benjamin said, knowing that he could well forge Heidi's signature.

'She must bring it herself and sign it in front of the officer. Together with her own photograph.'

'But she's ill,' Benjamin quickly improvised. 'Can't I do it for her?'

The official stared at his desk and shook his head. 'Impossible unless she presents herself,' he said. 'You must wait until she gets better.'

They took the forms and left the offices.

'They won't be able to go,' Benjamin said. There was a measure of relief in his voice. But he knew that that relief was selfish, that however heart-breaking it would be to part with his children, it would be less heart-breaking than exposing them to the fire that he knew would burn out their future. 'What am I to do?' he said.

'The Bindels have bribed frontier guards before,' David said. 'Let me take them anyway. It's worth that chance.'

*

When the day of departure arrived, Benjamin awoke in terror. It was a school-day, and the children were dressed in their school-uniforms. Benjamin had surreptitiously packed a suitcase of his children's clothes and stored it in the boot of David's car. They had breakfast together. Normally Heidi slept late, and the children would go to the bedroom to kiss her before going to school. But that morning, Benjamin insisted on her rising, and she couldn't understand this sudden change of routine. But she came down to breakfast, not wishing to displease him. The children too were unnerved by Heidi's unaccustomed presence.

'Why are you up for breakfast, Mummy?' Aaron asked.

'Daddy wanted it,' she said.

'Why, Daddy?' Jakob asked.

'I thought it would be nice if we were all together to start the day.' He was almost weeping with the shame of his deception. For a moment he weakened and decided that he would not let them go. Then he caught David's eye and his father's, and both spoke to him with an understanding of his pain.

'It's the same for me,' David said.

'What's the same for you?' Heidi asked.

'My coffee. Black, like Benjamin's,' David said quickly.

All the while Leon had kept his eyes on the children, drinking in their four separate voices, imprinting each image on his mind's eye, images to last him for the rest of his life. David saw tears start in his father's eyes and marvelled that out of his sheer will-power, they did not drop down his old cheeks. His restraint had a touch of nobility. When they rose from the table, he held them all in one embrace.

'Be good at school today, my children,' he managed to say, then quickly he left the table and hobbled through the French windows into the garden.

David gulped his coffee and rose from the table.

Benjamin followed him to his car. He did not want to witness

Heidi's unknowing last farewell. He kissed Sarah goodbye, but said nothing, and when the children came towards him, he did as his father had done. He held them all in one embrace, unable to let them go, knowing he would lose them for ever.

'We'll be late for school, Daddy,' Aaron said, and David touched his brother on the shoulder. 'We must go,' he said.

He settled the children in the car, then came back to Benjamin. 'It's for the best, brother,' he said. 'It means their survival. Soon we shall all be together again.' That Bindel phrase once more. Would there ever come a generation of Bindels when that phrase would never be called upon? Would there ever come a time when to leave was not to flee, when to part was not to die?

'I shall be back at the end of the week,' David said, and he got into the car, and drove down the drive. Benjamin watched them out of sight, then he went quickly back into the house, grateful that Heidi was not to be seen, and he took his coat and made for the door. On his way through the dining-room, he caught sight of his father in the garden. He was smelling the first of the roses, caressing them with his cheek, and Benjamin knew that his father's heart, like his own, was breaking.

He went straight to the hospital. Once there, he went to his room, locked the door and allowed himself to weep. After a while, he rinsed his face and made his rounds of the wards. He tried not to think of Heidi or of the hour when the children would normally return from school. He was afraid to go home, yet he knew he must be there by the time school was over. Then he would break it to her and take his punishment. Now, because of the great hurt he had done her, very slowly his old love for her returned. He watched the clock most of the day, timing his children's journey. Venice was almost 500 miles away. It would take two days of hard driving. They had been on the road for six hours. Allowing time to pick up the Biedermayers and to negotiate the centre of Leipzig onto the main road south, Benjamin reckoned, they must have reached the Austrian border. There would be no trouble at that frontier. That country had been annexed to the Third Reich. It would be like passing through Germany. David and the family would probably spend the night on the outskirts of Vienna. It would be sometime around noon on the following day that they would reach the hurdle of the Italian frontier. At three o'clock, he left the hospital and made his way home.

Heidi was sitting in the drawing-room. She told him that Leon did not feel well and had gone to bed shortly after lunch. She looked at her watch. 'I must get the children's tea,' she said. 'They'll be home soon.'

Benjamin did not look at her. Instead he went upstairs to see his father. He crept into the room and saw that he was sleeping. It would have been unfair to wake him up, so he tip-toed out of the room and went downstairs to the storm that awaited him. He heard her preparing the tea in the kitchen. Through the door into the dining-room, he saw her set the table. Four places, laying the knives and plates in meticulous symmetry. He watched her and he could say nothing.

The time passed. It was after four o'clock.

'The children are late,' Heidi said.

'They'll be home soon,' Benjamin heard himself saying. He didn't know how to tell her. He did not believe that there were any words in any language to inflict such pain. He watched her out of the corner of his eye. She seemed composed, but after about ten minutes she began to get restless, and she walked to the window that overlooked the drive.

'I wonder why they're so late,' she said.

'Traffic perhaps,' Benjamin said. It was not that he lacked the courage to tell her. One didn't need courage to break such news. It was simply that he didn't have the heart for such cruelty. But now it was too late. She had to be told.

'They've never been this late before,' she said.

'Don't worry,' Benjamin said almost to himself. 'They'll be here soon.'

He trembled as the time passed. At five o'clock, Heidi began to panic. 'I'm worried, Benjamin,' she said. 'You must ring the school. Please,' she said.

'But the school's closed,' Benjamin desperately played for time.

'Try them,' she almost shouted at him.

He actually got up and made for the telephone. Then he knew that he could delay it no longer. He turned to Heidi and held her at arm's length.

'They're not coming back, Heidi,' he said. The words were so simple, he thought, so easy to deliver, as easy as sliding an oiled dagger into a presented heart. It's over, he thought, and there was some relief in that.

'What do you mean?' she whispered.

'David took all the children to Venice. They'll take a boat from there to Palestine. Sarah and the Biedermayers are with them.' It was a comfort to add that rider. It guaranteed, if nothing else, the physical caring of their children.

'They're not coming back?' The words were unintelligible, but the eyes were burning in each terrible syllable.

He shook his head. 'It's only until all this is over,' he said. 'Then we shall all be together again.'

Benjamin had murdered many people, but none of them had

316

looked at him with hate. Now, for a crime that was possibly equal to all those heights he had measured, he saw on her face a look of such abject loathing that it stabbed his heart with her pain. Then she let out a scream, so silent, yet so piercing, that dogs on the outskirts of Leipzig might have pricked their ears at her call. It was a sound that stemmed from the bowel, that same sound that Benjamin had often heard from women in the last stage of their labour. But this sound would have no end, no relief or fruition. It would echo from the regions of her fractured heart for the rest of her life. He held her in his arms and she struggled like a wild creature to free herself. Finally he let her go. Whatever residual affection lay beached on the shores of their tormented wedlock was now engulfed by a tidal wave of loathing that swallowed it whole, and without trace. She screamed still, and still silently, with the occasional whimper which shrouded her shattered world. She stumbled into the garden, still screaming, then he saw her pause by a rose bush. But she did not smell the blooms. Instead she crushed them one by one in the palm of her hand, tearing the skin on the thorns of their stems. Then he saw her collapse on the lawn in merciful oblivion.

He went to her and gathered her in his arms. He carried her upstairs to the bed and laid her gently on the pillows. Then he took a syringe and gave her a sedative. He wanted her to forget for a while the gross deprivation he had inflicted upon her. He wanted to postpone the retribution that would surely come. He covered her with a quilt and crept out of the room. He sat in the drawing-room, wide-awake to his cruelty, while his father and his wife dreamed of the children they would never see again.

*

On the journey, the Biedermayers had regaled the children with stories of the adventures that lay ahead. The long boat trip through the Adriatic and the Mediterranean. Then the port of Haifa. They omitted any mention of the hazards they would encounter on the journey. They had heard stories of less than sea-worthy boats that had been tossed through the Black Sea and the Aegean, laden with refugees, dodging the attempts of the British Government to prevent their entry into Palestine. It was on such a boat that they were destined to travel, and they could only hope and pray for safe arrival. So they told the children stories of Palestine, a land which they themselves had never seen. David made many stops on the way, so that they could stretch their legs and take refreshments, for the car was somewhat over-crowded, and during the course of the day, the children caught the spirit of adventure.

They crossed the Austrian border with no interference and in the

317

early evening they stopped at an inn about ten miles outside Vienna. That night when David took Sarah to bed he said, 'This will not be our last night together,' but they both made love knowing that it was possibly for the last time.

They set off early in the morning for the Italian border. As they approached it, David was more and more nervous. He had money enough for bribery, and he had heard that the Italian guards were happy enough to look the other way in return for grease on their out-stretched palm. Even so he was afraid, for his instinct prompted him that the border crossing would not succeed. He slowed down, needing to delay his possible failure, and slowly the car crawled towards the Austrian frontier post. The barrier was lifted without any questions asked, and he was soon 200 yards away from the Italian hurdle. He thought of Heidi and her heartbreak, and of Benjamin, guilty and unforgiven, and for a moment he hoped that they would not let the boys pass.

'All out,' the frontier guard said as the car approached the barrier. There were no other cars waiting, and plenty of guards about with nothing to do. It was a relief for them when a car came through and allowed them to busy their idle hands. One of the guards directed David and his passengers to the passport office on the side of the road. He asked for the keys of the car-boot. Meanwhile, he told David, he would search their luggage.

David went first in the line, taking Aaron's and Jakob's hands. In his wallet in his pocket, he had a wad of ready notes, and behind that wallet, the legitimate passports of his wife and children. He allowed the Biedermayers to present their papers first. The official checked on their faces with a cursory glance and wished them a good journey. David approached the counter. He placed everything on the counter-top, the passports, the car documents and his wallet. This last he opened as if seeking something inside. The wad of notes protruded from the pocket. He left it open and looked the official in the eye. But the clerk seemed to read no message in his display. His face was a bureaucratic blank.

'Children with you?' he asked.

David nodded. They were invisible behind the counter. The man rose from his feet and came around to where they stood. It did not take him long to deduce that the number of passports and the number of children did not tally.

'Four children, two passports,' he said, spelling it out as if it might come as some surprise to David.

'I know,' David said, and he reached for his wallet and fingered the bribe in the pouch.

The official watched the gesture but said nothing. Then David was forced to speak.

'I can pay,' he whispered.

'Pardon?' the man said, having heard well enough.

Then David knew that he had the ill-luck to encounter an honest official. Nevertheless, he pressed on. 'I can pay,' he said, a little louder this time.

'I'm not in that market,' the man said, 'and I could well charge you for attempting to bribe an official of the Italian Government. But I see your family are in a hurry.'

'Thank you,' David said, and he put his wallet away. There was nothing more that he could do. He must consider himself lucky that he was not charged.

'I don't know what to do,' he said. 'I can't leave two children here.'

'Where are you making for?' the official said. 'Apart from Palestine.'

'Venice,' David said.

'You could drive back to Vienna. There are trains direct to Venice from there.' He retrieved the Biedermayer passports, and inserted a note that they had been stamped in error, so that there would be no problem when they re-crossed the border by train. The official was very accommodating, with a courtesy that matched his incorruptibility.

They returned silently to the car, and David found himself relieved that he had failed. Although he would now not be able to see his family onto the boat in Venice, he would at least be taking Benjamin's children home. Sarah too was relieved, and overjoyed for Heidi's sake. 'It's a good omen,' she said. 'It's a sign that they will survive.'

'We could try another post,' Mr. Biedermayer suggested. 'We could go west through the mountains. It might be easier there.'

'We would take a risk,' David said. 'If we should fail, we risk losing the boat altogether. We have little enough time as it is. We are some hours from Vienna.'

On the way back through Austria, the Biedermayers told Benjamin's children that they would be going home to their mother after all. Aaron and Jakob feigned disappointment because that was what they thought was expected of them, but their hearts were leaping with joy and relief.

It was early evening when they reached Vienna's railway station. They had two hours before the Venice train, time for a farewell celebration. David had been to Vienna many times on business, and he knew the whereabouts of the Jewish quarter. They would feel safer there. He drove across the city and found the area without needing to ask direction. He was saddened by what he saw. Most of the shops were boarded up, and daubed with yellow stars. Some were in the process of reconstruction with the legend 'Under New Management' across the hoarding. But they did find a restaurant that was open, with a brave proprietor beaming a welcome in the foyer. Or perhaps he wasn't brave, David thought. Perhaps he was an ostrich like Heidi who would not allow herself to believe that anything had changed.

Apart from a couple at a table at the far end of the room, the restaurant was empty. The proprietor guided them to a large family table in the middle of the room and hovered for their order.

'Order anything you like,' David said, though he knew that, although they had not eaten since lunch time, only the children were hungry. He ordered wine straightway to inject a little cheer into their farewell. David invited the proprietor to take wine with them. The presence of a stranger at their table loosened the tension between them, and they were able to talk of things that had nothing to do with the parting that, within the hour, would be over. Nothing that is, until the proprietor asked them their business in Vienna.

'My wife and children and her parents are taking the train to Venice,' David said.

'Palestine?' the man whispered.

David nodded.

'You're lucky,' he said. 'And very wise.'

'You could leave too,' David said.

'My mother is eighty-eight years old,' the man said. 'She is too ill to travel. How can I leave her? She has no one else. And my wife will not leave as long as I stay. But our son is in England. We advertised for a family to take him. He's in London. He goes to school there.'

'My father won't go either,' David said. 'I stay for the same reason as you.'

'Do you ever pray for him to die?' the proprietor asked. He had no shame in the question. It seemed to him that his mother was old enough to qualify for death from natural causes. He loved her without blame. He needed no more time for reconciliation. If she died that day, no guilt would prolong his grief. He could not understand that God was preserving her for the unnatural end that he feared awaited them all. These feelings he offered to David, taking a seat at his side, while the waiter placed their orders in front of them. In return for his confidences, David was able to confess, though in a whisper, that indeed he did pray for his father's death, and for those very reasons.

'We ourselves will go to the fire because we would not leave those we love,' the proprietor said.

'Perhaps that is as it should be,' David said, because after all, was that not the heart of the Bindel inheritance? The proprietor

320

was not an ostrich after all, David thought. He was a hero of sorts, and he wondered how many old Jews in the Third rotten Reich were pinning their children to their invalid sides, through no fault of their own, but through the invisible inheritance that bound them, a reversed alimony from children to parents, the loving payment of an account which nature was too tardy to settle.

For the rest of the meal, David kept his eyes on his two daughters. He was not without hope that he would see them again, but he knew that it was likely that he would miss out on the whole of their childhood. Now he knew how great-grandpa Jakob had felt when he had said goodbye to the milk-brothers. But after all those years, they had been re-united, and David had to cling to that possible reunion in order to overcome the pain of their absence.

'We have to leave,' he said. Now he wanted the parting over and done with. Within the hour, alone, he could release the silent scream inside him. Then he remembered that Aaron and Jakob would be with him, and he was suddenly glad of it. The house in Leipzig would not be childless, and as the milk-brothers had done in Odessa, they would share their children.

They reached the station and David was glad that the train was already waiting. It was five minutes to departure, a departure for which five years was too short, and five minutes too long. He settled them on the train. Sarah held him.

'Don't say anything,' she said, fearful of the traditional Bindel farewell. 'I shall write as soon as we arrive. Then I shall write daily, and so will the children. We shall all be together from day to day,' she said.

He kissed her then held the children together with her in their embrace. Then he turned and left the train and, holding Aaron's and Jakob's hands, he waited on the platform and prayed that the train would leave on time. Sarah hung from the window It was clear that she was smiling with great effort, that she too would turn, and in the confines of the carriage release her silent scream. The guard blew the whistle and the train shunted slowly away. David waited there long after it was gone from sight, viewing the empty railway track and the distant clouds of evaporating steam.

'Come on, Uncle David,' Aaron tugged at his sleeve.

David crouched down by their sides and held them in his arms. 'Come,' he said after a while. 'Let's start for home.'

Once on the road, he wondered whether he should telephone Benjamin and let him know of his failure. But he decided against it. His failure was neither good news nor bad, and such news should be told face to face, the evidence presented, and the outcome, whether of joy or of sorrow, should be shared. He considered driving through the night, and reaching Leipzig early in the morning before Benjamin went to the hospital. But he himself was weary with sorrow, and needed to be alone for a while. Some twenty miles out of Vienna he found a small hotel where they put up for the night. He settled the boys in their beds and was glad at last to be alone. It was fitting for him to cry then, away from Sarah and the children. He thought of Benjamin and he knew that, for whatever reason, whether for the presumed loss of his children, or for the shame of the hurt he had done, his brother was crying too.

*

In fact, Benjamin was pacing the drawing-room. He had had no sight of Heidi since he had carried her from the garden. She'd locked her bedroom door, calling out she was all right and wanted to sleep. She was deaf to Benjamin's constant entreaties. He wondered how it would all end. He'd gone to the hospital that day and thanked God for the work he was able to do. He worried constantly about Heidi. He feared that in desperation, she might take her own life. So every half-hour during the day, he telephoned and talked to his father, or the housekeeper.

That morning Leon had gone to the cemetery. Whenever he was troubled, he would visit Greta's grave and find some solace there. It was summer and the flowers were in full bloom. He sat on a bench alongside her grave. I'm eighty-two years old, he thought. I'm strong enough in limb, and young enough in spirit to run once more. For only in my fleeing will my children survive. For himself, he knew that his flight would be simply one to a natural grave, and it seemed to him that Palestine was a ridiculously long way to travel just in order to die. Yet when he'd seen Heidi's face he had felt chock-full of blame, and that day he had come to Greta's grave to say farewell. He had made up his mind. Although he knew that his sons stayed with him out of love, they would probably not live long enough even to view that love as sacrificial. He would go to Palestine, he decided, together with his sons, and, he hoped, Heidi. He stooped and put a pebble on Greta's grave, then another and another, until he had built a small pyramid of remembrance. In Senghennyd, in Cardiff, in Leipzig, he would leave his loves' triangle. He sat down once more and drew a circle on the gravel with his stick, his memories absorbed in an old man's geometry.

On his way home, he began to grow excited at the thought of David's return. He would ask him to lose no time in making arrangements for the emigration of the rest of the family. He would try once more to talk to Heidi. Now, with her children gone, she would rush to join them. He quickened his pace and for the first time in many years, he recaptured his boyhood spirit of adventure.

*

David began his homeward journey early in the morning. He wanted to time his arrival with Benjamin's return from the hospital. They crossed the Austrian border at lunchtime, and were able to take a leisurely meal before starting the last lap home. David was surprised at his own cheerfulness and he knew it was because of the children's company. He was glad that he had failed. He hoped that Benjamin would feel likewise.

'Did Mummy know where we were going?' Aaron asked suddenly. He was barely six years old, yet already he had a nose for deception.

David did not know how to answer the question. He did not want to presume on his brother's authority, or to tell a lie where Benjamin might have told the truth. 'I don't know,' he said.

'She'll be glad to see us anyway, won't she?' Jakob said. Both of them clearly knew that their mother had been duped. 'I bet you she's been crying all the time,' Aaron said.

'We'll be home soon. Then you can comfort her,' David said. 'Grandpa Leon too. He will have missed you.'

'Do we tell them where we've been?' Aaron asked.

'They'll know,' David said.

Thereafter they drove in silence. David thought of Sarah and his little girls. They had boarded by now, and were probably miles out at sea. He dared not think of the hazards of the voyage.

It was just over five o'clock in the afternoon when they reached the outskirts of Leipzig, and the children began to get very excited.

'I've got an idea,' David said. 'When we drive into the driveway, you crouch and hide, and I'll get out and tell them you've left. Then we shall surprise them.' It was a ruse to keep them out of the way to give David time to tell Benjamin and to preempt the sudden shock of re-union. He was particularly worried about the effects of such shock on his father.

As they approached the driveway, the children slunk to the floor of the car. David pulled up and went into the house. 'Papa?' he shouted. 'Benjamin?'

Benjamin rushed into the hall. He looked haggard, with the same guilt-riddled look he had brought with him from Buchenwald. 'I have committed a crime,' Benjamin said.

David shook his head. 'It didn't work,' he said. 'They're hiding in the car,' he smiled.

'Heidi,' Benjamin screamed, and he darted up the stairs. 'Heidi,' he shouted at the door. 'Our children are home.'

Almost immediately the door opened, and for the first time in three days. He was horrified at the way she looked. Her hair was uncombed and the layers of a three-day-old make-up were caked with dried tears. She rushed past him down the stairs, breaking into a whimpering hysteria.

'Where are they?' she cried.

'In the car,' David said.

Benjamin caught up with her, and managed to take her hand and together they went to their children. David and Leon remained in the hall.

'We shall have children in the house again, Papa,' David said.

'But not for long,' Leon said. 'You were right. You have been right all the time. I have decided to leave.'

'Papa,' David said, hardly believing. 'We are saved. All of us.'

They heard the children laughing in the driveway, and soon they were inside.

'Has Papa told you, Benjamin?' David asked. 'He's decided to leave.'

They all looked at Heidi. 'It depends on my parents,' she said. It was the first time she had offered an excuse for her stubborness, other than her manic optimism. 'I'll think about it.' It was the beginning of Heidi's surrender.

*

The following day, David made contact with his illegal immigration agent. The next sailing was due to leave just a month hence, in the first week of September. Its port of embarkation was Naples. He advised David to prepare the family's passports and to realise what capital they could. David was satisfied. Within the month he should hear from Sarah of her safe arrival and of a base perhaps in Palestine where they could settle themselves. Over the next week, each member of the family waited in the long lines at the passport office. Even Heidi went, declaring that a passport was always useful and didn't commit her one way or the other. But she signed for the children without argument. Since their return, she and Benjamin had re-captured some of their former affection for each other. Indeed they appeared to be very close, as if the man who had brought Heidi to the brink of destruction, and he who had finally saved her, were one and the same. She had grown closer to Leon too, and now replaced Sarah with her kindness and small services. Her parents had signalled that they were too old to leave. They too had replaced their optimism with a more feasible excuse, but they understood that, at her age and that of the children, it was wiser to find a home elsewhere. Meanwhile, David made an attempt to sell the fur business and the stock. But there were no buyers. It was clear that legal confiscation of Jewish property and businesses was only a matter of time, and no one would pay out good money for a concern that would soon be theirs by right of race and title. For the same reason, there was no interest in buying the large old family house. David realised what assets he could. He kept regular contact with his shipping agent, and after a little while, was given the firm date of September 5th for a Naples sailing. It would be advisable, the agent said, to arrive one full day before the scheduled departure. The Bindels said no word of their leaving. Only Hans and Inge were told. Hans received the news with both sadness and relief. He would miss Benjamin profoundly. His children, too. And, those last few weeks, they spent much of their time in the Bindel home in the manner of a long farewell.

Towards the end of August, David received the long awaited letter from Sarah. The post-mark of Tel-Aviv indicated that they had arrived and were safe, and he took the letter to the shop to read it privately. She wrote first of how she and the children missed him, and entreated him to persuade Leon and Heidi to make the move. Especially Heidi, she added, for Palestine was a land for children. She wrote about their journey, and although she said little about its hazards, it was clear from her reticence that the voyage was far from smooth. It had taken three whole weeks before they had sighted the Palestine coast-line. There they had lingered for many days, dodging the British sentry boats that scoured the shore. Eventually they had beached along the sands of Haifa. They had been warmly welcomed and well-accommodated. They had been housed altogether in a kibbutz on the Upper Galilee, a fishing settlement, where work had been found for all of them. The children had started at the kibbutz school, and she herself was attending Hebrew classes. She missed him, she wrote yet again, as he surely did her, and she hoped he would find some consolation in the thought of their safety. The children had appended their love and kisses and a drawing of their dormitory, and the Biedermayers assured him that all was well and that they missed him too.

He put the letter away. Now he longed to be gone from this place, and he counted the days to their departure. Just over one week. He had not yet sold the house or the business, but Hans had been persuaded to move into the Bindel family home with Inge and his mother, and to hold it for them until and if a sale was possible. He could do nothing about the business, but he had packed the remainder of his dwindling stock and hoped to turn it into capital on arrival in Palestine. Now all they could do was wait. An uneasy waiting-time, for rumours of war were rife.

Two days before they were due to leave, the German armies invaded Poland. The Bindels panicked and called Hans to drive them immediately to the station. When they were settled on the train, that, with two changes, would take them to Naples, they firmly believed that they could safely get away. But they got only as far as the Italian frontier.

It was early morning when the train came to a sudden standstill and they were shaken awake by a crackling announcement on the station tannoy. The language was Italian which none of the Bindels could understand, but two of their travelling companions were seen to grow pale at the news, and one of them started to scream. Then since it was a German train that had so abruptly stopped at the station, the announcement was given in German. It was cold, unadorned, and stated quite simply and without rhetoric that England and France had declared war on Germany. All transport out of the Third Reich was now suspended. This same train would return whence it had come.

For the Bindels the announcement was a sentence of death. They were now trapped in quicksands, beyond any means of escape.

CHAPTER TWENTY-TWO

And so it was that the Bindel family returned to Leipzig, and the fears that had prompted their flight were now magnified by their failure to get away. For with the borders open there was always the possibility of deliverance; closed, they were trapped beyond bribery or prayer. Their fears were confirmed too, for over the next few months oppressive measures against the German Jewish population were intensified. The fur-store, like all Jewish businesses was requisitioned by the government, and David was forced into idleness. He was profoundly depressed. He could no longer expect any communication from Sarah, and he tried not to believe that he would never see her again. The Jewish hospital was still allowed to operate, and Benjamin secured a job of part-time orderly for his brother. Every morning David would take Benjamin's children to school. One day, as he approached the gates, he saw a number of children leave the building and make their way home. On enquiry, the headmaster told him that five of the teachers had been arrested and that the school was obliged to close. David drove home with terrible premonitions of what was to become of them all. There were rumours that the hospital too would close. It seemed to him that the Bindels, like all Jewish families in Germany, were submitting to house-arrest by instalments, to enforced idleness and fear. It was a dismal time for them all.

But Heidi flowered. She was not afraid, and no terrible rumours, confirmed or otherwise, would disturb her. Benjamin had never told her the details of his Buchenwald experience. Those he had shared only with Hans and his father, without fear of their exploitation of his tale. But Leon wanted Heidi to know them, and to know them in their gruesome detail. For such knowledge could not help but shift her stubbornness a little. So in secret he told her everything. Her response was two-fold. She grew even closer to Leon by virtue of his trust in her, and that which he had told her could no longer permit her intransigence. She understood then that no one of them was exempt, and that one might as well fully espouse that Judaism of which one stood accused. So it was Heidi, she who had hitherto eschewed the Jewish community, who urged the Bindels back into the orthodox fold. It was she who organised the regular family attendances at the synagogue, and no Jewish festival would pass without her celebration. Amongst the Jewish community as a whole, the period marked a general return to the fold. The synagogue became the central meeting-place, for the exchange of rumour, hope and despair and, on the Sabbath, the Bindels would linger in the courtyard long after the services were over, finding comfort and a small security in the company of others in the same desperate plight. Out of this newly-strengthened community, grew a number of societies which concerned themselves with the study of the Jewish tradition. The Bindels began to attend Hebrew classes, and the children went on organised picnics, and sang songs and heard tales of Palestine. Each member of the community, old and young, now luxuriated in a dream which for most of them had come too late, and which for all of them now would never be fulfilled.

Like all European Jewish communities, there existed at the head a Council of Elders responsible for the administration of the law and custom of Jewish life. This body, the *Jüdische Gemeinde*, was now commandeered by the government as a liaison body between themselves and the Jewish communities of each town. The system was an exact replica of the function of the *Kahals* in Czarist Russia. Whilst such a system functioned within its own sphere of community welfare, it performed a function vital to the cohesion of the Jewish group. But once interfered with by a hostile alien hand, it protected itself in ways that hitherto would have been unthinkable. Thus, like the *Kahals* before them, the *Jüdische Gemeinde* became available to all manner of bribery and corruption. For despite the country's concern with the war, there had been no relaxation in the treatment of the Jews. It had taken Germany only three weeks to conquer most of Poland, and stories that leaked from that desperate Jewish community dared not be believed, for fear of their travel and translation. Wherever the jack-boot trod, Jews trembled, and by the summer of the following year, with the fall of France, almost the whole of Europe was Nazi-controlled. Jews went out and never returned to their homes. Sometimes the storm-troopers came to collect them, and nothing was heard of them again. Nothing except rumour, too terrible to repeat, for its telling might give it some tinge of credence. The word 'Auschwitz' was often whispered in those rumours, slicing each story like a guillotine. Yet despite all evidence to the contrary the Jews of Leipzig for the most part, went about what was left of their business as if nothing untoward would happen to them. It would happen to other people perhaps, even to those who lived next door, but the ever-present danger gave each individual an imperative sense of his own immortality.

Towards the end of 1940, when the war had been raging in Germany's favour for over a year, David Bindel was invited to sit on the *Jüdische Gemeinde* of Leipzig. Of the twelve men who ruled the Council, two had died of old age, a matter of some surprise, for a death from natural causes seemed almost illegal in the circumstances in which they lived. David was happy to accept the responsibility, for it would give him access to news otherwise restricted. Above all, he hoped through their offices to find some means of communication with Sarah and his children. One of his first duties, on orders from the Government, was to compile a census of the Leipzig Jewish community. It was a sinister directive. Even if there were to be an election, Jews were not allowed to vote, and the Jewish census was not part and parcel of a national survey. It was exclusive and its overtones were ominous. The SS had their own files on the Jewish population, but since the mass emigrations they were somewhat out of date. This did not allow any loop-hole for cheating since the figures were checkable against the number of issued passports and travelling papers. It would be difficult to slip through their enclosing net. But David Bindel was going to try.

The opportunity presented itself the following week when the preliminary lists were passed to him for his attention. Many names had been underlined, and the reasons were given in parenthesis. *Deceased* or *Emigrated*. The Bindel family were listed in one group. Greta was the first to be underlined. David seldom thought of his mother. During her lifetime she had been much closer to Benjamin. She had always regarded her younger son as her very own. She seemed to have donated her first-born to Leon, and this was indeed the case, in memory of his first David, though Greta's sons knew nothing of that namesake. But when David saw her name there, and the bracketted '*Deceased*', he felt tears pricking behind his eyes. It was not so much her death that grieved him, but the manner of her dying. And that had been terrible. He tried not to think of it now. He traced his finger down the Bindel line. His own Sarah,

Esther and Zelda, were legitimately underlined as '*Emigrated*', and that gave him a measure of comfort. He himself, Benjamin, Heidi and Leon were all listed next as alive and living in Leipzig. For a moment he thought that Aaron and Jakob had been omitted. He did not at first connect them with the Hermann and Heinrich at the bottom of the Bindel list. That era seemed so many years ago. Tentatively he underlined their names. Those names were indeed dead. Even Heidi had long since ceased their use. The children themselves would now be startled at such appelations, and probably very ashamed. At that moment he recalled their little faces when he told them that they would not be going on the ship to Palestine. That they would be going back home. And how they had feigned their disappointment, while their hearts thundered with relief. But on paper, they had sailed.

In a careful hand, he wrote *Emigrated* after each of their names, and he prayed that the SS would take his word.

At the end of the following year, in 1941, the Japanese attacked Pearl Harbour and America entered the war. This new and formidable participant changed the complexion as well as the course of the hostilities. Action was intensified on all fronts. Part of this intensification was the appointment of Heydrich to organise and administer the Final Solution, and by the end of the year the mass deportations had begun.

The first round-up in Leipzig took place shortly after David's census-doctoring. A directive came from the Town Council that fifty Jewish families were to assemble at the Leipzig bus station in two weeks from the date of the order. Guidelines were given as to how the selection was to be made. Those to be expelled were the unemployed, the sick, and the poor. Their destination would be a 'Jewish Settlement in the East', where they would find work and comforts. The *Jüdische Gemeinde* was content to believe that such a residence was the point of the expulsion. And at least they could keep families together. They called a meeting for the painful discussion of selection. The Bindels were neither poor, unemployed, nor sick, so they did not qualify for the round-up, and David went to the meeting without fear, but with a certain shame that he would be party to the expulsion of those of his own kind. None of the members of the Board qualified for the round-up, and each of them nourished the illusion that they would never qualify, whatever the conditions. But David was not deceived. Sooner or later his turn would come, along with the other Bindels, comparatively rich, healthy and employed.

The list of fifty families was drawn up, and each member of the Committee shared in that responsibility. Notices were sent out to each address, giving the time and the place of the assembly. Each family, according to the order, was permitted to take one suitcase, and this allowance confirmed their trust in the promise that they were indeed going for settlement and that the suitcase guaranteed some kind of future.

On the appointed day, David went to the bus-station. He could have wept when he saw them all assembled there, obeying the command, waiting in line, their cardboard suitcases, most of them bulging and secured with string, at their patient feet. Most of them were from the Jewish quarter of the town. Many of them were from the very orthodox sect, bearded, ringletted and kaftaned. A group of storm-troopers herded them into line, pulling the odd beard if its wearer was tardy. There were no buses in sight and David wondered as to the method of their transport. Soon afterwards a large truck rolled into the station. David gauged its size. There was hardly room inside for 30 people, but the contingent numbered over 300. The storm-troopers ordered the ramp to be lowered and they herded their charges inside. It was soon full, and most of the families still lingered outside. The troopers pushed them in, beating them on their backs to hurry them. There were cries from children who had been separated from their parents. Suitcases burst open in the crush and their contents were kicked aside by the guards. David saw a pair of black leather phylacteries roll into the gutter. He turned away, appalled. He could hear cries, and then the barring of the truck door. All was silent then, and he dared to turn and look again. The bus-station was empty, save for a few guards as they directed the truck on the start of its journey.

David got into his car and followed at a safe distance. He wanted to ascertain which road it was taking, whether indeed it was going eastwards or whether they were to be dumped outside the city and left to suffocate in the transport. In any case, if they were indeed going to the east in such conditions, they would never reach it alive. He prayed that, if they had to die, their deaths would be quick and merciful. The truck stopped at traffic-lights and he was obliged to pull up close behind it. He turned down his window and from the back of the truck he heard a sound that curdled his heart with pain. The mourning tones of the *Kadish*. They were already celebrating their dead. The truck moved on and David followed. They were approaching the road which gave out to highways leading to the east and west. At the junction, the truck turned westwards. After a mile or two, it turned down a side-road, and it was clear to David that it was making for the old Leipzig railway station, long since out of service for passenger use and used now only for cattle and freight. He stopped the car. It would have been folly to allow himself to be seen as a spectator, and he knew that whatever spectacle was about to be presented, it would be one that could do without witness. But he was curious. He swerved off the road and parked the car in a cul-de-sac of warehouses. Then he walked back to the station. He concealed himself behind a wooden fence which shielded the railway-yard from the road. He stood on tip-toe and peered over. There were hundreds of deportees in the yard, and many trucks, their ramps down, and emptied. He held his breath in horror. A freight-car stood on the sidings, its sliding doors open. The Leipzig truck had come to a halt, and the guards opened the doors. Bodies fell out, one on top of the other, and some of them rose and made their bewildered way into the fresh air. But some lay on the ground, either too weak to move, or simply dead. From where David stood it was hard to tell, but he saw the truck emptying and the body of what looked like an old man on the floor inside. Someone had covered him with a prayer-shawl. The children were crying, many of them lost. Families desperately regrouped themselves, finding in their kinship some sort of comfort. The ground was littered with broken suitcases, and even now their owners sought to re-assemble them, to re-tie the string with meticulous care. David saw one of them actually smile, an old Rabbi, as he managed to get the sides of his case to meet and to secure them with string, displaying for all to see that great Jewish talent for parcel-making, learned over centuries of enforced and sudden flight. He was actually smiling and David stared at him with a strange delight, for he symbolised for all time the stubborn and almost offensive optimism of the survivor.

David waited while the pathetic throng milled in the sidings, sniffing at each other's fear and bewilderment. He wondered where the other contingents had come from. They were not all sickly-looking, and many of them, by their mien and their dress, looked prosperous. Every remaining Jew in Germany would have his turn, David knew and he trembled at the thought of their future. Most disheartening of all, was the sight of so many children. Most of them were crying, and those dry-eyed, stared vacantly with fear. They were all too young to have armed themselves with weapons for survival, too young indeed for that word to have entered their hearts and find some meaning there. Too young to survive, but old enough to die, they clung to their fathers' and mothers' hands, and wondered why those once so strong and reliable hands were now trembling.

The guards had begun to herd the deportees onto the freight-car. They prodded them with their batons as if they were cattle. Those already in the van stretched out a helping hand to the old and the frail. Mothers hoisted their children onto the van then climbed in after them, hurriedly dodging the batons that now laid upon them indiscriminately. It took a long time to load them all. Most of them clung desperately to their suitcases, as if the ownership of tools, clothes and prayer-books would vouch for their future, a future in which to work, to take one's leisure, and to pray. At last no deportee was left on the siding and the heavy sliding-doors were closed. David dared not think of the despair behind them. A plate-worker idled on the siding.

'Where's that train going?' he asked one of the guards.

'To hell,' the man said. 'One way.'

David got back into his car and drove home. He would not tell his family what he had seen, nor any of the members of the *Jüdische Gemeinde*. If they had illusions about settlements in the east where work and leisure was to be found, it would be folly to shatter them. They would be forced to live in day to day dread of their future, to live with those fears that now plagued David every moment of his days and nights.

Some weeks later, another round-up was ordered, and this time the edict contained no directive as to the category of the selection. The request was straightforward and without reservations. Two hundred Jewish families. A meeting of the *Gemeinde* was called. David was loathe to attend. The lack of specific orders for selection would make him party to choice, and it would be like sending people to their death of one's own volition. Yet he was afraid not to attend, lest his own family be part of the list. His presence at the meeting would at least delay that catastrophe. Every member of the *Gemeinde* Board were of the same disposition, reluctant to sentence another, yet fearful in their absence of their own sentencing. All but one, a Mr Hugo Stern, a retired Hebrew teacher, widowed and without family. He saw his role as that of quota-filler, not out of any sense of sacrifice or nobility, though he was a noble enough man, but because he felt that his life had been fully and usefully lived, and that no one would now be burdened by the grief of his absence. When he offered his own person to the Board in this capacity, they would hear none of it. They saw his offer as a threat, as a hint to sacrifice on their own part. Besides, as a member of the Board, Mr Stern was entitled to those unspoken, unwritten privileges of a community leader. Like captains of a sinking ship, they would be the last to leave, and possibly thereby, would stand a chance of rescue. Hugo Stern's offering threatened that privilege and could not be allowed.

They sat at the board table with the copy of the order in front of them. Two hundred families. No more and certainly no less, ordered for employment and settlement in the east. No qualifications necessary. 'How shall we choose?' the Chairman of the Board asked, though he expected no reply, for no one was willing to take the initial responsibility for the sentencing of others. There was silence around the table.

'We must think of some kind of system,' the Chairman said after a while.

'Have you any suggestions?' one of the members asked.

'We could select by streets,' he suggested. 'Or professions. Or within a certain age limit.'

But to David all these suggestions smacked of deliberation. They were guide-lines as much as those they had received from the first round-up, the directives of unemployment, poverty and ill-health. Except that those qualifications were laid down by others. These they would be submitting themselves. The cap fits he who wears it, even though it be the black cap of execution.

'Why don't we have a lottery?' David suggested. It sounded cruel to play with people's names as if they were dice, but at least their choice of list would be arbitrary, without their interference and dependent only on chance. Even the hand that drew the name could not be held responsible.

They understood that David's suggestion would help assuage their consciences and they readily agreed. So they set about writing the names and addresses on separate sheets of paper of the whole Jewish community of families. They divided the work between them, but even so, it took most of that day. By early evening the papers were folded and there was the question of a covered receptacle to hold them. They settled on a dustbin, an appropriate lodging, David thought, mindful of that gruesome sight at the railway siding. To most Germans, Jewish names were rubbish and waste, and their consignment to a dustbin, even in lottery, was a fitting enough start to their journey to the dumping-grounds. The dustbin was filled, the lid secured, and it was rolled on the floor to give every name a chance to lose. Then Hugo Stern offered to make the draw, but even that was denied him, for the Chairman declared that that responsibility, such as it was, must be shared between all members of the Board. 200 families. Ten Board members. They would be obliged to twenty draws apiece.

The Secretary took down the names as they were called. She herself enjoyed the same unspoken immunity as members of the Board, but with each drawer, she feared for the names of her relatives and friends. Forty families had been selected and it was David's turn to draw. He put his hand under the lid and turned his face away. He wanted to shut his ears to the names he had drawn, but he had to share the responsibility at least of that knowledge. All the names were strangers to him, but that was no comfort, for he felt them part of his family, nationwide, and all doomed. The last name he drew was Ernst Mayer, a member of their Board. There was a ripple of consternation. Ernst Mayer slumped in his seat. The Chairman was quick to invoke their privilege, now spoken for the first time.

'We are exempt until the very last,' he said. And to David, 'Draw again.'

The unhappy family was called Zukker.

The bin was passed to the next drawer, Ernst Mayer, the reprieved one, and his hand trembled as he plunged it inside. Eventually the quota was filled. On the following day letters would be sent to all of them requiring their presence at the Leipzig bus-station at ten o'clock in the morning of a week hence. The promise of work and settlement was the same and so was the suitcase allowance. One for each family.

Once again David drove to the bus-station at the appointed time and once again he was sickened by the deportees' obedience. This time he noticed that the suitcases were of a generally better quality and there was little string in evidence. But there was the same meek servility, a desire almost to please. After all, were they not being offered work and settlement? None of them wanted to make a nuisance of themselves. Some were even on the verge of gratitude. Like their predecessors, they were herded into a truck that could by no means accommodate them. They were stuffed inside like old rags, the ramps were raised, the doors bolted, and they were on their way. David followed them. The same road, the same by-pass of the eastern highway. The same destination of the old Leipzig railway. He parked in the same cul-de-sac and peered over the same fence and viewed a facsimile of the original picture of a month before. Hundreds of obedient non-Aryans bowing to an Aryan code which they dared not think was bad for them. Herded together, clinging to their kin, they already looked as poor and as ill as their predecessors. Like them, they shared the same obsession with their suitcases, their insurance for a future. David did not want to see them in transport. He was no longer curious as to the manner of their travel or their whereabouts. To have stayed to witness it a second time, would have been to relish and savour his own survival. In time, all their turns would come.

At home, he dreaded every telephone-call, fearing a summons to another selection. After the second round-up there was almost a month's grace, and David began to believe that the Nazis had had their fill. Then suddenly they started again, and new and indiscriminate round-ups were ordered every week. The committee used the same method of lottery, and each member was aware of the growing hollowness of the bin. Over the last few months the lottery had sent thousands of people to the sidings. In Nazi terms, Leipzig was almost '*Judenrein*'. At the end of one of their meetings the Chairman said, 'We have to face the fact that we on this committee can no longer escape our turn. We must prepare our families. I want to thank you all for helping me,' he said. 'Perhaps our next meeting will be our last. Ours has not been an enviable task.'

The next meeting was indeed the last gathering of the *Jüdische Gemeinde* of Leipzig. The last round-up was by way of a mopping-up operation. No single Jew was to remain in Leipzig. The Board met and sentenced itself to deportation. By that time, rumours from the East had confirmed the lie of 'settlement'. The members of the Board had no expectation of a future. They knew that the suitcases were a mockery, that death called for no special change of clothing.

'We will meet a week's hence at the bus-station,' the Chairman said. 'We will be the last Jews to leave Leipzig.'

All but two, David thought, and suddenly panicked. The SS had not questioned Aaron's and Jakob's emigrated status. Now their discovery would be as dangerous as their deportation. He could no longer postpone telling Benjamin. He could not take the responsibility on his own. He reached home in time to kiss Aaron and Jakob goodnight. I'll wait until they're asleep, he thought, and then I'll tell the family. By the time he'd told them a story – David's nightly task since the departure of his own children – it was supper time. I'll wait till after supper, he thought. He had to tell them then. Tomorrow the official letter would come from the *Gemeinde* and they must not be caught unawares. Though it would come as no great surprise. On the Sabbath, at the synagogue, they could not ignore the empty pews, nor turn a deaf ear to the whispered rumours. They never pressed David for information, but they knew by his positive and continuing silence that sooner or later, the Bindels, like all the others, would be sent from Leipzig. Often during supper that evening, David opened his mouth to speak, but each time he swallowed his food on words that he couldn't find.

In the middle of the meal, the telephone rang. Benjamin went into the hall to answer it. From the dining-room, it was difficult to hear his conversation and David was nervous, lest the news that he had to divulge would be discussed as if it were already known. After a while, Benjamin called Heidi. It was her mother calling from Berlin. He returned to the table and David relaxed. Heidi was some time on the telephone, and when she returned to the table, she was smiling. 'D'you know it's our wedding anniversary next week?' she said to Benjamin. 'Don't worry,' she said, putting her hand on his, 'I'd forgotten too. But mother hadn't. She's sending us the silver candelabra. You remember it, Benjamin? It was my grandmother's.'

A premature legacy, David could not help thinking, hardly merited by an ordinary wedding anniversary, and the news disturbed him. But what was to follow disturbed him even more.

'They're going away for a month,' Heidi went on. 'To Wiesbaden. For the waters.'

335

'A month?' Benjamin said. 'That's a long time in a spa.'

'I thought so, too,' Heidi said. 'But Mother says they might stay even longer. Father needs a long rest, she said.'

David trembled. Heidi's mother had telephoned to say goodbye. She, with Heidi's father, had an appointment at the Berlin bus-station. They too were bound for 'Eastern Settlement', which, for her daughter's sake, she called a spa in Wiesbaden. The legacy of the solid silver candelabra was not so premature after all. Now was certainly no time, David thought, to broach the matter of the impending journey, else they might link it with Wiesbaden and wonder. They must speak of something else first, and David scratched in his mind for some topic of conversation. The war? That was rarely a subject of conversation in the Bindel household. Win or lose, it could make no difference to their present situation. They were fighting their own battle, and they knew it was a losing one. The Final Solution would conquer them all.

'Would you look at my foot after supper, Benjamin?' Leon suddenly said. 'I tripped on the stairs today. I think I may have sprained it.'

David was dismayed. Now was no time for one's health to falter. His father was eighty-five years old, but still young in his years, and fit. Always had been. David could not remember one day of sick-ness in his father's life. How ill-timed such a change, he thought.

'Why didn't you tell me straight away?' Benjamin said. 'Let me look at it now.'

'It'll wait,' Leon smiled. 'After supper.'

Now he could tell them, David decided. The dubious echoes of Wiesbaden had been safely dispersed. Now was the time.

'Our turn has come,' he said suddenly.

'Turn?' Heidi asked. 'For what?'

'We are to be deported,' David said. 'We are on the next list. We will be the last Jews out of Leipzig.'

'We won't be here for the candelabra,' Heidi said. 'What will happen to it?' Then she realised the implications of David's statement. She shrugged her shoulders. 'Well, it's only a cande-labra,' she said.

There was silence then around the table.

'We have survived worse,' Leon said after a while. 'What a pity about my foot. Look at it, Benjamin,' he said. Now in his mind, his foot had become a stumbling-block to survival. It was imperative that Benjamin cure that before his last battle would begin.

'All of us?' Benjamin asked, and he thought of his children and the boat that had sailed without them.

'I took Aaron and Jakob off the register. I marked them as emigrated. The SS accepted it. They don't have to go.'

'But where . . .?' Heidi whispered. Her face was white with fear.

'They must be hidden,' David said.

'That's impossible,' Benjamin's voice was trembling. 'Where should they hide? We cannot ask of anyone to hide them. Harbouring Jews is punishable by death. We've known it to happen. In Holland, in Norway, in Denmark, they've been caught and publicly hanged. We can't ask anyone to take that risk. We have to take them with us.'

'Hans?' Heidi dared to whisper. 'He's their godfather.'

It was astonishing, David thought, how she, whose former intransigence had prevented her children's flight, was now perfectly prepared to hand them over for their safety. She must have understood at last that deportation meant death. Her choice was very simple and now she was desperate to make it.

'Impossible,' Benjamin said. 'We cannot ask our closest friend to put himself at such a risk. Or Inge. Or his mother. It's impossible.' He kept repeating its impossibility, shaking his head but with each repetition he pondered on its possibility. Then finally he decided against it. 'No,' he said vigorously.

'They're coming over later on,' Heidi said.

Almost every evening Hans would drop in after supper. Because of his specialised job in radar, he was exempt from army recruitment.

'We must say nothing to them,' Benjamin said.

'But we must tell them we are leaving,' David said. 'We cannot just disappear from their lives without warning.'

'Why not?' Leon said. 'What is gained by telling them?' He was thinking of Heidi's parents' journey to the Wiesbaden spa. Their non-farewell. 'They will understand,' he said. 'Now take a look at my foot.'

He left the table and went into the drawing-room and Benjamin followed him. The door-bell rang.

'That'll be Hans,' Heidi said. She made for the front door, then turned. 'Do we tell him or don't we?'

'We say nothing,' Benjamin said.

Hans was alone. Inge was tired, he said, and had decided on an early night. 'I heard rumours today,' he said as he took the armchair that Heidi offered him.

David went to the drinks cupboard. 'Would you like a drink, Hans?' he said. He didn't want to hear Hans' rumours. He knew well enough what they were. He poured him a brandy. 'Your health,' he said, giving him his glass.

None of them cared to ask him what the rumours were. Then Hans knew that they were true. 'Are they sending you away?' he said.

Benjamin was examining Leon's foot. 'Can you stretch it, Papa?' he said.

'Well are they, or aren't they?' Hans asked. His voice was raised.

'Yes,' Benjamin said. There was now no point in denying it.

'All of you?' Hans whispered.

'The house will be empty,' Leon said. 'And yours if you wish.'

'Not mine,' Hans said. 'Mine for the caretaking. I'll look after it till you return.'

No one of them took him up on that. For it was clear to them all, including Hans, that they would not see Leipzig again.

'Is there anything else you want me to do?' Hans said. 'Your investments, your dealings with the bank, insurances?' He wanted to give himself jobs as caretaker. He wanted tasks to perform on the assumption that they would return.

'I shall put everything in order,' Leon said, 'before we leave. There's Greta's grave,' he added. 'I would like you to take care of it.'

Hans went over to the old man and embraced him. 'I'll come back in the morning,' he said. 'I'll help you with all the arrangements.'

'What about your work?' David asked.

'That won't run away,' Hans said.

It was clear that Hans was in a hurry to leave. He was shocked by the news, and needed to be alone to assess his loss. They did not try to keep him.

'I'll see myself out,' he said.

They heard the front door close.

'Poor Hans,' Leon said, neatly shifting their own despair.

'What about the children?' Heidi said. The subject had lingered in the drawing-room during the course of Hans' visit, unspoken yet on the tip of all tongues.

'There's nowhere they can hide,' Benjamin said. 'We shall take them. We shall all go together.' He looked at Heidi. 'I don't want to talk about hiding any more. Tomorrow we shall tell them we are all going on a journey.' He returned to the examination of Leon's foot. 'It's sprained,' he said after a while. 'I'll put a bandage on it. But you must rest it as much as you can.'

He went upstairs to the medical cabinet. He looked at the array of bottles and a terrible thought crossed his mind. In the hospital he had access to drugs that would painlessly and swiftly put an end to them all. But who would administer them? Who would dole them out to his children? He thought of Buchenwald and the six-foot high aperture in the wall. No more, no more, he said to himself. I am innocent. He looked into the mirror above the cabinet. 'We will survive,' he said. 'We must. All of us.'

He took the bandage downstairs and dressed his father's foot. Heidi was clearing the dining-room table and David was helping her.

'What must we take with us?' she asked him.

'We're only allowed one suitcase,' he said. 'For all of us.' He didn't want to tell her that even one suitcase was superfluous. Yet he suspected that she knew. So did they all, but it was important for each of them that their knowing should not be known, else they would have to give way to their despair.

Over the next few days until their departure, and for the days that were left after that, they would, each one of them, play the game of survival.

'You should go to bed, Papa,' David heard Benjamin say.

'I'm not tired,' his father said. He did not want to be alone at that time. He needed the comfort of company even if that company were silent. And silent it was, for the rest of the evening. When Heidi and David had finished in the kitchen they returned to the drawing-room.

'Shall we have a night-cap?' David suggested.

The Bindels rarely drank unless it was wine with meals, but now seemed a time to break with custom, to question habits of a lifetime, to risk change, since there was now little left to lose.

'I'll have a cognac,' Leon said.

'Me too,' Benjamin and Heidi said together.

David poured and held the glasses to each of them. He saw his father raise his glass and he trembled at what futile toast he had in mind.

'To survival,' Leon said. 'Of all of us.'

And so the game started. They sat around the fire until the clock chimed midnight, and all were loathe to leave each other. When the front door-bell rang, piercing the silence between them, they all trembled. Was it possible that the troopers had come for them, that even a week's grace would be denied them?

'I'll go,' David said.

'Ask who it is,' Heidi whispered. But David did not want to know. Not until he had to. He was trembling. So were they all. He opened the door.

Hans stood there with Inge.

'It's Hans,' David shouted in the direction of the drawing-room, and in their delighted relief they all came into the hall to greet him.

'Take your coats off,' David said, glad that their retirement could be further delayed.

But neither Hans nor Inge made a move to disrobe.

'We want to hide the children,' Hans said. 'Please,' he added, anticipating their objections. 'They'll be safe with us. And happy.

As happy as we will be to have them. We'll move into the country. Near Halle. I will arrange everything.'

'But you and Inge. And your mother. It's dangerous. You know what happens if you get caught,' Benjamin said.

'We've talked about it. Mother too. We know the risks. But we cannot stand by and do nothing.'

'Take off your coats,' Leon said.

Now they were prepared to disrobe, for it seemed that they might come to an agreement. David poured them a drink. Hans raised his glass.

'To Aaron and Jakob,' he said. 'And to your return.'

Heidi began to cry. She cried with sorrow that they would soon be parted; she cried with joy that her children would live. There was no need for words between them, words of gratitude or comradeship. Hans' and Inge's act of friendship could well involve a sacrifice that was supreme, and such knowledge could only be digested in silence.

Inge put her arm on Heidi's shoulder. 'Try to remember that they are alive and well, and to them you will always be their mother. And Benjamin their father. I promise you that. The war cannot go on for ever. Soon you will all be together again.'

That Bindel phrase again, and now uttered by one who, by her own perilous choice, had asked for admittance to their family.

'They will have to revert to Hermann and Heinrich again,' Hans laughed. 'We're lucky that they're both fair. Don't worry. We won't send them to school. We'll teach them ourselves at home. We'll take no risks, I promise you.'

'What shall we tell the children?' Heidi asked.

'We'll tell them the truth,' Benjamin said. 'We'll tell them all the truth we know.'

David was glad then that he had not taken Benjamin to the railway-sidings. The truth that Benjamin would, in all his honesty, tell his children, would allow for their possible re-union. Time and their growth would ease their pain. He thanked God that their childhood had been a happy care-free one.

When Hans and Inge had gone, all four Bindels were suddenly anxious to retire. It had nothing to do with fatigue, but for the need now to be alone, the need now for each one of them to make their solitary entry into the land of grief and sorrow.

340

The following morning Benjamin went to the hospital early. Rumours that the hospital would soon be closed had been confirmed in a letter from the Authorities. Arrangements were being made to send all patients home, even those who would die if withdrawn from treatment. They would die in any case, because home was only a stop-over before the railway-siding. He did his ward rounds, comforting as best he could. So often in his Buchenwald days he had wished he'd never qualified in medicine. Now he wished it again, disgusted by its waste and terrible abuse.

'I shall be going home tomorrow, Doctor,' one of his patients called from his bed.

Benjamin went towards him. 'You'll like that,' he said. 'You're getting your own way at last.'

Mr Zeider, a cancer patient, ignorant of his terminal condition, had daily begged to be sent home. And daily his ailing wife had visited the hospital and begged them to keep him, for she herself was not strong enough to care for him. If God were good, Benjamin thought, He would take them both into His keeping, and soon. But clearly in these terrible times, if there were a God at all, His back was turned.

He finished his ward rounds and was now anxious to get home. There were six days left before they had to keep their appointment, six days in which to feed his eyes on his children, to print indelibly on his mind's eye an image of them that would last until that day, he dared to hope, when they would be together again. But first he and Heidi must tell them about Hans and Inge and their new country home. He must look too at his father's foot.

He let himself into the house and heard his children's voices from the drawing-room. They were laughing. He followed the sound. They were sprawled on the drawing-room floor, with Hans who was working their train-set.

'Uncle Hans keeps calling us Hermann and Heinrich, Daddy,' Jakob laughed as his father entered the room.

'Where's Mummy?' he said.

'She's making lunch,' Aaron said. 'Uncle Hans is staying.'

Benjamin went into the kitchen. He was not surprised to find his father there too and it heartened him. Ever since Sarah's departure, Heidi had grown closer to his father and he to her. He was glad that, however they would journey and wherever their destination, they would at least be unburdened by family strife.

'How's your foot, Papa?' he asked.

'I've been resting it,' Leon said.

Benjamin bent down and undid the bandage. The swelling had eased a little, but the pain persisted, Leon said, whenever he put his foot on the ground.

'It will go,' Benjamin said, re-bandaging. 'Just keep resting it.' He eased on his father's shoe. It was an ill-timed injury. They would all need their health and strength to weather the impending journey. The eastern settlements were hundreds of miles away and the journey would be wearisome. Then they would have to adapt themselves to new surroundings, new work, new friends. Sometimes Benjamin firmly believed the Nazi promise of happy re-settlement and he would not admit to his mind that there could be any other interpretation. Then why, he said to himself, am I leaving my children behind? He knew well enough, but would not give it voice. Such thinking was confusing and totally illogical, but he believed it devoutly and so did the thousands of others who went to the railway sidings. Because, even with one's penultimate breath, death was an event that happened to other people.

'When shall we tell the children?' Heidi asked. She took his hand and fondled it, knowing that there was little time to make up for the loving that had been lost between them for so many years. He kissed the top of her head. 'After lunch,' he said.

David was called from the garden where he had spent most of the morning, sweeping the first of the autumn leaves from the lawn. For a time he had managed to forget about the impending journey, to concentrate on the leaves and their symbol of season. Their golden colours were herald to winter, and the snow on the lawn, through which snowdrops and crocuses would insist on their time in their season, and the laburnum would flower to shelter them, till it would shed its golden rain as a prelude to the full splendour of the summer roses. And this time next year he would sweep the leaves again to make way for the snows and the snowdrops and the laburnum and the roses and he would be part of nature's cycle for all eternity. When he heard their call for lunch, he saw the railway-sidings again and he plunged the rake's fork into the ground with monumental rage.

He was glad Hans was at the table, and the children were hanging on to each syllable of his stories.

'I've bought a house in the country,' Hans suddenly announced.

'Oh can we go there, Uncle Hans?' Aaron said.

'Please, Daddy,' Jakob echoed. 'Can we go and stay with Uncle Hans?'

The children were doing it for him, Benjamin thought, leaving on their own account. For a moment he dared to consider that the suggestion of a holiday with its inbuilt impermanence might be the only way to part from them. Yet it would be a monstrous deception, a trick that they might never learn to forgive.

'Why not a little holiday?' Leon said, quickly picking up on that solution, and sanctioning its deception. 'They could help Hans with the moving.'

'We'll go on Thursday,' Hans said. 'Is that all right, Benjamin?'

'I think that's a lovely idea,' Heidi said.

Was it all over? Was it all done? Had they separated without a single tear? Had they orphaned their children so swiftly with this splendid and base deception? What happened when the holiday was over? To what home would they return?

'How long can we stay, Daddy?' Aaron asked, as if prompting the truth from his father's lips.

'Perhaps for a long time,' he said. 'Listen to me, children.' He looked at them tenderly. Six and seven years old, he had to remind himself. What could they understand of pogrom? 'You remember,' he said, 'when you had to leave your old school, d'you remember why?'

'They didn't like the Jews,' Jakob said.

'That's right. And now they're going to send all the grown-up Jews away. We don't know where, but it won't be very far, and it's only until the war is over.' He was allowed a little licence, Benjamin thought, for pity's sake. Time would heal the scar of their absence, time too, the wound of their non-return. 'You are going to stay with Uncle Hans and Aunt Inge, and you have to pretend that you are not Jews. That's why you have to be Hermann and Heinrich again, because they're not Jewish names.'

He stopped. He had told them everything, he thought, except perhaps the terrible truth of which he himself was not sure.

'Is Grandpa going too?' Jakob asked. His voice was tearful. It wasn't going to be a holiday after all.

'Yes,' Benjamin said. 'And Uncle David too.'

'Is that why Aunt Sarah went to Palestine?' Aaron asked.

Benjamin, David and Leon knew at that moment that wherever they looked, it must not be at Heidi. They heard her sobbing. Perhaps for the first time she realised the terrible price of her former stubbornness.

And so the Bindel children were gently orphaned, and each one of them round the table, including Aaron and Jakob, turned away from the unspoken truth that filled the silence because none of them could face its fearful dark.

There were four days left of parenting. David, Leon and Heidi did not leave the house at all. Benjamin went to the hospital early each day, until the last day when there was no work for him at all. All the patients had been sent home and storm-troopers had arrived to commandeer the building.

It was the night before the children were to leave with Hans and Inge. Heidi had packed for them, and made a celebration supper. All of them were at pains to make it a festive occasion. Tomorrow the house would be childless, for the very first time since Leon had returned to Leipzig and started his second family. When the meal was over, the boys helped Heidi clear the table, and while they were in the kitchen, Benjamin turned to his father.

'Papa,' he said. 'I want my children to inherit.'

Leon smiled at him. 'Let's go upstairs to Zelda's room.' It was in that place that he had bequeathed to his own children Grandpa Jakob's litany. Of all the four traceable Bindel inheritors, Aaron and Jakob were the youngest, and Leon wondered what they would make of it all. He recalled the bluebell wood where he had bequeathed to his first David the prayer for survival, and how, in all his thirteen years, the boy had understood. He recalled too, the forest behind the Odessa tavern where he and Aaron had inherited, and he himself in his thirteenth year. He remembered that he had understood it too. And his own father, Benjamin, the milk-brother, with his unleavened bread in his baggage and terror in his heels, in all his ten years he had accepted the weaponry of survival, and in time he had understood its power. He rose from the table and called his grandchildren. 'Come. Let us all go,' he said.

They went upstairs.

'We will share in the bequest,' Leon told them. 'First, I have to tell you a little of the history of the time.'

So between them, Leon, Benjamin and David, they told of the milk-brothers' years in the tavern, of Meisels and the *Kahal*, of the child-recruitment and the milk-brothers' miraculous return. Leon watched the light flicker in his grand-children's eyes, with the wonder and the excitement that a fairy tale promotes. And suddenly he could not bear to break their spell. He could not tell them the story of that gentle Leon after whom he himself was named. Neither could he tell them the story of the fire. But he told them about survival in his own simple terms.

'Life is sometimes very hard,' he said, 'and sometimes we give in. We don't fight. I want you to fight to live, my children. Whatever names men may call you, whatever harm they try to do to you, you must always fight to live. We call that surviving. It is a difficult word to understand, and it is a word as long as the history of the Jews themselves. But as you grow older, you will learn its meaning. 'Aaron and Jakob,' he said slowly, 'I want you to survive. Now go to bed, my children.'

They came towards him for his embrace, and he held them long in his arms.

'Grandpa,' Aaron said. 'You must survive too.' Leon turned away his face, and he knew that they had understood.

*

That night Benjamin took a large piece of paper and wrote in his best hand the exact words of Grandpa Jakob's legacy that he knew by heart. On another sheet, he wrote the story of Leon and his Siberian imprisonment, and he wrote, too, the story of the fire. He folded them into a large envelope which he addressed to his sons. In the morning when Hans came to fetch them, he gave it into his keeping, as his Last Will and Testament. Hans put it away without a word.

No farewells were made until the children were settled in the car. They all came out into the driveway, and in turn they leaned into the car and kissed the children goodbye. Heidi was the last, and Benjamin held her body close to his to still her trembling. They smiled, all of them, as they waved the children goodbye, and Aaron and Jakob saw their mother turn her back and they wondered at it for they could not see her tear-stained face that she didn't want them to see. The car reached the end of the driveway and turned into the street, the children still looking behind them. Then Leon, David, Benjamin and Heidi held each other close and returned to the childless house to begin their mourning.

When night fell, Heidi suggested that they organise their packing. With the allowance of only one suitcase between them, it was important, she said, for each one to choose his own essentials. David knew the fraud of those suitcases, but suddenly he was anxious to make his own luggage contribution. To go without luggage of any kind was to abdicate entirely.

'I'll take my new grey suit,' he said. Not only would he pack, but he would prepare himself to be dressed for occasion. Benjamin too, decided on his best suit, and Leon likewise. They all went upstairs to collect their choices and bring them to Benjamin's bedroom where Heidi packed them with great care. Benjamin took the suitcase down into the hall, together with his newly-stocked medical bag, then he and David took their father to his room. Benjamin noticed that he was still limping.

'How's the foot, Papa?' he said.

'It will be better tomorrow,' Leon said. It had to be better tomorrow. Its cure was the first stage of his renewed survival, that survival that his seven-year-old grandson had ordered.

345

None of them slept that night. They tossed on their restless beds and wished for the morning. When it came, they rose, bathed and breakfasted as if it were an ordinary day. They each put a package of food in their pockets, then they left the house together. David had arranged that Hans would pick up the Bindel car at the bus-station. Benjamin helped his father into the front seat.

They were early for their appointment, but when they reached the bus-station, it was already crowded. They were horrified to note the number of infirm, those in wheelchairs, or simply carried on the arms of relatives. And children, infants-in-arms. Benjamin caught sight of a mother whom he had delivered of a son only a week ago. The baby was feeding at her breast and on her face was a look of bewilderment at the world into which he had been born.

The trucks began to pull into the station. Four of them, David noted, many more than he had seen on his former witnessing, but still hardly enough to accommodate the growing crowd that frantically surged onto the bus-station, fearful of missing their transport. The troopers began to load the first truck and there were those who rushed towards it, no doubt hopeful of better accommo-dation. But David held his family back. It was better to be last on the trucks. The danger of suffocation was less on the tail-end, and there was a small ventilation from the slats on the doors that could well mean the difference between life and death. They watched as the invalids were wheeled towards the ramp.

'No chairs,' a storm-trooper shouted, as one old man was wheeled towards the truck. 'You have to carry him.'

His escort, probably his son, David thought, was old enough in years, and looked hardly able to carry himself. He looked around helplessly for some support. But those about him looked away. Benjamin made to go to his help. But Leon pulled him back.

The storm-trooper grew impatient with the escort's feeble attempt to lift his patient. He pushed him aside, lifted the old man from his chair and practically threw him into the waiting truck. There was a scream of horror from the waiting spectators, but it was quickly stifled lest they themselves receive the same treatment.

David held his family back until the third truck began to load. He knew they would underestimate its capacity, even by their own cruel reckoning, and that it would be the last truck that would bulge with the uncontainable overflow. He waited until it was almost full, then he urged his family forward. Heidi took Leon's arm, and Benjamin noted again his father's limp. He took his other arm, and David took the suitcases on which he was now beginning to believe all their lives depended. They were fortunate to be the last ones on the third truck, though they were shoved in brutally by the guards and those behind them fell in confusion, for by the time

346

the doors were bolted there was room to shuffle about and to find some breathing space. Twice before David had taken this route and each time in his own empty car, with no discomfort except the fear of what he followed. He knew the road by heart, and when the truck swerved, he knew that they had by-passed the route to the east and were on their way to the railway sidings.

'It won't be long now, Papa,' he whispered to Leon at his side.

'I'm fine, I'm fine,' Leon insisted. 'Don't worry about me.'

He would not have said that, Benjamin thought, if there had been no cause for concern. His foot was hurting him and he was at pains to hide it. When Benjamin had re-bandaged it that morning, the swelling had almost disappeared, yet still his father limped as if he was in no hurry to meet his end. Death had lurked so often in many corners of his life and had lost its appetite for the kill. Now it could wait until the prey, in the natural order of things, would limp towards it. The dodgers, the wily, the arrogant and the cunning, it would pursue, but for the halt and the lame it would wait, for their arrival, though tardy, was inevitable.

There was silence in the truck, the hush of bewilderment and fear, the silence of those who were ambushed. A baby cried and was quickly put to the breast, lest its whereabouts, though known and monitored by all, should be discovered. The truck slowed down and David could hear the gravel under the tyres. It was drawing into the railway-siding. Suddenly it stopped, and its frightened cargo girded itself to alight. But the doors remained bolted. David listened intently. He could hear no noise on the outside, though there must be at least two truck-loads parked on the siding. The storm-troopers had changed their tactics and he felt cheated. Shortly afterwards, he heard the arrival of what he assumed was the fourth truck. He heard the grinding wheels on the gravel, the screeching of brakes, and again the silence. They waited. Then they heard the sound of heavy sliding-doors and David knew that they were preparing the freight-car for entry. Shortly afterwards the truck doors were opened, and the deportees tumbled out, grateful for the air and life-reprieve, no matter how short its duration. But alas, it was short enough, for straightway they were ordered towards the train and bullied inside. Again David held his family back, and for the same reason. He looked around. It was the same scene he had witnessed twice before from behind the fence in the cul-de-sac. Except that this time, there was a difference.

A crowd of spectators had gathered on the perimeter of the railway-siding, looking down on the arena, salivating for spectacle. They were but a few of those thousands of Germans who, in later years would claim a total ignorance of the inhuman drama of the Final Solution. Some were cheering and jeering; others were silent, drinking in each detail of that story that they would forbear to tell their children.

The Bindel family watched as the deportees were man-handled into the car. Soon those doors would be closed on all of them, on that stage of the drama that David had not witnessed. Until that time he had been able to guide his family along the lines of his own experience, but once behind those doors, they would all dwell in the same black ignorance.

He delayed their boarding as long as he could. Then a guard made his way towards their group, his baton raised. They dodged him, and hurried towards the car. Benjamin and David helped their father to board first, then Heidi, while the blows rained down on Benjamin's and David's backs, urging them to hurry. They were the last to board, and scarcely had Benjamin's foot slipped over the platform, than the doors were slid shut, and there was total darkness inside. The train shunted forward, and a woman screamed. Her cries were the signal to the release of all the pent-up moaning and sighs of the human cargo who must have smelt the death in the car, that sour odour bequeathed by their brethren who had journeyed before them. Children sniffed at their parents' fear, and whimpered with desertion, and the bowels of old men melted, those who were too old for tears.

After a while, they grew accustomed to the dark and they could see the faces around them. They shifted about, trying to find room for themselves. Benjamin sat his father on the suitcase, and David was glad that he had not advised them against baggage. For most of the cargo there was standing room only, though some held their children in their arms, for fear they might be trampled underfoot. Apart from the whimpering and the moaning, the truck was strangely silent, and Benjamin was reminded of his journey to Buchenwald, when the prisoners had kept that same silence, the silence that shrouds the non-question, that turns away from curiosity, lest the information received would be unbearable. All of them on the train knew enough from their present situation, and nobody wanted to know any more.

'Is there a doctor?' someone suddenly shouted into the dark.

'Yes. Here.' Benjamin's response was automatic. 'Where are you?'

'Here,' a man's voice shouted. 'By the wall. My wife's having a baby.'

The people around Benjamin squeezed together to allow him a narrow passage to the wall of the train. He held his medical-bag high above his head.

'Here, here,' the man called, and guided him with his voice to where his wife was crouching.

Benjamin bent down at her side. 'Lie down,' he said to her gently. The people around made what room they could for her, and they turned their faces away, stricken by the thought that a life could begin on such a journey, when there was such a little way for it to go.

'It's our first,' the father said, crouching by his side. Benjamin examined the woman as best he could. She was in the last stage of labour. He decided to stay by her side. She was a young girl, Benjamin surmised, probably twenty years old. Her body was healthy. She would survive. Her face was twisted with pain, but she stifled her cries, aware of her lack of privacy.

'Have you decided on a name?' Benjamin asked, wishing to engage her in conversation to allay her fears.

She shook her head. 'We're waiting to see whether it's a boy or a girl. Will I be all right, doctor?' she asked.

'Of course.' Benjamin held her hand. 'And so will the baby.' He wondered what was the point of it all.

The girl gave a small scream which she could no longer contain. 'It won't be long now,' Benjamin said. 'It will be painful, but during the pain you must keep in mind that soon it will all be over, and you'll hold a baby in your arms. If it helps you to scream, then scream aloud.'

But her shyness and strict sense of privacy overcame her need to cry out. She clenched her teeth and gripped her husband's arm. 'It's time to push,' Benjamin whispered in her ear. He prayed for a normal delivery. He had no equipment for any other. 'Have you got a shawl of any kind?' he asked the father.

The girl's head was resting on their suitcase, and gently the man prised it open and withdrew a white woollen shawl. They had set out on their journey well-prepared, full of hope and expectation of a new life, and a new life with whom to share it.

'Another push, my dear,' Benjamin said. He had begun to love this girl, this total stranger who, in her quiet pain and labour, was gently affirming survival, giving the lie to the death that lingered in the wagon, and their weary journey of no return. 'Push,' Benjamin said. 'It's almost over.'

He marvelled at her silence. He even detected a small smile on the wrinkled pain of her lips. He pressed his hands on her abdomen and saw the beginnings of the child's head. Although, in his time as a doctor, Benjamin had delivered countless children, that very first vision of a new-born always appeared to him as a miracle. At the sight of this one, this impudently ill-timed arrival, he almost laughed with joy. 'Push,' he whispered. The head emerged. It was going to be a normal birth and he thanked God for it. He clasped the baby's skull with both hands, and carefully withdrew it from its nest, the comfort of which the child was never likely, in its life, whether it be long or short, to enjoy again.

'It's a boy,' he whispered, and laid the child on her stomach, and took her hands and the hands of the father in his and gently he placed them on the child for their caress. Then he lifted the baby and cut the cord, thus giving it life on its own account, its inalienable separateness, its inviolate, untouchable solitude.

'Mazeltov,' he shouted into the car. 'We have an extra passenger. A baby boy.' As he spoke, he wrapped the child in the shawl, cleaned its eyes and ears with swabs of cotton-wool, then handed the bundle to the mother. She was smiling. Her husband cradled her head in his arms.

'You must start thinking of a name,' Benjamin said.

'What's yours?' the father asked.

'Benjamin.'

'Then that's how he will be called. Benjamin, the son of my right hand.'

'I'm honoured,' Benjamin said, and he embraced the young man. 'I wish you joy of your son,' he said, and meant it, although he was aware of how short-lived that joy might be. He poured a little brandy from the bottle in his medical kit. He urged the new mother to sip a little, then the father, and the baby was toasted into a world bent on its destruction.

Benjamin returned to his family, and gave his father a sip of the brandy. He took Heidi's hand. 'It's a lovely little boy,' he said. 'They've called it Benjamin.'

'What's to become of us?' she whispered. Her eyes were full of tears. He held her close. 'Think of our children,' he said. 'We must live for them.'

The train shunted along in the darkness, pulling up sharply from time to time, as if the driver was teasing his cargo. At those times there was much confusion in the freight car, and crying and raging against the helpless inconsideration of other passengers. Towards evening, the real nightmare began. They sniffed at it in the darkness. The most private pursuit of all, that which proclaimed the body's waste had, from want of privacy and facility, been publicised. And not a single one of them, in their own and natural time, would be able to escape it. During the night the smell was overpowering, and many were sick where they stood, and cried for air of which there was none. Some there were who cried for death, and those cries were more obscene than the odours that prompted them, and they were quickly shouted down. 'We will get used to the smell,' Leon said quietly. He was hungry, but he did not trust his digestion. The sight of food would have sickened them all. He dozed a little, leaning on Heidi's thigh, and for the first time in many years, he dreamed of Senghennyd and his first-born. He woke with calm and peace of mind, knowing with absolute certainty that he would soon join him.

'Where can we be?' David whispered. By his watch they had been travelling for sixteen hours.

'If we're going east,' Benjamin said, 'we must have crossed the Polish border by now. Even though this train is very slow. It can't be much further.'

But eastern settlement as the Nazis had promised could, at that time, have meant Russia too, much of which land was already German-occupied. He dared not think of the distance they might still have to travel. He made his way to the wall of the car to see his namesake. He was suckling at his mother's breasts between bouts of sleep. He asked her how she was, and explained about the milk and how soon she would lactate. She offered the baby for him to hold, and as he did so, he was overwhelmed by a sudden longing for his own children.

'I have two sons,' he told her.

'What are they called?' she asked.

'Aaron and Jakob.' But now he realised that they were Hermann and Heinrich, for that was the spelling of their safety. It was also the spelling of their infancy. He had held Hermann like this one, and Heinrich in his time. He thought of their Aaron and Jakob years and the beginning of his own awakening. And then he thought of the rescue ship his children had not taken and of Heidi who then still slumbered in her false hopes. He had almost forgiven her, and if his children survived, that pardon would be whole. But would he live to see the evidence? He must forgive her now, totally and completely. He returned the child to its mother and went back to his family. Heidi was crying. Her clothes were wet with her waste and her shame. He comforted her, and spoke to her words of love, and his tenderness frightened her.

'What will become of us?' she said again.

He poured brandy for them all.

Suddenly a cry was heard from the end of the wagon. Not a cry of pain, nor murmur of despair, but a chant of lamentation in which sound, Benjamin detected a rogue note of joy. It was the *Kadish*. Someone in the car had died, and his death had been merciful. The song sounded like a thanksgiving. Gradually those men in the car began to hum, until the song was a chorus of glorification, a hosanna of praise. Benjamin looked at his father. His face was stern and his lips tightly sealed. 'We must not celebrate death,' he said, his voice breaking. 'Never. When one of our people dies, our greeting to the bereaved is almost an order. I wish you long life, we say.' He raised his cup of brandy. 'Le'chaim,' he said. 'To life.'

Night fell once more. Neither David nor Benjamin could sleep, but they linked arms and rocked against each other with the motion of the train.

'What are you thinking of, brother?' Benjamin asked.

'I have the same thoughts as you,' David said. 'We are both thinking of our children.'

In the morning the stench in the car was piteously severe, the odours of human waste now mixed with the smell of vomit. In time, Benjamin thought, the corpse at the end of the car would decompose. He wondered if one could ever get used to the smell of that. In the late afternoon, they heard the *Kadish* again, distant now, and doubly-spoken, for somewhere in the rear of the car, two human beings had been delivered.

'I wish you long life,' Leon said.

Another night passed, and in the morning, waking to the stench, they wondered how long they could still be alive, and they marvelled at human endurance, and began for the first time to have faith in their survival. Then suddenly the train stopped and did not start again.

'We shall have air,' someone cried. 'God is good,' and the crowd echoed his thanksgiving. That's all they wanted from life. Not food, not water. Just air. And suddenly the doors slid open.

They were blinded by the light, and intoxicated by the astonished air. Some fainted where they stood, and some were trampled on by those in frantic rush for escape from the car. The Bindel family were among the first to alight from the wagon, and they breathed deeply of the biting and cold air. Benjamin waited at the doors helping the passengers alight, and waiting for the mother whom he had delivered and a new sight of his namesake. She came to the front of the wagon and handed him the baby. Then her husband jumped to the ground and lifted her down. 'Where are we?' she said, as she gulped for air.

Benjamin looked at his surroundings for the first time. They were bleak and reminded him fearfully of Buchenwald. For this was a camp too, though on a vaster scale, its perimeters beyond the eyes' reach, and despite the noise and cries of the new arrivals, as silent as the grave. Some storm-troopers leapt onto the wagon and hurried the remaining passengers outside, beating them with their sticks if they were tardy. 'Where are we?' a woman screamed, her eyes blinded by the light. 'Auschwitz,' a guard said, and that was the first time that many of the arrivals had heard the word, a simple German bi-syllable. A place and a name.

'Auschwitz,' Benjamin repeated to himself, the so-called eastern settlement.

He rejoined his family and they were herded into a line that was moving slowly towards the gate. The Bindels kept closely together. It was difficult to see what procedure was being followed on entry to the camp, but clearly there was some hold-up there, and Benjamin could see a group of guards at the front directing the human traffic. As they neared the gates, he could see that this traffic was being divided into two lines. He noticed, but as yet without any realisation of its import, that the one line consisted mainly of old people and children, while the other was made up of able-bodied men and women who looked as if they could work. But by the time the Bindel family arrived at the gates, each of them knew instinctively that the division of traffic was a very simple one. To the right meant to live, and to the left meant to die. As they walked forward, Benjamin noticed that his father was limping very badly, but worse still, that Heidi, on whose arm he leaned, was limping too, perhaps to facilitate her support. Her gait was not lost on the guards. One of them shoved Leon's and Heidi's shoulders with his stick.

'Left,' he ordered.

Leon turned and looked at his sons as the guard prodded them with his baton.

'Right,' he shouted.

It was a clear moment of farewell, too sudden, too stark, too terrible to believe. They looked across the space between them, that no-man's land of limbo. A mere few feet separated them, but it was a yawning chasm of despair. Benjamin looked at Heidi and tried not to convey to her his terrible fears on her behalf. But she knew. She smiled at him. 'Look after the children,' she said.

Leon was smiling too. 'It's all so ridiculous,' he managed to say, then a guard prodded him on his last journey.

Benjamin and David watched them go. Then suddenly their father stopped, turned and shouted across the miles that separated the quick from the dead.

'Remember Grandpa Jakob,' he shouted at them, his voice cracking with the exertion. 'Survive.'

The word echoed across the camp and lingered on the foul air like a blessing. Benjamin and David watched them out of sight. No tears. There must be no tears. Survival was dry, without lament, without mourning. Benjamin turned to his brother.

'I wish you long life,' he said.

'And I to you,' David answered, and because Benjamin had been twice bereaved, he added, 'A long life twice over.'

They stood as the death column moved slowly forward. Amongst them, the young mother Benjamin has so recently delivered, his namesake in her arms. She was alone, and her eyes were full of fearful wonder. Just about now, Benjamin thought, her milk would be coming through. He turned away, trembling. David took his brother's arm, and in a plaintive chant, they chorused the *Kadish* together. 'O Lord, what is man,' they prayed, 'his days are of grass; as a flower in the field, so he flourisheth. For the wind passes over it and it is gone.' They heard the echo of their father's words. Survive, he had called out to them. From generation to generation, their inheritance foretold, there would be a minstrel to sing that stubborn song of survival. Everywhere and at all times there would be such a troubadour, and somewhere, someone would hear his song. Now it rang in the brothers' ears, though the minstrel, like the salmon which spawns its future and dies, that minstrel had forfeited his life with his song.

CHAPTER TWENTY-FOUR

Millions of people perished in the German concentration camps, and they died in all colours. Red for politicals, yellow for Jews, mauve for Jehovahs' Witnesses, blue for emigrès, green for convicts, black for asocials, brown for gypsies, and pink for homosexuals. A pariah's rainbow.

Libraries of words have been written about them, based on the Nuremburg trials of the accused, or on the testimonies of those who survived, or on the diaries and journals that were found amongst the ruins. But millions of words were also never written. The basic lack of equipment was one reason for the prisoners' silence, a pencil and some paper; there was too, the sheer suspicion of one's own terrible words, that one could actually be dwelling in the hell of which one writes. But, above all else, the tale was untellable.

Out of that welter of unpublished alphabet, there follows the fragments of the unwritten spasmodic diary of one David Bindel, prisoner in Auschwitz, 1943. Aged 34. Registration tattoo, 796702. Classification, yellow star. Jew. Inferior race. The pencil with which the diary is written, never existed. Neither the paper on which it is recorded. For in truth, there exists no pen for such calligraphy; no paper that would not ignite in the terrible fire of each syllable. But in God's sight, if His eyes were open in this place, every syllable of every word was true.

*

It must be winter because it is snowing. Though which winter of what year, I am not sure. Hunger plays havoc with the memory. Perhaps it is the second winter in this place, because I remember being warm once, or was that a long time ago in the house in Leipzig. I must ask Benjamin. There is a calendar in the so-called hospital where he works ... I work in the munitions factory. I pack shell-cases. There are hundreds of us in the plant. We say nothing but we think all the time of sabotage for any Nazi enemy is our friend. Sonia talks about it to herself. I've noticed lately that she hides things under her blouse. Then she wanders off somewhere, hands clasped around her breasts. After a while, she comes back, her arms swinging and she goes back to work with a smile. Ada does the same thing. Her tattoo is 131313. Three thirteens. She says she'll be lucky.

I shall have my picture in the paper. I weigh 85 pounds. They picked me out with seven others to be photographed for *Der Stürmer*.

Today Ada and Sonia keep wandering out of the factory when the guards aren't looking. There are four other girls doing the same thing. I don't know their names. But I wish they would all stop doing it.

I saw Benjamin today. He's been sent to work in the medical experiment centre. Under a Dr Mengele. He's obsessed with twins, Benjamin says. All kinds of experiments. Mainly injections for instantaneous death. He had this notion that if you inject one of the twins, the other will die too. Telepathic genetics, he calls it. He keeps trying but it takes an awful lot of twins to prove anything.
Dr Mengele has children of his own.
Benjamin slipped some aspirin into my hand. He knows about my headaches.
He asks me do I ever think of my children. I think he was talking to himself.

I looked at my body today, and I wondered to whom it belonged.

I told them not to do it. At least I told Sonia and Ada. Tomorrow they're going to be hanged. Six of them. There's a prisoner works in the gas-chambers. He had a plan to blow them up. The girls were smuggling dynamite out of the factory. The prisoner was Sonia's husband. They buried him alive.

In the roll-call area, they're rigging up a platform for the orchestra. They play while the gallows are being erected. The guards say we have to watch it. It will teach us all a lesson.

Every morning outside my hut, there's a pigeon. It chooses to live in this place. It's a dove really, they tell me. A dove? Here?

At the foot of the gallows, I turned my head away. And so do many of the others. I'm beaten on the shoulders and forced to look. The orchestra plays the overture to *Meistersinger*. I am ashamed, but I confess to enjoying the music. I know it is the overture to hanging, but can I help it if the sounds please me? The spirit corrodes in such a place as this, and once corroded, it is divisible. Thus an SS guard will lovingly stroke his child's hair with one hand, while with the other, he scalps a Jew for a lampshade. It is possible.

Dear God, if that is so, let me not be made of Man.

To punish myself I look hard at the girls as they are led to the gallows. God be thanked, the music sours on me.
Ada is first, her three lucky thirteens hidden by the rope that ties her hands. Then Sonia. Then four others. I wish I knew their names. All of them are crying. All of them are afraid.
Great-Grandpa Jakob would not have applauded them. There is no cause on earth worth dying for . . .
There are six guards on the platform, one for each noose.
They string them roughly around each girl's neck.
I think that's the extreme of injustice. They might be gentle, oh so gentle, at such a time. It's quickly over. The band goes on playing and so do the guards, swinging the bodies to match the *Meistersinger* rhythm.

I don't know why I don't cry.
I don't know how I can sleep.
But I do.
I thought of my children today, and I wondered who sired them.

I am sent to the crematoria today to fetch back the towels for washing.

I can't write any more.
Never forgive. Never.

There's a girl in the laundry. I think she's beautiful. She looks at me and I at her with a mutual remembrance of all those old longings that we can no longer translate with our hungry emaciated bodies. I want to hold her, to kiss her sunken cheek, to stroke her stubbled head. But kindness is cruelty in this place, for it is a reminder of our living past.

I saw Benjamin today. I notice that we cannot bear to look at each other. We see death in each other's eyes, and it is a reflection of our own. But we touch each other. All the time. I have never loved him so much. He told me they had a selection at the hospital. Everyone is ordered out of bed. They have to strip, then the guards make the selection. They keep the pretty women, but the others they send to the gas-chambers.

I still cannot shed one tear.

I laughed today. I cannot remember why.

There are two women guards here. Bormann and Grese. Whenever I see Bormann she's with two alsatians. There's a party of women coming back from the leather factory. One of them walks slowly. She cannot keep up with the rest. Bormann sets the dogs on her. They lay her low on the ground. Then Bormann orders the dogs to the woman's throat. 'Good dogs, good dogs,' she says when they are finished. She actually nuzzles their noses with her lips. I walk away quickly. If you are to survive, you must not look at such things. I pass the spot later on, and the woman, or the pieces of her, still lie there.

I still cannot cry.

I have to start thinking of my children and my wife. Sometimes I cannot recall their names, and all their faces are a blur. Benjamin has children too, I think, though he never talks about them. I think of Papa all the time. I can remember *his* face very clearly. I think of the little jokes he played on us when we were children. That must have been why I laughed the other day.

Benjamin looks worse every time I see him. He told me about the sterilisation. He has to pretend to give women internal examinations. While he's doing it, he has to inject a chemical irritant into the uterus. Dr Mengele looks over his shoulder. They have women there with beards, he says, from Mengele's experiments. I'm glad I didn't study medicine. Poor Benjamin. We touch each other again.

Lately I dream a lot of Papa, Mama, Uncle Aaron.
All dead.

In the morning when I awake, the air in the barracks is foul, polluted by all our death-dreams.

Why don't we do something? Why do we let this happen? There are so many of us. But we are weak and hungry. Our hunger is greater than our rage. They are starving our vengeance. They are fasting our fury. For a meal, a bath, a change of clothing, many of us would, for a moment, forgive.

It is better we should starve.

Today a man tries to escape. He runs to the fence by the crematoria. He doesn't have the strength to climb the first few feet of wire. He *knows* he doesn't have the strength. He knew it when he started to run. He knew it even when the thought of running occurred to him. But he had to do *something*.

He had to make a gesture. He is a survivor who finds offensive his talent for endurance.

The guards look at him and laugh. His un-fused, un-earthed body, galvanised with current, burns spread-eagled across the wire.

I still cannot cry.

Today I see Benjamin again. He says, 'Don't worry about me,' and I say the same to him. It is our way of declaring our love for each other.

Today in the munitions factory, the supervisor tells me I am a good worker. I will be promoted. Tomorrow I begin work as a Sonderkommando, a special attendant, to work in the gas-chambers.

Promotion.

Last night I didn't sleep at all. It pleases me, for I think my rage returns.

In the crematoria today, I learn how Papa and Heidi died.

Never forgive.
Never.

When I was a child, we had to write an essay on what our fathers did for a living. My marks were the highest in the class. The teacher said it was because I went into great detail about everything. Detail. Cling to detail. Embrace particularity. It is an escape-route from what is real. For if I itemise everything I do in this job, I can shield myself from the horror of its totality.

Itemise. Itemise without adornment. It is the only way to survive.

This morning outside the barracks, the pigeon isn't there.

My place of work. Birkenau. Part of Auschwitz.
Five crematoria.
Four gas-chambers.
Each chamber holds fifteen hundred people.
Multiply.
Six thousand souls migrate in one firing.
Three firings a day.
Genocide.
The dressing-rooms. Signs on walls in German, French, Dutch and Danish.
Tie your shoes together.
Fold clothes neatly in a pile.
Authorities cannot be held responsible for loss.
One cake of soap per person.
One towel.
Hot coffee will be served after the showers.
Our generous captors.
Direct access from dressing-rooms to 'baths'.
The bath.
Sprays all over the ceiling in parallel rows. Blessed clean hot water. Try not to look at the floor of the chamber.
There are no drains.
Heavy doors both sides of the 'bath-house.'
Lock and bolt.
Hydrocyanic gas to be released through shower-heads.
Estimated duration of dying. Three to five minutes, depending on the gas supply.
Causes of death. Rupture of the lungs. Shattered expectations.
Despair.
Deaths out of season.
Unripeness is all.

So now I know how Papa and Heidi died.

Today I think of my children. I recall their names. For the first time since I have been in this place, I cry. I do not sleep and I am able to shed tears. Second by second my rage is fed.
I am alive once more.

But what can I do with all my rage?

My job. My promotion. I am part of the squad that services the gas-chambers.

Survive, so turn your ears from the screams and the whimpers behind the bolted doors. Wait patiently until the doors are opened.

Scan the bodies for any sign of life.

Watch it clubbed into peace.

Drag the bodies out.

Cut off the hair.

Place in neat bundles, according to colour.

Examine all fingers for rings.

Remove them. Lead us not into temptation. Collect them in bags.

Wait for dentists to extract teeth.

Gold-prospectors.

Stack bodies neatly in piles of ten each.

Shove each pile into furnace.

Time and motion study.

My job.

My pror tion.

At night I lie awake. I think of all the millions of people in the history of mankind, who have died by others' hands. Every day, I witness mass-murder. Thousands of us go to our unripe deaths every day. Probably by the time they've finished with us, millions.

But why is this holocaust more offensive, more foul, more malignant, more grievous than anything that has happened in history before?

It is not a question of numbers.

Millions of black people have been slaughtered in their history.

Millions of aborigines.

Who can count the Armenians?

Who dare count the American Indians?

No. Not numbers.

This genocide is different from all others. It is different because of its sublime and obscene efficiency. Mass murder when not a minute is lost. Mass burial where nothing is wasted.

Human skin for reading-lamps.

Human flesh for soap.

Human hair for pillows.

Man's teeth for investment.

No waste.

It is a system meticulous in every detail, long pre-meditated, planned and co-ordinated, administered with the most sophisticated and satanic technology.

360

It is an artistry of murder, that achieves a certain beauty in its symmetry.
That is the core of its obscenity. That is why it is different.
In the whole history of murdering man, among all its victimised peoples, there has never been a more accomplished, a more ingenious, a more cunning or more terrible cavalcade of cruelty.

Dear God: Let no one ever forget that. Ever. Ever. Ever.

Yet how will we be remembered?
Those who survive will write about us. Even those who were never here will write about us too.
Some will say that silence is the only way to report this tragedy, and those who promote silence will be the most vociferous of all. In time, when the facts are exhausted, and repeated to the point of boredom and non-belief, we will become fiction. We will graduate to the stuff of metaphor and symbolism. Our story will be polluted by literature. Sooner or later, we will be reduced to a rhyming couplet, or at best, a nursery rhyme, sung down the generations by innocent children long after its provenance is forgotten.
Finally we will become a myth. We have to. For in order to survive himself, man can find no other weapon but mythology, to confront the flesh and the blood of our tragedy.

A new supply of gas arrives today. It is delivered in a red-cross ambulance. Once again I laugh a little.

Another transport today. Those sent to the left at the railway terminal, line up outside the dressing-rooms.
All unripe.

If the Allies bombed those railway-lines, and all along the rails that lead to Buchenwald, Bergen-Belsen, Maidenek, Ravensbruck, Treblinka, Flossenburg, Mauthausen, Lublin, Saschenhausen, Orianenburg, Theresienstadt, Sobibor, all those sad miles of steel cortège, there could be no transports.
So simple.

Tomorrow there is to be another selection within the camp.
The hospital is almost empty now.
They won't be needing Benjamin any more.

Today the sun shines in this place. Unashamedly in this Place and a Name. I feel it on my back as I watch the selection assemble. All in tidy lines. Obedient. The meek that inherit the gas-chamber.

My heart turns over when I see Benjamin in the line.

I stare at him, but he does not look at me, although he knows I am at my usual stand. He does not look at me because he cannot bear my bereavement.

Great-Grandpa Jakob's legacy.

There is no cause on earth worth dying for. No principle worth one's martyrdom. No God worth one's sacrifice.

Only in the name of love is death worthy.

I shall not stay here. I shall not stay to sift my brother's gentle body from the carnage. I shall not shave his frail and beautiful head. I shall not tidy his bones.

I go to where he stands and I take his hand.

I wonder where God is. *If* God is. I think of all those millions of people across the earth who kneel, lie or simply stand at the invisible feet of some or other deity.

A universal deception.

A consummate swindle.

A Machiavellian fraud.

Now I know what to do with all my rage, with all my burning wrath. I hate God with it, with every shred of it, and that anger will see me through the chamber and annihilate my fear.

Shema Yisroel . . .

I squeeze Benjamin's hand as he moves towards the furnace. I know that somewhere in this inferno, there is a minstrel, although I cannot hear his stubborn survival song. Perhaps it is because I myself am singing it, crooning my quietus like a swan. I pray God that there are ears to listen. Somewhere, somebody will hear. Great-Grandpa Jakob promised us.

We move into the dressing-rooms and leave our clothes in tidy piles.

We do not bother with the soap and towel, Benjamin and I. We are old hands in the business of deception.

We say the 'Shema' together as we go into the showers.

I see my children again, and by the triumph in his eye, so does Benjamin.

Safe. Alive. The Bindels survive.

I feel a slow sickness.

Benjamin falters and turns towards me.

We embrace each other. Meeting of bone on bone.
We love each other in this moment as neither of us have ever
loved before.
The soles of my feet tremble.
Benjamin's hand loosens in mine.

Shema Yisroel Adonai Elohainu . . .

*

*So ends the unwritten and fragmented diary of one David Bindel, prisoner in
Auschwitz 1944, Registration tattoo, 796702, Classification Yellow Star,
Jew, Inferior Race. Fourth of the traceable generations of Bindels, from the
Ukraine to Bessarabia, from England to Germany, one of the millions who
died in those camps, and one of six million of his own kind.*

Never forget. Never.

CHAPTER TWENTY-FIVE

It was May 1945, and the war was over. The conquerors moved in
on their quarry and divided the spoils. Much of East Germany fell
to Russian occupation, and in amongst all the lootable terrain, lay
Leipzig, city of furs and fairs. Despite the war-weary misery of its
citizens, the conquered came out onto the rabble-strewn streets and
cheered the victorious Russian troops with the same welcome as
they had afforded their German predecessors. Those who for years
had hidden in lofts, attics and underground, now emerged from
their hiding-places, and viewed what was left of their city. Amongst
them, two small children, brothers, aged ten and eleven years old,
who had grown to answer to the names of Heinrich and Hermann,
but who henceforth would be freely known as Aaron and Jakob
Bindel.

It was almost two years since the brothers had seen daylight.
Their concealment under Hans' and Inge's direction, had been
complete. Every night after dark, Hans would take them into the
field behind their house in the country and instruct them to run
twice around the perimeter, before going back into hiding. Even in
the summer, when the light lingered, Hans had insisted on that
routine, and it was often close to midnight before the brothers could

go to bed. They slept in the attic of the house, which could be reached only by ladder, which, when not in use, was hidden under the stairs. The trap-door to the roof was camouflaged with a false ornamental light-fitting which Inge or Hans removed for their constant access. For the brothers spent almost all their time in the loft, which Hans had furnished with a sense of adventure as if he himself were still a boy. It was in the attic that they ate their meals, and where Inge tutored them in daily classes of reading, mathematics, history and French. In the beginning it had all been a game for the brothers, aided and abetted by the Dreiser family, a game of continual concealment, that seemed to have become a way of life. Until one day, they began to question it, and have niggling doubts about their parents' safety. Where exactly had they gone? What were they doing? Why didn't they write? For a few weeks the Dreisers avoided their questions. The game continued and the brothers ceased to enquire. Then one evening when Hans went to collect them for their field exercise, he found them both crying on their beds. They didn't want to play the hiding-game any more, they told him. They wanted their father and their mother.

Hans called Inge to the attic and together they told them once again the story of their family's deportation, the reasons for it, and the hope that those reasons would soon cease to be. They had gone to a camp, Hans told them, many miles away, and they were not allowed to write.

'Why not?' Aaron said.

'Hitler doesn't like Jews,' Inge told them. 'He doesn't want to give them any pleasure. Like writing letters for instance.'

It was the truth that they told the children, the truth that they knew, and within that limitation, the Bindel family were still alive, though far away, and there was every likelihood of a family re-union. Hans said it with fervour, for he dared not think of any alternative.

But Inge was less optimistic and she tried to school the children for bereavement. 'We hear it's a hard life in the camp where they have settled,' she said. But she couldn't continue. She had already given them stuff for nightmare.

For the children, the game was over. All that was left was its fearful and monotonous routine. The brothers cried piteously that night. Inge took a camp-bed into the attic, and for the next few nights she slept at their side, to allay their fears and terrible dreams. For a while they began to hate their foster-parents, as if they had abducted them from their reluctant family. They would not answer to those names they had been dubbed with. Hermann and Heinrich did not belong to that place where their parents had gone. They shouted 'Aaron' and 'Jakob' in their hide-out, so that it reverberated through the house like a fire-alarm. This phase of their desolate rebellion lasted only a few days, and it was almost a year before they enquired of their parents once more. By that time, rumours from the camps, which for so long had been hear-say, began to be confirmed. Camp guards came home on leave, and one of them lived in Leipzig. His brother was a laboratory technician, one of Hans' employees in the Halle plant. He was more than willing to relay his brother's stories, and though Hans was reluctant to hear, he encouraged him in his telling. His brother worked in a camp called Auschwitz, he said, one of the so-called eastern settlements near Cracow. Full of Jews, the technician said. Mainly from Poland, but there was a German contingent there too. 'He told me stories you wouldn't believe,' he said.

'I'll try,' Hans told him, his heart sinking.

The technician was delighted to find an audience, especially one in authority, and he regaled his employer with minute details of gas-chambers and mass-killings.

Hans turned away.

'It's terrible,' the man said, and for that at least, Hans was grateful.

By the end of that week, fed by the same source, everyone at the Halle plant was talking of the gas-chambers. All over Germany, camp-guards came home on leave. All had fathers, mothers, brothers or sisters, and all of those had friends. A nation-wide grapevine. Yet when the war was over, only a few Germans chose to know about the terror, and some to this day will deny that it ever occurred.

Hans did not tell Inge of what he had heard. But now, when he looked at the brothers, he saw them orphaned and he felt ashamed that he should be privy to information which was inalienably theirs. For many weeks he stifled that guilt in his heart, bursting with its need for release. Finally he told Inge. 'Let us wait,' she said. 'There's still hope. They cannot kill them all.' And although until that time, they had loved the Bindel brothers without stint, now they began to love them with a deeply protective passion, and the children sniffed at the change and they were afraid.

At about that time, early in the spring of 1944, old Mrs Dreiser, who had been ill for many months, died. It was an event that put the Dreiser family and the children at risk. Hans' friends lived in Leipzig, and though some of them were very intimate, none of them knew of the hidden children. Hans, and Inge too, had made a point of making no friends in Halle, for they didn't want callers. It had worked. No one ever came to the house, except the occasional tradesman. But a funeral could not pass unnoticed, without spectators or even a sympathetic caller. That day, the brothers were enjoined to absolute silence. They were sorry that old Mrs Dreiser had died, though they hardly knew her. They saw her only occasionally, and usually in the dark in the cellar of the house during an air-raid warning. She never climbed the ladder into the loft, and she was usually in her room when they sneaked into the field for their evening exercise. But they cried for her nonetheless. They were crying for Uncle Hans, whose mother had died. All day they sat in the loft, and not a whisper passed between them, and when night came, Inge brought them a supper of all their favourite foods, and Hans played with them till well into the night. Now with Uncle Hans as an orphan, there seemed to be a new bond between them, though they didn't know why, and thereafter they lost their fears in Hans' and Inge's frantic embrace. They knew that things had changed, that it was a new kind of loving, that loving that had nothing to do with kin, and it was that loving that would score their future.

During the whole course of their concealment, Mrs Dreiser's funeral was the only day of risk. Thereafter the house was silent once more.

Occasionally Hans would go to Leipzig. Each time he would call at the Bindel family home. He would linger in the large house and remember the happy times he had spent there. He wandered round the garden. Since the Bindels had left he had employed an old man to keep the flowers and the lawns in season. He had never not anticipated the Bindel's return. Even now against all the evidence, he dared to believe that the Bindels would come home and find everything in its place and season. And so he continued to believe, until one day, on one of his rare visits to Leipzig, he went to the house and found a number of government cars parked in the driveway. He hid behind an oleander bush, trembling, and had to accept that the house had been commandeered. It shocked him, but surprised him less, for most of the houses and apartments, especially the grand ones that had belonged to Jews, had long since been taken over by Party officials. This requisition depressed him profoundly for it seemed to confirm that Leon, Benjamin, Heidi and David Bindel were no more. He went home but he did not tell Inge what he had found.

The tide of war was beginning to turn. In June of that year the Allies invaded Normandy. It marked the beginning of the final collapse of the Third Reich. Hans and Inge listened to each news bulletin with growing and illegal excitement. After each broadcast, they were tempted to convey the good news to the brothers in the attic, that the war would soon be over and that they could come out of hiding at last. But how good would they find such news? Once out of hiding, to what should they return? Only to the undeniable proof of their family's murder. So they said nothing to the boys, afraid of what questions might ensue.

Conditions for the German people were worsening. There was a great shortage of food, and Inge had more and more difficulty in stretching their meagre rations. They had only two legal food allowances, and often they went hungry in order to feed the children.

At the end of April there were rumours that Hitler was dead. That he had suicided in his bunker. For many days the rumours were hotly denied, and there was a total black-out on news bulletins. The black-out was the rumour's final confirmation, and when a week later, Germany surrendered to the Allies, it could no longer be concealed.

On the 9th of May 1945, Aaron and Jakob Bindel came out of their hiding-place and asked to go home.

'In time, in time,' Hans parried.

He went to Leipzig and found the Bindel home deserted. He let himself inside and in every room he found evidence of a quick getaway. The house seemed to be shivering with the after-effects of burglary, with the shame of intrusion and assault. Yet little had changed. The antique furnishings were still in immaculate condition, but the garden had run to seed. Hans was glad of it, for they had left one part of the Bindel estate untouched, uncontaminated, and he walked in the long grass, and touched the profusion of unpruned roses, prematurely over-ripe. The apple tree was in stubborn blossom again, despite the fact that, in its shade on the lawn, there still lay traces of its last season's fruit. He wondered whether he should re-settle in Leipzig and bring the children back to the family home. In many ways it would represent a security for them, but in other ways it would remain a house of mourning. He would make no immediate decision, he decided. He would wait, and somehow or other, weather the brothers' impatience to return.

But the next time he went to Leipzig and visited the house, he found it requisitioned once more, this time by officials of the Russian occupation administration. Once again he hid in the oleander bush and watched their cool appropriation, and he wondered whether life under the Russians would be any different from the old and terrible regime.

Every week he went to the Leipzig Town Hall to make enquiries in the missing persons department. They told him that the Bindel family would take time to trace. The concentration camp records, such as could be found, had not yet been collated. Months later it was the offices of the International Red Cross that gave Hans the final confirmation of the Bindel deaths. It was recorded that some time in November 1942, Leon Bindel and Heidi Bindel had been gassed at Auschwitz, and that in January, 1944, David and Benjamin Bindel had suffered the same fate. The official showed Hans the names on the list. They told him nothing he hadn't already known in his heart, and now he could no longer delay telling the children.

That night he returned to Halle scheming to himself how he would break the news. There was no way he could cushion it, except to omit the details of their gruesome deaths. That they would learn in their own time.

'When are we going home, Uncle Hans?' Jakob said at supper. It was his daily question. He had almost begun to ask it for form's sake, and always it was a source of irritation to his elder brother, who knew that there was no such thing as home any more and never would be, for the armature of their family unit was broken.

Hans didn't need any cue to break the news. 'The house doesn't belong to you any more,' he said. 'The Russians have taken it over.'

The brothers paled.

'That's not fair,' Jakob shouted. 'It's ours.'

But Aaron had understood the implications of the take-over, even as Hans had understood them when the Germans had first requisitioned.

'Mummy and Daddy are dead,' Aaron said in a loud and clear voice. 'And Uncle David and Grandpa too.' He did not look to Hans or Inge for confirmation, but Jakob refused to believe one word of it. He raised his little clenched fists and punched his brother about the head.

'It's not true,' he shouted, the tears running down his face. 'It's terrible to say things like that. I'll tell Mummy and Daddy on you. I will,' he screamed. 'You wait till they come back. I'll tell.'

Inge took him in her arms, nursing his sobs. No one had denied what Aaron had said, and now Jakob knew better than to ask questions. They were dead. He knew it. He would never see them again. He tried to remember what they looked like, but he could only see the backs of them as they had turned back into the house when they had driven away in Uncle Hans' car. He wished they would turn round so that he could see their faces. But his mother and his father had turned their backs on him, and for a moment he enjoyed the relief of hating them. But it was short-lived. He went over to Inge and buried his face in her lap. In future, Aunt Inge and Uncle Hans would have to do.

*

And so the Dreisers stayed in Halle, and day by day they felt the harsh impact of the Russian occupation. They were issued with new food cards which entitled them to less than they had had before, but at least now they had one card for each person. There were daily round-ups of Nazi leaders and those known to have had Nazi sympathies. People disappeared and were never heard of again. The Russians lost no time in implementing their ideologies. Farms were seized and collectivised. There was no freedom of speech or information. The one-party system controlled everything, the law, education and the press, and, when the German citizens chose to think about it, the Russian system of government was little different from the Fascist regime they had known. Only for the Jews was it better. Except that there were no Jews left in Germany. Those very few who had managed to hide out the hostilities, left that hated land as soon as possible after the armistice was signed. But they were fortunate enough to live in the Western zone. Those handful of Jews left in the East were now trapped yet again.

This ban on emigration, which affected all German citizens in the eastern zone, played a great part in the discussions that Inge and Hans had about the brothers' future. Amongst the Bindel papers, Hans found Sarah's address in Palestine together with the addresses of other Bindel relatives in America, and he wrote to both, informing them of the fate of the Bindel family. He expressed his desire to continue his role as the brothers' guardian until such time as the children could make their own choice as to the location of their future provided that emigration would be possible at that time. Soon both Chaya and Sarah replied, each of them offering homes for the children whenever travel would be permitted. Both agreed to Hans' continual guardianship with overwhelming gratitude, and praise for his courage and show of friendship.

As for the children, they never mentioned their relatives. They seemed happy enough to accept their new family as permanent. They had settled in their new school, and had begun to make friends. The daylight still astonished them, as did the publication of their names, their fourth changeover in their young lives. 'Aaron and Jakob are for keeps,' Hans told them on their first day of school. 'You will never change them again. And Bindels you will be always.'

Their favourite lesson was Russian, a subject newly introduced into the school curriculum. Both brothers excelled in it, as if their old Odessa genes, long dormant, had begun to stir. Their French, thanks to Inge's tutoring, was far above the average standard of the class, as was their history. Hans looked at their school reports with pride and wonder.

'You are a credit to all the Bindels,' he said.

Life in East Germany was hard in those years. There was a desperate shortage of food, and potatoes, which had been a staple diet of most Germans, were suddenly a luxury. The Russians seized the crops for the distillation of vodka. The soldiers of the occupying army, and their families, lived like kings. Members of the German Communist Party were also favoured, and many joined their ranks for the supplementary food allowances that went with the card. But Hans made no move to affiliate. Though his father had died in that cause, he had lost his appetite for politics. The children and his work occupied all his time and his energies.

The Siebel Aircraft Corporation, where he worked, had always been under heavy guard and supervision. But nowadays it was like a fortress and he had to show his identity at least a half a dozen times before he could gain entry to his quarters. The place was swarming with Russian technicians. Hans was asked many questions about his work and, from their enquiries, he was able to deduce that, in his own special field of radar technology, they were far behind. This fact gave him some small pleasure, though he was careful not to show it.

One day, on one of his visits to Leipzig, a friend told him that the equipment of five large printing works in the city had been dismantled and sent to the Soviet Union. Some of the most specialising technicians had been more or less shanghaied into going too. Hans returned to Halle that night and he began to have fears for his own future. Fears that were confirmed for, during that winter of '46, it was known that hundreds of scientists and technical workers were deported to the Soviet Union from East Germany. And from the West, too, in a nocturnal wave of kidnapping. There were protests, representations from the West, deploring the Russian manoeuvre. So to counteract those protests, the Russians decided to found an organisation which was legal within the area of their own administration. Its name was Operation Ossavakim and it legalised the deportation of men and the shipment of machinery to their own country for full exploitation.

In the winter of 1947, the Russians re-opened the trade fair at Leipzig. Many visitors came from all over Eastern Europe, and factory visits were organised for those visitors with specialised interest. The Siebel Aircraft Association in Halle was the focus of many tourists' attention. Once again Hans was obliged to explain his work, and was pleased once more to note how backward they were in his line of research. But now this fact frightened him. The logical outcome of such an unbalanced situation was unthinkable. Yet he had to think about it. Scientists in his own line of work had been spirited away without warning or further trace. At least, since the founding of Ossavakim, notice was given and families were permitted to accompany their menfolk. Even so, the prospect of Eastern settlement in no way excited Hans and Inge Dreiser, but there was nothing they could do to change it.

So it came as no surprise when, about a month after the Fair had closed, the removal men moved into the Siebel plant. At the same time, 400 specialists who worked in the factory were given notices of deportations. Amongst the names was Hans Dreiser. Their families would be allowed to accompany them, the notices read. Their children would receive the best education, and each family would be provided with living-quarters. A whole train compartment would be allotted to each unit to take their furniture and effects. The train would leave in two weeks from the East Berlin station of Friedrichsfelde. Removal expenses would be paid by the Soviet Military Administration.

The Dreisers prepared for their departure. The brothers were excited at the prospect of a new country, especially one that had belonged to their forefathers. They were too young for that old Bindel-scruple of bone-desertion. Besides, apart from their grandmother, the bones of those they loved were untraceable, of no marked grave or honoured resting-place. Somewhere in the 'eastern settlements' their ashes had hovered on the wind for a while, without urn for memorial.

'What names will we use in Russia?' Jakob asked.

In Hans' ears it was an earth-shattering question, but he was glad that the children could still be amused by their constantly-juggled nomenclature. Was there anywhere in the world, he wondered, where the names of Aaron and Jakob would be given safe or even welcome passage? In Palestine perhaps, Hans thought, though now that proposal was even more remote than it had been before. But they must not live a lie again.

'Aaron and Jakob,' he said decisively. 'And Bindel. That name will be for ever.'

Before they left for Berlin, Hans took the children to Leipzig to see their Grandma Greta's grave. During the war he had done his best to keep it in order. On every visit he had brought flowers, and built a pyramid of pebbles against the gravestone. Now Aaron and Jakob Bindel added to the pyramid, with extra stones for Grandpa Leon and their parents.

'Now we have buried them all,' Hans said and he took their hands and left the cemetery for the last time.

The removal van came to Halle for their furniture and effects, and the following day, the Dreisers and their adopted family took the train to East Berlin. Hans Dreiser was one of 8,000 men and their families who were forcibly deported to the Soviet Union under the aegis of the Ossavakim Operation.

Thus Aaron and Jakob Bindel, fifth of the traceable Bindel generations, from the Ukraine to Bessarabia, from Bessarabia to England, from England to Germany, returned to the land where the bones of their forefathers lay, and hoped that they might call it home.

PART FOUR

The Book of Aaron and Jakob

CHAPTER TWENTY-SIX

It must have been snowing.

It was winter when the Bindel brothers of the fifth generation arrived in the land of their forefathers. It was almost a hundred years since they had been buried there, the pieces of them from the tavern fire. Much had changed and much was still the same. Many changes had come about in the matter of names and labels. The country itself was now known as the Soviet Union. The name of the Czar had disappeared too, and had been replaced by President. There was no longer any anti-semitism in the country. That too had another name. In the fifth traceable generation of the brothers Bindel, it was called anti-Zionism. What remained the same, immutably unalterable, were the Bindel names. Aaron and Jakob. Perhaps after all their bids at survival, the names were change-weary. They fulfilled no other purpose at that time than that of labelling. They were no act of defiance, no call of pride in inheritance. For indeed, the Bindel brothers, now in their thirteenth and fourteenth years, had still not inherited, a fact that disturbed Hans and Inge Dreiser. Year by year, as the brothers grew firmly in their Russianhood, without a fraction of Jewish self disturbance, the nature of their inheritance grew more and more irrelevant. For there was little Jewish about Aaron and Jakob Bindel. Not for many years, since their enforced involvement in the Jewish school in Leipzig, had they heard a word of spoken Hebrew. Jewish schools were not permitted in the Soviet Union. Neither of them had been barmitzvahed, nor had they entered a synagogue for many years. But on each of their identity cards was the word '*Jew*', which proclaimed their inherited faith. When they viewed their bodies in the shower, their mark of difference was attributed to reasons of health, as their parents had been at such pains to demonstrate.

*

In 1948, Israel proclaimed its independence, and that event prompted illegal stirrings in the hearts of thousands of Russian Jews. At the same time, the M.V.D. as the Ministry of Internal

Affairs was called, arrested four hundred and thirty-one Jewish intellectuals, poets, writers, musicians, party officials and charged them with the crime of 'National Bourgeois Zionism'. They were put in chains and sent to concentration camps. When Hans Dreiser first read this news, he hid it from the children. He did not want to frighten them but, at the same time, he felt guilty of depriving them of news that was theirs by a kind of birthright. Once again he thought the time was ripe for their inheritance, and once again he postponed it. He was temporising like any true Bindel, who would delay to arm for survival, lest it tempt the onset of battle. Over the next few years he followed the story of the convicted men wherever he could, but little was written about the fate of the victims. There were rumours that the majority of them had perished in the camps. Rumours that turned out to be sadly true for when, four years later, the accused were secretly tried, only thirty or so were brought to the court- house, and all were found guilty and executed. Still Hans held his tongue. He thought very often in those days of his father, and in many ways he was glad that he had not lived to see the reality of the cause in which name he had died. He was sickened by the gross deception of his innocent father's life, and sometimes, for solace, he would share his disappointments with Inge. But outside the confines of their own privacy, he would never voice them. He went about his daily work at the aircraft factory where, over the years, much progress had been made in his field of research. He was satisfied with his work, and so was Inge who had gone back to her old profession, as an assistant almoner. Their Russian was halting and would never be fluent like that of their adopted children. At home they still spoke German so that Aaron and Jakob would not forget their parents' tongue. Hans took no part in politics which seemed to be part and parcel of the social life of his friends. So the Dreisers led a comparatively isolated life centred about their work and their children.

*

It was 1953, and in that year occurred one of the most sinister events of Stalin's reign of terror. It was known as the Doctors' Plot and, unlike the earlier arrest of Jewish intellectuals, which was secret and clandestine, it was given the widest coverage in the press. A group of physicians, most of them Jews, were arrested on a charge of plotting to kill Soviet leaders. The newpaper *Pravda* claimed that the doctors were connected with an international bourgeois Jewish organisation, established by American Intelligence, with the aim of subversion. As it turned out, some years later, the 'Doctors' Plot' was an anti-semitic fabrication, engineered by the M.V.D. but, at the time, it rang with the most demonic and almost medieval overtones. Widely publicised, it was the current topic of conversation in factories, schools and at party-meetings. Jakob Bindel, who at that time was in his last year at school, listened in to the vicious spread of anti-semitic utterance and some irritant of a Bindel gene suggested that he himself was the target of such abuse.

Often the brothers would quarrel between themselves on the subject of their unpractised yet natural faith and their talk would ring with bitter echoes of the old Leipzig dialogue between Benjamin and David.

'Why must we be so exclusive?' Aaron would argue. 'And think we're so different from everybody else?'

'But *they* think we're different,' Jakob said, 'and nothing's going to change that. Jewishness is in the eye of the beholder. Maybe we *are* different,' he whispered and he would turn away.

Often they would bring the argument to the family table, and Hans and Inge were unsure how to council them.

At about that time a letter arrived from their Aunt Sarah in Israel announcing that she would be coming on a visit to Moscow. It was thirteen years since the brothers had seen their aunt. She had corresponded with them regularly, but for them she was part of a life that they rarely recalled, for it was the life of their parents and the memory of it was painful. Yet they were excited at the prospect of her visit. Especially Jakob who was curious about her port of embarkation. He wanted to learn about Israel, to know it and to love it, so that there could be some rationale for his groundless but insistent sense of Jewishness.

A week before Aunt Sarah's arrival, Stalin died, and Aaron, along with his school fellows, went into public and official mourning. But secretly Jakob rejoiced, as the milk-brothers had done almost a hundred years ago on the wild Siberian wastes, when the forbidden news had filtered through of Czar Nicholas the First's demise.

'Do not hope for too much,' Hans told Jakob, taking him on one side. 'There is no shortage of Stalins. Tyrants grow on many trees, whether they are called Czar, Chancellor, or President. In school you must feign sorrow, and mourn like the others. Stalin was their God, and they will punish you for any lack of respect.'

So Jakob took his bereaved face to school and it melded easily with the looks of sorrow and loss of the other students, but when he looked at Aaron, he pitied him for the sincerity of his mourning.

The whole family went to the airport to welcome Aunt Sarah.

'I've forgotten what she looked like,' Aaron said, as they scanned the curious and bewildered faces of those who had come to a land that half the world labelled Utopia. Through the glass partition that separated the customs area from the airport foyer, they looked for a woman who would be their mother's age, had she lived, each brother using this criterion independently of the other, for, in both their childhood memories, Aunt Sarah had shared their Leipzig home, had sat at table, her place next to their own mother, facing Grandpa Leon and their father at the end of the table. Aunt Sarah was the sole survivor. And in the heart of each brother was a rustling of resentment.

'There she is,' Hans shouted. Hans was in Aunt Sarah's age-group and as such had less problems with recognition for, in monitoring his own passage of time, he had taken into account that of his contemporaries. Sarah had worn well, he thought. Though her face was lined, and she was heavier than he remembered, her look was one of a young girl, with that dynamic curiosity that belongs to the faces of children.

She caught his eye and waved, and then she saw the brothers alongside him, and her face was seen to suddenly grieve as she held them for a moment in her gaze, seeing in their faces the undeniable Bindel image that her own children had not inherited. She stared at them. Aaron, though older than Jakob was the shorter of the two, and took after his father Benjamin. He had the same rigid air and, when he smiled at her, she sensed it as a production of his features. Whereas Jakob's smile was swift and wondrous. He has a slight Benjamin look too, she thought, and probably from his father's later years, when, having learned his lesson, the stubbornness was replaced by sheer bewilderment. In both their faces lay their father's history. True Bindels they were, and in their amalgam, she saw David Bindel, exactly as she had seen him for the last time, when he had stood on the platform at Vienna railway-station, holding those two boys for his comfort.

She rushed through the barrier, longing to embrace them, to catch perhaps from their image some tremor of the happiness of her past. Wordlessly she approached them and held them close, looking into their faces, hoping that the David she found in their features would be in their hearts too.

Sarah turned to introduce her nephews to one of her travelling companions and, out of the distant past, from the back row of an enforced Jewish classroom in Leipzig, the brothers heard the echoes of a strange tongue, of a language they had thought dead and which now, with an aggressive vibrancy, rang throughout the airport reception. 'D'you remember that Jewish school?' Aaron said to Jakob smiling. 'They actually speak it,' Jakob said, marvelling at the sounds.

They shook hands with their Aunt Sarah's travelling companion who greeted them in German. She too had come from Leipzig, she

378

told them, and she remembered their father very well, for he had delivered both her children. This reminder of their father from a total stranger, and in their mother-tongue, shipped them back into their childhood and the remembrance of how quickly it had soured. They knew that Aunt Sarah's visit would prompt those memories in abundance and it disturbed them, for they knew too the price of their recall.

For in truth the Bindel brothers of the fifth generation had been deeply damaged by their orphanhood. The deaths of their parents had been unnatural enough. But, in the eyes of the world, or of those who cared to look, they were but two of six million, and this continual promotion detracted from the particularity of their loss. Tragic and obscene as that number was, it was a national cause for mourning and sorrow by those uninvolved and undisturbed by its catastrophe. For Aaron and Jakob Bindel the holocaust was the definition of the deaths of three special people, their parents and Grandpa Leon, and they did not care to have them shrouded with six million others, for it somehow diminished their special sacrifice. Moreover, there had been the sudden change of guardianship, loving and familiar though it was, yet granted by neither law nor blood. That had required re-adjustment enough. But in addition there had been those two long years spent in darkness, and in those shadows, for survival's sake, and in the names of Hermann and Heinrich, they had buried their Judaism. And though the brothers had survived, through the Dreisers' care and cunning, those remnants had remained in the German darkness, unwanted on voyage. Yet their shadows still haunted the brothers, especially Jakob, who, when he recalled them, felt a sense of terrible betrayal. Now Aunt Sarah had come to invoke those spirits they had left behind, to nudge them without reprimand, into the open, to shift them under their noses, to stir their scent for their accommodation. Aaron saw her visit as a threat to his security, but Jakob felt no threat, for he felt no security that could be shaken. Hans and Inge had long anticipated this disturbance in the brothers' lives.

'Are we far from Odessa?' was Sarah's first question.

'About 600 miles,' Hans said. He smiled at her. She would lose no time in leading the brothers into their pasts, on a journey of such terrible and rich confusion, that it could well cause a small earthquake in their souls.

'I want to go there,' she was saying, 'I want to see where the Bindels began. David used to say that one day we would go back with Grandpa Leon. A pilgrimage, he said.' She looked at Hans, smiling. 'It's one of the reasons I came.'

It was at that moment that Hans decided that, during the course of Sarah's visit, the Bindel brothers of the fifth generation would claim their inheritance. He would not wait for a crisis or catastrophe in their lives that would prompt their bequest. He would give it to them in Sarah's presence, which would donate to their history some authenticity.

And as it turned out, the opportunity for so doing presented itself that very evening. They had finished the festive welcoming supper that Inge had prepared. 'I have photographs,' Sarah announced, and she went to her case and brought out the family album. Inge gathered together her own assortment.

Aunt Sarah started with a display of her children which stretched from their Leipzig infancy to their Israel adulthood. Esther and Zelda, now both almost twenty. They both resembled Sarah, and Aaron and Jakob were keen to know of them, of their likes, their dislikes, and whether they would ever come to Russia.

'Perhaps you should go and see them in Israel,' Sarah said, though she did not pursue the idea as if she were keeping that in store as a suggestion for their future.

'What's it like in Israel,' Jakob asked.

'I'll tell you about it later,' Sarah said, turning the pages of the album. She did not want to dwell in the present. It was the past she sought and all the links of which her David was a part. 'These are my wedding-photographs,' she said, stretching the double-paged spread of the album.

Now is the time, Hans thought. He remembered David's wedding with meticulous recall. It was the day that Benjamin and David had perforce inherited. He remembered his own part in the battle when he had gone out into the streets and faced the hooligans alone. He wasn't afraid at the time, but afterwards he had wondered why none of the other guests had come outside to support him. When he'd returned to the reception he was in time to see a white-faced Leon manhandling his two grown sons up the staircase. Then and there, in their full-grown years, and one of them already a groom, their father would teach them the lesson of their history. Hans recalled it now with a smile, and he hoped that Sarah would tell his Bindel boys the story of the wedding and ease them into their shared past.

'It was an unforgettable day,' she was saying. 'You remember it, Hans?' she asked. 'Look, here's a picture of you. You're not there, Inge.'

'We hadn't yet met,' Hans said. 'But she knows the story. You tell it, Sarah. Tell it to Aaron and Jakob.'

'The reception was in Grandpa Leon's house,' Sarah began, and from the collection of photographs she pointed out and named the guests, and, as a codicil to almost every name, she added, 'Auschwitz.'

'What's the story?' Aaron said impatiently. He wanted no reference to that burial-ground.

'That's all part of the story,' Sarah said, and the tone of her voice was inflexible. 'Auschwitz is only a name. A place and a name. But such places have mary names. Babi-Yar, the Katyn forest, Lidice.'

Aaron and Jakob did not quite follow her, and they were unnerved by the zealous look in her eye.

'You want to know the story of my wedding,' she went on, 'but first I must tell you a little of the history of the time.'

She spoke like any true Bindel.

It was late into the night when she neared the end. 'Now it's your turn to inherit,' she said, and slowly she recited the Patriarch's litany.

Hans and Inge listened and with a sense of peace, as they were slowly relieved of the burden of the Bindel bequest. Now they would put away Benjamin's letter, that Last Will and Testament that he had pressed into Hans' hand as he bade farewell to his children. Now those brothers, too, had inherited.

'It's time for bed,' Inge said at last.

No more words were spoken then, and neither brother slept that night. The secrets that had seemingly been left behind in the attic in the Dreiser house in Halle, had now been given release and public domain. Aaron, for his part, would have been happy for them to remain secrets for ever, but Jakob was elated by what he saw as a sudden enrichment of his life, and by all its strange disturbances.

In the morning they were both too tired to go to school, and Hans, who had always been very strict in that department, that day relented. He said that they could stay at home in honour of their Aunt Sarah's arrival, but in truth he hoped that they would spend it in bed and, through sleep, gather the strength to accommodate the uneasy changes that Sarah's story had wrought.

The brothers did not rise until late afternoon and the house was empty. Inge had taken Sarah sight-seeing. Aaron started on his homework, but Jakob was unable to concentrate. He wandered about the house and stole into Sarah's room. His aunt intrigued him. Though she was not of their blood, she was more at home in Bindeldom than he. It was that home he wished to enter, whose history he wished to probe, and of which finally to become a part. Aunt Sarah could help bridge those gaps between his orphanhood and his present state of alienation. She would tell him about his parents, and revive in his memory Grandpa Leon's stories.

The photograph album lay on the table. He leafed through its pages. Apart from those of Sarah's and David's wedding, many of the photographs were duplicates of those that Hans and Inge had collected from the Bindel home in Leipzig. But there was one that he had never seen before. It was a photograph that had been taken in a photographer's studio many years ago. Its colour was sepia and its edges were frayed. There was no clue in writing as to the identity of the subject of the portrait and this omission, as opposed to all the meticulous labelling of the other photographs, added to its mystery. The picture was that of a young boy, perhaps thirteen or so, Jakob thought. He wore a loose brown boiler-suit of sorts and on his head was a tin helmet. In his hand, he carried a small lamp and it seemed to Jakob that the boy was an actor playing his first role, that the photographer had recorded for posterity. Jakob looked closely at the boy's face, and in his features he saw distinct traces of the Bindel image. Alone, at the back of the album, with a page all to himself, the portrait had an air of a secret mystery.

*

That evening Aunt Sarah told them about her life in Israel. Aaron excused himself, pleading fatigue, but Hans and Inge knew that Israel was a subject Aaron dared not risk. It was part of that Jewish exclusiveness that so disturbed him. He did not want it rationalised. He needed it as part of his defences against Jakob's eternal pessimism.

'Tell us from the beginning,' Jakob said.

Sarah started her story at the railway station in Vienna. 'D'you remember that station, Jakob?' she asked.

He remembered it well, not so much for the scene of parting, but for the raging passion with which Uncle David had held him and his brother as the train had pulled out of the station. He hadn't understood it at the time. But from the carriage-window, Sarah had seen the embrace and though it was the beginning of her story, she knew then that it was also its end, and, on the long and weary ride to Naples, as her parents tried to comfort her, she slowly gathered about her the weeds of her widowhood, because she knew that she would never see David again.

'The boat was already overcrowded by the time it docked in Naples,' she said, 'and there were hundreds of us waiting to go on board. It took about three weeks to reach Israel, or Palestine as it was then called, and we stood on our feet most of the way. It was a silent journey. Most of us were too ill to speak, or we were listening for sounds of approaching danger, a British patrol ship that might turn us back, or the cracking of the ship's bows under its heavy load. But no one complained. We'd been given a chance to survive, and for that we were grateful. I really don't remember too much about that journey,' she said, looking up at Hans and Inge. 'It's easier to forget about it. But I remember the landing,' she said. 'It was at night somewhere along the Haifa coastline. We'd been skirting the shore for days. It seemed the captain was waiting for a signal. And one night we saw lights flashing from the beach, and we knew that our journey would soon be over. Then it all happened very quickly. The boat beached on the sands, and I remember seeing pieces of wood splitting from the bows as we came to a stop. Nobody moved. Nobody believed that we had come to the end of our journey alive. Though some had died on the way. We saw young people wading into the sea then, reaching up their hands to greet us and help us out of the boat. It seemed hours before we reached the beach and the row of huts hidden behind the trees. They were singing and dancing, needing to celebrate our safe arrival, but all we wanted to do was to sleep. My father was not well and we asked for a doctor. They took him off in a truck to the hospital along with many others who were suffering from the journey. I remember seeing him lying in the back of the van and then we lay down on the grass and stretched our bodies for the first time since leaving Naples.'

As she spoke, Aunt Sarah stretched herself as if to relive that moment of her intense need. 'I shall never forget it,' she said. 'It was all any of us wanted to do. We lay there in our hundreds and nothing on earth could move us. It was light when we awoke, and they led us to the trucks and drove us through the countryside, but we were all too exhausted and too astonished by our survival to look at the scenery. They took us to a kibbutz on the shores of Lake Galilee.'

'A kibbutz?' Jakob asked.

'It's a communal settlement,' Sarah said. 'It was our first home and we stayed there for ten years.'

'What happened to your father?'

'He got better and joined us after a few days.'

'And now?' Hans asked.

'Now we all live in Jerusalem. We have a little shop. Newspapers, sweets, cigarettes. That sort of thing. We all live together. But my parents are retired now. I run the shop with an assistant. He's taking care of it now.'

'And the children?' Inge asked.

'They're both at University,' Sarah said. 'After that they have to go into the army. And then, who knows?'

She had come to the end of her story, yet it seemed to Jakob that she had told them nothing.

'What about Israel?' he said.

She smiled at him. 'It's too long a story,' she said. 'I'm tired. Tomorrow perhaps.'

They knew she refrained because Aaron was not there, but they knew too that, if the subject of Israel were raised, Aaron would continue to absent himself.

'When am I to go to Odessa?' Sarah said suddenly.

'Can I go with you?' Jakob asked.

'You have school,' Hans said.

'But next week is half-term,' Inge reminded him.

'I'll wait till then,' Sarah said. 'We'll go together. Will Aaron come too?'

'He usually goes camping at half-term,' Hans said. 'I don't think he'll give that up for Odessa.'

'Then I'll take Jakob,' Sarah said, and she was suddenly excited. On behalf of David, she would be exploring his past, and with a Bindel for company, the country of his past that he had never seen, those bones of his forefathers that for him were the stuff of fairy-tales. She would go to Odessa and prove that the past in which she dwelt had a past of its own. That proof of David's history would at last absolve her from grief.

*

Immediately on their arrival in Odessa the following week-end, Sarah urged Jakob to enquire the whereabouts of the Jewish cemetery. He was nervous. To evince any interest in Jewish life was to betray some hint of unpatriotic allegiance. Sarah noted his hesitation. 'Or let us ask for the synagogue,' she said. 'We can ask there.' Jakob shook his head. Such an enquiry would be a greater risk than that of the cemetery. A passer-by might forgive a request for the whereabouts of the Jewish dead, but he could not admit to his Russian consciousness the thought of living Judaism. Or any other religion for that matter. If he himself went to church, as did thousands of his compatriots, he did not advertise it or ask where it could be found. The State frowned on competition of any kind, either from man or from God.

'I'll ask for the cemetery,' Jakob said.

They walked a little, while he scanned the faces of the passers-by for one who might be Jewish, but he was not enough of a Jew himself to recognise others of his kind, and not sufficiently Christian to sniff them out for scapegoat.

A bearded gentleman was seen to walk in their direction.

'There's a Jew,' Sarah whispered.

'He could be Greek Orthodox,' Jakob said.

'Well at least he believes in God. Ask him.'

'Excuse me,' Jakob whispered as the man came alongside them. 'Do you know the whereabouts of the Jewish cemetery?'

The old man smiled. 'You are standing on it,' he said. 'The

384

whole of Odessa is a Jewish cemetery. On the 23rd of October, 1941, 19,000 Jews were massacred here by the Germans. My wife, my children amongst them. Who knows where they are buried?'

Jakob and Sarah had got more than they had bargained for, and more than they wanted perhaps, for the old man took Jakob's arm and told him that he would lead him to where the dead Jews officially lay, those whom God had taken in His own and natural time.

'Come,' he said.

Sarah followed them, nudging Jakob for explanation. He gave it to her in his childish German, regretting the loss of the old man's rage in his translation.

'Does your mother speak Yiddish?' the old man asked.

'She's not my mother,' Jakob said. 'My mother died in Auschwitz.' He surprised himself. He had never in his life confessed in such fashion to the nature of his orphanhood, but he gave it to the old man as a common denominator for their loss. They had both been robbed, though in reverse generations, by the same agent.

'I'm sorry,' the old man said. 'She's a friend then?'

'My aunt. She lives in Israel. Her husband died in Auschwitz too.'

The old man stopped walking and turned to face them. 'It all happened so many years ago,' he said. 'Yet we never cease to mourn. It's because we never buried them.'

Jakob translated for Sarah. She smiled, nodding her head. The old man had exactly defined the nature of her sorrow. They walked on.

'Whose bones do you seek now?' the old man asked after a while.

Jakob told him the story of his Odessa beginnings, and he was glad to tell it, for it was new to him, and he thrilled to the adventures of his forefathers.

'That will be the very old cemetery,' the old man said, 'though it has been desecrated many times, and most of it now is covered with long grass. I'll take you there,' he said. 'It's not far.'

'You must not trouble yourself,' Jakob said.

'It's no trouble. It's my pleasure. The history of one Jew is the history of us all. We must share it. I shall help you find your forefathers' bones, and I shall mourn them with you as if they were my own.'

Jakob translated for Sarah. 'Has he nothing else to do?' she whispered. 'Aren't we taking him away from his business whatever it is?'

'He wants to come,' Jakob said. 'I think we're doing him a favour.'

They walked together and the old man was silent most of the time. He walked slightly ahead of them, looking behind occasionally to check their progress. To a passer-by he might have looked like a priest leading his small flock.

'Is it far?' Sarah asked Jakob after a while. 'He's an old man. We should take a taxi.'

Jakob passed his aunt's suggestion to their guide.

'It's not far,' he said. 'Just over the top of the hill. What's it like in Israel?' he asked over his shoulder.

Jakob translated for Sarah and she was about to give a short answer when the old man continued.

'I wouldn't go there,' he said. 'I could not be a Jew there. The essence of our faith is the Exile. The Diaspora is the core of living Judaism. Only in our homelessness will the Jewish race survive.'

Jakob stopped walking. He didn't quite understand the full import of the old man's words yet he sensed that it was a point of view that required serious consideration. Slowly he translated it for Sarah, checking occasionally with the old man as to the exact words he had said. He knew they were important, and he needed Sarah to know that too. But Sarah was not bewildered by his opinions. She had clearly heard that argument before.

'Some of us had no choice,' she told him.

Jakob translated her response, but the old man was not interested. He hurried forward, eager for bones, anxious to dwell in the past as comfort for his loss, as proof of his history and stubborn continuity.

They reached the brow of the hill. From the top the old man pointed out the burial-ground, and from where they stood it looked like an overgrown field. They picked their way down the slope. Jakob was wary lest the old man lose his footing and he hurried forward to take his arm. But the old man snatched it away.

'I can manage,' he said brusquely.

He did not want to appear frail. Not in this place. He was dying, he knew. He was naturally old enough for that. But dying had nothing to do with death. He knew that too. He had watched his own mother die for many years and when death came, it had had nothing to do with those painful years. For dying is mortal. Only death can grant us immortality.

They reached the burial-ground. It was less overgrown than it had appeared from the top of the hill, and it was possible to decipher the head-stones of many of the graves.

'What's the name?' the old man asked.

'Bindel,' Jakob said.

The man wandered off among the stones. Jakob regretted giving him the name. He didn't want him to discover the Bindel bones. It was not his right, whatever he said about universal history. 'I'll find them,' he shouted after the old man. Sarah too had taken her own way and was pausing by the gravestones where the legends were still legible, though she could not read them. So Jakob too went on his private search, hurrying a little, fearful that the old man would poach on his Bindel past. Any Jewish past would do for their guide, whatever its surname. Jakob looked across the sea of broken stones and saw him crouched beside a grave, in deep meditation, and there, it seemed that he was prepared to stay. He was in no race, and his old face was suffused with such peace that Jakob chided himself for his ungenerous thoughts.

Jakob looked up, and then he saw it. He was standing right in front of the Bindel tomb. He had seen the old man pause there, and pass it by, and he was enormously grateful for his acknowledgement of the privacy of their search. 'Aunt Sarah,' he called. 'It's here.'

She picked her way across the headstones, avoiding the graves with meticulous care. Then she stood by Jakob's side. 'Read it to me,' she said.

Jakob crept towards the stone, peering close. He read it aloud in the Russian that was engraved, and then he translated it for his aunt. 'In Memory of Jakob and Esther Bindel, and of their children and their children's children, who died in the Tavern fire. Passover 1871.' He looked at his aunt and saw tears in her eyes. But they were not tears of sorrow, for she was smiling too.

'It's just as your uncle David told me,' she said. 'His grandfather is in that tomb, Leon's father, Benjamin, along with his milk-brother, Reuben.' She sat down on the grass beside the grave and wept with such copious tears that Jakob wondered whether she had ever cried for her husband before. He made no move to comfort her, for he sensed that she was comforted enough by her release.

After a while the old man called out to them. 'May I join you?' he asked.

Jakob crossed over to where he sat, and helped him to his feet. Then he led him along the path to his own history. The old man stood and read the legend. '1871,' he said, over and over again. 'Almost a hundred years ago. Yet they survive, and will survive still, so long as their bequest is not destroyed. We owe them that, as our children will owe us. Magnified and Sanctified be Thy good Name in the world.' The old man sang the first words of the *Kadish*. He was surprised that Jakob did not join in the prayer, but he continued on his own, for his own dead as well as for those who lay at his feet. Jakob listened in wonder and, though he had never in his life heard that song before, the melody stirred a quaver in his heart and, despite its mournful tune, he thrilled to a sudden joy of awakening, as if he'd been re-born, singing.

The old man had started to move away. He did not wait for his fellow-mourners, nor motion them to follow him. But as he passed them by, Jakob noticed a small smile on his lips. He was humming to himself as he made his way across the burial-ground and slowly up the slope of the hill. They watched him out of sight, and then they made their way together, Jakob's arm in Sarah's, without words, until they reached the crest of the hill.

'I am ready now to go back to Moscow,' Sarah said. 'We have done our business here.'

Jakob was happy to agree with her. The experience at the burial-ground had shaken him, and he needed silence and privacy to contain it. They made their way to the station.

The same train that had brought them overnight from Moscow, was about to make its day-journey back to the capitol, and they boarded it and found a compartment to themselves. Though they had slept soundly on the train the night before, they were soon asleep again overcome by an emotional fatigue that had drained them both. It was as if they had called on sleep to seal the profound changes in their hearts, to enclose and preserve them for ever.

They slept for a long time, and the train was a mere thirty miles out of Moscow before both of them awoke. Sarah's waking thought was a resolve to tell the Bindel brothers all about Israel, its life and its history, its struggle. For the first time since her confused widowhood, she began to envisage a future. In that Odessa burial-ground she had visited the uneasy country of the past. She need never dwell there again.

Jakob woke with the image of a photograph on his mind's eye, the sepia portrait of the small boy in Aunt Sarah's album. He knew that that, too, was a story that belonged to the Bindel past, an unknown soldier of unknown grave. He needed now to know it, for it was part of that lineage he had so recently discovered was his own.

'I was looking in your album, Aunt Sarah,' he began, 'and I saw a picture of a young boy. It's on a page of its own. He has a sort of helmet . . .'

'David,' she said, interrupting him.

'Uncle David?'

'No. That boy was the first David after whom your uncle was named.'

'The *first* David?' Jakob was curious. 'Who was he?'

'It's a secret,' Aunt Sarah said. 'But I shall tell it to you. You shared the second David with me. Now I shall share the first with you. You remember your Grandma Greta?' Sarah asked.

'Of course.'

'It was she who told me. We were very close, your grandmother and I, and perhaps she felt she could unburden herself to me, for it was a secret that she never told her own children. Your father Benjamin and Uncle David died without ever knowing it, nor, had they lived, would they ever have known.'

Although they were alone in the compartment, Aunt Sarah spoke in a whisper and Jakob leaned forward to catch her words.

'Before your Grandpa Leon married Grandma Greta, he had been married before.'

'To whom?' Jakob asked excited. 'And where?'

So Sarah told Jakob the story as she had heard it from Grandma Greta that day when Leon had returned from Cardiff and Zelda's funeral. He had kept to his room all day in a black mood of desolation. Greta knew that his mother's death had affected him deeply, but she knew too that it was not only Zelda whom he mourned. Her death had awakened in Leon's heart all the pain of his first-born's non-burial, and Greta did not know how to comfort him. In her anguish she had told Sarah the Senghennyd story, and Sarah remembered it by heart and, word for Greta's word, she gave it now to Jakob. The train was pulling into Moscow as she came to the end of her story and, during its telling, the image of the helmetted boy had stippled itself on Jakob's eye like an engraving.

'He too is part of our past,' Sarah was saying.

When they reached home late that night, Hans and Inge were surprised at their swift return.

'We did our business,' Sarah said. 'We saw what we had to see.'

'Did you find the graves?' Hans asked.

She nodded, but they did not tell him how, or of the old man who had led them to that place. Indeed, in their eyes, the old Jew had already become a shadowy figure, and each of them wondered whether he had been a figment of their imagination, a guide sent from nowhere to signal to them their pasts, and thus to open a gate to their future.

*

Over the next few days, Sarah relaxed into a holiday mood. She visited Hans in his laboratory, and met many of the Dreiser's friends and slowly she gathered the background against which her nephews were growing into men. She thought of the old man's words in the Odessa cemetery. *Our past survives so long as its bequest is not destroyed. That is a debt we owe to our forefathers, and our children to us.* His words seared her mind, for, though she could in no way fault the care and the loving Hans and Inge had lavished on the brothers, she could not envisage their future as one that perpetuated the Bindel bequest. That day, she started to tell the brothers about Israel, and as each day passed, she familiarised them with

389

the land that she hoped would one day be their home. Jakob never tired of her stories, but Aaron listened only out of politeness. Until his Aunt Sarah's visit, he had given the country of Israel little thought. Now it actually frightened him. Its sheer presence in his consciousness was a threat to his future. He was a Russian. The Soviet Union was his nationality, his faith, his land and his living. Let Jakob do what he pleased. But he feared that Jakob's preference might cast a shadow on his own chosen life-style, that his friends would suspect the infection of brotherhood. But he did not question that fear, for the fear itself frightened him, and he secretly looked forward to his Aunt Sarah's departure.

When, at the end of the month, she left for Israel, she knew that her visit had wrought many changes in the brothers and, though such changes could not be harmful, she had a nagging fear of their consequences. Hans and Inge were left with the same apprehension. Aunt Sarah's visit was a milestone in all their lives, but none so much as in her own.

CHAPTER TWENTY-SEVEN

Over the years that followed, Jakob and Sarah kept up a regular correspondence. Occasionally his Israeli cousins would write to him, but their letters, though friendly, were without enthusiasm and Jakob had the impression that his Aunt Sarah stood behind them while they wrote. But he was always glad of Sarah's letters, for in them she kept alive his curiosity and interest in a country with which he sensed an indissoluble spiritual connection. He did not consider that he would ever live there. The words of the old Jew at the Odessa graveyard had made a lasting impression on him. The survival of Judaism was guaranteed only by the Dispersal. But it had to be a dispersal in which the laws of Judaism were known and practised, and Jakob had no means of learning them, and even less of putting them into practice. Amongst his friends at the University, there were few who admitted to being Jewish, and though he felt close to Aaron on almost every other issue, that of Judaism continued to divide them.

At that time, Jakob was in his final year as a student of mathematics at the University of Moscow. Aaron was due to qualify as a doctor at the School of Medicine. Hans and Inge viewed them both with pride, both for their sakes, and vicariously, on behalf of Benjamin and Heidi. But though they had done well, though both of them had inherited, Hans and Inge were still uneasy about the future of the Bindel line, and the possibility that its inheritance would come to an end, with the next generation, deeply disturbed them. So they were delighted when one Saturday morning, Jakob announced that he was going to the synagogue.

Amongst the articles that Hans had collected from the Bindel family home in Leipzig, was Grandpa Leon's prayer-shawl and this he now gave with joy to Jakob.

As he walked to Archipova Street Jakob thought of Leipzig and the weeks shortly before his parents had been taken, when every Saturday the family would go to the synagogue. He remembered little of the ceremony inside the temple, but he recalled the recreation time in the yard when the service was over, the games they played with the other children, and the sense of freedom that they shared that they no longer had to go to school. He wondered now how many of those children had survived. As he approached the synagogue, he grew nervous, and excited too. He felt as if he were returning to his home after a long absence. As he went through the doors, he heard the singing, and that sound shipped him straight back to his Leipzig childhood, and those few years when he had had perforce to accept his faith. He quickened his pace towards the swing-doors, donning his cap and prayer-shawl as he went. But his heart sank as he entered the Temple. A sprinkling of very old men sat there, no more than a dozen in all. He raised his eyes to the women's gallery, but it was empty. Now he wanted to leave. He felt suddenly burdened, as if the whole future of Judaism lay on his own shoulders. If he were to stay in this place he would be accepting that responsibility. As he turned to leave, an old man called to him in a whisper and motioned him to come and sit by his side. Jakob hesitated. It would have appeared rude to decline the invitation, so reluctantly he made his way to the pew where the man worshipped. The old man noticed that Jakob had no prayer-book so he gave him his own and pointed out the place in the service. He knew it by heart, he said. Jakob looked at the left-hand page for the Russian translation, that side of the page where in his childhood the German had been written. But the language of the translation was neither Russian nor German but in English which Jakob couldn't read. 'It's illegal to print Jewish prayer-books in Russia,' the man whispered, seeing Jakob's consternation. 'These are smuggled in by friends from England and America. You must learn Hebrew, my son.'

'Where am I to learn?' Jakob whispered, though he was fast losing his appetite for his return to the faith.

'Ask the Rabbi after the service,' the old man said.

But when the service was over, Jakob hurried from the synagogue, angry and disappointed. Judaism in the Soviet Union was clearly moribund and it was certain that, within a generation, it would expire. Yet it lived in places like England and America as the prayer-book testified. He was thoroughly confused. He wished he was like Aaron who was never irritated by elbowings from his past. He wished too that Aunt Sarah had never come to visit him, and that he had never set foot in that Odessa burial-ground. He decided he would not write to her any more.

He noticed how the old men left the synagogue without even pausing in the yard to exchange words with their fellow-worshippers. Even that post-service conviviality did not exist here. Perhaps that too would be frowned on by the authorities. He recalled the stories Aunt Sarah had told him about life in Odessa in great-great-grandpa Jakob's time. The Czars were tyrants and anathema to Jews. Yet in their time Judaism had flourished. Synagogues were freely open and full, festivals were celebrated publicly and without shame. Yet in this land of equal opportunity, of fair shares for all, the spirit of man had been equalised too, hatching shares of atheism for all, and faith so diluted by equal distribution, that it ceased altogether to exist. Jakob quickened his pace, anxious to avoid the old worshippers. He resented them for the monopoly they seemed to assume over his faith. He resented too, their neglect of bequest, but most of all he resented their old age, because their inheritance would be buried with them.

Many years were to pass before Jakob entered the synagogue again, and until that time Jakob did his best to keep away from the promptings of his past and to immerse himself in his studies.

*

On graduation, he secured a job at a Middle School Polytechnic in a suburb of Moscow. At about the same time, Aaron acquired a post in the Moscow National Hospital. The brothers saw little of each other in those days. As an intern, Aaron lived in the hospital and went home only on the occasional weekend. He and Jakob had little to say to each other, and those few words were usually in argument.

Since he had started in the teaching profession, Jakob had become more and more disillusioned. He himself had been through the Russian state school system, so he was not surprised by its methods. But as a teacher he was beginning to question them. During his schooldays, Jakob had conformed to the learning-method with no thought of rebellion, but from behind his desk as a teacher, he understood the shallowness and tyranny of the system.

As a schoolboy, he had, from time to time, been publicly repriman-
ded and shamed by a teacher in front of the whole class. That too
was part of the system, and he had, in great humiliation, accepted
it. But now as a teacher, he saw it as brutal and diminishing and he
hated himself for being a part of it. But he kept silent and he hoped
that he would never cease to be aware of the silence he was keeping.

Hans and Inge were sympathetic. 'It's not only the schools,'
Hans said. 'The schools are just part of the system. It's the system
that doesn't work.'

'Generally speaking, it does.' Aaron was angry. 'It's a good
system. It's fair. Why shouldn't it work?'

'It may be equal,' Hans said. 'More or less equal,' he added, 'but
it isn't free. Man is not free within it.' He heard himself whispering.
'See how I whisper,' he said. 'Man is not free in this country,' he
shouted, and shouted again, as if testing the gods to strike him.

'Sh,' Inge said.

Hans looked at her. 'See how frightened we all are,' he said.

Jakob was amazed at the force of Hans' reaction. He had noticed
how often, in those days, Hans would talk about his own father,
and Jakob knew that somehow his anger hinged on those memories.

Two years before, Hans had taken part in a small demonstration
against Russia's invasion of Hungary and had spent two nights in
prison for his pains. He had spent all that time thinking of his
father, and thanking God that he had not lived to see that day,
because Fascism had killed his father who had died in the name of
Communism, that same name in which his son now mourned him.
He thought too of leaving, of taking his family to America, but to
apply for an emigration visa was to risk refusal, which would
jeopardise his future livelihood. Hans had begun to hate the Soviet
Union with a passion, and, unlike some of his Russian friends at the
air-craft plant who were disillusioned in their own secret ways, he
did not rejoice in their compensating love of the Russian tongue, of
its drama, its landscape and its poetry. Even Jakob, with all his
disenchantment, could find some compensation in the Russian
spirit. His language was perfect, and Tolstoy was closer to the tip of
his tongue than Goethe. Sometimes Hans felt very isolated, even
from his children.

'I've never felt any lack of freedom,' Aaron said.

Hans turned towards him. 'If you wanted to be a practising Jew,
you would feel the lack of freedom,' he said. 'If you wanted to stand
up and protest against our system, you'd feel it too.'

'But I don't want to practise as a Jew,' Aaron said angrily.
'Neither do I want to protest. I'm in total agreement with our
system. I think all religions are a sop to the masses.'

He's brainwashed, Hans thought, and sloganised too, exactly as the Hitler youth had been.

'Let's go out,' Inge said, anxious to avoid argument. 'It's a lovely day.'

The others were eager to agree. It was a bright summer Sunday, a traditional walking day for Muscovites, who would gather in parks and squares and mingle with the tourists, in a state of either envy or pity, but always with avid curiosity. The nearest square to where the Dreisers lived was Mayakovsky and, as they approached it, they saw that a large crowd had gathered there. On enquiry they were told that a statue of the poet was to be unveiled, so they joined the crowd and watched the ceremony. After the formal speeches of Russian dedication to the Arts, the statue was unveiled, and a group of poets on the platform began to read their verse. The crowds were silent, hanging on to each syllable, as if for the first time in their lives they had entered a new dimension of the spirit. Hans too was similarly affected and his sullen mood dispersed. By his side, Jakob listened with wonder, smelling a forbidden freedom in the event, not so much in the words themselves, but that they were being spoken at all. He was not surprised when, after the official readings, a number of poets amongst the crowd took their verses to the platform. The crowd roared their approval, eager for more, and the light was beginning to fade before they dispersed. But not before one on the platform suggested that they meet again, and share their poetry with each other.

As the Dreisers left the square, Hans looked at Jakob and sensed a profound change in him. 'Will you go again, Jakob?' he asked.

Jakob nodded.

'Poetry lifts the spirit,' Hans said.

'It was more than a poetry-reading,' Jakob said. 'It might well be the beginnings of a revolution.'

*

After a number of such meetings in the square the authorities smelled rebellion amongst the crowds, and read dissent between the spoken lines. Moreover, when the readings were finished, the crowds did not disperse, but lingered in groups and talked of matters beyond the stuff of poetry. Mayakovsky Square had become a free Sunday club for those who grew offended by their own silences. There were random arrests and warnings until, finally, after a few months, the so-called poetry readings were officially banned. But not before Jakob had found an avenue of release for all his questionings, a camaraderie amongst those equally frustrated. These he found. And love too.

He had been a regular attendant at the readings, ever since the statue's unveiling. Each time he had noticed a young girl standing at the foot of the plinth, her hand fidgeting in her pocket, possibly with her verses, Jakob thought, that she was too shy to reveal. Sunday after Sunday he watched her standing there, happy to keep his distance, and to feed on her beauty which was considerable. She had long black hair, the style of which never varied. It was plaited into a thick pigtail which seemed to take off from the crown of her head, then hung in sheer perpendicular down her back. Her posture was strikingly erect and fearless, yet in her eyes was the timidity of a hunchback. For several weeks Jakob watched her as she stood immobile at the plinth, her body still and serene, but for the continuous fidgeting of her hand. One Sunday he placed himself by her side, and in an interval between the readings, he asked her if she herself were a poet. She trembled a little as she answered.

'I write a little,' she said.

'Why don't you read them then?' he asked.

'I don't carry them with me,' she said.

He smiled at her. 'Then what *do* you carry in your pocket?'

She withdrew her hand. Inside it was a small white mouse. She stroked it with the fingers of her other hand and looked up at him and smiled.

He was embarrassed by his poor guesswork. 'Well, it's a kind of poetry, I suppose,' he said. 'What's its name?'

'Moses,' she said.

Jakob trembled.

'It's Jewish,' she said, and laughed.

'Doesn't look Jewish to me,' Jakob said.

'Do I?' She looked squarely at him.

'How d'you feel?' he said.

'Jewish.'

'So do I.' And with those few words they had signed a treaty of alliance, and both, from each other's look, knew that neither of them would break it.

It was on the following Sunday that the police broke up the readings for the last time but, by then, Deborah and Jakob had seen each other daily and had found their own meeting-places rather more private than Mayakovsky Square.

Deborah was in her last year at the Moscow Film Academy. In the summer she would qualify as an editor and she hoped to specialise in documentary films. Despite the team-work that her job necessitated, she was, like Jakob, a loner. And for the same reasons. She was a doubter, a questioner and could find no one with whom to share her uncertainties. At the film school she had sought clues to frustration amongst her colleagues but, finding none, she had learned to hold her tongue, a habit encouraged by her parents out of fear for her future. She, like Jakob, had sniffed a promise of freedom in Mayakovsky Square. Deborah could retrace her heritage for five generations from the Magareks of Moldavia. Emanuel Magarek had dealt as a timer-merchant in Kiev at the same time as great-great-great-grandfather Bindel had traded in his tavern in Odessa. The Magarek family had never left Russia. They had survived pogroms, wars, dispossession and banishment from one province to another. But most of them had eventually returned to the Ukraine. Deborah's parents had settled for Moscow, because her father too was a film-maker and the centre of that industry lay in the capital. Her parents were indifferent to the concept of Judaism. They celebrated no festivals, neither had they ever been inside a synagogue. That aspect of Jewishness played no part in Deborah's doubts and she was surprised to find that it was the very core of Jakob's discontent. In the course of their daily meetings Jakob told her about his aunt Sarah and her tales of Israel. He told her what he knew of Jewish history, but he refrained from taking her to the synagogue, for it had dampened his own willing heart, and he would not inflict such a let-down on Deborah. But she warmed to his stories of Israel, and slowly she began to accommodate the notion of Jewishness within the arena of her doubts and uncertainties.

Once she took Jakob to her cutting-room at the film school. She was editing a government short on army training and, as the sound-track boomed the virtues of defending the sacred motherland, with its notions of equality in all things, she put her finger to her lips, because there were others in the room.

'See what I mean?' she whispered.

He saw it exactly and he understood, too, that the silence he was keeping in his own classroom was the same fearful silence that she kept here. It was a silence that could lead to collusion. They must fight against that, both of them.

Deborah was much at home in the Dreiser household. Hans and Inge welcomed her, glad for Jakob's sake that he had found a kindred spirit. Even Aaron was fond of her, despite her leanings towards rebellion. He even brought her a matching white mouse from the hospital laboratory. She would call it Aaron, she laughed, not for his sake, but that Aaron was Moses' brother. Likewise Jakob was welcomed in the Magarek household. Deborah's father was an established film-maker, highly thought of by those in the profession. As an artist, he was the recipient of many privileges unavailable to the ordinary Russian worker. His apartment was roomy. He was allowed far more space than the eight square foot per person that was the State allowance for urban living. Its furnishings were sumptuous. Both the Magareks were well-dressed, having access to the special department store available to the privileged class. Food was plentiful on their table and of a variety that Jakob had never seen before. There was clearly no cause for personal discontent in the Magarek household, and Jakob wondered at the source of Deborah's rebellious thoughts. Sometimes he talked to her father about the system under which they lived, but Mr Magarek felt himself in no way indisposed. He was allowed to travel freely to film-festivals all over the world. He did not feel his freedom restricted. Of course he realised, he said, that he was one of the chosen citizens, and in the same breath he urged Jakob to take into account the bonuses of a system that was fair and equal for all. Mr Magarek was not a man one could argue with, but Jakob liked him well enough to leave him with his illusions. Occasionally he would broach the question of the Magareks' Jewishness but, in this subject too, it seemed to Jakob that they dwelt in cloud-cuckoo-land for Mr Magarek asserted that he was a Jew only by accident, that he was first and foremost a Russian, a status that claimed his total allegiance. He protested over-much, Jakob thought but, once again, he left him with what he considered his illusion.

One day Deborah suggested that they go to the synagogue. Because it was she who had proposed it, Jakob was not averse to a second visit, and the following Saturday he took out his grandfather's prayer-shawl once more and set out to give his faith another chance.

Deborah had never entered a synagogue before, and had to be conducted to the women's gallery by an old man, who looked at her with some surprise. She was puzzled by his reaction, and understood it only when she reached the gallery and found that it was empty. She edged herself into a seat in the back row but, once seated, she could see nothing of the proceedings on the ground-floor, so she sidled into a seat a few rows from the front from which vantage-point, she could see the worshippers below. She picked out Jakob first of all, sitting with a scatter of very old men, their heads buried in their prayer-books, and the sight of Jakob among them, in his young years amid their hoary age, marked him as a beacon, a torch to illumine the future of his tribe. And because of the love between them, she too felt that responsibility. She looked along the benches for a prayer-book, but found none. She noted the long-gathering of dust on the foot-rails, the plush on the seats, once so clearly worn down by worship, but now filmed with grime. She listened to the rumbling from below but she could make no sense of any of it. Its sound stirred no lingering memory in her mind. Yet she did not feel in any way alien to the strange murmurings of prayer. Not as alien as she had felt in a Russian Orthodox church on the one occasion she had attended a friend's wedding. She wondered what a wedding would be like in this synagogue. She wondered too whether Jakob would ever ask her to marry him. She looked at him again, and saw how his neighbour was pointing a gnarled finger along the lines of the prayer-book, and how Jakob nodded and smiled. But not once did he look in her direction. Nor did any of the others. From long habit perhaps. Perhaps their women-folk were dead, or they were keeping the home while their men kept the faith for both of them. She fingered the mice in her pocket. Moses and Aaron. Closet Jews in the dark, like these men in the Temple mumbling their fearful faith behind closed doors. She brought them out of her pocket and let them slither along her hand. They blinked their pink eyes in astonishment. Moses, used to his black shelter, crouched against the warmth of her palm, but Aaron, so lately used to scurrying across experimental floors, darted from her hand and down her leg, and shortly disappeared along the floor-boards. She dared not move to search for him for fear of the noise that could draw attention to the gallery. So she sat quite still, her eyes darting along the floor for a white sight of him. She put Moses back in her pocket, but he writhed with a sudden sense of loneliness, so she cupped him in her hand in the dark lining. She hoped the service would soon be over.

Jakob was standing now, along with the others, and singing. She watched his mouth and from the precision of its movements, she could guess that the song was well-known to him, and was probably an echo from his Leipzig childhood. She stood herself, waiting for it to be over. Then she saw the men doff their shawls and fold them so slowly and so carefully into velvet bags. And then Jakob looked up at her for the first time. She smiled at him and tried to mouth the news of Aaron's disappearance. He could clearly make no sense of it, so she pointed to her pocket, scurried the air with her fingers, and shrugged her shoulders with helplessness. The message was then clear. He signalled that he would join her in the search. The synagogue emptied, and shortly afterwards Jakob reached the gallery.

'It's Aaron,' she said.

He smiled at her. 'I can't tell the difference. Can you?'

'Of course,' she said. 'Aaron looks much younger.'

'How does an older mouse look?'

'Bit like you,' she said. 'Worried.'

He laughed and crawled about the steps, making scratching noises with his finger-nails. Deborah did likewise. Then suddenly they saw its pinkish tail in the groove of the boards, and both put their hands over the little body as it slithered along the wood.

398

Deborah picked it up and stroked it, then returned it to Moses for companionship.

'Would you come here again?' she asked as they walked down the gallery steps.

Jakob stopped and took her hand. 'I'll come here again to marry you,' he said.

*

The wedding took place on a Sunday, and the synagogue was full. Jakob had invited all the regular worshippers, though he knew none of their names, and they rejoiced in the crowded congregation, even though most of them were not of their kind. But the host of celebrants reminded them of the youth of their barmitzvah days, and later of their own marriages, and caused them to weep a little for those partners who had gone before them, and the weeping itself was a pleasure, for it confirmed their own survival.

The two families gathered under the canopy. Aaron was the best man. He was happy for his brother, and as he stood there, clutching the ring, he began to wonder whether he himself should take a wife, and he cast a sidelong glance to find Sonia. He had no difficulty in picking her out of the crowd, since her beauty was remarkable, and those on each side of her sat apart a little, as if to give her framing. She looked at him, but without smiling, afraid that at this time and in this place, a smile might be construed as a declaration of her own expectation. But he smiled at her nonetheless. For he had made a decision. He would propose to Sonia after the ceremony.

Aaron had known Sonia for almost two years, yet he had never brought her to the Dreiser home. He was wary of Hans. Sonia was not Jewish, and Aaron knew that Hans' welcome would be cold. Not on his own behalf, but for the memory of Benjamin. Aaron knew how acutely Hans felt the responsibility of fulfilling what would have been Benjamin's wishes for his sons, and Aaron knew too that his foster-father had, thus far, executed that responsibility with diligence and love. He was grateful to his younger brother for marrying within the faith, for it helped to give him licence to choose elsewhere. The hurt to Hans would possibly be minimised. He would bring Sonia and Hans together after the ceremony. He turned to look at Deborah, and he wondered where on her white pocketless person, she had secreted Moses and Aaron, since it was known that she never went about without them. Then he caught sight of a small white silk purse, hidden in the blooms of her bouquet. The purse was wriggling a little, and Aaron was glad that they had come to the wedding.

Inge was crying a little, remembering Heidi and Benjamin, and

Hans comforted her, saddened himself by the desolation of all their pasts. Then Jakob pledged his troth according to the Law of Moses and Israel, and crushed the glass under his foot. A cry of 'Mazeltov' rose from the congregation, and Hans sighed with joy and relief. The Bindel line could now nudge itself forward to a new generation. He was at peace with himself, having discharged the moral burden of the Bindel fostering. Or almost discharged. He knew about Sonia and her friendship with Aaron. He knew it would not please him if their friendship resulted in marriage, and when, later on at the reception, Aaron asked him to meet his intended bride, he tried to hide his displeasure. But Jakob had noticed it, and once the introduction was over, he took Hans aside.

'You look worried, Hans,' he said.

'Your father would have been worried too. It is something that has never happened in the Bindel family in all its generations.'

Jakob thought of the portrait of the young boy in Aunt Sarah's album, and of the story of Grandpa Leon. It was a secret between him and Aunt Sarah, a secret that he had not even shared with Aaron. But at the look of pain on Hans's face, he knew he had to share it with him, to lift the guilt from Hans' heart. So he sat down with him and told him about Grandpa Leon's first marriage. 'So you see,' he said, when he had finished his tale, 'it won't be the first time, and it certainly won't be the last. Yet we survive, we Bindels,' he said, 'and that's the whole of our inheritance.'

'Does Aaron know this story?' Hans asked.

Jakob shook his head. 'There's no need,' he said.

'May I tell Inge?' Hans asked. 'She has the same guilt as I.'

'Of course,' Jakob said. Then he put his arm around Hans's shoulder. 'You have nothing to be guilty of,' he said. 'I have loved you and Inge as much as I could ever have loved my own parents. You know that. Aaron too. He has more difficulty in showing it, that's all.'

Jakob was right. Aaron was sometimes cold to the point of indifference. He had never accommodated the death of his parents. In the eyes of a child, death is the most extreme rejection of all and, since his orphanhood, he had trusted nobody. Jakob wondered whether Sonia loved his brother enough to allow for his distance and untouchability.

And presumably she did for, within six months, they were married. Theirs was a strange coupling. Sonia's way of life represented all that Aaron strived for, that Russianness to which he was not born. As an adolescent, Sonia had lisped her way through Tolstoy, Gorki and Pushkin, writers whom Aaron read with a foreigner's second-hand relish. Her father was a high-ranking government official, a staunch Party member as was his father before him. Sonia's mother had died when she was a child, and Mr Koskin had never remarried. In his privileged position he was entitled to a housekeeper and a governess for his child. He had had a series of mistresses who, after serving their term, had been discharged from their duties, usually on the plea that the Party claimed his total allegiance. Or almost total. His love for his daughter was greater than any loyalty he owed to his Party, a love compounded by the guilt of his neglect and his sundry infidelities. He would have forgiven her anything. But Sonia had always been an obedient child. Even as she grew, there were no signs of rebellion in her. She was exactly the stuff of Aaron's day-dreams. A life with Sonia would confirm the lie of his own, and in time would teach him to accommodate it and even find it comfortable.

His first meeting with his prospective father-in-law had been cordial but cool. Mr Koskin took no trouble to hide his disappointment that Aaron was not a Party member. 'We'll remedy that,' he had said, but with little conviction. He refrained from enquiry as to Aaron's background and parentage, as if he feared that investigation into that quarter would not please him either. He toyed with the name of Bindel, finding it foreign and of dubious extraction. On the whole, despite the fact that Aaron was a doctor, he thought his daughter could have done better for herself. But he did the right thing. He welcomed Aaron into their small family in his well-endowed quarters facing the Kremlin, but he took care not to introduce him to his friends. To this end, he insisted on a quiet wedding. So Aaron and Sonia were married in a State Registry Office, in the presence of the Dreisers, Jakob and Deborah, and Mr Koskin himself. When the ceremony was over, Sonia divided her bouquet into two sections and, with Aaron on her arm, took the bridal car to Lenin's Tomb. There she laid half of her bouquet. They walked down the slope to the tomb of the Unknown Soldier, where she deposited what was left of the flowers. She thus did her duty as a young Russian bride in her homage to her past.

*

To Hans' regret, Aaron made little effort to maintain contact with him and Inge. From time to time, Hans would drop into the hospital on his way to work, finding some excuse to talk to him. He was saddened by the distance that had grown between them. Only on the level of his work was Aaron willing to communicate, and Hans grasped at this thread to avoid a total estrangement between them.

Aaron had begun to specialise in immunology. He had his own laboratory in the hospital, and was slowly acquiring a reputation in that field. Once, on the occasion of Hans' visit, Aaron had shown him an article that had appeared in an American medical journal, written under Aaron's name. Hans was excited. He wanted to know the matter of the dissertation; he wanted it translated word for word, and Aaron did it for him gladly in his childhood German. Hans could understand very little of its technicality, but he understood the introduction, and he puffed with pride. 'Aaron Bindel,' it said, 'at the age of 27, is a brilliant young immunologist whose future work in the field could well revolutionarise present attitudes.'

'Your father would have been very proud of you,' he said. 'As I am.'

Aaron shrugged it off. To give to anybody, alive or dead, was for Aaron too burdensome a responsibility. But beneath the shrug, Hans could sense the anger.

'Aaron,' he said. 'I've never tried to replace your father. I have been your guardian. I have loved you as any father would his son. But you are a Bindel.'

'I am happy enough to be a Dreiser,' Aaron said.

How like his Uncle Aaron he is, Hans thought, that stern unbending man after whom he was named. And how like gentle Grandpa Leon Jakob was. Hans went towards Aaron and dared to touch him. 'Your parents are dead,' he said to him. 'They died in Auschwitz. No one can give you proof. The only evidence is my guardianship.' He paused. 'I remember when Inge and I told you in Leipzig,' he went on. 'It was Jakob who cried. But you were angry with disbelief. You're still angry, Aaron.'

'I know they're dead, Hans,' Aaron said quietly, and Hans was moved by that so rare use of his name. 'But it wasn't my fault. I refuse to bear the guilt of the survivor. That's what Bindeldom is all about. That's our inheritance. Let Jakob carry the torch of suffering. It's not my burden.'

Hans was deeply distressed at his words, and Aaron saw the sorrow on his face. And for the first time that Hans could remember, Aaron touched his guardian's head with a caress so tender that it seemed to make up for all the years of his cold indifference. 'Why do I need anyone more than you and Inge?' Aaron said.

Hans held him in his arms without fear, then quickly he left the laboratory.

Thereafter Aaron and Sonia were regular visitors at the Dreiser household and, though they had never sought or encouraged it, Hans and Inge accepted Aaron on his Dreiser terms.

*

In those days, Hans was a contented man. Deborah was about to deliver her first child. That morning, Jakob, who lived close by,

402

had borrowed Hans' car to take her to the hospital. Inge had waited by the phone all day for Jakob's call. Now it was evening, and Hans was with her, stifling his excitement at the thought of his putative grandfatherhood.

'Have they talked to you about names?' he asked.

'No,' Inge said. 'But I suppose it will be Benjamin or Heidi.'

'I hope so,' Hans said.

Then the phone rang, and both hesitated before answering. Hans nodded to Inge, feeling that it was her prerogative. She picked up the receiver and Hans watched the smile break over her face as she listened.

'It's a boy,' she shouted. 'Everything's fine.' She arranged with Jakob that they would go to the hospital in the morning. Then the two of them drank a toast to the new Bindel, that child whose life they themselves had enabled.

The following day was one of celebration. In the morning they were to see their grandson, and in the afternoon Hans and Jakob were going to Mayakovsky Square. After years of silence, the poetry-readings were to recommence. The first reading was not advertised, but word of mouth from poet to poet and reader to reader, would ensure a large enough gathering. That Sunday in the spring of 1961, marked the anniversary of Mayakovsky's suicide, so it was an auspicious time to hold a reading that proclaimed a perilous freedom. But it was a dangerous time too, for two days before Yuri Gargarin had made the first ever space flight, and such an exploit was the cause of great celebration amongst the Russian people. The authorities would not look kindly on any event that might sour such an achievement. Hans and Jakob were slightly apprehensive, but nothing would hinder their attendance at the Square.

In the morning, Hans and Inge went early to the hospital, and were surprised to find Aaron there. He excused his presence on medical grounds, but Hans knew that curiosity and a certain pleasure had driven him there.

'What will you call it?' he asked, as he passed the baby to Inge and Hans for their inspection.

'Benjamin,' Jakob said.

Aaron said nothing, and his lack of response signalled a positive disapproval.

'That's as it should be,' Hans said quickly. 'It's the meaning of continuity.'

Aaron let it pass. His children, when they came, would enter the world without any premeditated burden, for with a name like Benjamin, so highly-charged, went highly-charged expectations too.

'He's beautiful,' Inge was saying, and she sat next to Deborah on the bed, and asked for details of the birth and hospital care. They talked in whispers, and the men around the bed took the hint of the women's need for privacy and they sought a subject of conversation for their own.

'I think there'll be quite a turn-out at the Square this afternoon,' Hans said.

'You mean the reading?' Aaron asked. 'You're not going, I hope. There'll be trouble.'

'If we're orderly, there won't be trouble,' Jakob said.

'But just being there, orderly or not,' Aaron said, 'is an anti-Soviet statement. You're asking for trouble.'

'In what country in the world is poetry-reading such a crime?' Hans asked, though he did not expect a reply. 'You ought to come with us, Aaron,' he said. 'You would find it uplifting.'

'I have better things to do,' Aaron said. But he was smiling. 'In any case,' he added, 'my father-in-law will probably have many friends there. Keep out of their way,' he laughed.

Hans laughed too. He saw Aaron's joking attitude as a sign of a small thaw in his stubborn patriotism.

'Well maybe next time,' Jakob said.

'If there is a next time, and I doubt it,' Aaron said.

Inge had overheard the exchange. 'Maybe Aaron's right,' she said. 'Perhaps you shouldn't go.'

'Of course they must go,' Deborah joined in. 'What better way to celebrate? In any case, I want a first-hand report of what happens.'

'Well be careful,' Inge said. 'I'll stay with my grandson a little while. But come back here after the meeting. I'll see you here.'

Jakob held his son for a while, then he left the hospital with Hans. Aaron accompanied them to the carpark, where they went their separate ways.

Hans and Jakob reached the Square an hour before the proceedings were due to begin, but even at that time the area was crowded with people. They recalled Aaron's warning, and knew, perhaps, that, with such a crowd, there could well be danger; and no doubt each member of the crowd knew it too, for there was a sense of defiance amongst them, and already a slight sniff of victory. Amongst the crowd, Hans could spot those whom Aaron had called his father-in-law's friends. Plain-clothes KGB men, but in all ways uniformed. For they were dressed alike, in grey crimplene trousers, black leather jackets, and each carried in his hand a rolled newspaper. They were immediately recognisable for what they were, and indeed intended so to be, for their presence was meant to be a harassment as well as a warning. They did not attempt to mingle with the crowds, for they would have been given short shrift

404

by the square's audience, so they hovered on the fringes, pausing from time to time to talk to each other; then they would amble around, striking their legs with their newspapers. They, as well as the spectators, were impatient for the proceedings to begin.

Hans and Jakob mingled with the crowd and were quickly infected by their excited anticipation. There were rumours of names who would be reading their works, and Jakob recognised them as some of the most foremost poets of the time. Then one of them was indeed seen to be making his way towards the plinth, followed by a group of men and women, their verses in their hands. A hush fell on the square as they approached the platform, and one of their number made a short speech of welcome. Then he called upon Anatoly Shchukin, the renowned poet, to open the proceedings. Shchukin's first poem, though untitled, was clearly about freedom and, with every syllable of each audacious word, he confessed to the crime of individualism. The words echoed through the tannoy and collided head-on with the police cars at the entrance to the square. The officer-in-charge gave his orders through his radio-set, and drove off. Shchukin got away with three more inflammatory verses, before the snow-ploughs, their shovel-mouths agape with astonishment at such unseasonal duty, spluttered towards the square. Shchukin bravely went on reading, and most of the crowd, out of loyalty, stood their ground. But some panicked and tried to get out. In the scuffle, Hans and Jakob were separated, and neither could find the other.

Hans found himself on the plinth, and he shouted Jakob's name across the square. But not even he himself could hear it as it left his lips, so raucous was the panic amongst the crowd. Then miraculously he caught sight of him, standing with his back to the gaping shovel-mouth of the first plough that had entered the square. Jakob clearly could not hear its approach, for the din of the mob muted its rumble to a murmur. Hans looked at the gaping jaw with horror. He practically flew off the plinth and plunged through the mass to where Jakob stood. Then, with his two hands on Jakob's back, he lunged him forward into the crowd in front of him, putting some distance between his son and the jaws of almost certain death. But in the great force of his propulsion, Hans himself fell to the ground, and seconds before he surrendered consciousness he felt the steely and loveless embrace of the machine. Then he screamed aloud, but did not hear his screaming.

But Jakob heard, and all those who stood about him. They turned, and, when Jakob saw Hans' inert body in its iron nest, he knew who had pushed him so violently and with so much love. And, oh my God, he thought, with so great a sacrifice. The snow-plough grinded to a halt, and from nowhere two stretcher-bearers appeared in the crowd. They bent down over Hans' body and murmured to each other. Jakob watched, unable to move, transfixed in terror to the ground. He watched the orderlies unfold a blanket. I'll wait, he thought to himself, and see how much of Hans they will cover, and if they cover his face, he decided, I shall kill them both with my bare hands. But they stopped short of Hans' sleeping countenance, and tucked the blanket under his shoulder. Then Jakob stepped forward full of love for those men who had not pronounced Hans dead. He walked alongside them.

'I'm his son,' he said.

'We'll take him to the hospital,' one of them said. 'He's bad, I'm afraid.'

Then Jakob saw the blood seeping behind Hans' shirt-collar.

'One of the forks caught the back of his neck,' the man went on.

'Murderers,' Jakob screamed across the square. 'Murderers.' Some of the crowd who followed the stretcher tried to comfort him. Jakob began to pray. He did not know what God was made of, nor indeed whether He existed at all. He did not want to pray to that same God who had turned His back on Auschwitz, yet he had heard that there was no Other, and that His ways were mysterious. So he prayed fervently, or rather ordered, abjuring Him to leave Hans to the living. 'You've taken one father of mine,' Jakob screamed into the depths of his soul. Then he felt the tears streaming down his face, and he tried to tell himself that they were for a previous mourning, and had nothing, absolutely nothing to do with the pale figure whose life lay on the stretcher before him, bleeding to its close. He knew that he had to get hold of Inge. He didn't know how he would tell her. He'll be all right, he would say. Absolutely all right, he repeated, shouting it out loud, challenging its denial.

'Where are you taking him?' he asked one of the men as they loaded the stretcher onto the ambulance on the fringe of the square.

'To the National,' the man said.

'I'll go and fetch my mother,' Jakob said. 'We'll go there together.'

The man touched Jakob on the shoulder. 'You'd better hurry, son,' he said gently.

The National was where Aaron worked, but only now, for the first time since the accident, did Jakob think of his brother. It would be almost harder to tell Aaron than Inge. Inge's love for Hans was pure, constant and blameless. If he were to die, she would in desolation mourn him, but she would give time, time to heal the wound, for no guilt would prolong her grief. But Aaron's life would be shattered by a second orphanhood, by the death of one whom he had always viewed as a usurper to the Bindel throne, even though he himself found that throne so uncommodious and uncomfortable. But Hans would not die, he must not, Jakob wept inside himself, else for the rest of his life he would carry the blame of his demise. It was he who had insisted on their attendance at the reading. It was because he himself had so much wanted to go that Hans had accompanied him. 'Oh God,' he prayed again, 'let him live.' And as he prayed, thinking of Inge, Aaron and his poor blameworthy self, he ran and ran, unaware of his speed or breathlessness. He turned the corner of the Dreiser street and saw Inge coming out of the apartment building. She carried a bunch of flowers, clutching them in her hand on her way to see Deborah. Then Jakob who, for the last hour, had forgotten his new status of father, now remembered his son. The Lord giveth, and the Lord taketh away. Blessed be the name of the Lord. He stopped, frozen by the thought, and waited for Inge to reach him.

'What are you doing here?' she asked as she approached him. Then she stopped and trembled. 'Where's Hans?'

'There's been an accident,' Jakob said and put his arm around her. 'It's all right, it's all right,' he whispered. 'He'll be all right. It was just an accident.'

'What happened?' she screamed at him.

'We must get to the hospital,' he said, taking her arm, and almost in the same breath, 'it was a snow-plough. They sent them into the square. It ran over him.'

Inge stopped and forced Jakob to face her.

'How bad is it Jakob?' she asked.

'It's all right,' he sobbed, his voice breaking. 'It's all right.' He saw a taxi in the distance and with some relief, he flagged it down.

'To the National Hospital,' he told the driver. Then in a whisper, 'Please hurry.'

But Inge had overheard him. She settled in the back of the car and put her arm around Jakob.

'Whatever happens, Jakob,' she said, 'you are not to blame. You must never think that. Never, never, never.'

Then he put his head on her lap, as he remembered doing all those years ago when she had told him that his father was dead. He wept now as he had then and, as Inge had done in the Leipzig days, she cradled his head in her arms. They were silent for the rest of the drive and, by the time they reached the hospital, Jakob had steadied himself, and he took Inge's arm and ushered her into the waiting-hall.

The receptionist lost no time in checking Hans' whereabouts, for she read the urgency in Jakob's eyes. They took the lift to the third floor. The ward-sister, learning of their kinship with her patient, was very solemn, and told them as gently as she could that

Mr Dreiser was in a critical condition and was not expected to survive. The injury to his skull had been considerable. 'But go and sit with him,' she said. 'He is semi-conscious.'

Jakob let go of Inge's hand and she went into the little annexe where Hans was lying.

'I have a brother here, Sister,' he said. 'Dr Aaron Bindel. Could you page him please and ask him to come?'

'I'll do that immediately,' she said. Then she laid a hand on Jakob's arm. 'I'm very sorry,' she said.

Jakob crept into the annexe. He stood at the end of the bed. Hans' head was bandaged and his eyelids fluttered a little.

'Hans,' Inge whispered. 'Hans, Hans,' over and over again, as she held his hand, massaging life into his fingers with a tenderness so acute that it bordered on violence. Jakob sat by her side and took Hans' other hand in his own. He wanted to call him too, but suddenly the name of Hans seemed to have become, at that time, Inge's inalienable property. It would have seemed to trespass on her spousal state to voice it himself. So he said nothing and he put Hans' hand to his own cheek and caressed it. So they sat there, the two of them, watching him as his life ebbed away, listening to each breath that he savoured, sparingly and with relish, as if he knew of its rarity. He looked transparent, as if the shadow of sheer living had been lifted to point death its undarkened way. He lay, his breathing quivering like a humming-bird, a faint burring sound, a polite chorale in death's overture. Available to his passing he was, without rage, without struggle. Just a terrible sadness at all the love for him that he would leave behind.

After a while they felt a presence at the door and, turning, they saw Aaron, his face white and drawn with sadness. He tip-toed to the other side of the bed and gently took Hans' face in his hands. The eyelids fluttered as if in prelude to opening wide. Then Aaron spoke one word.

'Papa,' he said.

Tears veiled Jakob's eyes. From where had his brother plucked that word? From what hidden source had it echoed through Aaron's troubled heart? Had it lodged there since Auschwitz, on parole, as it were, waiting for its final release? And now the word had dropped from his brother's lips as if it had never been incarcerated at all.

A smile played erratically around Hans' mouth.

'Papa,' Aaron said again.

Then Hans opened his eyes and all those at the bedside knew that it was for the last time. Inge bent to kiss him.

'Love, love,' Hans whispered. Then he stared at Aaron and Jakob, and with the last traces of his smile, he said, 'My two dear

Bindels.' Then his eyes closed, though the smile still hovered on his lips.

Aaron took his hand and let his fingers creep around the wrist searching for the pulse that no longer beat. 'Papa is dead,' he said.

Jakob took Inge in his arms. 'No,' he said. 'He lives still in my son, for Hans will be his name.'

Only that morning Hans had rejoiced in the name of Benjamin as a symbol of continuity. That continuity was what Hans, in his Bindel guardianship, had laboured for most of all. Whatever the provenance of that principle, whether the pungent smell of gas in Auschwitz, or the small sniff of freedom in Mayakovsky Square, whether it was clothed in the name of Hans or Benjamin, it mattered not. For however it was called, it was a celebration of survival.

CHAPTER TWENTY-EIGHT

After Hans' death, Jakob and Deborah moved into the Dreiser apartment to live with Inge, and the presence and growth of the little Hans did much to alleviate the sorrow that had clouded all their lives. Aaron managed to secure Inge an administrative job in the hospital where he worked, and there she was able to make new friends whose diversion eased her wounds. Aaron hoped that in time she would marry again, and indeed Inge hoped it for herself. Her partnership with Hans had been a happy and fulfilled one. She liked the state of marriage. She felt it was of her nature, and to continue to live alone, even with the company of little Hans, seemed to her unnatural. So when, some eighteen months after Hans' death, she met Ivan Treger, a widower and one of the almoners in the hospital, she did not view him in any way as Hans' replacement, but as his continuation. They were married in the summer of that year, and Inge went to live in Ivan's apartment in the old city.

That time in Moscow, the mid-sixties, was a period of fervent dissidence. The poetry readings at the Square had been officially banned, but the protest movement flourished. Writers managed to publish their works. Two of them, Andrei Sinyavsky, and Yuli Daniel were brought to trial on the charge of disseminating anti-

Soviet propoganda through their writings. Synyavsky was sentenced to seven years' hard labour, and Daniel to five. The punishments were severe; the sentences made clear that the authorities would brook no opposition. Jakob and Deborah followed the trial from day to day, and each of them eavesdropped in their respective places of work, to pick up the opinions of their colleagues. But the subject was surrounded by silence, either because of indifference or ignorance, or because of the fear of voicing sympathy for the accused. Aaron maintained the same silence when Jakob broached the subject with him, but one day during the trial he warned Jakob that dissidence should be none of his business. Aaron was more than irritated by Jakob's interest in the rebels. He was downright angry. He saw his brother's dissident connections as a serious threat to his own career. Earlier that year he had been elected to the Academy of Sciences, a highly distinguished honour for one so young. His work in immunology was well-known to all practitioners in that field throughout the world. It was mooted that he would soon be awarded the privilege of a country residence, and numerous other bonuses for which the Russian elite were eligible. A rebellious brother might well interfere with his prospects of promotion and advancement, and often he considered cutting himself off from Jakob entirely. But since Hans' death, he had grown much closer to his brother, and it was because he loved him that he angered him so. 'I hear you went to the trial,' Aaron said with displeasure.

'Yes,' Jakob said. 'I thought it was an historic occasion. Your father-in-law was there too. On the other side, of course. He actually smiled at me,' Jakob said. 'But I ignored him. I suppose he told you.'

'He mentioned you were there,' Aaron said. 'He was not pleased.'

'I am not in the business of keeping your father-in-law happy,' Jakob shouted angrily. 'He and his kind are my enemy.'

'I urge you to be careful, brother,' Aaron said. His use of the sibling term was rare, and it rang with a combination of concern and warning. Its overtones of caring helped to offset its anger. Then, as if to underline his concern, he touched his brother's arm. 'Sonia's pregnant,' he said.

He turned to go. 'I'd like you to be around for the birth, Jakob,' he said, 'Don't get yourself into trouble.'

*

The baby was born in June. Aaron telephoned late one evening to give Jakob the news of the birth of his daughter. 'Hans has a cousin,' he said. 'Her name's Heidi.' The announcement was over very quickly, pre-empting questioning or comment. Jakob understood that, and enquired after Sonia's health and the baby's weight. He was glad for his brother. Aaron had made a certain peace with his past. With his calling of the dying Hans as Papa, and the naming of his daughter as Heidi, he had finally accepted his orphanhood and, in burying his parents, he had felt the itch of continuity. Jakob now felt free to attend meetings once more and to play his part in his inherited battle of survival.

In the following summer, Deborah had another child and, to Jakob's joy, it was a son. He named him Benjamin. Now he had donated to his tribe yet two more brothers Bindel, and it seemed as if a small burden had been lifted from his heart, a burden of which he had hardly been conscious until it had been discharged. The second event of that summer, which was to conscript Jakob into the dissenting ranks, was the six-day Israeli war.

Jakob had never ceased his correspondence with Aunt Sarah, although over the years it had become irregular. But her letters had kept alive Jakob's appetite for Judaism and for a knowledge of his past. The War reports on Russian radio and television were disturbing. They pointed to a total Israeli defeat. According to their bulletins, at the end of the six days it would have appeared that Israel had been annihilated. But it was still possible to tune into the BBC World Service and, between the jamming and the static, the truth could be learned. After a few days even the Russian News Agency could no longer mask the Israeli victory but, in their ham-fisted attempts to do so, their hostile anti-semitic face had been clearly shown. They called it anti-Zionism, but no Jew was deluded by that euphemism. The official press carried cartoons of the Israeli victors that recalled for Jakob those that had appeared in the Nazi paper *Der Stürmer*, when he was a child. The effect of the war on Jakob, as on thousands of Russian Jews, was one of stunning change in his life. He began to think seriously of emigrating. Deborah was of his mind, and they wrote at once to Aunt Sarah informing her of their considerations.

It seemed to Jakob that, during those days, Aaron was avoiding him. Whenever Jakob invited him over, he pleaded prior engagements, and one day Jakob dropped into the hospital after school and sought him out in his laboratory. Aaron was clearly not pleased to see him, but he tried to hide his displeasure.

'It's ages since we met,' Jakob apologised as he took the chair that Aaron offered him.

'I've been busy,' Aaron said.

He was prevaricating, Jakob knew, so he came straight to the point. 'What do you think of the war?'

'I don't think about it too much,' Aaron lied, for the war and its victory had threatened him profoundly. 'But as you know, I'm totally against nationalism. It leads to Fascism. We've seen it in our own lifetime.'

There was no way Jakob knew how to argue with him. His brother's premise was so brain-washed, so personally-projected, that to argue with him would have been futile.

'I'm thinking of going to live there,' Jakob said.

He was surprised at the violence of Aaron's reaction.

'That's impossible,' he said, his face flushed with fury. 'It would be an outright anti-Soviet act. It would be treacherous.'

Again Jakob felt he couldn't argue, and for the same reasons as before. 'How's Heidi?' he said.

'You mustn't go,' Aaron said, almost pleading. 'It will bring shame to all of us.'

'I'm sorry about your father-in-law,' Jakob said, and he left the room.

Thereafter Aaron telephoned him almost daily, ostensibly to exchange news of work and family, but all the news was sub-titled with Aaron's anxiety as to his brother's considered future. Jakob, for his part, was happy not to argue with his brother, and exchanged with him the same trivia of domestic news. The subject of Israel was not raised again for a very long time.

During that time, both Deborah and Jakob achieved promotion in their jobs. Deborah was appointed chief editor of the State Documentary Film Unit, and Jakob was promoted to Head of his Mathematics Department. These changes delayed their decision, even though many Russian Jews to their knowledge had already emigrated to Israel. Their treacherous defection appeared often enough in the press as a warning to those who were considering a similar course.

The Soviet authorities, worried at the increasing numbers of applications for Israel, called an international press conference. Forty prominent Soviet Jews were invited to attend to testify to the freedom and good fortune of the Jews in the USSR. The event was heavily covered on radio and television, with many repeats. One evening, Jakob and Deborah had turned on their set to view an old film that had been made by Deborah's father. But the programme had been changed and in its stead was yet another re-run of the press conference. Those taking part were introduced around the table. They were Russia's most prominent Jews in the fields of government, arts and science.

'Uncle Toms,' Jakob muttered, turning away.

Then he heard the announcer's voice behind his back.

'Dr Aaron Bindel of the National Hospital of Moscow, foremost immunologist of international repute.'

412

Jakob could hardly believe what he had heard. He looked at Deborah and saw confirmation in her disgusted glance. Then turning, he saw his brother in full close-up, and smiling as he acknowledged the praise of the announcer's introduction.

'Turn it off,' Jakob said.

'You turn it off if you don't want to listen,' Deborah said. 'It's horrible, but I'm curious.'

He sat by her side. The first to be introduced was a very high ranking Jewish government official, who swore that his religion had in no way impeded his promotion. He had never in his whole life encountered anti-semitism in the Soviet Union. This opinion was echoed by other token Jews around the table: a world-famous violinist, a ballerina, and a clutch of writers. Shortly it was Aaron's turn and Jakob was ashamed. Aaron reiterated much of what had already been said. But he went further. He attacked Israel for being anti-Soviet, and he suggested that rumours that Jews wished to leave Russia were sheer anti-Soviet propaganda. The Jews had every reason to be grateful to Russia who had, after all, delivered them from the evils of Fascism.

Jakob turned the television off. He was sickened by his brother's treachery.

'His father-in-law wrote that speech,' Deborah said.

'Yes, but Aaron delivered it. I don't want to talk to him again.'

'We must try and change him,' Deborah said.

'Hans used to tell me my father was like that. Stubborn, ostrich-like. He never believed that Hitler would stay in power.'

'Yes, but he changed, didn't he?' Deborah said.

'He changed all right,' Jakob's voice was bitter, 'but it was too late.'

Jakob was deeply depressed by the television interview, and the mood lasted for many days. The following week an incident took place at school which aggravated his depression. He was taking a class of fifteen-year-olds, when suddenly he was interrupted by the arrival of the Headmaster.

'I'm sorry to disturb you, Mr Bindel,' Dr Kumysh said, 'but I'd like a word with the class.'

Jakob stood to one side. By the stern look on the Headmaster's face, he knew there was trouble, and by some intuitive instinct he knew it was related to anti-semitism. When the Headmaster asked Isay Salmon to stand up, his guess was confirmed. Young Isay was one of Jakob's more talented students, but it was not on account of his promise that he had been singled out in class. He was also a Jew and known to Jakob to have Israeli sympathies. Jakob shuddered on his behalf. He marvelled at the boy's coolness. Isay was clearly aware of why he had been called. He knew the cause and he was aware of its effect. He eyed the Headmaster with a certain disdain.

'It has come to my notice,' Dr Kumysh said, 'that there is a student in this class who is the son of a traitor. He stands before you. His father has relinquished his Soviet citizenship and has applied to go to Israel, that country that is bent on maligning the highest ideals and principles by which we live in this blessed land. I have come here simply to make you aware of the treachery in your midst. As you know, one of the bases of our ideology is the strength and the power of the collective spirit. Traitors must learn their lesson, and it is the collective that is often the teacher. You may sit down now, Salmon,' Dr Kumysh said. Then he turned to Jakob. 'Thank you, Mr Bindel,' he said, overpolitely. 'I was delighted to see your brother on television.' Then he left the room.

Salmon was still standing, holding on to his status of outsider, proud to be considered such, and in such a cause. If there was any fear in him, he was certainly hiding it. Indeed a flicker of a smile played on his lips as if in challenge.

'Sit down, Isay,' Jakob said gently. 'Now let us get on with the lesson.'

It was the last lesson of the morning, after which came a playground recess and lunch-break. Dr Kumysh had timed his visit well. The break would come while the self-righteous anger that he had instilled in his pupils was still hot upon them, and they were ripe for vengeance. They would lose no time in venting their spleen. Jakob dreaded the bell that would signal the end of the lesson. When it came, he asked Isay to stay behind. He did not know what he would say to him, but he knew that he would need some protection. Jakob's authority as a schoolmaster might guarantee that protection, but that schoolmaster was also a Jew, a factor that might well cancel out his authority. He waited until the boys had left the classroom, and through the frosted glass of the window he could see their shadows hovering in the corridor outside and hear the murmur of their war-like voices.

'Where d'you eat your lunch?' Jakob asked.

'In the playground usually.'

'I go to the park. D'you want to come with me?'

'I'm not afraid of them,' Isay said. 'In any case, you can't always be around. They'll get me one way or the other.'

'I've never met your father,' Jakob said, 'but he has all my admiration and respect. And I don't mind who knows it.' Jakob almost shouted this last remark, and there was a certain joy in it, for at that very moment he had finally decided to take his family and to leave the Soviet Union.

That evening he told Deborah of the school incident, and she insisted that he rang Isay's father to enquire about the boy.

'You're right,' Jakob said. 'But I would prefer to go to his house. I have his address. In any case, I should like to meet his father.'

'Be careful,' she said. 'They're watching his house, I'm sure.'

Deborah was right. One of Aaron's father-in-law's friends was idling outside Salmon's house with little attempt to disguise his purpose, nor the small camera that recorded Jakob's entry. Jakob even smiled for him. Having made his decision to leave the country, he was aware of a sudden sense of freedom, and a total absence of fear. He knocked on Mr Salmon's door. He heard scuffling behind it, and then silence. He waited, then knocked again.

'Who is it?' a woman's voice asked.

'Jakob Bindel. Isay's schoolmaster.'

The door was opened almost immediately by Isay's mother, who welcomed him. 'Isay has told us about you,' she said.

'Is he all right?' Jakob asked.

'He's in bed. It's not too bad. A black eye and a cut lip.'

'He put up quite a fight, I think,' Mr Salmon appeared behind her. 'It's good to meet you,' Mr Salmon said, giving Jakob his hand.

The tiny hall gave off into two rooms. The one they entered was the kitchen-living quarter, which also doubled as a bedroom, for a large divan took up one corner. Mrs Salmon offered Jakob tea and some sweets and biscuits from a small tin box.

'You are good to come,' Mr Salmon said. 'And brave too.'

'No, not brave,' Jakob said. 'I have decided to leave too. I've come for your advice.'

Mr Salmon stared at him. 'Are you sure?' he said. 'It's a big decision and, once you apply, they don't make it easy for you. You will lose your job. That's an automatic effect of application. Have you got savings?'

'A little,' Jakob said. 'How soon do you expect to leave?'

'There are no rules,' Mr Salmon said. 'Some people wait for months. Others get exit visas immediately.'

'D'you have relations in Israel?' Jakob asked.

'I have a sister there. She left Moscow ten years ago. She was widowed and alone. It was easy to get a visa in those days. She's married again and lives in Tel-Aviv. I want Isay to go to the Hebrew University.'

'D'you know Hebrew?' Jakob asked.

'We've been taking lessons for a year. There's a good teacher nearby. I could give you his address. But you must keep it quiet. It's illegal, you know, Hebrew lessons. Not officially of course, but they harass him regularly. Raid his flat, take his books, papers and threaten him.' Mr Salmon shook his head. 'We live in sad times, my friend. But since I applied, you know,' Mr Salmon went on, 'I've never been happier. I've never felt more free. My wife is the same and so is Isay, despite the lesson they try to teach him. But now they've made their point, they'll leave him alone. Since I applied to leave, I've made many new friends. And lost some too. We all do. You can't blame them. They're just afraid to associate with us. But we know most who apply for visas. We're a sort of secret fraternity. We compare notes. Some people apply secretly, and don't even tell their children.'

'I shan't keep it a secret,' Jakob said.

'Then I wish you luck, as I wish us all. But you must be in touch with us,' Mr Salmon went on. 'We shall probably meet at Hebrew lessons. Wednesday is the beginners' class.'

'I shall be there,' Jakob said. 'And my wife too.'

*

The following day was a Wednesday and Jakob's classes did not start till mid-day. He used his free time to go to Kolpachny Lane, the offices of OVIR where emigration details were processed, and make his application for himself and his family to leave the land of the free. The official gave him the forms, his lip curling with contempt. Jakob filled them in with meticulous care, then he handed them back to the official, who gave him another set.

'These must be filled up by your parents,' he said. 'And the parents of your wife. You need to have their permission to leave.'

'But, by God,' Jakob said, 'we're over thirty.'

'I don't care if you're over seventy. If your parents are alive, you cannot go without their permission. It's the law.'

'My parents are dead,' Jakob said.

The official looked up on him. 'We can check on that,' he said.

'Then check at Auswchitz,' Jakob said. 'In the gas-chambers.'

Jakob left the desk. Behind him was another applicant and Jakob hovered on the sidelines to overhear their exchange.

'You again, Mr Levertov,' the official said with a smile. 'You were here only last week.'

'And I'll be here next week, too, and the week after that, and every week until I get my visas. It's over a year now since I applied.'

'Tell me, Mr Levertov,' the official said leaning forward, 'why are you so impatient to leave this country of ours?'

Mr Levertov sat down and he too leaned forward. It was clear that the two men had a relationship of long and tolerant standing. 'Why do I want to leave, Volodya? I'll tell you. The trouble is I'm tired of being happy here.'

Volodya looked at Levertov for some elucidation.

'You see,' Levertov went on. 'I see a queue. I join it. I wait two hours and at the end of it, I can buy a pair of shoes. So I'm happy. I join another queue, and after an hour I can buy a lemon. Again I'm happy.' He paused. 'Listen, Volodya,' he said. 'to tell you the truth, I'm tired of being happy.' He looked at the official with a smile, then sternly he said, 'I'll be back next week.'

Jakob followed him out of the office.

Levertov knew he was being followed. He had seen Jakob fill in his emigration forms. Even so, he did not trust him. The KGB had singular means of disguising their agents. After a whole year of being followed and harassed, after a year of nurtured paranoia, Levertov trusted nobody. He darted down a side street, out of Jakob's vision, then looked around furtively and saw that he had lost him.

But Jakob had seen his detour and understood his flight. It saddened him that these were times when men were so wary of one another, an age in which suspicion had become a weapon for survival. He criss-crossed through a maze of streets to reach the river, where he could walk along the embankment which would eventually lead him to school. There were few people about. Most of them were women, balanced on each side with empty shopping-bags, on the look-out for a queue and the promise at the end of it of something to eat or to wear. But, coming towards him, he saw Aaron. At first he was surprised, wondering what his brother was doing on the embankment, until he realised that his hospital was just across the nearest bridge. He did not want to meet with Aaron, but there was now no way to avoid him. They had had no contact since the press conference affair. Both brothers, for their own reasons, had avoided each other. But as Aaron approached, Jakob saw that he was smiling, obviously pleased to see him. But Jakob felt no such pleasure and he was glad that Aaron would take small delight in knowing where he had been and Jakob would lose no time in telling him. Aaron clapped his brother's shoulders.

'What are you doing in these parts?' he said.

'I've just come from the OVIR offices,' he said.

Aaron's hand dropped from Jakob's shoulder. His face was white. 'What for?' he asked, though with little hope, for there was only one reason why a Jew should go to OVIR.

'We've applied for emigration,' Jakob said.

'But you can't leave,' Aaron shouted. 'What about my work?' He hadn't meant so crudely to reveal the cause of his objection. He could have by-passed it for a while. But his anger was sublime. He knew that anyone who applied for emigration was automatically victimised, and that victimisation often extended itself to his innocent relatives.

417

'I wouldn't worry about your job,' Jakob said with contempt. 'They won't touch you. They need you. You're one of their token Jews. You proved it yourself at their conference. I'm late, I must go,' and with no leave-taking Jakob left his brother agape on the embankment. When he reached the bend in the river, he looked around and saw Aaron still standing there, his shoulders hunched in despair. Jakob felt very sorry for him. Then suddenly Aaron straightened and set off at a brisk rate, and it looked from his gait that he was smiling.

Which indeed he was. For he had had a very simple idea. He made his determined and delighted way to the OVIR office. There was no one waiting at Volodya's desk, and Aaron went straight towards him.

Volodya raised his eyes to the ceiling. 'Another one,' he said.

'Another what?' Aaron said, on his dignity.

'Traitor, if you want it straight. I suppose you want to emigrate.'

'No,' Aaron said. 'On the contrary. I like it here. I've come about my brother.'

'It's your brother who wants to emigrate.'

'Yes. He's already applied. This morning. Name Jakob Bindel. Wife Deborah Bindel. Two children. Hans and Benjamin.'

'Yes, I remember him well. He was here just now,' the official said. 'Parents died in Auswchitz. Your parents too, of course.'

'Yes,' Aaron said, 'but I am his older brother and, therefore, since we have no parents, I am his guardian. Yes?'

Volodya was not quite clear as to the direction of the argument.

'I do not give my permission,' Aaron said.

Now Volodya understood. He'd never known a case like it, but there was little question in his mind as to its legality, and if necessary the law could be stretched to accommodate it. 'You are a loyal Soviet citizen, sir,' he said. 'Here is the form. You should fill it in and send it to this office with a covering letter stating the nature of your guardianship.'

Aaron collected the papers and made to leave. He felt Volodya staring at him.

'Didn't I see you on television the other night?' the official asked. Aaron nodded.

'You see, I was right. You are a loyal citizen,' he said.

Suddenly Aaron felt uneasy. Over the past few weeks, with the continual re-run of the conference on television, he had often been recognised in the streets and praised for his contribution. Always it had pleased him. But now he found the official's compliment faintly offensive, that it had come from such a source perhaps, that same source that had so lately maligned his brother. 'Thank you,' he said quickly and he gathered the papers and left the office. He found himself slinking along the wall outside, hugging the shop-windows so that he would not be seen. He didn't know exactly how he felt about himself, but he did know that it didn't please him.

*

The OVIR office did not inform Jakob of his brother's injuncion. Nothing from that office on the matter of emigration was ever put in writing. Volodya expected the younger Bindel to return to the office about a week after handing in his application. They always did, the new ones. For the first six months or so, they would call regularly once a week, then it would fall off to a monthly visit, and then, when a year had passed, there would be a clutch of desperate visits in a very short time. After that, from time to time, their steps would lead them automatically towards that place that they had come to hate with all their hearts and, on the OVIR threshold, despair would slacken their pace, and they would turn away without entering, unable to face yet another refusal.

But as Volodya had predicted, Jakob Bindel, the younger one, the sudden ward of his elder brother Aaron, arrived at the office exactly one week after his first visit, on a Wednesday and at the same time.

'Have you any news for me?' he asked.

'Name?' the official said, though he knew well who it was, but there were certain formalities that had to be observed.

'Bindel,' Jakob said impatiently. 'Jakob Bindel. I sent the forms of permission from my wife's parents.'

'Yes,' Volodya said, checking needlessly on the file. 'We've received those and they are quite in order. But it seems that you have been forbidden to leave.'

'But my parents are dead,' Jakob said. 'I told you that last week.'

'Yes, I know,' Volodya said. 'But you are still forbidden.' He wanted to spin the tale out for all its worth. He wanted to endow it with suspense, to keep Jakob Bindel on the guessing end and for as long as he could.

'Who forbids it?' Jakob shouted.

'You have an elder brother,' Volodya said slowly, 'and since you have no parents, he is your legal guardian. It is within his rights to forbid you. Or of course,' he added, 'to give you permission to leave. But I doubt he would ever do that. He is a loyal Soviet citizen. He came here and I was proud to shake his hand.'

Jakob was trembling with anger and disbelief. 'Does that mean,' he spluttered, 'that I cannot leave? Ever?'

'Not until your brother gives his permission,' Volodya said. He leaned forward, confidentially. 'Mr Bindel,' he said, 'why can't you take an example from your brother?'

419

Jakob opened his mouth to try to begin to tell him, but then he suddenly didn't want to involve this enemy with his family, even though there was enemy enough within. But Volodya's enmity was official. It was paid for, it was even, by dint of his upbringing, absolutely sincere. It was an enmity far cleaner than Aaron's. For Aaron's was expedient, self-seeking and treacherous. Jakob tried not to hate him.

He left the office quickly. The need for fresh air was paramount, for he felt a nausea throughout his body. He darted into an alley near the office, and retched his heart out. The tears streamed down his face, but he did not bother to ascribe them to his retching, for he knew that they spelled out quite a separate despair. He leaned against the wall and took deep breaths to steady himself. He wondered what he should do. His instinct was to go straight to the hospital and upbraid his brother. But when he thought about it, he knew that that was what Aaron was expecting, and that he would be well prepared for it. He needed urgently to see Deborah, but he was already late for his classes. It would have to wait till evening. Somehow or other he would have to get through his day.

That evening, he was almost ashamed to tell Deborah. What his brother had done was, in his mind, so monstrous, so against fraternal nature, that he would have wanted to keep it a secret for ever. But in time, Deborah would have to be told the reason for their refusal. Besides, he needed her comfort.

When she had heard his story, she saw how it hurt him and, because of that, her heart filled with hatred for his brother. And anger too, for she knew that his refusal to sign would bind them to the Soviet Union for ever.

'I want never to see him again,' Jakob was saying.

'No,' Deborah said. 'You must see him. You must try to persuade him. It will be detrimental to ourselves if you cut yourself off from him. He expects you to come to him.'

'He's waiting for me to beg,' Jakob said.

'And if you have to beg,' she said gently, 'is that so terrible? It would make the whole difference to our future. I would go to him,' she offered, 'but it's you he wants. It's you he wants the loving from, even if he has to torture you to get it.'

'Then he'll have to wait,' Jakob said.

'Yes. Let him wait a while. But eventually you must go to him. Plead with him if necessary.'

'Never,' Jakob shouted.

'Then you sentence us all to life in Russia.'

'I'll find another way,' Jakob said. 'I'll ask around. There must be loop-holes in the law.'

'Of course there are,' she said. 'In every law, but not for people like us.'

*

Over the course of the next few weeks, and their occasional meetings with other exit-visa applicants, Jakob discovered that his case was unique. There were sundry examples of parental injunction, but no one had heard of the elder brother manoeuvre, and all sadly agreed that there was no way of getting around it. In itself it was a loop-hole in the law, which the KGB would happily exploit to their own advantage. Jakob's friends advised him to go to his brother and persuade him to change his mind. But privately they had little hope of it. They too had seen Aaron on television. But finally they managed to persuade him and it was now a question of choosing a venue for their meeting.

He decided against Aaron's apartment, for he did not wish to include Sonia in the encounter. He thought of going to the laboratory, but that choice would not appeal to Aaron for its lack of privacy. They could meet in Gorki Square, he decided. It was large enough and peopled enough for privacy, and was not as yet suspected as a focal point for dissidents.

'When will you telephone him?' Deborah asked.

'Tomorrow,' Jakob said, as he had said every day for a week, and his procrastination only served to nurture his rage against his brother.

'Shall I phone for you?' she asked, knowing that that offer would spur his decision.

'I'll do it,' he said, and he went to the phone and dialled his brother's number.

He was relieved that Aaron himself answered. There were few words to his request, but each of them was so heavily-laden that they would not bear repetition. 'Can we meet?' Jakob said.

'Of course.' Aaron had clearly been waiting for the call. 'Where? When?'

'Gorki Square. 3 o'clock. Sunday.'

'I'll see you there.'

Jakob put the phone down. He considered that the worst part was over. His pride had been forfeited in the overture on the telephone. The meeting need only deal with argument. Yet he dreaded Sunday, and all that week a cloud lay over him so that, when Sunday came, he greeted it with a relief that it would soon be over.

Jakob arrived early at the square and so did Aaron, as if both were anxious to get the meeting over and done with. They came towards each other.

'How are you, brother?' Aaron said, his hand on Jakob's shoulder.

'How should I be?' he said, shrugging the hand away. 'But you look well enough.'

'I've had good news,' Aaron said. 'The government has given me extra finance for my research. A very large sum in fact.'

'Did that surprise you?' Jakob asked with disdain.

'Of course,' Aaron said. 'It came out of the blue.'

'You sold your brother for it,' Jakob shouted at him.

Aaron was shaken, but quickly recovered. 'Rubbish,' he said. 'One thing has nothing to do with the other.'

'They'll be giving you a country house next,' Jakob said. 'It flatters me in a way, to think I'm worth all that. A country house, a research award, maybe in time even the Order of Lenin, just to keep me and my family in the Soviet Union. It's really rather pathetic, isn't it, such behaviour from what we are told is the freest country in the world. I pity you, Aaron.'

He shouldn't have said that, he knew. That was a remark reserved for parting, and most certainly when the battle had been lost. Thrown into the arena at so early a stage, it could only serve to sour and any further conversation.

'I've come to ask you to change your mind. To give us permission to leave.' There was no other way he could ask him. No innuendo, no threat, no pleading, no flattery. Just the simple words of a straight-forward request.

'I can't do that,' Aaron said. 'I don't want to do it. And even if I did, for what reason should I suddenly change my mind?'

'Tell me, Aaron,' Jakob said. 'Why do you want me to stay? It surely can't be brotherly love.'

Aaron ignored the question. 'I think you're misguided,' he said. 'Israel is an enemy of the Soviet Union, and to take Israel's side is to be a traitor.'

'Then let me be a traitor,' Jakob said, 'and let me go.' He touched his brother's arm. 'You don't mean all that, Aaron, do you? You're too intelligent to talk like that.'

'Let's walk a little,' Aaron said. He took Jakob's arm. 'Don't you see,' he said, 'how my hands are tied? You forget who my father-in-law is.'

Jakob had to laugh. 'You're not serious,' he said. 'Is he going to rule your life for ever? Is he going to cost you the love of a brother? What's happening to you, Aaron? They're laying a trap for you, don't you see, and with all kinds of bait, department grants, cars, medals. And what for? You have no more faith in this country than I do.' His voice was raised and Aaron squeezed his arm in fear.

'Sh—', he said.

'You are already afraid, brother. See how you tremble in this great country of freedom of ours. You are one of us. Leave this place. Come with us.'

'You are mad, brother,' Aaron said. 'I believe in this land. I do,' he shouted.

'Why are you shouting, Aaron?'

Aaron stopped and looked around at those passers-by who eyed him with wonder at his protest. He grabbed Jakob by the sleeve. 'Stay away from me, brother,' he whispered.

'How frightened you are, Aaron,' Jakob said. Then out of the corner of his eye, he saw the non-uniformed figure of a plain-clothes KGB. He did not recognise him. All he knew was that he was not his personal tail. Over the last few weeks he had come to recognise his own shadow. They even had a nodding acquaintance. But this one was someone he'd never seen before, and there was no doubt in his mind that this new one was his brother's keeper. He wondered whether he should tell Aaron, but he decided against it and again pity for his brother welled in his heart.

They parted where they stood and, as Jakob crossed the square, he turned and saw his brother hurry towards the underground crossing, and hurrying behind him, his rolled newspaper in his hand, was his keeper.

On his way home, Jakob wondered what had been achieved. Despite Aaron's refusal to retract his letter, Jakob had the feeling that their meeting had little to do with his proposed emigration. The meeting had exposed Aaron's own fears, his own ostrich-like attitudes, and above all his vulnerability. And, understanding all these things, Jakob found it very hard to dislike him. Indeed he regretted that Aaron had ordered him to keep out of his way. He wanted to see him, because he wanted to help him, and he knew that there would come a time when his help would be needed if not called upon. All this he explained to Deborah when he reached home, and all that she understood, but, in understanding it, she was made more desolate for there seemed no way that Aaron could be swayed.

'We must keep applying,' she said. 'We must make nuisances of ourselves. We must not give them rest. We will take it in turns to go. I wonder sometimes,' she said helplessly, 'whether anybody outside this country has any idea of what's going on. When you think of Stalin's time, when millions of people rotted and died in camps, and nobody outside the country, or even inside, ever knew. Could it happen to us, Jakob, d'you think?'

'We're not in any danger of our lives,' Jakob said. 'The worst that can happen is that we have to stay.'

'What about all those dissident trials, the prisons, the labour-camps and exile? People still disappear and are never heard of again.'

They were silent then, then Jakob said, 'I'll leave it for a month or so, then I'll go and see him at the laboratory. He can't refuse me. We won't talk about emigration. I'll talk about his work. And there's nothing to stop you seeing Sonia. You know,' he went on, 'I wonder if your parents were aware of the risks they were taking when they gave you permission?'

'Probably,' Deborah said. 'But despite Papa's status and his privileges, I think he is secretly sympathetic.'

'I hope to God they leave him alone,' Jakob said.

'Oh Jakob,' Deborah said suddenly. 'What did we do when we opened our mouths?'

'D'you regret it?' Jakob asked. 'D'you want to withdraw? We will if you want. I don't want to do it without you.'

'No,' she said, without hesitation. 'We must think of our children.'

He held her close. 'It will happen,' he said. 'Sooner or later, we shall be free.'

They went to bed early that night, and fell asleep in that sweet safety that loving provides. But in the middle of the night, the phone rang. Jakob crawled out of bed to answer it. There was a curt apology for a wrong number. Jakob replaced the phone in its cradle. He knew that their term of harassment had begun.

CHAPTER TWENTY-NINE

The telephone was the least of it. When they remembered, they took it off its hook when they went to bed. It was an irritant that was dealable with, unlike the other forms of harassment that were to follow.

About three weeks after Jakob's application, he was dismissed from his job. There was no explanation, no period of notice. Just a summary dismissal. It came as no surprise. Job dismissal was automatic after application for an exit visa. Deborah knew that, eventually, she too would be deemed unemployable. Neither of them were particularly worried. They had always saved money and they put aside a fund for the family fares so that they could leave as soon as permits were granted. For there was never any question in their minds that in time the visas would come through. The delay was part of their harassment. Both of them were surprised at their lack of anxiety. Indeed, instead of being constrained by the uncertainty of their livelihoods, they actually felt liberated, and this sense of freedom drove Jakob once more into the fray. He mingled with others of his kind, and learned how they, too, sensed that freedom, that having relinquished their Soviet citizenship, they no longer felt responsible for its oppression, although they were constantly the target of its harassment. There was a common ground in the problems they all shared.

The dissident movement had been alive and active for many years in the Soviet Union, but the refusenik element was comparatively new. 'Refusenik' was the term applied to those who had applied for exit and, for numerous reasons, had been refused. Most of these were Jews and, by the Law of the Return promulgated by the State of Israel, any Jew who so wished was entitled to Israeli citizenship. Though in its beginnings, the refusenik movement was becoming a cause of international interest and concern, a fact that gave no pleasure to the authorities. For the Soviet regime was acutely concerned about its image abroad and, when in that summer of 1972, Richard Nixon, the then President of the United States, was paying a visit to the Soviet Union, the authorities were much concerned with the impressions he would take home. They could afford no leakings of discontent during his visit. So they went to some lengths to restrain those possible trouble-makers. Internal passports of malcontents were temporarily withdrawn, so that those living outside the capital were unable to travel to Moscow to demonstrate their protest. Those who lived in Moscow were warned to keep to their homes. But there was also a known hard core.

Some months before Nixon's visit, a group of activists had written an open letter to the American President, asking for a meeting during the course of his visit. There were fifty-seven signatures to the letter, and among them, high on the list, for it was signed in alphabetical order, was the name of Jakob Bindel. The authorities had been keeping a wary eye on him since his first appearance had been noted in Mayakovsky Square. Now, prior to the President's visit, their harassment increased.

*

One morning, Jakob was on his way to see a fellow refusenik. He travelled by underground. In the same compartment, he noticed two men and a woman, who were eyeing him with undisguised surveillance. He alighted at Kursk station, and saw that they were following him. He was not easy with their shadows, and he quickened his pace, a groundless guilt in his speed, and though he was not surprised when he felt a hand on his shoulder, he trembled with fear. He stared into the face of the militiaman, then saw at his side his three shadows from the train. The woman was crying uncontrollably, mouthing unintelligible curses between her sobs. Her two escorts were looking at him with disgust.

'These witnesses,' the militiaman said, 'saw you molesting this woman. Come with me.' He grabbed Jakob's arm and marched him off to the station militia department. There he awaited the van that would take him to the court. Since his arrest he had said not a word. He knew they had manoeuvred a trumped-up charge, and no denial on his part would change the course of their injustice. Over the last few weeks he had heard of many such charges. Most common of all were those of drunkenness, and there was always a witness to hand to testify to disorderly behaviour. But he had not heard of the accusation of woman-assault, and although it had a far more offensive ring than the charge of drunkenness, that aspect of his arrest did not worry him. But he worried about Deborah. He asked his guard if he could make a phone call, but his request was brusquely refused. They bundled him into a van and took him to the Kalinsky District court. There the woman and the two witnesses testified to Jakob's molestation. As he listened to their story, Jakob could not help but admire their bare-faced audacity and the fluency with which they each told their tale.

'I watched the accused leering at my friend with a look of such lecherous intent that I felt a shudder run through my whole body. I did nothing at the time, because I thought that that leer might be a natural look of his, and I wished to give him the benefit of the doubt. But I mentioned my fears to my friend.'

At this point his friend continued the story, reading it unashamedly from a sheet of paper in front of him. 'I shared the same feelings of revulsion as my friend,' he read, 'and as we approached Kursk station, the accused, on rising from his seat, shuffled towards our companion.'

At this point in the narration, the woman gave a cry that simulated a painful recollection, and she was offered a seat and excused from testimony. The second witness then continued his tale.

'As we were pulling into the station, the accused grabbed our companion by the buttocks' – this last in a stage whisper in deference to the feelings of the woman beside him – 'and rubbed his body against hers. Then the train came to a stop, and the accused ran away down the platform.'

The magistrate turned to Jakob. 'Do you have anything to say?' he asked.

'I am innocent,' Jakob said, and he heard the utter futility of his words as they echoed through the court-room.

The magistrate sniffed and sentenced him forthwith to fifteen days for hooliganism. By the time of his release, the Presidential visit would be over. Two militiamen took him from the dock, and as he turned he saw Deborah rush in through the court door. 'Jakob,' she shouted.

A policeman took her arm and spoke some words to her, and Jakob saw her laugh in his face, then he was dragged away from the court. On his way to the cells, he began to giggle, infected by Deborah's distant laughter. The ruse that they had played was so desperate and so amateur, it could only be an object of mockery. But though he laughed at it, it incensed him too, and by the time he reached his appointed cell, he was filled with such a rage that he longed for a private place in which to scream aloud.

But there was no privacy in the cell. He took time to count the men who were already in residence. Because of their shaven heads, at first glance they all looked exactly the same, cloned from a single cell of despair. They stared at him in silence, and their looks betrayed nothing at all, neither of curiosity nor sympathy, and Jakob knew that, even when the guards were gone, they would maintain their silence. He was shown his bunk, the bottom slab of a two-tier arrangement of which there were four in the cell. The guard threw a uniform on the bed, and told him to change his clothes, and seven pairs of lethargic eyes watched him as he undressed. The clothes were many sizes too big for him, and he had to roll up the trousers and the jacket-sleeves. He hung his own clothes in the cupboard by the wall, and waited for further instructions. Then he was taken by the guard to have his head shaved. As he looked at the hair on the floor, he recalled Aunt Sarah's story of the milk-brothers' recruitment, and how the pious ringlets of the child-soldiers lay curled on the bath-house floor. Aunt Sarah had learned the story from Uncle David, who had learned it from Grandpa Leon, who himself had heard it from his father Benjamin the milk-brother. Jakob marvelled at the tenacity of such an oral tradition, and he resolved that he would tell it to his own sons as soon as they were ripe for inheritance. The shaving did not disturb him. Indeed it gave him a measure of relief, for now he would be no different from his cell-mates, and perhaps his like anonymity would loosen their tongues. But he returned to a silent cell, to a silence broken only by inward curses and cries in the dream-filled nights. In a way Jakob welcomed the silence, but he was unnerved by the looks of suspicion each man gave the other. Then he remembered how a friend of his, Ivan, another refusenik, who had been imprisoned on a trumped-up charge, had discovered that one of his cell-mates was a planted KGB agent, and when, on the second day of his incarceration, one of the men gave Jakob a sickly smile, he shuddered at the thought of how that smile was sub-titled and he turned his face away, and prayed that the smile was not a true offer of friendship.

Three times a day they were released from the cell for their meals, and once in early evening for exercise. Apart from these sorties, the men remained in their cells all day with nothing to do but to stare through each other, or at the floor. It was uncanny how the silence persisted and how its germs of suspicion and mistrust invaded each man's spirit and found uneasy accommodation there. It was a time for contemplation, or putting one's thoughts from one's mind, both activities requiring equal concentration. On Jakob's part, his thoughts of Deborah and his children were a welcome solace in his wretched situation and he tried to keep them in the forefront of his mind. Not only for the comfort they afforded, but that they acted as a bulwark against any thought of Aaron, who, ever since his arrest, had hovered on the tip of his memory, not to be denied. He did not want to think about Aaron, because he knew that in this cell, he would begin to hate him.

He found himself staring at his cell-mates. He realised that it had taken him but two days to become like them. He was no longer the one to be stared at. He, like them, did his own staring, and though he stared at them, he, like them, saw nobody. He did not know how much longer he could stand their unseeing company. That night he heard a noise in the cell, and it was not one that could be associated with dreaming. It was a voluntary sound, fully conscious of what it was doing. He listened carefully and he deciphered it as sobbing, and though its sound was desolate, he heard it with symphonic joy. It proved that, even in this place, the heart could still throb with sorrow, even though the tears of that pain were congealed.

The following day, two prisoners from his cell were released, and were not replaced by others. The silence that persisted, now seemed less oppressive, less confined, at home in the spaces the men had left behind. On the seventh day, three more men were given their release, and now Jakob was alone in the cell with the single remaining prisoner and he knew then that the silence would be broken. He knew, too, with some survival instinct, that it must not be he who broke it. The man watched the cell-door close, then turned to face Jakob. The stare was gone from his eyes. Now he was simply looking and seeing what he saw.

'My name's Isaac,' he said, and he held out his hand.

A Jewish name, Jakob thought, a little too Jewish perhaps, and he looked at the man's face and examined it closely for the first

428

time. The absence of a frame of hair facilitated a careful examination of the features, and there was nothing clearly Jewish about them. The man's hand still floated between them, and Jakob looked down at it and turned away. He hoped by that gesture to make it clear that he knew that his cell-mate was a liar.

'We've got a lot in common.' The so-called Isaac was not put off by the snub. 'I was on my way to Pavel's too when I got picked up.' Pavel Revich was Jakob's contact for the Presidential demonstration. He was a known refusenik. Jakob had visited him often, but never had he seen this man there.

'I'm new to the movement,' Isaac went on, as if reading his thoughts. 'They picked me up on a fake charge of drunkenness.'

Jakob gave no response. He wondered how much longer the man would continue to seek his co-operation. He was inept at his job, Jakob thought, like all of his kind. They were not trained to be subtle, they did not even care if their real motives were discovered. Their job was to harass, to frighten and to intimidate, and Jakob was aware that on those levels he was effective enough. He had almost another week to serve, and he began to fear the man's company. He debated now as to the best way to handle his presence. To continue to ignore him might lead to a dangerous antagonism. Such petty men could be vicious when thwarted. So he would be polite, he decided, and give nothing away.

'Who's Pavel?' he said. He was surprised at the sudden sound of his own voice. For over a week now, apart from the occasional acknowledgement of food and exercise, he had not spoken at all. The sound pleased him and he wished to hear more of it.

'Pavel Revich,' the man said. 'He's a friend of yours. He told me so.'

'I don't know any Pavel Revich. What does he do for a living?' Jakob asked.

'He's like us. Unemployed. A refusenik.'

Until that moment, the word had rung like a tribute in Jakob's ear. It sang of a certain courage, stubbornness and fraternity. Now as it dropped so casually, so rehearsed from this man's lips, it was suddenly sullied, and Jakob wanted to strike him. But instead he said, 'I don't know him. I was simply going to the park, and they picked me up on the underground.'

That night Jakob couldn't sleep. He went over in his mind each word he had given to his companion, over and over again, to ascertain that he had given nothing away. Towards dawn he fell into a deep sleep, and was awakened not by the usual clanging of doors and keys, but by a gush of hot air on his face. He opened his eyes wide to see his companion's face close to his own and breathing heavily upon it.

429

'The President comes tomorrow,' he said. 'What a pity we shall miss it all. Pavel had great plans for us.'

'You lose no time,' Jakob said, sitting up and brushing him aside.

'I'm getting out this morning,' the man said. 'And I need to know where we were supposed to meet. Pavel said he would tell me. But I never got there. Where is it?' he asked. 'Who am I supposed to ask for?'

Jakob stared at him and couldn't help laughing. 'You mean they faked a drunken charge on you, and they're letting you out before the President's gone? Anyhow, how am I to know where you're supposed to meet? I've never heard of this Pavel you keep talking about. But if you hurry, you might still catch him,' he laughed.

His companion's lower lip drooped into a sulk. 'We Jews should stick together,' he tried one more time.

The word 'refusenik', out of his mouth, had been offensive enough. But Jew was a far more insolent affront, for it embraced the whole of his tribe, and Jakob had the courage and the anger to call his bluff.

'You're a Jew like I'm a KGB man,' he said.

'You wait,' Isaac said, never a man to give up, 'we'll meet again on the outside. We'll meet on the same demonstrations. We'll run into each other in the same prison cells. And you'll be sorry,' he shouted.

At that moment the cell door opened and Isaac was called outside.

'I hope you find your Pavel,' Jakob shouted after him, and the door closed and, for the first time in over a week, he was alone. But he was afraid. He began to fear the next Isaac they would thrust upon him for company. All that day he waited in fearful anticipation, but that night he slept alone, and the following night, and slowly his fear left him, and he began almost to enjoy his solitary state. During that time, he put his fearful thoughts from his mind. He thought of Aaron with less and less anger, and of Deborah with more and more love. He thought too of his own participation in the refusenik movement, and those thoughts led him to think of Hans. At the memory of Hans' death, he grew angry, and he resolved that, thenceforth, he would commit himself totally to dissidence, and that thought gave him a surprising sense of peace.

A peace that was rudely shattered on his last night of confinement. Another 'Isaac' was let into his cell and, though he wore the convict's uniform, this one hadn't even bothered to shave his head. Nor did he bother with any preliminaries.

'Who were the leaders of the demonstration?' he shouted.

'They demonstrated?' Jakob smiled. Somehow or other his friends had made a protest.

430

'I'm asking the questions,' the man said.

'Why do you bother to put on convict's clothes?' Jakob asked. His recent decision on total commitment had given him courage.

The man hit him across the face. 'I told you I'm asking the questions,' he said.

His cheeks stung with the blow and he was enraged. But he tried to keep calm. He did not want to be injured so early on in the struggle, and by such a paltry opponent. So he sat on his bunk and breathed deeply to contain his pain and his anger.

'I asked you who were the leaders,' the man said.

'I don't know,' Jakob's voice was steady. He knew very well who they were. All of them. And he regretted this knowledge and he prayed for the courage to conceal it. But he couldn't understand why they were asking him. They must have known. All of the leaders were known refuseniks. All those who had managed to avoid arrest must have been at the demonstration. It was possible they were all now under police guard.

'Well, if you don't know, my friend,' 'Isaac' said. 'I'll tell you.' He took a piece of paper from his jacket-pocket and read out a list of names. Most of them known to Jakob, and he winced when he heard those names of particularly close friends. 'We know of their plans too,' 'Isaac' went on. 'The protest at Gorki Square next Thursday. They won't be there. Any of them. And I've come to make sure you won't be there either.'

He opened the cell door and admitted two men. He nodded to them and left the cell, his duty done.

The men took no time to examine their target and, in one swift movement, they enveloped him in the dark of their black boiler-suits, so that he was blind to their assault. He felt a sudden spurt of blood, and then a quick stab of pain, a pain so unbearable that his consciousness obliged by leaving him. Later, when he opened his eyes, he found himself alone in his cell, crouched on the floor, with his blood and pain for company. He located the pit of his stomach as the seat of his pain, and he felt on his groin the lingering imprint of a vicious knee. He touched his face with both his hands, feeling for the source of the blood. But it seemed all over his features, and he was glad that he could not see himself. He knew he had to lie there and absorb his pain in deep and measured breathing. He wondered what time it was. He recalled that when the thugs had been let into the cell, it had been twilight. Now, as he slowly raised his head to the window, it was twilight still, and wondered whether only a few minutes had passed since their visit, or perhaps a whole comotose night. If the latter, then he would be released very soon. But the pain in his groin and the print of the knee were so acute that he thought they must have been of recent infliction. It was still

431

night, he decided, and he could sleep till morning. But even as he closed his eyes, he heard his cell door open.

'Time's up, Bindel,' a voice shouted. 'Leave your clothes on the bunk.'

He made to rise, but the movement was so painful he feared he might have an acute internal injury. The thought angered him, for it would put him out of combat for a while and, for him, the real battle had only just begun. He was determined now, at whatever cost, to devote himself totally to the refusenik cause, and his first battle-ground would be on Thursday at Gorki Square. He crawled to the bunk, and hoisted himself upright, and tested himself to stand without support. Then he tried walking, but his progress was slow and painful. He would call on the doctor, he decided, on his way home from prison. Then he thought of Aaron, and tried hard to disconnect his brother from his wounds. But it was difficult to dismiss the thought that his injuries were part-payment for Aaron's department grant, and he wondered for how long he would have to go on paying.

He undressed slowly, and every movement was painful. He was shocked at the bruise on his upper thigh. A large spread of uncertain blue stretched from the knee to the hip-bone and he could see the pulse throbbing beneath the mottled skin. He was glad he had some proof of his pain, and evidence too of the assault, though there was no one, he realised, to whom he could complain. That thought fed his anger once more, and now he was impatient to get out of the cell and throw himself into the fray. No more fake charges, he decided. If he were to be arrested again, it would be for a good and valid reason. Then, out of nowhere, came the thought of his inheritance, of great-great-grandpa Jakob's litany, tolling in his memory like a tocsin bell. There is no cause on earth worth dying for, the old Patriarch had said. Only in the name of love is death worthy. And friendship. In that light, Hans' death was less painful in his memory. Of all the traceable Bindel generations of which he knew, none of them had volunteered their lives in a cause. From their very Bessarabian beginnings, death had volunteered *them* in another's crusade. To survive, in Bindel terminology, was to live solely in order to bequeath, for it was that survival that ensured continuity and, to that end, one's life, at the cost of everything except love, must be preserved. The greatest revenge on one's enemies was to live. He had a sudden longing for Deborah, and he hurried with his dressing, despite the pain of every single movement.

The prison clock in the vestibule showed six o'clock in the morning. Earlier he had washed his face and noticed how the water had run red. He'd managed to stem the small amount of bleeding,

432

but he felt swellings all over his face and he guessed at their uncertain tinge of blue. He lowered his head as he passed the mirror on the side wall. He knew that the sight of himself would depress him further. A warder stared at him as he approached the gates that led to the outside, and he could not disguise his look of horror.

'Don't want to see you again,' he said, as he said to every out-going prisoner.

Jakob stopped and looked him squarely in the face. 'In my case,' he said quietly, 'it's entirely up to you and your lot.'

The warden unlocked the gate. He had to have the last word. 'You can take it from me,' he said, 'just in case you don't know, but you're not a pretty sight.' Then he shoved Jacob through the gate and bolted it after him.

The bright light of the early morning, and in such large expansive measure, dazzled him, and he could not recognise the figure of a solitary man waiting at the end of the prison drive, though his outline was painfully familiar. Even as the figure started walking towards him, all he could decipher was its intense familiar-ity. Then, by his voice he knew him, for he called aloud, 'Jakob,' and in the sound, Jakob heard his brother. He was astonished that anyone had come to meet him, and Aaron most of all. As he waited, he could not deny his joy at seeing him, nor could he help being moved by the care and concern that Aaron showed in his coming, and by the risk that he certainly took in the brazen and public association with one who, in the eyes of all those who watched from the prison-windows, was nothing but a trouble-maker. He waited for his brother's approach and, as he neared him, he saw the look on his face, and he realised that his countenance must have seemed a battle-ground. Aaron stood in front of him. He did not offer a hand in welcome, or touch any part of him. The concern that Jakob had seen on his face in the distance was now diluted into anger.

'Look what you've done to yourself,' he shouted.

'It's part-payment for your research grant,' Jakob said. He knew that he shouldn't have said it. He knew that his brother's rage was compounded of his own guilt and concern, and of his love too. Yet he too was entitled to anger. He stretched out his hand to off-set the cruelty of his response, and he touched his brother on the shoulder.

'I must get you to hospital,' Aaron said with his stiff unyielding body, and he led the way to the car. He did not help his brother as he slowly and agonisingly manoeuvred himself into the front seat, but Jakob noticed the painful concern on his face, so painful that it seemed to disallow a helping hand. But Aaron did close the passenger-door when his brother was settled, then he rushed to the driving-seat and drove off. Jakob wondered whether Aaron would be brazen enough to take him to his own hospital, but he noticed that they were not on that route. They were making for the outskirts of the city, and shortly they pulled up at a small building which Jakob knew as a private clinic for the privileged. Jakob was uneasy.

'*Must* we go here?' he asked.

Aaron ignored his objection. 'I have friends here,' he said, 'We won't have to wait.'

He strode into the clinic with an air of authority, and immediately arranged a series of X-rays and examinations for his brother. None of the doctors asked any questions. Aaron had explained to them that Jakob had spent fifteen days in prison, and that information was enough to account for his condition. They made no comment. Indeed it seemed that they would have preferred not to have known anything at all. The examinations showed that nothing was broken, but that there were bad bruises all over his body. The bones of his nose were intact, and the swellings would subside, they said, though it might take some weeks. They prescribed rest and quiet. 'Keep off the streets,' one of them said.

In the car on the way home, Aaron asked, 'Who did it to you?'

'Friends of your father-in-law,' Jakob said. Again he knew he shouldn't have said it, but he didn't want his brother to go home and feel that he had totally squared his account by his care and concern for his physical well-being.

'You should listen to that doctor,' Aaron said. 'Keep off the streets.'

Jakob turned to face him. 'Stop the car,' he said. 'I want to talk to you.'

'We can talk as I'm driving,' Aaron said.

'Please stop the car,' Jakob said. 'It's important.'

Aaron pulled into a side-road. He looked in the driving-mirror before he stopped. Jakob had noticed how often, during the drive, his brother's eyes had been raised furtively to check on shadows.

'Are you being followed, Aaron?' he asked as he brought the car to a halt.

Aaron laughed, rather too heartily. 'Of course not,' he said. 'Why should anyone follow me?'

'Because of the company you keep,' Jakob said, and he laughed too, hoping to establish some affection between them, for what he had to ask of his brother required a mood of friendship as its setting. He came to the point straight away. 'We've got to get out of this country, Aaron,' he said. 'You have to withdraw your veto. I beg of you.' He hadn't meant so to précis his request. He had wanted to serialise it, to give it style, cadence, and turns of phrase

434

that would all have softened the nature of its demand, that would have muted its overtones of desperation.

'I won't do that,' Aaron said with some finality, and he turned the ignition key in the lock.

'Why not?' Jakob practically screamed at him.

'We're Russian citizens,' Aaron said in a measured voice. 'Our allegiance is to the Soviet Union. If you disagree with certain aspects of the system, you can fight if from within.'

Jakob laughed aloud. 'With what can you fight?' he asked. 'With free elections? With open protests? Why, if you open a dissenting mouth in this place, you get clapped into gaol. And even if you keep your mouth shut, you're not safe. Look at me. All I did was to go on the metro.'

'Yes,' Aaron said quietly. 'But whom were you going to see?'

Jakob wondered whether he should argue with him. He wondered whether it was simply a question of political differences. Whether Aaron sincerely believed in his argument or whether it was a cover-up to protect his own livelihood and reputation. But was it even that, Jakob thought. Was Aaron so cold that he could value his reputation above his sibling concern? Or was it more than that. Much more. Was it a self-hate, one that had been born all those years ago, when their parents had turned their backs on the drive-way of the Bindel home in Leipzig? Had such self-hate been nurtured in those years in the dark attic in Halle, and sprouted into full and poisonous flower when Inge and Hans had gently confirmed their orphanhood? And if all that were true, when in the name of God would his brother forgive God and His dark and mysterious ways? He put his hand on Aaron's arm.

'Do you love me, brother?' he asked.

Aaron raised his foot from the clutch and put the car into a jerky forward motion. He pressed the accelerator, revving the engine, so that its noise would drown his brother's simple plea, and the shrieking silence of his own reply. Jakob let his question hover, for no amount of engine noise could mute its elemental quest. For that was the only question that mattered between them, and both of them knew it, and knew too that politics and repute were only avenues of postponement, of detour, desperate clothing for their own nakedness that neither could show to the other. Not even myself, Jakob thought. Not even I can declare my love for him, for his own rigid reticence stills my tongue.

They drove in silence. After a while, Jakob asked, 'How is your work?' He did not want totally to estrange himself from his brother and he could only maintain contact on levels which were non-partisan. But even as he asked the question, he realised that there was little neutrality in the subject of Aaron's research projects, and again as so often with his brother, he regretted the question. But Aaron skirted its grey overtones.

'It's exciting,' he said. 'There's an American immunologist arriving next week. We're working on the same lines. I'm really looking forward to meeting him.'

Jakob noticed how his brother's body slowly relaxed, how the muscles of his face were less taut. He was even smiling, safe in that area of his life that he could happily deal with.

'How will you manage for money, Jakob?' he asked.

The rare use of his name indicated to Jakob yet another easy area for his brother and he anticipated an offer of financial help.

'I could let you have some money,' Aaron said.

Jakob smiled. As long as you had it, money was the easiest thing on earth to give, and the most comfortable, for it squared the conscience and took little time. The essence of generosity was the giving of one's time, of sharing one's thoughts and spirit, pursuits that for Aaron were alien and unexplored.

'Thank you,' Jakob said. 'But Deborah is still working. And I have some savings. They will keep us for a while. I have money, too, that won't be touched. Enough for our fares to Israel.'

'Will you get another job?'

'I shan't look for one,' Jakob said. 'I'm not planning any future in this country. I'm going to spend all my time and energy getting our visas. You could help, you know,' he added quietly.

There was no response, and Jakob turned angrily towards him. '*Why* won't you let us go?' he asked, but again, both brothers knew that it was no question, but simply a confirmation of the no-man's land between them.

As they approached the district where he lived, Jakob noticed again how his brother kept glancing in the driving-mirror. 'Thank you for meeting me, Aaron,' he said, for he was again conscious of the risk his brother had taken.

Aaron pulled up well beyond Jakob's apartment block. Jakob made no comment.

'Thank you,' he said, and he struggled to get out of the car, delaying his movements a little to give Aaron time to suggest another meeting. But Aaron was silent.

'Goodbye,' Jakob said. 'And thanks again.'

Aaron drove off in silence, and as Jakob crossed the road, he had to stop to let a car pass, a KGB car that had taken off from the kerb in shadow of his brother. Jakob watched both cars out of sight and again he felt grateful for his brother's visit.

He expected to find the apartment empty, and would be glad of it, to rest himself, and to make himself more presentable by the time Deborah came back from work. But as he put the key in the door, he heard her singing from the kitchen. He opened the door and called her name. She rushed out to greet him.

'Jakob,' she cried. 'What have they done to you?' She held his face in her hands.

'I'm all right,' he said. 'I've seen a doctor. Nothing broken and the swellings will go down in a few days.' He held her close and, knowing the answer, he asked. 'Why aren't you at work?'

'For the same reasons as you.' She smiled. 'They fired me a week ago. It's nice, being out of work,' she said, leading him into the living-room. 'It gives me time to clear up the mess those thugs leave after their visits.'

He looked round the room. It was tidy enough, over-tidy in fact, but without the usual signs of their living and loving: the books, strewn on the table; the records, half-expectant from their sleeves. He looked at the book-shelves and they were denuded, as was the table that had once held the turntable and speakers.

'They took the equipment,' Deborah said. 'They said it could all be used for Hebrew linguaphone. They took our Hebrew books and lots of others too. The Beethoven symphonies as well,' she laughed. 'I suppose they're dangerous too.'

'When?' he said, enraged at the intrusion.

'The night they arrested you. They didn't lose any time.'

'Where were the children?'

'In bed. They slept through it all.'

'What did you tell them in the morning?'

'The truth. Where you were and why. It's better that they know everything.'

'Has there been trouble at their school?' Jakob asked, sickened by the sudden memory of Isay Salmon and how he had been scape-goated for his father's so-called treachery.

'So far, nothing,' Deborah said. She looked at him. 'Oh Jakob, how much longer will we have to wait?'

He took her in his arms. 'Cry,' he said. 'Cry it out. We must not smother our feelings. We may have to wait a long time, and we must not allow the waiting to drive us mad. So cry,' he urged her. 'I'm home and we have each other.' He held her for a long time. Then, 'Aaron met me outside the prison,' he said.

'I don't want to hear his name.'

'He's in trouble, I think,' Jakob said. 'He's being followed.'

'Of course he's being followed,' Deborah said, But not like you. He's being protected. He's one of their token Jews.'

That thought had not occurred to Jakob but even now that Deborah had suggested it, he gave it little credence. Aaron's kinship with his brother had in itself stained his reputation. They were watching him to decipher the nature of that kinship, its intensity and its endurance. By interfering at all with his visa-application, Aaron had made a great mistake, for he had publicly acknowledged that kinship, and had taken a stand. Had he ignored it, he would possibly not have been suspect. Perhaps now, Aaron regretted his intrusion, but to recant at this stage would have drawn greater attention towards himself. Jakob felt very sorry for him. 'I think he regrets what he's done,' Jakob said.

'That's easily remedied,' Deborah argued. 'He could withdraw his letter and give you permission.'

'Then he'll have the same harassment as us,' Jakob said. He did not want to talk any more about Aaron, and he let Deborah lead him to the bed and gently undress him.

'You must rest,' she said. 'Tell me what it was like in prison.' He was glad that she had asked him, as he would have been displeased had Aaron made the same enquiry. He felt the need to talk about it, to share it with another person, to record it and thus give it credence, for he was already doubting the silent events of the last fifteen days. He told it to her in as accurate a sequence as he could fashion, but days that were filled with silences and non-events did not lend themselves easily to accurate chronology. He had an idea that Deborah was not listening, that she had asked him the question simply for his own sake, that she had understood that he had to record it, in detail, else retrospective fantasy might blur the edges of the truth. When the story was told, she let him sleep, and then she phoned Inge and Ivan and invited them over that evening for supper. From Jakob's loyal defence of his brother, she sensed he had need for family, and Inge, with her love, untrammelled by expectation, would be solace for him.

That evening, she kept the children up for supper. At that time, in the summer of 1970, in the first year of their father's application, they were eight and nine years old. Jakob hoped that the remainder of their childhood would be spent in Israel, and that, in their manhood, they would inherit in the land of their fathers. We shall all be going home, he thought. Perhaps old Grandpa Jakob's litany from the Odessa tavern would be obsolete once and for all. For surely home was no battle-ground for survival. That arena lay in the Exile. Home was safe. Home was for living. He raised his glass to the company around the table. 'Next year in Jerusalem,' he said, and with such fervour and confidence that it was difficult to gainsay him.

CHAPTER THIRTY

That Jerusalem toast, unfulfilled, tolled the passing of many years. Hans and Benjamin, the Bindel brothers of the sixth traceable generation, remained in the land of their buried forefathers and lived out their childhood there. It had been seven years since Jakob Bindel had first applied for an exit visa, and his brother Aaron's veto still stood. But soon there would be a greater threat to their departure. Unless the Bindel brothers could get a study deferment, they would, in two or three years, be eligible for conscription, and as children of refuseniks, study-deferment was likely to be denied them. Jakob and Deborah hid their panic from others. They maintained an outward face of optimism but, in private and alone, they gave way to their despair. Money was short. Their savings had dwindled. Over the years, Jakob had taken a variety of menial jobs, but even from these he was fired as soon as as his employers felt the pressure of the KGB. But their nest-egg for travel remained intact. Untouchable. From time to time, Aaron offered them money but Deborah had seen the offer as a purge for his guilt, and she would not give him that release.

At that time, Jakob had been unemployed for three months, and the ominous threat, the newly-invented charge of 'parasitism' hung over him, that charge that related to continuous unemployment, a state intolerable in a Communist society.

One morning, Jakob set out on his usual search for work, when he was picked up by two security officers and taken to the district court. His appearance was immediate and brief. The charge was parasitism and the magistrate gave him fifteen days to find employment or to suffer the consequences, and he hinted at the same time that, since the accused's political record bordered on the subversive, those consequences might be very severe.

Jakob was desperate. The penalty for parasitism was prison and, in some cases he had heard of, a term in a labour camp. The thought of a further postponement of his emigration and a separation from his family filled him with a profound despair, and out of that desperation, he went to Aaron to ask for his help. There was always a vacancy as a menial in the various laboratories of a teaching hospital and, though it cost a great deal of Jakob's pride to ask a favour of his brother, he was confident that Aaron, for the sake of his own conscience, would oblige. When he entered the laboratory, he was relieved to find Aaron alone. Aaron was glad to see his brother, and since there were no witnesses, he was effusive in his welcome. 'I hope at last you've come for money, Jakob,' he said.

Jakob shook his head. 'I want a job,' he said simply, coming to the point of his visit straight away.

'What kind of job?' Aaron was on his guard.

'Something here. In a laboratory, I thought. Anything.'

He saw his brother stiffen.

'I'm desperate, Aaron,' he said.

'I'd rather give you money.'

'I don't want money,' Jakob fairly shouted. 'Money won't help me. You know the charge of parasitism.'

'I can't help you,' Aaron said. 'It's impossible for you to work here.'

Jakob stared at him. His flat and swift refusal brooked no argument or pleading, and Jakob deeply regretted that he had asked at all. He had seen very little of his brother in the past few years. Jacob did not wish for complete estrangement from Aaron, but now the bonds of their brotherhood were sorely stretched. He turned and made for the door.

'Are you sure you don't want any money?' Aaron almost pleaded with him.

Jakob turned, and looked at him with disdain. 'I pity you, brother,' he said.

For a while Jakob walked aimlessly about the streets, envying those who went about their business. He didn't know where to turn. He joined a long queue of people outside a shop to give the appearance that he was doing something, and while he stood there, he made a sudden decision to give up the struggle. He would go straightway to the OVIR offices, withdraw his application for exit visas, and confess the folly of his ways. He would resign himself and his family to a safe if joyless future in a land not of his choosing. And never, never again would he set eyes on his brother.

He left the queue and made for the OVIR offices, and he noticed how his body sweated, and how his pace accelerated, translating the fever of his limbs. It all seemed to be happening outside himself as if he were viewing a stranger's raving. He watched himself jostle people aside, he heard his loud exaggerated apologies, he thought he was probably laughing, though his body was buckled in a silent coiled scream. In his mind he heard the rehearsal of his confession. 'I'm sorry. I was foolish. I can't imagine why I ever thought of leaving. There is no country in the world freer or fairer than the one in which I am privileged to live.'

He noticed how people stared at him as he made his demented mouthing way through the streets. By the time he reached Kolpachny Lane, his skin was crawling with the worms of his deception.

The office was crowded with renegade applicants, and Jakob was silenced by the sight of them. His eyes slowly focused on Volodya, sitting behind his desk, his face wreathed in a contemptuous smile. He was talking to an old Jew, who was hunched over his desk, in a tone of infinite disdain. 'My son's in Israel,' the old man was pleading. 'I want to join him.'

Jakob rushed towards the desk, pushing past those who were waiting. Volodya looked up at him. 'Bindel,' he said wearily. 'Again? You'll have to take your disgusting turn.'

'No,' Jakob said. The sweat was streaming down his face, and he drew his sleeve across it, then examined the material, and noted with some bewilderment that the sleeve was dry. 'No,' he shouted. 'I've got something to say. I've got something to say,' he kept saying.

'Well say it for God's sake,' Volodya said.

'I've got something to say,' Jakob faltered. 'I know I've got something to say.' In his raving mind he knew it, and he knew too that what he had to say had nothing to do with his street-rehearsal. 'Listen to me,' he whispered. 'Listen to me,' Over and over again he said it, until a woman, sniffing the fever on him, took his arm gently and led him outside onto the street. 'Listen to me,' he kept saying, and she left him there, leaning against a lamp-post, craving audience. And they gathered, one by one, hearing the pleading in his voice and the promise of an earnestness and urgency of his message. And as the crowd grew, so did the volume of Jakob's plea. He viewed the blurred sea of faces before him, and prophet-like he thundered into their midst. 'Listen to me,' and his voice was a trumpet, a last post for his despair. 'We are living in a cursed land,' he shouted. 'A land without freedom. A land of torture and oppression. A land where men are in chains.'

The crowd thinned suddenly, terrified to be caught eavesdropping on such subversion. They panicked, tumbling over each other, anxious to flee that polluted area, until within seconds it was emptied, but vibrating still with his perilous and passionate syllables of dissent. But Jakob Bindel no longer needed audience. He needed only himself as an ear, to hear his own shame that he had, even for one moment, been tempted to desert his cause, an ear to hear and to bear his rage, an ear to echo the Aaron-hate in his heart.

'No country is free if you cannot leave it,' he thundered across the streets. 'I want to leave. I want to go to Israel with my family,' he cried. 'Let me go. Let me go.'

And in his sobbing plea for freedom, he was rudely taken. Two security officers, who had all the while been listening as they stood at the entrance to OVIR, grabbed him, one on each side, and bundled him into a car that had silently pulled up at the kerb. The crowd that had fled to the sidelines now re-assembled for the kill, their anger and fear giving way to pity. 'He's mad, poor devil,' was the general murmur amongst the crowd, though some there were who had heard an unerring ring of truth in his words, and who pondered on the nature of insanity.

In the back of the car, Jakob settled himself between his two guards. He made no protest. A surge of relief welled through him, that he had said all that he needed to say, and that the fever had left him. He tried to recall in detail that series of events since he had left his brother in the laboratory, but they were confused in his mind. But above all that confusion, he was aware of a sudden sense of freedom, that freedom that belongs to those who have nothing more to lose.

They took him to the police-station and to the cells with which he was now familiar, and he had a strange sense of home-coming, as if the natural dwelling of the freedom that he felt was behind bars. Now he leaned with ease against those bars, and re-capped once again on the events of his day. It was not yet over, but in the course of a few hours, he felt that he had aged many years. In the short time since he had left home in his daily pursuit for work, he had flirted with hate, treachery and madness. He examined each of them, and each in their chronological order, for Aaron had first to be dealt with, since the burden of that hate outweighed all other considerations. Now he no longer needed to disguise his hatred of his brother, nor to chastise himself for it, nor to find any excuses for Aaron's behaviour. He had asked for his brother's help, and his brother, for whatever irrelevant reasons, had turned his back. 'I hate him,' Jakob whispered aloud. 'I shall never see him again.'

He shuddered with fear for his future. He needed desperately to see someone, someone to whom he could explain his aberrations. But no, he mustn't use that word, nor even think about it, for that was a terrible charge, and its penalties inhuman. But he knew from past arrest-experience that he could ask to see nobody, that in the course of the day, towards tea-time, when the children would come home from school, Deborah would begin to wonder where he was. She would make a few coded telephone calls to friends, and then, with her arrogance-wrapped fear, she would go to the police-station and learn what had befallen him. Then she would go to Inge for comfort, and it would be Inge who would tell Aaron. And it would be Aaron who would tell nobody how he had turned his back on his brother. Let him live with that, Jakob thought, and with the consequences of his neglect whatever they might turn out to be. But of those he dared not think, because they made of Israel a pipedream, and of his family's future a nightmare. He paced his cell to give himself something to do, measuring its length with his tread. But soon he saw the pointlessness of that pursuit, for it was hardly worth his while to familiarise himself with this dwelling for he knew it would not be his for long. As he was pacing, a warder came to his cell with a bowl of soup and a hunk of bread, and instructed him to eat, for there would be nothing until after his examination. The word was ominous. Examination was not trial. It was a word that pertained to medical care, an area so dark in the Soviet legal system that it could not bear scrutiny.

'What examination?' he dared to ask.

'You'll see,' the warder said and he locked the cell door after him.

Jakob had not eaten all day and, until the warder's announcement, he had longed for some food. But now his appetite had evaporated. He looked at the thin gruel that the warder had placed on the floor and he toyed with it with the metal spoon. A slither of onion and cabbage floated in the greasy water, and a knob of mutton that he knew was inedible. He forced it down, together with the bread, for he knew that hunger must be assuaged by whatever means, for hunger could unhinge a man's mind. But that thought too, was not permissible. It belonged to that area of examination that the warder had promised him. He nibbled on the hunk of bread, chewing it slowly, and he tried to clarify his thoughts in preparation for the examination to come. But he knew how futile that was, that clarity of mind in this society had nothing to do with sanity, that here, in the land of freedom and equality, dissent was a diagnosable disease, and there were plenty of dissenting words still echoing in Kolpachny Lane, to prove his malignancy. He felt already condemned with no means of self-defence.

Shortly after his so-called lunch, they came for him. He did not bother to ask where they were taking him. He did not want to give them the satisfaction of ignoring his enquiry. In any case, he didn't want to know. It would only add to his fear. But he knew shortly enough and his fears were confirmed.

The police van drew up at a large building which Jakob recognised as the Serbsky Institute of Forensic Psychiatry. Even had he not known it, its perilous purpose was blazoned across the entrance portal. I am sane, he kept whispering to himself as they shoved him in through the door. I am sane. But he knew that norms were different in this place, that what he had shouted in the streets, were words of disordered reason, unseasoned in this time and place, signals to a raving mind that should, for its own and society's sake, be safely put away.

There were three doctors in the examining room, and they

treated him with courtesy. The preliminaries were as Jakob expected: blood pressure, pulse, heart, all formal postponements of the serious business of diagnosis. Although they kept their findings to themselves, moving aside occasionally and whispering to each other, Jakob was in no way worried about his physical condition. He knew he was fit, and that all his bodily functions were in good trim. He knew too, that findings in that area were irrelevant to the charge for which they had to find symptoms. They asked him to sit down opposite them and he placed his chair at the end of the table to avoid the triple wall of accusation. Aslant, the view of them was not so formidable. The doctors saw his move as significant, and one of them noted it on the pad before him. Jakob knew it was a bad mark, and would do well as a sign of the category of madness they had designed for him. They would interpret his manoeuvre as fear, lack of self-assertion, a need to conceal himself, out of an obsession that he was being pursued. All that would do very nicely for the diagnosis of paranoia, which medical condition they probably had in mind for him. He realised that whatever he said or did would have nothing to do with the cause or the truth of it. and that all would be tailored to fit the unspoken, unwritten order from the authorities.

In front of the central doctor was a written document which he now perused. After a while, he looked up at Jakob and said, 'It appears you think there is no freedom in our country.'

It was a question and he waited for a reply. Jakob knew that to answer in the affirmative would be an outright self-condemnation on political grounds. An answer in the negative would point to his mental instability, for if he said it, how could he not think it? There was no safe way to reply. So he remained silent.

'Yes or no?' the doctor asked.

'I'm not sure,' Jakob whispered. He thought it was the safest thing to say, and again the note-taking doctor scribbled on his pad. Another appropriate symptom, Jakob thought.

'Tell me something,' the interrogating doctor continued his probing. 'What were we fighting against in the last war?'

'Fascism,' Jakob said, safe in the knowledge that that answer could in no way incriminate him.

'And what were we fighting *for*?' He paused. 'Was it freedom?' he asked him, giving his patient a clue.

Jakob nodded. He did not trust his words any more.

'Did we win?' the doctor asked.

Again Jakob nodded and again the doctor smiled. 'Well,' he said, 'if we were fighting for freedom, and we won, then we have freedom.' He paused. 'No?' he enquired.

Unanswerable. Jakob held his head and his tongue. He could not help but admire their brand of logic that could be fashioned to sentence anybody of any crime.

The doctor consulted the document once more. '*We live in a land of torture and oppression,*' he quoted from Jakob's speech. 'Torture? Oppression? Where is there torture and oppression?'

No. He would not answer that one, Jakob decided, neither with word nor gesture. Only silence could cover that reply, and again that lack of response was misjudged on the doctor's pad.

'Do you remember the last dream you had?' the third doctor opened his mouth for the first time. It was clearly his job to pose the only question that was marginally related to a psychiatric investigation. Automatically Jakob shook his head. He knew better than to offer any material for their partisan interpretation. Again the scribbling doctor made a note on his pad. Jakob imagined his diagnosis. *The patient did not remember his last dream. Amnesia? Unfit to plead.*

'That's all,' the central doctor said suddenly, rising from his chair. The examination was over. It had taken them less than twenty minutes to diagnose their patient's mental aberrations, and in the course of that twenty minutes only one token question pertained to a man's state of mind. The whole charade was a mere formality for the benefit of court evidence.

The warders bundled him back into the van and returned him to his cell. This time they gave him his convict's uniform, as if he had already been tried and sentenced. For a whole week he languished there, ignorant of anything that took place outside his cell. Each day he waited for someone to come and read a charge to him and to tell him the date of his trial. Every day he asked his warder if there were any news, and the warder said he knew nothing, and in the strict hierarchical privilege of the Soviet legal system Jakob believed him.

At the end of the week, the warder came to his cell and told him he had a visitor. Jakob was overjoyed at the prospect of seeing somebody, anybody who could give him news of the progress of his charge. But above all, painful as it would be for both of them, he wanted to see Deborah. The warder took him to the visitor's room, and there she sat, behind the table, with an officer standing at her side. Her face was pale and she looked frightened. Not of the guards or the prison. Jakob knew that, but of the knowledge that she held and feared to impart, because she could barely look at him as he came towards her. She stood up as he approached and he went to embrace her. But the guard held out his hand.

'No touching,' he said.

Jakob snatched at her hand and kissed it. He desperately needed some contact with her body, however small. The guard overlooked the gesture and told him to sit down.

'How are you?' he whispered. 'How are the children?' They appeared to him to be very personal questions and he did not want the guard to hear.

'No whispering,' the guard said.

'I'm fine,' Deborah said in a loud protesting voice. 'And the children too. They send their love, and all our friends,' she stressed. 'They wish you well.'

Am I ill then? Jakob feared. And if so, with their positive messages, are they wishing me recovery?

'When is the trial?' he asked.

And it was then that she turned her eyes from him, and the pallor returned to her face.

'When is it?' he asked again.

She looked up at him. 'It's over,' she said. 'I've just come from the court.'

'But I wasn't there,' he shouted. 'I wasn't told. I had no lawyer.'

'Yes,' she said. 'You had a defence lawyer.'

'But I never met him,' Jakob practically screamed. Now the charge and his sentence seemed very secondary to the gross injustice of his trial and it seemed now almost irrelevant to enquire about the judgement that had been passed on him.

'What was the charge?' he asked wearily.

'Anti-Soviet agitation.'

He trembled. From the despair on Deborah's face, he knew he had been found guilty, and in his mind he catalogued the punishments for such a crime. Banishment, a long prison-term, or detention in a labour camp. All were unthinkable. He was afraid to know his sentence. If only he could hold Deborah's hand. Her fingers were creeping along the table towards him. At the same time, she looked up at the guard, begging his permission, and he, knowing the terrible words that she had to say to him, nodded and looked away. She took his hand and caressed it against her cheek.

'They judged you insane,' she whispered. 'The doctors said you suffered from creeping schizophrenia.'

Out of Jakob's mouth came a sound that a listener, who did not know its source, would construe as laughter, but in truth there was little amusement in it for it was compounded of derision, fear and total disbelief. But fear most of all, as he slowly understood that they could not send him to prison for his lunacy, nor a labour camp. Nor into exile. A far far worse fate awaited him, because there need never in his lifetime be any end to it. 'What will become of me?' His voice broke on the question, and he gripped her hand.

'They're sending you to a psychiatric hospital. It's in Minsk,' she added wearily, for she knew that its location would make little difference to the pain of his sentence.

'For how long?' he asked as if to punish himself further, for he knew that there was no time-limit on such a judgement.

'Until you're better,' she said.

He stared at her. For a moment he feared that she might really have believed in their judgement. 'But I'm not ill,' he shouted.

She nodded her head.

'I know,' she said, and she gripped his hand, and that certainty of hers heartened him, for he himself had, for a moment, become unsure of his lucidity.

'When are they taking me?' he whispered.

She could barely answer, but she kept her sad eyes upon him. 'Now,' she said.

Jakob looked up at the guard, who once again nodded and turned away. Then he stood and took Deborah in his arms.

'Soon we shall all be together again,' Deborah said.

That Bindel phrase once more, and she, not even a Bindel.

'I love you,' Jakob said. He held her close for a while, until the guard tapped his shoulder. Then he held her at arm's length. 'Kiss the children,' he said.

'Next year in Jerusalem,' she whispered.

Then they took him away, and she was glad that he did not turn again to look at her.

He held the Jerusalem toast in his ears, and her sad face in his eyes, and the taste of her lips on his own, and there they would all remain until they were together again.

*

When Deborah reached home, she was relieved that the children were not there. They were with Inge. Now on her own, Deborah was able to give release to those tears that all day had seethed behind her eyes, during Jakob's mock trial, the prison visit, and the final separation. Once inside her front door, she let the tears flow, and with no preamble. No chair for her comfort, no support for her pain, but standing in the small hallway, and still in her hat and coat. Her heart-break needed no setting, no backdrop, no direction. Simply timing, and that she had rehearsed the long day through. She knew that she must wring out her sorrow, just this one time, and then, dry-eyed, she could face her children, and together they would weather the years of separation. As she wept she reached into her pocket for a handkerchief and felt the familiar fidgettings of her mice. Moses and Aaron. She took them out and let them scurry about her hand, and as she watched them she knew that they were no longer part of her. They did not belong to the woman she had become, that person who, in this one long and terrible day, had aged a hundred years. They belonged to the days of her poetry and

Mayakovsky Square and a freedom of a sort. They had no place in a cold and mean psychiatric ward that her vicarious world had now become. She took them into the kitchen. In the far corner between the skirting and the floor was a regular mousehole, a legitimate sortie for food forage in the winter months. Somewhere beyond the skirting, there must be a colony, and Moses and Aaron, with initial astonishment, would find their own tribe. She slipped them both into the opening, and they were gone before she had time to mourn them. She returned to the hallway and took off her hat and coat. The long plait slipped from her beret, and in the mirror she suddenly saw it as a foreign graft on her person. That too, like Moses and Aaron, belonged to another country, another time, a strange anachronism in her present self-reflection. She took a pair of scissors from the drawer and, without style or production, she cut it off, plaited as it was, and she wondered where to put it. She knew that if she kept it, tissued in some drawer, it would be an invitation to nostalgia and perhaps regret. Unlike mice, there was no natural habitat for one's own child-hood. Except in the mind. So she wrapped it quickly and threw it in the dustbin, stuffing it into the rubbish, beyond retrieve. And so Deborah buried her childhood, casting off the last defence of her despair.

That evening, she took her sons in her arms and told them what had happened to their father. She explained it all, and she told them, too, as much of the Bindel history as she had learned from Jakob, for all of it was relevant to their present dilemma. But she did not mention the inheritance. There would come a time for that telling, and the story would be told by Jakob.

*

In time, the story of Jakob's arrest reached Aaron and he went to see his father-in-law. His relationship with Mr Koskin was cordial but distant. As a high government official, Koskin was host to many parties in his sumptuous apartment in the Hotel Ukrainia, but Aaron was never invited. Indeed Koskin discouraged any visits, pleading Party business. But he would often go and see his daughter in her own apartment, and he made a point of visiting during laboratory hours, when Aaron wasn't there. But on the rare occasions that they did meet, Koskin was polite and reticent. But Aaron knew his father-in-law kept an eye on him, and if not his own, then those of his minions, for how often in the driving-mirror of his car had he seen them following him. Only once had Mr Koskin directly referred to his reservations concerning his son-in-law's family. He had commented on Jakob's application for an exit-visa with some disgust, and had hinted that it might well

448

jeopardise Aaron's career if he did not do something quite positive to show which side he was on.

But he had had nothing to do with Aaron's letter of veto. That had been Aaron's own idea, and he had written it with little thought of the consequences. When the government grant had come his way, he desperately tried to find other reasons for their generosity, but in truth he could not help feeling ashamed. Thereafter things had gone completely out of control, and at times he hated Jakob for having forced him into such an equivocal position. Now that anger was transferred to his father-in-law.

He rang the bell of his apartment with a certain fury and, as he heard its echo, he realised that he had made no appointment and, even if he had, his father-in-law would have suggested another venue. It was not a good beginning. Koskin was surprised to see him, but less displeased than Aaron had anticipated, for he was alone and seemingly unbusy. Yet his manner was businesslike.

'There's something you want to discuss?' he asked, leading him into the drawing-room.

'My brother is in trouble,' Aaron said, coming to the point straight away.

'I know,' Koskin said. 'I know all about it. But I wouldn't call it trouble. Your poor brother is ill. He's very fortunate that he will receive treatment. In time he will be cured.'

'There's nothing the matter with my brother,' Aaron screamed at him.

'I would be grateful if you kept your voice down,' Koskin ordered in measured tones. 'I am not to blame for your brother's madness. I'm sorry for him, of course. It is especially hard on relatives to have to accept a strain of insanity in their blood. It worries me too. Believe me, it worries me for Heidi.'

'You're crazy,' Aaron whispered.

Koskin ignored that comment, or perhaps he didn't hear it. 'Take heart,' he said. 'Your brother will get better. We have cured dissidents before.'

'You cannot really believe in the bottom of your heart that dissidence is a mental disease?'

'What else?' Koskin said. 'How else can one describe it? We live in a society of equality and freedom. If one speaks out *against* equality, against justice, against freedom, then surely one is deranged. What is normal about injustice, inequality, imprisonment?'

Aaron opened his mouth to argue with him, but then he realised that his father-in-law was totally sincere in his belief. He had come to plead with Koskin to engineer Jakob's freedom. Now, there seemed no logic in that plea. Nevertheless, he could not go away without asking for some concession.

449

'Can't you use your influence?' he asked.

'To do what?'

'To free him, of course,' Aaron said, his voice raised once more.

'Do you want your brother to get better?' Koskin asked. He put his hand on Aaron's shoulder in a first-time gesture of contact with the man who had married his daughter. 'Believe me,' he said, 'he's in the best of hands. One year, maybe two, and he'll be amongst us again. We mustn't blame him, Aaron,' he said. 'That's the trouble with mental illness. We think it's their fault and we want to punish them. But it is an illness like any other. If I caught pneumonia, you wouldn't blame me, would you?'

Again the logic, Aaron thought, and again based on a totally illogical premise.

'But if you could get his release,' Aaron begged, 'I could talk to him. I could make him withdraw his application for a visa. He could go back to work and become a normal Soviet citizen.' Whatever that meant, Aaron thought. He heard the futility of his argument, and he heard too how he diminished his brother by assuming that his waywardness was abnormal. It was Koskin and his kind who were crazy, brain-washed and brain-stormed.

'Curing a disease is a professional job,' Koskin was saying. 'We should leave it to the professionals. I know it's hard on you,' he said, touching his shoulder once more, but now Aaron felt it not as a gesture of sincere concern, but the ungentle touch of a KGB official. Had he imagined it, or was there a small hint of pressure in Koskin's touch, a pressure that had nothing to do with affection, but which bore the weight of warning? He was relieved when he took his hand away.

He got up to leave. There was no point in prolonging the meeting. In any case, he wanted to be by himself for a while to decide what he must do. For he had to do something. He wished now he'd never sent that letter of veto, but now, with Jakob incarcerated for an indefinite time, there would be little point in withdrawing it. He recalled their last meeting in his laboratory. In his mind he went over it in the greatest detail, and he knew that his rejection of his brother, had, for a while, unhinged his reason. There was no doubt in his mind that he himself was entirely to blame. He must somehow make amends. But how? He had to accept that there was no way in which he could help his brother. He could offer his support to Deborah and the children, but she would, with good reason, reject it. He could ask his father-in-law to use his offices to get him a visitor's permit to the hospital and perhaps talk to the doctors there. He did, after all, have some standing in the medical profession. But he had heard from various sources, and with little surprise, that the doctors at the prison hospital were employed by the MVD and the KGB, and answerable to those authorities. Their diagnosis and their treatment were conditioned by their direction. In any case, it was more than likely that Jakob would refuse to see him.

He found himself nearing Mayakovsky Square. He rarely visited that quarter of the city, and he found it strange that, as he was walking and deliberating with himself, his steps should have taken him to the scene of Hans' death. Certainly he had not been near the square since Hans had died. Perhaps he had been avoiding it, but now it seemed to him to be the right setting for his deliberations and for some form of self-confrontation. For he knew that he was powerless to do anything about Jakob and he had to deal with the pain of that conclusion.

He sat on the stone steps beneath the statue on the Square. He wondered at what spot Hans had made his sacrifice. He missed Hans terribly. His death had double-crossed him in orphanhood and sometimes he hated Hans as much as he hated his true father, and both for the same reason, that they had died on him. But Hans he could mourn and miss; his own father lay still uninterred in his heart. He knew as he sat there, with his mind full of questionings, that he was on the perilous brink of self-confrontation, a precipice he had assiduously avoided all his adult life. Now, at this time, and in this place, such confrontation was in season and without fear, and he took himself back to the attic in Halle, where his torment had begun, that dark breeding-ground of all his pain, of all that fury that had finally sent him to war with his brother.

He thought of Jakob, probably at this moment handcuffed to a guard, huddled on a train on his way to Minsk. Was it possible that the guard was like Koskin, that he too viewed his prisoner as a dangerous lunatic who must be cured of his irrational thought, whose mind the devil had entered and planted questions therein, questions that were not supposed to be asked? But he himself had sometimes, in secret, and in the dark, and in the still small hours of the morning, when he would awaken with sudden fear, he too would ask himself those questions, but unlike Jakob, he could not run the risk of their reply, and he would turn to the woman sleeping by his side, and put his arms about her for his comfort. And wonder who she was. For she was a stranger to him. And always would be. For the first time, he confronted his reasons for marrying Sonia and he knew that though he loved her, none of them had anything to do with loving, but that all of them were ammunition in the war against his brother, that man who had accepted the suffering of his tribe, that suffering that Aaron couldn't stomach; that man who had so peacefully accommodated his martyred inheritance, that inheritance whose words Aaron knew by heart, and each syllable of

451

which stuck in his throat. That sibling who had buried his past in his first move towards continuity. That brother of his. That offensive survivor.

Again he thought of Jakob on his cheated train journey into their thwarted terrain of recovery. He smiled to himself. He could be relied upon, that brother of his, to resist their cure. The devil's questions would not be dislodged from his heart. Yet he would survive. For if Jakob had any disease at all, it was that of survival, and for that condition, there was no known cure. As he thought of Jakob, he saw the train going through a tunnel, yet it was he himself who was in the dark, and in that darkness he felt tears behind his eyes, and he rose quickly from the steps and went on his blind way, because his self-confrontation was threatening to destroy him.

He picked up a passing taxi cab, and gave his home address. He knew he should go back to the laboratory. He had work to do there, work that until that time, had totally involved him, that work that was his own home-made second-hand survival-kit. Now he saw that weapon as futile, as unavailing as felling an oak with a razor-blade. He felt he had lost his footing. Or rather, that the ground itself was shifting. He needed to talk to Sonia, though he knew that such an encounter could well engender an earthquake.

She was surprised to see him, at that time of day, troubled too by the worried look on his face. 'Is anything wrong?' she asked.

Everything was wrong, he thought. He was wrong, she was wrong, their whole life together was wrong. Yet there was comfort in that mutual incompatibility. She was a million miles from his Bessarabian beginnings, but in that unspannable distance there was a frenzy of excitement. Above all she was a daughter of the KGB, and there was a fearful eroticism in the rotten stock from which she came. He held her to him.

'What's the matter, Aaron?' she said. Sonia was aware of the friction between the two brothers, but it was a subject that Aaron assiduously avoided, and she knew it was too raw to touch. But now she sensed that his unease lay in that quarter, and she asked, 'It is about Jakob?'

He wanted so much to tell her, but if he were to tell her the whole truth, she would hear their marriage crumble.

'I went to see your father,' he said.

She was surprised. There must be matter of some urgency if he had made such a call. He must have needed a favour, and to ask that of her father must have cost him some pride, and such a price would only be paid in the name of his brother.

'Is Jakob in trouble?' she asked.

So he told her the whole story. He didn't even hesitate to tell her how Jakob had come to him for a job and how he had refused to help. He was relieved that he was able to tell her that part of the story, for it was the one aspect of that self-truth that had been hardest to face in Mayakovsky Square.

'I am to blame,' he told her.

'No,' she said. 'What was he charged with?'

So he continued with his story, of the fraudulent psychiatric evidence, of the verdict and the judgement of the court. And when it was told, he turned to her and said,

'What do you think of all that, Sonia?'

He was asking her a simple direct question, without any loop-holes for escape or innuendo, for he felt it as basic and as elemental a question as 'Do you love me?' Which, in effect was exactly what he was asking. Its answer would determine the course of his future life. He hoped she would pause to consider before answering, that, in her consideration, she would understand the desperate import-ance of her response, and how much it could fray or ease their loving. But she did not hesitate as he held his breath.

'What can one think?' she said. 'Jakob is mad. I have always thought so, and thanked God that you were so different. But thank God too that he is in good hands. The Minsk Hospital is excellent, I have heard. In a year, two years maybe, he will be well. He'll be back at work and you two can live together in some kind of normal relationship. I know it's hard for you now, Aaron,' she said, 'but in a way it's a blessing that it's come to a head. Otherwise it would have been too late to cure him.'

He stared at her, astonished, yet unsurprised by what she had said. Her father's daughter. He went upstairs and packed a bag. As he folded his suits and his shirts, he was aware each moment of exactly what he was doing. He stowed his underwear in the separate compartment of the suitcase and checked that the drawers were empty. Then he left the room. As he closed the doors behind him, the thought came to him, that in that room they had together made Heidi, and it was his only thought that touched on nostalgia.

He stood at the door of the living-room, his suitcase in his hand.

'May I see Heidi once a week?' he asked. 'I could collect her on a Saturday.'

She stared at him, dumbfounded, astonished and bewildered by his move.

'What's the matter with you, Aaron?' She swallowed her words in her panic.

'Is it possible you don't know what is the matter?' he said quietly. Surely it was not possible, he thought. He stood there in the doorway, his body sweating with hatred. Was it possible she could not smell the stink of it upon him? He turned.

453

'I'll be here on Saturday,' he said. Then he left her. He stood for a while on the threshold of their apartment. His tears flowed freely now, and stung his cheeks with their truth. He knew that much had changed in his life that day, that priorities had shifted from their stubborn planting, that his past could no longer be denied, that the time was ripe at last for mourning. And for loving too.

CHAPTER THIRTY-ONE

The psychiatric colony of the Minsk hospital was once a prison. It is called a hospital for its implications of sickness and cure, but in effect it is an even more punitive institution than that of a prison. For once inside, the so-called patient loses all his legal rights. There is no avenue of protest, no machinery for redress. It is a place for toeing the line, for any protest only serves to confirm the initial and fraudulent diagnosis.

From his last incarceration, also fraudulent, Jakob Bindel remembered, above all, the silences, but in this place, if he should survive to recall it, it would be in the context of noise. Continuous noise, cacaphonic, demented. The treatment in the hospital, and its strident orchestration, was designed to drive its patients mad. He noticed the noise on his first entry, as his guard led him down the long corridor to the receiving quarters. He tried to isolate the sounds, and found that they came from no human source. There were clanging of keys, slamming of doors, a buzzing of bells, the discordant sounds of efficient and rigid administration.

He was led into the medical room for his initial examination. The doctor asked him to sit down and to make himself comfortable and Jakob was angered by his excessive politeness.

'Why am I here?' he asked. 'There's nothing the matter with my mind.'

The doctor picked up the charge-sheet. 'I see from here,' he said gently, 'that your views are socially dangerous. That's why you must be put away.'

'But my views have nothing to do with psychiatry,' Jakob said.

'It is part of your mental condition that you should think that way. You are a mathematician. That is your profession. To engage in other activities as you have done is a sign of a split dissociated personality. Your mind is split, Mr Bindel. You are rational and irrational at the same time. You dwell in fantasy and sometimes you cannot distinguish that from what is real. We call it schizophrenia.' He pronounced the word slowly as if he were speaking to a child. 'Once you change your political views, you will be cured. The cure is up to you, Bindel,' he said.

Jakob opened his mouth to comment on the utter stupidity of such an idea, but his instinct prompted him to hold his tongue. It warned him that to begin to argue on such a premise would give that premise some credence. That he must ignore their speeches and hold his tongue. And if possible, avoid their treatment.

But it was clear to him on arrival at the ward that such avoidance was impossible. A line of patients waited at the drug-trolley. A nurse handed a pill and a metal cup of water to the orderly beside him. The orderly would then place the pill on the patient's tongue and offer him the water. Then when the pill was presumably swallowed, he would examine the inside of the patient's mouth in case he had managed to avoid the dosage. With such a procedure, the doling out of drugs took some time, but the patients did not seem to mind the waiting. Indeed, some even appeared to be enjoying it, and later on in his stay, Jakob understood why. Because waiting for drugs, though intensively passive, was one of the few activities of the day. Jakob's guard showed him his bed, then pushed him into line and waited beside him, the order for his treatment in his hand. When, after an interminable wait, it was Jakob's turn, the warder handed the prescription to the nurse and left Jakob in his care. When his turn came, he asked the nurse what he'd been prescribed.

'You're new,' the nurse said with a smile. Old-timers knew better than to ask questions. 'Take it,' he said. 'It will make you well.'

He was on the point of declaring his perfect health, but such a declaration would have been taken as a common symptom of his illness. He took the pill obediently with a terrible fear that, by the time he got out of this place, he would be mad indeed.

When the trolley was wheeled out of the ward, Jakob took time to look around him and at his company. He hoped that amongst them might be a familiar face, one that he had met in Moscow in the various clandestine meeting-places where the refuseniks gathered. One or two of them seemed faintly familiar, but their shuffling gait and faintly zombie-like appearance obscured the particularities of their features by which Jakob could have identified them. One of the possibles was shuffling his way.

'We met at Victor's,' he whispered, and his speech was drawled, and with great effort.

Jakob held out his hand. 'Jakob Bindel,' he said.

'Grigory,' the man offered, but was clearly too tired or perhaps too unsure of his identity to offer anything further. There were so many questions that Jakob wanted to ask, but he could see from his friend's drawn and pale countenance that further conversation would have exhausted him. So he put his arm round his shoulder and squeezed it lightly, delighted that he had found a companion. Grigory put his hand on Jakob's and held it like a child. Then he led him slowly down the ward to his bed. He almost collapsed on it and motioned Jakob to sit by his side. They looked at each other for a while, and then with enormous facial effort it seemed, Grigory gave him a smile. Jakob tried to recall the details of their meeting. It had been some years ago, he thought, in the house of Victor Yakir, a refusenik, who since that time had been lucky enough to emigrate. There had been about half a dozen of them there, and he tried to recall the specific purpose of the meeting, and to locate Grigory in the kitchen where they were talking. Then he saw quite clearly in that picture a bearded man, slapping the table to make his point clear. A short brown beard he had, Jakob recalled, and a shock of brown curly hair. He was certain Grigory was that man, that man of fire, audacity and courage. He had never seen him again. He was told that he was in a labour camp for distributing illegal literature. Could this Grigory be the same? Jakob stared at him.

'Did you have a beard?' he asked.

Grigory nodded.

'And a shock of hair?' He looked at his almost hairless head with fear, and a faint hope that he was mistaken.

Grigory nodded and in his eyes he could see the faint flickering of the old fire.

'Were you in a labour camp?'

Again a nod.

'How long have you been here?' Jakob dared to ask.

'Two years,' Grigory answered slowly. And then, after a long pause, 'I think it's two years,' he said.

His slow unsure postscript was profoundly depressing, and Jakob raised his hand to his own head, stroking the hair gently as if he was touching it for the last time. He looked around the ward and was relieved to see some patients with a good enough head of hair, and some even had beards, but all seemed to share Grigory's vacant look. He noticed how some of them made moves to come towards him, but after a few steps in his direction, they would return to their cots, exhausted. He thought that later on he would do a round of the wards and talk to each patient in turn, while he was still physically able to move around with ease, but he knew that in time he would become exactly like them.

'What drug do they give us, Grigory?' Jakob asked.

'Triftazin,' Grigory said.

It was the only word that had rolled with ease off his tongue. He was more sure of it even than his own surname, for that identity in this place had become irrelevant. Of that former identity, that self that he had once known, there were now few traces, but of the drug, of triftazin, the evidence abounded, and tormented him day by every day.

'What's it for?' Jakob asked.

'Punishment.'

That word too rolled off the tongue. In his time, Grigory had been in prison, in a labour camp, and now in a psychiatric hospital. He was familiar with every facet of the Soviet penal system. He lay back on his cot and closed his eyes. 'Morning,' he drawled. 'Only time to talk.'

From that information Jakob deduced that the effects of the drug were less acute in the mornings. He looked around the ward and saw that most of the men appeared to be sleeping. It was only early afternoon and he wondered if all their days were spent like this one and how long a healthy mind could withstand such abuse. He did not know what to do with himself. He listened to the continuous din of administration noises. The patients seemed totally unaffected by them, the only bonus that the drug afforded. He walked to the end of the ward where the orderly had assigned him a bed. He felt a drowsiness creep over him but he tried to ignore it. He was imagining it, he decided. He had been affected by the other men's lethargy. Nevertheless he would sit on his bed, but not for long, in case his imagined drowsiness would lead to sleep. After a few minutes he forced himself to stand, but the action of pinning his feet to the floor called for great physical effort. His whole body was exhausted but he knew that it had nothing to do with fatigue. He was confident that if he lay on his cot, he would not allow himself to sleep the day away. I must not, he thought, because that way madness lies. He lay down and felt the weight of his eyelids, so heavy that they could not close. What in God's name am I doing here, he thought, and then that same survival instinct prompted him to speak those thoughts aloud and thus release them into the air, else they would gather in his head and ferment there, and in time addle his brain. 'What am I doing here?' he whispered aloud, dispersing that terrible thought into the air already polluted by other men's whispered fears. 'They will not drive me mad,' he said, over and over again, until he felt his tongue weighing heavily on the floor of his mouth. He longed for sleep, but he knew he must resist it, for sleep would swaddle his perilous thoughts into the cradle of his mind, and nurse and foster them there. 'I will not be driven mad,' he drawled. The effort to speak was painful, but he forced his declaration from his lips, over and over again. A nurse passed his bed, and watched and listened.

'Talking to yourself?' he said, his face benign with deduction.

Condemned, Jakob thought, but this thought he kept to himself, for to give it to the nurse would only confirm the diagnosis on the charge-sheet. He raised his feet on his cot, pushed his feet to the ground and forced himself to take a few steps. Slowly and with infinite effort, he ambled around the ward, but the weight of his eyelids was unbearable. He made for his cot again, lay back and put his hands over his eyes, as one would cover the stare of the dead. He felt them shutting and it was as if their closure had unturned the key of a projector, for it was then that the pictures began to run.

At first, as if in a pre-title sequence, he saw himself in Aaron's laboratory. In the background of his mind he could hear the hum of the projector that seemed to be intensified by the silent nature of the film. And the film was not only silent; it was in slow motion too, as Aaron turned his back on him in prolonged, interminable, unremitting rejection. Then the scene shifted suddenly to the attic in Halle, where he and Aaron, in the guise of Hermann and Heinrich, crouched silently on their beds, while below they carried the coffin of Hans' dead mother out of the front door. The film stuttered for a while as if a sprocket had broken, and then a big black car came slowly into focus. He sat with his brother in the back seat, and through the window he could clearly see his parents as they turned their backs and walked up the drive of the house. It is enough, it is enough, Jakob cried in his mind, but the film recall was relentless. Vienna station now, and the departing train that robbed them of their freedom. In the tunnel, the film went black, and it was then that the silence ceased. Hermann, Heinrich, he heard his mother calling, and Aaron and Jakob from the gentle lips of Grandpa Leon. Oh, if only these doctors knew how split I really am, Jakob thought, and he longed for his eyes to open, to blind him to his cleft past, for that re-run, in this place, he couldn't bear. He must have slept then, for the screen whitened and there was silence.

When he awoke, his body was light and his mind clear. He heard a bell ringing, and saw the men around him make their way to the drug trolley, the second drug round of the day. Their walk was sprightly and full of hope, and now would have been the time for talking. But the trolley waited, to slacken their steps, to numb their senses, to still their tongues.

He joined the line next to Grigory.

'How often do they drug us?' he whispered.

'Three times a day. 1 o'clock, 5 o'clock, 8 o'clock. Mornings are good here. Don't waste your talk now. In the morning we will be human for a while.'

Jakob took his turn with the others, resenting his own obedience. But he knew that any alternative would be to ask for trouble and that only mindless and blind obedience could work in this place, and that, if not overdone, would be the only behaviour from which they could draw no sinister conclusion. He straightened his back like a good boy, and took his medicine. Shortly afterwards, he was again overcome with drowsiness and his mouth was very dry. He asked for water, but it did not seem to assuage his thirst. He watched as the other men's gait slowly turned to a shuffle. Some sat on their beds, and stared with disgust at their ineffective feet that had lost their function. There was much sighing, and of a terrible resignation. He made for his cot and he lay there. And though he struggled against it, he entered once more the picture-house of his past. When the film had run its nightmarish course, he slept in the uneasy dark, and woke, purged and clear, once more to join the numbing line. After that last dosage of the day, they were given a supper of thin broth, a few sprats, and a hunk of bread, and though he was hungry, the effort needed to raise the spoon to his mouth was greater than his appetite. He put on the nightgown that the hospital had issued. It was white but stained with all the colours of sickness, mostly with the brown of despair. He wondered who had worn it before him, and whether he had died in it. Such thoughts were not conducive to sleep, which he now so craved, and he longed for a drug that would take his mind off his mind for the duration of his stay. He reached out for a mug of water, and in his trembling and fragile holding, it dribbled down his chin. He felt very old then, decrepit and disintegrating. But he did not give way to self-pity, because he knew, with that old Bindel survival instinct, that the loss of self-esteem was the beginning of despair, and perhaps even of the madness that they had prepared for him. In time, he fell into a mercifully dreamless sleep, and so ended his first day as a government-licensed lunatic.

*

When he awoke in the morning, he wondered where and why and who he was. He took his time with his considerations because he sensed that their outcome would be depressing, and when his fears were confirmed, he took some comfort in the clarity of his thoughts and knew that this was a state of mind to be savoured, every second of it, for it would not last for long.

He bounded out of bed and, looking round, saw that most of the men were already dressed and in conversation. He didn't want to miss one minute of it. There was so much he wanted to know, information that could only be gleaned from those who had experienced the hospital routine. He dressed quickly and went to join Grigory.

'Good morning, friend,' Grigory said as he approached. 'We meet for a short time in the land of the living. This is Yakov, Mikhail and Ilya.' He introduced the three men about him. 'All from Kiev,' Grigory went on. 'There was an epidemic of schizophrenia in Kiev a few years ago.'

'A few years?' Jakob asked, frightened. 'How long have you been in this place?'

'Two years,' Ilya said. 'All three of us. We came on the same day.'

'Yuri over there,' Grigory said, pointing to a man at the end of the ward, 'he's been here almost four years. He's very stubborn,' Grigory laughed. 'He just refuses to get any better.'

'What does better mean?' Jakob said.

'It depends,' Ilya said. 'Every six months they review your case. Then it's up to you.'

Jakob refrained from asking for a clarification of Ilya's last remark. He had a shrewd idea of what it meant, with its overtones of surrender and abdication. That's why these men had been here for two years or more. They were, in their own terms, stubborn. He skirted to safer ground and asked about the hospital routine.

'We go to the dining-room for a so-called breakfast,' Grigory said, 'and then there's an hour's exercise in the yard. Then a so-called lunch. Then after that we get on the old drug roundabout, and we don't come off till morning.'

'Is that all the treatment we have?' Jakob asked.

'It's enough,' Mikhail said. 'The less treatment we get, the better for our sanity. As it is, one can go mad in here.'

'Remember poor Evegny,' Ilya said.

Jakob used the time before breakfast to discover how they had come to this place and on what trumped-up charge. Their stories were similar. All of them were refuseniks, some of them of six years standing. All of them had been charged with anti-Soviet propaganda, and in each of their cases the court had been generous and declared them insane.

'How does one survive here?' Jakob asked.

'We have each other,' Grigory said.

Just then an orderly called them into line, shouting at them to hurry.

But the men took their time. Mornings and their clarity gave them the courage to dictate their own tempo as part of that self-assertion that soon enough, would be anaesthetised. There was a refreshing arrogance about their gait, and Jakob caught it and ambled at his leisure by their side. Then he was horrified to see the orderly crack a whip which he carried by his side. The men's pace quickened a little but, in some cases, not enough, and those whose courage outweighed their discretion felt the crack of it on their shins. Jakob saw their faces wince with pride and pain.

'But they're not allowed to do that,' he said to Grigory who walked by his side. 'We're supposed to be ill.'

'That's a dangerous thought, my friend, and you must put it from your mind if you are to survive. Whatever they choose to think, we are not ill. There is nothing wrong with our minds. We are saner than all of them.'

Jakob looked at the orderly and was unnerved by the uniform he was wearing. It was that of a convict, exactly the same as he himself had been obliged to wear during his silent prison-term.

'He's a convict, isn't he?' he whispered to Grigory.

'Yes. All the orderlies here are convicts,' he said. 'They're sent from prisons to work here. It's a plum job for them. They can beat us up as a change from being beaten themselves. And they do. Believe me, they do. Keep out of their way if you can.'

The line began to move and converge with the others on their way to the eating hall. There were about ten lines in all, and some of the men, Jakob noticed, looked very ill indeed, their bodies thin, and their faces yellow-pale, with hardly enough strength in their limbs to shuffle along the corridor. They frightened him, for they posed a picture of what he might in time become.

'Some of them look so ill,' he whispered to Grigory.

'They are,' Grigory said. 'Too long on the drugs. They have no mornings any more in their lives. They are riddled with lethargy.'

'Who are they?' Jakob asked.

'They are dissidents like us,' Grigory said. 'But they're not refuseniks. They don't want to leave this country. They want to right its wrongs. There are 100,000 political prisoners in the Soviet Union today, in labour camps, prisons, psychiatric hospitals. Only a small part of them are Jews. They just stick the Jews together.'

There were several long tables in the eating-hall, and at the end of it a counter where the meal was dispensed. Jakob took his turn in the line, holding the metal plate and the cup that the orderly had given him. When his turn came, he was given three sprats, a hunk of bread and a cup of thin gruel, together with his sugar ration for the whole day.

'Eat slowly,' Grigory said as they moved towards a table. 'It will satisfy you longer.'

An orderly was posted at each table, and he watched his charges with a superior eye. He was probably a thief or a murderer, Jakob thought, but probably in this place, and for the first time in his wretched life, he enjoyed a sense of being a class above the others, he who all his life, had slunk on the bottom untouchable rung of society. And he was going to make sure that these lunatics knew their place. He barked at them to hurry with their food, almost before they were seated on the benches. But the men took their time nonetheless, and most of them simply because they could not eat quickly. Their teeth were loose, or decayed perhaps from long lack of care, and their stomachs were shrunk to such proportions as to inhibit a swift intake of food. Indeed some of them, Jakob noticed, had difficulty in swallowing even the tiny rations they were allowed.

'We're not allowed to talk during exercise,' Grigory said. 'So tell me about yourself and why you are here. And after our walk, you can give all of us news of the outside.'

So Jakob told him his refusenik history, and as he unfolded the events, he found them more ridiculous and more incredible than he had viewed them at the time. But Grigory was not surprised. It was a tale similar to hundreds of others.

'I remember when I first came here,' he said, 'I thought I was unique. I was caught distributing the *Chronicle*. Like you, I was taken to the Serbsky Institute. They said I had paranoid delusions of reforming society and that I was suffering from something they called schizo-dissension. I thought they'd invented the word just for me. Then when I arrived here, it seemed to be a condition of epidemic proportions and I didn't feel so special any more. But for the first time since I'd been active, I realised how nation-wide our movement was. And that was heartening. It's the brotherhood that keeps us sane.'

'What happened to the one they call Evegny?' Jakob asked.

'It's nearly exercise time,' Grigory said quickly. 'Finish your food.'

He must not ask about Evegny, Jakob knew. Grigory's lack of response had been for Jakob's own protection. Nevertheless Evegny's fate nagged at him. In time, he would ask one of the others.

Most of the men took the exercise-hour very seriously, and they used every part of their bodies with as much vigour as their health would allow. But towards the end of the first half-hour, most of them had flagged and were leaning against the walls, their faces bitter with disappointment. For long and constant drugging had abused their bodies as well as their minds, and some men, knowing the pitiful outcome of their efforts, forebore to exercise at all, thus avoiding the disappointment. Jakob's body was fit, and he could, with ease, have spent the whole hour in strenuous exercise, but after half-an-hour he felt ashamed to put his rude health on show, and he lolled against the wall with the rest of them. He was glad when the hour was over.

They returned to the ward. Some of the men lay in their cots in sheer exhaustion. Their 'mornings' were over. Other read or wrote letters. That was a freedom that Jakob had not expected in this place. But when he asked an orderly for writing-materials, he was refused, for a month had to pass before he was allowed to make contact with the outside world. He looked around for Grigory, but found that even he had retired. He, who had promised him those 'mornings', was fast asleep on his cot. Jakob was afraid. How long would it be before he was like them, before his body would betray him, and follow his mind into numbness.

'No, no,' he shouted.

It was an involuntary sound. Had he thought about it, he would have kept his panic to himself, but it was already noted on the nurse's pad. He thought of Deborah to take his mind off his fears, and thoughts of her helped him for a while. He wondered how he could pass a whole month without contact with her, and he prayed that when permission was given, he would still have the strength, and more crucial, the appetite to write to her.

There was a shelf of books at the end of the ward. From his bed he could count them. Twenty-three in all. He resolved that he would read every one of them, word by word, however weary their matter or their style. I will start with the first book on the top shelf, he thought, and he made his way across the ward.

It was a history of Marx and Lenin. He gave a cursory look at the other titles, and they were no more promising. No matter, he thought. They will keep my mind active. They will jog what is left of my memory when the effect of the drugs wear off. He took down the volume with some eagerness, grateful for the first item of curative treatment that he had been offered. He took it back to his bed and opened the first page. He read every word. The name of the publisher, the copyright number, the dates of the first to the twelfth printing. He read the small paragraph of acknowledgements, over and over again, needing to memorise each meaningless name. Then he turned to the first page of the text. It was clear from the first paragraph that it was a purely academic work, turgid, heavy, and earnest to the point of distraction. He forced himself to read on, and when he came to the end of the page, although he had understood each word, he had no sense of its totality. He read it once again, and as he came to the end of it, he felt his eyelids grow heavy, and he realised that reading such matter was counter-productive, for its effect was the same as the drugs.

He was woken by a slight shove on his shoulder. An orderly gave him his lunch soup, and already a trolley was being wheeled through the wards. My life is passing by, Jakob thought, shrinking in sleep and idleness. I shall go mad here, he thought, and wondered again about the man they called Evegny.

That day passed like his first, and thereafter many days, until he could reckon them in weeks. Each sleep was deeper and his dreams were terrible. The exercise hour became a penance for him, for it proved his growing frailty. Men left the ward and never returned, and he was too afraid to ask where they had gone. Then one morning he woke to find writing-paper and a pen at his bedside, and suddenly he was alive once more, and he remembered Deborah and his children to whom he realised he had given no thought for many days. Now the thought of them gave him a small strength, a sense of his own being, so long dormant. He was a husband and a father, and much more than the wretch who slept his days away, and who peppered his nights with terrible dreams. He grabbed the paper and took the pen in a trembling hand.

My darling Deborah, Hans and Benjamin.

Their names were a shock to him. His status as husband of which he had lost sight, was now real and proven, and his rank of father, likewise. But who were these people whose names he wrote with such fluent familiarity? For he could not remember their faces. My God, he thought, and this is morning. Clarity time, conversation time. The pen shook in his hand. Yet he could find no words to write, no style to couch his fear, no grammar for the truth of his amnesia. He tried to picture Deborah in certain events of their lives together, standing at the plinth in Mayakovsky Square, under the wedding canopy in the synagogue, in the hospital bed after Hans' birth, but even in these identities, as lover, bride and mother, he could not evoke her features. But when he thought of their last meeting, that encounter he had tried to shift from his mind, it was then that he saw her, as she gave him his verdict. It was then that he heard her parting Bindel phrase, 'soon we shall all be together again', and it was then that his fingers steadied on the pen, and he began to write.

Soon we shall all be together again, my loved ones. It acted as a sudden injection of his heritage, and it gave him strength. *You remember the toast we give each other every year. That hope in time, will be fulfilled.* He was mindful of censorship. The word 'Jerusalem' would certainly not travel well from this place, but he need not elucidate to Deborah and the children. *My life here is calm and unmolested.* Both were close to the truth, though he had occasionally been beaten by a vindictive warder for his keeper's pure diversion, and the calmness of which he wrote bordered on despair. He was glad that there was a limited space in which to write, for though he had volumes to tell Deborah, for his own safety, and for the sake of her sanity, he would tell her nothing. For if he were to describe the daily hospital routine, she would be driven to despair. He wrote in unusually large letters, so that his permitted space would soon be filled. He told her about the book he was reading. Its title would happily pass the authorities, but then he regretted having written it, for Deborah might deduce from it his abdication. Indeed there was nothing at all that he could write that would not feed her anxieties. *Remember our toast*, he wrote yet again. Even though he could give small grounds for hope, they had to hold it in their hearts. *Write to me with news of our friends. And others.* He rounded off his letter. He wanted mostly to hear about Aaron. But he could not bring himself to write his name, and he hoped that Deborah would know that he was the 'other' of whom he wanted news. He sealed the letter and went to the end of the ward and put it in a box for that purpose. The box was half-full, and he wondered how long the letters had been lying there, bursting with their truths half-told, their longings and their pleas.

'When are these collected?' he asked the nurse on duty.

'Every Monday,' he said.

He had no idea what day it was, and he refrained from asking the nurse for he had learned to fear his note-taking pad. Grigory was dressing and he went over to his cot to ask him.

'How should I know what day it is?' Grigory laughed. 'I only know it's morning.'

Thereafter Jakob visited the letter-box every day on waking, and after three days, he knew that it was a Monday. He thought he would make a note of each day as it passed, or write a diary perhaps, since he now had writing materials. That thought cheered him a little and he went back to his cot to begin. But the problems he had with letter-writing were far more acute in diary-form. For they were but a confirmation to himself of the daily wastage of his life, of the constant threat to his body and spirit. To write of such things, to oneself, precluded another's sympathy, another's encouragement not to give way to despair, another's view of possible recovery. So he quickly abandoned the idea of a journal, and instead he wrote on the top of the page, *Monday*. That page he would keep under his pillow, and make of it a calendar, day by day. Thus time would tick through his sleep and his dreaming, and chronicle the passing of the days, and afford him some anchorage in the timeless sea of his despair.

He noticed that Ilya's bed was empty, and he could see him nowhere about the ward. Grigory was dressed now and coming towards him.

'Where's Ilya?' Jakob asked.

'He's gone for his examination. They took him before you woke up.'

'Might he be released?' Jakob voice was full of hope.

'I doubt it,' Grigory said. 'It's his fourth examination since he's been here. He's not very good at passing. If he passes, he'll come back soon to say goodbye.'

'And if he fails?' Jakob regretted his question, for he knew that Grigory would not give him a straight answer.

'He'll be back in a few days or so.'

Jakob asked no more, but all that day, he waited for Ilya's return, and as night fell, he accepted the fact that Ilya had failed again.

A whole week passed before Ilya returned, and he was almost unrecognisable. It was morning, but the zombie-look, that clothed all the men after the first trolley, had now settled on Ilya's face with hints of permanence. He walked very slowly as if in great pain. The men went forward to welcome him, gentle with their embrace, for they knew that his body was bruised. But no one asked any questions, because most of them had had examinations and all of them had failed. Until that time, Jakob had itched for the review of his own case. Now he dreaded his failure. But that same day, he had a letter from Deborah, and it was as if he had been suddenly released. He fingered the envelope in his hands delaying its opening, for by the weight of it, it was brief and possible censored, so he wanted to prolong the simple pleasure of receiving. He put it under his pillow and let it lie there for a few minutes, each second a teasing temptation. Then he lifted the pillow, but first entered the day they had reached on his calendar. It was a Friday, and in his terms, marked the end of a week. So he drew a line underneath. Then he opened Deborah's letter.

He noticed first the authorities' deletions. They were blacked out and unreadable. About half the letter was thus censored, and he noticed how his knuckles whitened as he clutched the paper, and he felt the anger rise in him. But he knew he must contain it. The recent sight of Ilya was testimony to where anger and indignation could lead.

My darling, he read, and was suddenly grateful to the authorities that they had not blotted out that token of love. *Words from you at last made us all so happy, and we have read and shared your letter a hundred times.* There followed a blacked paragraph, one that Jakob surmised spoke of reactions of friends, and perhaps of 'others'. But the following lines lifted his spirits once more. *Every night the children and I make our toast, and Inge and Ivan are often with us. I have applied for a permit to visit you. I am told that it is straightforward. I long to see you once again, to bring you kisses from our sons, and to hold you in my arms.* Another deletion followed, and this one puzzled Jakob most of all. He could not imagine what greater passion she could have expressed after her last sentence, so he supposed that it was a postscript of sorts, and such a cataloguing could only concern the subject of Aaron. He was convinced that she had written news of him, and it was that news that the authorities wished to suppress. And that made him more curious then ever.

When they were summoned to breakfast, he joined the others to help Ilya into line. Ilya knew that he had to eat to preserve what strength was left to him, but he needed a great deal of assistance to get to table. They walked each side of him, crowding him to protect him from the warder's whip, and Jakob on the outside, lent his vicarious back to the convict's flick-happy wrist. In time they reached the dining-hall and the serving-counter. Grigory held Ilya's tray, and they all urged him to eat. But he picked at his food with little appetite.

'I'm so terribly hungry,' he whispered.

He made no attempt to excuse himself from the exercise hour. He had to nurture his body once more after the terrible assault it had suffered. Once in the open air, he was seen to rub himself gently, all over his limbs, and the guard took it for exercise and turned a blind eye. Towards the end of the hour, when most of the men were leaning exhausted against the wall, one of the guards told Ilya to run around the square. Ilya made no manner of protest. He picked up one leg after the other, and with monumental effort, paced them around the exercise-area. It was his last act of obedience, for when the drug-trolley appeared on its first round of the day, Ilya refused to join the line. He would not move from his cot, and none of the men did much to dissuade him. For they knew, as well as Ilya knew, that with more drugs in his present state, brain damage was not far away. They knew too, that the punishment for drug-refusal might well be worse. But Ilya, on his two unsupporting legs, was making a small stand for his rights as a human being, which was why no man dissuaded him. But they themselves stood in the line and looked at his cot with fear.

It took little time for a guard to note his disobedience. He strutted across the ward, taking his time, no doubt savouring the prospect of a victim. The men saw a small but noble sign of struggle in the cot, and then Ilya was dragged bodily across the floor, his still-booted feet scraping a scream along the lino. The guard got him into the line, and tucked him under his arm, where Ilya lolled like a rag-doll, and waited his reluctant turn. When it came, he refused pill and water, using what little strength he had left to clamp his jaws shut. But another guard came to his side and, together with his mate, squeezed Ilya's nose until he was forced to open his mouth. Then they held it wide with their fists while the nurse put the pill on Ilya's tongue and sloshed some water after it. But he got it all back in his face for his pains, while Jakob stood with the other men, watching, helpless on the sidelines, and his heart heaved when he saw the nurse's face and the earnest promise of punishment that it held. He slapped Ilya hard across the face, and blood was seen to trickle from his nose.

'Once more,' the nurse said to the guards, and they fisted his mouth again, while the nurse applied another pill. This time he added no water, and the guards clamped Ilya's mouth closed, gripping it in a fist-hold for a while. Then they opened it again, as if it were an inanimate box, inspected its raw insides, and were satisfied. Then Ilya fell to the floor, and some of his friends ran to gather him up and to carry him back to his cot.

Jakob dreaded the next trolley-round. But Ilya resisted again, and again on the last round of the day, and each time he gave and received the same treatment. In the evening, when the men finally carried him back to his cot, Grigory urged him in whispers to give in. 'You will not survive another day of this,' he said.

'I have to try to do it,' Ilya whispered, 'else I won't survive at all.'

But the following morning, a doctor was seen to enter the ward and approach Ilya's bed. After a while, a stretcher-trolley was wheeled to his cot and Ilya was carried out of the ward. Jakob wondered whether they would ever see him again.

'Thank God,' he heard Grigory say. 'They will take him off the drugs and give him proper treatment.'

'What's proper treatment in this place?' Jakob asked. 'And what drugs are there to cure his courage?'

'Courage he has, my friend,' Grigory said. 'But he also has inflammation of the liver. I heard the doctor tell the nurse. Two years ago, Ilya Yakir entered this hospital a whole and healthy man. Even if he ever gets out of here alive, he will never be whole again.'

'Is it worth it?' Jakob asked, and he whispered the question, for it was more of a question to himself than one which required an answer.

But Grigory had overheard. 'Don't ever ask that question again,' he said, and for the first time since Jakob had met him in this place, his voice was raised. 'People make choices,' he said. 'And those choices are private. Next week it's my turn for examination. I have failed three times. Perhaps next time I shall decide to pass. And if I do, I shall come and say goodbye to you without shame. We all choose our own ways of survival.'

Jakob was stunned by the reverberating echoes of the Patriach Jakob's litany. Grigory was its true inheritor, and he wondered whether when his review time came, he himself would have the courage to surrender.

But when, in the following week, Grigory was taken for his

examination, he did not return to the ward and Jakob wondered whether his shame was too great, or whether he had found another way to survive. One week later, he shuffled back into the ward in the fashion of Ilya's return, zombied, fractured, but unbroken. Jakob was ashamed at the pleasure he took in seeing him again, for he had missed him terribly. For the next few days, he sat by Grigory's bed, and did his best to comfort him. Unlike Ilya, Grigory obeyed all the rules. He dragged his fragile body to the drug-trolley three times a day and he took his medicine. He lumbered around the exercise yard with no complaint, though his pain was clear for all to see. Sometimes Jakob would notice a glint of triumph in his eye. 'Why do you do it, Grigory?' he asked one evening at his bed-side. 'My friend,' Grigory said, 'the sweetest revenge is to live well, and to survive at all is revenge enough. One day I shall live well too. That will come, Jakob. It will come for all of us.'

The case-review examination that Jakob had dreaded, yet in many ways had been impatient for, came much earlier than he had expected. He was told that his first review would take place a week hence, barely three months after his arrival at the hospital. Grigory couldn't understand it, and could only ascribe it to pressure from the outside. At this suggestion, Jakob thought immediately of Aaron, who perhaps was using his stained connections in order to free him. And immediately he grew antagonistic, for he did not want his brother's help, from whatever source, for his brother was different, and so were his sources. They were the 'others'. They were not friends.

That same day, when they appraised him of his review, he received a letter from Deborah. It was a short letter and completely uncensored, and it announced that she had received a visitor's permit and hoped to arrange to see him within two weeks. The children were well and sent their love, and she, hers.

Her visit might not be necessary, Jakob thought, since his examination would precede it. Or would she come, and find him zombied, like Ilya?

He went over to Grigory's bed. 'What kind of examination is it?' he asked. 'Blood? Heart? Pulse?' he said hopefully. 'They don't touch you,' Grigory said. 'They only ask questions.' Jakob knew that he must not enquire further. As Grigory had told him, survival was a private matter. But he worried about Deborah's visit. He wished she were coming sooner. The brevity of her letter offered the promise of much news to impart on seeing him. He needed to sniff the outside world on her, to smell his home and his children, for as the drugged days passed, their pictures floated in his memory as in a developing-tank, swimming in and out of focus. He tried not to think of the impending examination. He thought now of his Bindel inheritance and repeated to himself the old man Jakob's litany. There is not a cause on earth worth dying for, he had said. No God, no country, no ideology. Death was worthy only in the name of love and friendship. Ilya was on his way to dying, and there was no doubt that the altar of his sacrifice was cause and ideology. Did that make him less of a lover? Less of a friend? In his dying, he was marching for millions of people whom he didn't know. Did that mean he would not sing that same march of death for one he knew and loved? Jakob was confused. As Grigory had said, survival was a private matter.

He took his calendar from under his pillow. Almost two months had passed since his first entry. Each week's end underlined and, as was his daily wont, he counted the days of his hospital past. But that morning, he did something very different. He began to count forward, adding the days until his review. It was the first time since he had been in this place that he had envisaged the future, and thus the beginnings of hope.

CHAPTER THIRTY-TWO

When Aaron left Sonia, he moved into an apartment near the hospital that belonged to a doctor friend who, at that time, had been seconded to a medical unit in Leningrad. He fully expected trouble. Koskin was not a man to let him get away with the desertion of his daughter. His revenge would take time perhaps, but when it came it would be sublime. But nothing happened. His job remained secure, and when he looked in the driving-mirror of his car, as he did all the time from force of habit, he found no shadows there. It seemed that his father-in-law had let him off the hook, but he regarded it as the lull before the storm.

He was very lonely. His sights were fixed on Saturdays, which day he would spend with Heidi. He missed Sonia too, he had to confess to himself, and each time he saw her, the old forbidden longings were aroused. She was always polite to him, and very controlled, and he sensed that she was close to tears.

Aaron's desertion had in fact shattered her. She had kept it from her father in fear of his wrath and revenge. But after a week of painful loneliness and deliberation, she considered asking for his help. She was convinced that the central cause of their quarrel was Jakob, and the fact that he was in trouble. If Jakob could be released, set free, not only from the hospital but also from the country, Aaron's guilt would leave him, and he would return to their home. She was surprised by her father's reaction. She had expected anger, and salivating plans for revenge. But he was deeply distressed by his daughter's desolate state. Although his relationship with his son-in-law had been distant, he had secretly grown fond of him, and he had much respect for his achievements in his field. Dr Aaron Bindel and his discoveries had often been talked about in the various official functions he had to attend, and although he would never volunteer his connection, he would admit to it whenever a Bindel-admirer enquired whether he knew him personally. But he had little room for that brother of his, and quickly dismissed Sonia's suggestion that he use his good offices to engineer his release.

'In any case, as you well know, my dear, he is ill. In his own interest he should not be released until he is better.'

'But that might take years, Papa,' she said.

'The law must take its course.'

She began to cry then, and he realised how deeply distressed the parting had left her. 'I can do nothing for his brother,' Koskin said, 'but I can see to it that Aaron is left alone to continue his work.'

She was grateful for that. Harassment would only feed his antagonism towards her.

'What am I to do, Papa?' she asked.

'Wait and see, my dear. He will come back. You just have to give him time.'

He had little confidence in his words, for he knew that Sonia was right. The core of Aaron's discontent lay with that offending brother of his. Koskin's whole being was revolted by the opinions such a man held. But his daughter's plight moved him and, when she was gone, he deliberated how he could intervene for Jakob's release. But she must never know it was his doing. As few people as possible would ever know, for Koskin had his own interests to safeguard. As a considerably influential Party official, he had the seniority to act on his own authority, and, forthwith, he contacted his opposite number in Minsk, to whom, by nature of his capital assignment, he was superior, and he ordered him to go to the hospital where Jakob Bindel was held and to instruct the doctor in charge that suitable reasons must be found for the release of that patient. He stressed the importance of the latter. Reasons had to be found. Bindel was on no account to be given a free release. That would totally invalidate their system of psychiatric treatment. There must be nothing in writing, he told his Minsk contact. 'Do the job, comrade,' he said. 'Keep me informed, and when it is done, I want to hear no more about it.'

He put the phone down, satisfied.

The following day he phoned Sonia from his office simply to maintain contact. A few days later his man from Minsk telephoned. It was too soon, he reported, to manoeuvre Bindel's release in any disguisable way. Three months was the minimum stay before a case-review could be considered marginally legitimate. The doctor in charge had suggested that as soon as three months had passed, the Bindel case would receive sympathetic review.

Koskin was satisfied. In time, Dr Aaron Bindel would return to the fold that, by virtue of history and national consciousness, did not belong to him. But Koskin's daughter loved him, as he himself had once so deeply loved her mother. Such love, he knew from his own philanderings, was never repeatable.

*

Some weeks passed, and Aaron was restless. The lull had begun to unnerve him. He should have been relieved, he knew, but there was something within him that *needed* trouble, trouble that would lead to punishment or at least, reprimand. It was his only present way of drawing near to his brother. So he went to the OVIR offices, and withdrew his letter of veto. While he was there, the thought occurred to him to make his own application for an exit-visa too, but that, at this stage, would have been too drastic, and the thought of Heidi precluded any idea of emigration. One thing at a time, he thought. The withdrawal of the veto was the first stage. He left the offices and waited for the clap of thunder. But even with that provocation, it never came.

It took little time for the withdrawal to come to Koskin's ear, and he was much relieved by the news. For he had it in mind to engineer the granting of exit-visas to Jakob Bindel and his family as soon as possible after the hospital release. And Aaron's veto would have been something of an impediment. So he was pleased with Aaron's move, although he was aware of its guilt motivation. He knew that only if Jakob were allowed to leave the country would his brother's guilt be finally assuaged. Then perhaps he would return to Sonia.

A few days later, Aaron telephoned Deborah. He had not seen her for many weeks and he asked if he might call. She was welcoming, and suggested he come that evening for supper.

'Will you bring Sonia?' she asked.

'No. I'll come on my own.'

Deborah went out to forage for food. For two hours she waited in line for a small piece of meat, and she was overjoyed at her success. When he arrived, he handed her flowers. It was the beginning of his peace-offering, and in case she should refuse them, he said straight-way, 'I have withdrawn my letter of veto.'

She threw her arms around him, unable to speak, so great was her relief and happiness.

'I shall write and tell Jakob as soon as I am able,' she said. 'I shall have to wait for a month, then he is allowed to write to me.'

'Do you hear anything about him?' Aaron asked.

'Nothing,' she said. 'I know people who have been in the Minsk hospital, and I avoid them. They avoid me too. I think they are afraid of the questions that I am too afraid to ask.'

He tried to find words of comfort for her, but knew none. So he took her hand.

'I want to help all I can. Though there's little enough I can do,' he said, and almost in the same breath, for it was reason enough for his inability to help, 'I've left Sonia,' he said.

Deborah was shocked by a mixture of feelings compounded of relief and concern. But relief was uppermost. That Aaron had left Sonia was not merely a case of a husband leaving his wife. It was a greater desertion: that of ideology. And in Aaron's case, more than that even. More positive than that. It was a gesture of love towards his brother.

'You did all you could for Jakob,' she said. 'And even if it didn't work, you did it. That's all that matters. What about Heidi?' she said after a while.

'I see her every Saturday. She's upset, of course. I'd like to bring her over to see the boys. She hardly knows her cousins.'

'You must do that next Saturday,' Deborah said. It was Aaron who needed family, she knew. In his aloneness, he'd suddenly felt its loss.

'Does Inge know?' Deborah asked.

'I wanted to tell you first. But I shall go and see her.'

'She'll come on Saturday,' Deborah said. 'We'll have a family reunion.'

*

Thereafter Aaron was a frequent visitor at Deborah's apartment. Once a week he brought Heidi, and Inge and Ivan would join them. But the comfort that Aaron found, within the family circle, only served to underline his monstrous part in dis-uniting them, and he wondered how he could do penance for all the wrongs he had perpetrated. He knew that, ultimately, he too must join his brother's struggle. But he knew, too, that the insurmountable impediment to that final move was his continuing love for Sonia. He knew that there was no way that they could be reconciled, short of a radical change in Sonia's outlook. But he knew that that was impossible. He himself had tried, had flirted with an alien creed, had thrilled with shame to its taboo, but finally he had returned to

473

the fold because it was more comfortable there. But the fold had its pitfalls, too, the yawning terrain of the past that had to be accommodated, that inconvenient Bindel past with its blackmailing dictum of survival. To remove himself to Israel was clearly his logical course. But there was Heidi, and Heidi tied him forever to Moscow. Indeed, though Aaron did not know, his own Grandfather Leon had once found himself in the same trap of loving, in the name of one David in the Senghennyd valley. Death had released him from that trap, else he too would have been tied to a comfortless alien history.

A few weeks later, Deborah told him that she had received a permit to go to Minsk and visit Jakob. He was happy for her and envious, too, for he wished he could go with her. There were almost two weeks before she would go, and during that time he spent many hours with her, and Inge too, recapturing for her his childhood in Halle, and Jakob's childhood too, which was what Deborah delighted to hear.

'When you see him.' Aaron said, 'I want you to tell him everything.'

'I've already written that you have left Sonia,' Deborah said.

Aaron laughed. 'I think that would merit their blue pencil,' Aaron said.

He was happy while he was with them, but when he returned alone to his borrowed anonymous apartment, he felt very lonely and he longed for Sonia, and during that time he immersed himself in his work and he was grateful that it was still open to him. Most of the time he thought of Jakob, and he would have been happy and ashamed to know that, most of his idle time, Jakob thought of Aaron.

Especially on that morning of his appointed examination. He was as nervous as he used to be at school in the Leipzig days before he was orphaned. And Aaron used to hold his hand and lead him into the classroom, and tell him not to be afraid. Now more than at any other time he needed a big brother, and those childhood memories stirred such fraternal love in his heart that, for a moment he forgot how diligently his brother had sought to destroy it.

They came for him very early, while most of the men were still sleeping. He felt a slight touch on his shoulder, and he wondered why the guard was being so gentle.

'Wake up, Mr Bindel,' he whispered. 'It's time for your examination.'

Mr Bindel? Jakob thought. He who from that same guard had never merited a name of any kind except 'scum', 'traitor' or 'criminal', names which in the guard's terms could apply to any one of the patients. But suddenly there was this gentle awakening and the courtesy of the summons. Jakob was now more nervous than ever.

He was taken to the examination room, that same room he had entered when first arriving at the hospital. Since it was morning, his mind was relatively clear, and he thought he recognised the same three doctors who had initially received him, the questioner, the scribbler and the diagnostician. But this time, there was no pad in sight, and no interrogating table. Instead, the doctors were seated in arm-chairs and they invited him to take one too, as if they were going to partake in pleasant conversation.

'It's good to see you, Mr Bindel,' one of the doctors opened the proceedings. 'You're looking well. And how are you feeling?'

'As well as can be expected.' Jakob was polite but distant. He wanted none of their proffered friendship.

'What does that mean exactly, comrade?' the erstwhile scribbler asked. 'As well as can be expected. Are you referring to the gravity of your mental condition?'

'Not at all,' Jakob replied without hesitation. 'I am as well as can be expected considering the drugs I am obliged to take.'

'Obliged?' the diagnostician asked. 'They're prescribed for your own good, and by the looks and the sound of you, they have ameliorated your condition.'

'Mornings are different,' Jakob replied. 'The effect of the drugs wear off for a while. There is a certain clarity of mind.'

'Then we are fortunate to have caught you in the morning, my friend,' the interrogating doctor said. 'We can have a pleasant discussion together. When you arrived,' he said quickly, 'you showed all the signs of what we term creeping schizophrenia. Now, Jakob, you're an intelligent man.'

Jakob was sickened by his use of his familiar name and he couldn't understand his friendliness.

'You had delusions of reforming society,' the doctor went on, 'an obsessive mania for truth-seeking. It was temporary, I'm sure of that, and yours was only a mild case. Which is why we are reviewing your situation earlier than is usual. The treatment you have been receiving should have had the desired effect by now. Let us say that your disease was a mild form of dissent. How have your opinions changed since you came here?' He had delayed the vital question for as long as possible. He had created an atmosphere of friendship and equality, a comfortable setting for the questions that had ultimately and legally to be asked. He waited for Jakob's reply, and he was unnerved to see him smiling. It was not a good beginning. For not only was Jakob Bindel smiling, he was close to derisive laughter.

'Why should my opinions have changed?' he asked. 'On the contrary, in this place they have been mightily confirmed.'

The doctors shuddered with dismay, knowing now that release was impossible. Even the MVD would understand that.

'When I was arrested,' Jakob went on, 'it was on the charge of saying that there was no freedom in this country. For what reason should I have changed my mind about that? The whole country's a prison, and parts of it are called psychiatric hospitals. It's a farce. It's you who are diseased. Not I. It's you whose brains are addled, stormed and washed. And you and your kind dare to call me insane.'

'Thank you, Bindel,' the diagnostician said. The 'Mr' had been quickly dropped. 'That is enough.'

But Jakob was unstoppable. As he spoke his mind was racing with the words of the Patriarch Jakob's litany. That old and venerable namesake of his would not have approved of his tactics. 'For whose love are you making this sacrifice?' he would have thundered. 'For whose friendship? You are committing yourself to confinement in the name of a Cause. That is called martyrdom, and that is not what I bequeathed you. My legacy was survival.' But perhaps the old man had been wrong, and in this place and at this time, Jakob thought he would have said the same. For he would have known that personal survival was secondary. That what was predominant was that ideas should not die, that notions of freedom must be kept alive for one's children and their future.

'I may not live to see freedom in this land,' Jakob went on, 'but it will come. In time the whole world shall hear of your evil and . . .'

One of the doctors, his face white with rage, clapped his hand over Jakob's mouth and screamed for the guard. His anger was sublime.

'Take this scum away,' he shouted. 'Cell 4C.'

Grigory would have known that location and would have shuddered at its name. So would Ilya and countless others. And the one they called Evegny. They, like Jakob, had refused to get better. So they had punished them.

It was called the 'roll-up'. Once in the cell, Jakob was thrown on to a bunk by two attendant guards, who then proceeded to roll him from neck to foot in strips of wet canvas, and so tightly that it was difficult to breathe. When they had thus embalmed him, they fastened him down to the bunk with rubber belts. Then they stood back and viewed their handiwork. They were smiling.

'Enjoy it while it lasts,' one of them said, 'because it won't last long.'

Then they left him, bolting the door behind them.

Jakob was afraid. He wondered what they had meant by enjoyment, for his present situation was uncomfortable enough. When occasionally he had been punished by the guards, he had resorted to deep breathing to contain his pain. But now, strapped down and swaddled, it was difficult to breathe at all. He closed his eyes, though he knew that sleep was impossible. It was very hot in the cell. He twisted his head towards the window but it was closed and barred. Despite the wet cold canvas that swathed him, he felt a fever in his body and his heart palpitated and he was afraid. He kept thinking of Grigory and Ilya. Now he knew how and where they had spent their absence from the ward. Yet they had returned, both of them, to protest and survive once more. They had not died in their swaddling clothes. He would survive too. As he lay there, the canvas seemed to tighten around him, and he realised, for the first time, the point of the punishment. As the canvas would dry, so would it tighten itself around his body. Now he understood the guard's parting phrase. 'Your enjoyment will not last long!' Now, he knew it could only get worse, and as the canvas would tighten he would surely die of it. He knew he must not lose consciousness, for that state was the carpeting for death's entry, and the thought of great-great-great-grandfather Jakob came to his mind, as if that venerable begetter of history would safeguard his survival. As he lay there, his body felt as if in a vice. He prayed that the canvas was by now absolutely dry, because he knew he could not bear it much longer. His heart thundered its struggle, and he felt a sickness in his stomach. He thought he saw the cell door open and the doctor approach, the diagnosing doctor who had been so disgusted at his lack of co-operation. He was not sure it was he, nor even whether he was there at all. He felt or thought he felt his hand on his wrist as if he were taking his pulse. Then he saw the guards and felt the bonds loosen. They let him lie there for the rest of the day, while his body breathed and stretched itself. But the pain of the recovery was unspeakable. It was too quick, too sudden. The muscles sprung back to their accustomed span, tearing his body like nails. He thought how endless man's endurance was, offensively so, and he could not help but wonder what he had achieved by his martyrdom. For that's what the Patriarch would have called it, and would have pointed to his canvas crucifixion as proof. But Grigory had come back, and so had Ilya, and countless others no doubt, and lived to tell the tale they would not tell.

That night they brought him some soup to his cell, and a hunk of black bread. He forced himself to eat it, though he feared vomiting. But he forced that down too. He daren't not weaken himself through lack of food. It had been days that Grigory and Ilya had been absent from the ward. He wished now he could remember how many. He was sure that there was more punishment for him to come.

And as it turned out, he was right. For six successive days they treated him to the 'roll-up', and released him only when his pulse threatened to surrender. On the seventh day even those heathens rested, and returned him to the ward.

Grigory helped him to his bed, a smile of joy on his face. 'We know how you feel,' he whispered. 'Don't talk. Just rest. Trust us. We'll look after you.'

He plumped the pillow under Jakob's head. 'Sleep now,' he said. But Jakob could not close his eyes for the sleep he so craved.

'Grigory,' he whispered. 'What happened to the one they call Evegny?'

Grigory clutched Jakob's hand. 'After the "roll-up",' he said, 'Evegny went mad, really mad, the sort of madness they don't treat here. He hung himself with one of the canvas strips they used to roll him.'

Jakob sighed and closed his eyes. Though saddened by Evegny's fate, there was a small satisfaction in knowing that he had now been fully accepted into that stubborn fraternity of refuseniks. He had paid his dues. He slept then, and the pain eased from his body.

On the first trolley round, he dragged himself across the ward and, on reaching his turn, he noted how the nurse checked on his treatment-card.

'It seems you need more treatment,' he said. 'The doctors report that you're not responding. I have orders to double the dosage.'

Jakob opened his mouth obediently while they slid two pills inside. Helplessly he washed them down with water and, as he did so he knew that, from that time, his life would be robbed of mornings.

*

Over the next few days, he became like Ilya, as if permanently zombied. It was an effort for him to speak and, though he was always tired, he could never sleep. He had continual headaches and his mouth was always dry, with a thirst that no amount of water could assuage. Often, in those days, he wanted very much to die. It was during that time that they came to his bed and told him that he had a visitor.

'I can't,' he whispered.

'It's your wife,' the guard said.

He knew it was Deborah, which was why he couldn't see her.

'Get up,' the guard shouted. 'She's come all the way from Moscow. You have twenty minutes. You're wasting time.'

Jakob dragged himself out of bed, straightened his hair and tried to compose himself. Then he shuffled behind the guard to the visitors' room. He wished he could walk upright with the brisk tread that she had last seen. He wished he had a mind to talk and an ear to listen. He wished above all that she hadn't come. Yet his heart raced to see her.

As he entered the room, he registered the look of horror on her face when she saw him.

'Jakob,' she cried, and ran towards him, holding his body gently and wondering where all its flesh had gone. For now, even holding him loosely, her own hands overlapped each other on his back. She took them away quickly, afraid that his frame would crack. She helped him to a chair. It seemed pointless to ask how he was. It was plain from his appearance that he had been abused, maltreated, and possibly tortured. She would not ask him. 'Don't talk,' she said, taking his face in her hands. 'Let me do the talking.'

She took a chair and sat alongside him, holding his hand the while as she spoke, caressing his cheek with her fingers and her lips. He was totally without response seeming almost not to recognise her. Though he was staring at her, Deborah felt that he did not see her, that her face was but a blurred interruption of his vision of oblivion.

'Aaron has left Sonia,' was the first piece of news that she gave him.

He heard the words, and the fact that they had spelled out, but his mind, fuzzed by drugs, had lost the talent of deduction, inference or perception of innuendo. His brother had left his wife. A piece of information.

She realised, as she looked at him, and by his complete lack of response, that he had no idea of the import of that news. She tried again. 'He has withdrawn his letter of veto, Jakob,' she said. Again he heard it as a piece of information, but he could not consider its cause, and certainly not its effect.

'That means we'll get an exit-visa when you come out.'

It was her last phrase that registered with more clarity than any of the others. He understood that he could never come out, that principle, a bond stronger than any canvas roll-up strip, was binding him there, unbreakable, unstretchable. How could be tell her that? He nodded his head as a signal of his understanding.

'Pavel has gone,' she was saying. 'They rang him up and told him he had forty-eight hours to get out. He was astonished. They had a farewell party.'

She looked at his non-registering face. 'You remember Pavel,' she said, reminding him of his closest friend. 'The engineer. They were holding him because he's had access to government secrets. All of seven years ago. You remember Pavel? And Mikhail's gone too. You remember Mikhail, Jakob? They kept him because he only had an uncle in Israel. Not sufficient kinship, they said.' She was trying to remind him of all the aspects of the refusenik struggle, to confirm that once he was part of it, and would be again.

'There was another letter from Aunt Sarah,' she was saying. 'She looks forward to our coming. Jakob,' she pleaded, gripping his hand. 'Don't lose hope. Don't despair.'

The tears rolled down her cheeks, and those he saw with blinding clarity and clear deduction. He wished that she would go away. He could not bear her pain. He could not bear the humiliation of his own frailty.

'I love you,' she was saying. 'However you are.'

Inference. Deduction. What did she mean by that? However I am. Does she too begin to believe that I am mad? He looked at her, painfully focussing his eyes on her face, and the name that went with that face, struck his tongue.

'Deborah,' he said, and there was a small relief in saying it.

'Deborah,' he whispered again. 'Please go. Please.'

Those were the first words he had spoken to her.

She rose. 'The children are well,' she said. 'They send their love.'

He hadn't asked about them. He had asked no questions at all. But she knew that later on, when he was alone, he would wonder about his home and those he had left behind, and he would be glad that they had not forgotten him. She took his face in her hands and kissed him gently. Then she watched him being led away, with half his visiting time still to run.

The guard who had eavesdropped on the one-sided visit, was angry. Once out of the waiting-room, he gripped Jakob's arm.

'She came all the way from Moscow,' he said.

Jakob was grateful for that rare show of concern, for that, he knew, was the cause of the guard's anger. 'I'm ill,' he said.

*

Whether that guard called the doctor, or whether it was a routine visit, Jakob never discovered, But shortly after he returned to his bed, a doctor arrived and gave him an authentic physical examination. He ordered the ward nurse that Jakob be kept in bed for a week, and that he should be taken off all drugs. He was adamant about that order, shouting it at the nurse, as if Jakob's condition was entirely his fault. The doctor was clearly disturbed by the state of his patient. In a supposedly remedial institution, it did not do to have too many deaths on their hands. Even if dissidence was a State-licensed disease, it was hardly fatal, and death, from its cause, carried uncomfortable overtones of murder.

'No drugs,' he ordered again. 'And extra rations. And don't let him leave his bed.'

All this, Jakob heard in a blur of sound, deciphering the occasional word and its meaning. Out of it all, he experienced a surge of gratitude, that they would save his life in this place, they who had been so bent on destroying it, pill by numbing pill. He would survive, and that word, that anchorage to his past, suffused him with joy.

For a whole week he lay there, fed, undrugged, and undisturbed. From time to time, he saw Grigory's face hovering above him, his lips moving with words of comfort. At the end of the week, Jakob woke, stretched his limbs and got out of bed, knowing that his 'mornings' had returned. At least this morning; for later that day the drug-trolley, that for the past week he had not heard or noticed, now wheeled its way across the ward, and the nurse shouted to him that from today, he was back to normal. Jakob smiled. Normal, he said to himself. Language was so abusable, he thought. Fashion could dishonour it, and manners, but most corrupting of all was ideology.

For the first few days after his rest cure, before the normal course of drugging began to take its toll, Jakob experienced a sense of physical well-being and a clarity of mind that he remembered from his pre-hospital days. During that time, he thought a great deal about Deborah's visit, and always with terrible soundings of regret. He knew that she would understand, but he knew too that she had returned to Moscow in despair. He recapped all that she had told him. All the facts of it had registered, but now, in his clear state, he could understand the ramifications of the news that she had given him. Aaron had left Sonia and had withdrawn his letter of veto. Now he could read the sub-titling of those news items and from them he could understand that his brother had returned to the fold. But Deborah's face as he had left her, or rather as he had sent her away, remained to haunt him. He thought of his inheritance, and for some reason it was Deborah's face that crystallised its whole meaning. She was love, she was friendship. Only in her name would he die. No other. No other, he kept repeating to himself. The old Odessa Patriarch had been right. Survive, he had said, in order to fight. In order to win. Survive, he had ordered the milk-brothers before they had entered the pagan service of the Czar. They will force you into baptism, he had said, and you must not resist them. Let them sprinkle their holy water on your brows. Let them flood your bodies with their purging priesthood. They cannot lay hands on your Jewish soul.

His words sang in Jakob's ear. The old Patriarch might well have been talking to him, his great-great-great-grandson who had taken his name, on the threshold of his examination, his case-review. Because, in a way, to claim that he was better, that he had changed his views, was to admit to a baptism of sorts. And there would be a joy in deceiving them for their baptism too would not touch his spirit. At his next case-review, he would recant, and he would return to the ward and say his farewells without shame.

Then he caught sight of Grigory walking towards him. It would be hardest of all to part from Grigory, and he wondered how long that old activist would hold out in this place. Perhaps he should tell him about Jakob's litany, and recruit him into his own brand of subversion. But Jakob knew that finally it was a question of language that divided them. Both of them coloured words according to their needs. Words like principle, cause, commitment, even the word survival itself, could be manufactured in different colours.

'I have news for you,' Grigory said as he approached. 'I have another review of my case.'

'Have you decided this time to be cured?' Jakob whispered.

'I want to see my wife and children,' Grigory said.

'They are cause,' Jakob told him. 'They are principles, they are ideals, they are love, they are friendship. They are worth lying for and perhaps dying for. But lie and live, my friend. We have both of us paid our dues.'

They made their way to the drug-trolley.

'Pavel has gone, you know. And Mikhail,' Jakob said. 'We have to join them.'

'If I choose to leave this place,' Grigory said, 'will you shake my hand and wish me well?'

'As long as you offer it without shame,' Jakob said.

*

A week later, Grigory returned from his case-review. His face was wreathed in smiles.

'I've passed,' he said, 'and they were delighted with their cure. They fell over themselves with gratitude. They called me "comrade", that word I so often use to you with all my affection. Words, my friend,' Grigory said. 'We're all of us in the cut-throat business of words. The only truth is silence.'

He held out his hand and Jakob clasped it.

'Farewell, my friend,' Jakob said. 'We shall meet on the outside. I too am in the word-business.'

'Then do a deal,' Grigory said embracing him, 'and we shall meet again in Jerusalem.'

CHAPTER THIRTY-THREE

Deborah returned from the hospital visit in a mood of deep despair. Apart from their total lack of communication, she was profoundly disturbed by the state of Jakob's health. He had lost much weight and, it seemed, all of his spirit. She was anxious to get home and see Aaron. Over the past few weeks he had been a frequent visitor, and she had grown very close to him. She had wanted to tell Jakob how Aaron had changed, giving him all the details that indicated a turning-away from his former assumed life. For Aaron had changed radically. He was becoming like Jakob in many ways, Deborah thought, as each day he released the Bindelhood within him and allowed it to assume its natural contours. He was gentle, supportive and repentant, but Deborah knew that his guilt still nagged at him, and that he continually sought ways of assuaging it.

She telephoned Aaron as soon as she returned to Moscow and arranged to meet him that evening. She lied to the children about their father. She told them he was well, and had every hope of his release. She hated herself for the deception, but she did not wish to burden them with her own profound pessimism. But to Aaron she told the whole truth. He was able to comfort her a little by explaining that his condition, as she described it, was wholly due to the drug that he was obliged to take. He had made enquiries as to its nature, he told her, and he stressed that though the effects were worrying, they were not irreversible. He stressed that factor over and over again, as much for himself as for Deborah, but in his heart he feared he might be wrong. When he left her, her spirits had lifted a little, but his own had sunk considerably. He knew from Deborah's description that Jakob's health could not withstand such treatment for very long. He wished he could see him. Just to be with him. He wished most of all that he could share his sentence.

He hadn't known why he'd never thought of it before, that simple solution to his guilt. That he himself must enter the penance that he himself had wrought. The following morning, before going to his laboratory, he walked with determined and almost euphoric stride to the offices of OVIR. And there, in a loud voice, and to the very official to whom he long ago handed his letter of veto against his brother, he announced his application for an exit-visa. It was how his brother had entered the struggle. He filled in the required forms and returned to his laboratory. He opened his drawers and packed a few personal belongings. He had left Sonia and he had withdrawn his letter of veto. And Koskin had all the time held his tongue and his power. This last move, this visa-application, Koskin could not ignore. Aaron would be summarily dismissed from his job and his struggle would follow his brother's course. He worked that day in his laboratory, convinced that it would be his last.

But Koskin had other plans. Words came to him soon enough about his son-in-law's application. He knew Aaron's motive. It had nothing to do with leaving the Soviet Union. It had less to do with going to Israel. It was his bid to join his brother, to penalise himself and thus lodge in his brother's skin. So he issued orders that Dr Aaron Bindel's latest move was to be ignored, Moreover, he once again telephoned his minion in Minsk. Koskin knew in his heart that nothing short of Jakob Bindel's release, and possibly nothing short of his emigration – and he would engineer that too – would ease Aaron's heart and possibly urge him back to Sonia and Heidi. Sonia's unhappiness did not seem available to time's healing, and almost every day she came to his apartment or even to his offices and begged him to use his influence for Jakob's release. Each time he refused, and with all the ideology that he could muster, for he dared not let her know that he was using his powers to weaken the system that he served. He carefully covered his tracks with each move. He had no intention of jeopardising his position on account of Aaron Bindel. Though he had to admit to a certain fascination with the man, a certain pride, a certain excitement in the taboos that clothed him. Like any self-respecting racialist, he had to have his pet Yid, and Aaron fitted that role exactly. In fact Koskin's attraction to Aaron was on the same level as Aaron's to his daughter, the taboo and forbidden level, and had Aaron been a woman, Koskin would have loved him.

He made a note on his file and dated it. October, 1978. Two months from Christmas. By that time he could effect a family re-union. Jakob Bindel's release could be scheduled for November. Meanwhile he could start cutting through the bureaucratic tape of his emigration plea. But by Christmas Sonia would smile again and he could boast of his son-in-law at official functions. He read the notes he had made, memorised them, and tore them up into tiny pieces.

Meanwhile Aaron waited. He went every day to his laboratory expecting, minute by minute, an indignant visit from the hospital director. He even arranged a chair for him though he doubted whether his words of angry dismissal would have been at ease in a chair. Day after day he waited, and after some weeks he had to accept the fact that they had chosen to ignore his trespass. He was after all, their token Jew, as Jakob was always so fond of calling him. He was their Uncle Tom, their pet Yid, their Iscariot, and such tokens could get away with anything. But he would think of something. He would find a manner of trespass that they could not ignore.

He went to the stationery department of the hospital and collected a sheaf of chart-papers and, together with selotape, he wrapped them furtively under his coat, and returned to his apartment. All that night he roughed out his design. *Free Jakob Bindel* was his first attempt. But somehow, in his eyes, it lacked something. It was too impersonal and, as such, minimised the seriousness of his plea. *Free Jakob Bindel from Hospital*, was his next example, but that too, though more specific, was still neutral. It was not until the morning light broke over his balcony that he found the word he had been seeking. Though indeed he had never lost it. It was a question only of its release. He roughed it out on a piece of paper. *Free my brother, Jakob Bindel*. It said everything he wanted to say. Above all, it associated him undeniably with dissidence.

It took him some time to paint the letters, boldly and with clarity, so that they could be read by the passers-by from his balcony only two floors above street-level. When it was done, inscribed across four large sellotaped sheets of graph-paper, he gummed each side to batons of wood that he had bought for that purpose, and stood it against the living-room wall to judge its effect. Its design did not bear too close an examination, nor did its calligraphy. But its message was loud and clear. They could not ignore it. Not even Koskin. It was too public a protest. He waited for the hour when people would start going to work, then he secured the banner across the balcony, returned to the room, put on his overcoat in readiness, and waited. After a short while he heard murmurings in the street and he crawled to the balcony doors and peeped outside.

Across the road he could see that a small crowd had gathered, and he watched for a while as the crowd grew. It would not be long now before the police would arrive and the plain-clothed uniformed KGB in their wake. He returned to his arm-chair and waited. He knew that he would not have to wait for long. He listened with joy to the crowd noises outside. He listened to their cries of disgust with infinite pleasure, and when he heard the boots outside his door, he almost rushed forward to let his captors in.

'Open up,' they shouted.

But Aaron was already at the door, his hand on the knob. He turned it quickly and opened the door wide. Three of them stood there, jack-booted in fury.

'Aaron Bindel?' one of them said.

'Yes,' Aaron said. '*Dr* Aaron Bindel,' he insisted. They were not arresting a nobody, he wanted them to know. They were taking into custody their system's token Jew, who had stood them in good if misguided stead in the past. 'Dr Aaron Bindel,' he said again. 'Fellow of the Moscow Academy of Sciences.'

The thugs were unimpressed. Two of them grabbed Aaron by the arms, while the other stormed to the balcony and tore down the offensive protest, stamping it with disgust under his foot. Then he closed the balcony doors, and joined his colleagues. Together they shoved Aaron into the lift and down into the street where a police van was waiting. They took him straight to the Kalinsky District Court, where he was arraigned on a charge of anti-Soviet agitation.

When the magistrate realised the identity of the accused, he ordered the court cleared and a defence council to be called. He summoned the advocate to his desk, and suggested that, in view of the reputation of the accused he should plead for mitigation of sentence rather than seek an acquittal. To take the latter course would involve many hearings, and could not escape public attention. The former course of action could be dealt with without any delay. He promised a light sentence. And so the defence lawyer, without a word of consultation with his client, by whom in any case, he had never been appointed, agreed to the validity of the charge and asked for the lightest sentence that such a charge carried. The magistrate was satisfied and he sentenced Aaron to prison for six months. He was to be held in Moscow.

They put him back in the van and handcuffed him. He was astonished that it was all so quickly over and that the wheels of Soviet law grinded with such speed, that any possibility of justice must be by-passed. He looked at his watch. It was barely two hours since he had first stolen out on his balcony and erected his protest. They had been quick to hush it all up, out of the public eye. He did not doubt that the speed and the cover-up were on account of his reputation and he regretted it. But he had no doubt that in time Deborah would hear of it, and certainly Sonia, who might hear of it on that very day from her father. But it was Deborah most of all that he wanted to know. Because, through Deborah, Jakob would hear of it, and would know at last that he had asked forgiveness.

When they reached the prison, they speeded him through all the formalities and then stowed him solitary in a cell. He sat on his bunk fingering the rough serge of his prison uniform, and for the first time in many years he felt at peace with himself.

*

That evening, Koskin himself came to Sonia's apartment, and broke the news. Again he stressed that he could not use his influence to free him. That his act had been too public. It would jeopardise his own career were he to intervene. But he suggested that Sonia apply for a visit.

'Believe me, my dear, prison life is so dull and monotonous, he will be glad to see you. Although I disagree with all he's done, you're still his wife and you owe him your support,' he said.

'Everything he did was because of Jakob,' Sonia said. 'If only he were free.'

She began to cry uncontrollably. He sat by her side and whispered, 'I am doing what I can. But not a word. Never, never. Or I shall end up where Jakob Bindel is, or your husband.'

She looked up at him and smiled.

'No questions,' he said quickly. 'And if you love your father, not a word to a living soul.'

She shook her head vigorously.

*

A month later, Aaron was called from the prison-workshop.

'You've got a visitor, Bindel,' the guard said.

Aaron hoped it would be Deborah. That was a possibility. He dared not hope for Sonia for he knew that she would not come. Although he preferred to think that she could not. Since his sojourn in prison, Sonia had been his ever-present thought, coupled with a sense of total hopelessness. There was no future for their togetherness, yet their years with each other had been an expenditure of such passion that it was unlikely that either of them could find a loving future with anybody else. He could not live with her unless she changed, and if she changed, he would no longer love her.

When he saw her there, sitting in the visitors' room, he saw the unavoidable trap that she was, and he its powerless victim. He went towards her, full of forbidden love, and wondered at her courage that she had come at all. 'It was brave of you to come, Sonia,' he said. He dared not touch her. The heat of her body would have sent him to sure and swift recantation. But she touched him, running her long fingers along his hand, and her touch seared his skin with longing.

'I know you only did it for Jakob,' she said.

Her first words to him, and each syllable of them was wrong, misguided, misunderstood.

He shook his head. 'It was more than that,' he said. 'You see, I'm not like you. I don't believe there's anything wrong with Jakob. If a man wants his freedom, that doesn't make him mad. I didn't do it just for Jakob.' He had to make that very clear to her, though it hurt him, for he knew that as she looked at him, she saw their future fade. Then he took her hand.

'Then what am I to do?' she said. It wasn't a question. It was a declaration of a future without him. 'What will you do when Jakob is released?' she asked.

'There seems to be little chance of that,' he said.

She held her tongue on her father's manoeuvres, as she had promised him. 'But what will you do, Aaron, when you are free?'

He shrugged his shoulders for he really didn't know.

'Do you honestly want to go to Israel? I heard about your application.'

He didn't know that either, but to admit to it would cast doubt on his visa-request and thus prove that he had done it solely for Jakob's sake, for his penalising alignment with his brother.

'Would you leave Heidi?' she asked.

He gripped her hand. 'It would be harder to leave you,' he said. 'And that's the truth.'

Her eyes lightened. 'We could come with you,' she said.

He had to laugh at that, because he could not bear the shattering inference of sacrifice in her offer.

'Your father wouldn't give you permission,' he joked.

'He would,' she said. 'And I'm serious. We could go with you.'

'Then it would be you who would be living a lie.'

'What does it matter?' she said helplessly, 'as long as I'm with you.'

'It would matter,' he said, as he knew full well to his cost.

She stared at him, the question on her lips that she knew she must not ask, but had, for her own confusion, to put to him. 'Will you never come back?' she said.

And with utter honesty he said, 'I don't know.'

For in truth Aaron was confused. He wasn't sure that he wanted to go to Israel. If he had to leave the Soviet Union, he would prefer to emigrate to America. From a work point of view, it would have been more exciting. And for Sonia, too, America would not necessitate the impossible re-adjustment that Israel would demand. But he knew that finally places of settlement were only peripheral to the choice and commitment to identity, and it was that area that lay still undefined and blurred and sometimes tormented in his spirit. No. He didn't know, and that was the truth of it and that truth he gave her, and if she chose to take hope from it, that was her risk.

'I don't know,' he said again. 'I really don't know.' He smiled at her, hoping to offset the pain of his non-commitment. He had a sudden desire to make love to her, and not to look at her face, not to know who she was, not to smell their past on her. Oh God, he thought to himself, I wish that she would go. 'How's Heidi?' he said.

'She's well. She misses you. I often take her to Deborah's. She gets on well with Hans and Benjamin. I'm getting closer to Deborah too.'

He smiled though his feelings were ambivalent. He was happy with the idea of family contact, but he could not help but suspect its motivation and he hated himself for such doubts.

'Have you told Heidi?' he asked.

'She knows where you are, and why. She's old enough to understand. The other day she said to Hans, "My father's a refusenik too".'

Both of them in their own ways, Aaron thought, were leading him back into his fold, even though it might cost them their own isolation.

'Has Deborah heard from Jakob?' he asked.

'Yes. I saw the letter. It was censored of course. But he's much better now, he says, and he's recovered from the illness he had when she last saw him.'

'Recovered? Illness?' Aaron asked. 'Do you never stop to think, Sonia, what all that means?'

'I'm different from you, Aaron,' she said. 'I was born here, I went to school here. All my life I have known no other way. I have not been taught the ways of other people.'

Aaron heard her words with a sudden flash of understanding. The whole massive body of the Russian people knew no other way. Why should they not think, then, that that way was right? It explained much of what he considered to be their bull-headedness. They had no access to knowledge of any other choices. Nor ever would in their entire lifetimes.

'In his letter Jakob sent you his love,' she said quickly.

Then he took her face in his hands and kissed her for the great gift she had brought him.

'Time's up,' the warder said, and Aaron was grateful for, after that piece of news there really was no more to say. They rose together and he kissed her once again.

'Shall I come again?' she asked timidly.

He nodded. 'There will never be a time when I wouldn't want to see you,' he said.

He watched her go, relieved, yet impatient for her next visit, and he returned to the prison workshop and thought about the gift she had brought him. Jakob's love. It had been worth all his torment.

*

So the two prison-widowed women waited in their separate apartments, the one knowing the exact duration of her widowhood, but unsure of its outcome. The other, Deborah, waited with only hope for company, for she knew there need be no end to Jakob's incarceration.

But in the Minsk hopital, some weeks later, Jakob was inwardly rehearsing his second case-review. For the warder had told him that he was to be given another chance. Those were the warden's exact words. He, like the doctors, made no attempt to cover the speciousness of the examination. If he was prepared to be better, then better he would be. And on this premise, Jakob rehearsed his apostasy. He had been wrong in his criticism of Soviet society. He had seen the light. As he spoke the words to himself, he heard the Patriarch Jakob prompting him and saw how he nodded his head in benign approval. 'Survival,' he kept whispering. 'Remember that. Each word is given in its name.' So when the time came for Jakob's review, he walked to the doctors' room, his mouth chock-a-block full with the vocabulary of recantation, and he prayed to the Patriarch to use his cunning wisdom to guide his lies from his throat.

They welcomed him as before. The long examining table had been removed and arm-chairs were in its place. They resuscitated the 'Mr' of his name, and asked him politely to sit down. Once settled, they joined him.

'We're going to have a bad winter this year, it seems,' the scribbling but padless doctor opened the proceedings.

Jakob was unnerved by this introduction to the examination and was afraid to react to it in any way, lest they diagnose from his reaction some further aberration of his mind. So he said nothing.

'Well, it will have its advantages,' the diagnostician said. 'It will be easier on the police. There'll be less demonstration. People do not like hanging around in the streets if they are cold.'

So that's what it's all about. So childish, Jakob thought, and he risked looking at them, hoping that the hatred and contempt that he felt did not show on his face.

'How are you feeling, Mr Bindel?' the third doctor asked.

'Much better, thank you,' Jakob said.

'Better than what?' the doctor pursued.

'Better than when I was here before,' Jakob said. He was as wary of their game as they no doubt were of his.

'D'you want me to read you the speech you made in Kolpachny Lane?'

Jakob manufactured a shiver.

'No,' he said.

'And why not?'

Jakob was grateful for the easy cue. 'I would now be ashamed of those words,' he said, and the sound of his sincerity sickened him.

'How do you now regard your former behaviour?' the scribbling doctor asked.

'I regret it,' Jakob said. He was going to add, 'With all my heart' but he curbed his enthusiasm, for over-protest often betrayed a lie.

'If you regret such behaviour,' the diagnostician said, 'you are not likely to act in the same way again.'

'Never,' Jakob said, 'I do not hold those opinions any more. The doctor was right,' he said, 'when he first examined me. In the war we fought for freedom and we won. Therefore we have freedom,' He thought he heard the Patriarch chuckle in his ear.

'Then we can assume that, when you return to Moscow, you will withdraw your application for an exit-visa?'

Jakob was prepared for that question, the hardest of all to dissemble. But he did not hesitate, for hesitation at that point would have given the lie to all the lies he had already told. 'Of course,' he said. 'I want to stay in the Soviet Union.' Say anything, he thought, just to get out of here. Grigory had told him that. The point, he had said, is to get out, if only for a while, and resume the struggle. At that point the Patriarch must have put the thought of Deborah in Jakob's mind and the prospect of reunion with her and their sons was worth all the falsehoods he could muster.

'There would be no reason now for me to leave this country,' he added for good measure.

They smiled at each other, clearly satisfied. No questions remained to be asked. Jakob Bindel was cured. He had entered hospital with the disease of dissent, and their clever and constant administration of drugs had destroyed his intellectual capacity to the extent that he was now incapable of holding dissident opinions. And that they sincerely believed. They rarely questioned it to themselves, possibly out of fear of discovering its flaws. Now they had satisfied themselves with the state of his mind, it only remained for them to check his physical health.

'Would you open your jacket?' the examining doctor said, putting his stethoscope to his ears.

He gave Jakob a cursory examination of heart, pulse and blood-pressure, and pronounced him fit.

'Normally,' the doctor said, and Jakob shuddered at the word, 'you would have to re-visit the Serbsky Institute in Moscow for your check-out, and then appear at court for your discharge. But all that will be waived in your case. You are free, Mr Bindel,' he said.

What a farce it all was, Jakob thought. Yet there was some justice in it. He had been charged and sentenced in his absence. It seemed right and proper that his discharge did not require his presence either.

The doctors showed him to the door, proffering their hands. He shook them each in turn.

'You will be given a train-ticket back to Moscow,' one of them said. 'And we rely on you to uphold the honour of Soviet citizenship.'

Jakob nodded his head in false promise. He could hardly suppress his feelings of joy. As he was leaving, one of the doctors put his hand on his arm.

'Ilya Yakir died, you know,' he said. 'Yesterday. Inflammation of the liver.'

Jakob was glad that they had not given him that information in the beginning of the interview, for all of the Patriarch's wisdom could not have persuaded him to hold a truthful tongue. His heart was leaden. 'I'm sorry,' he said. 'He was a friend.'

'You will no longer have such friends,' the doctor said.

Jakob clenched his fist, pinning it to his side lest he strike him.

*

The warder returned him to the ward where he collected his clothes. He sat on his bed. The news of Ilya's death had deeply shaken him. He was offended by the futility of it all, the indignity of such a death for a man of such honour and nobility. He looked around at the other men in the ward. Most of them were sleeping, some ambled around aimlessly, pinning each step to the ground, and it was still only morning. He couldn't bring himself to say goodbye to them. It wasn't because of shame of his recantation. That had not humiliated him. It was because of Ilya's death. That news had numbed his tongue to farewells.

In the train he could not put Ilya from his mind. Even thoughts of Deborah and his children could not erase the Ilya image on his mind's eye. He had known the punishment that had killed his friend, that remedial 'roll-up' meant to squeeze all dissidence out of the body. But Ilya had known it too, and many times before, yet still he had returned to it, defiant, stubborn, proud. Yet finally it had broken him. He wondered what the Patriarch Jakob would have thought of Ilya. Did he die for love, he would have asked? or friendship? Indeed, Ilya had died for all those, Jakob thought, for he had loved and befriended mankind, and for the first time in the lie-riddled day Jakob felt a pang of shame. He was glad to be alone in the compartment for he needed no witness to his guilt. He tried to sleep, but Ilya's face haunted him behind his eyes, After a while, he did not try any more to blind himself from it; indeed he came to be glad of it, for he needed that beautiful vision for his own resolve. Soon he fell asleep, and woke as the train was pulling into Moscow station, and for the first time that day he could think exclusively of Deborah and his sons and, though he was impatient to see them, the prospect frightened him a little. She would not be expecting him. His arrival would be a shock. Somehow or other he must cushion it.

As he stood outside his apartment door, he decided he would not use his key. His entry would be too sudden. He knocked on the door.

'Who is it?'

He heard Deborah's voice.

'Jakob.'

There was silence then and in the silence he heard her fear. He remembered, then, that a knock on a refusenik's door could be a prelude to a search, an interrogation or an arrest.

'It's Jakob,' he said again.

Again a silence, then after a while, with a voice full of hope, she said, 'I don't believe it. Jakob has his own key.'

He took it out of his pocket and inserted it in the lock. Gently he turned it, knowing that she stood terrified at the door. 'It's Jakob,' he kept saying as he turned the key. 'It's really Jakob.'

Then he opened the door wide. Proof of him. Proof of the recanted Ilya-laden Jakob Bindel.

She stared at him.

'Hans, Benjamin,' she screamed, as if she needed protection, protection from her own overwhelming bewilderment, relief and loving. The boys ran from the back room, and rushed towards him without any crippling astonishment, and embraced him lovingly. Then they made room for Deborah. And now that he had the family print upon him, it proved him real to her, and she went to him and took him in her arms.

'I don't want to know why they freed you,' she said. 'It's enough that you are here.'

She knew of course and that he understood. For she knew that in a psychiatric colony the doctor diagnosed the sentence and the patient pronounced the cure. She knew he had had to pay a price for such a freedom, but she didn't care. She would help him to live with it. I have to tell her about Ilya, Jakob thought. Then she will understand everything.

She prepared a festive supper and asked for his help in the preparation, easing him back into his domestic scene. She gave him all the news of all the events of his absence, news of the children, Inge and their friends. But she did not mention Aaron. He would know nothing of his story. Certainly not in Minsk, for even in Moscow the trial and the sentence had been covered with silence. No newspaper had reported it and, outside the family, few people knew that it had happened at all. His sentence had been short enough, so that by the time people had missed him and begun to enquire as to his whereabouts he would be free and it would be as if nothing had happened. Which would have pleased Aaron, for he had not made his protest for publicity's sake. He'd made it only for himself and that it should come to Jakob's ears. And now it was for Deborah to inform him. But she waited. She was waiting for Jakob to enquire of his brother. But on that subject he was silent too, and it was not until late that evening, when the supper was cleared away, and the boys were in bed, that he sat by her side and asked about Aaron.

'A great deal has happened to him since you left,' she began, and slowly, step by step, she told him Aaron's story.

*

The following morning, when the boys had gone to school, Jakob told her something of the life in the hospital. It was a relief to share it with another, one who didn't find it unbelievable. For even as he told it, he found it hard to credit and he wondered how he had managed to survive it. Jacob told her the story of Ilya, but he refrained from telling her about the one they called Evegny. That story was under the seal of a fraternity of a 'roll-up' brotherhood, and he would share it with nobody. As they were talking, the telephone rang.

'It must be for you,' Jakob said. 'No one knows I'm home.'

Deborah went to the telephone. 'Hallo,' she said, and waited, while Jakob saw her face grow pale. 'Just a minute,' she said. She turned to Jakob, trembling. 'It's for you,' she said.

'Who is it?' he whispered.

'I don't know the voice,' she said. 'I was afraid to ask.'

What do I have to fear? he thought to himself. I've just been released. I've been in no trouble. But just to be Jakob Bindel and in this place, was to be in trouble. Deborah took his arm and led him to the phone and watched his face for clues.

'This is Jakob Bindel,' he said.

There was a long pause while Jakob listened and while Deborah watched and on his face she saw a mixture of total astonishment and pleasure, but both reactions laced with concern, and she hovered impatiently until he put the phone down. Then when he had finished he turned and looked at her.

'That was OVIR,' he said.

She gripped his hand.

'The exit-visas have been granted. I've to pick them up. They're giving us 48 hours to leave the country.'

'It's eight years,' she said quietly.

She held him, and heard the sobbing in his body, and she knew that, though much of it was excitement and relief, more of it was sorrow.

'How can I leave Aaron?' he said.

She knew he expected no answer. He was simply stating his pain. He would leave Aaron, and he would know that he would never see him again, but he would leave, nonetheless, because he was a Bindel survivor.

'You go now to OVIR,' she said. 'I'll ask Sonia to arrange a visit. And I'll ring Inge too. And my parents. I'll ask them to come this evening. And Yosif and Gadaly and Irena and Abram.'

*

When that was done, and Jakob was gone, Deborah toyed with the idea of ringing Sonia, but then decided against it. There was little scruple in speaking to friends from one tapped phone to another, but Sonia's phone was clean, and it would be safer to visit her, so she took a tram-trolley to Sonia's apartment.

Sonia listened as she told of Jakob's sudden release from hospital and the equally sudden granting of the exit-visas. Deborah was surprised at Sonia's reaction. She had expected pleasure, but Sonia's delighted response was overwhelming and, as she embraced her sister-in-law, Deborah sensed that her pleasure was less on Jakob's behalf than on her own, that in Jakob's freedom and absence she saw an avenue of encounter with Aaron. Then she understood why Aaron had left her, why he had made his protest, and she understood, too, that Jakob's suspicions of Koskin's hand in the events were more than confirmed.

Sonia said that she herself had a prison visit that afternoon, but she would gladly waive it and arrange for Jakob to go in her stead.

'He comes out soon,' she said. 'Another two months.'

'Come this evening,' Deborah said, 'and bring Heidi. We have a farewell party.' She turned to leave.

'Wait a minute,' Sonia said. There was pleading in her voice and its tone was unavoidable.

Deborah went towards her. 'What is it?' she asked.

'What shall I do?' Sonia said helplessly.

I have to get the money, Deborah thought. I have to pack. I have to arrange a party. I have . . . Yes, a million things. Yet the story that had prompted Sonia's plea had made each one of those million things possible. She sat Sonia down on the couch. 'I don't know,' she said. She didn't want to hold out any hope. When Aaron had left Sonia, he had relinquished a way of life. Yet he had chosen no alternative. He was in a limbo, a tenuous arena for Aaron's and Sonia's kind of loving.

'I don't know,' she said again, but she knew that politics were irrelevant to Sonia's present pain. She thought of how desolate she herself would be if she were to lose Jakob's love. She took Sonia in her arms. 'I shall miss you very much,' she said.

On her way home, she went to the Savings Bank and withdrew the money that they had safely guarded for their fares. And once having taken that money out, that untouchable almost holy sum, she realised for the first time that they were leaving, and her heart filled with sadness. She would miss her parents, and Inge. Especially Inge. She would miss Aaron too. And Sonia. But most of all she would miss Russia, for whatever its cruelties, its nostalgic hold was painfully irresistible.

Jakob was home when she returned. He was examining the permits closely. He could still hardly believe that they were his. He showed them to Deborah, the object of all their waiting, all their torment. She took them and put them with the money.

'You must go to Aaron,' she said, 'and I must start to pack.' She behaved in a business-like fashion, a totally uncharacteristic trait in her, but both of them were so close to tears that the whole day could have passed in regret.

'Give my love to Aaron,' she said.

*

Jakob stood outside the prison, that same prison where he himself had been silently incarcerated almost eight years ago. He stood still on the gravel path leading to the prison-gates and he remembered how Aaron had met him there on his release, that stern unyielding man, full of concern and rage, rigid in his suit of self-deception. He longed to see him, yet he lingered, in postponement of a meeting that would probably be their last. For Aaron was fettered to this land as Grandpa Leon had been bound to the valley of Senghenydd. What a legion of partings had littered the Bindel line, he thought, and had bred that hopeful coda of 'Soon we shall be together again.' He walked slowly towards the prison-door.

'Bindel,' the warder shouted in the work-shop. 'A visitor.'

Aaron rose, excited, stirred by a passion that he knew would evaporate at the sight of Sonia, and that would surely return when she had gone. As he neared the door of the visiting-room he began to tremble and, when the guard opened it, he gave an audible cry of delight for, however much he wanted to see Sonia, there was no one on earth with whom he more wanted to be. He practically flew to Jakob's side.

'Where have you come from, brother? And why? And how? You are free at last.'

'I am more than that,' Jakob said, embracing him, and he led him to a chair at the table. 'But tell me first how you are.'

'No, no,' Aaron said sitting down but not letting go of Jakob's hand. 'There is nothing to say about me. They treat me well here, and I shall be free shortly. But you, Jakob, what has happened?'

Jakob noticed how his brother's body trembled and he was filled with such pain for him, for all the love that Aaron was at last able to release, his rigid body thawing with the agony of a sudden and intense defrost.

'I was freed yesterday,' Jakob said, 'and this morning they telephoned from OVIR to say that the visas had been granted. They gave us forty-eight hours to leave.' He paused then. 'We leave tomorrow,' he said, as gently as he could. He thought it best to tell him straight away, so that Aaron would know from the beginning that they were not likely to meet again.

Which was exactly Aaron's deduction, for Jakob saw his brother's eyes fill with tears.

'I'm glad,' Aaron said. 'I'm glad for you. I'm glad for all of us. I'm glad for the Bindels. The line will be secure.'

How radically he had changed, Jakob thought, and how dearly he had paid for the transformation.

'What will you do Aaron? Will you stay here?'

Aaron shrugged. 'I really don't know,' he said. 'But I'll tell you a story. Some years ago, when Sonia and I were first married, we were invited to dinner at Koskin's apartment. There were just the three of us. It was his birthday, I remember, and he opened a rare bottle of wine. No Georgian stuff for him of course. It was imported and the very best, as he and his kind are privileged to acquire.' He smiled with a twist of irony. 'It was a Claret, a Chateau Mouton Rothschild. The wine was superb, but what fascinated me was the label on the bottle. Old Koskin couldn't understand my fascination with its design, but he gave me the label to take home. I have it somewhere still amongst my papers. Let me describe its pattern. It's in the form of a shield. A red shield, which is a direct translation of the family name. Within the shield are five arrows that branch in different directions. Old Mayer Rothschild, the founder of the firm, had five sons and, when they grew, he sent them to different parts of Europe to establish in each place a branch of the Rothschild banking tree. Frankfurt, Vienna, Paris, London, Rome. It was his way of ensuring continuity. You see, that old man from Frankfurt, old Mayer Rothschild, knew about survival. We're not Rothschilds,' Aaron said, 'but our history is as long. Our wanderings are as world-wide. Go to Israel and be happy there.'

'And you?' Jakob asked again.

'I don't know. I really don't know,' Aaron said. 'My application might have been just a gesture. I'm beginning to understand, but I'm still confused, you see. Then there's Heidi. There's Sonia. There's all of my loving.'

Jakob looked at him tenderly. 'You mustn't turn away from that,' he said.

For a while there was silence between them, then Aaron asked, 'Will you go via Vienna?'

'Yes,' Jakob said.

'I remember that railway-station so vividly, and how glad I was that I was not on that train, and that I was going back to Leipzig.'

'I shall think of you on that platform,' Jakob said.

'D'you remember how Mama hugged us when we returned, how she held us in her arms and wouldn't let us go? D'you remember . . . d'you remember? There are so many memories I'm now ready to share with you. Will you write?'

'Of course,' Jakob said. 'And so will the boys, to Heidi.'

And again there was silence between them, but each unspoken moment was a cementing of their brotherhood and it was as audible and as resonant as words between them. So that, when they heard the guard's voice, it was as if he had interrupted their conversation.

'Time's up,' he said.

They smiled at each other. They had said all that they needed to say. They held each other close and for as long as the guard allowed. Then he tapped Aaron's shoulder. Neither Aaron nor Jakob could turn his back on the other, so they walked away from each other backwards, holding each face in the other's eye. Aaron to prison, Jakob to freedom. Then they stood for a moment on their distant and separate thresholds.

'*Shalom*,' Aaron shouted, plucking out of his enforced Jewish childhood that word that would do for greeting or farewell, but which in either context meant to come or go in peace.

'*Shalom*,' Jakob said.

Outside the prison, Jakob stood for a while and said his own farewell to his brother. Inside the prison-workshop Aaron was doing the same. Soon we shall be together again, each said to himself. Over every generation, from Russia to England, from England to Germany, and from Germany back to Russia, no Bindel could part from another without that phrase. Over the years it had lost its overtones of re-union. It was stated simply as a confirmation of Bindel continuity.

CHAPTER THIRTY-FOUR

They were catching the night-train to Vienna and Inge and Ivan saw them off at the station. Inge could not hold back her tears. It was a terrible parting for her. It seemed to her as final as Hans' dying. Which it was, for she was unlikely to see them again.

'You still have Aaron,' Jakob said.

'I'll look after him, don't you worry,' she said. 'Sonia too, and Heidi.' In her heart she had re-united them and that gave Jakob a measure of comfort.

The journey was long and they slept most of the way. They reached Vienna early the next morning. Jakob stood on the platform and breathed freedom. Yet the last time he and Aaron had stood on that same platform, it was not freedom that they breathed, but captivity. The official from the Israeli Embassy, who met all trains bound from Moscow, was there to greet them.

'Welcome to freedom,' he said, and for some reason, Jakob felt a shiver of resentment. What did this man know about freedom, he wondered, he who had probably never known bondage? He thought then of all those friends he had left behind in their involuntary servitude, and he thought of Aaron, too, in his own thrall, and he hoped that he was sleeping.

They travelled El Al to Tel-Aviv, and when, four hours later, the plane touched down, the pilot made an announcement. He gave it first in Hebrew, only a few words of which Jakob could understand. But a German translation followed in deference to the plane's port of embarkation and from it Jakob gleaned the message. He translated it for Deborah and the children as the pilot was speaking.

'He apologises,' Jakob said, 'but there will be a delay in passing through Customs and Immigration. There has been a bomb scare in the airport, and it is being cleared. The police are searching the area. The delay will last about two hours. Meanwhile passengers will be taken to a building on the far side of the airport, and given refreshment.'

'What bombs?' Benjamin asked.

'Palestinians,' Hans said.

They knew about the PLO. Over the past few years, Russian radio and television had given much time and praise to the activities of the Palestinians, not so much that they applauded their cause, for in truth they cared little for their fate, but that they were a convenient peg on which to hand their incessant anti-Israel propaganda.

'What a welcome home,' Hans said.

They were taken by bus to a building on the fringes of the airport. It seemed to be a conference room of sorts, for it was huge and richly appointed. The Bindels took chairs at the far end of the room, away from the other passengers. Jakob wanted to sit privately with Deborah and his sons. Coffee was brought to them and refreshments. It would be a long wait, the server told them.

Jakob looked at his two sons. Fifteen and seventeen years old, uncircumcised, too late for barmitzvah, and still uninherited. What was there Jewish about them, he thought, except a vicarious and fragile thread from their past? Yet, alien as they were, they were going to a land that by virtue of that same history was their home, their family, and he pondered on the wisdom of their uprooting.

'It was safer in Moscow,' Hans was saying.

'That's stupid,' Benjamin said. 'What is safe in not being free? At least in Israel we're home.'

'It's the Palestinians' home too,' Hans said with some indignation.

A terrible peal of warning bells chimed in Jakob's ear. For in his children's argument, he heard the rumblings of that fraternal conflict that had dogged every generation of Bindels since the milk-brothers, whose love for each other had not been clotted by fraternal blood. His children had to learn that Bindel history. They must be told. They had wandered for so many generations over the earth's surface, and had finally come home, and even before entering they were threatened. It was surely the time, and certainly the place for his children to inherit.

'It's not safer in Moscow,' he said again, 'nor ever was. Nor in the whole of Russia. The Bindels knew that generations ago. It was from Russia that they started their wanderings.'

'Where? And who?' Benjamin asked.

'It's a long story,' Jakob said smiling.

'Then tell us,' Hans said. 'We've plenty of time.'

Jacob wished that Aaron were with him, that they could bequeath together, in the same way as the milk-brothers had together consigned their inheritance in the wood behind the Odessa tavern. At that moment he felt very much alone. He took Deborah's hand.

'It all started, as far as is known, over a hundred years ago in Odessa. But first I must tell you a little of the history of that time.' And as his father Benjamin before him, and Grandpa Leon before his father, and as Benjamin the milk-brother had spoken to Grandpa Leon, Jakob began his story.

'The Bindels have come a long way from Odessa,' Benjamim said, when the long tale was at an end.

'Yes,' Jakob said. 'But now we're home.'

'Then we're safe,' Hans said. 'We need no longer struggle for survival.' He saw his father's questioning look. 'Well, need we, Papa?' he asked.

'I can only answer you with another question,' Jakob said. 'Why are we waiting here? Perhaps, in each and every step from Odessa, the struggle for survival was only a long and gruelling rehearsal. For the real battle begins at home.'

'We're ready now,' the steward called the passengers. 'The bus is waiting to take you to the airport.'

Thus Hans and Benjamin, of the sixth traceable Bindel generation, from Bessarabia to England, from England to Germany, and from Germany to Russia, entered the land of their forefathers, not of their bones but of their spirit. Jakob followed them. He recalled the old man who had led Aunt Sarah and himself to the graves of their past in Odessa. Living Judaism belongs to the Diaspora, he had said. Did survival too? Jakob wondered. He thought he heard the minstrel singing.

EPILOGUE

Come, stranger. We have eaten of the bread of affliction and the bitter herbs. We have recounted the plagues of Egypt and given thanks for our deliverance. Now between us we may break unleavened bread, and share the feast that celebrates our freedom. We will be here next year too, and every year to come. 'In every generation each man must regard himself as if he himself had gone forth from Egypt.' That phrase will echo in many places and in many tongues, that refrain of the minstrel's song, that tone-poem of almost six thousand years of Jewish history. Know, stranger, of our survival. Know, stranger, of our stubborn continuity. Know, stranger, of our chronic permanence.

Then come, stranger. Any year, any place, any tongue.